y reading

John Sandamore

THE HOLLOW

THE HOLLOW
A Trilogy
Part 1: Lucinda

John Scudamore

Book Guild Publishing

Sussex, England

First published in Great Britain in 2010 by
The Book Guild Ltd
Pavilion View
19 New Road
Brighton, BN1 1UF

Typeset in Baskerville by
Ellipsis Books Limited, Glasgow

Printed in Great Britain by
CPI Antony Rowe

A catalogue record for this book is available from The British Library.

ISBN 978 1 84624 450 6

To
Lucinda, Celia & Alice
Thanks for coming
To the party

1

The Screen

Lucy was for the moment a little weary and, to tell the truth, her feet were sore. Perhaps Celia was used to all this activity and attention and frivolity; she her self was not.

Yet it had been a good evening, even though she had not initially been looking forward to it. Now that was nearing its end, she was glad she had come, although her original reservations were not entirely dispelled. Yes, she had met some charming and even one or two handsome young men as her cousin had promised. She had received much attention, again as Celia had promised, although she had not earlier been convinced of either possibility when the ball was first discussed. But no 'tingle'.

'You need to get out of your self,' Celia had said. 'Besides, there are some very nice young men who are sure to be there,' and proceeded to describe several of them whom Lucy could not fail to find, at the very least, worthy of her interest. 'You might even (giggle) find your self head-over-heels in love by the evening's end.' So said Celia as she spun in her skirts so that they appeared as a halo of colour about her pantalooned legs. Lucy had smiled politely, and said nothing. She did not *want* to be swept off her feet. 'In love' indeed! She was only eighteen to her cousin's nineteen, nearly twenty, and that year-and-a-half seemed to make all the difference somehow.

Besides, with her father, only just . . . And at the first sign of tears Celia had stamped her delicate slippered foot; 'stop that at once do you hear; or I declare, you shall just have to stay *at home*.' Lucy had to smile, for she knew her cousin did not mean it. Besides, she quite evidently intended to show off her 'beaux' to Lucy; how they all flitted and flirted around her like moths 'round a candle – and occasionally got just as burned.

1

And they did, flit and flirt that is, somewhat to Lucy's surprise, for she thought her cousin's radiance more than a trifle forced. But if it was, the young men did not seem to notice. To the contrary; they swarmed thicker than ever. Lucy, not knowing any of them, was her usual quiet self; if any thing, even more reserved, despite Celia's urgings and nudgings. Nor did any of them give her that 'tingle' that Celia had been so descriptive of with several of them. So explicit in fact of the feelings of her body that Lucy was quite embarrassed by it all, not comprehending much of what Celia was describing, but too shy to admit that she had never experienced any thing like that in her own feminine self.

Now after standing up with three different partners five dances in a row, she was in need of a little customary solitude, as well as being a trifle too warm. Making her excuses in a sufficiently vague manner to her party, she left the ballroom and strolled to an adjoining room with many portraits around the walls. She made a pretence of studying them, for there were several other guests in the room, and she did not feel like conversing at that moment. The usual set of family portraits; doublet and hose, beautifully adorned women, and Russian wolfhounds. There was even one that she immediately recognized as a colonel in the Hussars, just like her father. Handsome, too, like her father and at the thought of him, tears welled up in her eyes before she could control them.

Oh dear, the last thing she needed now was any sort of fuss from her hostess the Baroness and, without further ado, she slipped through a door in the panelling that was already slightly ajar, closing it softly behind her. She leant there, fanning her self and dabbing lightly at her eyes with the little square of delicate Alençon lace that she carried, controlling the emotion that she knew was most inappropriate, for she would not be able to appear again in public that night if she failed. 'Deep breathing, that is the secret to control,' Celia had told her, knowing that it would never do to have a weepy cousin by her side, even one as pretty as Lucy.

At the thought of sweet Celia, who seemed to a have a recipe for every circumstance from tingles to sniffles, she had to smile. Now more composed, she looked about her. She was in a short corridor in which were several doors, all closed. But straight ahead there appeared to be a narrow circular staircase leading to a small balcony. It was mostly in darkness, for the few candles in the corridor did not reach that far out or up, and she strained to see more.

At that moment there was a new murmur of voices in the gallery whence she had just escaped. She was in no state to be discovered, at least not until she had repaired the damage to her face. She probably looked a fright. Yet for a further moment she hesitated. Would she be intruding? No, all seemed quiet, except for the salon behind her.

Suddenly she felt a thrill of energy from the very stillness of the place. It was like being alone in her very own castle; and she tiptoed down the corridor to the foot of the staircase. Peering up, she could see no more than before, rather less in fact because the balcony was now over her head. Her heart was beating faster with the excitement of it all and, lifting her skirts, she carefully made her way up. Thank goodness those dreadful hoop skirts were no longer the fashion, or she never would have made it to the top.

It was indeed a small balcony, big enough for only one chair and straight ahead a door, slightly ajar. She paused again, listening intently. Nothing; except the loud pounding of her heart. Nothing for it now but to lead on, to whatever lay ahead, and again she felt that slight tightening of her chest. In three steps she was inside and closing the door softly behind her, leant against it to ease her breathing and survey where she was.

The room was small and perfectly octagonal, with an octagonal carpet, and an octagonal moulded ceiling painted with cherubs. The walls were in what appeared to be a pale pink satin, delicately patterned, and set in framed panels. Directly ahead was an oval mirror in which she could see her self, and illuminating it, two candles in crystal holders on a table on which also appeared to be ladies' ornaments; hand mirror, brushes – all the things she would need. Perfect. Strange, she thought, that she should be led to just the right place in her moment of need.

Moving closer, she studied her appearance. Her eyes were indeed red and moist and only time would improve them, so she would need to take it. But the application of a little powder helped her cheeks, which had become distinctly flushed. That accomplished, she studied her reflection gravely. The dress, which she had at first refused to wear because it was so low cut, was, as Celia had insisted, quite becoming. She was simply not used to displaying any where near so much of her bosom in her own village as they did here. But Celia was correct, too, that it was even modest by comparison with some she had observed in the ballroom.

Celia said she had only worn it once her self, and nobody at that ball would have seen it. Still, to be on the safe side, she had asked Alice to decorate the bodice with tiny seed pearls, add a little ecru lace to the short sleeves, and change the lacing in the front to a deeper peach. A final touch was a real rose in its little silver holder, fastened just at the point where – and she blushed again at the remembrance of Celia's description of what that did to the young men.

The cream satin was just right for her lightly tanned complexion, too, and the slightly puffed sleeves did show off her shoulders rather nicely; her best feature she had always thought. Alice had also swept up and pinned her hair in a quite alarming style, but despite her worst fears, it was still in place. The ruby-drop earrings her aunt had so graciously presented to her and her own single-strand pearl necklace completed the picture. Passable, she thought, with only a touch of modesty.

She was feeling much better now and ready to return to the ball. Just a last flick of the powder puff – when a slight rustle froze her in the act. Slowly replacing it in the bowl, she turned to the sound. At first saw nothing, her eyes being still dazzled by the candles in the mirror before her. Gradually she made out a triple silk screen and, partly behind it, an oil painting of what looked like a lady reclining on a chaise. Otherwise, silence.

She moved quietly forward to the painting and, putting her hand on the screen, observed that it was indeed a lady, draped – or rather undraped – on a sofa couch, for she was quite spectacularly naked. Again that slight rustle. This time she moved only her eyes and saw a dim figure at the far end of the screen, sitting in a chair, holding some thing in its hand.

Had she not been holding the screen, she might have cried out. As it was, she held her silence, though her heart was pounding furiously, and the screen shook slightly with the grip of her tense fingers. As Lucy stared into the dimness, the figure unfolded it self to become a tall man. Even in the shadow she could see that he was well dressed; a guest like her self, perhaps.

When fully erect he took a step forward, gently uncurled her unresisting fingers from the screen and, raising her hand to his bowed head, kissed it tenderly. He remained holding it to his lips, the while gazing intently into her eyes then returning it gently to her side. Before she could open her mouth to speak he reached to take her other hand, leading her gently yet firmly back to the mirror.

First he laid the object that he was carrying on the table and she could see that it was a sketching pad, on which was the outline of the lady of the painting, performed in charcoal. Unfinished, though quite distinct as to what it was, Lucy could appreciate that it was a very good likeness, although somewhat embarrassing to her self, its graphic physical detail being already marked in. Yet she could not help admiring the grace that he had achieved in his subject.

Next he pulled out a low stool from under the table, which Lucy had not noticed, and she wondered how he knew of its existence. Then, standing behind her and taking hold of her shoulders, he gently lowered her onto the stool, guiding her into the position he was seeking, at a slight angle. Now he rested his hands lightly on her bare shoulders, and stood gazing at her in the glass.

Returning his gaze, Lucy was immediately aware of several things simultaneously: his hands were cool, his fingers were long and soft in their touch, yet her skin burned on the contact; his eyes were a pale clear blue, and his strong simple face was quite handsome. He turned her shoulders slightly to one side, reached over to pinch out one of the candles, picked up the sketching pad, tore off the half-finished drawing, crumpled it, and threw it contemptuously to the floor as if in rejection of his own work – or was it of the subject? Then he reached into his pocket for his charcoal, and commenced sketching, still standing behind her.

All the time not a word was spoken. When he saw her looking at him, he indicated with his eyes that she should look at her self. Complying, she found that her own were no longer moist and red; rather they were bright and sparkling. Thus it was with some surprise that, when several silent minutes later he propped the sketch against the mirror in front of her, she saw that he had captured the moment of their first meeting. It shewed a wide-eyed, apprehensive, somewhat sad Lucy, which portrayal was startlingly accurate.

On a second glance she noted that the figure in the drawing stopped at the waist, with shoulders and arms bare. No slightly puffed sleeves. The earrings were there, as was the pearl necklace, but there was no bodice; just white paper. His pale blue eyes were now burning into her green ones, and she felt, rather than saw, his hand, his long fingers on the bare skin of her shoulder. A pause, then the sensation made its way slowly downward across her chest, downward, over her exposed upper bosom until it at last burned its way inside her bodice and lay cupped, hot and searing, on and under her right breast.

At the touch, her heart, her breathing stopped, absolutely. She could neither move nor talk; only her eyes could speak. And in answer to his, questioning, they said a reluctant 'no'. His response was not immediate. For a long moment, an eternity it seemed to her enthralled body, he, too, was still. Then slowly, ever so slowly, his palm left her softness, pausing as his fingers gently massaged the already hard bud of desire, some thing she had never experienced in her whole life, swelling it even greater as if to hold those searching fingers to her self, sending a sharp thrill deep into her inner being. Even more, this was matched at that same moment by the equal swelling of her left breast. Then the hand retreated up and out of her gown, until it rested once more, burning still, on her shoulder. But his eyes continued to smoulder into hers. At last, with great reluctance, he picked up the pad and with a few deft strokes, sketched the line of her bodice, shaded in the upward curve of her exposed bosom, the deep shadow of her cleavage thrown by the single candle, the tiny seed pearls and, finally, the strategically placed rose in its silver holder.

The speed and deftness of his actions left her motionless still. Then, with a flourish of the pad before her, he bent and kissed her bare shoulder, and turned silently away into the shadows. She did not even hear the door close. But though he was no longer in the room, the fire of his fingers on her body and his lips on her shoulder, and the desperate throb in her bosom and now throughout her entire body, even to her toes, were more fierce than ever.

And it was a long, long moment before she could move, all the while willing the burning of her bosom to quieten, which it did, eventually, though her cheeks were still heightened by a blush that had nothing to do with that applied at Celia's insistence that all young ladies would be similarly adorned.

Lucy would have slept late, but Celia would have none of it, demanding that if she did not come down *this instant*, then she, Celia, would be up to see to it her self. When she did finally arrive, breakfast was almost over. Not that anyone noticed or minded. Celia just wanted to brag a little of her conquests to the other more distant cousins that Aunt Charlotte had invited for the ball and to stay the night. Besides, Lucy could not eat a thing, though she tried.

She caught Celia looking thoughtfully at her on several occasions during slight lulls in the conversation. But when some one did ask her a question as to how much she enjoyed the evening, her murmured comments were scarcely out before some one else rushed in with their own passionate response. It was giggles and laughter among the young ladies for the rest of the morning.

After that, it was all hustle and bustle while they packed up and the young people rushed around saying their 'goodbyes' and how much they had enjoyed it all and how they must do it all again soon and that *they* were going to have one soon at *their* place and how every body *must* come and visit and it would be a marvellous and wonderful time again, and on and on. The adults were more circumspect, but it was quite apparent that the weekend had been an overwhelming success.

In the midst of every thing, Lucy managed to slip away while they were still busy, having said her brief farewells to most, well, some anyway. The lake was her special place when she wanted to be alone for a while. But this morning she was almost desperate in her desire for time to think. She hoped she hadn't been rude but, for the most part, she just could not match her cousin's exuberance, this particular morning especially.

So it was with great relief that she found the boathouse deserted. Her favourite was a little red and yellow punt not much bigger than her self. It was tied up where she had left it, and a quick push along the dock, a final heave against the last post and she was underway. It was only then that she remembered that one usually put the oars in the boat first. Never mind; there was nowhere to go, and she placed the cushions on the seats and stretched out to look at the sky.

Where to start? That was the most difficult question. She hadn't slept very well; in fact, she had slept hardly at all. Strange, troubling dreams that seemed to have no beginning, no end, no purpose and that she could not remember – except that they had disturbed her greatly, then and still. When she brushed into the reeds that fringed the centre island she lay back again to try to work it all out. She would be missed some time and some one would come and rescue her. If not, then she would have to paddle with her hands. It wasn't that far.

Whether it was the gentle rocking of the boat, or the cooing of the doves, or the warm sun flickering through the overhanging willow could not be told, but she was soon in a deep but troubled sleep. She was in her little boat, *sans* oars, but now she was on the river, the boat was spin-ning 'round and 'round, the river running faster and faster, and she was rocking wildly and threatening to capsize. She kept calling out but there was no one to hear her. She tried and failed to grab bridges as they sped by, and when she did see some one they took no notice of her, as if she did not exist. Then there came the sound she had been dreading; the waterfall, and she could not swim. Faster and faster, nearer and nearer, until the horrid roaring was almost more than she could bear. And just as she went over the edge, falling over and over, getting wet from the spray, *he* was there, catching her in his strong arms, holding her tight, ever so tight, until she could scarce breathe. And his hands were burning her skin and his lips burning hers, and he was calling her name over and over. Lucy! Lucy! That was strange, because how could he know her name?

She had fallen off the seat and was lying in the bottom of the boat, which had more than a little water in it, dirty water, as is the usual way with boats, and she was wet right through. That was going to be humil-iating enough, going back through the house dripping water like a drowned rat. But worse; it was Celia calling her name from the boat-house bank! How would she ever live it down? She would not ever dare show her face here again. *Never to come here again!* That was simply too awful to bear. Never to have even the *chance* of seeing him again. And at that crushing thought, all her pent-up emotions released in one gush, and she simply laid her head on the gunwale and cried as if her heart would break.

She never heard the other boat come alongside. Knew nothing, felt nothing, until some one lifted her head onto a soft shoulder. Nothing was said; not a word exchanged. She was simply held until she could cry no more. Held 'til the tears turned to sobs, and the sobs to little hiccups, until they too mostly ceased. And even then until she was once more able to lift her head, Celia simply held her and stroked her and comforted her, and said nothing except a few cooing sounds, a few 'there, theres' and such-like.

Then Celia tied the little boat behind hers and quietly rowed to the boathouse with scarcely a splash. Quickly she helped Lucy into the boat-house, up the stairs to the neat storeroom above it, and sat her on a chair, brushing her hair back out of her eyes and, holding her head between her hands, kissed her gently on the eyes and the forehead and on each cheek. Then she took up a towel from the pile kept there for when it rained or some body got wet from catching too many 'crabs' and briskly rubbed Lucy's face until it was rosy red; until they both laughed from the joy of it.

Still cradling Lucy's head against her, Celia now talked softly as if to her self. 'Now, let me see; how to get back to the house without anyone seeing me. I could go in through the pantry, up the servants' stairs, right to the top, then come down the west wing staircase, and straight into the bathroom. Should be plenty of hot water, still. Then ask Alice to wash the clothes without making too much of a fuss about it, and explain how I slipped in the boathouse. That should do it fine. Nobody's business but mine. Then I can rest until my *headache* is better.'

By this time Lucy was feeling a little more of her old self – though in truth she still looked quite dreadful. So as they both rose, she reached out and hugged Celia as if her very life depended on it. And, who knows? – maybe it did. And Celia hugged her back just as fiercely as if she understood it all, and maybe she did. At least Lucy hoped so, for she did not understand any of it. Nothing at all. Not even a teeny bit.

From then on the two cousins were rarely apart. Lady Etheridge, Celia's mother, tried on several occasions to explore the subject of their sudden fondness for each other. Separately, each just smiled, and said nothing, or gave some off-hand remark. Together, they would simply look at each other and smile. Or on occasion, roar with laughter to such an extent that they had to be sent outside to recover. *Most* unladylike behaviour was all Aunt Charlotte had to say about that!

But she was not displeased. Her own – and only – daughter was somewhat on the wild and reckless side. Her late brother's daughter was much the quieter, more sensible, shy almost to a fault. Moreover, since she had been with them – over a month now – Celia had settled down, become in some strange way almost a big sister to Lucinda. Aunt Charlotte much approved of the given name, for it was in fact she who had suggested it. But she could be flexible on the point, if only for her brother's sake, for 'Lucy' is what he had always called her. And at the thought, she was obliged to dry her moistening eyes, ever so gently.

If Celia had changed for the better, so had Lucy. She did not smile enough, and often, caught alone and unawares, was quite sad. She read a lot, which was good, though her taste ran to the romantic more than was perhaps good for her. But she got Celia to reading, too, which was quite remarkable for she rarely took a book let alone read it. The two of them would spend hours together, reading quietly from Jane Austen – of which her ladyship greatly approved since she had pulled them from the library shelves her self to leave them scattered about. Sometimes they talked quietly – about what Aunt Charlotte was never able to discover, though she hoped it was the excellent taste and decorum on which those novels were based.

In discussions with her young cousin, Celia never again referred to the incident of the boat, or for that matter to the ball – except in the most general of terms. For that, Lucy was eternally grateful. The only single remark that Celia made on one occasion was to the 'tingle', on which she regarded her self as some thing of an authority. Lucy had made no reply; did not even look up from her book, but the deep blush on her half-hidden face said it all. And shortly, after a deep silence, Celia rose and crossing over to Lucy, gently kissed the back of her bent neck. Lucy reached out and took Celia's hand, still without looking up, and gave it a hard squeeze and nothing more was ever said. But from that moment, their friendship deepened until they were as inseparable as twins.

It had been a wonderful summer, which made it all the more sad when the moment Lucy had been dreading inevitably arrived. It was time to leave. She and Cousin Celia had done *every thing* together. Riding, hunting, rowing, country house parties, countless soirées, even a weekend ball with distant cousins. But, search as she might, she had not seen *him* again.

Celia had been watching intently, too. But though she had her mother arrange more parties than ever in the excuse of keeping Cousin Lucy engaged, nothing. And she would have known. She had in fact kept her own diary of every one who had attended any ball to which they had been invited. Still nothing; and it baffled her, for she knew all the eligible young men for miles around. Liked to keep most of them on a string. Still nothing. Now they had come to the last day. Twelve whole weeks, and it would soon be over, perhaps forever. And she had to wipe away a few tears her self; most unusual, for she was not given to that sort of thing.

The goodbyes were unusually solemn, and little was said. Lucy's face was set with a fixed expression that forbade any reference to the future. Even Aunt Charlotte was subdued. Alice, sweet little Alice, made the most fuss, giving her a deep curtsey and handing her a little present, then rushing off wiping her eyes. That made every thing even worse. So when the coachman opened the door, Lucy stepped up, gave a little nod, and was driven away without another word. Celia simply stood in the carriageway, looking after the coach, long, long after it had disappeared, too sad to even wave, too sad to do any thing but walk in the gardens until tea-time. Too upset to eat, to speak even. Then she went to her room before dinner, and sent a message with Alice that she had a headache and would not be down. Her mother responded by sending up a tray with Alice, but when checked a little later, nothing had been touched.

Never in all her life had Celia reacted in that strange way – since she had grown up, anyway. She usually shrugged off these things, got over them if any thing a little *too* quickly. But this was different. By the third day of eating little or nothing, her mother was worried enough to call Dr. Jamieson; not that it did any good, for Celia refused to be examined by him. Sent him away with a flea in his ear, so the below-stairs gossip went. Some thing more drastic would have to be done.

Celia her self was not so much unhappy, she wasn't the unhappy sort. But suddenly she found that much of the joy had gone out of life; as if part of her was missing. She had never had a sister, and her brother was much older. Had spent most of his time away at Harrow and Oxford, so she saw him only during the hols. Then almost straight out to Delhi as an aide to the Governor-General. Besides, they were never very close, somehow. But Lucy? That was different. She had in some strange way become part of her life, part of *her*. And though she would have fiercely denied it if challenged, she had learned much from Lucy. It *was* better to be a little on the quiet side; the young men of her acquaintance seemed to like her better that way, too. And the ones who did not, well, they were the ones she cared less for, anyhow.

But deep in her heart, Celia finally came to know why she felt the way she did: she had failed her cousin, completely and utterly, and she was not used to that. And upon that realization, her self-pity began to give way to a healthier and much more useful feeling – determination. A plan was beginning to form in her mind, one of which she thought Lucy, the more serious of the two, would be proud. It was to be two-pronged, and she would start the first this very afternoon.

So it was that at tea, Lady Etheridge was surprised and relieved to find her daughter looking her self again. Well, not quite, for there *was* a difference about her; a new determination, a new seriousness of which she wholeheartedly approved. But she said nothing, for she had learned to wait to find out what was in the offing.

'Mama,' began her daughter. Promising, for that was exactly how she was addressed when some thing important was to be broached. 'Mama, I think we should do some thing nice for Cousin Lucinda.' Lucinda? That *was* a new approach.

'And what did you have in mind, my dear?'

'Well, Mother, you remember how when Lucinda was here?' A brief pause.

'Yes, dear?'

'Well, you remember what a jolly time we had?' And as her mother nodded, she went on, 'I thought it would be nice if she could come . . . come, and visit us again, but,' more hesitation, 'but this time, spend . . . spend, a little longer with us, perhaps . . . perhaps . . .' But Celia could no longer continue, and suddenly she was in her mother's arms, sobbing uncontrollably, a child again. 'Just as well I wasn't holding my teacup,' thought her mother, as she held her daughter tightly, until her sobs had lessened.

'Mother,' whispered Celia, looking up at her. 'I miss her so, Mother. Could she come and stay? For always, I mean. Could she, may she, Mother?'

'Well, my dear, I am not sure if . . .', and perceiving a look of pain in Celia's eyes, hastily continued, 'but I think we could perhaps arrange some thing. When winter is over – and Lucy is willing, of course. If that is what you would like, and what her guardian wants and will agree to?'

'Oh, I *know* she will. And pooh! to the old guardian,' replied Celia, fiercely, her spirit returning. And her mother just smiled.

'Why not go and wash your face and come back and drink your tea, and we will talk about it.' But Celia was content to lie in her mother's arms for several minutes more.

And talk about it they did; then, and for quite a bit of the next day, when Lady Etheridge wrote a long letter to her solicitor.

2

Winter

For Lucy, it was quite the worst winter of her life. Never had she known it to be so gloomy or November to be so wet; and when it wasn't wet, it was damp, and always cold and drear. The house was now just an empty shell. She barely remembered her mother, but the signs of her father were every where, even after the most obvious things were gone. His chair was still in its accustomed place in the study, as was his dining chair. After all, you could not take all the chairs out of a house, could you? She could still catch the scent of his special aromatic brand of tobacco he had sent down from London. At times, even thought she heard his voice, and would raise her head to answer his half-caught comment.

Christmas was close at hand, and still she dined alone. She had had plenty of invitations, but found her self quite unable to accept any of them. 'Perhaps in time,' she would reply. But in her heart, she knew that time would never come. It seemed that winter, the one outside and the one in her heart, would never end. Perhaps that was the way it was now meant to be.

She did not think about the time at Etheridge Hall. Did not think about her cousin or her aunt. And most of all, she did not think about *him*. It was as if it had never happened. Perhaps it was a dream. Perhaps she had never left her house after all. Probably she would always stay here.

Her guardian was well meaning enough, but what could he know, what could he understand? Her father's solicitor had prepared all the papers for her to sign, and she understood that the house was now hers. But what did she want with an eight-bedroomed house, most of which was now locked up? She should think about selling it, he had said. He was probably right, but she did not think she could bear to part with her father's house while his presence was still all around her. Not for quite a while, anyway.

It was at this, perhaps her darkest hour, the very week of Christmas, that she had an unexpected visitor. It was a distant cousin, Emily; distant in the sense of relation only, for though residing a bare half-day's distance by carriage, she was an infrequent caller.

'My dear child,' exclaimed Cousin Emily, as she swept in, 'I just had to call and say how sorry I was to hear the news. I have been away you know, in Italy,' Lucy nodded, 'and I have just heard the dreadful news. You poor child,' and she gave Lucy a brief embrace and a kiss on the cheek. 'But let me look at you.

'Dear me, child, you do not look well at all; positively peakéd. And I must say, my dear, you do not look at all well in black. You must amend that just as soon as you are able.'

Lucy did not quite know how to respond to this depressing statement, but she remembered her manners sufficiently to ask if Cousin Emily would care for tea. 'Just a cup, my dear, for I must not stay long. I have so many things to do, being away most of the summer, and Christmas almost upon us, you know.

'So what do you do with your self?' now on her second slice of cake and third cup of tea. 'It must be so dreadfully lonely for you.'

In response, Lucy indicated the spinet in the corner. 'Excellent,' approved Cousin Emily. 'I know just what music can mean at a time like this. But did you not have a pianoforte?'

Lucy replied that indeed they had; however her father was in the act of getting a new one. The old one had already gone to make room for the new one in the Music room, when . . .

'Well, my dear, that is quite wonderful,' broke in Aunt. Then seeing Lucy's shocked expression, hastened on. 'I mean it is wonderful because I have just been bequeathed one by an old aunt of mine. I have two already, you see; and I have been looking for a good home for it, and I remember how wonderfully you play. I will have it delivered immediately, and it can remain as long as you choose.

'Goodness. Is that the time?' as the long case clock in the hall struck five. 'I must go; I am already late.' And she departed in a swirl of skirts and a clatter of hooves, leaving the house and Lucy dark and silent once more.

To Lucy's considerable surprise – for Cousin Emily was wont to be ebullient but not eminently reliable – on the second day after the visit, Mrs. Hollett, the housekeeper, announced that a cart with a piano had just pulled up in the carriageway and the men wanted to know where to put the instrument.

Lucy went to investigate, half expecting a dilapidated relic. But again, to her surprise, discovered that it was a full grand, which meant she would have to open up the Music room again, for it would simply not fit in the Parlour where she tended to pass most of her time these days.

So it was that on Christmas Eve, when the room had been cleaned and aired, she was able to pull up the piano stool and sit at the new piano. She had not noticed until the moment of trying to lift the stool, that it was in fact a double one, and also astonishingly heavy. The first discovery lowered her spirits, for she and her father would often of an evening play duets together, and that moment was very poignant. But the second was a far more brightening prospect, for the excessive weight was due to each half of the very deep storage seat being packed full of music books and manuscripts of all kinds.

Thus it was with a somewhat lighter heart she was able to pass Christmas Day playing carols and hymns (although the instrument was not in the best of tone). These produced many a tear, until Mrs. Hollett was quite worried at the constantly streaming face – and the steady flow of handkerchiefs to be laundered and ironed.

Early January was if any thing even more bleak, with alternate snow and rain producing slush that made venturing outside quite impossible. Thus the piano became her constant companion. By now it was in such poor tone as to be almost unplayable, and she was obliged to request the services of the piano tuner, Mr. Feldman. He advised that it needed a complete set of felts, several action replacements, a number of new strings, and it was three full days before he had it restored.

Mr. Feldman had initially told her that it was indeed a fine instrument and that it was a pity for its owner to have let it get into such a poor condition. Lucy had her doubts on that score, for the overtone echoes were severe and disquieting. But when he finally had it tuned to the satisfaction of his discriminating ear, the difference was quite astonishing. He also played exceeding well, and she was more than a little sorry when he departed and she was alone once more.

So it was that Lucy spent most of every day with her new companion. At first it was the Beethoven she had found in the stool. Some of his darker pieces – especially the Funeral March – suited her mood perfectly, and she would play them hour after hour, over and over, until she scarcely needed the music sheets. The Bach choral works also matched her disposition, for nothing could pierce the cloud over her heart.

As winter dragged on, even the snowdrops were late. She had thought that the crocuses (or was it croci, as her Latin tutor had insisted) never would get there; and nary a sign of the special tulips that her father had planted last year. But her piano playing continued unabated, although she had advanced up the mood scale to Haydn.

One dark day in late winter, she received an unexpected visit from her guardian. 'Would you consider,' he had said, 'going to spend some time with Cousin Celia at Etheridge Hall?' She had been invited by Her Ladyship, and 'was welcome, expected even, to stay as long she chose, their house to be regarded as her own'.

Lucy thanked him politely, and asked him to call back in a day or two when she had had time to think about it. And think about it she did, over much heavy pounding of the piano. But winter was still in her heart. The only smile she managed to her self was when she thought about Celia's 'tingle'. If it was never to be again, then what was the point of returning to any where? So when he called the following day, she gave him the decision that she 'did not feel able at this time to accept Lady Etheridge's most gracious offer, and would he please convey her most sincere thanks for the occasion'.

The guardian was considerably surprised, but said nothing, and he wrote the message as given. Lady Etheridge was even more surprised, and quite disappointed, for she genuinely liked Lucinda, though she said nothing, except to inform her daughter of the sad news.

Cousin Celia initially received the news quietly, but inside she was as angry as ever she could remember, and said much when she was on her own, far from the house. Every tree on the estate heard about it, as well as those whose job it was to care for them, and the stories that were shortly told below stairs cast some doubt as to the young mistress' balance of mind.

If she had had an obligation to Lucy before, Celia now had a crusade, for she had sworn to the trees that she would not rest until whatever it was that made Lucy refuse was resolved. Time for putting pen to paper and, though spring was close at hand, Celia refused all offers of hospi-tality; all save one, that is. But first, she would write to Lucy her self.

Thus it was only a week after her refusal to the guardian that Lucy received a Poste-haste letter, addressed in Celia's rather untidy hand.

'Dearest Lucy,' she read, 'I was greatly disappointed to hear that you are not yet able to come and visit us.'

A somewhat formal opening for Celia, to be sure, Lucy thought, but she read on.

'I have been busy, and now that spring is nearly here, I do have a plan for solving the "mystery". Of course, as none of the Great Houses are open for at least another six weeks, I cannot really make a start yet. However, although I have written down what I know, that has not been as fruitful as I had hoped, as there is so little to go on.'

So little to go on! What could Celia know? Nothing! She did not know any thing her self, and she had *been* there!

'If we could work on it together I am sure we could solve it.'

How could Celia solve any thing; she did not even know what *it* was!

'Please say you will come, I miss you greatly.

Your loving cousin,
Celia.'

It was almost more than Lucy could bear. She would answer it tomorrow. Now she would rest – after the salve of a little more Beethoven.

But by the morrow she could clearly see the futility of it all. Celia knew every body in the *County!* If she had not succeeded, in some thing she knew nothing about . . . Oh! the whole thing was too preposterous to even think about. If she went she would only make a bigger fool of her self than she had already. She could never actually tell anyone about it; not even Celia. Perhaps *especially* Celia, for she would only think her a silly child. After all, what *had* happened? Nothing! A strange man in a strange room (in which she had no right to be!), had made a simple charcoal sketch of her. That was all – except he also briefly laid his hand on her, accidentally, probably. How long had she been there; twenty minutes? thirty minutes? Certainly no longer, and mostly by her self. What kind of a thing was that to get worked up about?

It was really all too ridiculous, and the sooner an end were made of it the better. And drawing a sheet of notepaper from her letter writer, she set out to pen a reply. And that night she wept bitterly over her piano.

Celia received the letter with great disappointment, although she was not entirely surprised, for she knew that her argument was not a convincing one. What really hurt though, clear to her heart, was the cold tone that Lucy had used. She had not expected any thing like that, and a cloud gathered over her mind and soul. Now she knew that only the most immediate and determined of actions would suffice to cure the ills to which Lucy was prey.

When Celia did not appear for luncheon, Lady Etheridge sent Alice to look for her. She was soon back (for Alice usually knew where to find her young charge), reporting that Miss Celia was well, she was rowing on the lake, and she would be back for tea. So Lady Etheridge dined alone. Time to worry later, if there was really any thing to worry about. She knew her daughter well enough to know that when the moment was right, she would be asked for her opinion or judgment.

And she did not have long to wait; teatime to be exact.

'Mother,' said Celia, slowly and solemnly, 'is it all right to do some thing that is not quite right, if the *result* is right in the end?'

'Hmmm,' replied Mother. 'Do the ends justify the means? What exactly did you have in mind?'

But Celia was ready for that; she had not wasted her lunch hour.

'Well, supposing you said some one was pretty when they were quite plain?'

'That would be flattery,' replied Lady Etheridge, not quite liking the direction this conversation was taking. 'And flattery rarely achieves any good.'

'But Mother,' persisted Celia, 'supposing there *was* lasting good. Supposing that the plain person really became quite beautiful after being told? After a little while.'

This was indeed a strange conversation; too oblique for comfort. But she knew her daughter well enough – or she hoped she did – to know that she would not do a bad thing though sometimes her judgment was a little reprehensible.

'In that case,' replied her mother carefully, looking directly at her daughter, 'if that were to be the case, then it *might* be justified. If she really did turn into a beautiful person, and no-one else was hurt in the process.'

Celia's response was instant, and quite astonishing; for she leapt to her feet, rushed to her mother to give her a fierce hug and an even fiercer kiss, and left the room in a whirlwind of motion.

'Celia!' cried her mother. 'For heaven's sa . . .' but she was talking to the air. Lady Etheridge shook her head. 'Oh, dear. I do hope I shall not live to regret this little *tête-à-tête*.'

Celia, meanwhile, was in the Morning room, at her mother's writing desk, composing a letter.

If Lady Etheridge had changed her inflexible habit of spending the next thirty or so minutes in the Drawing room, and visited the Morning room, she would have observed Celia's activities, how she was writing and what she was writing, she would have concluded without any shadow of doubt that her daughter had inherited criminal tendencies of the most dreadful nature. And for that, people went to jail.

It was with some surprise, and not a little apprehension, that Lucy received the note on Lady Etheridge's personal notepaper, a few days later. She did not open it immediately, for she was fearful of its contents. Instead, she put it in her pocket and went into the garden, to sit at the little rustic table where she and her father had spent so much of their time together when the weather was fine.

The tulips that she had quite given up on had thrust their little green heads through the soil the day after she had replied to Celia. She knew now that her letter to her devoted cousin had been cruel and hurtful; deliberately so, which made it so much the worse. Celia had been doing what she could, trying to find a way to help, in what for her must have seemed an impossible circumstance. Still she tried, in the spirit of friend-ship and love, and for her pains had been refused even the comfort of a polite response.

Since writing the letter, Lucy had, in some strange way, begun to mend. Perhaps it was finding the tulips responding to the inevitable tug of spring, and perhaps her heart was responding to the same call. Perhaps that had also led to her choosing lighter piano pieces and thence to Beethoven's sonatas, of which she relearned special delight in the 'Moonlight'. But she aspired to the grandeur and feeling in his so aptly named 'Appassionata', and gave it as much feeling as she was able as she learned its so well-known passages.

Lately she had rediscovered the joys of Mozart and Scarlatti, though she would have preferred to play the latter on her old harpsichord. She was beginning to recover her naturally light spirit, and the music reflected her mood. If only she hadn't written that dreadful letter, she might have been able to rise above the dismal winter entirely. Now she realized, too late, that she had struck away the one hand that reached out to her – her very special cousin, in whom she had taken much pleasure.

The tulips were starting to flower for the very first time, and she could see why her father had chosen them. One was the most gorgeous shade of dark purple-red, with a velvet-like texture to its petals. Another was a quite vivid orange; and a third a vibrant yellow, with red spots and stripes. There were going to be dozens and dozens of them, in a huge circular bed all around her. Her father would have been very pleased indeed with the array, for he had been proud of his garden, and had done much of the work him self. But she knew he would not have been pleased with his daughter or proud of her work, for inwardly she knew she had unexpectedly turned cold and heartless.

In her pocket the letter from Lady Etheridge was probably to advise of her Ladyship's own displeasure at the thoughtless and needless hurt she had caused to her cousin. It would be a most deserved reprimand for, with the advent of the spring as foretold by the glorious display around her, the winter in Lucy's soul was beginning to lift. If only . . .

She had to read the letter, and take her punishment. But first, she had to speak to her father, and she turned to the garden shed.

About two years earlier, he had work carried out to the Dining room, to put in the terrace where they spent summer mornings having breakfast. That was why he had planted the tulips there, too, so that they could see them from the same spot. Left over from the work had been a small stained-glass window, with a curved head, and she had asked that it be put into the side of the garden shed. At times, of a summer evening, the sun would shine through one of its roof-lights, right onto the back of the stained glass, and it would glow as if a beacon in the gathering dusk.

Thus it was to this window into the world of beyond that she bent her head and silently asked for his forgiveness, for his understanding in this,

his garden. Then she dried her eyes, and took out Lady Etheridge's letter, resolved to understand, to accept, whatever reprimand it carried.

Horror of horrors! Celia ill? And it was certainly all her fault. How could she ever be forgiven for that? She must leave at once, and just hope she was in time.

At first Celia had been her old cheerful self. But then, as the days passed, she had grown withdrawn and quite agitated, until her mother was once more concerned.

'Whatever is the matter with you, child?' she exclaimed at breakfast.

'Nothing, Mother,' was her daughter's reply. But some thing clearly was, for she was quite pale and trembling. At tea-time, Celia appeared just as pale, but a trifle more composed.

'Mother,' she started; 'we may have a visitor soon.' Lady Etheridge raised her eyebrows in response, but waited for her daughter to continue.

'Yes,' she said; 'Cousin Lucy may come for a visit.'

'Really?' responded her mother. 'And why would that be; she has already declined the invitation.'

'Well,' said Celia, swallowing hard, 'because I invited her. Or, rather, you did.'

'I know,' replied her mother, rather tartly, 'and she declined.'

'No, mother, you do not understand; I invited her, on your behalf.'

'And you think she will accept?' said Lady Etheridge, not quite understanding what 'on your behalf' meant. 'What makes you think she will accept this time?'

Celia swallowed hard again and the constriction in her throat made it difficult to speak. 'Because I said, or rather you said, that I was ill. Very ill,' and this last was barely a whisper.

Lady Etheridge was beginning to understand – that some thing was very much amiss. There were undertones here that she did not like the sound of at all.

'Let us get this clearly understood. You wrote on my behalf to your cousin,' and Celia nodded. Now the question her mother was dreading to ask. 'By what means?'

'On your personal note paper,' barely audible now in response.

'You wrote, on *my personal note paper*? But your handwriting is nothing like mine.'

'I know,' whispered her daughter, 'but I made it look like it.'

'You,' and she had some difficulty saying the word, 'you *forged* my hand-writing?' Celia nodded, 'and my *signature?*' Celia nodded again, hardly able to look at the anger in her mother's face, but equally unable to look away.

The stony silence was scarcely bearable. 'I think, young lady,' her mother began, 'that you had better go up to your room. You will not be expected for dinner.' And with that Celia was dismissed.

Lady Etheridge was completely stunned by what she had just heard. She could not conceive what had got into her daughter. A forger? A *common criminal?* Simply too appalling for words, and she continued with her tea, without any recollection of doing so. She was going to have to take some advice on the matter. How was she going to explain the falsehood to Lucinda? And for the first time in many years, she wished the General were there to guide her.

At breakfast, Lady Etheridge was not surprised that her daughter did not put in an appearance. Still, the matter had to be resolved. 'Alice,' she called, and when Alice appeared, 'please visit Miss Celia and see whether she is coming to breakfast.'

'Yes, Madam,' responded Alice, with a little curtsey, and left the room.

She was back more quickly than Lady Etheridge had expected, and when she did return to the Breakfast room, there was a look of concern on her face.

'Well?'

'No, Madam, she will not be down for breakfast.'

'I see.' But Alice did not retire, as expected.

'Begging your pardon, Madam, Miss Celia is not well.'

'Really, Alice?'

'Really, ma'am,' and Lady Etheridge looked straight into Alice's eyes.

There was some thing about Alice, some thing quite different from any servant she had ever had. She could never put her finger on it, but she had a very high regard for her as a person. She had never known her to be in the slightest dishonest, in word or in deed. Although Alice must have overheard various personal matters during her almost nine years with the family, there had never been an occasion when that trust had been betrayed.

'Begging your pardon, Madam,' went on Alice, with another little curtsey.

'Yes, Alice, go on.'

'Begging your pardon, Ma'am, but I think Miss Celia is ill. Quite ill.'

'Truly?'

'Yes, Madam.' A pause, then, 'I think Your Ladyship should visit Miss Celia to see for her self.'

And her ladyship did that without further hesitation, for when Alice used that term of address, some thing was very seriously awry. On the way out she asked Alice to tell Cook to see that breakfast was kept warm, and then to join her in Miss Celia's room. Another little curtsey of acknowledgement and Alice disappeared, by which time Lady Etheridge was nearly at the top of the main staircase.

When she entered her daughter's bedroom, she was shocked almost beyond belief. Celia was undoubtedly ill. Her face was completely white, her eyes appeared huge, and were surrounded by dark circles. She looked as if she had been crying most of the night, and seemed utterly exhausted.

'My goodness, child, whatever is the matter?' and she moved to her daughter's bedside. Celia tried to raise her self, but appeared simply not to have the strength, and fell limply backwards. She did not even seem to be able to speak or lift her hand, which her mother reached to pick up.

'Good gracious, she is burning up. Alice! quickly, Cook, hot chicken soup, immediately.'

And Alice was gone almost before she had arrived – and was back almost as quickly.

'A cold cloth; and then send Robert immediately for Dr. Jamieson. No excuses. Go!' And she turned to gently wipe her daughter's burning face and arms and chest, and then dry her just as gently with a soft towel, and repeat it over and over. Suddenly Alice was back again, hot and flustered and dishevelled, to take over the cold cloth and towel.

Lady Etheridge turned to the window, and studied the newly budding trees. What had she been thinking of! If she hadn't been so concerned with her own self-righteousness she would have seen that her daughter was already ill, consumed by some dreadful thing that she thought she had done. Now it seemed of so little consequence that she found her self surprised that she had ever considered it important, and she prayed that she would be forgiven for her personal failure of compassion.

A booming voice from the hall below told her that the good doctor had arrived. 'Out, every body out,' and she and Alice found them selves outside on the landing while the doctor examined his patient.

At the bottom of the staircase, Lady Etheridge turned and said, 'Alice, please ask Cook to make tea for three and then bring it into the breakfast room. We will not be requiring the breakfast, after all.'

In a few minutes, Alice returned with the tray, and turned to leave.

'Just a moment, please, Alice.' Then she turned to pour out two cups. 'Alice, I would like you to know just how much I appreciate what you have done. Not just now, this morning, but for all the mornings. I would like you to join me in partaking of a cup of tea,' and she handed Alice the second cup.

Alice, however, would neither sit nor drink, so Lady Etheridge rose again and put out her hand to take Alice's.

'I understand, Alice. You may take your tea into the kitchen if you prefer, but please, do me the honour of taking this cup with you,' and she released Alice's hand. At the door, Alice turned again, this time with a deeper curtsey, and a 'Thank you, Madam.'

'No; thank *you*, Alice.' And as she turned to go, Alice's dark eyes were sparkling.

Lady Etheridge had barely seated her self and picked up her cup, when Alice was back, more excited than ever. 'Madam,' she almost squeaked, 'Miss Lucy, Madam, she has just arrived!'

'Thank you, Alice, please bring her to the Morning room,' and she rose again to go there her self. She was hardly in the hall when Lucy her self burst in.

'Lady Etheridge,' she cried, 'I am so sorry; it is all my fault, I just know it is, I must see her at once,' and with that she threw her self up the staircase, narrowly avoiding the descending Dr. Jamieson.

'Who, or rather, *what* was that?' pleaded the good doctor, after the departed whirlwind.

'*That,* my good sir,' she responded warmly, taking his arm, 'that was the cure to our patient's low spirits,' as much of the past weeks' difficulties suddenly became crystal clear to her, and her worries over her daughter's health evaporated. Stopping at the doorway, she turned again to Alice, a little wearily, but with a smile.

'Alice, my dear, would you be kind enough to ask Cook to prepare us some fresh tea? And then you may check on our patient, if you wish. And perhaps, when you have a moment, you would see to Miss Lucy's room and her cases.' Alice replied immediately with her curtsey, and a wide smile of appreciation for the acknowledgement of inclusion.

'Now, Doctor, let us discuss my daughter,' as she closed the Morning room door behind them.

The first week had passed in a blur, with the patient regaining strength almost by the hour. And, to tell the truth, when Lady Etheridge had the chance to examine Lucy discreetly, she had looked not much better than her own daughter. But the drawn appearance did not remain so for long. Within two days there were peals of laughter from her daughter's room, and Lady Etheridge knew enough to leave them to their own healing magic. Dr. Jamieson had prescribed some dark, foul-tasting medicine which he had impressed on them that Celia must take if she were to recover her full strength. Lady Etheridge nodded, and handed the bottle to Alice. And that was the last that was seen of it.

Alice was in fact the go-between, and her ladyship received a full report every morning of the progress of both patients.

'Alice,' asked Lady Etheridge, one morning, 'are things well with you?'

'Yes, Madam,' replied the faithful Alice.

'And my *two daughters*?' continued her ladyship.

'They are well, Madam, *very* well.'

'They must be quite a handful for you, Alice; are you sure you can manage both of them?'

'Oh, yes, Madam, quite sure.'

'But you will let me know, if you need any assistance?'

'Yes, Madam, I shall,' replied Alice carefully, making it very evident in her tone that she would rather cut off her right arm than admit anyone else to the care of her charges. But her ladyship took note to amend the situation.

In some strange way, Alice seemed to draw strength from them – and they from her in return; outside, yet a part of the relationship, somehow a member of a triad sisterhood. Not that much older than her own daughter, in age anyway – certainly less than thirty – yet possessing wisdom well beyond those years. One day she must find out more about Alice and whence she came.

She remembered only that Agnes, her then elderly personal maid, had received a request from Cook to employ an additional scullery maid – although the Household was at that moment complete. Apparently, Cook had noted that the young woman – then about 20 or so – who appeared at the kitchen door hoping for employment, was in a very poor physical and emotional state and took pity on her, providing bread and soup as the very least she could do for a fellow human being.

After that, Alice had spent the next two nights and, with hot water and soap and some decent food inside her, recovered enough to impress Cook with her general manner and deportment, once decently dressed in one of the maids' cast-off uniforms and her own rags burned.

And it was done, although she her self did not see the newcomer for at least several weeks. Really quite amazing when she looked back on it all.

With that introspection complete, she realized that she would never understand that sisterhood any more than the magic that flowed between and from her two daughters.

She was simply eternally grateful that she was able to apparently do so much, while actually doing very little, for her brother's only child.

3

The Sisterhood

It was a day in early spring some three weeks after Lucy's arrival, and they lay in the Summer House. It had not been much used in recent years, but this season the cousins had it filled with plants and flowers, and fitted out with lounging chairs and rugs against chilly days, and with a thick carpet and cushions on the floor upon which to lie. The Conservatory would have been far more convenient, for it was attached to the house it self, while the Summer House was all of one hundred yards away. It was close enough to be usefully in contact, yet far enough to be their personal refuge. They had in fact christened it 'Haven Hill', for it was on a little rise. Alice was the only other person allowed to go there; and even she had a signalling system to let her know when she was needed for some chore like tea, or when she should join them for instructions.

Lady Etheridge wisely kept her distance; if there was any thing important she needed to know, she was sure Alice would inform her. She made her contribution to the well-being of the two young ladies by adding a scullery maid to the staff, so that Alice's attendance in – or rather absence from – the kitchen did not cause any ill feeling. Nothing was said by her ladyship or Alice, except that on the third day of the addition the two of them met in the relative seclusion of the upper stair hall. Alice presented a deeper curtsey than usual, together with bowed head and a 'Thank you, Madam,' then she was gone, and no mention was made of it again. But they both knew.

As for the two cousins, they had long since forgiven any disagreeable things that might once have come between them. All it had taken was a tight hug, a long thoughtful silence, and it was gone, as if it had never been – and in a sense it never had. They were as one again – except for one particular, which Celia was determined to remove. The plan she had conceived – and fervently hoped perfected – was ready for implementation.

On this particular morning, Celia, now entirely recovered, had brought with her a brightly coloured box decorated with her own drawings, one that Lucy had not seen before. 'This is the day,' she announced boldly, 'when we plan our *Season*,' and she drew from the box a number of pieces of paper cut out of her large scrap-book.

'Now, dearest cousin, you must try not to mind me, but I do have to run through these things with you or we shall not have a good Season at all. But if you do mind, you must tell me *straight away* and I will stop and do some thing else.'

So saying, she rolled over to Lucy and looked long and deep into her eyes, then kissed her gently on the cheek, before rolling back to her place. Good thing her mother did *not* visit HH, for she strongly disapproved of young ladies rolling on the floor.

'Now, where shall I start?' – this more to her self. And in answer to her self, 'I know, let's review those parties from last year that you liked or did not like.' She pulled out several sheets of paper with much writing on them and read off where each one was located, when they were there, what they wore, and who had been there to the best of her recollection, which did not leave very much out. Then she made a new list of the ones they would make an effort to attend *this* Season, and those they would try to avoid without being rude.

'But supposing we aren't invited?' interjected Lucy, much impressed by all the work that Celia had already done, but momentarily ashamed of past doubts as to her cousin's sincerity.

Celia, watching her casually but carefully, had seen the slight shadow cross her cousin's face, was indeed half expecting it, but this question was quite a surprise. 'Not be invited? *Not be invited!* Oh, you silly goose, there has not been a dance or an outing or a ball in the *past five years* to which I have not been invited to, if I wanted to *be* there.' And she roared with laughter and rolled on the floor until Lucy joined her. But she had unintentionally mentioned a word that she had studiously avoided up 'til now; Ball. And she had caught a sign of that shadow again. 'Luncheon,' she cried gleefully, and she raised the signals for lunch and for Alice to join them. But, until it arrived, Lucy was off in her own world. After lunch, Celia promised her self, there would be the *dénouement.*

'Alice,' said Celia, looking up from the cold collation Cook had prepared, 'do you only wear black and white?'

'Celia!' replied Lucy, a little sharply; 'you know the answer very well,' picking up immediately Alice's discomfort at the question.

'No, I do not,' stoutly retorted her cousin. 'If we are going to all these dances and things,' waving her sheets of paper, 'we are going to need some one to help us. It could be Alice; but we can not take her if she only dresses like *that,*' pointing to her crisp outfit.

Lucy stopped eating, while Alice sat bolt upright in her chair in the corner. That was the first that Lucy had heard about anyone going any where with them; Celia had *indeed* been planning. All Alice could accomplish was a little squeal. 'Me?' she managed at last to get out.

'Perhaps,' replied Celia, offhandedly. 'Of course, we could find some one from the Houghton estate; Georgina says they have lots of maids. I have seen any number of *very* pretty ones there, my self,' she added to Lucy. Then looking Alice and her outfit doubtfully up and down.

'You would do, I suppose, but only if you were *really* capable of it, of course.'

Alice rose immediately in defence of an opportunity under her very nose. 'Of course I am,' she replied, spiritedly, stung by the 'very pretty ones' remark, and then remembered where she was. 'I mean, yes, Miss, I would like to try, if I might be permitted.' It was only then that she noticed the twinkle in Celia's eyes, and she dropped her head, blushing deeply with embarrassment at having been taken in so completely.

'Now look what you have done,' cried Lucy. 'You are a mean brute, Celia.'

'Yes, I am,' replied her cousin, easily, and reaching out took hold of Alice's hand to give it a squeeze. 'I am a mean pig,' she intoned. 'Please forgive me, Alice.'

Alice, still blushing, said, 'Certainly, Miss Celia, and I *would* like to do it.'

'Capital!' responded Celia, 'I will speak to Mother about it, right away.' And for the rest of the meal there was silence, each of the three with her own private thoughts.

'This afternoon, Alice,' said Celia, as she lowered the signals, 'we are going to have some private, *secret* discussions, my cousin and I, so we must not be disturbed.' Then, noting the slight flicker of disappointment on Alice's face at the exclusion, she added, 'but if you are determined to be better than the Houghton beauties, please think about colours and styles that you like, and that will make the most of your form – which, now that I look at you, is not unpleasing.' Another deeper blush from Alice here.

'As I think of it, you know those ladies' gowns' journals on my dresser?' to which Alice nodded dumbly. 'Well, take some of those, and look through them. You may do it in my room, if you like,' she continued, thinking of the ribbing that Alice would get if she took them to the Servants' Hall. Alice nodded again gratefully, all the while searching her mistress' face for signs that her leg was being pulled once more, but all she saw there was openness and sincerity. Satisfied, she jumped up, gave a little curtsey and a 'Thank you, Miss,' and rushed out; then remembered she had forgotten the luncheon tray, and had to rush back in again.

'Alice,' called Celia, rising and indicating to Alice to put down the tray, then taking both her hands.

'Yes, Miss?'

'I do mean it, Alice, really,' which flustered poor Alice even more, so that she could only stammer, 'Yes, Miss, thank you, Miss. I will try very hard to be worthy of you and Miss Lucy, really I will,' and then she was gone, the tray wobbling precariously.

Lucy had taken all this in with increasing amazement, quite forgetting her own troubles in the exchange she had just witnessed. 'But will Aunt Charlotte approve of what you have done?'

'I think so,' replied her cousin, taking up her accustomed position on the red cushions.

'But the cost,' countered Lucy, settling in to her yellow ones.

'Oh, I do not think that will cause a problem,' Celia replied, again with a great deal of self-assurance. Lucy continued to look doubtful, but said no more. What she did not know, what nobody knew, outside the immediate family circle, was that Celia had a substantial private income; was indeed a wealthy young woman. She could have employed Alice as her own private maid, had she wished, and bought all the dresses needed. In fact, probably *would* pay for them; that was only fair.

But for Lucy, all this self-assurance was some thing of a shock. This was a side of her carefree cousin of which there had never been even a hint. But she had two shocks still to come, one she knew about and was dreading; the other that she was vaguely aware of but had pushed aside because she had no answer to it.

'Well, what now, dearest Cousin? We have made a good start, but there are two more things we have to write in before we can make our social rounds.' At this, she rolled over towards her cousin until their foreheads were nearly touching, and she was looking directly into Lucy's eyes. Taking both hands in hers, so that she could feel Lucy's racing pulse, she said simply: 'There are five Balls in this Season, of which we can only attend three; and we must settle what you are to wear.'

The pounding was so great in Lucy's own ears as Celia raised both her spectres in one simple sentence of doom, that she thought it might be heard at the house, while the panic that gripped her heart turned her face a deathly white.

None of this excess of emotions was missed by Celia, although the extreme pallor of Lucy's face was quite worrying. 'Let us take the Balls first,' she went on, as if nothing had happened, 'because that will affect your choice of the gowns.' She was deliberately returning to the more dreaded of the pair as she casually rolled away to pick up her paper and crayon, but resting an ankle against her cousin to retain a physical contact.

'Now,' she said, almost to her self, 'let's list the five, in the order they will occur,' consulting her papers. She glanced at Lucy in passing, noting that not a muscle of her features had changed. But at least she hadn't fainted dead away as initially feared.

'First,' she continued, writing away, 'comes Lord Houghton's, that is always first, by tradition, and a "must" for anyone seriously into The Season. That is at Houghton Hall, of course,' she added. Now looking at Lucy: 'You have already met Georgina, but not Geraldine and her brothers Geoffrey and Jeremy. Easy to remember; all "Gs", in sound, anyway.' And she turned back to her paper, having seen a slight lessening of the tension in Lucy's features.

'Then there is a choice: it is either the Debenham's, or Col. Fawcett. Can not attend both because they are too far apart. We have to spend at least four nights away, and that all has to be arranged. We will talk about which of the young men of the family you like most – or,' and she laughed – 'the ones you dislike the least, and that may decide it,' and she put a question mark against the two of them.

'Then there is the Hunt Ball,' she continued, in as easy a manner as she could muster, for she had detected a sudden tremor against her ankle. 'I am sure you remember; the one you attended last year, always held at the Greville Estate, although there are no more Grevilles; now it is Baron Otto Blackmoor – or was. His widow is Baroness Hilda von Schwartzen-heide, to give her the proper Prussian name. I hardly remember him, for he has been gone for many years, and spent the last of those in Berlin, as I recollect. They have no offspring, but her niece, Winifred, was at the Ball, although you may not remember her for she is a rather plain girl and quite shy.

'That really is a "must" – unless, of course, you'd rather not go back there,' with a glance here at the frozen face of Lucy, rigid once more. 'And last, and probably least, is the County Ball, but this year it is being held at quite the most dismal place in the County, so nobody will be going to that one.'

But Lucy lay there, as if she had not even heard, staring straight ahead, seeing nothing.

'In between there are lots of other fun things to do,' proceeded Celia, smoothly, 'that we will talk about once we have settled the major ones. So what do you think, Cousin?' and she rolled over until she was on her back looking up into Lucy's face, still staring straight ahead. As she did so, two large tears welled up in Lucy's eyes, rolled down her cheeks, and plopped onto Celia's upturned forehead, followed quickly by two more that landed on her cheeks.

'Why, whatever is the matter, you silly goose? Now you have made me all wet,' reaching down to wipe her face with the hem of her dress.

'You do not understand,' whispered Lucy, 'I can not go to *any* of them.'

'Can not go?' echoed Celia, sitting up abruptly and staring open-mouthed at her cousin. '*CAN NOT GO*? Of course you can go; *every body* goes during the Season. I never heard such nonsense in all my born days!'

But Lucy continued to shake her head. 'No, you do *not understand*. I haven't even *one* ball-gown that is suitable, much less three or four,' and the tears rolled down faster than ever, plopping onto the carpet.

'Oh, dear,' cried Celia, 'you really must stop that; you will have us quite flooded out in a minute, and we will both go floating through the door into the lake to be fished out like fat trout.' At this ludicrous picture, Lucy's solemn countenance broke into a faint smile.

'That is better!' cried Celia, 'we need a little sunshine.' At those words, the obliging sun really did break through the clouds overhead and stream through the glass roof onto them, causing Lucy to raise her tear-streaked face to its warmth and to give a real little laugh.

'Much better,' continued Celia, and she rose to drag two more cushions to where they lay, and placed them side by side. 'Come and lie down here, my little sister. For you are my sister, you know, because you need an awful lot of looking after.'

When they were lying comfortably facing each other, Celia continued, 'I can see that I am going to have to explain some things to you.' She took up Lucy's hand, which she found to be ice cold, and commenced rubbing it briskly. Then she reached for travelling rugs to spread over the two of them.

'There, that is better, is it not?' and was gratified to receive Lucy's nod of response.

'Firstly,' she started off, 'you do not *need* three or four ball-gowns; because . . . ,' she said carefully, and slowly, 'to the Hunt Ball, you will be wearing the cream satin. We will fix it up, of course, but that is very important.'

At the words 'Hunt Ball', Lucy's hand tightened its grip on her own. And when she mentioned the cream satin, the haunted look was back in Lucy's eyes, the colour draining from her face again, and the grip of her fingers so strong that Celia thought that one of them might actually be done an injury.

'Secondly,' she continued, as if she had noticed nothing at all, 'if you need ball-gowns, two or three or four even, then *I will get them for you.*'

The look of panic was instantly replaced by a wide-eyed one of amazement. 'You?' gasped Lucy. 'How can *you* get them for me?'

'Why, we will go to Town, of course, and have them fitted properly. It will be fun,' she said lightly, 'and we will stay with Aunt Julia and Cousins Emily and Charlotte, named for Mother, you know.' But Lucy did not know. 'You will like them,' Celia bubbled on, 'they are great fun, and Aunt puts on the most fabulous "Town" parties. They are quite different, you know.' But Lucy again shook her head. She did not know that either.

'Oh, quite different,' gushed Celia. 'They are ever so . . .' but Lucy broke in this time, her words coming in a rush of emotion and anguish.

'The outlay, Celia, I simply cannot afford that sort of thing. I have to be very careful,' dropping her eyes and voice in the embarrassment of raising such a personal matter as one's financial situation.

'Oh, that!' said Celia, easily, leaning forward to kiss her cousin's still damp cheeks. 'I mean that I will *buy* them for you, silly.' And Lucy's eyes popped wide open again in even greater astonishment.

'*You,*' she gasped again. 'How can you possibly afford *that*? They are very expensive,' she added, dropping her eyes again in continued embarrassment. 'And *London!*' popping them open again, 'they must cost the *earth* there!' She stared in wide-eyed wonder at this cousin she thought she knew, in the discovery that she barely knew her at all.

'Come here,' said Celia, putting a hand on her shoulder and drawing her closer. 'I have some thing to tell you. But first you must promise to tell no one. It is only known to the family; but you are one of the family now because you are my little sister. Promise? Cross fingers?' Celia felt down to the hand she had been holding. 'Now the other one?' And Lucy poked it out, crossed, from under the rug; smiling again at the ridiculousness of it all.

'Good,' continued Celia, seriously. 'You see, dear Sister, when I was eighteen, on my birthday to be exact, two of my uncles settled a quite large sum of money on me, in trust, and in my name solely because I seem to be the only girl in that side of the family. I had to sign a lot of papers, and it was quite exciting really. So, sweet Sister, I *really can* afford a ball-gown or two.'

'Really?' replied Lucy.

'Really and truly, little Sister.' And they hugged each other tightly for several minutes.

'One more thing,' said Celia, as they broke apart. 'As my sister now, I intend to see that you are happy. No more sad faces. And we *are* going to solve that little difficulty that you seem to have with that *cream satin dress!*

'Now what!' cried Celia, as the tears started down Lucy's cheeks again. But Lucy shook her head, 'Nothing,' she replied, 'I am just so happy.'

'Really?'

'Really and truly,' responded the now-glowing Lucy. And the tears on their cheeks mingled together as they embraced.

'Enough of that,' exclaimed Celia, jumping up several minutes later, 'we have things to do.' So saying, she rushed outside and began pulling on a large bell. 'Oh, where is that lazy girl?' she called out loudly.

'Do you not remember?' said Lucy, joining her in the doorway of the Summer House; 'you gave her the afternoon off.'

'Yes, of course,' said Celia, turning to look at her cousin, 'we did, didn't we,' stressing the 'we' both times. 'Come on, then.' She grabbed Lucy's hand, and rushed her across the lawn towards the house, only to meet Alice in the middle, rushing the other way.

'Where have you *been*, Alice? We have been waiting for *ab-so-lute-ly a-ges.*'

'But, Miss, you gave instruc . . . ,' then Celia interrupted her by grabbing her hand while Lucy took the other and they danced her 'round and 'round until they all fell in a heap on the grass, Celia and Lucy rolling over and over, laughing and crying at the same time. Finally, Celia put her elbows on the grass and said simply, 'You do not understand, do you, Alice?'

'No, Miss,' replied the utterly bewildered Alice.

'Never mind, Alice, you will, in time. You will.' And the two girls looked at each other and burst into laughter and tears all over again.

'Alice,' said Celia, when she had finally regained some sort of composure. 'We are in need of a bowl of warm water and a cloth, and some other things for our faces, as you can see,' and Alice nodded. 'Would you please be good enough to bring them to the Haven, and then we will have some tea, and you can bring the pictures of dresses and shoes and ribbons and things that you have selected for your self and we will talk about it all. And, Alice,'

'Yes, Miss?'

'Please bring my silver high-heeled slippers, and a dress of yours in *any other colour than black!*'

Dinner was over, and they had just finished coffee when Lady Etheridge rose and addressed them both.

'Celia, Lucy, I would like you to join me in the Library.'

Without waiting for a reply, she rang the bell.

'Alice, please bring some fresh coffee to the Library.'

Then she led the way, the two young women following. Celia was surprised to find the fire already burning in the hearth, for they hardly ever used this room now.

'Please sit down, my dear,' this to Lucy, for her daughter was already plopped in a chair and comfortable. 'I wish to talk to both of you, but especially to you, my dear,' turning again to Lucy.

'You know that I invited you to come and stay with us, but at the time you were not able. Then there was . . . ,' she paused, briefly, searching for the right word, 'there was a change of . . . let us call it a renewed opportunity. It is not of the slightest importance as to what it was,' this last directly to her daughter, who smiled with nervous relief. 'Let me just say that I am glad,' continued her ladyship, 'very glad, indeed, that you *were* able to come.

'Now, I would like, personally, to renew that offer to stay with us for as long as you should wish, to consider this your home should you choose to do so,' adding with a slight frown in the direction of her daughter, 'I believe I speak for my daughter also, if that quite disgraceful scene on the south lawn this afternoon is any thing to judge by. I believe the staff will also welcome you in the house, my dear, for it is their home also. Especially that young tear-about, Alice. I do not know what has got into the girl since the two of you have made the Summer House into your second home!'

Turning now to her daughter once more, 'Oh, yes. I ran into Alice coming out of your room carrying several of the dress journals, and was advised that she had received your permission both to be there and to have them. I hope you know what you are doing on that score, young lady.'

'Yes, Mother, that is quite correct. And, yes, I believe I do.'

'Good,' responded her mother, without a great deal of conviction in her voice. And yet there was some thing in her daughter's manner that spoke of a new confidence and sureness of her self, some thing of which she thoroughly approved.

In the silence which followed, Lucy looked from her aunt to her cousin, then back again, unsure and not wishing to appear too eager in acceptance, but knowing that her life back home would be a dull affair indeed, and that she might easily fall prey once more to the blight of winter that she had only just shaken off.

Lady Etheridge broke the moment of embarrassment by adding, 'You may take as long as you like to decide, my dear; but there are two questions that must be addressed, and fairly soon: the legal position with your guardian, and the clothes left at your own house.'

'Aunt Charlotte, I do not see any difficulty with my guardian, and I could easily get my own things from home and be back when you choose to invite me.'

'No you jolly well could not,' broke in Celia, before her mother could speak again. 'You jolly well might not *come* back!'

'Celia!' retorted her mother immediately, 'what a dreadful way to talk to your cousin.'

'You do not know, Mother, what I have gone through, what I have had to put up with, just to get this silly goose of a cousin of mine to even be *sitting* here right now! And she is jolly well not going to get away that easily!'

'Well, that was rather impolitely put, my child,' chided her mother; 'but I think I *do* have some inkling,' this last with a twinkle in her eye. 'Perhaps I have more understanding than you give me credit for.'

'Aunt Charlotte, I thank you most kindly for the offer, but,' and here it was Celia's turn to go pale while she awaited the fateful words of rejection, in an agony of dread that she had pushed Lucy too far that afternoon. 'That is, if you are quite sure that I would not be intruding?' and receiving a shake of the head from her aunt, continued, 'Then I would like to accept your most generous offer.'

The explosion of sound from Celia's corner of the room was a combination of exhaled breath too long held and a loud 'whoopee!' as Celia bounded out of her chair and was hugging Lucy before she could move, and then the same with her mother, with a whispered 'Thank you, Mother, you have made me the happiest daughter in the world,' and was back in her chair in one almost continuous whirl of motion.

'Really, Celia!' exclaimed her mother, though not unkindly. 'You must try to control your self. Lucy, you must try to forgive my *other* daughter; she has still to understand the meaning of some words; like "decorum" and "deportment". You would be advised not to emulate her in many of her characteristics, for they are for the most part decidedly flawed.'

But she smiled, for she was not displeased, since Celia was also clearly improving in many ways as a result of Lucinda's presence.

'But I am quite delighted, my dear, at your acceptance, and we shall *both* try our best to make you feel at home here. This brings me to one final, somewhat delicate point. Please respond as you deem appropriate, for I do understand the sensitivity of what I am about to suggest.

'As I shall henceforth regard you as my daughter in every sense of the word, equal in every respect – except that I may on occasion prefer your quiet composure to that of my *elder daughter* – I would be honoured if you could find it comfortable to address me as "Mother", but I leave that entirely to you.

'Now, we must seal our little agreement.' She walked across to the liquor cabinet and drew out a bottle of brandy and several glasses.

'This was your father's favourite Cognac, Celia.'

Turning first to Lucy, who wrinkled up her nose at the thought of liquor, and then to her daughter, who did the same. 'Very well,' and she poured out three cups of coffee, before putting several drops from the bottle into each. 'Come,' she said, 'you will not notice this little amount.'

So they drank a toast in laced coffee. From Lady Etheridge; 'to my *two* daughters,' they adding to each other, 'to my new sister,' and Lucy appending, 'to my new mother.'

'Now, my daughters, I think that is quite enough excitement for one day. I suggest the two of you are going to need your beauty sleep if you are going to be the Belles of the Ball that I know you can be.' And she kissed and hugged them both at the same time, after which the two left with their arms around each other, giggling and laughing as they tumbled *up* the stairs, leaving the bemused Lady Etheridge to wonder whether a few drops of brandy could really work that quickly.

But the warm feeling that spread throughout her being as they departed was most assuredly not occasioned by the brandy.

Lucy was down rather late for breakfast, having been exhausted by the previous day's emotional excesses. But now she was feeling refreshed and eager for the day's activities. 'Good morning – Mother,' she said, a little hesitantly.

'Good morning, *Daughter*,' replied her ladyship. 'It does take a little getting used to, doesn't it?' And Lucy nodded. 'Did you know, my dear, that it was I who suggested the name "Lucinda"?'

This time Lucy shook her head; 'No, Mother.'

'Well, it was, and I liked it because it has such a lovely sound to it. But my brother, your father that is, he would insist that you were just his "Lucy". And so it has been.'

Lucy looked around but Celia was nowhere to be seen. 'Shall we wait for Ce . . . for my sister?'

'Oh, no, my dear; she had her breakfast long ago, before even I came down. She is out some where I believe. *Most* unusual.'

So Lucy had breakfast together with her new mother, which was probably a good idea now and then, if she were to get to know her better, and they chatted amiably about every thing in general and nothing in particular.

But remembering all the excitement of yesterday, she was anxious to get off and find out what her new sister was up to. Celia did not usually get up early; was in fact a bit of a lie-abed. Some thing was definitely 'up'.

As soon as she could decently leave the Breakfast room, Lucy rushed to the Haven; but found no sign of Celia. Nowhere to be seen in the grounds, either. Perhaps the lake; and down at the boathouse Lucy found signs of activity. The 'long boat', as they called it for it was certainly long, had been lowered into the water from its winter storage rack. The oars were ready in the rowlocks, and there were two folding chairs, a table, and a couple of sausage-like things in the bow. But no big sister.

She was hurrying back to the house, half-afraid that whatever it was might go on without her, when two laden figures rounded the corner and came towards her. It was Celia and Alice. 'Here,' called Celia, putting one of the bags she was carrying on the ground. 'If you are going to live here, you are jolly well going to have to earn your keep. I seem to have to do all the work around here!' And she stopped and waited 'til Lucy had reached them.

'Good morning, little Sister,' then added, 'It is all right, Alice knows.'

'Good morning, big Sister. Good morning, Alice. Lovely day.'

A curtsey, a smile, and, 'Good morning, Miss Lucy. Yes, Miss.'

'Well, I never!' responded Celia. 'Are you two going to stand there all day talking about the weather?'

'Is she usually this belligerent, Alice? Or only when she gets up early in the morning?'

'Sometimes, Miss Lucy,' replied the grinning Alice, beginning to understand how the two young 'ladies' behaved when they were together.

'Belay that you scallywags, or, shiver m' timbers I will have the lot of ye scrubbin' th' quarterdeck, afore walkin' th' plank. As for you, m' beauty,' rounding on Alice, 'I will have *you* rowin' the lake an even dozen, *in each direction!*' growled Celia. But all she got for her jolly buccaneer talk was a hoot of laughter from Lucy, and a broad smile from Alice.

'Ye gads,' roared Cap'n C, ''tis a mutiny afore we're underway!' Dropping the other things she was carrying, she strode empty-handed down to the long boat. 'Mr. Mate,' she called, 'I be awaitin' t' be piped aboard. Be lively about it, or 'tis m' cat o' nine tails ye mutinous squabs 'll be feelin'!'

But Lucy could only roar with laughter. At last, when she could catch a breath, she said to Alice, 'Shall we?'

'All right, Miss,' replied Alice, and they picked up the bundles, which really weren't that heavy and strolled leisurely down to the boat and stowed the cargo. Then Alice handed Lucy aboard, and Lucy returned the favour.

All this time the Cap'n was standing, arms akimbo, one foot on an upturned bucket, waiting to be piped aboard. 'Step lively there, Mister,' and Lucy moved to the bow while Alice took the stern. Now Lucy raised her hands to her mouth and called through them, 'Ready to board, Cap'n.'

'Cap'n comin' aboard,' was the response, and as soon as she put one foot on the gunn'l, Lucy issued a trilling set of 'pipes', which quite astonished the other two.

'Where on earth did you learn to do that?' said the captain, quite forgetting the sea-talk.

''Tis me secret,' replied the Mate, having learned bird-calls from her father, 'and it'll cost ye a pirate's ransom t' find out.' And the two of them laughed so hard that they nearly fell out of the boat. Probably would have done had they not held on to one another.

'Time to go,' said Celia, when she was seated in the stern, with Lucy in the bow, and Alice at the oars. 'I mean, "Shove off"', Mr. Mate. Let go, for'd,' and Lucy slipped the painter; 'Let go, aft,' and Celia her self pushed against the dock.

'Under way, Cap'n,' cried Mate Lucy.

'Avast there. Topside, Mr. Mate. Man t' Mains'l, Gallants, T'gallants, trim th' Mizzen,' shouted the Cap'n. 'Pull! you slovenly landlubbers, or by thunder I will have yer gizzards fer . . .' This was just too much for First Mate Lucy, who fell forward in a paroxysm of laughter, bumping Midshipman Alice just as she was about to drive the oars into the water, causing her to catch two crabs simultaneously (a memorable feat) and nearly drowning the Cap'n, who, giving a loud and most unmanly shriek, managed to get out 'you scurvy knaves,' before she, too, was doubled up in the bottom of the boat, convulsed with laughter. Fortunately, having only just been placed in the water, the bottom was quite dry, even though the Cap'n was not.

'Blackbeard's Cove, Middy!' bellowed the Cap'n, when some semblance of order was restored among the crew. 'You know where to take her in?'

'Yes, Miss.'

'Aye, Aye, Cap'n,' roared the Captain. 'Why, shiver m' timbers; I'll see the lot o' ye keel-hauled afore the sun is over the yardarm!'

'Aye, Aye, Cap'n,' replied faithful Middy Alice with a broad smile, rowing steadily and easily for such a large boat, while the others lay back on the cushions, quite exhausted from all the hilarity.

Around the back of the island, where Lucy had not yet been, was a little pebbled cove, marked with a crude sign that said: 'BLAKBeeRdS COVe'. Alice, with scarcely a backward glance, drove hard for this, beaching her expertly alongside a jutting flat rock, so that her charges could step out without getting their feet wet, then handing up the items for their outing.

'Shiver m' timbers,' said the still dripping Cap'n, 'that was a stormy passage, Mr. Mate; the wettest voyage ever!'

'I am very sorry, Miss,' replied Alice, quite ashamed of her perform-ance, only to receive a shoulder squeeze from Lucy as she was stepping out and a quiet, 'That was excellently done, Alice. Thank you,' receiving a little curtsey and a demure smile of appreciation in response, while Celia nodded and gave Alice an absent-minded wave of dismissal.

At this signal, Alice expertly shoved off the pebble beach and, with a few deft pulls, turned the long boat and quietly and effortlessly slipped out of sight.

The cove opened up to a clearing on the highest point of the island, which also had a dilapidated arrow sign pointing downward that declared: 'TReshuR', with the 'Rs' printed backwards, and a tattered Jolly Roger fluttering above it. Lucy smiled to her self in an understanding of where all the sea-talk came from and who had spent many a long day of preten-sions and digging for treasure. In a sudden flash of comprehension, she also understood that it indicated a lonely childhood and a longing for companionship. And she reached out to take her sister's hand to give it a good squeeze, as if to say that it was all now in the past.

When every thing from the 'Golden Hind' had been carried to a clearing just out of sight of the landing, the folding chairs were set up with the table. The 'sausages' turned out to be hammocks, which Celia took to the north edge of the clearing, after squinting at the sun.

'These will do nicely,' she said, pointing to several young trees fairly close together. 'I will use this one for the bow.' Handing one of the hammocks to Lucy, she added, 'You take the other tree there, and use a clove hitch, not too tight so that the tree can breathe, and then finish with a throat turn and a couple of half-hitches. You see? Just like that,' and turned to see how her sister was coping.

'Now that *is* interesting. I do believe you have invented a new knot,' giving the free end a quick jerk, whereupon every thing fell to the ground in a heap, narrowly missing their toes.

'I tried to follow, but you did it all so quickly,' apologized Lucy, morti-fied at the spectacular nature of her failure.

'Years of practice,' replied Celia. 'Never mind; just watch,' and seizing the rope, 'around here, like that, over here, under there, 'round the fixed end, through the throat with a little slack, and then the halfs. There,' and she stood back to survey her handiwork. 'Not bad,' she said, only half to her self, for she was enjoying her sister's amazement at her knots' skill.

'Now the stern,' and to Lucy's great relief, 'let's do these together. Not too bad, for a beginner,' she added, a little condescendingly. 'But the half-hitches have to lie in the same direction, there, like that, and a bit tighter. Now the other one. There, see how easy it is?' which only caused Lucy greater consternation.

'Now, those lashings, please,' she said, pointing over by the chairs. But Lucy could not find any thing that looked like a whip.

'There, you goose, those short pieces of rope, those are lashings.'

Lucy was beginning to feel distinctly clumsy and unwanted. 'Here,' she said, a bit grumpily, 'Nobody ever told me these things.'

'Oh, come here, you silly goose; do you not understand?' and gave Lucy a fierce hug. 'No? Well, how could you.

'First, one of the under-gardeners was on a Ship o' the Line at Trafalgar, and he told me all about it when I was little. That is how I know all about topgallants, and mizzenmasts and knots and things nautical. I once took a painting from the Library to the garden shed, and he pointed out the sails and spars and gave all their names. He was very excited about it, because it was the *Illustrious*, the very one he had served on. And told me tales of where he had been and how the sailors lived aboard, and the captain's quarters and the mess deck and things like that. And the battles he had been in, and the big guns and broadsides, and how they "cleared the decks for action" by completely dismantling the junior officers' quarters in a matter of minutes, and ever so much more,' she finished, breathlessly. 'And I have never forgotten it; maybe I should have been a sailor.' She paused, making a little face. 'But Daddy, he was *very* cross; he said it was a very valuable painting, and promised me a taste of the Gunner's Mate if I ever did it again.

'And second,' taking a long breath before giving Lucy a look from under her long lashes, 'second, because I am a mean pig. I have never had anyone to show off to, you know, except Alice, of course, but she doesn't . . . well, it is not the same. And now I do!' Then she seized Lucy's hands. 'I will try to keep it under control. Forgiven?'

'Forgiven,' replied her new sister, 'but neither did I, so watch out,' and laughed, and squeezed Celia's hands in return.

The two hammocks were lashed side by side, 'so do you now see why they are called that?' explained Celia, and then, 'so you will not fall out.'

Then she added the boat cushions, 'otherwise you will have a diamond back, like those snakes, you know,' at which horrid thought, Lucy shuddered and carefully examined the ground around her for any signs of movement.

'Now, I want to do a little sketching, and you can, too, if you like, for I have two of every thing. And there are several books to read, as well as some rather good poetry. Indeed, you might like to read some of those aloud to me while I work.

'And if it is fine tomorrow, we can try a little swimming,' at which Lucy made a face, but said nothing.

Celia stood back and surveyed it all. 'Perfect,' she declared. 'It only remains now to prepare my self for the Ball,' ignoring Lucy's puzzled look. First she put a large cloth bag on the table and opened it, pulling out two pairs of slippers. The pale green ones she put on one chair, 'match your eyes,' she said to Lucy. 'Mine are pink,' and put them on her chair. 'No, not my eyes, silly; but these are all I have.

'Now for my Botticelli impersonation,' and reaching under her long skirt, struggled to undo some thing.

'Botticelli?' said Lucy, puzzled.

'Yes,' said Celia, as her first petticoat fell to the ground at her feet. 'The one of Venus,' watching Lucy's eyes getting bigger by the moment. 'You know, on that big oyster shell,' and Lucy's eyes nearly popped out of her head as the famous painting registered and the second petticoat fell, and Celia's legs became clearly visible through her voile skirt.

'You are not going . . . you can not . . . it isn't . . .,' gasped Lucy, her open mouth now as big as her eyes.

'Decent?' teased Celia. 'No, I am not; not right now, anyway, but I might tomorrow!' she added wickedly, and proceeded to undo the buttons of her damp blouse. 'There, that'll do, for now.' And turning to the chair, put one foot upon it, raised her flimsy skirt up over her knee, undid her boots, rolled down her stocking, and pulled on a pink slipper.

'That is a lot better,' she said, as she completed the other leg. 'Now it is your turn,' and swung her self up into the hammock. 'Come on, I need you to balance the other side of this hammock,' as she wallowed dangerously to one side.

'I could not do that,' gasped Lucy, shaking her head vigorously, still not quite believing what she had just witnessed.

'As you wish, it is your body, but get up here quickly; this is most uncomfortable,' and she put out her hand to help Lucy on the far side.

'Ah, that is *much* better,' she sighed. 'And just in time, for here comes the sun.' As if on command, the sun did indeed gradually emerge from the edge of a cloudlet to pour out its warmth fully on them both.

'Pity to waste it,' she added a moment later, sitting up carefully. 'You never know just how long it is going to last this time of year,' as she undid the buttons on each sleeve, removed the blouse, and placed it on the hammock ropes behind her head to dry. Then she slipped off the shoulders of her under garments to bare her white shoulders, and pushed them down to generously expose her upper bosom, before pulling it back to a careful line.

'There, that is how it is done,' she explained, to no-one in particular, finally raising her skirt to above her knees. Then she closed her eyes, and settled back for a little sleep in the warm sunshine. Lucy, still fully clothed from ankle to throat to wrist, including her boots, said a little plaintively, 'What did you do that for?'

'Do what for?' responded Celia, sleepily, knowing full well what was meant.

'Well,' said Lucy, hesitantly, 'exposing your . . . your upper . . . chest like that.'

'Oh, that,' replied Celia nonchalantly, opening first one eye then the other. 'Well, just imagine you are in your new ball-gown, and it is *quite* low cut,' and Lucy nodded hesitantly. 'Good; then if your chest is a nice even brown – no strap marks showing, mind – it sets off your pearls beautifully. But, and this is the really important part, your bosom is still quite white, and if you get the line just right, then it looks bigger, and the young men notice that.'

'They do?' queried Lucy, in some wonder.

'They do,' opined Celia.

'And then?'

'Well firstly, the young men see that from the other side of the room as if it were a beacon. Then you get a lot more attention and requests for dances. After that it depends on you and how much you like the young man.'

'I see,' said Lucy, still a little puzzled by the need for it all. 'Do all the young ladies do it?'

'Only the ones with any sense; the ones who do not want to end up as old maids. Am I going to have an old maid for a younger sister?'

'No. That is, I hope not, of course.'

'So, that is why you have to do some thing about it, that only you can do. You are doing it for your self.'

'Really?' said the still doubtful Lucy.

'Really, little Sister.'

'All right then, I will try it just this once. Help me down.' And Celia held out her hand for Lucy to lower her self slowly to the ground. 'But you are not to look! Promise?'

'I shall be asleep in a minute if you do not hurry. I promise,' and in a moment or two Celia heard the rustle and slither of petticoats.

She was almost asleep, for she had been up a good deal longer than Lucy that morning and had been too excited to sleep properly into the bargain, when Lucy called from the far side of the hammocks. 'Help me up then, but keep your eyes closed!'

Celia felt for her sister's arm, which was bare, and her shoulder, which was likewise. 'Good, now copy mine to get that line just right, and let's get a little rest,' and promptly fell into a dreamless sleep.

Lucy was not so fortunate. She was at first quite uncomfortable and kept looking around to see if anyone was watching. But as Celia had pointed out, it *was* a private island in a private lake, and their property went all the way 'round it and much farther out than that. Celia was right about the sun, too; it did feel gloriously warm on her skin and gradually induced the sleep her sister was already enjoying.

It was almost an hour later when Celia stirred, and put out her hand to feel if Lucy were still there. 'Good,' she murmured, 'I thought you might have swum back to the landing.'

'You are being silly, Celia. Besides, I can not swim.'

'You can not swim?' said Celia, turning her head to look at Lucy, and giving an inward nod of satisfaction as she observed the carefully defined 'sunshine line'. 'Well, well. We will just have to fix that. We will have luncheon in a while, when I have wakened up properly. After that, I have told Alice to be back for Four O'clock Tea, so we have plenty of time to our selves.

After a most satisfying luncheon that Cook had prepared, Celia opined: 'Now I am going to do a little sketching of that rock over there, the one with the pretty tree hanging over it and the moss and flowers growing 'round it. Perhaps you would like to read me some poetry while I work. Tennyson will do nicely – or any thing that suits your fancy,' taking those very things from another bag that she had carefully set aside.

'But suppose Alice comes back and sees you like that?', indicating Celia's almost see-through garments, for she her self had slipped back into her under-things in the seclusion of nearby trees immediately upon rising – so she did not see Celia's deep frown and sad shake of the head as she had done so.

Celia's face registered considerable surprise at this question. 'She has seen me like this ever since I was a child,' raising her dress to the knee, 'every time she bathes me, silly,' giving a slight smile at Lucy's shocked appraisal of her sister's undeniable charms through the thin slip. 'Besides, who is here to see me like this?' spreading arms wide and twirling on one slippered toe in a tight circle, so that her skirt billowed out well above the knee.

'Mind you, I can think of any number of my admirers who would give their right arm to see before them what you are now observing,' hands on her hips, thrusting out her chest to emphasize what she knew to be her most attractive feature.

'Now to work,' picking up her prepared canvas and charcoal. 'But when we return tomorrow I intend to talk about those "tingles" that have been bothering you,' noting her sister go pale. 'And if you intend to understand it, I expect to see more of you than you are now showing,' at which her sister crossed her arms over her bosom as if to protect her virtue, although she was fully clad from head to toe.

'And it is no good looking like that, my girl. You'd better get used to the idea or we shall not bother to come', turning back to her canvas and commencing her sketching. Meanwhile Lucy remained unmoving, still shocked by the recent uninhibited display of her sister's barely concealed form.

Eventually she moved to pick up the book of poetry and seated her self, but it was quite a while before she trust her voice to read aloud, her thoughts still quivering as she tried to imagine her self as Celia had just been attired – or rather unattired.

But the inner vision was completely denied her and she knew that she could not make another visit to the island if that were the price of admission.

4

Secrets

For the next two days, the weather was cloudy and dull with light showers, so no trip to the island was possible. They were also decidedly tense days for Lucy, though she tried to act normally. Her new mother noted the difference immediately but kept her concern to her self.

As for Celia, she wisely kept busy in her studio, giving Lucy time to work out for her self what she was prepared to reveal of her inner feelings and her outer form.

But the third day dawned bright and warm and after breakfast, at Celia's suggestion, the two sisters strolled down to the lake. Seated on a convenient bench, it was a while before either of them spoke, and it was Celia who broke the strained silence.

'Well, what is it to be, Sister?' and lapsed into silence once more. It was a long while before Lucy replied.

'What is it that I have to do?' she finally whispered, although there was not another soul around to hear them.

Respecting her sister's reluctance, Celia replied in a similar whisper; 'Nothing much, really. First we must talk about some of the things that have been bothering you, and secondly we must talk about those tingles,' taking her sister's hand and gently stroking it.

'And that is it?' responded Lucy, at which Celia nodded. 'But do I have to . . . to dance about as you did that last time,' her voice now barely audible, at which Celia simply burst into laughter.

'Heavens, no! You act as you see fit, as shall I. But I suggest you be a little more casually dressed than you are now,' rising to show her own attire which was a much shorter skirt and a simple blouse and light open shoes, before reseating her self.

Finally Lucy rose and looked down at her sister. 'Well if that is it, I think I might accept your suggestion.'

'Very well,' replied Celia, 'I will see Alice about some luncheon and the boat while you go and change into some thing lighter, like mine,' rising also to face her sister, then giving her a light reassuring hug before taking her arm to return to the house.

Once back in her room, Lucy struggled with the question of whether she could be attired with as little on as her sister, though she had a blouse that was very similar. Eventually settled, though still uneasy in her mind, she was surprised to find Celia and Alice already in the long boat – unaware that it had all been arranged the evening before!

'Good,' was Celia's only response as Alice shoved off with an oar and rowed steadily, expertly landing and removing the few stowed bags, before departing as skilfully without a word being spoken.

With the hammocks already in place it was the work of a few moments for Celia to remove her undergarments, these being much fewer than the last time, though Lucy still required her sister to close her eyes before she was installed in her hammock.

'Now that we are relaxed and warm and comfortable, we had better talk about the coming Hunt Ball, for it isn't that far away now. First, though, we need to know a bit more about the last one.' At which, Lucy turned her eyes upward to the leafy overhead and remained silent.

Celia reached out to take Lucy's hand, only to find it clenched.

'Of course, you were only my cousin then, but now as your sister I had better tell you what I know, first. You certainly met some one.' Silence.

'A man, of course.' Silence, but she felt Lucy' arm stiffen.

'It was when you left us, and went into the salon with those family paintings.' This time she received the slightest of nods.

'But then you disappeared, for you did not come out again,' and Lucy's body seemed to go rigid.

'Must be a secret door in that panelling,' whereupon Lucy relaxed enough to look enquiringly at her sister, surprised by the level of Celia's insight, but she kept her silence still.

'Then you reappeared,' Celia continued, confident now that she was on the right track and that the mystery would soon be revealed, 'just as suddenly as you disappeared. By then, whatever it was, had happened,' and Lucy's pale face and bright eyes with a tightening of the hand were all the answer needed.

'So there is another room behind that room?'

But this time Lucy shook her head. 'A corridor,' she whispered, speaking for the first time, and it was Celia's turn to nod.

'A corridor with doors off it? He was in one of those?'

Again a shake of the head, and a whispered, 'A little staircase, that went up to a room,' then silence.

'Well, what sort of room?' prodded Celia. 'Big, small, round, square?'

Again the whisper; 'Octagonal.'

Lucy's intensely personal encounter had been bottled up inside so long that it was in danger of suppressing her own nature. In truth, she knew that she desperately needed some one in whom she could confide, some sympathetic soul who would not judge her for her actions, good or bad. If not her new sister, who else would be as understanding? And slowly, piece by piece, the story unfolded, with gentle questioning and nodding and a few 'and thens' and 'after thats'.

'Was there any thing else in the room?'

'There were a number of old paintings on the walls – you know, portraits of ancestors and suchlike. And a little modern one on the table titled "Die Aushöhlung" – that would be "The Hollow" in English, of course.'

'In Sachsen, eh? That is unusual; although the Blackmoors are indeed from that area around Prussia, and were originally called "Schwartzen-heide", as you now know, so that could explain it. Could that have been painted by him, you think? There is a place not too far from the Hall by that name. I haven't been there for a long time, but I will take you there one day if you like, and you can tell me if it is the same.' And Lucy nodded her acceptance.

'And what happened to the drawing?' asked Celia, returning to the most important element of her probing.

A moment's silence, then a soft, 'He took it with him. He was gone before I could say any thing.'

'What did he say while he was sketching?' Lucy shook her head. 'Nothing? Nothing at all?' and received another shake of the head.

'Goodness me, how strange. I suppose he *can* talk. Did you see him in the ballroom afterwards?' and was again rewarded with a shake of the head. 'Or since?' with the same response.

'So you have no idea who he is?' Another shake. 'Most peculiar. And you think he touched you where he did . . . because he wanted to draw you like the painting?'

Lucy nodded, adding, 'The top part, anyway.'

'Hmm. I think if some nice man that I liked wanted to draw me that way I would not object – if he was good, that is. After all, it was a fairly conventional arrangement; just the model and the artist, and you say he had already sketched that painting on the wall – which sounds like a copy of "The Naked Maya". I will show it you in my art books. So why did you not let him?'

Lucy's shock at the improper suggestion registered immediately; but Celia was not finished.

'Did you not *like* him touching you, especially there?' indicating with a hand on her own bosom. And Lucy's downcast eyes and flushed cheeks gave instant answer.

'So you *did* like it!' said Celia triumphantly.

'Was it very shameless of me to like it?' whispered Lucy, the awful truth finally dragged out for the world to condemn. 'To want him to go on doing it, even though I told him "No"?' she pleaded, relieved that some thing she had intended to keep secret forever was revealed at last, and she hung her head in anticipation of her sister's reproach.

Celia simply hooted with laughter.

'You silly goose, you are *supposed* to like it. That is the way we women are made, with bodies that have many curves and lots of hollows so that men can make love to each part. Think how awful it would be if you hated it and had to put up with it anyway!'

'But,' said Lucy, 'why do I have to "put up with it" as you say, and what is this about "men making love to each part"?'

'All in good time, Sister,' replied Celia, thinking to her self that this was a larger task than she had imagined.

Lucy stopped, not sure what to say next. Celia simply waited while her sister digested these new thoughts.

'Then it *is* all right to enjoy it,' Lucy said, mostly to her self, and a faint smile spread across her countenance, as Celia nodded and smiled with her. 'And all this time I thought it was quite awful of me even to have permitted it.'

Suddenly, Celia was serious again. 'Of course, it should only be with the one man. Otherwise, all the young men will want the same thing, and I hope you know where *that* leads,' she added, ominously. 'So you have to be very particular to whom you say "yes".' Fortunately for us women,' she added, 'we usually are only interested in the one man, so that is all right. With the young men, though, it is *quite* a different story, so you just be careful, little Sister. We will talk a lot more about what it all means, for I would not care for a sister who was a silly goose all of her life. Would you like that?' Lucy nodded. 'Then I will show you how to deal with it, but later. Right now it is time for luncheon.'

Slipping carefully out of the hammock to avoid rocking Lucy, she did not bother to put any thing over her bare shoulders. As she put the hamper on the table she frowned slightly and said, 'Let's see what Cook has prepared for us.' But in reality the frown was for her sister's continuing timidity, for out of the corner of her eye she observed Lucy behind a tree, slipping on one of her petticoats and replacing her shoulder garments before donning her blouse. This lesson in growing up was going to be quite difficult with still a long way to go. Even though she had made considerable progress, she was not out of the woods yet.

Aloud she said, 'Hmmm, hard boiled eggs, lettuce, tomato, cold duck, ham, brown bread. Gracious me, but I am starving. It has been *years* since I ate any thing.'

Before returning to her hammock after luncheon, Celia pulled some things from her bag to accompany her.

'Your turn now,' she called from the hammock, 'but please remove those extra garments and do not take all day about it. Lying like this is making me seasick already. Do not worry; I will keep my eyes closed.'

When they were ensconced again, she sat up and put a soft wool shawl about her shoulders and examined her self critically in a hand-mirror, twisting this way and that to study the effect.

'If a man wanted to draw me,' she said, to no one in particular, although aware that she had Lucy's full attention, 'that is how I would want to be. Except for my hair,' and she reached up and removed all her pins until the rich blonde flood poured over her shoulders and down to her waist.

Still not satisfied, she reached under the shawl to adjust some thing. Then taking up a soft brush, she proceeded to drape and brush hair around her self, first one side, then the other, with a studied look in the mirror. 'There, that is how I would want him to draw me,' as she shrugged off the shawl and drew back her shoulders. This thrust forth her bosom so that it showed through clearly in two important places, eliciting a gasp from Lucy, for under the veil of hair from the waist up her sister was apparently wearing nothing at all.

'Do you not agree?' she said, turning to Lucy who had gone quite pale at the thought that she might be required to do the same thing.

'Celia,' she exclaimed, 'that is not proper.'

'Well, there is no-one here but you and me – and I trust that *you* do not mind, for I should be *most* disappointed if you did. So . . .' and she laid down the mirror to pick up her hairbrush again and proceeded to brush the long hair down to her waist until it lay in a thick, golden water-fall over her chest. Then, rising and turning her back on Lucy, she tossed her hair over her shoulders once more and handed her the brush.

'Here, it has been a long time since I had a good brush at the back, but be careful not to lean forward or you will have us both tipped out,' leaning back her self to avoid just such a fate.

Lucy was relieved not to be required to look at her sister's front, fully exposed to the open clearing. That was simply too awful to think about.

When Lucy had finished, Celia said, 'Now turn around, and I will brush yours.' Lucy complied quickly before Celia could present her self in her direction. Nevertheless, she had to admit that she enjoyed it when Celia removed the pins and returned the favour to her own light-brown hair. It was going to be nice to have some one who could do that for her, and she thanked her sister profusely, although still without facing her directly.

Return favours concluded, Celia lay back, arranged her hair over her self, and brushed it down her body until she got the effect she was seeking.

'There,' she said, 'that is better; it feels so good after all my hard work. Now I am ready for another sleep, but first tell me about the "tingles" when he touched you. Was it strong here?' touching her own bosom under the hair with the brush. Lucy nodded shyly, still without looking at her sister. 'And here, was it hard, like this?' again touching her own barely covered prominence, hard from the brushing it had just received. Another slight nod.

'And down here?' she queried, touching her own lower belly. This time Lucy just blushed, so no response was necessary, and Celia nodded. 'Well, that will happen every time with him now, and each time it will get stronger and stronger until you can not stand it any more, and you just want to give your self to him.'

'What do you mean by that,' in barely a whisper from Lucy.

'Here, let me show you,' said her big sister, reaching over to open the hooks and eyes that enclosed Lucy. But before she could make a further move, Lucy put her own hands on her chest to protect her self.

'Oh, no, I could not be like *that*.'

'Like what?' replied Celia. 'You mean like this?' looking down at her exposed bosom. 'It happens every time I bathe, you know, and I do not think any thing of it then, so why should I now?'

'But that is different,' responded Lucy, averting her eyes; 'there it is just you. Here there could be any body.'

'But there *isn't* any body,' protested Celia, 'there is just you. Unless, of course, *you* object to seeing the undeniable charms of my upper body,' she continued in a voice of disbelief, cupping her self to emphasize just those charms.

'If *that is* the case, *Sister dearest*, then you are probably justified in averting your gaze, clearly demonstrating that it is too early for you, though I must say I am surprised at that,' and she lay back, carefully brushing to cover her exposure, then closed her eyes for a sleep in the sunshine once more.

Lucy was silent for several moments, but finally could stand neither the dismissal nor the uncertainty any longer.

'Too early for what?' she asked, in a barely audible whisper, resting on one elbow as she questioned her sister.

'Oh, dear,' came the grumble, 'and I was nearly asleep there. What is it?'

'You said it was too early. Too early for what?'

'Why, too early to talk about what we are talking about, of course; the feelings in your body, the feelings of a woman. You said you wanted to understand, and I am trying to show you, but . . .'

'But I would like to know about them and what they mean,' declared Lucy.

'That is what you *say*,' was her sister's petulant reply, turning toward her, 'but it is not what you *do*.'

'But I haven't done any thing!' protested Lucy.

'*Exactly*!' exclaimed Celia, also raising her self on one elbow, unconcerned that she was now fully exposed once more to Lucy's open gaze; 'which shows that it is too early; just why I am not sure, for it would not have been too early for me. I just wish *I'd* had a big sister to help me through it at the time. I am concerned that it is already getting very late.'

'Oh, dear,' wailed Lucy, falling back, 'now it might be *too late!* You are really making my head spin, Celia, with all this nonsense, when all I wanted was a simple explanation.'

'All right, all right. I will see what I can do to make it possible to grasp; but simple, it isn't!

'Where to start? Well, when you are young, you are a girl. As your body develops, you become a woman; but the *feelings* of that grown body come afterwards; sometimes shortly after, sometimes a good deal later. Mine came early, yours are evidently coming later. But they *will* come, and you must be prepared for them, otherwise their sudden emergence will take you by surprise and overwhelm the good judgment of your head and you will be in great danger. All right so far?'

'Yes, I think so, although you will have to explain the "danger" part,' replied Lucy.

'Good, and I shall. Now, we cannot talk about the feelings of a woman's body if mine shocks you and you keep yours covered up like a granny in a blizzard! You could not expect a doctor to tell what ails you if you remained fully dressed. Whether you like it or not, he must touch and probe to find out what he needs to know.'

'Yes, I see that,' responded Lucy in quiet disappointment, for it was the 'show' part that she was secretly dreading, although having now seen her sister fully exposed to her view, apparently without any reservation or embarrassment, she was beginning to understand how it might be for her own body – except that Celia's charms were so much more . . . well . . . abundant. Then to cover her own confusion, she added, 'But you said I was supposed to like it, yet it makes me very uncomfortable, just as the doctor does.'

'I know it does, dear Sister, and I do not pretend to have all the answers for you. But you can enjoy the touching and caressing by a man and still feel uncomfortable about it afterwards. You see, the body will almost always say "yes", while your judgment – that is the intellect – will almost always say "no", exactly as you have divulged to me before lunch, so that agrees with your experience to date.' Lucy nodded.

'Good. This is your self-preservation instinct, and thank goodness for it, or I should have been an abandoned woman long ago! Then there is the heart, which can tip the balance either way, but that is more subtle, so we will come to that later.

'Now, talking and feeling are two different things; that is why we need to discuss it thoughtfully between us, though I can only explain what I know, what I have discovered or read, or worked out for my self. I never had a governess who would tell me the first thing about it, and it used to make me so angry because *she knew!* All grown women know. My mother knows, but do you think she will tell me the first thing about it? Oh dear no. It simply embarrasses them, Lucy, that is why *I* am trying to get you to understand, because if *I* do not *nobody* will, and you will be the one to lose and all the adults will blame you for not knowing – especially if you get into trouble!' she added ominously.

Lucy was silent trying to comprehend all this, so Celia continued. 'I am sorry, dear Sister, I did not mean to rant on like that, but it just makes my blood boil at the way we *girls* are treated. We have to know, but no one will tell us!' and she paused to allow her hot temper to subside. Then she took Lucy's hand.

'Do you want to continue, or shall we leave it for another day?'

'No,' Lucy replied, with a shake of the head. 'I mean, please go on. If it must be addressed sometime, then we had better discuss it now. I am truly sorry that I offended you, Sister, with my reaction to your body. But I am beginning to understand what you are trying to teach me. I also see what you mean about it being a little early for me, and I believe you are correct. But as I am beginning to experience those "woman's feelings" you refer to, I certainly do not want to be taken advantage of because I am ignorant, and I also now understand what you meant by too late, strange as it seemed at the time. So, what would you like me to do?'

She raised her self again on one elbow to look directly at her sister, admiring once again the perfect form presented and wondering how she her self might be viewed in just such a 'state of nature' by an admirer – knowing exactly whom she had in mind.

It was Celia's turn to be silent, quite taken aback by the meekness and sincerity in her sister's voice, touched that she should exhibit such faith and chastened by the responsibility she had just assumed.

'Well,' she began, hesitating as she found her self unprepared for this moment, 'we could go on talking about women in general but, sooner or later, we are going to have to address the feelings in *your* body, and that we cannot do as you are now.' She paused again to consider her next words.

'So you would like me to undress as a doctor would require for an examination?' broke in Lucy.

'No, no, that will not be necessary,' said Celia, suddenly feeling very uncomfortable at the clinical nature of the discussion. 'Oh, dear, this is more difficult than I thought,' suddenly becoming very aware of why her mother, especially, could not bring her self to 'educate' her daughter. 'Perhaps we had better leave it for a more appropriate time and place,' she sighed, and sank back, closing her eyes briefly.

When she opened them again, Lucy was still leaning on one elbow looking at her in a very direct manner.

'This has all become very difficult for you, Sis, hasn't it,' she whispered, and Celia nodded, closing her eyes again. 'Why is that?'

The ensuing silence was heavy with anticipation, which the passage of time did not dissipate. Finally Celia said, with eyes still closed, 'I am not quite sure. I suppose . . . I suppose, that, I have too much respect for you to do any thing that might be hurtful and that might make you reject me because of it,' and she rolled over on her stomach in the hammock and buried her face in the pillow.

Lucy was silent for a minute before reaching out in reassurance, realizing in the instant of contact that before this moment she had never touched her sister, except as people often do – hands and face only.

'Do you know,' she said softly, caressing Celia's bare back, 'this is the first time I have ever touched you, the real you, that is? Until now, I was unaware how soft and warm you are and what silky smooth skin you have. And such silky hair, too,' as she ran her fingers through it.

Suddenly Celia turned around and reached up to put her arms tightly around her sister, holding her in a grip of iron, and Lucy could feel the tears hot on her bare shoulder, and the warmth of Celia's bare bosom against her own clothed one – and was further surprised by a slight 'tingle', apparently out of nowhere.

'I am sorry, I should not have done that,' Celia said, breaking free after several moments of tight embrace and wiping her eyes with her hair.

'Of course you should,' replied Lucy. 'How are we going to get to know each other properly if we can not do some thing unexpected every now and then? Besides, I liked it, and thought it very appropriate,' hoping that the slight blush that she felt at this bold admission did not show it self on her face.

'But I am quite embarrassed by my weakness when it was a time for a deal of courage,' responded Celia. 'Please forgive me.'

'There is nothing to forgive, Sister. We just have some thing difficult to accomplish between us, that is all. Now,' and her voice dropped to a whisper again, 'do you want me . . . dressed, or rather, not dressed, as you are now?' and she swept back her own hair and commenced undoing the hooks and eyes, head lowered to hide the inner feelings that she knew her face must show.

This time it was Celia who put up her hand to stop her.

'No,' she said softly, 'that will not be necessary just now. I think we can proceed a little more leisurely than that.' And she lay back and brushed her hair carefully in place so that she was no longer exposed. 'Why not lie down and first brush your hair as mine is,' handing her the brush. 'Then just undo as few of the hooks as you like, all right? I will look the other way.'

'All right, but there is no need to look away. I am now ready for that,' responded her sister, busy for a few minutes brushing and unpinning. 'Now what?'

'Now we have to return to where we were before lunch, when we were talking about your "tingles", but to tell the truth, Luce, I am having difficulty getting back into it.'

'You were saying that I was supposed to like a man making love to my curves and hollows, as long as it is only one man, and that you were going to talk more about what it means and show me how to deal with it.'

'Quite right,' said Celia, shaken at the accuracy of Lucy's memory and the directness of her expression. 'Yes, Tingles . . .'

Lucy suddenly laughed out loud, breaking the tension.

'Why, dear Sister, I do believe you are *blushing*. Surely you cannot be *embarrassed* at the subject?' and she gave another merry laugh.

Celia replied with a wan smile. 'Suddenly, I am. And for the life of me I do not know why.'

'I do,' responded her sister. 'It is because I have very foolishly turned it into a "teacher and pupil" exercise, when it should be some thing much closer to a quiet exploration of maidenly feelings between two young women who like and respect each other very much.'

'Sometimes, Sis, for the younger of us, you simply amaze me,' at which Lucy gave another merry laugh.

'And I also know how to get you in the mood again to tell me and show me these special things.'

'How?' responded her sister.

Lucy lay back in her hammock again, and brushed her hair in place once more before she replied. 'Why,' she said, lowering her voice, 'the way such things are always done, of course; by whispering.'

'I am ready as soon as you are, Sis,' when she had finished brushing and adjusting her clothing as she lay with eyes closed.

Celia raised her self on one elbow to study her sister carefully. Satisfied, she reached over to take the brush.

'Very well. And you are sure you are ready to be shown these special things, which will require me to touch you in certain private places?' Lucy nodded eagerly, for she was already feeling little quiverings and expectations of excitement inside her body.

'Good. Now what I would like you to do is just relax, become soft. Then imagine you are a little cloud,' at which Lucy's eyes popped open. 'No, keep them softly closed; for this is all going to be in the imagination. A soft, fluffy pink cloud,' she reiterated softly, brushing Lucy's hair down the middle of her chest, 'floating all by it self on high. It is feeling relaxed and very, very happy,' as she made a little white parting down the middle, finding to her pleasant surprise that Lucy had already loosened the undergarments all the way to her waist.

'Completely at ease, with palms up and fingers relaxed,' she continued, noting Lucy's clenched fists. 'That is it, quite relaxed, a little pink cloud that is very contented with it self, just floating and floating,' and she felt rather than saw the tightness gradually leaving Lucy's body, while she continued to brush lightly. 'So light are you that you feel nothing,' as she deviated from brushing the centre, 'except the feeling of floating it self.' She eased the garments gently from Lucy's soft and unresisting bosom, exposing it to the sunlight and noting its swelling, before laying the hair thickly over her again.

'Does that feel good?' she whispered, and Lucy nodded. Celia then gently brushed down from Lucy's forehead, over her shoulders, until there was a smooth and glossy, golden brown covering down to her waist.

'A little boy cloud has just come into view,' she said softly; 'he is blue and coming your way, now brushing up against you, because he likes you, very much,' as she stroked gently under the soft, white mounds, each in turn.

'Do you feel him touching you?' she whispered, and Lucy nodded. 'And you like him?' a slow sensuous nod this time. 'He is softly caressing you, exciting you as you swell toward his touch, to achieve the tingly feeling.'

'Yes, it is coming,' was the whispered reply, as Lucy began to move instinctively into the brush strokes.

'You see, if he keeps touching and caressing you here,' returning to the brushing of the hair, especially where the mounds were growing through it, 'the feeling gets stronger and stronger,' receiving an affirming nod. 'Then, when he moves away,' removing the brush, 'you want him to continue.' A clear nodding this time from Lucy, her body unconsciously seeking to restore the touch. 'That is the first of your safety signals, and you will be wise to heed it.'

Celia resumed the brushing, gradually applying more purpose and direction until the hard points of desire pushed through to seek the sunlight and its touch, until Lucy's head movements and the arching of her back against the brush to increase the contact at the crucial points of desire clearly marked her high level of excitement.

'If you do not heed it,' Celia whispered, 'if you let him excite you, some thing at which he is extremely skilled, for in these matters he knows your body better than you and where and how to have his way, if you let him get your bosom to this level,' circling and teasing the hard, swollen buds with the brush handle. 'Your body will be moving by it self – as it is now – against his body and your breathing will become difficult, as it is now. That is your second caution.

'Now you are perilously close to losing control, to preventing his access to the rest of your body, which is his goal, and the ultimate peril for you, as you must know. That is why you must use all your remaining willpower to say "No", for he must not overcome your resistance to that exploration. You must protest and protect, as if your life depended on it, and well it might. That is your final caveat, and it *must* be obeyed, otherwise you are lost.

'Do you feel some thing down here?' she whispered, sliding the brush handle inside Lucy's waistband to press it into her bare lower belly.

'Oh, yes, yes,' jerking in pleasure at the unexpected contact.

'It is extremely pleasurable,' Celia continued softly, returning to brush the hair aside so that Lucy's dark and swollen mounds were fully exposed and gently caressing them, 'and when you are sure he is the right man for you, that is when you really do not want to deny him, even though you know you should, yet you are sure that he will respect you when you wish him to stop,' and Lucy nodded, still moving to the sensuous touch.

'Yet this is where he really seeks to be,' sliding the brush slowly and sensually down her open body, under the waist band and beyond, holding it there for some moments. Then she used the brush to raise Lucy's thin skirt, exposing and gently stroking her covered inner thighs, 'and this is where your own body is now seeking him,' as Lucy's lower body began to move with the brush strokes. 'You have unwisely ignored the second warning, believing you can retain control, not realizing that he can and will do things to your body there 'til you cannot deny him.

'Soon you will submit to his touch here,' stroking higher and higher until Lucy was wriggling against the brush head, 'and the final warning has passed unheeded. Now you will not want any thing – especially clothing – between your body and his, nor can you now resist his ardour and his final demand of you, for now you are as desperately seeking him as he is you, to surrender freely your most intimate parts to him, your virtue irretrievably lost,' and, indeed, Lucy was barely able to keep her body and breathing under control, so violent had her movements become.

Now Celia gently lessened and removed the contact, returning to her upper body and gently soothed that area.

'You may now understand,' she whispered, gently wiping Lucy's brow with her lace handkerchief, '*some thing* of what a little blue cloud can do to a fluffy pink cloud to overcome all resistance, for the cloud used only a simple hair brush, and your lower clothing remained intact. *He* has two hands, a mouth, and the rest of his urgent body to apply against yours and once he has undermined your resolve by conquering your upper body, you are unlikely to be a match for them when they act all in concert to satisfy that which your own body is now also desperately seeking, desperately wishing unto it self.

'Whatever else you do, little Sister,' she concluded softly, as she restored Lucy's skirt to a more appropriate position, 'remember to keep your ankles crossed, or you will quickly surrender your self completely. *Never* forget that, and you may be saved that ultimate humiliation,' all the while gently brushing Lucy's hair 'til it covered her nakedness, brushing and soothing until Lucy's ragged breathing and agitated movements ceased, and she was once more calm, although still far from relaxed.

Taking Lucy's hand in both of hers, she gently stroked and relaxed it while saying, 'Now sleep for a while, and then we shall perhaps talk about it some more. After that, we shall take tea with Alice, and discuss her plans to assist us.'

Then Celia lay back and gently brushed her own hair into place as she fought to bring the urgent throbbing of her own body under control without revealing its agitation to her young pupil, until her pulse was near normal again, surprised by its strong reaction to a little suggestion of imagination to another being. And she gave her self a private smile at her success in freeing that special sister from her self-made bonds. Now they were united in body as well as mind and spirit, with only one more goal to achieve, but this in the interest of art. Then she recaptured Lucy's hand, and slept as soundly as her sister.

The following Monday morning Lady Etheridge said, 'After breakfast, children, I would like the two of you to join me in the Morning room.'

'Yes, Mother,' replied Lucy, immediately.

'Oh, Mother!' replied her elder daughter, 'We have a lot of things planned for this morning, and if we do not start right away we will never get them all done.'

'I am sure you do, my dear; nevertheless, I require your presence in the Morning room.' When they had all finished, she rose and led the way.

When they were seated, she opened, 'The two of you young ladies have been having a wonderful time, I have observed. However, I think it is time a little more was achieved than your own pleasure.'

'Mother!' responded Celia, 'I am keeping my new sister amused.'

'Indeed you are,' replied her mother, 'and I am indeed grateful for that; but it is time to achieve a little more than your own gratification.'

'What did you have in mind, Mother,' broke in Lucy.

'Well my dear, I believe you should get down to some serious things such as needlework, and painting and . . .'

'Mother!' wailed Celia, 'you know how I hate those things, and what is more I am no good at them at all.'

'You are very rude to interrupt, young lady. I shall thus address my further remarks to your sister, who I am sure has a greater sense of responsibility than do you. You may, therefore, leave us and do the things you had planned. Lucinda and I will continue without you.' With this she turned pointedly to Lucy.

'Yes, Mother,' replied Lucy, 'what things would you like me to do?' Celia, who had half risen, sat down again, but her mother ignored her.

'Well my dear, until quite recently my elder daughter was taking art lessons from a tutor, and I my self was instructing her in needlework. She has several needlepoint pieces half-finished. But she lacks determination and attentiveness, and I reluctantly abandoned the effort. However,' and she smiled at Lucy, 'you may choose to do some of these things as a way of bettering your self – unless of course you are already expert at them.'

'Oh, no, Mother,' quickly responded Lucy, 'I would love to do some of them with you.'

'Very good, my dear, I will set up the art classes for Tuesday and Thursday mornings, and perhaps Mondays and Wednesdays we can do needlework. Then you can proceed with that any time you have an hour or so to spare.'

Rising, she said, 'Come; let us start the needlepoint right away in the Conservatory. The light is best in there.' She led the way, with Lucy following, and much to the rear, an angry and defiant Celia.

Lady Etheridge took out the canvas and wools for the twelve chair seats that were being worked on. 'We have finished six as you see. These other three are in different stages, but I think you should start your own from the very beginning; then you can know that it was all your own work. Have you done much of this sort of thing before?' mindful that Lucy's mother had been laid to rest these many years.

'Oh, yes,' replied Lucy. 'When I was younger, I used to stay with an Aunt Alicia during the summer, and we did all the stitches. I still have a sampler some where. Would you care for me to look for it?'

'That will not be necessary just now; but I am pleased to hear you have experience. Why not use this finished one as a sample to follow; it is correct for it is my own work.' Then she picked up one that she had been working on, and they settled down to their needlework.

After a while in complete silence, Lucy asked a question about a stitch, and Lady Etheridge took the opportunity to examine her work.

'Very nice, my dear, I can see that you are indeed quite expert already; unlike another of my children.'

'Mother,' replied Lucy; 'May I speak to Celia – to my sister?'

'You may, my dear,' with a glance at her elder daughter. 'But do not expect to receive a civil answer, for I see her face is as black as thunder.' This last was a considerable exaggeration, for Celia was more hurt than angry, more anguished now at being excluded than defiant.

'Celia,' said Lucy, 'would you like to join us in a little embroidery? I will help you if you really need it,' but was rewarded only by a pained silence.

'Well, I did counsel you, my child,' said her mother, ignoring the scowl from her elder daughter, yet understanding that her own presence was hindering further progress.

'Excuse me for a moment, Lucy, for I must see Cook about the menus. I am sure you can manage well without me for a little while.'

'Yes, Mother,' responded Lucy, and busied her self until her mother had left the room, carefully closing the door behind her. Then she jumped up and ran over to Celia.

'Oh, do not be like that, Cel,' she said, using her pet name for her sister and putting her arms lovingly around her neck. 'I hate it when we do not do things together.'

'I know, Luce,' said Celia, 'so do I. But I really am no good at that sort of thing. You will see.'

'Then it will my pleasure to help you, really,' and she took her sister's arm and led her to the table. 'There. Now which one is yours?' and Celia picked up one of the covers.

'Would you like me to help you get started again?' and without waiting for a reply, picked up a needle, threaded it, saying, 'Let's start with this pretty delphinium here; it is just the colour of your eyes, except that yours are much the prettier.'

So it was that when Lady Etheridge returned to the Conservatory, this time quietly approaching the French doors from the South lawn, she was not at all surprised to observe them busily working away, talking softly, each to the other. So she left them to their own affairs and undertook those things that needed her presence elsewhere in the house.

After lunch Lady Etheridge spoke to her daughters.

'Let us take our coffee on the dining terrace, for there are some other matters I would like to discuss with the two of you,' nodding to Alice as they left the room.

'I think there is one more activity that I would like to encourage for the two of you, some thing that you can do together. And that is music.'

Celia said nothing, but Lucy responded with a bright smile. 'I would like that.'

'Good,' replied her mother. 'And what instruments do you play?'

'Pianoforte', responded Lucy, 'is my best. The violin, some; and then the flute, but that not very well yet.'

'Celia has played piano, as I do my self, but it has been quite a while for either of us. I also play the 'cello for accompaniment, and Celia plays the flute rather well, so we might be able to perform a little some thing. Let us go to the Music room and see what we shall see.'

The two girls followed her, Lucy leading her sister by the hand. 'This is going to be fun,' she whispered.

'First the piano, my dear,' to Lucy. 'Any thing that you care to play.'

Seated at the concert grand, Lucy lifted the lid and immediately exclaimed, 'Oh, my, it is a *Bösendorfer!* My music teacher had one, though not as fine as this. And he would let me play it sometimes, but only if I had prepared my exercises properly and was behaving my self into the bargain. He said it was the finest piano in the world with a special resonance from its single stringing and spruce-wood construction.

'Now; let me see. I must play only the finest music on such a beautiful instrument,' as she made her self comfortable. After a few scale and chord exercises to relax and flex her fingers, she sat still for some moments, waiting for that special inner joy of music that she knew would come in its time.

At last, 'A little Beethoven, then perhaps some Mozart, or Haydn,' she said quietly, mostly to her self. Then after flexing her fingers once more, the music flowed, and she became so carried away by the delight of making music once again, that her delicate rendering of the 'Pathé-tique' opening movement flowed into a passionate 'Appassionata' finale, and that into a lyrical portion of Mozart's 21st, one of her very special favourites, before finishing with a spirited Scarlatti. She was as one in a trance, not realizing that she had played for the most part of an hour.

When the last note died away, she folded her hands in her lap, and there was silence – for neither of the audience could utter a word – as the room and its surroundings slowly returned to her focus. At last she turned.

'Was that all right, Mother?' she asked, modestly.

Lady Etheridge had some difficulty finding her voice, before she managed, softly, 'That was *truly magnificent*, my daughter. And all from memory! I had absolutely no idea we had such talent in the family, or I would have asked you to play long ago. I am honestly at quite a loss for words.

'So, I hesitate to ask you about the violin, but perhaps you could give me a few bars, just to see how you get on.'

At that the happy Lucy laughed. 'I am very rusty at that. I have not played since Papa . . . and I . . .' And she fell silent. 'That is all right,' she suddenly broke in again. 'It is time I got back to it,' and opened up the proffered violin case.

'Why, it is a *Guaneri;* I have never even *seen* one of these!' she exclaimed in astonishment. 'My teacher said it was the very finest, with an exqui-site tone. And this one even has the sacred monogram of Giuseppe him self. Oh, my, how lucky you are to have such fine instruments to play any time you choose!' and proceeded to tune it and play a few simple pieces.

Lady Etheridge broke the next silence.

'I am sure you will soon get back to playing that, Lucinda, just as well as you do the piano. I will leave the two of you to practise together this afternoon, and I will expect you for tea. Then we shall talk about it all,' and she left the room.

'Well?' said Lucy to her sister, 'what shall we play together?'

But her sister just sat looking at her, still in stunned silence. 'Mother was right,' she whispered in awe. 'That was truly *magnificent*. I could not possibly sit at the same piano with some one as talented as you, Luce. Honestly.'

But Luce would have none of it, and dragged her sister to the piano. 'Come on,' she said, 'let us play Clementi duets for a start.'

And in no time the two of them were giggling when their fingers got entwined, until Celia fell off the stool, dragging her sister with her, and they rolled laughing on the floor, then lay there holding hands, staring at the ceiling, enjoying a quiet moment of mutual joy.

After a while, Celia rolled over, put her elbows on the floor, looked deeply into her sister's green eyes, and said, 'I have an absolutely *brilliant* idea.' And she did, and it was.

Over the next few days the details of the scheme were worked out and committed to paper. A separate list was made of all the places that they must visit.

'But of what use is that,' objected Lucy. 'We *know* where he is!'

'So what do you suggest, my dear Sister,' replied Celia sarcastically. 'That we stand outside the Hall and play away until he appears at an upper window, then you rush upstairs and into his arms?'

'Oh, my dear, I am so sorry,' as she saw Lucy blush and go pale at the same time. 'What a completely thoughtless pig I am,' reaching out to comfort her. Then she stopped.

'Wait a minute – that is it! A truly *brilliant* suggestion. Oh, Luce, you are an absolute genius!' blowing her a kiss and writing the item on her papers. Then, seeing her sister's continued puzzlement of her supposed 'genius', reached over and squeezed her hand.

'You are quite right; we know *where* he is – so we will *practise* there! That must do it for sure. Do not fret little sister, I know just how I am going to achieve it,' she gurgled happily.

However, there arose a problem that Celia hadn't expected. She was quite right that Georgina and Geraldine would think it was a wonderful idea. They had played music together many times in the past, and it was always great fun. What was totally unexpected was Lord Houghton's complete rejection.

'Unthinkable,' was the way they received his response.

'That puts a decided damper on the whole idea,' said Celia, when she heard the bad news. 'The thing just will not work without G & G.'

'Could we not get some one else to join us?' implored Lucy. 'There must be lots of young ladies around here.'

'The problem is that the others do very much what we do; piano, violin, flute, and not as well at that. And how many pieces do you know for two pianos and two flutes?' to which Lucy nodded. 'Rosalind plays the harp beautifully, but that means we would have to carry that around with us. What a bother. Besides, G & G are oboe, bassoon and clarinet. Now you know *lots* of pieces for those combinations.'

Again Lucy nodded, but not willing to capitulate so easily, added, 'So we have to get his lordship to change his mind.'

'Oh ho; you do not know *the Brigadier*. He would rather *shoot* the animal than change horses!'

'All right. So that is it,' concluded Lucy. 'A "do-or-die" effort; change his mind or get shot for our trouble,' at which they both hooted with laughter. With the mood considerably lightened, they hooked little fingers for luck and set out to ask mother to arrange a meeting of conciliation with His Lordship, as soon as possible.

In the meantime, they were not ones to let the grass grow under their feet, so they arranged to meet with G & G at a safe distance to discuss Celia's outline of practices and potential soirées.

'I hope we are not wasting our time,' said Georgina. 'Father is not one for changing his mind, you know!'

'I know,' said Celia blithely, 'But my sister and I have a *secret weapon*.'

'You do?' chorused G & G in unison.

'We do,' responded Celia confidently.

'And what about getting permission to practice at Greville?' added Geraldine, the younger of the two sisters at a mere seventeen. 'We do not know anyone there,' then she answered her own question: 'I *do* know – *Reginald!*' and the two Gs squealed with girlish laughter, while Celia frowned.

'Who is Reginald?' asked Lucy.

'Who *indeed*,' chorused the two Gs, 'just an old heart-throb of your sister, *that is* who,' added Georgina, younger than Lucy at eighteen.

'He is a cousin of the Blackmoors who sometimes stays on the Greville Estate when he comes down from Oxford,' said Celia, more informatively, 'but that was years ago. And, yes, I think he was quite fond of me, in a way.'

'Miss innocent! *Besotted* is more like it,' chipped in Geraldine again. 'Got him wrapped around her little finger, poor deluded young man,' and Celia blushed. They rather enjoyed the chance to get at Celia now and then because she was to them, at nearly twenty-one, practically a grown woman.

'All right, *children;* now that you have had your fun, let's get on with arranging some music,' said Celia, a little testily, for these two could be quite juvenile when they were together. Then she continued, 'I would rather we had a quintet, George. That will provide more flexibility in our repertoire than a quartet. Besides, if one is unable to perform for any reason, we would still have an acceptable group. Trios are quite difficult to cut back to.'

Georgina nodded in agreement and for a moment or two discussed with her sister whom they knew, concurring that Alexandra was the best choice. They informed Lucy that she lived quite close to Greville, the other side in fact, which made it a wise choice for practices.

'And she plays violin wonderfully,' added Geraldine.

'How about 'cello, Gerald, any chance of that?' added Celia.

'I do believe she does,' responded George.

And so the Silchester Quintet was launched – subject to his lordship's change of heart of course. But that would be assured according to Celia, by standing in a circle, little fingers locked together, eyes closed, wishing hard for two minutes.

'Are you sure your "secret weapon" will not backfire, Celia?' inquired Georgina, before they parted. 'Father is *very* determined, and he was *most explicit* on the point!'

'Absolutely,' responded Celia. 'Cross my heart,' making the appropriate gesture with her right hand. But the left one, behind her back, had its fingers crossed, just in case.

To say that the group was a success would be a considerable under-statement, for it was a veritable triumph. Lucy was undoubtedly the star soloist on piano, but the woodwinds were outstanding in ensemble. Alexandra, who was twenty, was a fine and sensitive violinist, who played 'cello even better, if any thing, and was at the same time a natural leader.

The music room at Greville Hall was large and convenient, with a side door so they could slip in and out without disturbing the household. There was only one problem: Reginald. He would insist on stopping in to listen more often than not. That made Celia self-conscious, and she would miss her cues. So Alexandra, the leader, asked him to either stay away (which was a little difficult, it being his house), or hide behind a potted plant.

In the second week, at only their third practice, their hostess was so delighted that she asked them to play at her niece's eighteenth coming-of-age birthday celebration, the following Friday. That turned out to be a large gathering of over one hundred, many from outside their area, and quite a number from Town.

After that the requests for their appearance grew beyond all possibility of acceptance, and Lady Etheridge had to step in to handle the delicate matter of to whom to say 'no' and to prevent the whole affair from getting completely out of hand.

The one thing that Lady Etheridge did not share with her daughters as the season progressed, were the invitations for the Quintet to play in Town and other major centres. That could cause more disruption than the family could handle, at least until further circle discussions were undertaken.

Indeed, it sometimes seemed that the social calendar for that season revolved around whether the Quintet was going to perform at a function. If they weren't, then the acceptances dropped off alarmingly, much to the irritation of the hostess, whose only recourse was to attempt to secure their services for the occasion – which request would almost certainly be answered by 'with regrets' from her ladyship.

And the quality of the invitations also rose sharply. Lady Etheridge – not to mention the Quintet – knew that the pinnacle had been reached when she received an informal communication that the Duchess her self would be pleased if the group could perform at the Steeplechase Ball she was giving at the end of the month.

That turned out to be some two hundred and fifty guests, and the young ladies had to stay for two nights – which also meant two new London-quality ball-gowns, plus a full complement of accessories for each of the players, which their mothers were quite delighted to undertake. These opportunities to parade their daughters in their very finest – at whatever cost – came rarely enough, and usually not at all, for the Duchess commanded only the highest of society at these functions – which naturally included the young scions.

And it was not only the Quintet that was delighted. For Alice it meant that an unattainable dream was actually coming true, for she invariably accompanied the young ladies on their soirées, her role being that of dresser, *coiffeuse*, and confidante for all five. When they stayed overnight, which was becoming increasingly frequent, she stayed with them, usually in an anteroom. On the one occasion that she was shown accommodation in the servants' quarters, Miss Celia had made it startlingly clear to the hostess that such a thing was as unacceptable as if she her self had been offered similar accommodation, and the 'oversight' was corrected with alacrity.

The purple velvet dress, lace trimmings and all – another impossible dream – became a reality, too, as did a gorgeous emerald *gros grain* and a *toile ecru*, each together with its appropriate accessories. Even the pearls, though they were not genuine, were more than real enough for Alice. She was in seventh heaven.

But woe betide any young man who – inadvertently or otherwise, whatever the rank – made any remark or implication of the slightest immodesty concerning 'her' young ladies!

By mid-season Lord Houghton was heard to grumble that he no longer saw his daughters, though he was secretly more than pleased at the fine compliments he received on their behalf and the connections made with the First Families far and wide.

The roués of the district were also heard to exclaim on more than one occasion that the Quintet was the finest stable of fillies that had been seen in the neighbourhood in many a long year. When the motherhood heard that, they tightened the security, and saw to it that the several escorts were left in no doubt whatsoever as to what would happen to their prospects if any thing happened, *any thing at all*, to their charges. For these all-male conversations, 'horsewhipped' was the usual starting point.

Nevertheless, the ladies of the neighbourhood were quite beside them selves at the exposure their daughters received, and in the most desirable of circumstances. As all requests to increase the Quintet it self were firmly resisted and the motherhood became aware of the opportunity for their own aspirations, the grapevine concentrated on which balls the group was playing – and then inveigled an invitation by any means, fair or foul.

It was a truly notable season, for nothing so fortuitous had occurred for as long as any of them could remember.

As for Lady Etheridge, she had more personal invitations than she could manage on account of her daughters' formative roles in the Quintet.

It was perhaps the happiest period of her life, excepting only when she her self was a young bride. A subject, she reflected when it struck her mind, that must be addressed soon with both her daughters.

For the players, the social side of the frantic activity was not without its benefits, either. The increasing number of extremely eligible young men attending the functions where they gave performances was quite head-turning, and at times Celia and Alexa had their hands full keeping the younger pair focused on their *raison d'être*.

As Celia succinctly expressed it on one occasion, 'We are here to play music, not the fool!'

They were usually escorted by one of the brothers Geoffrey or Jeremy, or Alexa's brother Charles, and sometimes by Reginald. Celia professed to discomfort at having him around, but Lucy knew that in secret, she was delighted at his presence, although she pretended not to notice.

But of *him*, not a sign, until . . . One afternoon they were practising and establishing their programme just prior to the Duchess's Ball. For the very first time Lucy missed a cue, and they all stopped playing and looked at her. She blushed scarlet, in embarrassment the group thought, before they repeated the piece, this time without a flaw. But Celia knew better.

When they stopped for lemonade she took Lucy for a walk in the garden. 'Well?' she said.

'Well what?' replied Lucy.

'Luce, you *saw* him! So do not tell me you did not.'

Lucy's face paled, and she nodded.

'Well, I could not be sure, you know,' she added, tentatively. 'There was some one behind the potted plant. I thought at first it was Reginald,' and Celia nodded. 'But then I saw his back as he walked away.'

Celia sighed. 'I know how it is,' she said wistfully. 'When some one matters to you, I believe you would probably recognize his little finger.' And cheek to cheek, they rested chins on the other's shoulder before returning to the music room.

It was the very next day that Celia decided the time had come to carry out the next piece of her plan; some thing she had been hoping to achieve for quite a while.

'As we seem to have a spare afternoon, Luce, why not take a picnic tea to the Hollow and you can tell me if it is the same as the picture. We shall just be our selves, because Alice will not want to go. I will explain that later. Besides, she has much work to do with our ball-gowns.'

This time they took the trap to convey their tea things, plus a sketch pad or two.

'It is only about three miles this way,' said Celia, 'although we could have been there much quicker on horse back.

'That is it, there,' pointing to a clump of trees in the distance, 'just off the side of the Common. Does it look any thing like the picture?'

'Very much. The colours were a bit greener, so it must have been painted in mid-summer.'

They drove until they arrived at an opening in one side where Celia released and tethered the pony to crop the grass at its ease.

'Before we get out the tea things,' said Celia, 'let me show you what is down here,' and she led the way into the grove and partly down into the Hollow.

Inside the ring of trees, Lucy noted that the 'Hollow' was exactly that, a pudding basin, though rather more oval, with short-cropped grass. But though open to the sky, it seemed to bear a decidedly dark character that did not sit well with the muted sunlight streaming in. Altogether a most unwholesome place, she thought. For her self, she was happy to give it a wide berth, but Celia took her hand and advanced down the slope a little way before stretching out her arms.

'You can really feel the silence in here. Now, down at the bottom here is a big round stone, you see,' as she advanced to place her foot on it, then turned to find Lucy still standing where she had left her. 'Is any thing the matter, Lucy?'

'I really do not know; but, somehow . . . I feel sort of . . . strange in here. And when you said I should listen to the silence, I could hear some thing else. Sounds, sort of voices, indistinct and far off. And a weird sort of . . . music.' And she turned and quickly retraced her steps to the trees and thence to the cart – and on the far side at that!

'It is strange that you should say that, Luce,' as Celia rejoined her. 'I feel it just as I said. But Alice would not go down there unless you dragged her. She says the place is haunted, and that sometimes people come in here and do not come out! I must admit that there are one or two old wives' tales about that, but I take that as idle gossip. But if you are not happy, Sis, let's go over to that little rise with old tumble-down cottage on it. Nobody's ever accused that of being any thing

71

other than what it is.' Meanwhile, she hitched up the pony and helped Lucy up.

'The old-timers in the village even say that the stone I was pointing out to you at the bottom – which I am convinced is an old well – is a trap-door to the underworld, and that is where Old Nick him self emerges when he needs another soul or two,' and she gave a merry laugh. But she felt Lucy's uneasiness and a distinct shudder against her shoulder so she switched the conversation.

'But let us talk of more pleasant things. We will have our tea at the old cottage next to that boulder, and then do a little sketching of the cottage and that gnarly old tree. It should make a grand picture if we are up to it.' She gave Lucy's shoulder a gentle squeeze of reassurance and, releasing the pony once more to roam and graze, spread the table-cloth on the grass by the cottage and laid out the tea things.

'There,' she said, laying her head on a cushion, taking her sister's hand, and staring at the soft clouds overhead. 'A perfect day for doing nothing; or at least, very little.'

5

The Professor

It was the middle of summer, and Lady Etheridge was sitting in the Conservatory after luncheon, with her accounts book and personal diary, and the special one she had prepared for the Quintet. She would normally have carried out these duties in the Morning room. But of late much of the daily activity had been transferred to the sunny space of this charming room. Because she wanted to encourage her daughters to behave in a somewhat more familial manner, the piano was moved in – thank goodness for double doors! – and had some rugs placed on the tiled floor.

The latter was some thing of a sore point. She did not approve of young people, over the age of ten anyway, lolling on the floor; that was why *chairs* were placed in rooms. For young ladies of any age beyond three it was quite unthinkable and forbidden on pain of . . . but here she had met her match and in a relaxed postprandial mood, fell to cogitating on what it was that 'inflicted' her daughters when they were together.

Separately they were 'normal' young ladies – if there were such specie. She was quite sure that Lucy had always been a quiet lady-like person; sedate, modest, and reserved. On the other hand her daughter Celia, before the arrival of Lucy, had been difficult and moody, at times barely controllable. Yet when they were together, two halves of a whole, a new energy seemed to infusion them, a new spirit that was not in evidence before. It was as if a river of a different consciousness flowed through them, uniting them, and *that* they followed and no other.

She recalled the mysterious force of magnetism. Its power was quite invisible to her, yet objects in its unseen path were inexorably moved by it. So it was with her daughters. And as evidence of their power over immovable objects, there was that strange episode of Lord Houghton

73

and the proposal for the Quintet. As she understood it, when Celia first approached his daughters they were excited by the prospect, as was Lady Houghton. But when His Lordship heard about it there was apparently a row of epic proportions. *He* was not going to have *his daughters* cavorting 'round the countryside *like a band of itinerant troubadours!* And that was an end to it.

Except that it wasn't, for Celia and Lucy requested an audience with his lordship and to her own immense surprise, it was granted. She had gone with them and spent a rather tense tea with Lady Houghton. Her daughters were admitted to his lordship's private study no less, a place that even Lady Houghton rarely entered.

What went on in there she did not ask, and was not told. Suffice it to say that when Celia and Lucy emerged more than an hour later with Lord Houghton, the three of them were laughing and he was quite playful. Then they all sat down to tea (some thing Lady Houghton confided to her later, he had never done in their entire lives together). And he talked about his military campaigns – some of them with the General, her husband – and about the Season Ball in preparation, which she and her charming daughters must be *sure* to attend and to join his party. Then he bade them a fond farewell at the main portico, with embraces and well-wishes all round.

With such apparent power at their command, to forbid them to roll on the floor – when they were in the mood to do so – would be to banish them from the house altogether, to 'The Haven', as they called the Summer House, or to their 'Treasure Island', whose allure she totally failed to comprehend; she her self had not been there for years. She did say that they could only do that in the Conservatory and only if no others than her self were present, with the sole exception, of course, of Alice. At which thought there was a tap on the door and that worthy appeared as if by the rub of a magic lamp.

'Yes, Alice?' she responded, trying to cover her astonishment.

'Begging your pardon, Madam,' and she came forward with the silver salver on which lay an elegant, silver-embossed calling card, which Her Ladyship read aloud:

Professor Manfred R. Werner, D.Sc., Ph.D.
Greville Hall

'Professor Werner is *here*, Alice?' she inquired.
'Yes, Madam.'

'Do we know a Professor Werner, Alice?'

'No, Madam. That is, I am not sure, Madam.'

'Come, come, Alice. Either we do or we do not. And what are all these strange initials after his name? I am not at all sure about this, Alice. Besides, this is a most inconvenient time to call.'

'Yes, Madam.'

'You are the only one to have seen him. Is he respectable? Young or old?'

'Yes, Madam; quite distinguished, about 30 or a little more, I would say.'

'Really? Most inconvenient.' And she was on the point of saying that Alice should ask the young Professor to call again, when she noticed that Alice biting her lip, not a habit she had seen before.

'You think I should see him, Alice?' she asked.

'Begging Your Ladyship's pardon,' a deep curtsey this time, 'yes, Madam, I do.'

'Well, you had better be right, Alice, or I shall be *very* cross at being disturbed. Please show the Professor in here, and advise Miss Celia and Miss Lucy that I may need them to meet this strange visitor.'

And strange he did appear. Very tall, slim build, but with unusually broad shoulders, a purposeful stride and manner, and a face that while not out of the ordinary, had at the same time a strangely handsome air to it. His dress was elegant and formal, yet in a distinctly foreign style; Sachsen, she thought, though the cloth was clearly of English origin.

His most powerful appeal, however, she was about to discover, for when he took her hand, it was to impart a formal kiss, but not that artificial French 'almost' sort. This was genuine and full of meaning, and accompanied by a little click of the heels. When he finally released it, she could feel the tingle remaining in her fingers for quite a time afterwards; almost a numbness.

'Lady Etheridge,' he began, in a pleasant baritone, 'I am most remiss in calling in an unannounced manner and at such an inconvenient time.'

Well, she thought, at least his manners are commendable.

'But I have been wishing to introduce my self to your household for some considerable time, and found that I could postpone that pleasure no longer.'

Well, well, this was indeed a *most* unusual person. 'You are staying at Greville Hall, I see from your card. You are related to the Blackmoors?'

'Distantly, Madam.' Now why did that 'distantly' sound so hesitant, and why was his speech so stilted, almost as if it were a foreign language?

'I am staying for an indefinite period, one that depends . . . on other circumstances.'

To break the silence that followed this unexpected reply, Lady Etheridge spoke.

'Will you take some tea, Professor?'

'Thank you, no, Madam. But if coffee were available, I should be glad to join you in that.'

Coffee? At teatime? That was certainly the first time she had received that request, and rang the bell for Alice.

'Perhaps you would like to meet my daughters, Professor,' she inquired – and suddenly knew why he had come. 'And ask Miss Celia and Miss Lucy to join us,' she added to Alice.

'Of what are you a professor, and where are you in residence?' she resumed, still seeking better knowledge of this man than she had at the moment.

'Astrophysics, Your Ladyship, but I am at the moment on an indefinite sabbatical.'

Whatever and wherever that is, thought her Ladyship, none the wiser on either score.

Alice knocked and entered, followed closely by Celia.

'Celia, my dear, this is Professor Manfred Werner,' as Celia moved forward to be greeted. 'Of Greville Hall,' she continued, but Celia had stopped dead in mid-stride, her face a frozen mask, hand dropped back to her side. 'He is an astro-some thing, on a saba-some thing.' To fill the awkward silence that ensued, she said to Alice, 'Miss Lucy?'

'She is not . . . not to be found, Madam.'

'Shall I see if I can find her, Mama?' broke in Celia, quickly regaining her composure.

'Very well, my dear, please do,' and she settled down again to discover what she could of the strange professor. But in the intervening period she learned little, except that he was a stranger in the land, yet seemed to know much about it. His speech was so peculiar, too. She could not place his manner at all; mid-European, certainly, but he hesitated often as if to find the right word to convey his meaning. Yet more than that, as if . . . as if he did not wish to use the *wrong* word. Even then his words were used in a strange and unfamiliar manner.

A welcome knock on the door again broke the silence, and Celia entered with – although it looked more like *dragging* – Lucy by the hand.

'My younger daughter, Lucinda; Professor Manfred Werner.'

Lucy said nothing, rooted to the spot. The professor said nothing, either. They simply looked at each other, and the atmosphere in the room positively crackled. *These two have met before,* was the astounding conclusion of which she was instantly aware.

At last Lucy moved forward. Not her usual relaxed self; no, this was a stiff-legged gait, a shuffle of distinct unwillingness as if she were being dragged by an unseen hand, by some sort of magnetic force. Still, they simply looked at each other. The professor had given Celia a much too bold look of appraisal on first entry, of which Lady Etheridge did *not* approve, even though her elder daughter was undoubtedly a very attractive young woman. But now he looked only into Lucy's eyes, and she unblinkingly returned his gaze.

'Lucinda, my dear,' she interjected into the palpitating silence, 'perhaps the professor would care to hear you play the piano?'

At last Lucy turned.

'Yes, Mother,' she replied, and walked stiffly over to the piano and, seating her self, lifted the lid, and took her position at the keyboard very deliberately. Then she turned to the professor, smiled, and spoke for the first time.

'Professor Manfred,' she began, most improperly, but now apparently fully relaxed, 'what would you care to hear?'

Now it was the professor's turn to speak for the first time in their presence.

'Whatever you choose, Miss Lucinda,' and looked as if he would have moved to the piano, except that some thing in Lucy's countenance warned him to stay where he was.

'Well, then,' she smiled, 'I will give you a choice of two by the master him self: the "Moonlight", or the "Appassionata"?'

'Miss Lucinda,' he smiled in response, 'I always prefer the passionate to the lyrical.'

In the silence that followed, while Lucy was settling her self again, her mother suddenly appreciated what had happened to Lucy. Awkward as she was when she entered, the moment she sat at the keyboard she was the master; there she had no equal, man or woman.

Lucy relaxed her fingers by playing a series of complex scales, guaranteed to get the attention of any audience. She even played the first twenty or so bars of the 'Moonlight', to the end of that first tremendous glissando, performed with a fluidity and grace her mother had rarely heard.

Now she was ready, and chose the final movement of the 'Appassionata'.

The rest Lady Etheridge could only recall as if in a dream. She had never heard fire poured forth from a piano the like of which her daughter was now producing. At one point she thought that the piano it self might disintegrate under the weight of emotion as it soared and deluged them with music. From the lyrical to the savage, it was all packed into that one movement, and when an eternity later the last notes finally died away, they seemed to reverberate around the walls as if the music would never cease.

It was Lucy her self who broke the spell, for no one else was capable of any movement at all. She arose gracefully from the piano secure in her conquering triumph, flowed to where her sister was seated, and raised her by the hand. Then the two of them, in unison and in silence, curtsied deeply to the professor, turned slightly and repeated the generous gesture to their mother, ran lightly to the door and were gone, almost as if they had never been – except for the girlish laughter in the hall and the last notes of the sonata still bouncing off the walls in their mother's head.

As for the professor, he looked as stunned as Lady Etheridge felt.

'There,' she said to him, ringing the bell for Alice, 'You have met my daughters,' and led him to the Conservatory door. 'Please call again, when it is *convenient*,' leaving the professor in no doubt, if he had any sense at all, that the *next* time he took a fancy to calling, he would please make prior arrangements. She did not want a repeat of the utter confusion that one had just caused!

'Thank you, Alice.'

It was some time before Lady Etheridge could overcome the feeling that the swirling music she had just experienced was truly over. When she did, she pulled the bell cord. 'Alice,' she inquired, 'you knew *some thing* of the professor, did you not?'

'Yes, Madam, I think I did.'

'But you were not sure until you knew a little more.'

'Exactly, Madam.'

'And just when were you sure, Alice?'

'When Miss Lucy entered the Conservatory, Madam,' and her mistress nodded.

'As I thought. And what were you then sure of, Alice?' But Alice deigned to respond.

'Alice, there is a circumstance to this, is there not?'

Again Alice was silent, but as her ladyship continued to look her straight in the eye, she made to reply.

'I am afraid that Your Ladyship must request that of Miss Lucy.'

'Very well, please ask them to come and see me.'

Alice did not move, but did respond.

'There is some thing, Madam, but I do not know what it is,' and still she did not move.

'There is more to this, isn't there, Alice. Much more.'

'Yes, Madam. May I have permission to speak, Madam?'

'Certainly, Alice.' Goodness, this was puzzling.

'Well, Madam, I have come to know Miss Lucy quite well, and with her they do say that still waters run deep.' At that, Lady Etheridge raised her eyebrows but nodded in agreement, for she was beginning to see. 'I could not help hearing the music, Madam. It was like Miss Lucy's soul was on fire. I do not understand it but I believe she was playing for him, for the professor.'

'Yes, Alice, I do believe you are right.'

'And one more thing, Madam.'

'Go on, Alice.'

'Well, Madam, this is a matter of such import to Miss Lucy that I believe we – begging your pardon, Ma'am,' and here a little curtsey, 'that we are not *meant* to understand. Yet if Miss Lucy is made to be upset, I mean very, *very* upset Madam, over whatever it is, then . . . then . . .'

'Yes, go on, Alice.'

'Then I believe, Ma'am, that Miss Lucy will leave . . . for a second time. And this time she will *not* return and we will lose her . . . forever.' And Alice's eyes filled with tears 'til they overflowed down her cheeks.

'Goodness, Alice, you mustn't upset your self like that. Here, come and sit down while we discuss this matter.'

She led Alice to a chair, and then seated her self. She waited until Alice was composed once more.

'You mean to say, Alice, that whatever this thing is between Miss Lucy and the professor, it is from the *first* time she was here?' she asked, incredulously.

'Yes, Madam, I am sure it was. Indeed I *know* it was because I can read Miss Lucy, Madam. Sometimes that is,' and she smiled again.

'I see,' said her ladyship, though she wasn't sure that she did. 'And you feel that, if it is not properly – not carefully – undertaken, that we might lose our new daughter?'

Alice nodded, 'Yes, Madam, I think we shall.'

This was indeed a matter of considerable moment, for if Alice was correct in the understanding of her younger daughter – and could she her self offer any thing half so perceptive? – it would require the most delicate handling.

'Very well then, Alice, please ask the young ladies, nicely, if you will, and if they are not otherwise engaged, to be so good as to join me on the dining terrace.'

And Alice's shining eyes were all the reward for her own understanding that Lady Etheridge needed.

'My children,' said Lady Etheridge, when they were all seated in the 'Haven', 'I want to thank you for accepting me into your own inner sanctum because I need to assure you that I want to help. And I have asked Alice to join us because she does not seem to be excluded from much that the two of you do.' And they both nodded and smiled at Alice, who remained standing.

'Firstly, my dear,' to Lucy, 'that piano playing was simply . . . I know I shall never hear its like again, if I live to be a hundred. Now, Lucy, this professor is important to you, is he not my dear?'

'Yes, Mother,' whispered Lucy.

'In fact, he is your whole life,' and Lucy could only drop her tear-filled eyes and nod.

'Have you met him often?' and Lucy shook her head, while Celia held up one finger. 'Once only?' responded her astonished mother, and Lucy nodded.

'Well, we must all see what we can do to further the cause of true love if it be that,' at which Lucy blushed deeply. 'But I must add, my dearest daughter, that I shall be checking on the Professor very thoroughly indeed, for *both* our sakes!' Then she rose.

'I suggest we all have a rest before dinner, and then perhaps an early night.' Putting her arms now around both her daughters, she added, 'So *that* was what was behind the Silchester Quintet,' and this time they both smiled and nodded.

'Well, if its purpose was to attract the fish and then to hook him, I am sure, if I am any judge of such things, that with your magnificent playing this afternoon, he is now well and truly in your net!'

And they all had a hearty laugh, a deep hug between the two girls, a little curtsey together to their mother (who marvelled at the excellent manner in which they achieved it always so perfectly in unison), before rushing ahead hand-in-hand to their rooms – one or the other!

But her ladyship and Alice were more sedate. She only raised her eyebrows questioningly in Alice's direction, whose shining eyes and beaming face were all the response needed.

'Thank you, Alice. You are a true friend, indeed.'

Alice blushed deeply and turned away to wipe her brimming eyes; but when they separated in the hall, offered a full, deep curtsey in gratitude at the complete acceptance of her contribution.

Manfred left in a frame of mind so different from the one in which he arrived, that he wondered how Lucy had managed to achieve it. An incredible performance by any standard, modern or old.

He mounted his horse so absentmindedly that he wondered afterwards why it did not throw him. He wasn't a very good rider yet – probably never would be – but every body else seemed to have been born in the saddle. Even the redoubtable Alice was riding, he had noted, though she obviously preferred to ride astride – when she could get away with it. How Lucy (no, Lucinda, he was going to call her that from now on, it was such a lovely name); how Lucinda and Celia rode side-saddle without falling off he had no idea. He had taken a few tumbles in the early days, and he had both legs to hold on with!

He loved to watch the two of them riding together, although he had to keep his extreme distance, and often wished he were with them, riding alongside. Maybe now he could be. But he knew that was going to be difficult, to say the least. Lady Black-moor, as he now addressed her and even thought of her (although he would rather have used the more appropriate title of Baroness) had made it abundantly *clear to him that she would not hesitate to use her authority if he stepped out of line.*

And it was an incredibly narrow band he had to operate within. She would have been entirely right to take action; finally he understood that. At first though, it had been a lot *different, the mores were almost like a strait-jacket. It was different now that he had met Lucinda 'up close and personal' as they used to say – or was it as they were going to say? He did not think he knew anymore, and he was supposed to be one of the experts on the subject!*

Thus caught up in his own wandering thoughts and that incredible performance he had just experienced – and he did not only mean the Beethoven – he paid no attention to direction. He was letting the horse have its head, it knew the way home probably as well as he did. So it wasn't until the buzzing in his head grew very loud that he looked up. My God, he was in the Hollow, and he jerked the horse up so sharply that he was nearly thrown.

It took all his new-born skill to get the animal back up the slope, afraid it might just take off straight through *the Hollow.* He *would decide when that was to be, not some damn* horse.

At the top, he stopped to get over his fright and to think a little, maybe a lot. He had had plenty of time this last year. Strange though, that buzz. He had been here a number of times early on, but there was not the slightest disturbance then. Probably hadn't been here in perhaps six months, so why now? It was about a year, and he dug out his watch from an inner pocket. He now kept it well hidden, it raised more questions and downright suspicions than he could possibly answer, for it was one of those digital jobs that told every thing; but not for much longer, for the cell must be about on its last legs.

Of course! That must be the reason. It was Mid-Summer's day; exactly one year, pretty close to the exact time, even. That was *exciting, and he considered going down into the Hollow, even took several steps, then backed up again. If he was going, he would take that lovely girl with him. Or could he; should he? It would be over his dead body if Lady Blackmoor found out. Damn it, his head was spinning out of control again. He was just going to have to get out of this place before he went crazy. One thing he knew now for sure: he wasn't going unprepared, and if that meant another year, so be it.*

He turned Johnson — its bullheadedness reminded him of the ex-president — and rode off so as to give the Hollow a wide berth before settling back into his reverie. Well, at least now he knew that it was a solar cycle, to the hour probably. One more piece of evidence. But why solar, he would have to think about that some more, try to rationalize it. Powerful pull though, really quite remarkable. His scientific instinct told him to go back and carry out some controlled experiments. Find out if the pull diminished over time and distance, if it was linear or quadratic, a point or a line, could even be spherical, though he doubted it. He could have thrown a rock or two through it to see what happened. Perhaps offered up Johnson as an experimental sacrificial lamb — better make that 'horse', but that would have raised more questions than he could answer!

He did not slacken his pace forward though, he noted wryly to himself, for his gut common sense said to stay the hell out of there. That place was dangerous, *and apparently not only to him, as he had heard rumours concerning it.*

The real questions he had pondered long and hard were why here? Almost self-evident, though not entirely because time and space weren't truly separate. In fact, Stephen Hawking had postulated that they were at right angles to one another. Pity he hadn't managed to make that connection before his 'trip'; Stephen might have had some good ideas to offer. Too late now. And he wished he had entered those esoteric discussions of parallel universes, or multiple co-existing universes as the latest advanced thinking postulated.

And why this particular period for 'destination'; no theories there yet. And, lastly, and most perplexedly, why him? He had some initial thoughts on that but they were too vague at the moment to publish. Publish? Who was he kidding!

It was all Carl's fault, Carl and his damn flow chart. His elder brother had always been a history buff. Who else would have visited the site of Waterloo at least once a year, sometimes several times? That is how Carl had run across Otto. The Family Tree was complete, so everybody thought. But not Carl! Too smart for his own good that one. 'If it ain't broke, don't fix it' was Manfred's guideline, but not Herr Carl Werner.

But then he would not have met Lucinda, so it wasn't all bad. Still, he could not have missed what he did not know. That reminded him of one of his former professors: 'Let us start by listing the unknowns,' he would say to the assembled students in his first lecture. And there were always a few who would spend several moments staring at their notebooks, about to write some thing, before they realized that every one else was laughing.

The way Carl explained it, it was the birth dates; Helga's, which of course everybody knew, and then out of the blue, Otto's, her twin who nobody knew of except smart-aleck Carl. Should have kept it to himself. The Rolls of Honour for Waterloo were the key, combined with the accidental browsing through a Debrett's one innocent day on the Web. And there it was: Otto von Schwartzenheide 'Baron Blackmoor' in translation.

'You are going to England,' Carl had said. 'You will be in London for at least a week at the conference' (all of which was true). 'Take an afternoon off to clear out the dead cells, and visit this lovely country estate.'

'OK,' he had responded, 'I might,' although he had no intention of doing so.

'Good,' Carl had replied, 'I have written and told them you are coming, and they wrote back and said they would be delighted to see you and you can stay over the weekend.'

'Damn you Carl, for wasting a good weekend for me,' he had retorted. He remembered that he had got very angry with him. He had been hoping to find some nice young thing at the conference and try his chances at a little . . . whatever. He might have got lucky.

But he had to be honest. He had enjoyed meeting Cynthia Blackmoor, a very attractive woman perhaps a year or two older than himself. She even spoke a little German and lived in the gate-house of the estate, the main house being in a rather poor state of repair.

'But I mean to restore it one day – if the wealthy side of the family could see their way to assisting, of course. Trouble is . . .' and she had left it dangling. 'Unless, of course, I can manage to catch me a rich husband,' giving him a wide smile.

Then he had shown her Carl's computer printouts of the gap he had established in the Tree; she had dug out her Family Tree, and they could see the beginnings of a fit, so they drank a toast to the venture before he went to shower prior to dinner. He had invited her to dine out, but she preferred to eat in. Besides, it was already in the oven. Perhaps another time? – which sounded most promising.

It was after dinner over a glass of Schnapps, that Cynthia had mentioned the Hall.

'Would you care to see it?' and he had nodded. 'I usually do not show it because it is not in a very good state. The roof has leaked badly in several places – though I have had that taken care of – but it has left some of the plasterwork – especially the ornate ceilings – looking rather dreadful.

'But in some way I feel your connection to it, almost as if you had been here before. Perhaps it is the Family Tree.

'It is a bit late now, but I could ask the caretaker tomorrow to open up some of the windows for light and a little fresh air. Then perhaps we could wander round after lunch.

'And if you insist on a meal out, there is a very nice restaurant on the river that serves an excellent Sunday lunch of fresh-caught trout and salad – not forgetting my favourite strawberries and cream.'

'You're on,' he had replied with the enthusiasm he genuinely felt. 'Trout with strawberries and cream sounds delightful,' and she had laughed at that. A very musical laugh he remembered. 'We could then perhaps study the two Trees together in the very building in which it was happening all those years ago.'

They'd drunk a little skol to that, talking animatedly late into the night about his work and hers as a web designer. He had shown her a couple of his sketches of the conference, while she had pulled out some of her excellent watercolours.

As he settled in his solitary bed, he found that he was quite looking forward to the venture, after all. He had wondered why he felt so comfortable here in this house with Cynthia. He was usually quite a bit more reticent than that. But there was a welcoming feeling about it all, some thing he could not put his finger on. And he recalled having had very strange dreams that night; of travelling but never arriving.

He had done a quick charcoal sketch of her having breakfast on the terrace, because he had been so taken by her striking appearance. The previous night she had been in her demure business attire of long skirt, high-collared blouse and wearing high-heeled shoes. At breakfast she was in modish shorts and a matching, nicely cut halter top, *showing a fine tanned figure with plenty of midriff and quite excellent legs ending in open sandals. Indeed, the best prospect he had met in a very long time, decidedly gorgeous – especially when she leaned over to pour him a second cup of coffee, shewing a clearly excited right breast. If that was deliberate – as he suspected – and he played his cards carefully, well, any thing could happen.*

The sketch had turned out rather well, and she was pleased when he signed it and presented it to her with a solemn bow.

Then, 'I have a suggestion for you, Manfred,' she had said. 'Why not take your pad over to the village and sketch the old church, for it has a lovely spire? I could meet you there and explore together the old stone Priory, then we will walk by the river to the restaurant. We would be back in plenty of time to look over the Hall.

'As you will be off in the morning, I could show you my plans for renovating the cottage, then I'd like to try a sketch of you on the terrace. We could have an early dinner with a nice wine I have set aside for a special occasion. Then perhaps a quiet evening together, sketching, or whatever else comes to mind.' She had smiled openly at him as she said these last bland words, but they seem to include a promise, too.

He had agreed that it was a fine suggestion and 'he would be happy to fit in with her plans for the evening,' with an answering smile of acceptance of . . . whatever.

'As a matter of fact, I would like to do a sketch of you after dinner, when we are more relaxed. Some thing less formal,' and he had taken the liberty to walk around her, examining her from head to toe, as artists are wont to do. 'You have a wonderful figure, Cynthia,' ignoring her faint blush, 'and I believe I could do it justice, given the appropriate setting,' leaving her – he hoped – with a clear indication that it would be in her bedroom with little if any attire. In response she had just smiled, but it carried with it a strong hint of acceptance.

They shared a common bathroom, and her door into it had been left ajar, so he had taken a peek. A very feminine room with a queen-sized bed, and he now believed that the open door was an invitation to share it. Indeed, his hopes were raised when he had found her skimpy night attire and robe still on the hook behind her bathroom door.

He was finding that he could grow fond of this distant cousin – in the genealogical sense, for her warmth toward him was most clear. His departure could even be delayed a day or two, if she chose to find that an agreeable prospect. He certainly did.

But his trout and strawberry lunch was to be postponed indefinitely.

He had been crossing that hollow on foot, wondering idly why it was there, though in truth his thoughts had been more on his hostess and the 'quiet evening' to come; whether she was more of a Giorgione than a Goya. Either way, he would enjoy that moment of truth.

All he could remember after that was a flash of light in his head, a loud noise, and then he was on the ground with the charcoal hot in his fingers, so hot that he dropped it. The time was burned in his memory because his watch had stopped at 9:31:29, at least until he gave it a sharp tap, and it was certainly still Mid-Summer's day, yet suddenly every thing was different. The trees, the grass, even the shape of the Hollow.

He had thought then that he must have had a small stroke, for nothing else seemed to fit the circumstance. But the heat and the stopped watch? That had been a complete mystery. He remembered seeing two young ladies in period costume riding side-saddle in the distance and thought not much of it. Somebody making a movie probably, so he headed back towards home; probably better to rest than sketch. He could sketch the church tomorrow – if he was correctly reading his hostess. Besides, they certainly would not want a tee-shirt-and-jeans clad figure strolling across their expensive period landscape. Now he realized that it must have been Lucinda and Celia he saw.

He couldn't understand where all the houses had gone – though the church was still there. But the closer he got to home, the worse he felt, until by the time he staggered through the door he had been almost out on his feet. He had managed to find his way to his room (his room, indeed, to them he was a complete stranger, an intruder), only to find that all the furniture had been changed, before he collapsed on a bed.

They told him he had been unconscious for six days, delirious much of the time. What he could not understand at first was why they were all wearing those movie set costumes. But gradually he was left with only the one conclusion. What was it Sherlock Holmes said?

'When you have removed the possible, whatever is left, however unlikely, must be the truth.'

Some thing like that, anyway. Now he realized that the old sleuth was onto some thing. They weren't *dressed in funny clothes,* he *was.*

His jeans were certainly strange in cut, though they must have known the fabric because the French sailors wore it as trousers, out of sailcloth – de Nîmes *to them, denim to him. It was the zip and pop fasteners that blew their minds. And his watch positively scared them. Silent, no 'tick', yet showing the correct time, to the second, always. Just as well they did not work out that the '01' meant* 2001, *or they might have strung him up for being in league with the devil. Not literally – at least he hoped not.*

It was the German that saved him, for only Baroness Hilda von Schwartzenheide and one very strange manservant spoke German. She was also a very intelligent and attractive woman.

At first he was unable to discuss any thing at all with any sort of rationality, for the Baroness naturally had wanted to know by what happenstance he had arrived at her door. By then he had learnt to be most circumspect in discussing the nature of his 'trip', so he only spoke of his intention of visiting the village church, all of which she took in her stride.

It was when he mentioned the Hollow that her countenance underwent an abrupt change as she became quite pale and motionless.

He said nothing, knowing – too late – that it had been a bad move.

Then after a very long pause she had regarded him sombrely and, addressing him in her quaint German, warned him that he must never speak of it again on penalty of . . . and she had made that crystal clear by drawing her finger across her throat in a most unpleasant gesture. And it never was.

When they finally got a framework for discussion sorted out – though that had taken a couple of weeks, she told the staff – which automatically meant tout le monde – that he was a distant relative of Sir Otto, from the old country, implying 'back in the hills', a little . . . you know. That was a good approach, because it relieved him of much responsibility. Whenever he did some thing strange, which was most of the time – to them anyway – they could shake their heads and knowingly tap their foreheads. Well let 'em; he was improving all the time.

It was somehow a code of honour that he and the Baroness spoke only German, although she had difficulty understanding his. Hers was a strange and formal Prussian, which he quickly learned to adopt – and suddenly he understand why, as he recalled an event from his early life.

As a young boy – about five or six as he remembered – he had spent a couple of summers in the country whilst his parents were on sabbatical in Wisconsin. They had taken Carl with them, but thought he would be better staying with old friends on their farm near the East German border.

Just across the fields – where he freely roamed, guarded by his new companion, Reinhardt, their large but friendly Alsatian – was a small, dilapidated farm. Herr Heine was at least 85, probably more like 90, grizzled, taciturn and some thing of a 'loner'. He kept a few hens, a small flock of geese, two or three pigs, a horse for ploughing, and a pony for the trap to take him to the village to sell a few vegetables, eggs, and the occasional side of bacon, for he cured his own.

Manfred remembered that he had loved those carefree days, quickly learning to call the old man 'Opa' – the familiar for Grossvater, or Grandfather. And that wasn't the only thing he learnt; for the old man spoke in a strange dialect, which wasn't much like the traditional German he was used to. But with the enthusiasm and lack of inhi-bitions of the very young, he had dropped easily into understanding and using it – much to the dismay of his hosts for they neither understood nor approved of it, so that he kept it mostly to himself. But with Opa – with whom he spent most every day, sharing the homespun lunch – he spoke nothing else. Strange how that had so prepared him for this moment, almost as if . . .

The Baroness accepted, after a fashion, that he had arrived from some where else, been transported in some unusual fashion from a faraway place in Germany, though she did not know that word. To her München (where Carl lived) was in Bavaria, and his home base of Magdeburg and college town of Leipzig were in Sachsen.

He hadn't got his Doctorate in Science with his Dissertation in Chaos Theory by being slow at things. Thus he quickly learned to compartmentalise, to separate the 'old' (by which he meant the chronologically later) and the 'new' (the earlier or here and now). For example, Poland, to the Baroness, was almost a non-place, while Prussia, much of which to him was in Poland, was the centre of the universe almost. At first the Baroness insisted that he stay indoors, out of sight, but gradually allowed him more freedom – provided he watched his tongue! She provided him with clothes that had been her late husband's, old-fashioned and country in style to shield him from too much mixing with the local population.

His English was good, but here they spoke a different dialect of it, and in a strange and formal manner. But this he learned, too, for he was good at languages, having spoken passable Russian.

He also adopted their mannerisms, styles of speech and address, and their social customs – to the best of his ability, for they were just there. The Baroness discouraged his meeting with her peers for fear he would disclose something embarrassing of his background and previous life. But he adapted, reforming himself the best he could by watching visitors, softening his normal somewhat dominant manner – as much as he was able – to remain low-key.

But he was no wiser as to why he was here, for what purpose, and for how long.

He had been there about eight weeks when the Hunt Ball took place. It was made clear that he was not expected to attend, in fact, he was to be 'invisible' and he would please remain in his room. And he did. He had a very comfortable one with a partially screened balcony overlooking the entrance carriageway and, through a panel, an octagonal anteroom that gave him access to the house interior. That is where he was sketching, behind the screen that covered the door to his room, when some one entered the room.

By keeping quiet, he had hoped that they would leave him undiscovered. And it would probably have been so had not the sketchpad rustled. The next thing he knew was that he was looking into the startled eyes of the most beautiful young woman he had ever seen. Her skin had that translucent quality so renowned of his own famous Meissen ware. He simply could not forgo the opportunity to sketch her.

That he was powerfully moved by her presence was undoubted. Why, was more difficult to fathom. Seated now in front of his opened private storage chest, he wondered whether, as she was the first person he saw on arrival – although from a great distance – there wasn't perhaps some sort of pattern imprinting, like baby ducks.

But back then it had been quite different. Then, he only knew that he must capture some aspect of her ethereal beauty. Why had he touched her? He did not know that, either. Impulse, certainly, but it was deeper, much deeper than that. She touched some chord in his soul, and up to then he wasn't even sure he had a soul. It seemed that he touched hers, for although her eyes had said 'no', the response of her silken body was quite to the contrary.

The Baroness had given him the small chest, making it clear as she gave him the only key, that he was to lock away certain things that could cause 'difficulties'; things like the strange device he wore around his left wrist, the equally strange keys in their little elephant skin wallet. Then there were the keys for the Avis car rental, and he wondered briefly whether it was still sitting in the driveway of the gate-house. That had changed hardly at all.

Surprisingly, it was his wallet *that caused the most consternation. They must have looked at it while he was still unconscious. It was innocuous enough to him: the usual stuff – driving licence, a few D-marks, some Pounds, a Shell credit card, a Master-Card and a Visa card for he always carried the two, some German airmail stamps, Munich subway pass, and a few business cards. These last would have been understood by the Baroness, with their Magdeburg and Leipzig addresses in Gothic script, and that was probably his badge of acceptance, or heaven knows where he might be now!*

He could see when he looked at it now with his new understanding, that the credit cards, with their embossed ciphers, must have looked for all the world like some Merlin's travel kit, and that maybe they would suffer a horrible death for having even touched them. The Munich pass was indeed to the 'underworld', a special privileged card to enter Hades – and to return! It even had his likeness on it. The stamps could be an evil magic designed to blight your manhood.

He had never liked his driving licence photo, and come to think of it, it did make him look a little Mephistophelean – especially with that little beard he had then sported. Do not joke, he reminded himself, your very life might be threatened by that picture. And the credit cards. How could you explain to some one here that all you had to do was go up to one of these, uh, boxes, in the wall, stick in your card, punch a few buttons and out would come money! They could not know that you had to put it in there first! And they would not bother to ask, either. They would probably punch his buttons by swathing him in chains and giving him five fathoms of water to drink.

That is why he always made sure his door was locked and bolted before he took the chest out of its hiding place. But also locked up in that chest was Lucinda, first the charcoal sketch, distinctly recognizable but quite respectable. The second, constructed by a vivid imagination in the absence of the original model, showed a reclining Lucinda without the benefit of attire, au naturel *as it was politely phrased in his world. That one was dynamite almost certainly – for both of them.*

But now that he had seen the original once more, he knew that it did not even begin to do her justice, though it would have to do until he had the model her self to work with; and he vowed to make that soon.

Then he lay down to rest before dinner, and dreamed of a 5-D world, where time and space were as accessible as the other three, and populated by scantily clad maidens dancing around him with garlands and flagons of nectar, intent only on satisfying his every manly desire.

Except that Lucinda was not among their number.

6

The Balcony

It had now become customary for the young ladies of the Quintet to play at each of the functions they attended, and these were occurring at least twice a week, more often three times, and sometimes even four. As a result, insubordination was growing in the ranks, with Georgina and Geraldine deeming that the summer was passing by and they had done nothing but work at music, either playing or practising, all season long.

'Very well,' said leader Alexandra at their next practice, 'I think we have perhaps been overworking a little. From now on, only one practice session a week and no more than two performances.' And they all agreed. 'Also,' added Alexa, 'we will try to limit the performance to one session instead of two, and no more than one encore; well, two at the most. That should lessen the playing considerably.

'We have only two more performances before the Hunt Ball; they will have to be pretty much as arranged, although we can shorten them a little. If a guest or the hostess has a complaint we will simply say that we like to enjoy our selves, too,' (applause here from the younger pair). 'Now, I have a suggestion to make for the Hunt Ball. We will see if we can play early, so that from then on you can enjoy your selves with your favourites.

'Later in the evening, there will be a solo performance by Lucy. She can choose any piano piece that she wants; is that all right with you, Lucy?' That was the first she had heard of it, but nodded acceptance.

'Finally, we shall make our last performance about the end of September. After that we may have just one or two more if the appropriate special occasion is forthcoming.'

There were groans at this from the younger ones. 'But there goes our whole summer,' complained George, and Celia chipped in.

'Do you two *children* realize what a marvellous opportunity this is providing you, to meet the most eligible young men of the County? If you do not, just ask your mother for her opinion, and she will leave you in no doubt whatsoever. Besides,' looking at Alexa, 'we have agreed that we shall take a two-week break in July to pursue our neglected interests. Will that satisfy your appetites?' And the two of them nodded, looked at each other, and giggled.

'What piece will you play, Luce,' said Celia. They were sitting on the edge of the dock on a couple of boat cushions, dangling their bare feet in the water. Their mother would have been horrified. 'The Beethoven?' continued Celia.

'No, I think I have played that enough already.'

'True; besides,' concluded Celia, 'he has already heard it. A new bite requires fresh bait.'

'Oh, you are incorrigible,' said Lucy, yet she laughed. It was a strange thing, but now the mystery man had revealed him self, there seemed no longer the necessity to always be on the lookout for him or yearning for his presence at her side. Neither Celia nor she had any idea whether he was watching or not, but they both knew that he would return when he was ready.

Besides, they were having a wonderful summer. 'The best one ever,' Celia had said on more than one occasion. The Quintet enthusiastically agreed, for in what little spare time they had between recitals, they were individually deluged with invitations from all quarters – and from some *very* eligible young gentlemen!

'Cel,' she said to her sister. 'What do you think about Mozart's 27th? I know it is a piano concerto, but I have recently obtained a copy transposed as a sonata. I have not played it that much yet, but I have enough time, I believe, to practise it. And then for the encore I have a brilliant idea – I think. I would play the Rondo from his Sonata in A-major, but very slowly and without the repetition. I have been practising it that way, and it sounds very beautiful. Then for the return encore, I would play it again, but this time as fast as possible. What do you think, Sister?'

'For the encore, that is brilliant, Luce. The second one would have them on their feet cheering, without a doubt! For the rest, I was thinking some thing a little different. The same composer, perhaps, for the whole evening – or most of it, anyway, so that we have one thread running through every thing.'

'Well, we might, but whom do you suggest, Sis?'

'Well, Franz Schubert has composed some wonderful pieces recently. Although the last movement of that Mozart is very beautiful, and would certainly draw him out of his lair, I thought for the Quintet we might have one or two light pieces – the Minuet in G by Boccerini is always well received – and it would allow Alex to display her wonderful violin skills. Then perhaps the last movement of Schubert's Quintet in A major.

'For your solo, it would be a nice change to play a medley of love songs; things like "Traümmerei" and "Für Elise". They will suit the mood of the Hunt Ball guests perhaps better than the more serious music,' she concluded, 'and what better than the early promise of a love song!' At this, Lucy laughingly splashed water on her sister with her feet, receiving a shriek of protest and more splashing in return, requiring them to repair to their bathroom by the back route that Lucy remembered so well.

It was the afternoon of the Hunt Ball. Piano and other instrument lessons were concluded, and the music assembled.

Alice had a new lilac dress; the prettiest yet, she avowed. The young ladies were resting, trying to sleep a little for it would be a long night, but they were too excited – or thought they were, for Alice had to rouse them – every one.

Lucy's dress would be the cream satin, though why, her mother could not fathom. She had offered to have several sent up from Town to try, but Celia would have none of it.

'You will understand one day, Mother,' was all she would say. Alice had removed the 'pearls' and sewn 'emeralds' in their place, and the lace trimming was also changed to an *eau de nil*. The key element to ring the changes though would be the real emeralds. These were Lady Etheridge's, and were a matched set that consisted of a full necklace and solitaire drop, with long-drop earrings, together with an emerald bracelet for the left wrist and a full emerald dress ring for the right hand.

When Lucy tried on the dress for a final fitting, she also applied all the jewellery to assess the overall effect.

'Absolutely overwhelming, my dear,' remarked her mother, in some awe. 'I do not believe they ever looked better on myself! They match your eyes beautifully. But please remember, my dear child, that they were a present from your sister's father, when we lived in Vienna, and that they are very valuable. They are probably worth more today than the entire estate.'

Then turning to Alice, she said, 'Every time you look at Miss Lucy, you will count the pieces to see that they are still all there! I could not bear to lose a single one,' to which Alice nodded and curtsied.

Although the Ball did not begin until at least nine o'clock, they would be there by eight. That would give Alice sufficient time for the final dressing and last minute hair brushing and pinning. They also liked to eat a little some thing before the performance in a more relaxed atmosphere.

It had been arranged that they would entertain at about half-past nine or ten o'clock. Lucy would play her final solo some where after midnight.

Celia had never seen so many people at the Hunt Ball, and she had never had so many dances with so many different partners.

'You see?' she observed to Lucy during a quiet moment, 'I told you the "Sunshine Line" would bring them all running! Was I right?' And they both laughed.

Now she was quite exhausted and definitely over-heated, when she met Lucy in the same state. Together they made for the balcony that over-looked the portico and fanned them selves vigorously.

When they were a little recovered, Celia had a thought. 'Let's go and see if we can find "The Door" in the salon.' But search as they might they could not be sure which panel was the opening one, and there were certainly too many present to go actively tapping and pushing at the walls.

Reginald came looking for Celia because he insisted that this was his dance, at the same time that Alice sought Lucy to take a rest before her performance, and then to complete whatever *toilette* was necessary.

Back now on the terrace, Celia was glowing with excitement, for Reginald had just declared that he could not live another moment without declaring his love for her. She had replied that he had drunk too much of the excellent claret being served just then. He did indeed look very flushed. He said she had trampled on his heart and he was insulted by her callous indifference to his anguish. She pretended not to care 'a fig', as she indelicately put it.

Lucy was simply exhausted. The solo had been so well received that she had to perform *four* encores; would probably have been there all night had not the band struck up a waltz while she was off the platform. Then before she could rest she was waltzed off her feet by Geoffrey, followed by the very handsome young Guards officer for the third time, and after that Lord Houghton, who'd had too much to drink and held her much too close.

Geoffrey had brought some chairs so that they could be comfortable, but Celia ordered him to take away all but the two. They wanted to be alone at that moment and she waved off any number of young men who had the temerity to approach, deaf to their blandishments and entreaties.

'It was wonderful, Luce,' she said. 'The poor young man was tripping all over his tongue, then he accused me of laughing at him. Said he would never talk to me again as long he lived. But never take a young man at his word when he says things like that, for I do believe I see him making his way in this direction. Shall I dismiss him?'

'Now you *know*, Celia, that you like him, why do you torment him so? He is really a very nice young man; and you are very fortunate to have some one so devoted to you. He quite worships the ground you walk on.'

'I know,' sighed her sister, 'It is dreadful of me,' but she giggled. 'Though I noticed *you* melting in the arms of the Captain of Horse! That must be at least five times already.'

'I was *not* "melting" in his arms,' protested Lucy; 'I was perhaps just a little tired, that is all, and it was only twice as I recall,' but she blushed. 'Who is he anyway? Not that I have the slightest interest in him at all,' she said dismissively; but then had to lower her eyes against her sister's questioningly-raised eyebrows and penetrating gaze.

'I do declare you are a faithless strumpet, Miss Lucinda,' she was chided, in reply. 'He is a *very* eligible young man, quite the catch at this Ball as any of the young misses could tell you, for they have all set their caps at him. He is Captain Charles Allison, third son of the Earl. I have been watching him, and he has not been able to take his eyes off you all evening! It must be those emeralds on their "sunshine field",' she exclaimed, running a delicate finger along the 'Line', and they both laughed again.

'But, seriously, Luce, I do believe he is in earnest, for I was told by more than one person that he was enquiring of you. Mark my words; once he declares a serious interest – and he is not given to frivolity like some of the young jackanapes – he will be *very* difficult to put aside. So I think, dear Sister, you had better watch your step on *that* account. And

I was quite correct, here comes my faithful Reginald, and the Captain is watching him, knowing that he will find me, and where I am, you will likely be! So remember what I told you,' as she was swept away by her beau who would brook no resistance.

'Oh dear,' whispered Lucy to her self, 'whatever shall I do?' The Captain had seen Celia emerge from the shadows of the terrace, and was indeed making his way in her direction. His progress was impeded by the swirling dancers, but he would not be long delayed by them, and he had a most determined look on his countenance.

In a corner of the terrace, set back against the wall, was a large bush in a sizeable earthenware pot. Perhaps she could squeeze behind that, although it could be quite a disgrace if he found her hiding. How would that look! But she must try, for she was not ready to make any moves on that path until she had had time to resolve many conflicting emotions. She found her self strangely attracted to his aristocratic manner and generous conversation concerning her appearance – despite her denials to the contrary and her passion in quite another direction.

She had just squeezed into place when she felt a hand take her arm. She opened her mouth to scream, when a mouth close to her ear whispered 'Lucinda', and she was gently guided through a gate in the wall, which was then quietly closed behind them.

She would have spoken, except for the lips that were now passionately crushing her own. For the next moments she heard little except the pounding of her own heart, fearful that it would give her away, though that was unlikely, for her bosom was tight against his in fierce embrace. And the kiss lasted long after the Captain's puzzled and disappointed footsteps had died away.

Then she was led by the hand up a narrow walkway and onto a balcony where stood a familiar screen against the door from a room, a small table, two chairs, and a lighted three-branch candelabrum. As she turned to address her rescuer, she was swept into his arms again, his eager mouth was all over hers, and her eyes, her ears and even her throat.

She had never been kissed like that, in fact, had never really been kissed in her life, though she would never have admitted it to anyone. When he had to stop for breath, he held her tightly to him, while his hands explored her neck and back, down to her waist and beyond, pulling her into him in an incredible energy of passion.

When their breathing had returned a little to normal, he led her to a chair, which he pulled out, and helped her to be seated. Only then was she able to see that the shielded balcony overlooked part of the terrace and the portico below it. Still standing behind her, he put his hands on her shoulders and once more she felt their searing heat, before they slowly burned their way in perfect unison down over her upper bosom, and would have made their way inside her gown, except that it was too tight to give any but his fingertips access – though their reach was quite enough to send shards of passion down to her lower region.

She rectified this momentary pause in his exploration by placing her hands upon his with a fierce squeeze of approval, before releasing the top fasteners of her gown to provide admittance for his adoration. Unconstrained, her eager bosom swelled and hardened to greet and welcome his encircling palms and searching, massaging fingers burning hot in their worship of her body until she thought she would catch fire. And the earth stood still as his lips eagerly sought her upturned face and unshielded body, and she knew at last the thrill which Celia had promised – but of the warning that had accompanied it, very little remained.

But she did not care, for her body was in control and her mind would not obey any of the strictures Celia had implanted there. The more he opened her bodice and caressed her, even to her waist and beyond, the more her body craved and melted to his touch, and she wondered briefly if he would want more of her than she was already giving – and knew that she would not, could not resist if he did.

Where that passion would have ended was not, fortunately, to be resolved at that moment, because from behind them came a voice in the room beyond the screen.

'*Manfred, wo bist du?*'

Suddenly he released her body and stood upright. '*Hier bin ich, auf der Terrasse. Augenblick; ich komme,*' and, pinching out the candles in one swift movement as he turned, rounded the screen, and disappeared into the room beyond.

Lucy – shocked into full awareness by the peril of her fully aroused and barely dressed state – also wasted no time in rising swiftly and silently, carefully making her way in the darkness to the bottom of the steps. There she spent more than a few moments reassembling her clothing until every thing, she fervently hoped, was back in its proper place. Then she silently opened the gate and slipped through, thankful that he had not locked it, just as two dark figures emerged on to the balcony above her.

Now she could rest behind the large plant until her heart stopped pounding, and that was several minutes. She emerged just as Celia came up the steps from the ballroom.

'Where on earth have you been, Lucy, I have been looking every where for you.' Then, taking a better look at her in the light from the ballroom, added, 'My dear, whatever is the matter?' before answering her own question. 'I thought it might be some thing like that. Here, take my shawl,' and she carefully tied it around her sister's shoulders, adding dryly, 'You look a little "untidy", my dear. For now let's get you to the dressing room. I know a good way. But do not stop or speak to anyone if you value your reputation – and mine!'

Fortunately, Alice joined them on the way to make their passage easier. With the help of a screen, and a lot of head shaking from Alice, her garments were reassembled 'til all was as before, the emeralds were checked, and her hair was once more immaculate.

Now with a warning glance to Alice, Celia finally said, 'We will talk more about this; much more,' adding darkly, 'Like it or not, you shall return to the Ball, for the night is not yet half over. And no more for tonight, you understand?' but Lucy was silent.

'Alice,' charged Celia sternly, discerning her sister's thoughts to the contrary, 'I leave it to you that she is never out of your sight for one minute, or you and I will have a day of reckoning. Am I clear on the point?'

'Yes, Miss Celia, *perfectly* clear. I shall not fail, if I die in the struggle.'

As Lucy turned to Alice for support in her cause, she saw that she also was in as deadly earnest as her sister – if not more so. Goodness, *they* thought she was in the wrong, while she knew she would do it all over again if she had even one quarter of a chance.

'Come then, *Sister*, for you have many more dances to thrill to before this night is done,' critically surveying Lucy from head to toe, and nodding approval to Alice. 'The Captain has twice asked me to tender his compliments and entreat you to do him the honour of several more dances before morning. If I were you, I would oblige that request,' taking her firmly by the arm into the teeming Ballroom.

'There he is, on the other side,' she whispered as she piloted a reluctant Lucy across the ballroom, purposefully drawing notice of the intended liaison. 'At least the Captain will keep you out of *his* fatal embrace! Now smile, please.'

Then they curtsied and bowed to him in perfect unison in response to the Captain's nod of gratitude to Celia, and his smile to Lucinda was one of even greater admiration as he offered her his arm to join the dance in progress.

For Manfred, the evening was one of triumph turned to disaster. He was so close, so very close to achieving his avowed goal, when . . . Well, no good dragging that up; although he had to admit it had been a close-run thing. Another minute or two and who knows what scene the Baroness would have found on her balcony – and that did indeed give him a distinctly cold feeling, especially as he suddenly recalled the menace of her manservant, Horst, and his body gave an involuntary shudder. He knew she would be quite ruthless, as he thought back to Teutonic times.

He was going to have to be a good deal more circumspect than he had to date to succeed with the lovely and incredibly available Lucinda. Certainly her luscious body was worth a good deal of careful planning to make that conquest.

Tomorrow, he would start it in earnest. Meanwhile, he thought he now had what he needed to complete that special sketch of his heart's desire, as he locked and bolted the door.

They had slept late and it was well past noon when Alice rowed them to the Island. Neither had spoken much since they arose; Lucy because she recognized that her sister was very angry with her, Celia because she knew that to guide the conversation in the direction she sought would require privacy and seclusion. No high jinks on the way this time, for they were much too weary, including Alice, who rowed at a very modest pace.

'Come back for us at four o'clock,' said Celia, 'and bring tea with you, and we will discuss what we are going to do about our little sister here,' turning to Lucy, and giving her a severe look, while Lucy glared back defiantly. Meanwhile, Alice had quietly departed.

'No good looking like that, my girl,' said Celia as she removed her petticoats, donned the slippers, then climbed into her hammock.

'Are you going to stay like that?' as Lucy made no movement to remove even her boots. 'Are you so ashamed of your ravished body that you have to lie there fully dressed?' and Lucy blushed but said nothing. 'Very well, it is your choice. But we have several hours before Alice gets back, and we are going to have this out one way or another. Now let us relax and sleep for an hour or so,' and she established her sunshine line before closing her eyes.

Celia awoke first, and judged from the sun that she had slept for a bit more than that. Alice would not be back for a while yet, still plenty of time to debate the subject uppermost in her mind. Meanwhile, she opened her bodice and quietly brushed her hair until the tension in her bosom, created by the excitement of the previous night reached its peak and was released.

All this time Lucy was moving in her sleep, in the grip of some powerful dream, until Celia reached over and held her hand 'til she quieted and finally awoke.

'Are you going to tell me about your dream?' but Lucy shook her head. 'It was one of those, was it?'

Lucy blushed and nodded. 'Do you get them, too?' she asked her sister.

Celia nodded in return. 'Was it *very* real?' and again Lucy nodded, putting her hands to her chest.

'Would you like me to brush your hair for you?' but Lucy shook her head, closing her eyes in anticipation of the conversation she had been dreading.

'It would be much better,' continued Celia, 'if you got rid of some of those clothes together with the tensions in your body so that you can relax, but suit your self. In any event, you are going to tell me all about last night.' Still Lucy remained silent.

'Very well,' responded her sister, 'then *I* will tell *you*. When I left you to dance with Reginald, you were on the terrace and Captain Allison was on his way there, so you could not have left without meeting him. As I saw him some minutes later without you, you must have stepped behind that bush, and there must be a gate or door behind that where he was waiting, hoping to catch you alone. Right so far?' Lucy said nothing, but the colour in her cheeks told its story.

'That would lead up to the balcony overlooking the carriageway I seem to remember in daylight. So *that* is where his room is!' and Lucy finally nodded.

'He led you to the terrace, and there behaved as before, except that it was too dark to sketch.' Lucy hesitated, but still said nothing.

'Well?' continued her sister, 'I am waiting.'

Lucy hemmed and hawed, but finally whispered, 'Well . . . no; the bodice was too tight for him. So I had to . . . to . . . loosen it.'

'You *had* to loosen it?' queried her sister. 'It wasn't enough that he kidnaps you from the Ball; *you* had to make it easy for him by opening your gown? All the way?' but Lucy shook her head.

'I see,' continued Celia. 'You gave him the encouragement and he did the rest; exposing you right there on the terrace, so you were half-naked almost from the beginning of this sorry little affair.' Lucy simply hung her head as the tears began to trickle down her cheeks.

'Usually, my dear, a man makes many attempts before he succeeds to that degree in his quest – *if* he ever does, that is,' she continued, bitingly, 'but not apparently with my sister. She is so eager to be fondled and titillated that she undresses her self. *Very* comforting to hear, I must say,' and she exhaled loudly in sheer exasperation, unmoved by Lucy's obvious distress.

'Did you learn *nothing*, you silly girl, from our discussion of so recently,' she continued, angrily, 'right here where we are lying now? Did I waste my breath as it all went in one ear and out the other? And having granted him the favour of your full upper body, you were quite confident that you could stop him – and your self – before he went further?' And Lucy went a deep crimson.

'Are you quite, quite *mad*, Lucy?' misinterpreting the extreme embarrassment. 'You actually permitted him complete entrance to you on that open terrace!' said Celia in horror, 'in the middle of the Ball?' And for once Celia was speechless, for although Lucy was shaking her head in violent rejection, she could read in her sister's expression that was exactly where the 'exploration' was leading – and probably well beyond and she involuntarily covered her face with her hands in a state of complete shock.

It was some moments before Celia could regain her composure, finally to inquire caustically, 'So just how intimate did his adoration get?'

By now, Lucy was crying openly, tears running down her cheeks as she shook her head. 'Only a little farther than the top, I swear. Lady Blackmoor called him from his room, before he . . . he . . .' she sobbed, quietly.

'Far enough!' cried Celia, 'but heaven be praised for saving you from a much worse humiliation. If our hostess had been a little later arriving, even by a minute or so, she would have discovered one of her principal guests, her star performer of the evening, quite naked on the terrace with one of her own house guests. By then he would doubtless have been making love to you, considering the "resistance" you offered to his venal conquest. A pretty scene, indeed!'

Lucy sobbed all the harder at the brutally explicit picture her sister painted, for she could not refute one single word of it.

'I can see I did totally waste my time and my breath,' Celia cried, raising her face and arms to the heavens as if imploring their assistance. 'You have absolutely no intention of listening to any advice as far as *he* is concerned. Anytime he wants he can satiate his carnal desires with you. And in any place, apparently,' continued Celia, bitterly. 'One final observation, though, and then I will desist, for it is quite useless to remonstrate further,' and Lucy steeled her self for the blast.

'Did you remember, Lucy, whilst you were revelling in his adoration and ravishing of your body, that you were adorned with a *considerable fortune in emeralds*? If in that shared moment of abandoned and intimate passion a clasp had been broken, or even a jewel dislodged, you would never be able to replace it. Did you pause to think how you would approach Lady Blackmoor?' she continued, scathingly. "I am terribly sorry, Your Ladyship, but during a period of intimate exposure and its ensuing ecstasy with your house guest, I seem to have mislaid a priceless emerald necklace on his balcony",' and she gave a snort of utter disgust.

Lucy turned to her pillow, unable to take any more of the haranguing, and sobbed harder than ever. The trouble was, not a single thing her sister had said was in error. Only then did she realize the enormity of her wantonness, the disgrace she would have brought to all who had been associated with her. Celia would be completely ostracized – probably forever – and the shattered 'Quintet-cum-Trio' given a wide berth. Lady Etheridge – she could not bear to think of her as 'Mother' or even Aunt – would never have overcome the shock.

And she, her self, would have been required to quit the County immediately, never to return to that which she desired and had so grown to love. *Never to see any of them again.* As for Lord Houghton and . . . horror of horrors! Was *he* really worth all that? And she already had the answer to that question before it was even framed.

In the enormity of it all, she made to rise, but fell back, her head spinning wildly, as she felt the hammock sway and realized that her sister had departed. Then she faintly heard the splash of pebbles from the end of the island, as Celia vented her anger with them, before blackness engulfed her.

The hammock rocked once more as Celia returned, but Lucy did not respond, even as Celia spoke to her and shook her a little, thinking she was sleeping – or pretending to. With a start, Celia realized that all was not well with her sister for she did not stir even to a more vigorous shaking and a louder calling of her name.

Now more than a little frightened at this turn of events, she quickly but carefully stepped down, fearful her unmoving sister would fall out of the hammock on the other side, doing her self an injury, perhaps even . . . Then she swiftly picked up a towel, ran to the lake to wet one end of it, and as quickly returned to cradle Lucy's head in her arms and gently bathe her forehead and cheeks.

It was some minutes before Lucy responded, but gradually she stirred, then whispered, 'Celia, forgive me,' and was quiet again until her shallow breathing returned to normal – during which time her sister was mostly holding her breath.

Then, at last aware of her sister cradling her head, she turned to face her. 'What shall I do, Celia?' she whispered, hoping to forestall her renewed assault. 'I freely admit that I seem quite unable to help my self as far as he is concerned. It doesn't happen with anyone else at all; just him, and I do not know what to do about it. You must help me.'

'Quiet, my darling, rest a little 'til you feel better.' Then she replied softly, 'Well, dear Sister, I did try, or at least I thought I did,' and she took her sister's hand to find it as cold as ice, despite the warmth of the day, and she rubbed it briskly to return the circulation.

For several minutes both young women pursued their own thoughts, before Celia broke the silence.

'I am sorry, Luce, I spoke much too harshly to you just now, and I did not have that right. It was, I think, the frustration of realizing that I had failed to communicate the importance of the terrible dangers we women face in combating the fires of our own bodies. I am sorry it did not work; it may even have had the opposite effect, and aroused a hunger to experience the thrill of a personal encounter, but this time with a man, instead of an imaginary, innocent little blue cloud. I just do not know. But I am very sorry to have upset you so much . . . that . . .' and a tear dropped onto Lucy's forehead.

'Celia,' Lucy whispered, misjudging the cause of her sister's tears, 'am I very wicked; even beyond redemption?'

'Whatever gave you that foolish idea,' came the soft reply. 'Of course you are not wicked, sweet Sister; just terribly unwise, that is all. But in some thing that can only end in disaster if you do not curb your instincts. I was angry because I seem to be unable to help you parry his forays or sublimate your natural desires. Unless you are able to accomplish one of those, you must not meet him again, or there will certainly be no salvation, and I am very afraid for my beloved little sister.'

'Really?' said Lucy. 'Is it that bad?'

Celia nodded. 'Well, what will you do next time you see him? Fall into his arms, let him have his way, hoping this time he is not interrupted? No; I am sorry, sweetest, that was more than a little unkind. But can you truly say that you will behave as a young lady should and not even let him *touch* you? I had hoped somehow to make you understand, Lucy, that not only do you have to rebuff the advances of *his* body, but you also have to resist *your own!* You see, its innermost desires are on *his* side; they *want* his touch, his exploration, his adoration. Deep inside you are secretly, desperately even, wanting him, willing him to succeed. Yes, it is a battle that you will one day lose, but you have to make that surrender count as a victory for you, not a conquest for him. Do I make any sense?'

Lucy was silent for a long moment, before replying, hesitantly, and with a sigh. 'Yes, I think so.' Another pause. 'Yes,' she repeated with a stronger voice now, 'I *do* see what you mean. So it is up to *me* to work out an avenue of survival against the dual attack – external *and* internal. Yes, that makes a lot of sense, and I have only part of me to do it, namely my head, for my body will lose me the struggle every time – certainly as far as *he* is concerned – indeed, as it is doing now,' she concluded.

'You feel the tingles even now?'

Lucy nodded.

'Very well, we will take care of that later. But some thing has just occurred to me that I must confess to you. One of the reasons I was so angry minutes ago, was that I was perhaps a little envious,' at which Lucy's eyes opened wide. 'Not of the experience with him on the terrace,' she hastened to add, 'but of a different nature.

'You see, dear Sister, I have never had a beau who was as insistent as he is. Oh, I have had many a suitor who wished they could get to Step One – which is what I call the kissing stage – though not to be compared with what you have just described. I would have to label that One-x for extreme. A peck on the cheek is as far as most of them get, though one or two have been bold enough to kiss me on the lips, to which I have sometimes responded with pleasure.

'They, the young swains that is, would not have dared to attempt Step Two, which is access to the bosom, nor would I have permitted it – though

I freely admit never to have liked any of them sufficiently to even think of it.

'Step Three is the stage that you have already reached with Manfred; that is where he has free access to your whole upper body, to make love to you as he chooses, meaning that you would have no clothing to restrict him. And, believe me, he would make absolutely sure of that,' she added ominously.

'Step Four is access to your lower body – from which you were saved purely by chance. So whilst he is further enchanting your now naked upper body, he is relieving you of any remaining clothing. Remember, Lucy, that he is extremely skilled in this matter, and in the thrill of those precious moments, you would probably not even notice it. By now he would also have you lying down, stark naked for him to do to your body whatever he wished – and you would be loving every moment of it.

'Step Five, which we need not go into now, follows as surely as night follows day.

'If any young woman were to allow such indecencies, it might not happen at one time; but each time you provide him the opportunity, he advances another step toward that ultimate union of bodies – and your inevitable disgrace.'

During this whole telling, Lucy was becoming more and more tense as she recalled, Step by Step, what her lover (and she could think of him in no other manner now) had achieved in a matter of a few minutes – all the way close to Step Four. At the same time her face was becoming more and more pale, until it was dead white, and she was on the point of fainting, such was the agony in her spirit.

None of this was missed by her sister, but she held to her narration because the success – or failure – of what she knew must be achieved, was paramount if complete humiliation and societal rejection were to be avoided, though she did wipe Lucy's brow with the damp cloth and rub her hands to restore some sense of normality.

'Oh dear, I do seem to have made a complete disaster of every thing,' was Lucy's only response before lapsing into silence once more.

'Well, I cannot refute that, Sister dear, though it pains me to say so. But there are two things I still need to bring to your attention: one that I understand, and one that I do not. So let us talk about that.

'But before we do, a sudden thought occurs to me. Do you love Manfred – in the same manner that Reginald apparently adores me?' The silence was complete for some moments before Celia answered her own question.

'Obviously you do not.'

Much surprised, Lucy gave her own response. 'How can you possibly say that without knowing what is in my heart?'

'Because my dear girl, if you did, you would have answered in the affirmative immediately, without hesitation. It is the one thing that a young woman knows with certainty. Either she does love or she does not – there is no in-between – and you very evidently do not, for the heart is very clear on that subject.'

'Let us now move to the thing that I mentioned; the one that I understand that is, namely, young men. But first I must talk about our selves, young women. We are motivated by love. We wish to love a man for all his qualities of goodness, kindness, thoughtfulness, and so on, and seek to be loved by him in the same manner. And we seek that in one man only. Once chosen, we seek no other. I am speaking in broad terms, of course,' and her sister nodded. 'There are exceptions, but that is the general rule.

'So let us turn to the young men and their reasoning.

'They are motivated by their natural desires – again I speak broadly, but in almost every case it is true. The one exception is when a man is in love; then he is virtually as are we. He is dedicated to that one only – and here I would include Reginald. Note that Reginald wants to *marry* me, *not* to make love to my body. That would come later, of course, but not until he secures me at the altar. The marriage bed takes care of the rest. Even then, it may be many months before he has the temerity, and she the acceptance, Step by Step, until they mutually reach that ultimate unity of Step 5. Is all that clear so far?'

Lucy nodded.

'Now to the broad body of those others. Nature has made them the way they are. They really have no other course than to act as they are made. Is that also quite clear?'

Again Lucy nodded.

'Good. Now to show how great is the level of your understanding, suppose you tell me what you think that intention is.'

There was a long moment of silence before Lucy responded, and then only after much twisting of her handkerchief and a deep blush. Finally, in a whisper, 'Is it just me, my own *outer self*?'

'Hoorah, then you *do* understand. They seek only your body, ravishing it, step by step, until they reach their ultimate – and *only* – goal, the complete union of his body with yours in Step Five.

'Note, my dear Sister, that at no time have they talked of love, or if they have it is a false declaration – and any sensible girl knows when that is by their actions, their attempts to get to the next Step.

'Has Manfred told you that he loves you? Has he spoken of engagement, or even of marriage? Indeed, has he made *any* declaration? If I understood you correctly, he has rarely spoken at all! He seems to think of one thing only; that is his own carnal desire, his access to your body and its delights, before that ultimate insult to your spirit: Step 5. And after that, he no longer has any interest in you – except perhaps to repeat it in an even shorter time until he tires of your "delights" and looks for some new conquest.'

'Then that is what you meant when you said "I have to put up with it".'

'Exactly. You are still hoping that one day he will say those magic words, I love you, in a tone that speaks the truth. Yet the longer it takes to say that, the lesser the chance of it ever being spoken. In the meantime, he expects, *demands*, that you are to be there in your naked state for his every desire, of whatever type and as often as he chooses. There; have I painted a bleak enough picture?' and Lucy could only nod before turning to lie on her face and sob quietly into her pillow, while Celia gently stroked her back until she was calm once more.

'I am sorry to see you like this, my love,' as she looked into Lucy's tear-stained face. 'Yet there is one more thing we must discuss,' ignoring the shudder that went through Lucy's frame. 'But this time I shall need your assistance, for you know much more about it than I. Agreed?'

Lucy replied with a reluctant nod.

'Good. Now what I am about to discuss is not to be taken as a criticism of you or your actions. I am merely trying to understand some thing that puzzles me greatly, and it has two parts.'

Lucy nodded once more.

'Very well. You see, my darling, I do not know a single man who would *dare* to behave as your lover does with you, and he does it as if it were a *right*! I have already said more than enough about your unwise behaviour, but what of his? What madness makes him think he can ravish you in that open manner with no regard whatsoever for the propriety of it – let alone your feelings on the matter? It is as if he were a law unto himself. Do you have any insight into that?'

Lucy merely shook her head.

107

'Well, we know he is strange, clearly different in an aspect that I cannot define, which brings me to the second point. How is it that he got you to open your self to him so completely? What power is it that he possesses that makes you melt to his every desire? Do you know of any other young man for whom you would undress your self as you did for him?'

At Lucy's decided shake of the head, Celia continued. 'As an example, let us say Captain Charles Allison had taken you out on that terrace behind that convenient bush. Would you have let him kiss you in that wild fashion – and for you to return them in the same manner?'

Celia knew the answer, of course, but it was Lucy's countenance that she was watching, and it was one of complete shock.

'And suppose he had undone the top of your gown so as to fondle your breasts, would you have encouraged him?'

With a look of utter horror on her face, Lucy replied in an angry tone, 'What complete nonsense you talk, Celia. You know very well that such a thing is impossible. He would no more ask for that than I would permit it. And if he were to attempt such a thing, I would never speak to him again. And I thought that this was a serious discussion we were having!'

Celia simply smiled. 'But it *is* serious, my dear, for that is *exactly* what you would do if it were Manfred instead of the Captain. So I repeat; what is Manfred's power? By what means – and it certainly is not brute force – does he coerce, expect, require, seduce – choose your own word, to do exactly that to your body without uttering a sound?

'I judge from your silence that you do not have an answer, and neither do I, But the fact remains that he does possess such a power and *that* is what we must guard against. Now, we have talked enough. Let us relax until Alice returns.'

With that she removed her shoulder straps and combed the hair over her chest until she had achieved the feeling she was seeking.

Lucy was silent for a long while before she said quietly, 'I think I have grasped all that, dear Sister, and I have to thank you for taking the time to explain it to me. I shall, of course, have need for much time to digest its full import. But I know you are right, and I really will try to control my self, for now I realize that there is so much more at stake than just my own feelings and their gratification. I also see that you would all suffer most dreadfully – and all because of my foolishness.

'But perhaps there is one way that will assist in this dilemma.'

'Oh, and what is that?' turning to look at her sister.

'I could brush my self before any possible encounter, so that I do not have such a strong reaction to his nearness. Do you think that might work?'

'I can not honestly say I know, because I have never tried it; but it might. It is certainly better than your current way!' and Lucy winced at the reference to her emotional vulnerability.

'Let's talk no more about it for now,' responded Celia, more kindly now. 'We will perhaps return to the subject in a few days when we have put some distance between it and our selves. Let us relax until Alice comes, and then we can have tea.'

In the ensuing silence, Celia thought that her sister was sleeping, until Lucy slipped a hand softly into hers.

'Sis,' she whispered, 'have I become so wanton in your eyes that you could not bear to touch me?'

'What a ridiculous idea,' snorted Celia, 'of course not. You are my sister and will always be dear to me,' giving her hand a fierce squeeze.

'Thank you, Sister,' Lucy said quietly. 'The problem is that when I brush my self, it does not seem real, so it doesn't help – a bit like you cannot tickle your self, no matter how hard you try. But when *you* brush my hair over me, it is quite different, somehow. Then it has that special feeling, you know, when I was that little pink cloud,' and was gratified to see her sister nod. So she added, shyly, 'Would you comfort me, now? Please?'

'Yes, if you would like me to.'

She turned to observe the tears of relief at not being rejected welling up in Lucy's eyes. 'Of course; but not like that,' giving a playful tug at Lucy's blouse, buttoned all the way to her throat.

'All right,' she smiled in return. 'I shall not be long, so do not go to sleep,' and it was her turn to slip out of the hammock.

When Lucy returned only a minute or so later, Celia was dismayed to note the blouse buttoned to the throat. But as she climbed into her hammock, unhindered now by under-garments and moist from the recent ordeal, there was revealed a clear state of arousal that almost thrust it self through the thin, clinging fabric, heightened even further as she raised her arms to unpin her locks. Then she lay back and brushed the hair over her self.

'There,' she said, 'now I am ready, if you would not mind opening the blouse to my waist and brushing for me – but I can do it for my self, if you would rather,' she hastened to add.

'No, that is quite all right, Luce, you just relax properly,' and she took the brush and tenderly opened the blouse, wondering at the softness of her skin as she did so (realizing that she had never touched her sister in that way, either), smoothed Lucy's hair, and was not surprised to find her already hard and excited, willingly exposing her self through the hair curtain. Almost immediately she responded to Celia's gentle rhythm and skilled patterns by thrusting her self into its soft bristles; emitting little squeals of pleasure as she did so, until she was gasping for breath with the excitement of release, gripping hard on the hammock; and until she finally stopped moving and was still, though still breathing heavily.

'That was unbelievably strong, Luce,' whispered her sister. 'The last time you were not that hard nor did you react so quickly. That must have been all those pent-up feelings from yesterday and before. It is perhaps no wonder that you acted as you did if you are experiencing that level of emotion deep inside. Perhaps I understand a little better now what happened to you, and perhaps even why he is so insistent, for your inner-most feelings are so clearly shown by your body,' indicating with her brush the still-present thrust of the bosom.

Lucy nodded. 'Yes, that may well be so.' Then she added, in a whisper, 'However, you exercise me so sensitively and skilfully, dear Sister, that I am quite overwhelmed by the passion you engender in my bosom – and even beyond, in that other area. It was especially wonderful today, and I do feel much better now, as you said I would. That, and your sound advice, may yet be my salvation.'

'Now, in return for those wonderful feelings that are still running through me, can I do any thing for you?' picking up the hair brush.

'For me?' echoed Celia. 'I had not thought . . . Would you like to do that?'

Lucy's shining green eyes were all the answer needed, though she added softly, 'It will give me the greatest pleasure, sweet sister'.

'Very well, if you are sure . . .'

But Lucy was already brushing her sister's hair, parting it to expose her bosom, watching with fascination as each breast in turn swelled in response to the soft bristles, seeing the nipples harden as she teased them, learning as she remembered how Celia had done it, gaining expertise as her sister's body responded to the touch, until Celia was wriggling to the rhythm.

Indeed, Lucy was surprised at the enjoyment she her self was getting from the exercise, feeling her own body reacting once more as she increased the pace until Celia was uttering similar cries of pleasure, her movements increasing until her whole body was writhing. It was at this point when Celia seemed to be reaching a climax, that Lucy made her boldest move, swiftly opening the one remaining garment, exposing the whole lower body, brushing into the area of the inner thighs and that special private area until Celia was squealing with complete abandonment. Then with a final arching of the back and a loud moan, she was still, breathing ragged, but gradually returning to normal.

As a final act of mutual enjoyment, she placed her hand gently on Celia's breast, surprised at its softness and hardness at the same time. Celia's reaction was to put her own hand over Lucy's to hold it there until her body was quiet once more.

When all was still, Celia opened her eyes that, to Lucy's surprise, were filled with tears.

'Do I need to tell you how wonderful that was, Sis?' she said softly, at which Lucy shook her head.

'No, it is not necessary, I could feel and see for my self, it was that clear what you were feeling.'

'But I do need to tell you that I have never experienced any thing like that in my whole life, especially when you were teasing me down here,' placing her hand on her own lower body. 'I am glad that you were bold enough to try it, for that was truly wonderful,' giving Lucy's hand a special squeeze.

'Would you like me to do that for *you* next time,' and Lucy's sparkling eyes were all the answer needed.

'That is why I tried it for you, Sis, to see how you would react, what it would do for your inner spirit. Now I know, and will be happy to experience it for my self, so let's make that time soon.

'But there is some thing else I should add. Much as I enjoyed my "lover" (as I now think of him), when he plays with my body, it is not the same. Perhaps it is that with you I have no fear of discovery, or guilt, of worry that he will exceed the limits I have set for his exploration.

'All of those lay a heavy hand on my spirit, much as I enjoy his touch. With you, my darling Sister, I can be completely free, to express my self openly in enjoyment of the moment. And now that I think of it, some of the things you said about young men and their desires on capturing a woman's heart ring very true. Shall I show you one of them?' looking deeply into her sister's blue eyes.

'Is it pleasurable?' Celia replied softly, and Lucy nodded. 'Very well; you may go ahead.'

'Would you be upset if your younger sister showed you some things that you can only guess at?'

Celia smiled at this challenge to her supposedly superior knowledge. 'No, I shall not be upset. If it gives you pleasure, I shall be happy for you. Do I have to do any thing?'

'No, except to respond as you wish, as your sprit wishes. Then I shall start as he did, with Step One, move to step One-x then proceed to Step Two. All right?' and Celia nodded and closed her eyes.

After a moment's hesitation to compose her self, Lucy leaned over, put both hands on her sister's cheeks, and kissed her softly on the lips and withdrew for a few seconds. Then she repeated the kiss, but this time it was a little longer, and this time Celia responded.. For a third time Lucy repeated the kiss but much deeper and longer, finally receiving the same in return. Then she knew that she had succeeded, that her expectations of sisterly response were fully met.

Then she moved into what Celia had called Step One-x, her lips never leaving her sister's, receiving as eager a response as she was giving. Finally she decided it was the moment to add Step Two while maintaining and increasing One-x. Laying her hand on her sister's belly, she gently encircled her belly button, making the movements bigger and wider, and wider and higher until she was just under the breasts, then circled the left breast softly, moving inward until only her finger tips were encircling the hard nipple. Then she gently withdrew her hand to place it once more on Celia's cheek, gradually lessening the deep kissing until it, too, was withdrawn, and Lucy lay back quietly on her own pillow.

For some long moments there was silence, save for Celia's heavy breathing. Finally she spoke in a soft voice.

'Is that what he did to you?'

'Yes, and much, much more,' said Lucy. 'Do you wonder now why I could not help my self but be drawn into a whirlwind of love-making until I did not know my head from my heels?'

'Yes, indeed. Now I think I understand much of how he entraps the ladies of his choice. I do not believe any of the beaux of my acquaintance would be half as entrancing as that. No wonder he is so successful at seducing any young lady of his choice. And I, who thought I knew all about kissing can see that all his Steps have an "x" appendage!' at which Lucy gave a quiet chuckle. 'Now I understand his power, for he clearly comes from a society much more advanced in these special arts than any thing we have.

'Those kisses you showered on me and induced – nay, seduced me into returning – were unbelievable,' and here she paused. 'However, my dear sister, I believe we must keep those to our selves. It would never do to show any young man of our choosing that we knew more about the art of love-making than he did!'

Lucy laughed.

'You are quite right, Sister; it would indeed show us to be *too* knowledgeable, when we are all supposed virginal innocents.'

Celia gave her hand a squeeze of appreciation, and was about to close her eyes, when she held up her hand for silence as she caught the sound of an oar splash, and she waited for the grating of the keel on the pebble beach. But there was silence, except for another little splash.

'Is that you, Alice?' she called.

'Yes, Miss, and I have the Professor with me.'

Lucy sat bolt upright in the hammock, hands clutched to her naked chest, face white and strained. But Celia motioned for her to be lie down and be calm. 'Take the professor out onto the lake once more, and then come back *in ten minutes,* and call before you land.'

'Yes, Miss,' and they heard the oar splashes diminish.

'Whatever shall we do, Celia,' said the frightened Lucy, pulling her blouse tightly and revealingly against her aroused self.

'Why, get dressed, of course. But take your time, Sis, we have plenty of it; Alice will make sure of that.'

And indeed they had, for she was not back for fifteen minutes, to find the two young ladies sitting by the picnic table; Celia calm and relaxed, Lucy agitated and tense.

Before the professor could alight, Celia addressed him, stony-faced. 'Can we help you, *Professor?*'

He cleared his throat and responded, 'I would like to speak to Miss Lucinda, if I may.'

Celia looked in her sister's direction, and received a pale-faced nod.

'Very well, we grant you permission to come ashore on Our Island. However, that permission may be summarily withdrawn should you give occasion to displease anyone here, and that includes our companion, Alice.'

Celia and Lucy remained in their chairs while the professor sat on a cushion on a tree root. Alice busied her self laying out the tea.

'Professor,' Celia started, 'it is not the custom in these parts to visit young ladies unannounced, and even more so when they are not chaperoned. On this occasion, you will consider that I am the chaperon as well as the guardian, and that Alice announced you, as she most properly did. However, I can assure you that it will not be permitted again. Am I clear on that point?'

The professor inclined his head in acquiescence.

'Good. Now, you have disturbed my sister and I, much to our regret, when we were enjoying a mutually quiet moment. However, perhaps you would be so good as to advise the purpose of your visit?'

The professor looked uneasily at Lucy and Alice, and said, 'Well, I was hoping to discuss some personal matters with Miss Lucinda.'

'You may proceed,' instructed Celia, noting his discomfiture with considerable satisfaction.

'I was hoping for a more private meeting,' he said, tentatively.

'I am sure you were, *Professor*,' responded Celia, curtly. 'In which case you do not understand the role of a chaperon. There will not be a more private meeting than that in which you are currently engaged. Next time her ladyship will undoubtedly join the discussion, so I suggest you take this opportunity to say whatever is on your mind in this limited privacy, before it is altogether lost.'

'Very well. I agree, but some of what I have to say may come as a considerable shock to you. I hope you are able to accept that without undue anxiety.'

'As to that, we shall judge for our selves,' replied Celia. 'However, you should be mindful that I *know* what indecencies you perpetrated on my sister on your balcony last night, and Alice has only to put two and two together to get as much. Should others become aware of what took place – although I have no intention *at this moment* of making that so well-known then . . .

'However, I should stress that such incredible liberties, in normal circumstances, can have only one consequence. And if so known to those others, you would undoubtedly find your self involved in a duel of honour or some thing equally unpleasant. Am I clear on that point also, *Professor*?'

The professor sought Celia's face for any sign that she was exaggerating the matter, and found absolutely none. Indeed, there was present a hardness and determination that he had not expected in one so young and pretty.

'I came,' he said, swallowing hard, 'because I wish to declare my strong affection for your sister, and to explain that some things between us must be clarified before we can proceed further.'

'You may continue,' said Celia, but she did not like this 'before we proceed' opening at all.

'You are probably aware that I arrived here in an unusual manner,' began the professor. 'I was in Germany – what you would call Saxony – one minute, then I seemed to be here the next.'

He had decided that a certain obfuscating embellishment was preferable to the unvarnished truth, especially as he barely understood the so-called truth himself.

'How that was managed, I am not entirely sure. Perhaps I was administered a powerful potion, but when I awoke, I was here.' That was close enough to the truth, even to himself, for travelling in time made a lot less sense than potions; they were at least tangible and demonstrable.

'Things are quite different where I come from, the language, the customs, the style of living, every thing to me is quite strange, and therefore I must seem quite strange to you, although Miss Lucinda seems to accept me as I am.'

'So we have noted – to our considerable alarm,' commented Celia, dryly. 'Continue.'

'The greatest difficulty I have is that I am without any of my own possessions, nor can I readily get them here in any way that I can devise. Thus I seem to be without any of the normal accoutrements of civilization, although I own a large house and a . . .' (what was a sixteenth-floor apartment in Munich called), 'a small studio in the city, which I use when I work at the university. The problem that I have with a relationship . . .' – bad word, he realized, as he turned his gaze toward Lucinda; God, but she was exquisite! 'with continuing my friendship with Miss Lucinda, is that . . .' but here Celia cut in abruptly.

'Professor, I wish to make it utterly clear before you speak further, that you *have no friendship* with my sister, and until we receive greater assurance than we have already, there will exist no "relationship" as you call it, of any sort.'

As she paused, she observed the look of open physical admiration for her sister on the professor's countenance, while Lucy was white knuckled in her struggle to contain her emotions. She also observed the frown on Alice's face.

'I also require, *Professor*,' Celia continued harshly, before he could speak again, 'that you address your remarks exclusively to me. You are to regard Miss Lucy as being here in spirit only, not in the body you lust after so openly. I permit her to remain as a favour to her, not to you, which concession will be withdrawn immediately if you as much as look at her again.'

The professor opened his mouth to protest, then thought better of it. He could see, in a perverse sort of way that Celia was correct. She was behaving in a manner that was the norm to her; *he* was the strange one, and his views and opinions counted for naught. This interview, he decided to himself, was not going according to his carefully thought-out plan. Ultimately he might take matters into his own hands, for it was clear where Lucinda's emotions lay. She would share her glorious body with him soon enough, if presented with the slightest opportunity.

'Well . . . ,' he began, but Celia broke in more sharply even than before; and it was as if she had read his very thoughts.

'*Professor!*' and her voice cut into his mind like a whip, causing him to recoil. 'You will have the decency to treat my sister with the respect her innocence and position in society require; no, *demand*. Let me assure you with the utmost sincerity that if you do not satisfy Lady Etheridge *and my self* on certain important questions as to your background, prospects and intentions, then you are indeed seeing my sister for the very last time! Am I crystal clear on that point?'

'I am indeed sorry,' said the shaken and contrite professor, playing for time. 'Perhaps I could call on your mother, that is, on her ladyship and your self and request to visit your sister,' he concluded, hopefully taking the heat out of the discussion by changing its direction.

'Your apology is acknowledged, most reluctantly,' replied Celia tightly. 'As for your call, you will be advised when – and if – it is convenient. Until then, you will *not* be welcome. With respect to your request to visit my sister, I currently have reservations as to your intentions in her direction so grave that they are unlikely to be assuaged by any thing you can offer in explanation or mitigation.'

She stood up, the interview clearly over, leaving the professor shocked by the sudden failure of his gambit and at his unceremonious dismissal, for he was from then on utterly ignored.

'Alice, please take the professor to the boat house immediately and see that he is escorted from the estate. You will find Jackson in the East Orchard and ask him to see that this is done. He is *not* to visit the house on his way out, nor is he to ride faster than Jackson can walk. Then immediately return here for I have some important things for you to attend to. Am I clear on all these points?'

'Yes, Miss,' with a little curtsey, and turned immediately to usher the unwanted guest into the long boat, making sure as she rowed that at no point was he facing the Island until the landing was out of sight, then she shot forward as fast as she could pull.

As soon as Alice was gone, Celia walked to the hammocks and removed the unwanted clothing until she was comfortable once more.

'Is that wise, dear Sister, for Alice will easily see through that thin voile skirt and top, and jump to certain conclusions.'

'That is the intention, my dear. If we cannot trust Alice, then we can trust nobody. And I suggest you do the same before she returns. Now let us get to our delayed tea before every thing is stone cold.' Then taking Lucy's cold hand, she added more softly:

'I am sorry, my love, that a most beautiful and mutually enjoyed afternoon was so rudely interrupted.'

She reached to give her sister a gentle hug, which was returned by Lucy as a much fiercer one, so that for some moments, some thing of their mutual expressions of love returned to reunite them.

'But here is Alice,' as she heard a distant splash. 'Come, Alice, you are most welcome to join us.' And a few moments later, 'Now you may pour for us and lay out a little some thing to eat. You may join us if you wish, Alice. I am sure there is plenty here for Cook is always most generous.'

'Thank you, Miss, but I had some thing in the kitchen before I came,' which was untrue, but she preferred to keep the distinction of rank intact. Every one knew where they were that way – and though there were some drawbacks, it had its advantages, too.

'Alice, I shall not ask how it went with the professor for I know that you will have carried out my instructions most carefully. However, I was a little sharp with you when I dismissed the professor for I was quite angry with him. I hope you understand my reasoning.'

'Perfectly, Miss,' with a little curtsey, 'and no apology is necessary.'

'Celia,' began Lucy, as they settled to their delayed tea, 'I thought you were a little hard on the professor, for I am sure he is quite a nice man.'

'Are you indeed?' mocked her sister. 'Did you see the looks he gave you?'

'Yes, I did observe them,' responded Lucy, the colour rising in her cheeks.

'Exactly; and it was as I thought, for your own cheeks disclose yours. Am I wrong, Alice, or was that pure lust in the professor's eyes?'

'You were not wrong, Miss,' replied Alice softly, for she alone could see the tears forming in Lucy's eyes. 'But I think we may need to make some small allowances for the different customs – once, of course, we have made the professor aware what is required of him.'

'We will see,' was the only reply that her mistress allowed her self. 'But my sister is *not* going to be sacrificed on that altar,' and lay back on the boat cushions, while Lucy stared straight ahead, allowing the tears to course down her cheeks and to plop onto her skirt quite unchecked.

Alice rowed steadily and easily, barely making a ripple in the smooth surface of the lake. She took a much longer route than usual, wondering at the most casual state of dress – or was it *undress* – as she mused on the subject. Certainly there was a completely different air, a certain some thing between them – until the professor intervened, of course. And that took her thoughts to one who had once looked upon her in much the same manner. But that was quite different, for she had no position to maintain and little enough to lose – or so she thought then.

'Do not be too hard on her, Miss,' she said to her mistress, when they had a quiet moment together, 'for Miss Lucy needs understanding, not discipline.'

'Perhaps, but it seems to me that she needs to understand my view-point, which is that she is heading for disaster unless she is able to control her emotions.'

'Did she reveal the circumstances, Miss? I mean, did he attack her or force her in any way?'

'That is the astonishing thing, Alice, it was Lucy her self who invited it. The way she told it – and that took some considerable haranguing to achieve – was that he opened the gate from the terrace and immediately began kissing her in a manner that opened the flood-gates of her emotions. Thence to that balcony where it began again, a repeat of that last, but this time it was she who opened her bodice for him, so that in mere moments she was half naked and well on her way to . . . Well, you saw the state of her attire, Alice, so you may judge for your self. If our hostess had not called him at that moment, who knows where it would have ended – but I can make a good guess,' now with a grim countenance.

'The strange thing is the power he exerts over her. I asked if she would have permitted the Captain to kiss her and fondle her breasts on the terrace, and she thought I was mad to insult her judgment in that manner. Yet . . . But I must go to her,' moving quickly to the house, leaving Alice deep in thought.

It was some time later that she found a quiet moment with the still tearful Lucy.

'Try to understand, Miss, that it really is for your own good. If you behave properly, it may work out well for you. But if you are wilful, it will most certainly go against you.'

And there it rested until Celia was of a mind to accept the professor's assurances; and that would unquestionably be a very distant prospect.

But Alice was most uneasy, turning the matter over in her mind while she ironed the Misses' gowns and under-things.

James was cleaning brasses in the harness room of the stables when she surprised him, for he could not remember ever seeing her there.

'Yes, Miss Alice, c'n I 'elp yer?'

'Yes, James. I seem to recall your mention of a friend in the stables at Greville Hall; is that so?'

'Yes, Miss. 'is name's Andrew,' and Alice nodded.

'Does Andrew . . . has Andrew told you any thing of the Gentleman who was here recently from Greville Hall?

'Yes, 'm. Very tall 'e was, 'n I tend'd 'is 'orse Johnson. Andrew says 'e's strange. Visits t'ollow and speaks to 'er Ladyship in that for'n tongue, an't' same wit 'Orst, t' Footman. 'E is ev'n more strange; Andrew's 'fraid o' e! ses 'e's evil. An' 'e visits t'ollow many's a toime.'

'Thank you, James, you have been very helpful.'

''Tis a plesur, Miss Alice,' touching his cap, which she acknowledged with a nod, leaving James smiling, for he genuinely liked Alice and was pleased that he could be of service as he returned to his polishing, whistling a merry tune.

That *was* interesting. Clearly Manfred was a most powerful person in more ways than she imagined. Even so, that he could get shy Miss Lucy to bare herself almost completely in a matter of minutes, and totally in a few minutes more in order to satisfy his lustful desires – and without his saying a word! – was . . . Well, she did not know how to express it, even to her self.

Not only that, but his power was not just in his presence, for Miss Lucy would have been back in his arms in an instant given a sliver of a chance.

That Hollow was known to be an evil place, and some how she felt that his unseen powers came from there. She would need to be on her guard and keep a close eye on Miss Lucy if she was to be saved from utter disgrace.

But for the moment she would keep all that to her self and stay on her guard.

7

Jermyn Street

They had been in Town only a few days, shopping and seeing the sights, for Lucy had not been there since she was a child. Besides, the Quintet had called for a short break, and they both felt the need of a breath of different air, away from 'distractions'.

The professor (as Celia preferred to call him, certainly not 'Manfred'!), had been nowhere in sight, as far as either of them knew – the which her sister seemed to be accepting. Perhaps there was hope in that direction after all.

Now Celia was enjoying showing Lucy the many delights the city possessed. She was also glad of the opportunity to re-establish the harmony of their relationship which was now closer than ever, and it was all proceeding rather splendidly.

On the social side, it was also all measuring up to her expectations and the promises she had made to her sister. They had already been to several soirées, and now it was time for the first formal ball, with Lucy performing for the assemblage. For that she had a new ball-gown in pale green satin, and was adorned in the emeralds, including a new tiara-style one for her hair. For her self, Celia had chosen a yellow/red shot silk, and rubies – also with a tiara in rubies. Both were deemed by Alice, somewhat immodestly but without a trace of embarrassment, to be 'the prettiest young ladies in all of London'.

As they waited for their carriage in the hall with its several large mirrors, Celia acknowledged that they did both look rather splendid, and she felt it inwardly to be so. However, she could not but also quietly admire Alice's appearance – now in a pale blue organdie gown, and how it was becoming increasingly difficult to find any mark of difference between the two young 'ladies' and the ordinary 'servant girl'. Quite a remarkable and admirable achievement for one apparently without the benefit of that upbringing, and she promised her self to find out more about that one day.

On Celia's insistence, Alice's gown was quite low cut which, with the new and daring undergarments that were now all the rage in Town, showed off her full figure quite handsomely – as she had known it would.

Now thanking Alice graciously for the compliment, she added one of her own.

'While that may be so, Alice, I must advise that you also do us great credit in your choice of gown. You look most handsome indeed, and we are delighted that you are our companion, for I can find little distinction amongst us.'

Alice blushed deeply, unusually flustered by this surprising remark, casting her eyes downward with a little curtsey and a stammered 'Well . . . uh . . . thank you, Miss . . .' when the carriage arrived at that precise moment, saving Alice embarrassment of further speech. But her face was glowing and her eyes sparkling as she accepted Celia's insistence that she not be last to enter the carriage, where the darkness of the interior saved her from the emotional difficulty that was welling up inside her.

She was further elated on arrival – though more than a little apprehensive – to be introduced to her hostess as 'Alice, a friend from the country', adding *sotto voce*:

'You must remember, however, not to curtsey when we meet, so it may be more of a challenge than you think.'

'Thank you, Miss. I shall remember.'

Indeed, for Alice the whole evening was less of a challenge than she was dreading, for quite soon she spied a woman somewhat older than her self who was clearly in the same circumstance. At that she smiled as she joined her, for it was quite easy to distinguish the rank of those present. So she spent most of the evening with Martha, openly acknowledging that status, thus being able to talk of their respective households, the ladies that they served and so forth.

Several times she quietly checked on Miss Lucy to ascertain that her jewels and dress were all in order. And as the evening wore on, her confidence grew – after all, Miss Celia had found both her self and her gown most handsome with little distinction between them.

Thus with a new resolve to behave as she had been informed, and despite her declared strong reservations about joining the dance, on the several occasions when a gentleman requested her hand, she accepted with a smile, though inside she was trembling with doubt. It was not that she did not know the steps – for these were often performed below stairs where the music of the evening from above could clearly be heard, and on many occasions she was present as a serving maid so was able to observe them directly. And that sort of thing she never forgot.

No, it was rather that she had never danced in this setting, in the ball-room it self – and certainly never with a gentleman! So at first she was very hesitant and felt decidedly awkward. But after a little while, she resolved to set all that aside and just enjoy her self. And when she took the opportunity to freshen up a little, she was able to join the general conversation in the ladies' room, and her confidence grew even further.

Indeed, she was complimented on several occasions by older gentlemen on her dancing, occasioned, she suspected, by her figure – which the plentiful mirrors around the walls told her was indeed most handsome, as Miss Celia had informed her. All in all, she was very pleased with her self.

As for conversation, she invented a small village close to a well-known town in the country and made her self a widow, for she wore no rings – except one borrowed from Miss Celia on the right hand – and kept the discussion mostly on her 'very good friend', Miss Celia Etheridge and her lovely sister.

Miss Lucy performed her music in an exceptional manner, being roundly applauded by all present, and was required to provide five encores before the hostess stepped forward to thank Lucy most warmly, and invite the assembly to refreshment in the adjoining salon.

At that, Alice quietly led her to a small anteroom discovered earlier, so that she could recover in a quiet setting.

Of Miss Celia she saw little, being virtually isolated from all other guests, much to Miss Celia's clearly apparent delight, and to Alice's dismay and dislike.

But other than that little distraction, she had a wonderful time, one that she was indebted to her young charges, and one that she would certainly never forget.

Reginald had not been invited, and though he threatened to put in an appearance anyway, had not yet done so. Lucy was surrounded by admirers, as would have been Celia her self, except that she was monop-olized by the only son of the hostess, Lady Astoria. Lord Percival, or Percy, as he insisted she must call him, would allow no-one to come within talking distance of her.

Celia had met him at their first soirée in town. He was several years older than she, and reminded her then that they had met at a riding party many years before. Celia only distantly remembered the occasion, for she had been only eleven or so at the time, while he was a grown-up seventeen or eighteen. But she well remembered how handsome he had looked and how well he rode; and they now talked at some length on that subject, mutually delighted at their recollections.

She had thought of him many times since that first evening, and in her romantic chatter with her sister, confided that he was the only one on this visit to give her that special 'tingle'. To her cousins she remarked on how handsome he had grown, to which Cousin Emily replied 'maybe so', but added that she wasn't so sure that he was a suitable escort, for, she added darkly, she had heard several stories of 'distinctly unsuitable conduct with young ladies', a comment that Celia dismissed as perhaps born of envy at not being among their number.

To Celia's delight, Percy never left her side at the ball, except to allow her to dance with some of the special guests, such as Ambassadors to the Court of St. James, after which he recaptured her. They sat together at dinner, and she barely had a chance to talk to her sister or her cousins. Not that she minded too much, for she was having a wonderful time, and every time he took her hand or her arm, which was often, she felt the tingle growing in her. He also contrived, she noted, to 'accidentally' brush his hand or arm against some part of her upper body when it was not too conspicuous, and she had to admit that she liked the feeling it gave her. Reginald had never tried any thing like that, though once or twice she had half hoped that he would. It made every thing so much more exciting, and her eyes were sparkling at the attention she was receiving as well as the envious glances it engendered.

It was when he escorted her onto the terrace to admire the view that he was most bold. He had insisted that he first get her an evening wrap to cover her bare shoulders against the evening chill. When he tied it around her shoulders he managed to be 'clumsy' enough to touch her again, especially as he adjusted and smoothed it across her bosom, at which caress her heart suddenly quickened its beat, for this was no 'accident'.

But whatever his purpose in bringing her out, Celia had to admit that the view was indeed quite spectacular, showing the lights of the City and Parliament, and the river winding through it, and several of the bridges with carriages crossing them. Then, when he was pointing out the dark dome of St. Paul's, she was suddenly aware of the warmth of his hand on her waist under the shawl, gently massaging and soothing upwards until he encountered the outward curve of her bosom, which suddenly thrilled with a life of its own and grew under the encircling hold until it was hard, seeking and adoring the attention it received.

All the while he went on describing the scene before her as if he was not responsible for the fire that was consuming her bosom, causing her to stop breathing altogether, and her arm almost involuntarily to press his hand more tightly to its rendezvous.

Then almost reluctantly, she put her hand to his and gently removed it from her. This at least permitted her to breathe again, but she had only time to take a single breath, before she found that while he continued talking of the scene before them, he no longer needed to point, so that a hand found its way to mould and caress her excited bosom on the other side, while the one she was holding was now on her waist and below, squeezing it self fiercely into her softness.

She gave an involuntary gasp of surprise at the movement, combined with the deep thrills that it shot right through her, down even to her toes. Then he calmly released her and moved to the other side of the balcony to explain another feature of the view. She was ready this time to resist as she rejoined him, except that he made no move in that direction at all, as if he had lost all interest in her physical charms, which disturbed her even more and left her aching for contact.

She moved closer to him and turned pointedly in his direction to provide a further opportunity, but he suggested only that they rejoin the ball while carefully removing the wrap, this time with the gentlest brush of contact with her raging fire, while she inwardly longed for a firm touch and would have willingly remained awhile to encourage it.

Once inside, he apologized for taking all her time that evening, and that he had been unreasonably selfish in wanting her to him self, and that she should dance with some of the other charming young gentlemen present. Then he kissed her hand in a deep bow and was gone.

After that it was all she could do to suffer with whom he was dancing or conversing, and how pretty they were compared to her self. Thus it was with a special deep pang that almost at the end of the evening she saw him dancing with Lucy, her face glowing with delight, for he was a wonderful dancer, very light on his feet, making his partner feel like the Queen of the Ball, contriving to brush against her, quite evidently thrilling her sister, too.

At the very depths of this distress at the loss of a beautiful evening, there he was again, making his way toward her. With a deep bow, he took her hand, revealing that he had saved this – the last dance – for her alone, and Celia was not sure that her feet touched the floor the whole time she was in his arms, until the musicians ceased their movements, though the music played on in her head for a long, long time.

As he took her hand to wish her a safe journey home, he suddenly exclaimed, as if in a passion of agony at parting; 'Please dine with me at the Dorchester tomorrow, one o'clock. But keep it just to our selves, our little private secret,' and before she could even think, let alone reply, he kissed her hand, bowed deeply, and was gone, to bid farewell to the milling guests.

She slept badly, dreaming of many things – none of which she could remember. But around dawn, her decision made, she fell into a deep untroubled sleep only waking long after breakfast was over.

They were seated in a quiet corner in the rear, 'my own special table when I am with a beautiful woman, but none has graced it as you do', and she blushed at the compliment, and at the brushing of her inner thigh as he spread the napkin over her, recreating the fluttery feeling in her breast again.

The luncheon was delicious, although much too rich for her palate. Percy was his charming, fully attentive self again, laughing at her little jokes and saying how much he had enjoyed the evening, regretting only that duty had forced him to pay attention to some of his mother's other guests, although he had wished that he could have spent the whole evening with her alone.

Suddenly he called the waiter and asked for the wine list, although there was a bottle on the table barely touched, for she did not care for wine.

'This,' he said, 'calls for a little celebration,' ordering a bottle of champagne.

'No,' Celia protested, 'not for my self, thank you; I never drink it.'

'Just a taste,' said Percy, when the bottle arrived, and a little poured into her glass. 'You must,' he insisted, 'I cannot taste it for I ordered it, and the wine waiter will stay here all day until you approve or disapprove of it.'

So Celia had no choice but to sip it, and nod that it was acceptable, whereupon the waiter filled her glass and then Percy's.

'To your beautiful eyes,' he intoned when they were alone again and looking deeply into them, then raised his glass, waited until she raised hers, and then leaned forward to touch the fine crystal together to a bell-like ring. 'May the rest be as exquisite.'

At that moment he dropped his napkin, and when he picked it up, she felt his hand inside her skirts, against her stockinged thigh, where it rested then stroked where it should not, thrilling her deep inside, and she let it remain until the toast was drunk.

By the time dessert arrived, Celia was having difficulty controlling her giggles, although she did not think she had drunk much of the golden liquid at all. It was just that the bubbles kept getting up her nose and making her snort, which Percy found very amusing.

With luncheon over and most of the other diners gone, Celia found difficulty rising from the table, and she sat down again. 'Oh, dear,' she exclaimed, 'I do not think I could face walking through the dining room.'

'That is all right,' Percy whispered, soothing her hand in his so that he stroked her excited bosom in the same motion, sending new fire searing through her. 'Take your time; we can leave by the private exit when you are ready,' and he signalled to a waiter.

Outside a cab was waiting, for which she whispered her thanks.

'I have a thought,' said Percy, when she was comfortable. 'My Aunt lives just off Jermyn Street; you can stay there for a little while until you feel rested.'

Celia remembered little of the ride, except the soothing swaying of the cab, and the even more soothing feeling of Percy's arm around her, holding her tightly to him so that her bosom was squeezed against his chest, and she clung to him until the cab came to a stop.

He helped her down, then held her close to him as they mounted steps to a front door. She was a little surprised when instead of ringing the bell, he took out a key and unlocked it. Inside, it was silent and dim, for the curtains were drawn, and he led her into a sitting room, where he gently removed her coat and lowered her onto a settee where she relaxed while he lit a large candelabrum.

'There, that is better,' he said. 'Now you can rest for a while. But first let's make you a little more comfortable,' and raised her feet on a stool, then gently removed her gloves and stroked her hands, and finally removed her boots, making a great fuss of massaging her feet and ankles and calves, which Celia found very relaxing indeed.

'Isn't that better?' he inquired, and she nodded.

'One more thing,' and he rose and brought a wine glass filled with champagne.

'Where did you get this?' she whispered, sipping it gently. 'Will they not be upset at your stealing it?'

'Not at all,' he replied. 'They would only have to throw it away. Drink up,' he followed, kneeling in front of her, 'Now we have to finish the bottle.' And together they drained their glasses.

Celia had been feeling sleepy, and would willingly have taken a nap, but the new champagne seemed to revitalize her. That, and Percy's arm massaging her waist, his eyes looking deeply into hers, drawing her gently closer, ever closer, until his lips were on hers in a soft stolen kiss.

Suddenly it was as if the flood gates opened. All the pent up passion, unrequited since last night welled up and overflowed, and her lips responded with an ardour of which she had not believed her self capable, as she pulled him fiercely into her arms and sank back against the cushions.

It was many moments before her lips were even partially satisfied by his; by which time her bosom was in turn on fire, for his fingers had penetrated her gown to reach and stroke their throbbing tips to a new level of ecstasy. Then he leant back and gently and tantalizingly teased her white bosom free of her undergarments to gaze enthralled at their perfection, she all the time willing him to hasten before the burning passion, the urgent thrusting of her bosom was spent.

But she need not have worried, for when she was finally free of the constricting trappings of civilization, his cool fingertips on her bare mounds with their hard thrusting points of desire were almost more than she could bear, until she cried out in a mixture of agony at waiting and ecstasy at arriving. And she pulled his head towards her, desperately wanting his burning lips to soothe their fire.

But he was apparently not yet ready for this intimacy, for he raised her upright and, with her willing assistance, gently wriggled her gown down until it lay in a heap on the floor, then drew her into the hall to the foot of the stairs for another passionate kiss, while his palms teased her exposed upper body almost beyond endurance. As he led her slowly up the curving staircase, he stooped to swiftly remove a petticoat to fling it with an extravagant gesture on the floor below. Then he poured the last of the champagne from the bottle and bade her sip it.

A few more steps, another petticoat flung to the winds, another sip, and a bout of giggling from Celia, for she thought that she had never seen any thing as funny as her undergarments scattered to the winds.

At the last step, she found her self turned to face him, though he was on a lower step so that his mouth was at the level of her bosom, and at last, at last her greatest desire was fulfilled, and her spirit seemed to soar to heaven at the touch. Meanwhile his hands had found their way even to and under her bare bottom, pulling her fiercely into him self for long moments of further ecstasy.

The landing at the top seemed to Celia's legs to be very unstable, but her escort leant her against a wall, opened a curtain, and directed her to the broad shaft of sunlight now streaming in. She found her self looking into a large mirror, from which a pale figure stared back, one who seemed to have little by way of clothing. But even as she looked, the shadowy being behind peeled off the remaining upper garment until it wore nothing above the waist.

Then the hands moulded and teased her bare bosom and belly to their mirrored counterpart until she had to cry out again in the heat of desire, at which she was spun around and seated on a stool while he knelt before her, his lips and tongue burning and quenching her desire in turns once more, while soft fingers descended to massage the throbbing triangle between belly and thighs.

As suddenly, she was picked up in strong arms and carried to a dark room to be gently deposited on a soft mattress. Once more his lips and mouth and hands were all over her body, her face, her lips, her neck, her belly, her thighs, and still the passion burned hot within her as her body writhed and called out in response to hold him to her.

For a brief period he withdrew from her embrace, and there followed an interlude of much soft touching and stroking of her delighted lower body, together with a soft sound that she could not quite decipher, causing her to partly open her eyes. Even in the dim light from the closed curtains, her shocked gaze took in that he had somehow removed every single stitch of clothing except her stockings, and these he had rolled down to her ankles. No man had even had a glimpse of her bare bosom, let alone that state of total undress, and she had fully intended that none ever would, except for the one she had just married.

Not only that, but she also discovered the source of the rustling, for to her now fully opened and astonished eyes, standing beside her as he removed his last undergarment, was an equally unclothed and abundantly aroused Percy – a sight which informed and alarmed her naïveté even more, as she became newly aware of the manner and nature in which his next intention toward her open and unprotected self was to be carried through.

The titillation had been wonderful, although far exceeding what she had intended to permit and was now beginning to regret. But this, *this* was some thing too dreadful to acknowledge, though how to prevent the consummation of his passion within her innocent body she knew not.

She would have risen to prevent it, but the next instant he was upon her, grinding his naked torso into hers, while his mouth found her bosom once more. Now her cold body recoiled at the mortal peril she faced as it sank through to that little place of her consciousness that still remained un-blurred by the excess of liquor she had so foolishly consumed.

She had disregarded all the warnings she had impressed so harshly on her sister, save only one: 'Whatever else you do,' she had instructed Lucy, 'never forget to keep your ankles crossed,' and with that ultimate guardian of virtue at last alarmed, her passion died as quickly as it had arisen.

Yet the awakened sixth sense of survival also warned her not to make him angry, for she was certain he could and would enter her by force if he so chose, so her body consorted to keep him excited until, mercifully, he let out a great sigh, and lay heavy and still, his passion spent on her lower belly.

An eternity of agonized waiting later, without a word, he rolled off her, picked up his clothes, and left the room, while she remained motion-less and silent, scarce daring to breath, petrified in fear of his return as he whistled a merry tune from below. Finally, she heard the loud bang of the front door as he departed.

At last, brutally in full consciousness once more, only her shame remained to rebuke her degraded and soiled body, until it too revolted, and she was violently sick in the wash basin, before collapsing in a naked heap on the bare floor as cold and dirty as her own self.

The unclothed figure looking back at her now from the oval mirror over the basin was a truly dreadful sight. There were red marks that looked like bites around and on her bosom, belly and thighs as well as bruises in several other places, and she felt sore all over. How she had then managed to get to Aunt Julia's was some thing of a miracle in it self, let alone to her own room without being seen.

Her wardrobe yielded the garment she was looking for – a cotton robe, which she ripped from its hook and wrapped tightly around her as she reached for the bell cord. When Alice appeared, she gave two instructions; first to prepare a hot bath and then, while she was bathing, to remove all the clothing that was lying in a heap on the floor at her feet.

'Remove, Miss?' said Alice.

'Do you have trouble hearing, Alice?' replied her mistress, harshly, and the shocked Alice reddened. 'I want all of those things gone from my room when I get back. *Every thing*, you understand?' in a raised voice, and Alice nodded vacantly, understanding nothing.

'Furthermore, tomorrow you will take all of it to some place where they will appreciate it as much as I loathe it, though none of it is to be given to anyone I know, including your self.' Observing the total lack of comprehension on Alice's pale face, she snapped, 'You really must pay attention, Alice. Now hurry with that bath, and make it hot. I must be clean.'

And hot it was, so that it stung her skin as she entered the steaming water and lay back until it covered her chin, but especially where she was sore. A tap on the door, and Alice returned, pale and frightened still, convinced her mistress was ill.

'Well?' she inquired, 'Is it all gone?'

'Yes, Miss.'

'Every thing?'

'Every thing, Miss.'

'About time. Now tell Miss Lucy I want her, and then bring me some really hot water, for this is cold. And some strong soap; and a hard scrubbing brush. And do not dawdle on the way!' she finished sharply, and the troubled Alice scuttled away to do her bidding.

Another tap on the door and, when bidden, Lucy entered.

'Well?' snapped Celia to her sister, 'what do you think of your clever sister now? The one giving advice on avoiding the snares men set for unwary maidens.'

'I am sure I do not know what you mean,' replied the bewildered Lucy. 'Has some thing happened while you were out shopping?'

'Has some thing happened?' mocked Celia. 'Yes, some thing *has*. I went shopping for excitement, a little wanton titillation that I was sure I was grown up enough to manage, and was sold some thing I had not bargained for; a humiliating lesson in shame and degradation. Even if the other counsel went unheeded, let *this* be a lesson to you!' and she stood up.

Lucy gasped. Firstly, because she had never before seen her sister so completely unclothed, secondly at the marks so clearly evident, marks that had been exacerbated by the steaming water.

At that, Alice entered struggling with a large pitcher of steaming water, to gasp in turn: first at the sight of her mistress standing naked in the tub, and then at the marks so prominent on her otherwise smooth white body.

'Pour it in here,' commanded Celia, but Alice put the hot water on the floor. 'No,' she responded resolutely; 'I shall not.'

'Then give me those,' and she wrenched the coarse brush and floor soap from Alice's hand and, still standing, proceeded to scrub her self vigorously until her skin was a bright red.

'What is it?' whispered Lucy, but received no reply, for Alice had reached out, snatched the soap and scrubber from her mistress, and flung them angrily in a corner.

'How could you do that to your self, Miss Celia?' she said, which Lucy took to mean the marks, 'after the way I have looked after your lovely skin all these years! You ought to be ashamed of your self. Now lie down – at once!'

'I am, but not at my skin, only how it got like this,' replied her mistress bitterly, tears trickling down her cheeks to plop into the steam, but she did as bidden, re-entering the water until it was to her chin once more. Meanwhile Alice knelt in front of the tub and took her mistress' hand.

'Did she do that? To her self?' repeated Lucy, in an awed whisper, again getting no reply, for the other two were looking steadfastly into each other's eyes. A message was passing there, Lucy knew, but she had no idea what it was.

'Shall I, Miss?' said Alice to the silent Celia and, receiving an affirming nod, turned for the first time to Lucy.

'It was a man; or rather, a devil,' at which explanation Lucy was no wiser at all.

'Treating your self like that, Miss,' Alice said softly, returning to her patient once more, 'does no good at all. It is here that the problem is,' patting her own bosom, 'not here,' touching her mistresses reddened skin. 'You have to get rid of it from inside. The hot water just makes things worse.'

'What are you two *talking* about?' cried the exasperated Lucy, at which Alice turned to her and said softly, 'All in good time, Miss, all in good time.' Then she turned back to her charge.

'That is right, Miss, go ahead,' as she noted the tears rolling faster down Celia's cheeks. 'Just as much as you like, the more the better; and let me take care of it for you,' as she took the softest sponge and the softest soap that she could find, and gently and carefully washed her mistress all over, from the roots of her hair to the soles of her feet, missing nothing. Then she patted her dry, applied creams and ointment, and powdered her with a fine scented talcum.

'There,' she said, to no-one in particular, 'that is better, I am sure,' and she took up the cotton bathrobe to wrap her mistress.

'Not that one!' cried Celia, shrinking away from it. 'I never want to see that one again.'

Alice nodded and, to Lucy's astonishment, just threw it in a heap on the wet floor.

'I understand, Miss,' and turning to Lucy, 'please see that there is no-one around, Miss.'

She wrapped her charge in fresh, dry towels for the short walk to the bedroom when Lucy gave her the sign.

'Let me bring you some hot tea, Miss,' she said, when her mistress was tucked up in bed in a clean night-gown.

'Yes, please,' said Celia, 'and please explain to Aunt Julia that I seem to have taken a slight chill from the night air at the ball, and that we,' receiving an acknowledging nod from her sister, 'that we will not be down to dinner.'

It was difficult to say who shed the most tears during the telling of the afternoon's events, though Celia's were certainly the most anguished. And yet, with Lucy holding one hand, and Alice gripping the other tightly, the telling was not so awful or quite as humiliating as she had been dreading. But at last it was done.

'I do believe,' whispered the now exhausted Celia, 'that the very worst part was afterwards, when I had to go around that dark, deserted house, wrapped in just a soiled bed sheet, picking up all my things from where he had flung them. It was, as if . . . as if . . . he had flung *me* all over the house. Do you see?' she almost begged.

'I understand perfectly, Miss,' responded Alice softly, kissing her cheek, 'I really do.'

'One piece', she continued, mentioning a most intimate garment, 'was on the chandelier, and I thought at first, I thought . . . I thought . . .' and now she was sobbing gently again, 'I thought for a while that it might have to remain there for all to see and mock my shame, and that I must leave without . . . without wearing . . .' but she could not continue, and wept openly and bitterly on her sister's shoulder. 'I have been so wicked, Lucy, so . . .', and she sobbed as if her soul had been ripped from her body.

The hot, fresh tea that Alice provided did restore spirits a little, and the hot buttered crumpets improved them still further.

'Miss Celia,' began Alice, 'I have some thing that I would like to say.'

'Yes, Alice, please go on,' whispered Celia, in response.

'Well, Miss, you are *not* wicked. You were wickedly treated by an evil monster, who will get his just desserts, on that you may depend. But you are most decidedly not wicked your self. And I know what I am talking about.'

'You do, Alice?'

'Yes, Miss, I do, and we shall talk of it again soon, in a few days if I may, but tonight you must rest. I will see if I can get a key to the door between your two rooms as you may have a restless night.'

'Shall I, Alice?' inquired Celia, looking at her through red-rimmed eyes.

'Yes, Miss, I think you will, but Miss Lucy will be here to comfort you, and I can be here in a twinkle if you need me.'

'Thank you, Alice,' whispered Celia, 'you are very kind after the way I shouted at you.'

'That is quite all right, Miss,' was the soft reply. 'I know that it was your pain that was shouting, not you, and now that it is all poured out, you are already on the mend.'

It was Lucy who was most glad of the open door, for twice during that long night Celia cried out and moaned loudly in her sleep, so that Lucy had to visit and comfort her.

On the second occasion, the agitation was so great that Lucy climbed into her sister's bed to find her trembling violently, and jerking about as if trying to escape some terrible thing. So she put her arms around her and held her tightly until the trembling subsided and her breathing returned to a more normal state.

'You see, Lucy, what can happen to a young woman,' came the whisper when calm returned, holding her sister tight, 'even when she tries to be careful, even when she thinks she knows how men are,' and felt Lucy's nod of response. 'We two are just going to have to be more careful and look after one another, or we might both suffer the same fate,' and she drifted off finally to a soft, restful repose.

And thus they spent the second half of the night, entwined in each other's arms, which was how Alice found them in the morning, sleeping like babes.

It being Sunday, Celia and Lucy were able to spend the day without interruption. Alice had brought them a late, light breakfast, and had arranged for a simple luncheon also to be provided to their rooms later. Then she stated that she would like to take the rest of the day off for visiting and taking care of some of her own affairs, though she would not say more.

Lucy had managed to convince Aunt Julia that Celia was just slightly indisposed, needing only a relaxing day, and definitely *not* a visit from the doctor.

'Horrors!' Celia had gasped, when she heard that mentioned. 'I had not thought of that. He would have to examine me and Aunt Julia would of course insist on being present, and I would just *die* if that happened!' and she gave her sister an appreciative hug and a kiss on the cheek before they settled down once more.

With that dreadful fate averted, they talked of their own experiences, played a few games of chance, and ate their luncheon sprawled on the carpet, which certainly would not have been permitted if Aunt had any inkling of it.

As Monday was to be the last of the piano recitals that Lucy was to give while in London, a special lesson had been commissioned by her new tutor for two and a half hours that afternoon, with a final one the following day immediately before the recital it self.

She had been taking three lessons a week since arriving, and he was extremely pleased with her progress. While he had been congratulatory on her Beethoven, he expected considerable improvement in her interpretation of Mozart, and insisted on a great deal of practice. He made

great play of the fact that he had heard the Maestro play when he him
self was a student in Vienna, and had studied his playing technique with
great enthusiasm.

Now he had found one of the few pupils who could perform with
almost the same easy and delicate fingering. She certainly needed more
practice and guidance, of course, but he was gratified that so much had
been accomplished so quickly. Indeed, he had offered the opinion to Aunt
Julia that her niece shewed a good deal of promise as a recital pianist,
and it would indeed be a great pity if such innate talent should 'be born
to blush unseen', which poetry her Aunt dismissed out of hand. Such a
thing was preposterous and out of the question.

'I can assure you,' she said, 'that Thomas Gray was most decidedly
not referring to Miss Lucy; neither does she waste her sweetness. Quite
the contrary.'

He was however undaunted, for he had met such outright opposition
before and overcome it.

'You played that quite beautifully, my dear,' he praised when Lucy had
finished the last rehearsal. 'Tomorrow we will practise that second movement once more, and then you will be quite ready.' He bowed and clicked
his heels in a formal salute of farewell.

Thus it was with a light heart and a deep inner satisfaction that Lucy
returned to her room, carrying with her the tea tray. She entered through
her own room, and thence through the opened dividing door, Celia's
being locked, as one could never be sure what she would be up to by her
self, although she had been bidden to sleep if she could.

As it was, she found her lying on cushions on the floor, in front of a
considerable fire, in the new Chinese silk robe of red and gold dragons,
which she and Cousin Emily had purchased the previous week.

'Put the tray down here, and then come and join me in front of the
fire. But first take off and hang up some of those dressy clothes; for Alice
will be very upset if she has to iron them all again. You will find a silk
robe in your wardrobe just like mine, only in gold and turquoise birds
that Emily chose, and which I liked exceeding well.

'Lucy,' she said, when they had finished tea, 'would you mind getting
my hand mirror from the dresser, and that jar of ointment from the bathroom, the one that Alice used for those marks?

'Good,' she said, when they were handed to her. 'And that nice scented powder, too. You are a dear. Now let's see if its use has improved them at all, though the light is not very good. Still, I certainly do not want to add to my troubles by having hot candle wax dripped over me, so we will just have to do it by the firelight.'

She handed the jar back to her sister and said, 'You look, Luce; I do not want to until they are all gone,' and she closed her eyes and lay back on her cushions and opened her robe.

Lucy realized afterwards, when Celia revealed her self to be quite without any other garment, that she should not have been surprised, for she suspected during tea that her sister was wearing very little under her robe. But she was nevertheless startled, and her little gasp must have disclosed it, for Celia said immediately:

'Now do not tell me you are fully dressed under that lovely gown!' and she put out her hand to touch her sister.

'Good heavens, child, I do believe you are all trussed up like a turkey-ready-for-the-oven under that beautiful robe. I do not know how you can stand all that heavy material on you, suffocating your gorgeous skin, especially when you have that lovely soft silk to wear against it. Go and remove it this instant – or do not come back!'

As Lucy closed the dividing door behind her, she wondered how she was going to respond to her sister's request. No, not request, it was a typical big sister challenge, and there were only two ways to respond: to comply, and return as undressed as Celia, or to stay in her own room.

Celia was a great one at games. She had beaten her that morning in both chess games, and three out of four draughts. The backgammon was more evenly divided, but even there her sister had the edge, with better throws of the dice and a more cunning strategy.

Standing in front of her dressing mirror, now minus the gown but otherwise fully covered by under-clothing, she reflected to her image on the challenge before them.

'Face it,' her reflection was telling her. The trouble was that she was not used to undressing before the mirror. At night she always put on her nightgown before removing all her undergarments, so that she had actually never seen her self completely disrobed. Somehow it seemed . . . well, a little indecent. Now there was little choice.

As she slowly disrobed, one garment at a time, the real self gradually emerging to expose its pale body in the light of the candle, her reflection told her 'she has beaten you again; it is either this', running her hands over her slim form – which was no match for her sister's – 'or a lonely evening for self and sister'. But her mirrored self was unwilling to decide the matter.

Celia had waited so long for her sister to reappear, that she had quite decided that she wasn't coming at all. She had just reached out her hand for the ointment, when the door opened and Lucy was back, her robe wrapped tightly around her small waist.

'Well?' said Celia, 'is it not a nice feeling; that soft silk on your soft skin?'

'I have not had time to think about it,' replied Lucy, a little stiffly.

'Well, stand there and think about it. I do not know how anyone with such an appreciation of music and can play like Wolfgang Amadeus him self, could not but feel the greatest of thrills. Just think how long it took those Chinese women to weave those wonderful colours into that cloth, just so that *you* could show it off. But as I am the only one likely to see you in it, you had better show it to me. Turn around. Now the other way. Lovely!

'Now undo the bow and spin around.'

Lucy stood stock still.

'Go on,' repeated her sister, 'there is nobody here but us,' but still received no answering action. 'Very well,' she said bitterly, 'if you are going to be that way about it, come here and put some of this ointment on my ugly skin, or I shall be marked as a wanton woman for the rest of my life.'

Lucy did not always do Celia's bidding, and here again she had a choice. She knew that, despite her sister's brave face, she was still deeply pained inside, and it was part of her duty as a caring sister to do all she could to heal that hurt. Thus decided, she undid the bow, raised her hands high over her head and posed on her toes in the manner of a ballerina, so that the gown parted slightly down the middle to reveal a knee.

'That is better,' cried Celia, brightly. 'Now give me a spin. Left. Right. That is it. Now 'round and 'round to make the skirt billow.'

In the bright firelight Lucy's pale body and up-raised arms glowed a golden-orange, inside a swirl of golden-turquoise.

'Beautiful, truly beautiful,' whispered Celia, in awe. 'You present a picture more glorious than any thing Mozart ever composed. Velazquez him self could not have painted any thing to outdo it.'

In the silence that followed the swish of silk returning to its folds as she re-tied the gown – but this time more loosely – Lucy heard her sister sigh deeply, and then say in a harsh voice that cracked and ended in a sob:

'Now come here, and see what you can do for my ruined body.'

It was very late when Alice returned to let her self into the room; so quietly that neither of them stirred from where they lay on pillows before the fire, now only a dull glow.

Carefully removing Celia's gown, she was not surprised to note her lack of any other clothing. But as she made to put the night-dress over her mistress' sleepy head, Celia reacted immediately.

'No! I do not want any thing next to me. Nothing. Ever again.'

She flung her self on the bed and pushed under the sheets, which Alice then pulled up around her.

She led an equally sleepy Lucy into her room, and succeeded with the night-gown, although this time she was surprised. She had never known Miss Lucy to wear nothing at all underneath her gown, never, but accepted the night-dress before tumbling between the sheets. Then Alice returned to put more coal on her mistress' fire.

Twice during the night she returned to add more coal, to find on the second visit her mistress soaking with perspiration and sobbing softly, so she gently patted her dry, then took her hand and held it until she was asleep once more. Then she curled up in the armchair and tried to do likewise.

But the black dragon was still out there roaming free, and when she did manage to doze it was to encounter it her self, and she awoke as distressed as her mistress had been.

8

Mildred

'I swear you cheat at this game,' said Lucy, after losing her third game in a row at backgammon. 'I really do not know how you do it.'

'Some thing I was born with, I suppose,' replied her sister, 'So I cannot teach you – not that I would,' she smiled wickedly. 'I like being the best at the things I do.'

They were sitting at the table this time, for Alice had insisted that they present them selves for breakfast and luncheon in proper fashion. 'Or you will find your selves being asked more questions than you care to answer.'

Now she was back again; this time with a personal request. 'I have need,' she said, phrasing her words carefully, 'to go out for a little while.'

'But you were out all day yesterday,' said Celia, unmindful of the fact that that was really Alice's day off and she could go where she pleased. 'And I do believe it was three times last week.'

'Twice, Miss, and one of those was for Miss Lucy,' replied Alice.

'Well, all right then, twice. But today is a very important day. My sister has to practise and then be dressed for the recital, and you know how long her hair takes.'

'And yours takes even longer,' broke in Lucy.

Celia shook her head. 'No, that will not be necessary, for I shall not be going today.'

'*Not going?*' echoed Lucy. 'Of course you are going. You must be there to compose me. Besides, I *need* you there,' and she reached out over the game board to take her sister's hand.

But Celia withdrew her hand to her lap and shook her head again. 'No,' she whispered, 'I cannot. *He* will be there, I *know* he will; and I simply could not face that.'

141

'But you *must* face him,' replied her sister, hotly. 'You cannot hide for the rest of your life because some one who has hurt you deeply might also be in attendance. Do you not see that?'

'No,' said Celia, bitterly, '*you* do not see. Can you imagine how it is going to be – when he greets me with a dreadful smirk on his face, and I can do nothing, though I would wish to kill him! When I see him looking at me, *through* whatever I am wearing, seeing the natural me, *feeling* me, how I was, lying there without a stitch . . .' but here her voice broke, and for a long moment she could say nothing.

Then she whispered, 'I could not bear to know he was even in the same *room*, for then I would feel his evil eyes devouring my body all over again, his cold hands on my . . .' and she stopped, eyes wide, staring at nothing.

'*Oh my God, he did not just take advantage of . . .*' and suddenly she gave a violent shudder as the full horror and reality of her dalliance thrust it self upon her consciousness, whereupon she placed her hands to her face and collapsed on the table, scattering game pieces in all directions, sobbing bitterly once more.

She had been seduced. Deliberately and skilfully pursued with just one intent – her seduction – nothing less, and certainly nothing more. He had no interest in her at all, it was all a charade, a monstrously engineered scheme, and he had played her emotions as artfully as any harpist.

From the very first gay chatter at the soirée, to his monopoly of her at the Ball and the 'Sights of London' tour of her body, to the unrelenting titillation at 'our private secret' luncheon, every one of his actions had been a cold calculation of how to entice her to that dreadful house – which it turned out wasn't even close to Jermyn Street!

The intimacies so skilfully accomplished on the terrace tested her willingness to be pursued, to be excited, as well as her resistance to such exploration. Then came the ignoring to heighten the desire and strengthen the willingness to participate. After that, quite certain of his conquest came the intrigue of 'our little private secret', and he had only to ensure that she was befuddled enough by drink to accompany him and then with even more wine to procure her, his to titillate and play with in any manner he chose; her virtue for the price of a luncheon at the Dorchester!

What a stupid, gullible fool! What a complete idiot she had been to be taken in, even by a single word, by a single soft caress. Yet she had drunk it – literally – all in, swallowed his smooth patter like a naïve fourteen-year-old child, not the sophisticated 'woman' she took her self to be.

Mortified now that she could even have permitted those liberties, let alone revelled in such depravity, she knew she could never again hold her head up in public. Yet he, despite his monstrous deception, was free to pursue his evil sport with whomever he could entice into his evil web. Worse, she dare not make any issue of it; dare not breathe a word, for that would be to expose her self to utter contempt and humiliation. And she broke into weeping once more.

Bad enough as that was, an even more horrifying thought suddenly thrust its ugly self upon her. It was simple enough to avoid him, yet supposing he *insisted* that she meet with him again, that she provide him another opportunity to 'enjoy' her body, but this time to his full and complete satisfaction. Failing this, amongst his male acquaintance he would describe his triumphal tour of her nakedness, divulge the most intimate details of her innocent body, soon to be known to all by underground whispers. Then, on some pretext or other, they would conspire to sample her 'delights' for them selves. It had been so easy, so willing to participate was she. Equally she would be unable to refuse them when introduced by him with that knowing smirk.

To any who doubted, he could even offer proof: just ask the waiter at the Dorchester, or the coachman, they would verify that it was so, for every word of it was true.

And she suddenly realized this was his *modus operandi* with all whom he seduced. Always the same: Dorchester, waiter, coachman, his partners in crime, both well paid for their complicity in his evil conquests. They could even provide her name, for he had asked the wine waiter to pour 'Miss Celia' another glass. And doubtless the same with the coachman.

Then she knew for a certainty that he *would* come for her, perhaps this very afternoon at the recital, smiling and effusive as always, to require her attendance upon him, to secure her degradation and compliance once and for all, knowing that she dare not refuse.

In the long line of fallen women of which her cousin had broadly hinted, she was just the latest victim. That next 'private secret' would not be a request but an insolent *demand*, where he would be free to use and abuse her body at will. But this time it would be without the delight of the Dorchester, without the balm of the wine; this time she would be hungry, stone-cold sober – with no recourse but to accept and endure it, whenever, wherever, however and for as long as he chose, a naked and ravaged prisoner in that dirty and evil house, perhaps chained to his loathsome bed. It could be even in the next hour. And how he would crow. Oh, the humiliation!

She was truly, utterly lost, completely ruined, forever. Her only hope was to leave Town immediately, hope she could escape, never be in his path again, never dare to return to Town, and pray that he would not follow her.

With that bleak and hopeless future, that devastating picture of her despoiled body, a forever damned and disgraced woman now fully formed in her mind, she threw her self on the bed and wept even more bitterly – startling Lucy and Alice with the suddenness of it all, when they had thought it beginning to mend.

It required some considerable time and skill before Alice managed to coax out of her the reason for her demand that she leave Town immediately, rising even to pack her own trunks, insisting that she had not a moment to lose. But finally the cause of this new depression of spirit was understood, and they were both horrified at the power and evilness of his intentions toward her.

Fortunately, here again the recounting of the humiliation eased the pain a little, although her recovery was set back a long way, repeating her insistence that she must go without delay, for she now knew for a certainty what he would demand of her at the recital, what must be surrendered afterward, irrevocably and before the evening was through. He might even, to declare to all who were there, insist that she leave in the middle of the recital, she trailing after him in disgrace, a truly 'fallen woman', and at that terrible picture suddenly burned into her inner eye, she put her head in her hands to weep bitter tears once more.

Lucy, meanwhile, was attempting to digest this grotesque tale, seeing at last the *real* message that her sister had been trying to impart to her: the dangers of *any* relations with a man outside of marriage, how they could progress so rapidly to utter desolation, far from the pure and mutual romantic love with which she had imbued them.

Yet worse was the even greater threat he continued to pose. Now, with a cold sickness in the centre of her being, she recalled Elizabeth Bennet when she had said: 'She has thrown her self into the power of . . .' knowing now the full and terrible import of those words, of what she had innocently assumed was mere fiction.

There was yet more. 'How is such a man to be worked on,' had cried her heroine, and 'I have not the smallest hope,' and she never thought in her most terrible nightmares that her beautiful sister could be so entrapped. Indeed, Celia must be right; the only hope was to leave immediately, within the hour, as she suddenly understood what Jane Austen had meant by it all.

Alice, however, was strange in her attitude when Celia was done with her new understanding.

'Then it was his just deserts,' she muttered to her self, with what looked almost like a smile on her face, puzzling the two young ladies considerably.

While Alice went to fetch a fresh pot of tea, it took still some minutes for Lucy to calm her sister enough to talk.

'That is quite all right, sweet Sister, you will not need to come to hear me because I have decided not to go either, so every thing will be fine and we can leave together as soon as may be.'

Celia was still angrily shaking her head when Alice returned with the tea.

'Alice, will you please tell this foolish and misguided *child* that she *must* give her recital; that she has a *duty* to the invited guests of her hostess, even though I leave almost immediately.'

'No, I do not!' retorted Lucy, with a considerable flash of spirit. 'My first duty,' stamping her little slippered foot on the carpet for added effect, '*my very first and most important duty*, is to see that my beloved sister is well and whole and taken care of, and that is an *end* to the matter!' and she stamped again. '*And you can not make me go nor make me play.*'

The two sisters were now glowering at each other with an equal ferocity of wills that could have no happy outcome.

'Here is your tea, Miss Celia, and yours, Miss Lucy, and *two* slices of fruit-cake each that Cook baked specially for you this morning. And will the two of you young ladies please stop scowling at one another, ruining your complexions, after all the trouble I have taken to make you the prettiest pair London has seen this Season.'

This last remark lightened the atmosphere in the room, though only a little, until she added, with a little smile, 'Besides, you may both carry out your original intentions,' nodding to each in turn, 'because he will not *be* there,' at which it became positively *electric!*

'Who will not be there?' cried Celia, immediately echoed by Lucy's, 'Will not be where?'

'*He* will not, at the *recital*, this afternoon.'

Celia was the first to recover from her surprise. 'How could you possibly know that, Alice? Even if he is supposed to be some where else this afternoon, he will turn up at the last moment just to *humiliate* me, to demand I attend him for his final victory over my body.'

'Besides,' added Lucy, 'I am *not* going to perform if there is even the *slightest* chance of his being there, for I would have to stop playing the very moment he entered the room.'

'That will not be necessary, either,' said Alice, quietly. 'He will not be *any where* this afternoon; at least, not at any soirée.'

'Alice,' said Celia firmly, 'you cannot possibly be right unless you know some thing. Out with it.'

'Well, Miss, it was just some thing I heard – but whatever you do, you must *not* repeat it.' And the two of them nodded.

'Well,' she went on, 'I only heard this, mind you, but it seems that he, you know, *him*, was out in a carriage last night with a young lady, stopped in a quiet area close by some park, and he was, you know . . . misbehaving him self,' and she avoided looking at Celia here. '*Very* badly, I hear, when he was set upon by some, some, uh, *ruffians*, and they beat him, quite severely, and left him lying in the road. Then they helped the young lady to get home safely.'

The two looked at each other in astonishment, then back at Alice. 'How badly?' said Celia, followed by, 'Hurt where?' from Lucy.

'Well, I heard that he was severely beaten all over his face and body, with some broken ribs, and a very badly broken right arm and shoulder, and also one foot was broken. Oh yes, and he was apparently kicked quite severely in the . . . in the . . . well, let us just say that it will be a long, long time, if ever, that he will interfere with another young lady. So there,' and her eyes flashed with an angry, inner fire that they had never seen before.

'Alice,' said Celia, in a subdued voice, 'That wasn't very . . .' but stopped, not knowing quite what it wasn't very.

'After what the devil did to you, Miss Celia, after what he deliberately made you suffer,' she added, fiercely, and here her eyes positively glowed with hatred, 'I could have killed him with my own bare hands. If ever he dares even to be in the same room with you again, Miss, I shall make certain of it.'

Both of them were silent and recoiled a little at this incredible ferocity of feeling.

'You know,' as Celia said later to her sister, 'at that moment Alice reminded me of a tigress in defence of her cubs, even if it meant dying in the attempt.' And she had shuddered at the awesome power of the female spirit when truly aroused.

'But, Alice, how can we be certain, once he has recovered, that he will not return to seek his revenge?'

'Because, Miss, I took the trouble to visit that dreadful house and find out the name of the owner.'

'But how could you ascertain that, Alice, if it was empty?'

'Very easily, Miss. I simply went to the next house and inquired of the kitchen staff – who knew all about the goings on. Over a cup of tea, they explained that it was an elderly widowed lady of high rank who lives in Somerset, Coombe Down near Bath, where she has a large estate. Evidently, she prefers the society there, and rarely visits London. Besides, when she wishes to take the air, she has a manor house at Weston-Super-Mare.'

'My goodness, Alice, you do nothing by half-measures! And?'

'Then I bought a sheet of fine hand-woven paper and envelope and, in my best hand, wrote to her ladyship to tell her that her town house was ill-used by her grand-nephew for the purpose of disgracing young ladies in a most vile manner – and such like,' now with a sly smile. 'So you see, Miss Celia, he will not be tolerated much longer in London when her ladyship's views are made known on *that* score!

'Well, I must be going, now,' said Alice to both her charges as she arose, 'Remember, not a word,' and would have left the room except that Celia took hold of her hand.

'Very well, Alice. Then I shall stay in Town if you insist there is no danger to either of us. But where are you going? Will you be back in time for the coiffures?'

'I will try my very best, Miss, but it *is* quite a long way,' and in answer to Celia's 'but where', she replied, 'The East End, Miss, near the docks.'

'But that is *miles*, Alice. How will you get there?'

'I will just have to walk, Miss, for I can not afford to ride.'

'Here,' said Celia, handing her some silver coins from her purse, then changing her mind to give her the purse it self – which greatly surprised Lucy, for she knew for a certainty there were at least two gold guineas and three half-guineas in it, newly obtained in Thread-needle Street.

'That will easily be enough to get you there and back. Then you will be in time for our dressing.'

But she wasn't back in time for that, nor to accompany them as she always did to the recital to cope with emergencies; nor did they see her before they went to bed, very late, after a most successful and enjoyable evening. And no, he was *not* there.

It was mid-morning, and the household all upset at the failure of Alice to return. They were meeting in the Morning room and Aunt Julia was set to call on the Sheriff when a rather dirty young lad delivered a note to the kitchen door addressed 'Miss Celia Etheridge', before he ran off.

'Yes,' said Celia to the assembly, 'it is from Alice, and she is all right. But now I must have a little time to think. Come, Lucy,' and taking her sister's hand, led her quickly to her room.

'Is it bad, Cel?' said Lucy, when they were alone behind the closed door.

'No, I do not think so, but here, read it for your self.' And Lucy read Alice's rather neat hand aloud:

'Dear Miss,

I have had some trouble, and I cannot leave where I am at the moment. I will need to get some money, then I can return, but I am quite well as I write this.

Alice.'

'Well,' said Celia, 'What do you make of it?'

'I am not quite sure,' replied her sister carefully. 'It rather sounds to me as if she has been *kidnapped* or some thing.'

'That is about what I thought. Nor do I like the insinuation behind that "at the moment". Notice the address; I do believe that is not too distant. Time for action,' and she went to the writing desk where she took up her notepaper, swiftly penned a note and sealed it, and quickly ran downstairs.

'Aunt Julia, is there a maid who could take this note to Mr. Reginald?

He is staying not very far from here. It concerns Alice.'

'Certainly, my dear,' and called one of the kitchen maids, a reliable girl named Bessie.

'Now, Bessie,' said Celia quietly, when she had taken her to one side, 'You know where Mr. Reginald is staying,' and the girl nodded. 'Take this note, find him, and give it to him *personally*, you understand, *personally*.' Again the girl nodded. 'Do not fail to find him, *even if you have to swim to India*, do you understand me?' and while the harshness in her sister's voice startled Lucy, it almost terrified Bessie, who could not swim and had no idea which way was India, yet whispered, 'Yes, Miss.'

'Come back in less than 30 minutes and you shall have this shilling. Now go!' and Bessie scuttled out like a frightened rabbit.

'Would you mind if we waited in the Morning room, Aunt Julia?' asked Celia.

'Not at all, my dear, make your selves comfortable. I will have some coffee sent in, and then see that you are not disturbed.'

'Thank you, Aunt. You are very kind.'

'Not at all, my dear, I could hardly do less.'

The waiting seemed interminable. At last a knock on the door admitted a breathless and wind-blown Bessie.

'Well?' queried Celia.

'I found 'im, Miss, an' I give 'im your note, personal like.'

'And?'

'Well, Miss, at first 'e just stood there, a-readin' of the note it seemed like two three times, and a-pullin' on 'is ear, sort of.'

'That was Reginald, all right,' interjected Celia. 'Then?'

'Well, Miss, then 'e just sort of "exploded" and rushed around callin' a couple of names at the top of 'is voice, Miss, then they all rushed out the door an' vanished like.'

'Thank you, Bessie, that was very well done. Here is your shilling.'

'But I was gorn the bes' par' uv a 'our, Miss, so I don't deserve it,' replied the honest Bessie.

'Yes, you do Bessie, and here is another one for trying so hard.'

'Thank you, Miss,' curtsied the delighted girl, face beaming. That was almost a week's wages for her, and that new bonnet and pretty shoes became a reality in her head.

'Now what?' queried Lucy.

'I could beat you again at backgammon,' was the dispirited response.

'But you *lost* the last two games,' replied her sister, secretly delighted, because it was the first time she had ever won two in a row. 'And what *did* you put in that note to light such a fire under poor Reggie?'

'Oh, just some thing about Alice being held against her will, and suggesting that he take Geoffrey and Jeremy with him for "moral" support, and a few heavy law books, for Geoffrey is a junior in law, you know.'

'And, what else?' continued her sister, not yet hearing any thing that would have created a fire *that* hot.

'Well, there *was* some thing about if he did not succeed by luncheon, simply never to darken my doorstep again. You know; that sort of thing.' and she gave her sister a sly smile.

'You scheming little vixen you,' retorted Lucy. 'The *one* thing Reginald would give his very life for.'

'I know,' sighed Celia, unashamed, 'I am awful,' and for the first time in days they laughed uproariously and clung to each other for support to avoid falling down, but they finished up on the carpet, anyway.

The chess was worse than the backgammon, and Celia had lost her queen, both rooks and a bishop by the twelfth move. The game should have quickly ended in ignominious defeat, except for the fact that Lucy was only one rook better off, and neither of them could find a move to finish the other. So they simultaneously resigned their kings, and sat staring at nothing.

The mantel clock was in the middle of announcing the luncheon hour, when a tap on the door admitted Reginald and the two Houghton scions.

When she had received Reginald's answering nod that every thing was all right, Celia said to the others, 'Why don't you two go and find Cousins Emily and Charlotte, but please do not talk about the affair, for Alice's sake. You may get invited to luncheon, as neither Lucy nor I are hungry, so you are welcome to ours. And thank you very much for what you have done this morning.' And they departed thinking that a most splendid idea, for the female cousins were indeed *very* agreeable, to say the least.

'Now, tell us all about it,' she said to Reginald when the three of them were alone.

'Well, it went very much as you suggested,' and Celia smiled. 'They were very belligerent and obstructive and knew nothing, at first,' and Celia nodded. 'Then Geoffrey started reading all that stuff about "detention against one's will" being punishable by public flogging and 5 years in Dartmoor, and the crime of "kidnapping" being "punishable by deportation or public hanging." That is when they began to change their tune and thought that they just *might* have seen some one of that description around.

'But it was when Jeremy produced a hammer and started nailing a legal-looking piece of paper to the front door that Alice suddenly appeared.'

'Bravo,' broke in Lucy, clapping her hands in delight. 'How is she?'

'She is well,' replied Reginald. 'A little tired and dirty, that is all. But prepare your selves for a shock. There were *two* of them.'

'Two *Alices*?' said the now astonished Celia.

'No; well, yes, really. I never saw two souls more alike, though the other was much younger and called Mildred – and she has green eyes.'

'Thank you, Reginald,' said Celia, very softly, and she crossed over to where he stood, put both arms around his neck, and gave him a long lingering kiss on the cheek, making quite sure as she stood on her toes to reach, that her upper body was firmly in contact with his.

'Yes, thank you, Reginald,' echoed Lucy – but he never heard the second one, for his cheeks were such a flaming red that even his ears were blushing. 'Please ask Alice to join us in here for a few moments. Just Alice,' she added softly, as she pressed her self into him again and gave his still-red cheeks a kiss, first one then the other, followed by a brush with her soft lips upon his.

'Another "Alice", we are told,' said Celia, when they had seen that the real Alice, now with a clean face and apron, was not much the worse for wear.

'Yes, Miss.'

'Named "Mildred", we are also told.'

'Yes, Miss.'

'And she is a relative of yours?'

'Yes, Miss. My daughter, Miss' replied Alice, looking at the floor.

'And where did she come from?' continued Celia, not at all surprised, although her sister gave a little gasp.

'My daughter, Miss?' said the surprised Alice.

'No, Alice. I *know* where little girls come from,' said Celia with a smile, and Alice reddened, and resumed her downcast gaze. 'I mean, where has she been all these years, and why is she with you now?'

'It is a long story, Miss,' responded Alice, stiffly, 'and I would not wish to take up your time with it. But she is with me now and must remain with me, so we will have to stay here in London for a while.'

'But how can that be, Alice, for we are returning the day after tomorrow?'

'Yes, Miss, I know. That is why I will have to give you my notice today, right now,' her voice now so low that Celia had to strain to catch her words. 'But you do not have to give me any money because I cannot give you the proper notice. And I am afraid I lost the purse and all that money you gave me, so I really owe you quite a lot – far more than I can ever repay, though I will try when I get my self settled.'

Although Alice was still staring down at the carpet, Celia observed the two tears that plopped down onto it, followed quickly by several others.

'But you *must* return with us, Alice; isn't that right Lucy?' and Lucy nodded vigorously. 'We will not hear of it any other way,' she concluded firmly, 'and that is an end to it.'

Alice raised her tear-stained face to look directly at her mistress.

'No,' she responded firmly. 'I left my daughter once, and I will not abandon her again. We will be together, even if I have to sweep streets to make a living. And I will defend her against any body and any thing that comes between us for as long as I am given the strength,' and here her eyes flashed with the same fire they had so recently witnessed. 'I have acted wrongly and foolishly in the past, and I intend to make it up to her, every *bit* of it. Whatever the cost, Miss Celia,' she continued defiantly, 'I will *not* leave her.'

'Of course you will not,' responded Celia, taking up her handkerchief and wiping Alice's tear-stained face. 'Have I asked you to?'

'Uh, no, Miss,' replied the startled Alice, quite taken aback by both the action and the words, but not knowing yet what to make of them, or the smile she now observed on her mistress' face.

'You mean, Miss?' she gasped, when the truth finally dawned, 'that you do not *mind*; about Mildred, I mean?'

'Mind? Of course I do not "mind", Alice, you foolish thing. Do I look such a monster as to come between a mother and her child?'

'No, Miss, of course not,' blushed Alice'

'Well then, let's have no more of this nonsense about "staying in London" and "sweeping streets". The very *idea* of it, indeed!

'Now, is Mildred in your room?'

'Yes, Miss.'

'And nobody saw her go there?'

'No, Miss. Mr. Reginald took her up while the others were all making a fuss of me.' (Good for Reginald, thought Celia, that is another special kiss that I owe him.)

'Right, then. After dinner, please bring your daughter to my room, for I would very much like to make her acquaintance and to talk with her. If you are agreeable, of course?' she hastened to add.

'Oh, yes, Miss!' gushed Alice. 'I am very proud of her; she is a lovely girl,' and then blushed at her own lack of modesty.

'I am sure she is,' responded Celia warmly. 'In fact, she could not be any thing else with you as her mother,' and Alice went scarlet, and had to wipe her eyes and blow her nose.

'As for the money you say that you owe me, Alice, what was in that purse?'

'I cannot rightly say, Miss. I know it was a lot, because besides all the silver, there were at least two sovereigns and several halfs – or perhaps they were guineas. I am not sure, because I have only once seen their like. My mother had one on a gold chain as a present from father that was to come to me, but it had to go when . . .' and her voice trailed away into sadness.

'But I will replace those . . . given a little time, Miss,' now urgent in her desire to reward her mistress' kindness.

'And any thing else, Alice?'

'Uh, no, Miss, except a button from your cream dress that I was looking for to sew on again.'

'And that is all?'

'Yes, Miss,' replied the puzzled Alice. 'Other than those it was empty.'

'There was no love in it, tucked away, perhaps, in a corner? It was there when I gave it you,' but Alice merely shook her head in total incomprehension.

'Do you not see, Alice, that those few coins are as nothing compared to what they have brought in return,' but Alice was none the wiser, shaking her head once more.

'Not only have they returned our wonderful companion – that is you, Alice – but we are told that she brought with her as a part of the compensation for that loss, a wonderful daughter who is – if we are to believe but half of what Mr. Reginald expressed – as pretty as the mother her self,' and Alice could only lower her eyes, colouring with embarrassment mixed with pleasure at this double compliment.

'So, no, we are not upset at its loss, Alice, and, no, we do not wish to see it replaced, for we – and I will speak also for my sister here,' receiving Lucy's enthusiastic nod, 'we are more than delighted at the bargain.

'Perhaps the Bard of Avon said it best – as he did in most things – when he has Iago say: "Who steals my purse steals trash; But he that filches from me my good name . . . makes me poor indeed." I have shortened it a trifle to enhance the message, but if the loss of the first has prevented the loss of the second, I am rewarded even to a thousand fold.

'You see,' she added softly, raising Alice's chin with her forefinger, then taking both her hands in her own, and looking straight into her dark and luminous eyes, 'I know, somehow, deep down inside, that your current misfortune is intimately and directly connected to my rescue from that most recent horrid one. If I could not find it in my heart to welcome *your* daughter into our household – and I will explain it to her ladyship, have no fear – I would have to be the most heartless *monster* ever to walk this earth.'

"Now, let us have no more talk of this. Dry your tears,' presenting Alice her handkerchief, 'then go to your daughter and welcome her into the fold – as Miss Lucy and I shall later. We have a joyous evening ahead of us, so let us make the most of it, and we shall tell you both of Miss Lucy's wonderful recital. Had every thing and every one in a complete uproar, she did.'

And it was Lucy's turn to redden and look down at the floor, but immensely pleased, just the same.

'You were quite right, Alice, she is a lovely girl,' said Celia, once they had left the town and the green fields began to emerge.

'Thank you, Miss,' replied the anxious Alice. 'I confess I thought you would think her an additional burden to your household and that she might interfere with my duties. But I can assure you that she will not, Miss,' she rushed on, to make her determination clear that such an occurrence was unthinkable.

'Alice, before I respond, I wish to thank you once more for my rescue.'
'That is not necessary, Miss, I . . .'

'No, Alice,' raising her hand, 'please let me continue. I shall say this once only, although I shall think it all the rest of my life. As we all know. I was facing complete degradation – to put it mildly. You completely changed all that. We shall not speak of it again, ever, but I wish you to know, Alice, that you have my undying gratitude and devotion,' as she took Alice's hand in hers and kissed it, and to the silent observer, Lucy, the look that passed between their moist eyes was one of nothing but pure love, each to the other.

'Now,' with eyes dry once more, 'to return to daughter Mildred. Where is she going to sleep, Alice?' eyebrows raised to emphasize her concern.

'Well, in my room, Miss,' responded Alice in a hopeful but uncertain voice, 'for I really would rather she did not live in the village in lodgings.'

'But your room is no bigger than a shoe-box as it is,' laughed Celia. 'I do not think you could squeeze a cat in there, let alone a thirteen-year-old daughter almost as tall as you.'

'Oh yes, Miss, I could. I have been thinking about it. I would move the cupboard to the foot of the bed, then I would put a cot in its place, although the washstand might have to move to the passage,' shaking her head sadly. 'But I'd manage Miss, really I would,' she concluded eagerly.

'Alice,' said her mistress, 'Mildred is a little grown for a cot! And what about *her* clothes? No, I don't think that is appropriate at all.'

'But not the village, Miss,' said the agitated Alice, twisting the corner of her apron almost into a knot. 'I don't think I could bear to have her even that far away, Miss,' almost pleading now in her despair at the thought of being parted after so soon reunited.

'Alice, Alice,' laughed her mistress. 'You are turning into a real worry-wort. I have a plan that I think you will like. But here we are at our first Coach Inn. We can take a dish of tea, and you shall meet your daughter once more, unless she has fallen off, of course. Did you see anyone fall past the window, Lucy?' and they both burst out laughing as Alice quickly thrust her head out of the window – and the wrong side at that – to check if her daughter was still up on the box with Mr. Reginald.

They were all glad of the break in the journey, for although the coach was well made and quite new, the roads were in poor condition. There would needs be more such stops to rest the horses before they arrived home very late that night.

Celia was also glad that Geoffrey and Jeremy had decided to stay in Town a few more days, convinced she believed, by the undeniable charms of Cousins Emily and Charlotte where there seemed to be a decidedly mutual attraction. That had left the entire coach for just the three of them, for Mildred had elected to ride on top with Mr. Reginald.

Over tea and country cake, Celia asked Mildred, almost literally tucked under her mother's protective wing, how she was enjoying the journey.

'Luverly, Miss. I ain't never bin on a coach afore,' and Celia hoped that the wince she felt inside at the dreadful London accent was not too evident; for the pain of it was quite evident in her mother's face.

'Has Mr. Reginald been good to you?'

Mildred turned a glowing face and shining eyes in his direction.

'Wunnerful, 'e 'as bin, Miss. Ever so kin' 'e 'as.'

The recipient of this ardour smiled faintly back at Mildred, and then uncomfortably at Celia.

'So that is how it is, Mr. Reginald,' Celia demanded of her admirer. 'See, Lucy, the fickleness of the manly sex; "unfaithful" is their middle name. "Out of sight is out of mind", put them up on a box with a pretty young woman at their side, and their brains turn to mush,' and she flounced out of the Inn in mock distress and hauled her self up into the coach.

'But, Celia,' he began, as he followed her out.

'Do not "Celia" me, you faithless wretch,' she interjected. 'You watch, Lucy,' as he helped her into the carriage, 'how he hands Miss Mildred up onto the box, how carefully and tenderly he holds her; while my self, his avowed one-and-only-true-love, he allows to make her way as best she can,' and she turned her head away from him in pretended rejection.

'You should not make sport with him, Miss,' said Alice, as they got under way again, 'for Mildred means no harm.'

'I know that Alice, and I really can understand it. There she is with her mother at last after these many years, in serious trouble with some very rough men and not knowing what to do, when along comes this handsome young man who rescues her (and you) from a "fate worse than death". It would be surprising indeed if he were *not* her knight in shining armour,' whereupon both Lucy and Celia burst into peals of laughter.

This was not missed by the subject of their merriment above their heads, more miserable than ever over their hilarity at his expense. Just, he thought ruefully – her soft lips still burning his cheek from the morning kiss, and the warm softness of her . . . her . . . self – just when he was making progress in the matter of gaining her affections. It really was too bad; at which thought the subject of his dismay, Mildred her self, wrapped the blanket around their joint knees, slipped her arm through his, laid her head on his shoulder and cuddled *her* slight warmth against him.

'Miss,' reminded Alice, anxious to get the matter of her daughter's living arrangements resolved, 'You said you had a plan.'

'Yes, Alice, I do. But I have need to confer with mother before I take some thing upon my self that she would not support. It will be taken care of, Alice, and to your satisfaction, have no worries on that score.

'But now while we have some moments to our private selves, I do wish you would tell us some thing about Mildred's circumstances – if you have a mind to, of course. It will not pass beyond these carriage walls, save for the essentials I must present to her ladyship, on arrival.'

'Well, Miss, I do not mind talking about it, if you will not be bored or affronted by what is a common enough tale. To tell the truth, I have longed to tell it many a time, but was afraid to do so for fear of being even more rejected than I already was.'

'We would *love* to hear it,' broke in Lucy, already a little teary at what she suspected the story would reveal, although she did not guess even the half of it.

'Well, his name was Richard, Mildred's father, that is. His father was a Lieutenant in the Indian Army stationed on the Northwest Frontier. Richard, like most sons of army officers there, was educated after the age of eight or nine in an English boarding school, which is how we met because I was going to a school for young ladies close by. But I will come back to that later.

'Some thing happened, apparently, though Richard never quite found out what it was. Some thing to do with missing money from the Mess, and a senior officer's daughter who was with child. Richard thought that they made his father the scapegoat, because he was always on the outside, never having gone to the right schools, if you see what I mean. So he was cashiered, finished. It killed him, literally, for the army was his whole life.

'Richard's mother had died of a fever in India shortly after he was born, so he was an only child and he did not know where to turn. There he was, son of a cashiered officer, no money and no prospect of any, so his fine school turned him out. What he would have done if my mother hadn't taken him in, I do not know. He was only fifteen, you see.

'Now we come to my side of the story – am I boring you, Miss?' looking from one to the other.

'Oh, no,' exclaimed Celia, 'I am quite fascinated – although troubled – by it all. Please go on, and do not miss out a thing!'

'Well, it is very good of you to say so, Miss, for I am feeling stronger already for the telling of it. My father was also in the army, but he was in France and Spain, doing what he could to stop that madman, Napoleon. He was a Captain of Foot, and he was trapped in a siege, and those that were left at the end were imprisoned – which was almost worse than not surviving at all.

'My mother knew that he had survived the siege, but she heard nothing after that, and that is what broke her, simply not knowing, for she was never really very strong, and her only brother had been taken by that war some years' before. As it happened, father did not last very long in there, barely six months; but we did not know that for nearly four years. By then we were in a poor financial position our selves. I had to leave my school and stay at home to look after mother, for she was just skin and bones. I studied as best I could, but it was very difficult.

'Richard had been with us about two years by then, and so we studied together – which was perhaps part of the problem. He was a fine young man and was beginning to make some thing of him self – he had a lot in him, did my Richard. But with the war flaring up again, he had to go, you see,' Alice's voice barely a whisper, now. 'Within a month he was gone, forever. Then a winter chill just took mother off, and I was all alone. I had lost the both of them within two months, and I was not well. But we will also come to that later.'

The silence in the carriage was broken only by the soft sobbing of three women in the pain of loss; for both the younger two had lost their fathers through war, Lucy only recently.

'And Mildred?' Celia commented quietly, the first to recover some semblance of control through her sniffles.

'Well, Miss, Richard and I had been thrown together quite a bit, for it was a small house. We were the same, you see. We had both had a good education, up to a point, then it all fell to pieces for us in very much the same way – the loss of our fathers. That led to a downward path in our living conditions that seemed to have no bottom, and we could not get out of it.

'But the good of it was that over the years he was there, we came to love each other. He would like to have got away to set him self up properly, then he was going to come back and we were to marry. I was but sixteen then, and only fourteen when we first knew each other – not much older than my young Mildred,' and she smiled to her self at the thought. 'I hadn't met any other young men, and I did not want to, he was all I ever wanted, so I know what it is to be in love.

'Mother was quite ill by then, and rarely left her room, so we took things in to her. I think she could see how things were between Richard and me, and she was happy for us. I was much too young of course, she knew that, and I knew that. But I was growing from a girl into a young woman, and I had desires. I am sure you both know what I mean, Miss,' and they nodded, 'and I wanted him so badly, it hurt, especially as he was always there so close to me.

'We had the run of the house, you see, mother being in bed and all, and one day – well, I'd like to come back to that part in a little while, Miss, for that is the happy part.

'Anyway, Richard had to go to the war, and then with that, mother just sort of gave up, and faded away. I discovered I was with child the next week, so neither of them ever knew, you see.'

The silence was broken again by the gentle sobbing, until Alice once more regained the strength to continue.

'With more rent due and nowhere to look for it – for Richard was helping us from what little he had – they seized every thing bar our books which I had squirreled away, and I was out on the street with little more than what I stood up in, which was not very much. Then things got very bad, Miss, but I kept my self proper, you understand; I did not do what some women do when they get like that,' she added, fiercely.

'But I do not really want to talk too much about that, Miss, it really is very painful to me. Let me just say that after a little while I was lucky enough to get a job as a scullery maid, so I had to leave my baby with a cousin in London. She had a baby of her own of almost exactly the same age, so it was as if my Mildred had a twin sister, and I gave her what I could in return.

'Then some one told my mistress that I had a four-year-old child and she turned me out, without any notice. After all, who wants unwed scullery maids with babies when they can get them without,' she added, bitterly.

'That is why, Miss, I was so concerned if you found out, that you might feel the same way. I am sorry, Miss, I should not have said that. I am a stupid girl for thinking it even for one minute. I should have known you were not at all like that, but I was scared out of my wits with what to do, being held by those rough men and all.

'Then whose voice should I hear but your wonderful Mr. Reginald, just like you said, Miss, a knight in shining armour, and I just knew that he would not leave until I was safe, whatever he had to do and however long it took. That is a wonderful feeling, Miss. You really are very fortunate to have such a man as that devoted to you; just like my Richard.

'My cousin did a very good job of looking after Mildred instead of me, and she had as happy a childhood as could be expected in the circumstances. But what with her husband returning and Mildred beginning to grow up and . . . well . . . develop into a young woman her self – if you know what I mean – things of late had become very trying for her. So it is really better that it worked out the way it did. Really it is. I have to thank you two young ladies for making it possible for me to get back to London to see her. And now she is with me, thank the Lord. And that is the story, Miss, as far as it goes.'

'Thank you, Alice, for sharing that with us. I think we understand a lot of things much better now, and it makes it much easier to welcome your daughter, knowing a little of her father.'

While they were still drying their eyes and blowing their noses, the coachman called out that the next Inn was in sight, by which time they hoped that their respective appearances would not cause comment. As it was, only Mildred noticed any thing amiss.

'You are still happy riding on the top with Mr. Reginald, Mildred?' inquired her mother. 'It will be dark soon.' To which her daughter replied that she would enjoy that.

'Alice,' said Celia, when they were all comfortably seated again, 'I need to say some thing that I do not want you to take amiss, but I need to get it off my chest. I was not even Mildred's age when I met, you know, *him*, for the first time, and I can still recall how wonderful I thought he was; tall, handsome, grown up, and I was in love immediately. That you see is why I made such a fool of my self because, in a way, I was still that little girl, my head full of the childish dreams *he* planted there – and then came back these ten years later to pluck and consume the ripened fruit!' And she gave an involuntary shudder at her so apt analogy.

'Oh, Miss, I will call her down immediately if you think I should,' responded Alice, half rising.

'That will not be necessary,' said Celia, holding up a restraining hand; 'not with Reginald. You agree, Sister?'

'Oh, yes, indeed,' replied Lucy immediately. 'I hope you know, my dear, how lucky you are to have such a fine man as Reginald to adore you,' to which Celia gave only a somewhat quizzical look in response.

'We have no worries then on that score, Alice, but I just wanted you to know how it happened to me; for your daughter's sake, you understand?'

'Yes, Miss, I understand,' said Alice, softly, 'and thank you, Miss, for your great insight.'

'Now that you have given us a good cry, Alice, you were going to tell us the happy part.'

'I did not mean to make you sad, Miss, I am truly sorry for that.'

'We are not the slightest bit, Alice. It does us good to know that there are such misfortunes in the world. We who have not known lack of love or even discomfort *should* cry a little, now and then, for those less fortunate.'

It was almost dark in the carriage when Alice returned to the happy part of her tale. 'You see, Miss, this is what I wanted to explain to you the other day, after your "accident", you know. When you asked if you were wicked, and I said you weren't,' and Celia nodded in the gloom.

'I was remembering then about Richard, and how it was with us, how it was so much the same – forgive me, Miss, for saying it that way, but it was, and yet it was oh so different, oh so wonderful. The difference is the right man, you see, Miss, and *he* was just a wicked devil. When it is the right man, Miss, in the right circumstance, it is wonderful, truly, truly wonderful. Then you can give your self freely and be happy in it.'

Celia's eyes were full of pain, though none could see it in the darkness, yet both could feel its potent anguish.

'Shall I go on, Miss, or would you rather I stop?'

'Please continue, Alice, I believe I can bear it, and I do need to understand,' but she was glad when her sister took her hand and held it tightly.

'All right, Miss. Then here is how it happened. It was one evening, and

Richard and I had been sitting in the kitchen talking about the future, him saying that he was going to marry me, but that it would take time, for we were both so young, and he did not want me to accept him – as he knew I would – until he was able to provide properly for me and our children, for we had decided that we would have three, if God would grant us them. We knew then that he would soon have to go to fight, and hoped that he could be back soon, so that we could start our lives together properly.

'Of course he, being the older and wiser, was right. But I said that I did not see why we could not be married right away so that we could start our family right away. He said that was all wrong and we had responsibilities to the children we brought into the world; to see that they were properly clothed and fed and educated, as we had been by our parents before misfortune overtook us both.

'I got angry with him and said that if he really loved me he would not say that. He got upset with me and said that I was a foolish child for thinking that way, and I would understand better and see that he was right when I was older. I realized later that was what really got under my skin, being told that I was still a child, because I had the powerful urgings of a fully formed woman and was determined to prove it to him if he gave me the chance. So I told him he was the one being childish and that I was going to bed and he could do what he liked.

'Although we never really quarrelled, he did not like parting, especially at night, if we had any disagreement. I knew that he would soon come to my door to say good night, that he was sorry to have offended me, and that we would talk of it again in the morning.

'Usually I closed my door so that he could have some privacy because he had to sleep on his bed in a corner of the kitchen. But this night, after I had undressed right down to my skin – which I never did – I put my dress back on as if I had not undressed at all, but I left all the buttons – except the top one – undone down the back to below my waist. Then I opened the door again.

'I was combing my hair, which was also to my waist, when he came to the half-open door and stood there and said he was sorry that he had upset me, just as I knew he would. I told him that if he had any thing more to say to me he had better do it by the kitchen fire, as it was cold in my room and I might take a chill. So he came in and seeing me as he thought still fully dressed – for he would not have done so otherwise – took me by the hand to the warm fire, for I had added another log or two to be sure that we had a good blaze for the next part of my plan.

'Then I said that I was the one at fault and that he was correct, and that we should kiss and forget it – and that was his undoing, and mine. You see, Miss, before that night, our kisses were of the sister-to-brother kind, but this time I made it more, a good deal more, and held him squeezed to my bosom, so that he would do likewise to me.

'Of course, no sooner had he put his arms around me than he could feel that underneath my dress I had nothing on. But my design went further, for through my hair, the open dress allowed his hands to touch my skin, which had never happened before. Then as I knew they would, they were inside my dress and down on and under my bare bottom and, as he pulled me to him as I was doing, I could feel him come alive against me, just as I did against him.

'But I was not finished, for to tease him more, I pulled away to put up my hair into a topknot. But at the same time I undid the button, wriggled my shoulders, and my only shield from his astonished gaze was in a heap around my ankles. I stepped out of it, kicked it to one side and as naked as the day I was born, slowly and shamelessly finished fixing my hair in the over-mantle mirror, twisting and turning at the same time to make sure he would miss nothing for – though I say it my self – I did have a fine figure in those days for such a young woman.

'So I turned that unguarded self to him and said that now he could go to bed if he wished, but I needed to warm my self a little first.

'Then the one that he had thoughtlessly mistaken for a mere child knelt by the fire, close to him, pretending to warm my self by its glow, but half facing him and pretending to fix my hair again so that as I looked up at him, his devouring eyes could get an ample view of all my charms, those of a now fully excited "woman" – undoubtedly the first he had ever seen – at his feet and for his taking.'

There was utter stillness in the carriage as Alice paused, carried back in her memory to that glorious moment.

'That is when I was reminded, Miss, for take me he did,' she continued softly. 'One moment I was on my knees before the fire, feeling its heat, and the next it was the heat of his hands on my body, up and down and all over. Then it was the turn for his burning lips and his mouth. But these were all gentleness it self, and it was heaven. There was not a part of me that he did not kiss or caress and love with the utmost tenderness.

'Then it was me that undressed him, until we were both as God made us, and my lips were on his body, and we devoured each other in turn, until we could stand the separateness no longer and he was finally naturally and effortlessly deep inside me, and I wrapped my self around and clung to him as my body did every thing in its power to hold him and keep him there. It was the most natural and most wonderful thing in the world, just the two of us becoming one and remaining one until we slept in the utter joy of our union.

'It is some thing I shall remember and treasure for as long as I live – for it was the one and only time for me – and I am reminded of it every time I look at my Mildred, for there were just the two of us when we started the kissing, but three of us when we finished loving each other's bodies that night.'

The silence, previously as deep and quiet as velvet, was now broken by the uneven breathing of the two listeners, quite overcome in their emotions by Alice's gripping episode of true love played out to its ultimate climax. Neither had been taken to such a point of consent – although Lucy could understand the feelings of desire – and no word could be voiced by either of them.

'So you see, Miss Celia,' concluded Alice, her tearful voice floating softly in the total darkness that was the only thing that made the very telling possible, 'You must not blame your self for being led astray by a man, for your body is just like mine. It was made for being adored and loved by a man, and for making love to him in return. What is so important is that it can only be the right man. Every thing else is make-believe, or in preparation for that special, heavenly moment of final and complete coupling, of giving and receiving, in equal and total measure.

'Now Miss, perhaps we should rest until the next stop, then I think Mildred might join us, for she must be very tired.'

But relaxing was easier said than done. For her self, it was an unbelievable release, finally to feel free enough to relate such an intensely personal and tender moment, never shared with another living soul; although many a time in memory with her beloved Richard.

For Celia, she could scarce believe that this was the same quiet, timid Alice she had known for so many years, since her own childhood. She was indeed breathless with the sweep and depth of the powerful emotions that Alice had conjured in her own bosom, of yearnings to be requited, and could only hope some day to be so fortunate to want and be wanted in the same measure.

For Lucy, having had no-one to explain these things, it was a revelation, with awe that such things actually happened. And suddenly it dawned what her sister in her quiet way had been trying to awaken.

Those Island scenes were not merely idle pleasure play, their purpose of self-protection was well beyond what her innocence and, yes, ignorance had supposed.

Informed by Alice's most explicit description of the nature of true love, Lucy suddenly realized that her eyes were now fully open. She also saw that her beloved sister had only experienced – to her deepest regret – the evil side of love, which had in it no 'love' at all. And just as suddenly knew what Celia and Alice meant when they used the word 'lust'.

She then realized that it was her duty – no, that was not the word: her most heart-felt obligation, at the earliest opportunity, to demonstrate, as near as she could (for only a 'Reginald' could do that), to show her beloved sister the kind of love that Alice had so beautifully demonstrated.

Then, leaning her cheek against her sisters', she gave it a soft, lingering kiss to seal her undeclared promise of mutual affection. Next time, Celia would find her not only a willing and able partner, but one who could take the initiative, be the leader in this titillation and exploration, just as Richard had to his beloved Alice, giving and receiving in equal and total measure, as Alice had so aptly described it.

It was at that moment the coach halted, and Reginald spoke through the hatch to declare that the coachman thought it best to stop for the night at the next inn, for the horses were tired and would not be able to conclude the journey that night. Also, there was a good coaching inn only a mile or so further on.

After a light supper, they retired to their respective rooms; Celia and Lucy together, Alice and Mildred likewise, and Reginald by him self. And though Lucy had much to discuss with her sister, they were both quite exhausted by recent events. However, it was not so much that when they were both in their nightgowns, Lucy gave Celia a tight hug then stepped back, peeled off her own gown, quickly doing likewise to her sister so as to be equally bare – body to body, bosom to bosom enjoying its momentary thrill. Then, tumbling into bed, arms wrapped around each other, they fell into a deep sleep almost immediately.

The next morning after a leisurely breakfast while every one was readying to commence the journey, Lucy had a chance to talk to Alice alone.

'Alice, I want to thank you personally for providing us with your life story yesterday, especially when you described in such detail the pure love that could exist between a man and a women, each so much to give, and each so willing to receive.

'You cannot know the insight that I was granted by that story. You have given me much more than you could ever know, and for that I am deeply grateful,' and she gave Alice a kiss on the cheek as they parted.

For Alice, that was a quite startling confession, for that was not the Miss Lucy that she thought she knew. She could only believe that Miss Lucy was growing up in some mysterious way.

But she was more than pleased that her own enchanted love story, kept concealed for so long, had helped not only her self to become lighter for the telling, but her beloved charges, too.

9

The East Wing

'Mother, I have been thinking,' said Celia after breakfast, one morning shortly after their return.

'Well I should hope so, dear; but about what, particularly?' pausing momentarily in her letter writing.

'About re-opening the East Wing.'

'Re-opening the East Wing? What on earth gave you that idea?' replacing the quill pen in its holder so as to pay full attention, for her daughter's thinking seemed a trifle on the extravagant side this morning.

'Well, it would solve a lot of our problems,' replied Celia, calmly.

'My dear child, I was not aware that we had many problems. Besides, it might create some, too. Have you thought about that?' hoping to nip the idea in the bud before it got to full flower.

'Not particularly, at least not at the moment,' replied her daughter, still composed. 'I like to list the benefits first, then set the drawbacks against them later for fear that the former may grow stunted – or not at all if faced with a full mountain of obstacles to surmount at the very start.'

Indeed, thought her ladyship, this was well-reasoned.

'Well, perhaps you would like to enumerate them for me so that I can understand them, too.'

She could see that this was going to be one of those where the purpose was made clear only late in the conversation. Perhaps on this occasion she could get an outline of where they were going before they arrived. And she did, for Celia had been very thorough.

'I have in fact made out a rough list, so let us use that as a discussion point. First,' checking it off with her crayon, 'Lucy and I need new rooms,' and her mother's eyebrows shot straight up.

'You do? This is the first I have heard about that!'

167

'Of course it is, Mother. That is why I am bringing it to your attention now. You must surely agree that our current ones are getting quite
shabby. So, rather than do them up while we try to stay in them, why
not make new rooms out of the East Wing, *then*, when we have moved
to the new rooms, they can be redecorated as guest rooms.'

Lady Etheridge had to see the wisdom of that approach, except that
she did not yet see the need for two more guestrooms, and said so to her
daughter.

'That may be so,' replied Celia, 'but there are other advantages, too.
I have done some considerable thinking about it, and it seems to me that
both upper floors of the wing should be re-done.'

Good heavens, thought her ladyship; there is *more?*

'That will provide a room for Alice and her daughter,' Celia continued.
'In addition, we should seriously consider adding one of those new heating
systems that Jeremy, Lord Houghton's son, was telling me about while
we were in London. He is studying to be an Architect, you know, so that
he can properly look after the estate in later years.

'Jeremy has helped in the design of such an installation in one of the
largest houses in the County, not ten miles from here. He says that it is
very efficient and quite the latest thing. They are called radiators, and
are heated by hot water either from the kitchen stove – in which case the
extra costs are minimal – or by use of a special boiler. Either way, they
are quite safe.

'They also heat the water for the bathroom at the same time, so you
have cold and hot water in the pipes ready for use whenever you want
it. Further more, Mother dear, we would have enough hot water in the
system to put a radiator in the Dining room, which you have always said
was much too cold. Then the rooms stay much cleaner, too, because there
are no fires with their smoke and ashes to make the ceilings and curtains
dirty, to say nothing of the danger of a conflagration.

'So what do you think of all that, Mother?'

'Well, I do not quite know what to say,' responded Mother, almost
breathless from this grand scheme her daughter had concocted apparently out of thin air. 'Except that it will all be rather disrupting and quite
expensive, though it would be nice to have a warm Dining room. Just
how long have you been working on this "East Wing" scheme?'

'Well,' replied her daughter, 'while I was in London and ever since,
really. As I hope you can see, Mother, I have put a lot of thought into
it, and asked a lot of questions, so that I could bring to you some thing
that had been carefully considered.'

'Indeed, my dear, I am really quite impressed with the thoroughness of your proposal. Of course, it is all rather sudden – and *very* unexpected, for I had no idea that the Hall was wanting in so many ways, so I will have to think about it a good deal first.' But her daughter had noted the thoughtful nature of her questions, and was relieved at the apparent ready acceptance.

'So you think we should go ahead, Mother?'

'Well, perhaps we should get an idea first from some one as to what is involved,' hoping to slow her daughter down a little. But Celia was up to the challenge.

'Good idea, Mother. Lucy and I will ride over to see Jeremy tomorrow, and ask him to look into the matter. One further thing before we leave it. As it is largely for my benefit that we are considering refurbishing the East Wing, I think I should be the one to provide the funds, though you can perhaps take the cost of the new guest rooms and Dining room, although no-one other than our selves need know those details.'

And her mother simply nodded, quite dumbfounded by this new responsibility adopted by her elder daughter. She had indeed grown up, overnight it seemed, and she felt a warm feeling of love stealing through her, despite her desire to show caution. Clearly some thing important had happened in Town, although she knew well enough that she would be told by one of them – should it become necessary.

There was a good deal of conversation in the following weeks; much, much more than Celia had imagined. Some of it was quite heated, so that tempers became considerably frayed on more than one occasion. Jeremy, though, had been a brick, introducing his patron, Sir Richard Crimble, into the discussions with his many comments on the internal design, for it was Celia's requirement that the outer structure remain essentially the same.

It was, however, all finally decided, plans drawn and specifications written. Celia took it upon her self to keep her mother informed for she did not understand those squiggly lines at all. For her self, she found it all quite fascinating and clear as a bell. On more than one occasion she surprised Jeremy by her understanding and insight, pointing out weaknesses or flaws in the design that needed correcting, and improvements that might be incorporated, and he came quite to rely on her sound judgment.

So it was that the contract was drawn, and the work commenced.

It was Sir Richard's chief works assistant, Ralph Ponsonby, who was the greatest contributor, for he had become an expert on the new heating and piping system, having developed a number of its most important features him self. He was also a stickler for detail, and he would not approve the work as it progressed if it was not to his liking, which was often, for the heating contractor foreman had not installed a system of this type before.

There were several instances of strong disagreements over what was right, the most notable being when the foreman had the main header pipe installed. When challenged by Mr. Ponsonby that it was sloping the wrong way, he maintained that the drawing was not clear, and that anyway it would make no difference, and that if it was insisted to be changed he would expect to be paid for the extra work.

This brought the construction to a standstill for almost a week, while her ladyship fretted about the mess the place was in and how she wished now it had never been started. The Hall had been quite all right as it was, and 'well enough' should have been left alone in her opinion.

Cook was on the point of handing in her notice (or so she said), because her kitchen was turned completely upside-down (which was quite an exaggeration), and she had to cook on an old wood stove outside in a shed (which was perfectly true).

Celia was on the point of tears over the matter, for Jeremy said there were only two ways out: to pay the extra, or go to arbitration, which latter might take several weeks. There was no question of paying the extra, she replied – with some considerable heat – therefore she her self would visit the East Wing worksite and arbitrate the matter for her self.

'But the issue is very technical,' Jeremy pointed out, hoping to save Celia from the embarrassment of a disastrous retreat. 'Perhaps you should reconsider . . .' But she would have none of it, and he dutifully drew up the rear to save the situation as best he could.

After Mr. Ponsonby had recovered from his shock at what the young mistress was attempting, he patiently explained his position and showed her the drawings which, to his considerable surprise, she seemed to understand.

Griggs, the foreman, was quite dismissive in his attitude at this interference in his world of pipes on a matter that no woman – certainly not one little more than a child – could possibly understand. But he held his annoyance in check to point out that it made no difference anyway to the working of the new system, a position that Mr. Ponsonby vigorously rejected.

'Very well, I understand the respective positions,' said Celia crisply. 'Let us now examine the authorities,' addressing first the foreman. 'Does Mr. Ponsonby direct the work?'

The foreman hesitated for a moment, and Celia cut in:

'Yes or no, Mr. Griggs?' giving him a title to show no social differentiation between the parties to the dispute.

'Yes, Miss,' responded Griggs; 'provided them drawin's is clear.'

'I am coming to that. So, Mr. Ponsonby's instructions must be obeyed.' At the foreman's hesitant nod, she turned to the Architect.

'The drawings again, please, Mr. Ponsonby. Is this the system?' pointing to one coloured red, and Ponsonby nodded.

'And this is the pipe in dispute?' Again he nodded, as did the foreman when she turned to him.

'Then it seems perfectly clear to me, gentlemen, that the "Main Header" – as I see it is labelled on the drawing – slopes upwards from left to right.' Mr. Ponsonby nodded; Mr. Griggs was silent.

'And that is the one up there, the large one snaking its way through the roof, right above our heads?'

'Yes, Miss,' replied Mr. Ponsonby.

'Well, *that* one slopes *downwards* from left to right. Is that not so, Mr. Griggs?' and he nodded reluctantly.

'But 'er don' make no dif'rence, Miss, her'll work jes' as well,' Griggs hastened to add.

'Very well, Mr. Griggs, if you say so. I have no way of knowing my self, so we can leave it just as it is.' And here Griggs smiled triumphantly in Ponsonby's direction, while the latter opened his mouth to protest.

'Provided, of course,' she continued, with barely a pause, 'that I have your assurance that if it does *not* work properly when every thing is done, you will correct it – at your expense, of course,' she added, pleasantly. And Griggs' smile froze in place.

'Mr. Jeremy,' said Celia with an air of finality, turning in his direction. 'We should have a legal document to record that Mr. Griggs agrees to correct the Main Header pipe if it fails to function properly in any way after the whole work is complete. Do you think that Geoffrey could have some thing for Mr. Griggs to sign today?'

'That would be difficult, Miss Celia, for he is up to London at the moment. But I could have an agreement by the end of the week.'

'That would suit me fine, and you, Mr. Griggs?'

'Well, I d'no, Miss; wha'll 'er say?'

'Oh, some thing quite simple, Mr. Griggs,' she said, disarmingly. 'That we will leave the Main Header pipe the way you have installed it, sloping in a direction contrary to Mr. Ponsonby's drawing. But if it does not work properly, for any reason, then you will return and amend the slope of the pipe at your own expense, including repairing and refinishing all work damaged by the correction. Nothing very complicated. You see?' smiling at him and Mr. Ponsonby, which only the latter returned.

'Repairin' 'n refinishin' 'un?' said the foreman. 'But then 'er 'll all be plast'd 'n th' loike! T'would mean tearin' down t' new wall t' git a' tha' ther' pipe!'

'True, Mr. Griggs,' acknowledged Celia, nodding her head. 'But that will not be necessary you say, so you have nothing to worry about,' she concluded, brightly. 'But we better have that legal paper signed, just to be on the safe side.' She smiled warmly at him again.

'Jeremy, you go ahead and get it drawn up, and remember to include that the new floors and wool carpets will have to be included in case they get damaged during the repair,' and he smiled, and nodded.

''Ere, 'alf a mo',' broke in the foreman. 'I don't know nuthin' 'bou' fancy floors 'n wool ca'pits 'n th' loike. Reckon's I might 'ave a go t' fix 'er afore you lo' git t' aw tha' ther' truble.'

'But that might waste several days, Mr. Griggs,' wailed Celia, 'and we have lost enough time already!'

'Naw; us'll have 'er roun' t'other way afore ya' c'n blink, Miss.'

'Well, if you really think you should, Mr. . . .' but the foreman was already gone.

''Arry,' they heard him shout, 'git yer sen an't' boy up t' 'eader. I wan's 'er roun' t'other way afore y' leaves, y' 'ear!'

'Well, Mr. Ponsonby,' and she smiled sweetly at him, 'will that settle the matter for you?'

'Miss Celia,' responded he, shaking his head in astonishment born of admiration, 'that was as masterful an arbitration as I have witnessed in my entire life. I do not think we will have any more trouble from that quarter. But if you *ever* have a hankering to go into the business, Miss, just let me know, and I will have you set up in two shakes of a lamb's tail. You hear me, Master Jeremy?' to which that worthy smilingly nodded his agreement.

'Why, thank you, Mr. Ponsonby.' Celia smiled, 'You are most generous, but I rather think not. However, from tomorrow you might see if you can get the work speeded up a little?' at which he doffed his hat, bowed, and set off in Griggs direction, chuckling and shaking his head. 'Well I will be a monk . . .' which fortunately for her maidenly sensibilities, was the last word she heard.

'Was that to *your* liking, *Master* Jeremy? Was the *technical* side of things adequately addressed to suit you?' smiling sweetly at him, too.

'Miss Celia,' said Jeremy, 'I am bowled over! That was a performance to equal Portia's, without a doubt. The Bard would have been proud to know you and would undoubtedly have written a play around you. Today you taught me more about that aspect of the business than I have learned from any of my mentors.' And he bowed and kissed her hand before running off to witness the next exchange in the 'Saga of the Header Pipe', as he would later write it in his 'Memoirs of a Country Manor'.

Christmas came and went, and still the work was not quite finished, although it had been promised for the week before. All potential visitors had been warned to stay away because of the mess the manor was in. And all did, those that were informed that is, for on Boxing Day morn, the professor put in an unexpected appearance with a small present. It was a charcoal sketch of Etheridge Hall from the front, done, he assured a doubtful Celia, from memory.

'He must have a remarkable memory, for it seems to be accurate in every detail – including that south dormer window we have just added!' grumbled Celia to Alice, when he had gone. And gone he soon was, when Celia put a flea in his ear concerning their last conversation.

Lucy, though, remained in the background and said nothing, not even rising from her needlework Celia was glad to note. Nor did she react as strongly in his presence as Celia had expected.

'Perhaps there is hope yet, Alice,' she opined, quietly.

One by one the tradesmen finished: the carpenter with the handsome new skylight over the studio ('bigges' 'un I ever did' he said proudly); the plasterer with the walls and ceilings ('be'er mouldin's you never seen'); the joiner with the wainscoting, doors and cupboards; parquet floor man, the glazier, the painter, the carpet-layer, all in turn, until at last it was complete and the Hall slowly returned to its normal state.

Lady Etheridge was delighted with the new radiator in the Dining room, so that they were now able to have breakfast in its warmth. She had also taken the opportunity to have the room redecorated to lighter hues so that it had an altogether brighter aspect. To her further delight, Mr. Ponsonby had managed to incorporate radiators in the entrance hall and the upper staircase, though he suggested that the stone floors be covered with large carpets to improve their effectiveness. Her own bedroom was, regrettably, too far away to benefit from the new system; that would require a new boiler in the West Wing at some future date.

But she was more than satisfied, and was generous to her daughter in praise of every thing that had been accomplished.

Cook had grumbled about the mess in her kitchen before the work even started, until she found out that a new and larger stove was to be installed and a new, more convenient pantry constructed, then her opposition had melted like one of her raspberry jellies on a summer picnic. Now that it was finished, she was as proud as any body over the fact that it was *her kitchen* that provided the heat for more than half the house, so the maids could thank *her* that the chore of grate cleaning and filling was no more.

The only disgruntled one was Alice. After several temporary arrangements, Mildred was now sleeping on the cot with the washstand outside in the corridor, which was cold by the time they needed it to wash in the early morning.

'Miss Celia promised an arrangement that I would like, but I do not think much of this one,' she grumbled on more than one occasion to her daughter.

'But Mother,' responded her cheerful daughter, a quick learner to speak almost as well, 'You told me your self that this was your idea so that I should not sleep in the village. Really I do not mind, for I have slept in smaller spaces and I am with you.' She gave her mother a big hug, and had it returned in full measure, which made them both happy.

'Besides,' Mildred continued, 'you have forgotten how lucky you are, living in this big house, with plenty of warmth and good food and clean clothes and clean air. And all that green outside; the grass and the trees and the vegetables and milk and every thing. I would not go back to London even if I had to sleep standing up in that corner, so there!'

All of this brought a smile to her mother's face and finally a hearty laugh and another even bigger hug, which was the best part for both of them.

Alice did have a difficult time of it, for her mistresses were always into some thing new. First there were the new beds: should they be mahogany

– which Celia preferred, or walnut – which was Lucy's choice, or oak to match the new floors and woodwork. Jeremy settled that one in favour of harmony – the oak – provided it was golden and not red.

Then there were the furnishings. Curtains, bed covers, carpets, wall coverings and wall and floor tiles, ceiling decoration, and paint colours for sundry things. The new bathroom was another challenge for shape and size of the bath, the basin, and the separate enclosed toilet. Celia wanted the largest tub they could find, and she had it all tiled in so that the feet and the dirty space under it did not show.

But for Alice, keeping every thing the young ladies wore clean and well pressed with all the dust and mess created was decidedly more diffi-cult than ever.

'Up early tomorrow, Alice, for finally we move all of our clothes and other things to our new rooms.'

Alice just nodded, and said 'Yes, Miss,' for she did not like getting up early on these cold mornings. With her bed so close to the fireplace, she was afraid of catching the blanket on fire, so it went out quite early during the night, and there really wasn't much point in relighting it in the morning.

Thus it was with an armful of clothes that she entered Miss Celia's room for the first time.

'Oh, Miss,' she exclaimed to the room in general, 'this is lovely; and so warm, without even a fire being lit, and it a cold day outside. May I bring Mildred to show her?'

'Certainly,' replied her mistress. 'Indeed, why not ask her to give you a hand bringing the clothes; they will go much quicker that way.'

With another two loads now laid on the bed, Alice could show off her mistress' style – which she considered excellent – to her daughter by way of education.

'Do you see how it is done, Mildred? One day you may be lucky enough to live in a grand mansion like this, and do for a lady with impeccable taste, like Miss Celia.

'See how the curtains and bedspread match, and how the carpet uses the same colours. Then there are the silk drapes to the bed canopy that are the same shade as the red in the bedspread. Notice that the wall-paper has the other shade of beige, which is the same as the carpet. That, my girl, is some thing to be proud of, to achieve an effect like that.

Wonderful, Miss Celia, I am so pleased for you that it worked out so well.'

'So am I,' replied her mistress. 'With these things, one doesn't always know that one will succeed, so it is very gratifying when one does. I am certainly very pleased with it,' she finished with a smile, and she turned to the new clothes cupboard that had been built the entire length of one wall.

By now Mildred had all the doors opened, and was staring in amazement at all the hanging and shelf space, which looked all the more because it was still empty.

'Oh, Miss,' gasped Alice, 'this is wonderful! Is it all your own idea?'

'Well, other people had a few suggestions but, yes, it was my idea. I was so tired of that cramped space in those other wardrobes, which never had the right amount of space for any thing. That is when I decided that as I knew pretty well what clothes and other things like shoes and purses I possessed and of what type, why not construct the cupboards for just those things? Of course,' she laughed, 'we shall see in a little while after you have brought every thing in whether I was right!'

'Yes Miss, we shall, but if I am any judge I think you have made a wonderful job of it. What do *you* think, daughter dear?'

But daughter was too much in awe to say any thing at all, and simply stood there, agog.

'One day, Mother,' she said in a whisper, 'I am going to have a cupboard like that.'

'Well, look closely then, my girl, for you may never see its like again.'

'So, let's put the day dresses in this section,' said Celia, 'and the ball gowns in here. These middle two are for under-clothes and night-gowns and such like. Then over here,' walking to the end cupboard, 'these special racks are for the shoes,' at which Mildred was open-mouthed.

'Now the bathroom, Alice. These shelves are for the towels, this bin is for the soiled clothes, and this cupboard is for the bath oils, creams, talcum powder, and the like. Of course, you will have to leave room for Miss Lucy's things, for that door leads to her room as we share the bathroom.'

'This room is lovely, Miss. I do love the pale peach colour of the wall tiles, and the darker ones on the floor. 'Ooh, and you have a radiator in here, too, no wonder it is so warm,' she exclaimed, shaking her head in amazement.

'And a special one to warm the towels, too,' added her mistress.

'And look at that tub, Mildred,' she almost whispered, 'I should not like to carry the hot water for that one!'

'Fortunately, you do not have to, Alice, because the hot water comes all the way from the kitchen through this tap,' and she opened it until the water ran steaming into the tub.

'Did you notice the wash basin in the bedroom?' as she walked back to it. 'See, it also has hot water,' opening the tap until it, too, steamed. 'And the water just runs away by it self, so no more bowls of dirty water to carry away – and slop over the carpets,' she added, slyly.

Alice was simply too overcome by it to do any thing but just shake her head in amazement.

'Wonderful, Miss, simply wonderful. And does Miss Lucy have the same?'

'Just the same, Alice, except that her room is a bit smaller, because that was the way it was laid out when the house was built. However, we share that balcony on the East side there, which should be lovely on summer mornings, but I have this big one that looks out over the South lawns. I expect we shall spend a lot of time on it in the summer and autumn.'

'One last thing, and then you and Mildred can bring over Miss Lucy's things and put every thing away.

'Off the corridor here, we now have the art studio on the right, and the music room on the left. They used to be the small guestrooms, but we will take a look at them later. At the end of the corridor there is a new door, as you see, so that when it is shut, the East Wing is our private sanctuary, except of course, for this old staircase here. It has been redecorated, as you see. Have you been up here?'

Alice shook her head.

'No, Miss.'

'Come, then, let us take a look,' taking hold of Mildred's hand to lead the way.

The rooms were partly in the roof space, a larger and a smaller one, each with a dormer window, newly decorated and with a new wooden floor.

'You take a look at the smaller one, Mildred, while your mother and I look at this. Notice how cozy it is up here, Alice?'

'Yes, Miss, it is lovely and warm; such pretty curtains on the window, too. It looks out on to the same view as your balcony, Miss, only higher up.'

'Yes, and what else do you see.'

'Well, every thing is so clean and new and – ooh, there is a wash basin here, too, with two taps, and a waste water pipe, just like yours, Miss,' and she walked over to test the hot tap for her self. Yes, it steamed, and yes, it ran away by it self.

'And here is a large bed and dressing table with drawers and a mirror over it, and a clock ticking away on the wall beside it. Even a chair and table to write on. Oh Miss, your guests will have a fine time here. Many a lady does not have as fine a bedroom as this.'

She was about to speak again when Mildred ran back into the room.

'Mother, Mother,' she cried excitedly, 'that room has a radiator and hot water just like the one in Miss Celia's room, and a cupboard nearly as big, and a beautiful new black iron bed with a lovely soft mattress on it just like this one,' as she sat and bounced upon it. 'And I can see right out to the mountains.'

'Well, they are really just hills,' replied Miss Celia. 'Do you like it, Mildred?'

'Oh, yes, Miss Celia, it is wonderful. I could live up here for ever and ever and never leave it. It would be my castle tower, and I would wait for my prince to ride up on his white horse, and only then would I leave it. But I would come back to it every year 'til I was old and withered and...'

'Oh, hush, Mildred,' broke in her mother, 'Miss Celia doesn't want to hear you prattle on like that.'

'But I do,' laughed her mistress, 'I was a bit that way my self when I was her age. Anyway, if she likes it that much, she shall have it. It is yours, Mildred, you can move in as soon as you like,' and she turned to leave.

'Miss,' said the visibly shaken Alice, 'you should not make fun of her like that; she is only a child, and she might think you meant it.'

'But of course I meant it, Alice, or I would not have said it, would I?'

'Hurrah,' shouted Mildred, and rushed back into the room, where they could hear her bouncing on the bed.

'Mildred!' called her mother, walking to the adjoining doorway, 'stop that at once, do you hear me?'

'But, Miss,' she said turning to face her mistress again, 'she can not have a room all to her self; think of the mischief she will get up to with me over the other wing and her here.'

'That is true, Alice. Then maybe you should move here, too.'

'Oh, Miss, could I? That would be wonderful. There is plenty of room in there for the two of us, for it is more than thrice the size of my room now.'

'Very well, Alice, you may move right away, too. But I do not know why you would want to squeeze the two of you in there, when there is a perfectly good room here. We would put carpets on the floor, of course.'

'You mean, Miss, that I could have this great big room to *my self?* With Mildred in that room to *her self?*'

'Why, yes, if you want it. These quarters are not for guests, Alice, they are for Miss Lucy and my self, and we are certainly not going to have any body else up here but you – and Mildred, of course. So if you do not take it, it will just stay empty.'

'Oh, Miss, I do not know what to say,' as tears rolled down her cheeks.

'Then do not say any thing, Alice. I promised you an arrangement for your self and Mildred that I thought you would like, and here it is. I am sorry it took so long, but it could not be done more quickly. You seem to like it, or at least your daughter does!' as the bouncing resumed from the other room, and she turned to go.

Alice suddenly took hold of her mistress' hand and, with a deep curtsey, knee touching the floor, kissed it. 'Thank you, Miss, you are so kind to us, and we do not deserve it.'

'But you *do*, Alice, you do,' whispered Celia huskily in response, struggling to retain control, not trusting her full voice. 'It is *we* who should be grateful to *you* for all you have done for *us*.

'Now you had better go and take care of that daughter of yours before she breaks the springs of both your beds!'

As Celia reached the door, she paused to ensure that she could once more retain her composure, and turned to speak in a firm, business-like voice.

'Now in the centre drawer of the dressing table, Alice, you will find a little box that has a small memento in return for your service to Miss Lucy and my self. Mildred has one likewise, but hers is for the future rather than the past.

'However you must not open it until five minutes have passed; is that clear? The clock there will advise you when that is. Understood?'

Alice nodded.

'If you have need of me, I shall be in the parlour having tea with Miss Lucy and her Ladyship.'

'Yes, Miss,' with a little curtsey.

Celia had just picked her teacup when there was a tap on the door and in rushed Alice, followed by a smiling Mildred, and they presented a deep curtsey to her Ladyship, and another to Celia and Lucy. Celia had just enough time to put down her teacup before Alice, tears streaming down her face, approached her mistress and, with some thing clutched in her hand, put her arms around Celia's neck and kissed her on both cheeks.

'I do not know what to say, Miss,' she whispered. 'It is so beautiful, and I can not help crying – for joy that is. No-one has *ever* done any thing so beautiful for me – except Mother, of course, who gave me life it self, and Richard who gave me Mildred,' and she hugged and kissed her mistress again. Then, opening her hand again, she whispered,

'Would you put it on for me, please?'

'Of course, Alice,' tears now streaming down her own cheeks, and taking the proffered chain, hung it around Alice's neck, whereupon Alice kissed her mistress once more, stood up, eyes sparking and a big smile through her tears, which she wiped with a corner of her apron.

Lucy and their mother sat amazed at this display of affection, completely mystified by the tears of emotion from the two of them, for they were generally not given to this sort of thing. Her Ladyship could not recall ever seeing such a tearful Alice. But there was yet more, for this was followed by a smiling Mildred, who approached an astonished Lucy with a similar request.

By this time some composure had returned, so that Lady Etheridge turned to her elderly daughter.

'What is this all about, pray?' and then to a now beaming Alice. 'Is there a simple explanation for this, Alice?'

Alice turned to Celia, who indicated with a slight nod that she should explain the circumstance.

'Well, Madam,' approaching her and kneeling to show that around her neck was a golden sovereign on a fine golden chain – which meant nothing to her Ladyship – before doing likewise to Lucy, who understood perfectly, so that tears formed in her eyes and ran down her cheeks.

'You see, Madam, my father gave my mother a gold sovereign on a gold chain, exactly like this one, and when she passed on,' and here a pause to regain composure, 'she left it to me. But then I had to part . . . with it, when I got into . . . into . . . difficulties . . . Oh, Madam, I can say no more,' and, eyes streaming, turned and fled, followed by a still-smiling Mildred, who gave a perfect curtsey at the door, then closed it softly behind her.

For some moments no-one spoke, then a tearful Celia explained that it was a memento for the many things that Alice has done for her self and Lucy, but especially when in Town.

'And Mildred?' echoed Lucy.

'Well, I could not give some thing special to Alice and neglect her daughter, so I had a similar one made of silver, using an ancient silver shilling. Alice's is in newly-minted gold, of course. I made the gift from you, Lucy, because – well, there is a reason. We both owe Alice a great deal, Mother, and it seemed appropriate to do it that way.' At this Lucy rose and gave her sister a big hug and a kiss on both cheeks.

'This means a great deal to Alice, doesn't it,' said their mother softly, and Celia nodded, again becoming teary-eyed. Then she rose, indicating that her daughters do the same, and hugged them both tightly, adding:

'I am most pleased with you, my dears. I could not have done any thing as wonderful as you have, Celia. You both do me proud, and I would not wish for daughters more beautiful than I have today,' and their tears mingled together as they stood, hugging each other, heads bowed.

'And what is this "reason", Cel?' when they were alone together.

'Why, that Mildred should do for you, what Alice does for me. That is all.'

'Oh.'

'D or G, that is the question,' said Celia, bouncing into the Morning room.

'I beg your pardon?' responded her mother, not quite appreciating her daughter's lack of decorum upon entering the room.

'D or G, duck or goose, that is the question, whether 'tis nobler to pluck or to roast. I think we might have both, and perhaps a suckling pig or two as well, or even a gobbler. You see, Mother, I have been talking to Cook about the Spring Dinner we have to give to our friends and neighbours.'

'Have you indeed! And since when have you taken unto your self the ordering of social events in this household? But then,' continued her mother, dryly, 'since you seem to have the matter so well in hand, perhaps you should handle the entire affair.'

'No, Mother,' replied Celia, confidently, 'I believe that you do that sort of thing better than any body, so we will leave it to you. But Lucy and

I would like to be involved in the menus and guest list, and especially in the decorations and seating arrangements.'

'Would you, indeed,' replied her mother, eyebrows raised; 'and what kind of an occasion did you and Lucy intend for this "Spring Dinner" – for I have never heard of such a thing?'

'I thought some thing a little different. For the younger people that we know, perhaps fancy dress, or a masked ball,' said Celia, with a measured indifference. 'The dining arrangements would be less formal than they would have been at Christmas, of course. Indeed, perhaps we could have smaller tables in several places around the house, and we would make sure that we had an interesting group at each table. Either that, or we could have a guessing game or "blind man's bluff" or some-such as the deciding factor for who dines with whom.'

'Really!' replied her ladyship in some indignation, 'I can see some of our society responding *very* poorly to that!'

'Exactly, Mother. That is why I suggested it, because we do not want the same dry, boring gatherings that we have every year.'

'Thank you, my dear daughter, for your frank and depressing assessment of the nature of my dinner parties. I had always thought that you rather enjoyed them.'

'I do, Mother, I do. But just because I enjoy grilled trout, that doesn't mean I wish it every day of the week!'

'Grilled trout? What does grilled trout have to do with Christmas Dinner, even if it is in the middle of spring? I am not sure I understand what you young people are up to these days, really I do not,' and she resumed her reading of the Parish Magazine.

'That is settled then,' said her daughter, cheerfully, picking up her papers. 'I will get out the guest lists and menus and other details for you to look at in a day or two for a special Spring Fancy-dress Ball, with masks, on Friday, the Ides of March.'

In the pause that followed, the words echoed on the air.

'Fancy dress, on the Ides of what?' said mother, looking up, only to find that she was alone once more.

'Alice, I do believe we have a challenge before us,' Celia said softly, rising out of her night time bathtub and shaking the water drops from her body.

'And what is that, Miss,' responded Alice, wrapping the towels warmed on the radiator around her mistress, and steadying her as she stepped onto the bath mat. But her mistress put a finger to her lips and inclined her head in the direction of Lucy's room, and stepped through into her own room.

When Alice had closed the door behind them, Celia added,

'It concerns Miss Lucy, or at least her welfare, so we need to be circum-spect in our discussions. I shall also require your extreme discretion in the matter, as you will see later,' she added, with raised eyebrows in Alice's direction.

'Certainly, Miss,' replied Alice, with a little curtsey.

'Good. Now, I am feeling girlish tonight, so suppose you get me the pretty one with the lace gorge and cuffs and the pink roses on the front.'

'This one, Miss?' said Alice, retrieving a night-gown from a cupboard drawer.

'Yes, that is it, one of my special favourites,' adding, 'Thank you, Alice,' as it was slipped over her head and the ribbons tied at the back.

'Not bad,' she said, turning from side to side on tiptoe and addressing the mirror she had set into the corner of the room, so that she could see her self from all sides, then returned to the dressing stool for Alice to brush her hair.

This had become a nightly ritual for Celia. Alice would draw her bath, using one of a variety of bath oils and fragrances, and then help her undress and enter the water, talk about the day's events while she bathed her, select a nightgown, and finally brush her hair until it shone. Then they would discuss things of a more serious and personal nature.

It was the new room radiators that made all that possible. Instead of rushing the bathing to get in and out of the cold bathroom and the some-times not-very-hot water as soon as possible, it was now a relaxed and enjoyable affair, with as much hot water from the tap to indulge her self as she wished, without the embarrassment of asking Alice to go down to the kitchen to heat and fetch it, stumbling up the staircase with the large heavy jug on her return.

Similarly, in the warm bedroom Celia could wear her light cotton summer gowns 'so my skin can breathe' as she put it, instead of the hated heavy flannel that had been so essential before to avoid freezing. Nor was it necessary to get into bed as quickly as possible, a bed that was invariably cold, despite the two or three hot water bottles. She could now attire her self in pretty, frilly gowns and relax – for she had two easy chairs and a chaise longue in her room – Alice brushing her hair the while they talked of delicate and intimate matters, woman to woman.

Tonight she decided she would sit up in bed and they would talk from there. After Alice had bunched the pillows behind her, she said:

'Pull up that chair close to the bed, Alice, so I do not have to strain to see or hear you, and put out all the candles except the one on the dresser. Good. Now a question. Why can I not talk to Mother as I do to you?'

'I do not know, Miss.'

'Yes you do, Alice. You are just not trying.'

'Well, Miss, I think it is some thing to do with the questions you ask, and the things you want to talk about. Like last night, when you wanted to know what it was like to carry a baby inside you, and feel it moving and kicking, and what it felt like to have it suckling at your breast. Do you really think her Ladyship would welcome that sort of discussion or, for that matter, answer such a personal question?'

'Well, I do not really see why not, Alice; after all, we are both grown women, and I am certainly the proof that she has experienced all that. Is that not so?'

'Yes, Miss, but *she* was the one that bore you, and breast-fed you, and to her you will always be that "baby" – not the "grown woman" you propose. If she were to discuss such an intimate subject, you would once more become that suckling, not who you are now. Besides, her ladyship would want to know *why* you wanted to know, fearful that you had in mind going out and making one as I did; begging your pardon, Miss.'

She was afraid for the moment that she might have overstepped the bounds of decency in attributing such an outlandish thought to her mistress.

'Oh, that is all right, Alice, I am not offended in the slightest. Besides, how do you know I am not?' Celia added, with a soft Mona Lisa smile: but Alice only smiled in return, for she was now used to her mistress' sly humour. 'Now, what shall be the special topic for tonight?'

'You said we had a challenge, Miss, concerning Miss Lucy.'

'So I did. It has to do with the Ides Ball that we are arranging – and that "we" will include you, Alice, to a considerable degree arranging things with the serving maids and so on, so put on your thinking cap.

'However, at the moment I am mulling over the guest list, for it is bigger than ever since our Quintet debut. Most importantly at the moment is whom we *must* include, whom we *might* include, and those we would *rather* leave out – if we dare! So, directing your mind to that aspect, Alice, in which of those categories do the following prospective guests' names fall: *Captain Charles deWitt Allison,* and *Professor Manfred R. Werner.*'

The silence that followed her question was so complete that the ticking of the small French carriage clock on her bedside table was quite distinct.

'Well?' commanded Celia, looking directly at Alice, who lowered her eyes in response, but made no reply.

'Do you know what you are asking, Miss?' finally whispered the pale and shaken Alice.

'I think so,' replied her mistress. 'At least, I hope I understand it. What do you think I am asking, Alice?'

'I do not think I dare put it into words, Miss.'

'Come, come, Alice. You dared tell me the other night about the manner in which you and Richard made love – in quite graphic and explicit detail if you recall, the which I much appreciated, you understand, as my many Art books fail to do. Is this so much more daring than that?'

'Yes, Miss,' replied Alice, still in a whisper.

'But why are we whispering, Alice?'

'Because, Miss, you are really asking me to say which man Miss Lucy should marry, and to decide whether she would be happy in that marriage or not, and I could not presume to do that for Miss Lucy. You might just as well ask me if you should marry Mr. Reginald.'

'Well, for that matter, should I?'

'Oh, Miss, this is getting into very deep water. I am just a simple servant girl, Miss, and I know better than to advise my superiors on such matters.'

'Alice!' snapped her mistress, in rising fury, 'do not *ever* say *any thing* as *stupid* as that to me again, *do you hear me?*' and she was by now quivering with rage. 'If that is how you see your self, you can take *that self* out of my sight, right now, and *do not bother to bring it back!*'

'Yes, Miss, I mean no, Miss,' whispered Alice, frightened out of her wits, for she had never seen her mistress this angry. 'I am sorry, Miss, I truly am; I do not quite know what came over me, except that suddenly I was afraid, Miss, by the importance of the question you are asking – shall Miss Lucy be happy or unhappy in love, for the rest of her life! Do we have the *right*, Miss, to even discuss that matter without Miss Lucy knowing about it?'

Celia was silent for some further moments while she allowed her temper to cool to a manageable level before she snapped:

'Perhaps we do not, Alice,' but then continued in a hoarse whisper, 'but you see, that the question will not just go away. It will still be there in the morning, and who is going to decide then, if you and I do not? Shall we leave it to her ladyship, who will make the "correct" decision? We *know* what my sister will decide!'

Alice nodded, mutely.

'Well, it is getting late, so perhaps we should put it aside for the moment, but it *must* be addressed, and soon. Now, good night, Alice,' and she put out her hand for Alice to take, 'and thank you. I am sorry that I jumped on you so hard but, believe me, I understand more of your dilemma than you think I do.'

'Perhaps, you do, Miss. I will think about it, I truly will,' at which she snuffed out the lone candle, and dissolved like its light into the darkness; only the soft click of the latch signalling her true departure.

10

Dolly

At the knock on the door, Celia said loudly, 'If it is Alice, come in.'

Alice entered and stood waiting at the door. She did not proceed further into the room, for she had received strict instructions never to enter the art studio unless invited, and then not to look or comment on any work in progress unless specifically directed to do so. It was a rare exception indeed that anyone other than Alice was admitted (excepting Lucy, of course, although even she was circumspect in her use of her acceptance). Her ladyship knew better than to arrive unannounced and uninvited on any occasion.

Her mistress, still in her rosebud nightgown, was seated at the easel, which had its back to the door, so as to catch the north light, as well as to provide the artiste the privacy that they always seemed to require. And Miss Celia was no exception.

'Yes, Alice?' she said at last, without looking up from the easel.

'I have put the coffee in your room, Miss, as you asked.'

'Thank you, Alice,' looking up now but without her customary smile. 'Are you free now?'

'Yes, Miss, most of my morning chores are taken care of.'

'Good, then let us repair to my room,' and she led the way through the passage to her own room, where she lay on the divan, while Alice poured the coffee.

'Shall I take a cup to Miss Lucy?' she inquired, indicating the adjoining music room, whence they could hear Miss Lucy practising her part of Mozart's Flute Concerto.

'Perhaps later, Alice. Just now, I need you to brush my hair for I am all at sixes and sevens this morning; and it is all your fault!'

'Yes, Miss,' responded Alice, recalling the conversation of last night.

'I am still thinking about it, Miss, but I do not have an answer yet.'

'And neither do I,' replied her mistress, despondently, slowly drinking her coffee while Alice knelt on the floor behind the divan and soothingly brushed her hair for a good ten minutes.

'How would you like me to dress it, Miss?

'Is it long enough for me to ride like Lady Godiva, Alice, over hill and dale, to the far horizon?'

'I do not think so, Miss; that will take several more years.'

'Well, that will not do, then, will it? However,' sitting up and smiling for the first time, 'we could go for a more conventional ride, could we not?'

'Yes, Miss, we could,' glad that her sometimes temperamental mistress was coming out of her dark mood. 'Shall I ask Robert to saddle Sally for you?'

'No, but you can ask him to saddle Jasper.'

'But Miss, he hasn't been ridden for a while, and you know how wild he can be sometimes,' protested Alice.

'True,' replied her mistress, 'but that is what I want, what I *need* this morning, some thing a little wild to shake up this dull brain and even duller spirit of mine. And ask him to saddle the pony that you ride. Molly, is that right?'

'Dolly, Miss.'

'Get him to put a regular saddle on her, but do not let her ladyship see it; then we will ride out through the orchard. Oh, and please inform her Ladyship that we shall be out riding for some hours.'

'Yes, Miss,' responded Alice eagerly, eyes shining, for that meant she could ride the way she preferred, astride, the way the men did.

'I will be back directly, Miss,' and ran out of the room.

The orchard path led to the top of the slight hill behind the Hall, and from there through several farm fields until it opened up to the common, a great expanse of open upland, broken only by small copses, that stretched almost to the next county. Here they alternately cantered and trotted and walked their animals side by side along a slight crest for several miles until the house was far behind them.

Celia examined a number of the copses looking for some thing, but whatever it was, she did not find it – until they came to a stand of old oak trees to the right of their path. It was off somewhat to the side and leading downhill on the far side, surrounded by smaller trees and bushes, so that it was quite enclosed, and further surrounded by the remains of a much dilapidated fence.

'This looks inviting,' as she reined in Jasper and walked him in to where the sun was shining in a recent clearing. 'Perfect,' she exclaimed, almost to her self, and dismounted, tied him to a tree, and indicated to Alice that she should do the same with Dolly.

'Isn't this the most beautiful place, Alice?' draping her riding cape over a branch, and stretching her arms to the sunlit canopy.

'It is, Miss,' pausing in her dismount to admire her mistress' lithe figure in the dappled glade. 'So secluded, yet open to the sky, and so peaceful one could almost forget there was a world outside.'

'Most poetically put, Alice, I am impressed. Now, if you would please hand me my carry bag, we can make our selves comfortable,' and she took from it two soft towels, which she then spread on adjacent tree stumps. 'There, thrones fit for a queen and her hand-maiden,' and sat on the one that had a stately oak close to it. Next she took from the bag an antique silver-backed hairbrush, which she handed to Alice.

'But I have only just put it up, Miss,' complained Alice.

'True,' replied her mistress, 'but now I need it down – and brushed,' after which she took the brush from Alice and used it to brush her hair across her chest, while Alice took a seat on the other stump and watched the display, curiously.

'Oh, this will not do at all,' said Celia to her self in exasperation, after a little while, followed by, 'You may close your eyes or look the other way, Alice, or both if what I am about to do causes you any embarrassment.' And to Alice's amazement, reached under her hair, undid the buttons of her blouse and removed it to lay across her knees.

Celia ignored Alice's 'But, Miss . . .' and tossed her long blonde hair behind her to expose her smooth shoulders and soft upper bosom and bodice which, to Alice's open-mouthed astonishment, she also removed and laid on her knee, so that she was wearing nothing at all above the waist except her hair. Then she draped the blouse over her shoulders but left it quite open, pulled her hair to the front and proceeded to brush it over her bosom.

'Tell me, Alice,' she said innocently, 'what do you do when you feel like this?'

'Like what, Miss?' said Alice, jerkily, when she finally found her voice.

'Alice, do not tell me that you never feel this . . . this *tension* in your bosom, just here,' parting her hair with the brush to disclose the swollen pink against the soft white, 'this tingly feeling inside that will not go away until it is released? Because if you do, I shall just not believe you! So how do you satisfy its demands?'

Alice dropped her eyes and blushed.

'I am quite ashamed to admit it, Miss, but I no longer feel those "demands", as you call them. They died, I think, with my Richard. But you should not be doing that here!' looking around wildly to see who was watching the display, this uninhibited expression of female release in the middle of an oak glade. But there were no gaps in the early spring growth around them and nothing stirred save the leaves overhead, the horses nibbling the grass and the birds and bees busy with their own pursuits.

'Here,' said her mistress after a while, holding out the brush, 'you may do it for me, while I relax,' and she held it there until the reluctant Alice rose and took the brush. Then she leaned back against the tree trunk, closed her eyes, and thrust her body into the soft bristles as Alice stroked slowly across her arched body.

'You are very lucky; you know,' whispered Celia with a deep sigh of contentment, as she gave her self up to the wonderful feelings that were flowing through her with every stroke of the brush. 'You have Richard to think about when it is happening to you. I have nothing but wishes and dreams, all unfulfilled, so far.'

'One day, Miss,' responded Alice softly, 'one day they will come true, and you will know the wonder of it, too.'

'Have you done this before, Alice?' she whispered, as Alice brushed and stroked with the consummate skill of an artist, until her release was finally complete.

'No, Miss, I haven't, but I know what you are feeling, and where you are feeling it, and that makes it easier. And I can see, and feel even, what you are feeling inside. I will tell you more about it one evening.'

'Soon?' queried Celia.

'Soon,' declared Alice.

'One last thing before we depart this Sylvan Glade – for that is what it shall be called henceforth,' said Celia, as she arose, slipped off her petticoat, and put it and the other garments in the bag. Then she buttoned her blouse over her bare bosom, and strode to where Dolly was munching the grass.

'You can not ride dressed like that, Miss,' gasped Alice.

'You just watch,' she laughed, as she lifted her skirt above her knees, and mounted astride Dolly in one easy swing.

Once out of the trees, she dug in her heels and raced the pony along the ridge to its end, almost out of sight. There she stopped, studying some thing below the horizon, then turned and raced back again, her long hair streaming in the wind, almost as far in the other direction before she turned once more and trotted at a more leisurely pace to spare the winded animal.

'There,' she said, triumphantly, swinging her leg over the saddle and jumping lightly to the ground. 'You did not think I could ride like that, did you, Alice?'

'No, Miss, I certainly did not, though I knew you had the spirit,' and she could not help but admire her mistress' glowing cheeks and tousled hair, and the healthy thrust of her so-evidently bare bosom, as the blouse clung and moulded to its newly excited and damp form. 'You do look the very picture of health, Miss – though I am also very glad there is no-one else here to say the same thing!'

'Thank you, Alice, and you are probably right. Now that the body's desire is requited and the spirit resuscitated, I feel it, too,' said Celia, removing her blouse once more so that Alice could dry her bare moistness with the powder produced from the bag.

'Now, please put every thing properly back in its place, and let's go a-rovin' to determine what lies over yonder ridge.'

'There it is, Alice, behind that clump of trees, and the white building at the left end is the conservatory, where we used to practise, and hope to again, come the Season. But hold; what else do we have here? Company, I do declare,' as she observed a lone horseman come out of a small gap in the trees below them and make his way purposefully in their direction.

'Perhaps we should leave, Miss. If that is Greville Hall, and if that is who I think it is, we might do better to retrace our steps without delay.' It was true that she had seen little of the professor since that last near-disaster with Miss Lucy at the Hunt Ball, but she was not one whit less concerned about his power, and turned her mount to leave.

'Not so fast Alice, this might be just the opportunity we seek to answer our unsolvable question,' and she sat perfectly still on Jasper, waiting for the figure to reach them.

'Good morning, Miss Etheridge, good morning, Alice. May I have the pleasure of your company for a few moments?'

'You may, Professor, although I confess that if we are worthy only of a few moments of your time before you are bored with our company, perhaps we should decline so as to retain our self-respect. How say you, Alice?' turning in her direction, and ignoring the professor's obvious embarrassment.

'I think, perhaps, Miss Celia, that the professor meant it differently from the way he expressed it.'

'You really think so, Alice? For my part, I had thought the professor possessed of many parts and guises, and not given to any but the most careful expression of what he meant. However, as you may well be correct, and are certainly most charitable in your allowances for his manner of speech, let us then allow him the benefit of such doubt as may exist.

'Professor,' facing and addressing him once more, 'We are of the opinion that you may have misspoken in the breathlessness of your ascent of the hill beneath us, and we are thus inclined to allow you a further opportunity of our company,' and her bright blue eyes looked levelly and innocently into his pale blue.

The professor shifted uneasily in the saddle, and looked to his bridle while he prepared his response, for he knew that she was more than a match for him in repartee, besides having the uncanny – not to say frightening – ability to read his thoughts with deadly accuracy.

'I apologize most humbly, to you both,' he said, finally, 'and can only offer the most wretched of excuses, in that, as Alice so accurately divined, my words were meant to convey that I consider my self unworthy of more than the most fleeting of attention before you become unutterably bored with my ignorance and lack of grace,' with which he gave a low bow to Celia, and almost the same to Alice.

'Shall we accept, Alice? I do believe the professor is both genuine and abject in his submission to our forgiveness, and his words were most pretty to my ears.'

'I do believe he is sincere, Miss, and further, that we may do him an injustice if we proceed otherwise.'

'Very well, Professor, we shall inform you when we are bored with your company, and then invite you to leave us. In the meantime you may ride with us for a pace or two,' and she led the way leisurely back toward the oak glade, with Alice at her side, the professor trailing at the rear.

The professor was actually glad of the opportunity to relax out of direct view, for he found Celia a most challenging young woman. He had known quite a number of very bright ones in his college days, but she was more than their equal in every sense of the word. She always was able to best him with the utmost ease, making him feel as uncomfortable in her presence as he had ever felt in his life with anyone.

He knew that she was playing with him, as a cat plays with a mouse, but for the life of him he could find not the slightest weakness or chink in her armour. 'Armour?' Amour, that certainly was the better word, for right now she was looking more feminine and quite as desirable as any female he had ever met. Perhaps that was an approach; certainly nothing else seemed to work, and he knew that his chances of ever even *seeing* Lucinda again were close to zero if he failed to meet her challenge now.

His reverie was abruptly broken by Celia's voice as she reined in her horse, and half-turned to address him.

'So silent, Professor, and you trail in our shadow, I had thought you craved our company?'

'Indeed I do, Miss Etheridge, yet I find my self quite inadequate in it, and lack the courage to discourse directly.'

'Dear me,' said Celia, with a shake of her head, 'are we that fearsome, Alice?'

'I had not thought we were, Miss.'

'Well, we are at a rather pleasant coppice; perhaps we should repair there and rest our mounts for a brief spell,' and she slowly walked Jasper in to its interior, where she waited.

'You may hand me down, Professor, if you have a mind,' she said in a matter-of-fact voice in his direction.

The professor responded with alacrity, jumping from his horse and moving to where Jasper stood.

'I am much afraid that I have never undertaken this delicate task before,' he exclaimed, reddening with genuine embarrassment, for he considered him self capable of most assignments.

'Really?' said Celia, in some surprise. 'Well, the gentleman is supposed to hold the lady softly yet firmly at the waist, and lower her gently to the ground. It is really quite simple, and I am sure you will perform the task admirably.'

And he did, with more ease than he had expected, for she was light as a feather. It was, he reflected, a most enjoyable undertaking in fact.

Yet there was some thing he had *not* reckoned with. As he lowered her slowly and carefully, his senses swam at the softness and allure of her persona when she was on the ground but still held on her toes, his hands completely encircling her tiny waist under her cape, the scent of her hair and her warm body assailing his nostrils, her upturned smiling face no more than a few inches from his, her bosom almost touching his. It was overpowering beyond description.

'You may release me now, Professor, for I shall not fall over, I assure you,' and again he blushed, for her voice and demeanour were now soft and feminine in the extreme, leaving him quite weak at the knees, a feeling he had not experienced since he was a schoolboy.

'I do beg your pardon,' he exclaimed, breathlessly, his heart pounding furiously. 'To tell the truth, Miss Etheridge, I am quite overawed by your beauty, which this morning is entrancing beyond all description, and quite takes away my senses,' and it was Celia's turn to colour and lower her glance.

'Your flattery is becoming, Professor,' she responded demurely, 'though I should reject it. However, I perceive that it is genuine, and therefore I thank you for it, and for the truly delicate manner in which you assisted my dismount,' and her face lighted with a smile of unbelievable radiance.

'Alice, if you would be so good as to put some thing over these tree stumps we could perhaps sit for a while. Perhaps you would be good enough to assist me again, Professor,' and she held out her hand to him, and waited for Alice so that he might lower her to the towel.

'Goodness', thought Alice, as she spread the towels on the stumps, 'if he could have been here only thirty minutes ago, he would have seen some thing that men would give their inheritance for', and she was glad that her back was to him so as to shield her outrageous thoughts.

Celia, waiting with her hand in his, had much the same thoughts; except that she was excited by them in that he *could* have been a thrilled witness to her self-fulfilment and her wild and sensuous ride, and this sent the blood tingling through her veins, causing the professor's pulse to race.

The professor, finally seated on a blanket on the ground, was overwhelmed by the magic of the sylvan setting as well as the distinct air of excitement coming to him from both women, but especially from Celia, though he had no way of knowing its origin. He only knew that the atmosphere of enchantment was strongly in his favour for certainly the first and probably the last time, and his opportunity was now or never.

'Before you address us, Professor, I have a confession to make. I am glad we met so providentially for we, Alice and I, have a difficulty to which you can perhaps assist in finding a solution.'

'I am happy to oblige your self and Alice in even the smallest of services, and I am yours to command,' and he bowed his head to each of them.

'Thank you. It concerns my sister, Lucinda, to whom I believe you have both a certain attachment and a desire to make better her acquaintance.'

The professor nodded his head, 'That is quite correct, Miss Etheridge,' at which Celia held up a gloved hand.

'I hesitate to advise you on such a minor matter, Professor, but the correct form of address for my self is "Miss Celia". However, as we shall shortly have either a much closer family relationship or none at all, you may address me as to a sister, simply as Celia,' and she gave him a polite smile. 'Provided, of course, that we receive agreement from Alice, for she is my chaperon today. Alice?'

'Yes, Miss, but only when we are together in this manner. It must never occur when anyone else is present, especially Miss Lucy and her Ladyship. Is that quite clear, Professor?'

'That is perfectly clear, Alice, and I accept the conditions. You should in return, Miss, uh, Celia, call me Manfred, which I much prefer.'

To his surprise, she shook her head.

'That will not be possible, Professor, for that name must be reserved to one special person only.'

'I am naturally disappointed, but I understand,' he replied. 'However, I too have a confession to make, for it is not entirely by fortune that we meet today. From my window in Greville Hall there was a most glorious sight: a beautiful young woman riding a pony like the wind along the top of the ridge. I confess that at first I thought of you, but then realized that you always ride side-saddle and this rider was clearly astride her mount. Also, her hair was blowing magnificently in the wind while yours is neatly coifed, so I was mistaken. But I was so intrigued by the grace and skill of the young rider that I was moved to investigate – to my immense good fortune, as we see.

'Now, how may I be of service to you?'

Celia was so moved by the thoughts racing through her head that she had to feign examining the overhead canopy. So he *had* seen her, although not known it. And if he *had* been closer – perhaps *much* closer, a witness to her overexcited charms – what might he now be saying! And it was with much effort – and even greater reluctance – that she forced her self to return to the matters at hand.

'Professor, we shall be having an Ides Ball for our special friends, to welcome spring, as well as to celebrate the completion of the new East Wing. It is possible that you will be invited, but is by no means certain. If you are, and you accept, you will be expected to comport your self in a manner as befits a gentleman at all times.'

'I would most certainly accept, Celia, and will heed your advice.'

'Well said. But before you indicate your desires, there is one thing more for your consideration, Professor, and you would do well to ponder it conscientiously. Also invited will be a most eligible young gentleman of title and breeding who has privately expressed the *strongest* interest in my sister. Should he do so publicly, I confess that he would be acceptable on every possible ground, to my mother and to her advisors. And, I may say, to my self. Unfortunately or otherwise, Lucy's views on the matter carry little if any weight, and she would be almost bound to accept such an offer for her hand. In those circumstances, Professor, would you still accept? Think carefully before you answer.'

'Would I be permitted to meet and talk with Miss Lucinda before that occasion; or to my rival?'

'The former will not be possible, and the latter would be *most* inadvisable.'

'But if I cannot talk with her about certain affairs of the heart, Celia, how can I know whether we two are well suited?'

'One either knows these things, Professor,' said Celia, with a tightening of the jaw, 'or one does not. There is no room for in-between.'

'That is easy for you to say, for you know her well, but I have hardly even spoken to her.'

'That I accept. Nevertheless, you *know* my sister, Professor – in the classic sense – that your rival (as you refer to him) will not until the wedding night, giving you a benefit that he would consider of the grossest impertinence. And *were* he to be aware of that "knowing", you would immediately be challenged to a duel, with only one possible outcome for you, unhappily.'

'That may be so, yet I would still wish to meet my rival on equal terms so that Lucinda may have a choice. If I do not attend there can be no preference for her and, as I cannot surrender without a fight, I have no option but to attend.'

'Very well, I will see to it that you are sent an invitation,' said Celia, her face a set mask. 'But I am much disappointed in your judgment, Professor. This is not a battle, and my sister is not a "Helen of Troy" to be fought over. Only her happiness is at stake, and your responses may have put that in considerable doubt. Choice is not such a simple matter as you seem to make it. Some events are plainly preferable to others, but one accepts them as ordained. However, I will respect your decision.'

At these words she rose to her feet, this time unaided.

'Adieu, Professor, we shall not meet again until the day of the Ball, and then only as hostess and guest. Come, Alice, the sunshine has gone out of this place, and it grows cold.'

As he rode Johnson down the slope, Manfred knew that he had been beaten, again. He had learned enough of this society to know that Celia had indeed spoken the truth. No matter how strong Lucinda's feelings were for him – and his for her were of no account at all – she would not be permitted to indulge them in the face of a contender of genuine substance and position. Nor would a 'Lochinvar' rescue, much as he admired the Sir Walter Scott poem, have any but the most disastrous of consequences in this world – for both of them.

His final thought before he dismounted was the ephemeral nature of happiness. One moment Celia was effervescent and luscious beyond belief, and it was joyous just to be in her presence; the next a glacier had flowed through the clearing and between them, and all was in shadow. And he wondered how he could ever find happiness in this strange land to which he had been transported. Perhaps it was all in the nature of a challenge; a sort of 'Twilight Zone' through which he was expected to divine his way to win the golden apple – if that wasn't too mixed a metaphor!

If so, all his learning, all his training, even all his considerable experience of life – and he had lived it to the full – were as naught in his efforts to touch or even glimpse the elusive Lucinda.

Even that had him as thoroughly confused as he had ever been. This new Celia, of whom he received ample opportunity to examine so short a while ago, was so completely unlike the one he thought he knew. Her allure was quite unmistakable (recalling her assisted dismount and its powerful effect on his senses); one minute she was . . . was so . . . tantalizing, and the next . . .

And with his head spinning uncontrollably, he retired immediately to his room in a state of considerable gloom.

'It is done; but was it well done for my sister, Alice?' said Celia as she wended Jasper gently down the slope toward the orchard. She feigned a headache but, in truth, it was in her heart that she felt the most pain.

'I think it was as well done as it could be, Miss. It is clear to me where Miss Lucy's heart lies, and almost as clear from which quarter a marriage proposal might originate; and ne'er the twain shall meet.'

'Again very poetically put, Alice. Is there no hope then but unhappiness for my sister?'

'Well, Miss, I do not think it is quite that bad. I haven't quite worked it out yet, but have you noticed that Miss Lucy does not seem to miss the professor when he is not there? Is it her *heart* that wants him, or . . . you know, that other thing you were so desirous of so recently? – begging your pardon, Miss.'

'That is quite all right, Alice. And now that you mention it, she does seem perfectly happy practising for the Ides Dinner Concert, day after day, doesn't she? So perhaps it is "that other thing" – as you so delicately put it.'

'Exactly, Miss. When my Richard and I were . . . well, he was just never out of my thoughts, Miss, day or night, and I moped for him dreadfully. Still do, in some ways. But Miss Lucy, why she just seems to get on with things, and it is only when she observes him that things go amiss for her because that power he exudes just sweeps her off her feet all over again.'

'Except that he did not on Boxing Day Morn, which is very interesting.'

'But there we were together, Miss. Perhaps it is only when they are alone that he uses it,' to which Celia nodded.

'So do we just have to stop her ever seeing him again, at least alone?' said Celia as she dismounted. 'That would be a pretty tall order, Alice.'

'Yes, Miss, for it means she can never be out of our sight. That is why I said that I do not have it all worked out yet, for that piece just hasn't come into my mind. Maybe it will by tonight, Miss, when you bathe. Or maybe *you* will have the answer by then.'

'All right, Alice, let's dwell on it awhile. Perhaps I *have* been worrying a little too much over the issue. Now that you have cheered me up a bit, I think I will have luncheon after all.'

'Was it a good day, Miss?' as she rinsed her mistress' hair and bound it up in a warmed towel.

'Yes, Alice, I did a number of charcoal sketches that I quite like, and I have practised a new technique for shadow, that I like well. I also think I have worked out the sketches for the Ides pictures.'

'Here is one thing, Miss, that your new-fangled radiators cannot do; dry your hair. Give me a good old-fashioned coal or wood fire for that. Now we will have to let it drape over the back of the divan for a while, while I brush it lightly. Also, which gown would you like for tonight, Miss? You have not worn the cream one with the yellow roses for quite a while.'

'I do not feel like a gown tonight, Alice,' interrupting the brushing. 'What else do I have that doesn't have me all wrapped up,' and she rose to open the cupboard doors. 'How about this one,' and she pulled a voile square.

'But that is only a scarf, Miss.'

'Exactly, Alice, and here is one in blue,' and she walked over to the mirror. 'Here, Alice, you tie this lavender one behind me,' as she shrugged the bathrobe off her shoulders in a heap on the floor.

'But you can see right through it, Miss,' gasped Alice, shaking her head, 'it shows every thing you have . . .'

'Exactly, Alice; there. Now this other one down here, and that is it,' and she twirled in front of the glass, eyes sparkling. 'Oh, it was so wonderful, Alice, riding the wind this morning, just like the professor said. I could feel the breeze on my body as if my blouse were not there at all. But this is how I'd *really* like to ride, wearing just these two scarves and my hair down my back. That *would* be exciting.'

'Yes, Miss,' said Alice, dryly, 'and if the professor had come along ten minutes earlier, *he* would have been the one to be excited at your little exhibition, with your blouse *really* being not there.'

'Your problem, Alice, is that you have no artistic soul, or you'd see the human female figure for what it is, a masterpiece of shape and form. All curves and hollows and shadows and highlights. It is no wonder that the Greeks were forever trying to sculpt its mystery and capture its excitement.'

'My Richard did not need to be Greek, Miss, to appreciate the mystery of *my* curves and hollows or to create *my* excitement, so I do not see what that has to do with it. Now will you stop prancing around in those scarves, exposing the mystery of *your* sculpting in front of that mirror and come back here so that I can get your hair dry, or we will be here all night.'

'Do I have a nice figure, Alice, one that some one would truly admire if I showed it to him as you did so openly to your Richard?' as she ran her hands lightly over nature's gifts to her self.

'You have a gorgeous figure, Miss, and one day the right man will show you just how much he admires it, and you will be greatly astonished and delighted. Now stop that and come here or I shall leave you to do your own hair.'

'Oh, all right. But do not pull too hard. So, your Richard really appreciated the secret of your curves and hollows did he, Alice? Tell me about it.'

'Yes, he did, Miss, and I have already told you about it. Now lie still.'

'I can not, Alice. Well, tell me again, for I feel all jumpy tonight,' and she sat up. 'Here, take these scarves off; I do not want any thing on my skin tonight, except perhaps a little exotic perfume,' and she giggled.

'But Miss, you can not lie around with no clothes on, you will catch your death.'

'Did you find him exciting, Alice?'

'Did I find *who* exciting? Richard, Miss?' to receive a frown and a shake of the head in response. 'Oh, you mean the professor, Miss. No I did not! But he is trying very hard, Miss, to get *you* to like him, and you are quite harsh with him in return.'

'Yes, Alice, do you think I did not notice? That is why I was so angry with him. I tried being nice, but he only wants to get around me so that he can have his way with my sister, and ruin her life. And I will not have it, do you hear?'

'Yes, Miss, but it is no good getting cross with me.'

'I am sorry, Alice, I did not mean to shout at you; it is just that he makes my blood boil! If he thinks he can worm his way into my affections he has another think coming. If that is his little game to get to Lucy, I am more than a match for his wiles. Now, where is my bathrobe, I am freezing to death here, and my night gown, one of those flannel ones for I am going blue already.'

'Here you are, Miss; but I think he likes you for your self, not just because of Miss Lucy,' added Alice softly. 'I believe he finds *you* exciting, Miss, especially in the dismount when he was holding you much longer and closer than he should. And you seemed to like it a little, too, I think,' and Celia went crimson.

'I did *not* like it, Alice, and I *do not like him*. Will you please stop *saying* that? I hate him, do you hear me? How *dare* he use me like that. He really is too insufferable for words,' and the tears started rolling down her cheeks, as she threw her self on the bed sobbing, 'I hate him, I hate him, do you hear me? I do not want to see him again. Ever. You really are so *stupid*, Alice, sometimes,' and she pounded the pillow with her fists.

'Yes, Miss, then I hate him, too, Miss. Goodnight, Miss, sleep well,' and despite the continued sobs, she left the room, smiling in the darkness.

But she was not the least surprised in the morning to find the hated nightgown thrown in a heap against the wall; her mistress cuddling the pillow to her bare bosom and smiling in her sleep.

11

Models

'Put the coffee on the table, Alice, I have some thing to discuss,' said Celia, apparently still not in the best of moods.

'That man you hate, Miss?'

'*No*, Alice, I am not going to discuss him any more. He has simply ceased to exist as far as I am concerned; and as far as you are concerned, too, if you have any sense. The way you keep talking about him anyone would think that it was *you* that he was interested in. Is Miss Lucy in her room?'

'No, Miss, she is practising in the Conservatory with the young Houghton ladies.'

'Good. The person I want to talk about is called Mildred.'

'My Mildred, Miss?'

'Do you know another Mildred, Alice?'

'No, Miss.'

'Then she must be yours, Alice. What does she busy her self with?'

'Well, she helps in the kitchen in the mornings, Miss, peeling the potatoes and such like. Then she helps the maid clean the grates; and in the afternoon she does a little in the silver pantry, or some thing like that.'

'And when does she study?'

'Study, Miss?'

'Yes, Alice, study, as in "learn to read and write".'

Alice coloured, 'She can read and write, Miss,' she responded with some heat.

'And what else, Alice? French? German? History, geography, mathematics? How is your daughter getting on in geometry?'

Alice turned a bright red, swallowed hard several times, and finally responded in a small voice.

'That was a little unfair, Miss, you know very well she doesn't know any of those subjects. Besides, she is only thirteen.'

'Thirteen going on seventeen, I have observed.'

'I try to teach her, Miss, I really do, but I do not have very much time after . . .' and she stopped, realizing she was about to criticize her mistresses and how little time they left her after she had attended to their needs.

'Exactly, Alice! And what was it your Richard said about educating your children?'

Alice went red then white, and whispered, 'That is not fair either, Miss,' but her mistress had not finished.

'And what was it you said to us in London? That you would "make it all up to her"? You are not living up to either of those, Alice, and your daughter, and Richard's, is being given a very poor start in life; much worse, if I understand it correctly, than either her mother or her father.'

Alice was now white and trembling, her eyes swimming with tears. 'But I . . . I try to do my best, Miss,' she sobbed, 'what else can I do?' and she broke down and wept openly.

'We,' said Celia, going to her and gathering her in her arms, '*We* are going to take the matter in hand, Mother Alice,' and she held her tight until the sobs eased. 'There, you will find a wash basin and towel behind the screen.'

When Alice returned, still weepy but in some sort of control of her self, Celia returned to her subject.

'Sit down, Alice, while we talk about it. From my observations and discussions, Mildred is a very bright girl, and deserves the best education you can afford.' Alice opened her mouth to respond, but her mistress raised her hand. 'If you would like me to help,' and Alice nodded, 'then here is what I propose.

'Firstly, I admit to keeping you very busy helping me, not leaving you much time for Miss Lucy, and then there are our bedtime chats . . .'

'But I love helping you, Miss,' broke in Alice, 'especially at bedtime; then you are like my . . .' and she stopped, embarrassed.

'Like your what, Alice? Please go on.'

Alice swallowed hard. 'Like my . . . my daughter, Miss, for somehow I can tell you things that I cannot explain to my real daughter, just like you and her ladyship,' her eyes appealing to her mistress not to change that special part of her life.

'Do not worry, Alice, I am not about to change that; it is special for me, too; besides I like being your daughter for you tell me the things I must know,' and she smiled, which Alice returned with relief. 'No, I am going to suggest that Mildred help Miss Lucy in the same way that you help me, to the extent that she can, of course, considering her youth. But that will only be for a part of the day. The major part will be study, which Lucy and I will help with, but we do need a tutor for some of it.'

'Oh, Miss, that would be wonderful,' beamed Alice. 'I know she doesn't much like . . .' and she paused again, reluctant to put it into words.

'Quite right, Alice, I cannot think of a greater waste of talent than to have Mildred peeling potatoes and cleaning grates. She will cease that activity, immediately.'

'Thank you, Miss,' whispered Alice, 'I do not know what to say.'

'Then say nothing. I am sorry, Alice, that I had to be so unkind to you at the beginning of our talk, but I did want you to appreciate just how seriously I regard the matter. It was not just a question of a little more reading or a few more sums; I really want you to be serious about it, too. Your daughter – and Richard's – is far too important to be given any thing but the best,' at which Alice blushed deeply in embarrassment.

'Thank you, Miss,' was all she could manage to whisper.

'I could do no less, Alice, for one as faithful and as devoted as you to both Lucy and my self, and to your daughter. Oh, and by the way, I notice that Mildred has lost most of that dreadful London speech. Is that your doing, Alice?'

'Yes, Miss; well, no, Miss, not really. I have been teaching her, of course, but I told her to observe most carefully how you and Miss Lucy speak, how you use your words, Miss, and I must say she has taken it all up very quickly. I hope you do not mind, Miss,' she added hurriedly.

'Mind? Of course not, Alice. Indeed, I am a little flattered. Though I can see that I must watch my Ps and Qs,' and she smiled at the thought – as did Alice, for she thought her mistress already to be perfection in every respect.

'But now it is my turn to be embarrassed, Alice. You can have a good laugh at my expense, if you like, for I can think of only one person suit-able as a tutor,' and here she lowered her head and looked at Alice from under her lashes.

It took Alice a moment to comprehend the look; then suddenly her eyes opened wide. 'You do not mean . . .' and her mistress nodded. 'Now *you* can laugh or scold me, Alice,' she said quietly.

'Oh no, Miss, I think it is a *wonderful* idea, I am so happy for you,' and she leaned forward impulsively and gave her mistress a hug. 'I am sorry, Miss, I should not have done that, I was a little carried away with the wonder of it.'

But Celia leaned forward in return and hugged back.

'That is all right, Mother Alice, I liked it,' and they both laughed. 'But why should you be happy for me? It is Mildred who will get the benefit of his presence; it has nothing to do with me.'

'Yes, Miss, I know,' dropping her eyes as they got a little teary again, afraid that her mistress might glimpse in them the true reason for her happiness. 'But I did not like you hating him, Miss. That is not like your loving nature at all, if I may say so.'

Alice paused to gain a little more control of her overflowing emotions before speaking again, but did not succeed very well. Then, to Celia's surprise, added, 'Oh, Miss, I am so happy for you,' and she leant to bestow on her mistress a quick kiss on the cheek. Then she jumped up.

'Now I must go and tell Mildred, Miss, she will be so pleased,' and rushed out with tears in her eyes, but spun around at the door at the last moment and presented Celia a full formal curtsey, head bowed, which she held for fully five ticks of the long-case clock in the hall.

Then she was gone, leaving her mistress with tears in her eyes, tears of happiness, too – though for the life of her she could not think why she suddenly felt in such high spirits.

'Good morning, Miss Celia. I talked Cook into making your favourite scones for your morning tea. She grumbled a bit, but I would not let her say "no".'

'Thank you, Alice, But I am not sure what I have done to deserve such special treatment.'

'Oh, Miss,' responded Alice, eyes shining, 'You do not know even half of what you have done for me, and I shall never let you forget it.'

'Dear me,' said Celia, 'I am not sure I like the sound of that,' but she was smiling. 'How is our Mildred this morning?'

'Wonderful, Miss, thanks to you. I told her she must come to say "Thank you", but you know how young ones are, Miss. Well, perhaps you do not, but she really is very grateful.'

'That is settled then. I have spoken to Miss Lucy, and she was delighted, too, for she has been feeling a little neglected – all my fault,' she hastened to add. 'Anyway, she would like Mildred to start helping as soon as she is free. Can she sew?'

'Yes, Miss, she is now making her own dresses, and she sews them beautifully,' gushed Alice, then blushed at the lack of modesty concerning her daughter's accomplishments.

'That is all right, Alice, you *should* be proud of her. I would be. As for the tutoring, I have yet to arrange any thing,' and here it was Celia's turn to colour slightly. 'Perhaps you can arrange for them to meet some where casually, for I cannot do any thing formally until after the Dinner, you understand?'

'Perfectly, Miss, I would not want it any other way.'

'Good. But I do have another task for Mildred, although I hope it is a pleasurable one. Immediately after breakfast, I would like to do her portrait for the Dinner.'

'Paint Mildred, Miss?' squealed Alice, unable to contain her delight.

'Well, it will be in pastels probably, Alice, not oils.'

'That is wonderful, Miss. Fancy my Mildred having her picture painted; I *never* thought she would be famous like that.'

'Well, Alice, I am not Sir Joshua or Sir Thomas you know, so do not hold out too much hope for Mildred's immortality,' and they laughed together. 'That is Reynolds and Gainsborough, of course.'

'Yes, Miss, I know.'

'You do? Well, good for you, Alice. Now I see where Mildred gets it all.' And they laughed together again.

'Think of your self as a sprite, Mildred, can you do that?'

'I dunno, Miss; what's a "sprite"?'

'Some thing like a fairy, Mildred, but in the fields and woods. You represent "Spring", so you have to be light on your feet and feel as if you are floating, all right?'

'I will try, Miss, but I am not very good at floating, except in my dreams, of course. Then I can do it for miles and miles.'

'Just imagine that you are dreaming, then. Now, you are running through a field of Michaelmas daisies, and you have just picked one. Here, this artists' brush is a daisy. Got that?'

'Yes, Miss. Is a Mikle-what daisy like a regular one?'

'Yes, Mildred, only a lot bigger. Now,' looking thoughtfully at Mildred, 'Your feet should be bare, so shoes and stockings off; and you would be wearing a short dress rather like your petticoat, I expect. Would you mind showing me your petticoat?'

'No, Miss. I cut and sewed it my self; it is a lot like yours.' And indeed it was; a simple white under-dress, with narrow shoulder straps.

'So it is, Mildred, and how clever of you to notice,' for when she was in her studio working, Celia usually wore a simple three-quarter length ballerina's dress and shoes, with the minimum of under-things. 'If I am going to paint with a light touch', she was fond of saying, 'how could I wear ankle length dresses with three petticoats, lace-up boots, and six-button cuffs? Impossible!'

'Please slip off the shoulder straps and tuck them in so that they do not show. Good; you have lovely shoulders, Mildred. Not every one can say that. Also, it would be above the knee; yes, that is it. And hair, piled up on top of your head. Beautiful!' And to her self she was saying 'this child is a natural model, she makes it perfect the very first time she tries'.

'One last thing, Mildred; try to keep your chest in. Sprites did not have bosoms, because they never grew up, you see, so I am afraid I am going to have to paint you without one, is that all right?'

Mildred screwed up her face.

'All right, Miss, but I am glad I am not a sprite, for I want a beautiful body when I grow up,' unconsciously pushing forward her chest despite the request, 'just like yours, Miss. Mother says you have the most beautiful curves and hollows, and you are simply gorgeous when you are not wearing any thing at all,' she gurgled happily.

'Does she, indeed!' exclaimed Celia, self-consciously, although not displeased by this frank discussion of her natural charms. 'We must talk to your mother about that!'

'Oh! Please do not say any thing to her, Miss, for she will be very cross with me if you do. She says that I must guard my tongue carefully when it comes to the young ladies, especially now that I am going to be helping Miss Lucy.'

'Very well, Mildred; but that is very good advice, and you would do well to remember it.'

'I will, Miss. It is really that mother is so proud of you both, but especially you, Miss Celia, that she wants me to grow up beautiful and talented, just like you, and that I must never stop learning from you. How to walk, how to talk – she has a lot to say about that, Miss, but I am trying hard to . . .'

'Mildred!' broke in Celia, 'I do not mind you talking while I sketch, but you must keep still, while at the same time loose. That is better.'

'She also says, Miss,' she went on, scarcely pausing for a breath (although now in a relaxed but unmoving manner that quite amazed the artiste), 'that I must watch how you sit on a chair, how beautifully you get down and up again, that is. I am happy to learn any thing you want to teach me, Miss,' and her face positively glowed with contentment and an inner incandescence, which Celia proceeded to capture as well as she was able on her expensive, hand-woven paper.

'Nearly done, Mildred. I will put in the fields of daisies later, and a garland in your hair. But first,' and she crossed over to Mildred with her crayons. 'First, those eyes; they are an incredible green; nobody will believe me if I make them that colour. And those gorgeous dark lashes. How long have they been like that, Mildred?'

'As long as I have had them, Miss,' she replied with an impish grin. 'Mother says that Richard, my father, had eyes this colour, except mine are a deeper green and my lashes are longer.'

'Well, I have to colour as I see,' retuning to her easel, 'but nobody who doesn't know you, Mildred, will believe it. There, all done.'

'May I see my self, Miss?'

'No, Mildred, you may not look.' Then seeing her downcast face, 'It is nothing against you, Mildred. Artists *never* show their work until it is quite finished, and the model – that is you – is usually the very last. It is sort of – unlucky. But you can walk up and down for me. That is right. Now pose, arms up, down, twirl 'round, good. Now point, curtsey, on one knee, arms folded, head back. Wonderful; that is very good.

'Thank you, Mildred, we are finished for now. Please ask your mother to come and see me, when she has a moment.'

'Yes, Miss Celia,' and she presented a most graceful full curtsey, which she maintained with bowed head, then raised it to say earnestly, 'Thank you, Miss, I am deeply and eternally grateful for all you are doing for me.' Then, to Celia's astonishment, she ran forward lightly to kiss Celia's hand gently, retrieved her clothes, and ran on tiptoe upstairs to her room to dress.

When Alice entered the studio, she found her mistress slumped in a chair in the corner, looking at the wall behind the open door. 'Is any thing wrong, Miss, has Mildred done some thing?' her voice sharpening.

'No, Alice,' replied Celia, wearily, 'I am just feeling old, that is all.'

'But you are only twenty-one, Miss,' gasped Alice. 'What has happened?'

'Happened?' echoed her mistress, 'Mildred has happened, Alice. Come here; now turn around.'

Alice did as she was bid, and gasped, seeing the latest portrait by her beloved mistress.

'Oh, Miss, that is *beautiful*,' she whispered, in awe. 'I have never seen you do any thing so lovely.'

'It wasn't me, Alice, it was Mildred. I will explain later. Right now, bring me some tea in my room, please.'

Alice found her mistress stretched on her bed, a pillow over her face. 'Is any thing wrong, Miss? Please tell me what Mildred has done.'

'Mildred has done nothing, Alice,' removing the pillow, 'except be her self. I do not know how to explain it better than that,' and she sat up. 'Where is that tea – *two* hot buttered crumpets? Are you trying to turn all my hollows to curves, Alice?'

'Oh, no, Miss, I think you are just lovely as you are.'

'So Mildred tells me!' and Alice blushed deeply. 'But do not say any thing to her, Alice; I am not in the slightest upset. The question is, "what are we going to do about your daughter"?'

'*Should* we do some thing, Miss?'

'I am afraid we must, Alice, or we will both be failing her.'

'Has she been bad in some way, Miss? If she has, I want to know about it right away, and she shall be punished. She is a bit too forward, that one,' she finished, determinedly.

'On the contrary, Alice, she is too good, and for the life of me, I do not know what to do about it.'

Alice shook her head in bewilderment.

'I *still* do not understand, Miss; you are just going to have to say it to me in simple words.'

'In simple words, Alice, your daughter, Richard's daughter, is very, very talented. She has an incredible natural beauty of mind and spirit, although as she develops most men will see only the body, more's the pity. She has a natural talent and grace as a model, which could express it self as an outstanding actress or dancer. She is remarkably self-possessed and unself-conscious; and learns incredibly quickly, so she will probably turn out to be very intellectual. I promised to help you and I think I am out of *my* depth, Alice. Is that simple enough for you?'

Alice was silent in the face of the torrent of words that she understood individually but could not grasp collectively.

'How can that be, Miss?'

'I do not know, Alice. Perhaps it was the passion that you generated in Richard that night. I do know that I am right. I am a good artiste, Alice, but you saw that picture; I am not naturally *that* good. It was Mildred that somehow came through on the paper; the crayons seemed to come alive in my hand. And those eyes, Alice, I have never seen a green that brilliant; it was all I could do to reproduce them, even with every colour that is made in my box! Perhaps I will do her again, but this time in oils, perhaps as a bridesmaid, and we will see if I get the same result,' at which the startled Alice whispered 'my Mildred a bridesmaid?'

'Yes, Alice, and she will be beautiful. But perhaps there is one other thing I might do, and that is talk to the professor. I have a feeling he may be able to offer some help in deciding a course. Now I think I will sleep for a little while. Please say that I will not be down to luncheon and that I am resting in preparation for this afternoon's session with Miss Lucy.'

'Maybe we should try again tomorrow, Luce; I do not seem to have any feelings or spirit left after this morning's exercise with Mildred, and I do not want your picture to be less than hers.'

'Well, if you really think so, Sister, but there is only one week left, and still so much to do.'

'True,' replied Celia, 'but I have no inspiration. All I can see in my head right now is Mildred as a dancer or a bride – she will make a gorgeous bride, and I will want to design her wedding gown. Yet I am supposed to be painting my favourite sister, but suddenly I feel so clumsy and awkward. What am I going to do Luce?' and she walked over to Lucy and put her arms around her and dropped her head on her shoulder and shed a few hot tears while her sister comforted her, though from what ailment of spirit she knew not.

A pot of tea, produced by Alice at Lucy's request, and a little light sisterly chatter, restored Celia's spirits sufficiently to make a fresh start.

Seated again at the easel, she addressed her sister.

'Perhaps we should try a different approach. How do you see your self, Lucy? What picture comes to mind in your inner eye?'

'I do not know that I *have* an "inner eye", much less know how to use it,' protested Lucy.

'Yes, you do; every one has. Think about a piano sonata, or an operatic solo, and tell me which one you are.' But Lucy just shook her head in a puzzled fashion, as if to say, '*me, a piano sonata?*'

'All right,' continued Celia, but warming now to her own thought. 'Let's get to the roots here. Deep inside, are you Beethoven or Mozart – or perhaps Schubert?'

'Mozart, I think – if I have to be a man.'

'Never mind about that. Now a Mozart sonata or one of his operas?' but again Lucy shook her head.

Celia gave a little sigh of exasperation.

'You are not in the spirit of this at all, Luce. But that is all right; I am beginning to feel some thing. Let us say "opera" to see where that takes us.'

She was speaking mostly to her self now; looking at Lucy but 'seeing' her, in imagination rather than reality.

'Die Fledermaus? Noooo, bats are too black. Figaro? No; nor can I see you as a Barber. But you play the flute, so it could be "Die Zauberflöte". The Magic Flute. *The Magic Flute!* That is it! Hurrah, hurrah, hurrah! Of course. "The Flute Player". How clever of you to think of it.'

'But I did not, you did,' replied Lucy, in great surprise, for she had felt quite unable to contribute to this strange idea of being a Mozart opera!

'No, no, you did; I was simply thinking *inside* you, that is all. But never mind; the flute, quick! Get your flute before the inspiration fades! Oh, I have it, I have it, I have it,' and Lucy rushed out before some thing terrible happened to her sister's vision, for she never even vaguely understood the passion that Celia was able to bring forth in the visual side of art.

When she returned only moments later, Celia was muttering to her self.

'A pair! How *stupid* I am. Why was I born without a brain? The pictures are *complementary*. Dress; that is going to be the *most* important element. Dress; clothes; costume.'

Then she stopped, and looked down at her own simple outfit.

'Of course, the *very* thing!' And to Lucy, 'Quick, your Chinese gown, for you shall be me and I shall be you!' and Lucy fled to her room again in utter bewilderment.

Although gone no more than a few seconds, when she returned with the turquoise-and-gold gown, Celia's tunic-like dress was already stripped off and hanging over a chair back, and she was in the final act of removing her undergarments. When she stood in her bare skin she said,

'Good, now I shall wear your gown,' as she slipped it on and tied it loosely around her, 'and you shall wear my dress. It suits you perfectly,' holding it against her, 'although I may have to add a pin or two to get the right effect. But, first, off with those clothes.'

'You want me to undress? Here?' replied her sister, aghast at the thought of appearing, if only for the briefest of moments, almost as unadorned as she had just seen her sister, for she certainly had no intention of revealing her self so thoroughly or wearing nothing at all under a dress; that was simply too disgraceful to give it a second thought.

Yes, she had done just so at the inn; but in a moment of the passion generated by Alice's tale. Besides, it was in the semi darkness of a single candle, not in the full light of day!

'Very well,' snapped Celia, walking to the door and locking it, 'leave some thing on if you must, but if I can see it, or even *feel* it underneath, off it must come. When it is finished I want it to show *you* under that fairy dress, not a wardrobe of clothes! And I will turn my back if it makes you feel any better; but be quick about it.'

Lucy trembled at the intensity of the command and, swallowing her distaste, finished up nearly as bare as her sister had been before she put on the dress, although she did have to turn and face away to bring her self to do it.

'All right, you may turn now,' she said, finally, breathless from the rush to cover her self again, afraid that her sister would not play the game and look before she was ready.

'Beautiful,' said Celia, turning, and rushed forward to kiss her sister's cheek. 'I *knew* you could do it. Hair down, that is it, and on your shoulder, tumbling, like that. We must first bare that shoulder, though,' as she slipped one strap off, surprising Lucy with the warmth and pressure of her fingers on her upper body as she tucked it in and smoothed the delicate fabric across her bosom. 'And the other one, falling a little. There. But it is acceptable for *you* to have one, though,' smiling to her self at the thought of Lucy trying to draw in her shapely bosom. 'And we have need to pin it a little at the back and waist, as I thought,' reaching for her sewing lady. 'Now the flute, that is it. Splendid,' as she ran back to her easel to seize the crayons. 'Perfectly *angelic*.'

Lucy, glancing in the mirror to confirm her own severe misgivings, would have protested her sister's definition. *She* thought that the bodice was tight to the point of indecency for humans, let alone angels, regretting that she had acceded to her sister's wishes on the removal of critical underclothing; and would have loosed it considerably if she could have reached to do so – and if she had not feared Celia's wrath at disturbing her 'vision' before she had even started!

Celia simply smiled at her enigmatically, amused at the contrast in the unconscious reactions of her two models: Mildred striving to augment her slight upper body, Lucy trying to retract it altogether, and neither possessing that capability!

'Just relax, and I will set the scene for you. Now, you are doing something that you love to do; you are playing the flute. That is it, but raise it just a little higher. On your toes, and remember, this is a magic flute,' she began, sketching rapidly now. 'One of your sprites – that is Mildred – is dancing for sheer joy at its music, the beautiful music you are making. But you are not even aware of her any longer, for your thoughts are not here, they are far away, with your Prince, who is at this very moment riding to meet you on a magnificent white stallion, in this secret clearing in this very forest and, who knows, perhaps to make passionate love to you, for the very first time, as Richard did with Alice.'

Lucy's face coloured, though she said nothing. But as the tale unfolded, she slowly came alive under the garment, her eyes sparkling with an inner joy, lighting up her entire face. And the crayon in Celia's hand came alive in the same manner, as if possessed by its own free spirit, yearning to fully conquer the white surface.

'And now as your yearning for him grows ever stronger, your ear catches a sound, the sound of his horse swishing, swishing, through the forest leaves. You believe you catch a glimpse of him through the trees; you rise on your toes even higher, the better to behold him, while your flute plays its most beautiful love song to greet him and so that his heart is abundant with love for you. But you cannot cease playing, for that is forbidden; you must play on, even as he dismounts and approaches you, touches your arm gently, strokes your soft shoulder, his hands caressing you now more urgently in their quest of your hidden charms, exciting you, and still you cannot respond, although you crave him desperately, passionately. Your eyes alone express how much you cherish him and how much you hunger for him, even as he makes tender love to you, and your heart overflows with the joy of giving.'

And Celia's face shone as earnestly as her sister's at the joy of capturing the overflowing of emotion on her parchment, while her tears flowed even more copiously.

'Was I all right?' said Lucy shyly, lying completely submerged in the water. She had not intended her sister to join her in the bathroom, she never had before; but then they never locked the door between the rooms, so there was little she could do or say, except in rudeness. She wondered if Celia would remain while she bathed and if so, what to do when she wished to exit. Could she *really* tell her sister that she preferred to bathe in private; that she could not possibly get out until she was alone? It seemed too ridiculous a request between sisters.

'You were magnificent,' responded Celia quietly, sitting on the edge of the bath. 'I just hope I did you justice; but I think I did. I believe I achieved the same quality for both paintings.'

She rose and paced the room several times before facing Lucy again.

'Certainly the pair of them are the finest works I have yet done – and both on the same day.' she added with a smile of inner satisfaction. 'I admit to being rather pleased with my self, rather pleased.' Then slipping off her robe to disclose that natural self ready for her own bathing, she placed one foot in the tub. 'So slide up a bit, Luce, for I am jumping in there, too.'

Lucy opened her mouth to say that she would rather . . . but by then Celia was standing in the tub, and she had no option but to comply, embarrassed that her bosom was now almost fully exposed above the water even though she tried to protect it with the sponge – which was anyway much too small – until the presence of her sister sitting down uplifted it again to shield her modesty.

Celia gave a sigh of contentment as she splashed the hot water over her body.

'This is a wonderful way to end a beautiful day, Luce, one of the best days of my life, and much of it is thanks to you.'

'I am glad it worked so well for you,' responded her sister when her voice returned from the shock of having another person in the tub with her. The last time she could remember sharing was with her cousin at her Aunt's house as a child, many years ago. Now she was hoping that her sister would bathe first and withdraw first. She was due to be disappointed on both counts.

After closing her eyes and relaxing for several minutes, Celia said,

'That was good. Now,' and she reached for the sponge and soaped it. 'You can do my back for me. Good, but a little harder; that is it,' and turning and kneeling, added, 'and now my front. Do not be shy,' as Lucy was embarrassed at touching her sister's bosom – even with a soapy sponge.

'I am quite solid, you know, so you can give them a good rub, too,' taking Lucy's hand to do just that. Then raising her self, 'and the lower part, too,' but Lucy demurred there, with the whispered comment, 'I can not quite reach properly, so perhaps you had better do that your self,' and handed the sponge to her sister, and closed her eyes.

'Oh well, as to that I can do it easily enough. Always have. There, done,' reclining again to rinse her self.

'Now to share my happiness for your efforts, I am going to finish it by bathing you, Sister dear, so sit up,' and over Lucy's protests that she was quite capable of bathing her self, reached for the soap and sponge once more and applied it – though quite tenderly this time – to Lucy's upper body and arms. 'Now stand up so that I can wash the rest of you.'

Lucy initially thought she had no option but to comply, or look impossibly prudish, although she found the idea of exposing her self so utterly to her sister quite shameful, when the solution suddenly presented it self to her.

'I have already washed there,' she replied, closing her eyes to hide and remaining submerged as she was.

Celia regarded her with a distinct suspicion, before adding, 'Oh, very well, then you had better get out so that I can turn around and relax in comfort. These bath taps are digging into my back. Besides, I need some more hot water.'

And now Lucy's inspiration deserted her, so she rose and quickly reached for the towel to cover her self before stepping out, while Celia turned to the other end, adding more hot water 'til it covered her once more, the while studying her sister with a thoughtful air.

'Do you know, Sis, that you have very beautiful legs? I wish mine were like that,' and Lucy blushed, for the whole business embarrassed her dreadfully, even though she had turned her back.

Celia lay in the tub a while longer, studying Lucy as she discreetly dried her self and donned her robe while still quite damp in her haste to be securely covered.

'Lucy,' she said as her sister was about to enter her own room, 'I need to paint you once more, but this time it will be in oils – if you do not mind. All right?' and Lucy nodded. 'Good. Then first thing after breakfast, tomorrow, I'd like you to wear your Chinese gown when you come to the studio, but with nothing under it for I shall supply that.' Lucy's eyes widened and her mouth opened as if to say some thing, but the words she might have uttered stuck in her throat, and the moment to demur was past.

Celia gave her sister a kiss on the cheek as she stepped out, and said, 'Good night, dear Sister, It has been a good day, a most wonderful day, every bit of it,' and entered her own room, her wet body still dripping water, where Alice was waiting with a selection of three night-gowns.

'Which one would you like, Miss?' as she took the silently proffered towel and patted her mistress dry, to which Celia replied by crossing to the dressing table, returning and handing to her a puff and a box of jasmine-scented powder.

'Just that one, Alice, all over,' and she stood before the mirror with her hands clasped and raised over her head, on her toes, while it was gently applied, as requested.

'Now the bed,' and stood while the sheets were pulled back, and she slid her self in, Alice tucking them in after her. 'Good night, Alice, thank you for a wonderful day,' and she closed her eyes, sighed contentedly, and settled into preparation for a blissful sleep.

Alice brushed her hair gently onto the pillow for a few moments, pondering this strange new mood. She always bathed her mistress; yet this evening she had been invited to wait in the bedroom. And she had never known the two young ladies to bathe together, or even be in the room while the other bathed. This was indeed some thing new between them, as she extinguished the candles and wonderingly closed the door behind her.

Slowly mounting the staircase to her room she pondered the matter. Yes, some thing was in the air, most definitely. It was if a new era had begun, nothing ever to be the same again, one in which the professor had no part or opportunity to use that awsome power, and she slipped into her own bed almost hesitantly, as if even that had changed.

But, unlike her mistress, sleep was long time coming.

As Lucy entered the studio, robe tied tightly around her small waist, she was clearly nervous, for she had not seen her sister at breakfast. Celia was already at work behind the easel, preparing her canvas, when her head popped up above it and said, cheerily, 'Good morning, Sister; how is it to be?' to which Lucy made no audible reply.

'I think some thing classical,' continued Celia unabashed, as she crossed behind Lucy to lock the door. 'Greek, perhaps, unless you have some thing else in mind?'

On the chair beside her was a length of fine, soft white cloth, which she picked up and draped over her sister's shoulder and down across to her hip, where she pinned it, and then let it drape to the floor.

'That could do it, I think.'

There was an apple on the chair also, which she put into Lucy's hand, raising it over her head.

'There,' she said, and returned to her easel to study the effect. 'Do you want me to tell the story of what I have in mind, Luce?'

'Yes, I think so,' replied Lucy, and hesitated before adding, 'Can I leave my gown on?'

'Well, if you are uncomfortable without it. I will paint as if you weren't wearing it, of course, so I will have to imagine how you look underneath the robe.'

'Can you do that?' responded Lucy, hopefully.

'Yes, but it will be difficult.' Then she hesitated, biting the end of a brush. 'No, I have to be honest with you, Luce, it cannot be done. Well, it could, but the result would be so awful that I would just destroy it, and we would both have wasted our morning.'

'Then you would really rather I did . . . I did without it?' said Lucy, uncomfortably.

'No,' said her sister, suddenly. 'I am wrong, I should never have suggested it in the first place,' and she arose to remove the draped fabric and take her sister's hand.

'You see, Luce,' she said in a soft voice, 'I have been studying for some months now, especially when we were in Town. While you were practising your music, I was practising the art of drawing and painting the female form, and the best way to do that is naturally, without any obstruction, especially clothing or any thing that gets in the way, except for adornments, of course. I have a number of books with famous paintings by the masters,' and here she unlocked a cupboard, drew out a large folio, and showed a number of its plates to Lucy, who gazed at them wide-eyed.

'And you want to paint me,' she whispered, 'looking like that, *showing every thing*, that I . . .' pointing to Cranach's 'Nymph', as she plumped dispiritedly down on the chair.

'To tell the truth, no, for my style has more realism than Cranach portrayed there – although it is beautiful executed – but then that was three centuries ago.' Then she sighed, and paced back to lean on her easel. 'Unfortunately, my sweet Sister, the only way to succeed is to practise – just like your piano playing – and the female form is no different. I can no more prepare to paint you by drawing horses, than you can practise piano by playing violin.

'That is why the great artists had favourite models to pose for them. Some were painted many times by a number of the great painters, and became famous in their own right. That is because they were considered to have the most beautiful bodies. I do not have that luxury, and the only person I could ask is you, you see.

'But it was wrong of me to have put you in that position simply to satisfy my craving for an exemplary model. I can continue copying the best plates from the books. The trouble is, you can never know how good you are until you try a real, breathing original of your own; then you either capture her essence, or you do not, but you keep trying until you do – or conclude that you are a failure and take up knitting, or basketweaving, or some thing equally spiritless.

'I even tried a self-portrait in that mirror, but it was so dreadful that . . .' Then she smiled at her sister. 'I understand, Luce, believe me I do. Let's say no more about it and go and spend a fine, warm spring day on the lake. Anyway, it is too late to do an oil painting now,' and she removed the prepared canvas and set it against the wall.

'Oh, dear,' said Lucy, despondently, 'I did not mean to spoil your inspiration; perhaps you could manage some thing simpler in charcoal? It is just that I think I will make a terrible model, Celia. I really do. My simple body,' she continued in a whisper, 'could not begin to compete with those paintings.'

'Luce,' said Celia, kneeling now in front of her sister and taking both her hands into her own. 'I want to tell you some thing, and you will see in my eyes that I am telling the truth. God endowed you more bountifully than any painted in those books. Your natural charms, I am quite convinced, would have had the Masters lining up to paint you, any way they could, clothed or not, and that is a fact. But let us go,' as she rose to her feet, 'and enjoy the day.'

'But I ought to help you, Sister, if I can. Do you really want to paint me', her voice again dropping to a whisper, '*with nothing on, at all?*'

Celia laughed.

'No, as a matter of fact, I prefer you to be wearing some thing, that is why I found this cloth, which would represent a Greek gown, draped loosely over the shoulder and down across your body, the way they were so often depicted.'

'Well, perhaps we might try a little of it,' responded Lucy, rising and loosening the tight bow somewhat. She draped the cloth tentatively over her robe and studied her self in the mirror for a moment. 'Perhaps I could get used to wearing this, it has a very nice feel,' and Celia attended her, placing and loosely pinning it on it self.

As she resumed her pose, Lucy adjusted the tie still further and raised her arm, whereupon it parted slightly to reveal a thin sliver of her essential being from gorge to toes. But if she felt its exposure, she neither commented on it nor restrained it.

'That is lovely, Sis,' confirming Lucy's position and returning to the easel. 'Now I will set the scene for you, and leave the rest to you. But if you do not want to, that will be the end of it, all right?' and Lucy nodded.

'You are in your magic orchard, where no-one is permitted to come but yourself, because they know not the spell to unlock the iron gates set in the high garden walls. But you wish that the prince could learn the secret, for you are remembering yesterday in the forest, when you were playing your magic flute, and he was coming to see you. You are remembering and dreaming how you felt when you knew that he was going to make love to you, but you could not stop playing so that he could, because your gown was always between you, but you were made to play and could only express your love for him with your eyes and your music.'

As the spell was woven, Lucy's body began to respond to the message and her hands almost unconsciously went down to the bow to loosen it so that her robe fell open, while Celia's brush moved swiftly to capture the line of the figure before her.

'You are remembering him and yesterday with longing,' she went on, 'because he is intent on seeing you again today, and you are waiting for him in the apple orchard, dreaming of how wonderful it was when he touched you under the gown. But today you are free, unconstrained by the flute, free to embrace him, and you long to feel the warmth of his hands on your self, but the robe is a hindrance, and you let it slip from your shoulders to leave only the drape of the soft cloth so that it cloaks your modesty sufficiently that he still must seek, but does not remove the promise of your charms completely from his searching gaze.'

Lucy was woven into the spell so skilfully that she pushed the opened robe from her shoulders, briefly exposing her self while she adjusted the cloth in its folds. When she raised her arm again, the drape released her bosom partially so that one side of her body was exposed from shoulder to ankle, and Celia restrained her breath to a quiet intake at the exquisite beauty of the semi-covered form, before resuming her tale in the knowledge that she could not have draped the fabric as beautifully with her own hands, as they would have trembled too much at the first touch.

'The little white dove that has been watching from the high wall now flies down and settles on your shoulder, and you whisper the secret to open the iron gates before it flies away over the wall, and your heart goes with it to guide it to the prince and whisper the mystery in his ear.

'You know that your prince has heard your heart speaking to him, because the gate slowly opens and he enters and walks among the apple trees seeking you, for at first he does not see your inert form. Your heart beats faster and your bosom swells with excitement as he searches, and the waiting for him to discover you thrills your body 'til you can bear the torment no longer, and you pluck an apple from above your head and hold it out to him as at last he beholds and slowly approaches, entranced by the beauty of your exquisitely draped softness, waiting eagerly for his love, until at last you feel his touch, his questing spirit, his ardour against your abandon, until you wish that nothing shall come between you, as you slip the cloth from your shoulders, so that you may know the true wonder of his love.'

In the verbal silence that followed the conclusion of the tale, the only sound was that of the palette being set down, and that of breathing, broken by Celia's hoarse whisper.

'Done. I will fill in the background and details later.'

Lucy did not move from her position as the apple was carefully removed from her hand to be dropped onto her discarded robe and drape. When that was followed in turn by her sister's soft hands on her shoulders and an even softer kiss on her cheek, she was restored to some sort of normality, realizing only then as she embraced her sister, as her arms wrapped them selves around her waist and onto a very bare bottom, that at some point in the weaving of the tale Celia had dispensed with her gown, also.

The greater surprise, however, was in feeling, for the second time in her life, an unclothed body in intimate contact with her own. But this time it was borne of love, and it was from cheek to hip to ankle, and it was twofold. First, she became instantly aware that she her self was completely unadorned and, second, that she liked it. Indeed, it sent such an exquisite thrill through her that all else was swept away – and she was back in her dream world of love once more.

The wonderful feeling spread from her throat, down through her now hard, throbbing bosom in such intimate contact with her sister's that she could feel its hardness thrusting and probing into hers, coursed across and into her belly and beyond, down and down, even into her toes. All the while Celia tenderly stroked her quivering, embraced body ever so gently, though now with an increasing urgency of discernment and expectation.

As she dropped her head on Celia's shoulder, she felt her sister's hot tears on her own, and joined in the silent tears of a common joy as Celia's hands were now as hot and urgent as the prince's had promised to be, and as her own were on her sister in a searching response, following each thrilling moment of her sister's touch, joined together in a shared pleasure of joy, beyond joy.

'Celia? I have some questions that I would like to put to you, but you must tell me if you are uncomfortable answering them,' receiving an answering nod. 'I shall understand if they are difficult for you,' and again a nod, accompanied this time by a quizzical look. 'But first tell me how you thought it went this morning.'

They were on their private island after luncheon, lying in their hammocks which Celia had lashed together to form a single more comfortable unit, which also permitted a more personal togetherness. They had prepared themselves in the now usual manner for their afternoon slumber, with Alice being given strict instructions that they were not to be disturbed until teatime at four o'clock.

At her question, Lucy was quite astonished to see her sister's eyes fill with tears until they overflowed and coursed down her cheeks to disappear into her long hair.

'Whatever have I done,' cried Lucy, 'I had no idea you felt so badly about it. Are you *so* sad?'

Celia shook her head.

'No,' she replied, 'I am just too happy to contain it all. I thought Mildred's picture went beautifully and I was very happy with that. Then yours was equally as satisfying. But the two of them together were as naught compared to this morning. You were . . .' and she paused for words, 'there are no words to express it. I just hope I was able to capture even one quarter of what you were giving to the world at that moment.'

'To the world?' echoed Lucy, softly, 'Is the *world* going to see this one?' her eyes round as saucers.

'I was only speaking figuratively,' hastened her sister. 'This one will only be seen by me and your self, and perhaps only one other person in the world,' at which Lucy blushed prettily. 'You were magnificent. At the end it seemed as if you were actually *glowing*, from the inside. But what did you think of the "sitting", although "standing" is more like it?'

'I really do not know, Sis. You put me in such a trance that I did not notice any thing. I do not remember taking off my gown, at all, but I must have,' and Celia nodded. 'For quite a while,' went on Lucy, 'I must have been wearing only that drape, and then nothing at all, so that now I wonder why I made such a fuss about it, for it all seemed so natural when you told that magic tale, just like Scheherazade.

'But afterwards . . .' her voice dropping to a whisper while her cheeks coloured perceptibly. 'After you finished painting, that is what I want to ask you about – but you do not have to say any thing if you feel awkward about it.'

'Afterwards, what?' responded Celia, also in a whisper.

'Well,' whispered Lucy, 'afterwards . . . you know. I do not know when you removed your gown because of the spell you put on me, so I got quite a surprise when I felt . . . when I felt, you know,' she finished, lamely. But Celia simply looked at her, and said nothing. 'Well, you know, when you put your arms around me, and I felt your . . . your body, so smooth and soft, so hot against my own. Why did you do that?'

'Did you not like it?' responded her sister, with a private smile.

'You know I did,' replied Lucy, so softly that her words were almost inaudible, although her shining eyes divulged all the story that needed to be told.

'And so did I, dearest Sister,' came the reply in an equally soft voice, reaching to hold her hand.

'As to why, by the time I had finished sketching, your body was telling me as plainly as it knew how that it urgently needed release, as did mine. Do you think that you are the only one who gets all disturbed inside at a story like that? Do you imagine that I was not excited by my own tale, that I did not also long for my prince to come and take my body into his as your prince was intent on doing?

'So in order to assuage your passion, I took it upon my self to be your prince, trusting that you would be mine in the same measure. Do not forget,' she continued, 'I had not only to look at your beautiful body as you disrobed and adjusted the drape – 'specially as it was only half dressed at that – but I had also to capture it all in oils, every curve, every hollow, every excited bit of you and, believe me,' said Celia, impishly, 'you *were* excited.'

'I was? I mean, yes, I suppose I was. I could almost feel his . . .' and she stopped, embarrassed by the thought and the picture that accompanied it, but then she went on. 'Did you really paint all that?' with a barely suppressed squeal of excitement when her sister nodded. 'Can I see it when we get back to the house? I want to know how I looked just then, when the prince was supposed to . . . to be there, you know,' and she dropped her gaze briefly to cover her all too obvious exhilaration.

'Are you sure you want to?' inquired Celia, 'It is rather, well, *revealing*.' Lucy nodded, eyes shining in anticipation at the viewing.

'All right,' said Celia, 'When we get back, you shall be the first, after the artiste, that is,' and they both laughed.

'But you still haven't answered me,' went on Lucy, again in a whisper. 'Is it all right for the two of us to . . . to, you know.' Again Celia said nothing but raised her eyebrows in a query. 'You know,' said Lucy, a little crossly, but her sister shook her head. 'Yes, you do,' complained Lucy, 'to . . . to touch me, to *play with my body*,' and she blushed again as she finally got it out in a whisper. 'And for me to play with yours in return, although now I do not quite know what I did or why I did it?'

'But you liked having your body stroked and caressed,' whispered her sister in reply, noting Lucy's blush of response, 'that is why I did it; to give you the pleasure you wanted to be given. I was certainly very excited by what you did for me; even if *you* do not remember it, *I* certainly shall. Always. Here, let me show you what I mean.'

And removing her hand to rest it lightly on Lucy's hair-draped form, she parted the hair with delicate fingers to expose her excited bosom to the dappled sunlight.

'If *I* do not release these feelings that are now clearly showing them selves,' circling the hard mounds, each in turn, sending a readily discernible tremor through Lucy's entire body, 'who is going to do it for you? Who is going to let you express your self as openly as you are doing right here, without any embarrassment or distress?' Lucy remained silent, eyes closed, lips half-parted in a soft smile of self-indulgence. 'So, who better than your own sister? You *know* what happens when you permit some one else that intimacy, and the extreme danger it poses – just ask

Alice! And you do not even have to ask me for you already know how close it was.

'Does that answer your question, dear Sister? It is simply that we two can be together as we are now, safe in our private hideaway and giving each other love when we need to be loved, and without any hurt or failure to our virtue or our reputation. We can protect each other, by helping each other; it is as simple as that.

'Besides,' giving her sister a soft look from under long lashes, 'it is only fair to add that – despite the haranguing I gave you – I now desperately need you to protect me, and this seems to be the only way we can ensure that.

'Whether it is "right", as you inquire, I cannot say. I only know that any other course has proved disastrous to each of us, and it is either this approach or we lock our selves away and shun men entirely. We are, however, very fortunate in that we can find the pleasure we seek at the very same moment, each from the other, as we have just seen in my studio. Then, when the right man, *and only the right man* comes along, it will be his pleasure to surprise and release us, and that will be the very best love of all, as Alice has told us.'

At the mention of Alice, Lucy suddenly recalled her self-promise to accept her sister as mentor in these matters of the body, yet be willing and able to respond in equal measure. Clearly she had just done so under the spell Celia had so artfully woven, so why not now, openly, purposefully, in the seclusion of their own private world?

All this while, she was being gently caressed, until she was wriggling in her hammock.

'Now you clearly *feel* what I mean,' whispered Celia, as her sister moaned softly at the growing level of emotion. 'Just one more thing. You must remember to give as you receive, just as you did in my studio, whether it is with your future husband or your sister, for her need is as great as your own, and in just the same manner and degree,

Lucy nodded before raising her self on one elbow to smile at her sister.

'You have just read my mind, sweet Sister,' as she flicked her own long hair back over her shoulders to sanction full access to her sister's soft touch, to invite and encourage the gently resumed caresses. 'I do finally understand,' she said simply, 'and a special thank you for explaining, and now demonstrating to me so directly, so artfully to my needs. It was my natural shyness that prevented me from acknowledging it sooner.'

And to her self, she knew that now was the time for the second aspect of her promise, that next time Celia would find her not only an accepting receiver, but a dedicated initiator, one who took the lead, who was the generator in this titillation and exploration, just as Richard had to his beloved Alice.

As Celia would certainly have put it: 'If not now, when?'

'As I promised my self, so that you can forget that other thing,' she whispered in her sister's ear, 'shall I show what true love is between two people who truly respect each other, how it was achieved, giving and taking in equal measure?'

Before Celia could reply, to her quiet surprise and delight she found her own hair lifted aside so that her body was similarly revealed. But then Lucy removed the hair completely, letting it fall to each side so that her upper body was completely bare in the afternoon sunlight. Upon this, Celia felt a sudden surge of joy at the accessibility of her bosom, and her back arched in anticipation of the next touch.

She was not to be disappointed. First Lucy studied her sister's body as if she had never really seen it before, as one openly wishing to be loved. Then one hand slowly and softly first explored her belly, then her chest, all the while coming closer to the bosom as Celia was willing it to do, gently titillating with soft and inquiring fingers to test its reaction.

There was a pause while Lucy sat up to make both hands available, which then gently massaged both bare white breasts, from the soft underside and around, fingers then gently circling the dark rings around each nipple until they were hard as rock. Meanwhile Celia's breathing quickened as she was moving to the rhythm Lucy was creating, circling and stroking, caressing and squeezing 'til Celia was in an agony of anticipation.

But there was more, for as the fingers of one hand maintained their massaging, the other gradually descended to her waist, while the now-exposed nipple suddenly felt Lucy's gentle lips upon it and over it, consuming it, eliciting a gasp of surprise and delight from Celia. At that same moment, the other hand was gently massaging her soft belly. Then Celia felt her lower garments being gently opened and removed until none remained, the while receiving continued soft caresses to both upper and lower body from hands and lips.

Now, after a shy study and gentle massaging of that open lower body, especially that area almost as fair as Lucy her self, the gentle stroking continued until Lucy's probing fingers found what they were seeking, and she found her self thrilled at the softness of the triangle between the inner thighs, at which Celia gave a gasp of pleasure. It was, she thought, no wonder that men found this area so entrancing, for she delighted in it and its moist nature her self, and almost envied the man who could penetrate and find his release deep within it.

The next surprise for Celia was when she found Lucy's lips upon her own, first in a gentle kiss, increasing then in passion, breaking only to take a quick breath before the passion returned and increased while the gentle playing of breast and nipples, and especially that lower triangle, massaging with increased intensity and movement until it overwhelmed her whole body, which then arched it self and she cried out in an ecstasy of final release, then all was still in the sun-dappled glade, and Lucy returned to her own hammock, now totally bare from head to toe, her white form clearly showing its own excitement, while awaiting the return of her own skilful loving of her sister's body.

It took Celia some minutes to regain her composure before she was able to turn her attention to her sister, but Lucy was the first to speak.

'How was that, Sis, did you enjoy it?' and in return received a beautiful smile and a soft hand stroking her cheek.

'It was absolutely wonderful, Sister dearest. But where did you learn all those things that you did to my excited body? They had me so worked up I could scarce breathe!'

'Well, some of it from Manfred, of course. Then it was partly from my own imagination, but mostly from how I was feeling in my own self. I found that I could feel what you were feeling, then I imagined what I would like you to do to me, in what area and with what touch, and so on, and that is what I did to you. And it all came so naturally that it required no thought at all.

'But now I have a confession to make,' she said softly. 'After that memory of Alice's in the coach on how beautiful it was to be loved (and to counter that horrid thing in Town), I vowed to my self that the very next time the opportunity arose, I would become Richard and make love to you, to your body, just as he would, as he did to Alice. I would take the lead so that you could feel as wonderful as did she.'

'So that is what you meant by your promise to make me forget,' and Lucy nodded.

'And that lower area?' now in whisper. 'That was incredible. What led you to that?'

'Well,' whispering in return, 'I have never seen that part of you before, of course, but I found it quite deserving of special attention. And I confess that I now understand why a man seeks it, for it is incredibly beautiful to see and to touch; so soft, so fragile, yet moist and warm and so, so inviting, that I almost wished I were a man so that I could enter and create a new being out of passion deep within it,' this last with a distinct blush of embarrassment in it.

'That was most poetically expressed, sweet Sister, and now I understand what I must do in return. I shall be that man, Luce, eager and passionate, and wanting to give you every thing I can – as a woman, that is,' placing her hand on Lucy's belly, quickly running down to the inner thigh then up the bosom, so that Lucy wriggled in the anticipation of the enjoyment to come.

When she was ready, Celia took a lesson from her sister and sat so that both hands were free.

It was then that she found her self thrilled at being so close to see and feel the perfection of Lucy's slim body, hips and bosom less than her own, yet beautifully in proportion. An artist of any worth would be thrilled to paint her undraped – or semi-draped – symmetry. And at that thought, she vowed she would paint her sister in such a pose, with flowers covering that special part or some thing similar, as did the classicists.

Now ready to return that which she had so wonderfully received, she gently caressed each part from ankle to hips to waist to breasts, throat and face, while Lucy thrilled to each touch and was unable to resist the small cries of pleasure that forced them selves from her lips. Celia was so delighted at this immediate response that she took to tantalizing her sister. First was a gentle playing with the nipples, which hardened even more than they were already, then a soft massaging of the inner thighs and a light brush of the triangle, which elicited a soft moan from Lucy's lips in expectation of that final thrill.

Then she proceeded to repeat Lucy's skilful loving, action for action, part by part, until all were involved, awaiting that final special moment.

Alice had prepared scones and an apple tart freshly baked by Cook, together with the usual sliced meats and brown bread, and all was ready except for the kettle on the stove, yet to boil.

While she waited, she mused on her young charges, aware that there was some thing quite different about them when they set out. She could not quite put her finger on it, yet . . . And Miss Celia's stricture 'that they were not to be disturbed' had a clear sensuality to it. All rather puzzling.

And then their recent closeness – especially after the morning painting session when Miss Celia again required 'that they were not to be disturbed'. And when they emerged, arms around each other's waist, happiness clearly in each face – but especially Miss Lucy's – she thought she was beginning to understand, for she had never seen that before, and she did not miss much as far as they were concerned.

So she went up to their respective rooms, returning with a small canvas bag. She could be wrong, though secretly she knew more than she was prepared to acknowledge to her self.

Thus she approached the island carefully, mindful of the most recent time when she found them fast asleep with very little attire. And this time she did not beach the long-boat, but quietly tied it to the landing platform, leaving the tea things but taking with her the canvas bag, stepping quietly and tiptoeing to where the small table was positioned for their afternoon tea and sat on her usual tree stump.

There were only soft sounds coming from the location of the hammocks, but when she looked toward them she was so startled that she almost cried out, for there was Miss Lucy lying quite naked in her hammock, with an equally bare Miss Celia bending over her. It seemed at first glance that she was making love to her sister, and upon second glance this was indeed so for Miss Celia's hands and mouth were all over her sister's body, and especially in that most private area, while Miss Lucy was moaning in clear delight.

At first she was shocked at the sight of such intimate and naked bodily contact, both equally enthralled in their love-making and so absorbed that they were shamefully oblivious of her presence. Yet, as they continued their mutual enjoyment, she found her self quickly moving to a completely different frame of mind, returning in her inner being to her own young life with Richard.

Many's the time she had found her self consumed by a passion that she had no way of venting. If she had had a sister, might they have enjoyed a similar intimacy to release that urgent desire? Indeed, why not? It was innocent, private, did no-one any harm? Society would have been shocked, of course, but this was none of their business, and she smiled quietly to her self as she watched the engrossing scene: her two young ladies making passionate, intimate love, one to the other, doubtless now the other way round.

Meanwhile, they were coming to a climax in their own private world, and Alice was surprised, indeed astonished, to find her own bosom coming alive, which had not happened for many a long year. In that area of her current life, she considered her self now to be quite dead. But when she touched her own bosom, there was no doubt about it, for her own breasts were quite hard, their newly-released passion reaching to just where, well, just where Miss Celia had reached with her sister! And once again she was back there, in that time, when she and Richard had made love in just such a manner, as she had so recently related to the pair of them, her hand now of its own accord reaching to press her belly and beyond, while the other tried to quell her throbbing breast.

And suddenly Alice was envious of their mutual enjoyment, for nothing so fortunate had happened to her since, well, since Richard, and she found tears in her eyes, which, unattended, simply ran down her cheeks, for the ladies were simply re-enacting the very same scene she had so vividly described to them in that darkened coach,

At just this moment in her reflection, Miss Lucy's movements became quite agitated, until she gave a loud cry, followed by a soft moan, and then silence as both settled back in their hammocks. And Alice sat motionless as if in a trance, absorbed in the renewed feelings of her body, of making love with him once more and returned in full measure, for she vividly remembered that climax, that loud cry, the arched back, and him deep inside her.

And, yes, she was truly jealous of their situation, able to indulge themselves whenever and wherever they wished, provided it was private – and there were indeed a number of those close at hand. Perhaps that what was behind the new East Wing, and she suddenly saw it all quite clearly.

Miss Celia had it all in mind from the beginning. Their private quarters, quite separate, with all the facilities except a kitchen, and a door they could lock whenever they felt . . . whatever, knowing for certain that Miss Celia often painted with very little clothing to inhibit her movements and her artistic spirit.

Goodness, they must not see her like this and she quickly wiped her eyes but it was too late, for at just that moment, Miss Celia sat up.

'Well, hello, it is Alice,' at which Lucy sat up, too, hiding her bare self behind her sister. But that was only for a moment, for Celia stepped out of her hammock to stand quite unabashedly facing Alice so she must, perforce, do likewise.

'How long have you been there, Alice?'

'I am not sure, Miss, but I suppose it was about ten minutes.'

'So you saw all that we were engaged in.'

'Yes, Miss.'

'And were you shocked?'

For a moment Alice said nothing, thinking how to tell it, then decided the truth was the best explanation.

'Yes, Miss, at first. But then the more I thought about it, the more I could see the sense of it – especially when it was perfectly evident what joy you were both giving and receiving from it, and how excited you both were,' this last with a little smile. 'But standing with nothing on like that you will both catch a chill, so I brought you these lightweight robes because it is a warm day,' taking Celia's robe out of her canvas bag first and wrapping it around her.

Next came Lucy's, but she was folding her arms across her chest to protect her self, though she had to open them so as to permit Alice to put the robe on.

'Now I shall get the tea things.'

'How did you know to bring robes, Alice?'

'Well, Miss, I . . . sort of deduced that from when you came out after the morning art session.'

'Was it that apparent?' said the surprised Celia.

'Well, it was to me, Miss, but I do not believe anyone else would have noticed it.'

'Well, thank goodness for that. What did you think of our love-making, Alice? Was it good?' and Alice blushed.

'Yes, Miss, I thought it excellent. It reminded me so much of my own love when he and I . . . were together.'

'Now that I look at you more closely, Alice, I do believe you have been crying. Is that so?'

'Yes, Miss it was so. You see, you took me back to those days when I was with him and wished I could have achieved what you and Miss Lucy have just enacted.'

'And were you a little jealous?'

'Yes, Miss, considerably so.'

'And were you, perhaps a little excited, watching us being excited?'

'Yes, Miss, I was, and very much so, all over, every part of me. It was completely unexpected, for I have not felt that way for many a long year, indeed since Richard, for he was the last.'

'Thank you, Alice, for being so frank with us. And here is a hug for being so understanding of our mutually shared passion,' moving to hold her tight, even to arousal once more, at which the observant Celia whispered in her ear, 'Alice, we must explore these "unexpected" feelings of yours, as soon as maybe,' to which Alice smiled and nodded.

'Now let us get to our tea.'

It was some hours later that Lucy was able to talk with Alice privately.

'I want to thank you, Alice, for giving me the insight and the manner in how to cure my sister of that wicked thing in Town.'

'How did I do that, Miss?' quite unaware of having done so.

'It was when you told us the beautiful story of Richard and his making love to your body,' and Alice blushed at the remembrance of her frankness on that occasion. 'It was later that I realized that this was what my sister needed to make her forget that monster. That was pure animal lust – and evil into the bargain. What you told us was how beautiful true love could be, when equally given and received.

'Then, even later, I realized that if I were to make my sister forget that, I would have to be as he was to you, to play the part of a man. And that was what I did this afternoon – mercifully before you arrived – but it was much the same, for I suggested to my sister that mine (fashioned after your own), was the model for the way she should make love to me.

'So you see, Alice, not only were you the saviour of my sister in Town, but here in our own private castle by informing myself as to how it could, and should, be. And I wanted to make sure you understood that, that is all.'

'Miss, I think that is wonderful, and I am so happy that my own tale of joy led to your wonderful enjoyment of each other that I was witness to, giving and receiving in equal measure. Does that then mean, Miss, that you have given up . . .' and here she paused, fearing to tread where she should not.

'Do you mean, Alice,' Lucy said softly, taking her hand, 'that I no longer wish for Manfred to take me?' receiving a hesitant nod from Alice.

'Then the answer is twofold. First you are correct that I no longer wish for it; his power over my self, my body, is gone. But secondly – and more importantly – I know that in his selfish lust for my naked body, he could not possibly have given me even one tenth the ecstasy that my wonderful sister provided so recently that it still echoes through my being. And I can luxuriate in the thought that we may re-enact that at our common will – and may that be soon, and often.

'Thank you also for being concerned for my safety, Alice, but now I have unease about your self. Is it true that no-one has been . . . with you since that time?' and Alice nodded, downcast at the thought. 'But your Mildred – and now my Mildred – is twelve and more, so that it has been . . .'

'Yes, Miss, thirteen years. Thirteen and a few days.'

'So, though you considered your self past all that, our mutual exploration has re-awakened that spirit to its fullest?' and Alice nodded, head down, to hide the sadness in her eyes, but Lucy was nevertheless a witness as she lifted her chin.

'It was not intended, Alice, that you should witness our mutual explorations, but now that you have, we owe you some thing in recompense for your current and future emptiness. Perhaps . . .'

'And what are you two whispering about,' as Celia rounded the corner. 'Some thing about me, I will be bound.'

'It was indeed, sweet Sister. I was telling her how beautifully you made love to me. Do you mind?'

'Is that true, Alice,' replied her sister, doubting the whole matter.

'Yes, Miss – except that she also told me how beautifully she made love to you,' and with a deep curtsey to both she departed.

'Oh, well, it was beautiful as you said. But that reminds me of some thing that I promised my self.'

'And that is?'

'That I shall paint you in oils just as you were on that hammock,' and noting the shocked look on her sister's face, 'well, with a little bit of discreet cover, of course. But not too much,' she added, wickedly, 'for your body is too gorgeous to hide completely. And then afterwards, without the benefit of covering . . . ?' and they swung away, arms around each other.

As for Alice, she was saddened by her own unfulfilled satisfaction of the spirit, but happy that Manfred's power over Miss Lucy was at last broken. Now she must be aware for Miss Celia, in that he might switch his power of the Hollow to her as his next victim.

But that broken discussion with Miss Lucy reminded her of Jane Austen, where Edward had something of importance to convey to Elinor, and Willoughby likewise with Marianne. In each case that interruption was of the greatest import, blighting their lives, leaving her wondering what opportunity she had missed as a result. And try as she might, sleep was a long time coming.

12

Betrayal

The preparations for the Ides Ball reached fever pitch in the following week. The question of what to wear had been resolved by Alice suggesting that their dress be the same, each wearing the same wig of piled blonde hair and a highwayman's mask, so that it was difficult to tell them apart when they tried it all on.

'That way,' Alice whispered to her mistress, 'you may surprise one of them into declaring his love to you by mistake, as Herr Mozart is so fond of doing.'

'Alice,' responded Celia, 'you have a devious streak in you, but it may contain a stroke of genius, too; so you may dress us as you propose.'

By the evening before the Ball, all was as ready as could be. Even the tables were set out around the manor, although not yet laid for dinner. Cook had been hard at work, justifiably proud of her creations and the way her new ovens were functioning.

'I never 'opes to do better than this 'ere, Ma'am,' she told her lady-ship. 'Even if I lives to be a 'undred!'

Lucy and the quartet – for Celia was much too nervous to participate – completed their final practice with Lady Etheridge as their musical critic, and she declared her self more than happy with the quality of the efforts.

'I expect we shall receive offers for all your hands before the evening is out,' she declaimed, eliciting giggles and blushes all 'round – though not from her elder daughter.

Celia was unsettled; and the closer the day, the more distraught she had become. Even her nightly talks with Alice failed to calm her nerves. She was sleeping fitfully, rising tired and irritable, unable to paint or do much else.

Alice was concerned that her mistress was going to look any thing but her best on the special night.

'If you do not get a good night's rest tonight, Miss,' she had declared earlier that day, 'we will have to use some thing to colour your cheeks and cover your dark eyes, for even the mask is going to be inadequate.'

At a light dinner on the penultimate evening, Celia could not even finish her soup, leaving to go to her room to lie down. It was clear that it had to be resolved.

'Alice,' she declared through her tears, rejecting the food being offered her, 'I need your help. I cannot attend the Ball tomorrow, for I will ruin it for every body, especially my sister. You will have to say I am ill, but I cannot stay in the house for that would spoil it even more, so I must find some place to stay for a day or two. Where do you suggest I repair to?'

Alice, though shocked by the statement, was not entirely surprised, for she had seen some thing of the sort coming. But now she needed more time to elicit what was truly behind this malaise.

'It would be a pity if you did forgo it, Miss, though I can see you are not at all well. But before you do any thing irrevocable, perhaps you should inform her ladyship. She may have a remedy that would ease the difficulty.'

'How can that be, Alice;' misinterpreting the reply, 'I know all the places that her ladyship does?'

'Yes, Miss, I am sure you do. But do not forget that her ladyship is also your mother,' and at Celia's look of surprise at this strange state-ment, went on; 'You forget, Miss,' she said softly, 'that I am a mother, too, and sometimes we mothers have an insight into such matters. At the very least you should explain that you will be absent tomorrow. Indeed, as hostess to a number of very important guests, you must disclose that as a simple courtesy to her ladyship.'

'Do you really think so, Alice?'

'Yes, Miss. Now, you rest there for a while. I shall find her ladyship and return. Try to sleep a little to relax your nerves.'

'Yes, Alice?' responded Lady Etheridge to Alice's request for a moment of her time, in the midst of some last minute directions in the Dining room.

'Begging your pardon, Madam, would it be possible to speak to you privately?'

'Now?' said her ladyship, and Alice nodded. 'You can see I am very busy, Alice,' she said, a little crossly. 'Can it not wait until the morrow?'

'No, Your Ladyship. By tomorrow it will be too late, for the damage may have been done.'

'Really, Alice, you do speak in riddles. Very well, I shall be in the Morning room in a few minutes, please wait for me there.'

'Well, what is this matter of life or death?' as she closed the door behind her.

'It is Miss Celia, Madam; she feels unable to attend the Ball tomorrow.'

'Not attend? But that is quite absurd; the whole thing is her idea! I have never heard any thing so preposterous. Please tell her that I wish to see her right away. I will wait for her here and we will soon get to the bottom of this nonsense!'

But Alice did not move.

'Alice!' said her ladyship, sharply, 'did you hear me?'

'Yes, Madam,' with a little curtsey, 'However, it is not quite as simple as that.'

'Are you telling me how to handle my own daughter, Alice?' replied her ladyship, with not a little heat. It had been a very trying week all round. Now this ridiculous situation. It was all really too much!

Alice went scarlet, but stood her ground.

'If it please Your Ladyship, I am a mother, too, and this is one of those times when being a mother requires special awareness. So I beg you to reconsider, for Miss Celia's sake.'

'Very well, Alice, what is this mystery with my daughter that she would want to withdraw from the very thing she has been planning for weeks – and turning the whole house upside down, I might add!'

'It has to do with the guest list, Madam.'

'I am familiar with the list, Alice,' she replied tartly. 'What of it?'

'It includes the name of Professor Werner, Madam.'

'I am aware of that, Alice, and I did not entirely approve, although I did not insist on its withdrawal. Again, what of it?'

'As perhaps Your Ladyship is aware, the professor has a decided interest in Miss Lucy.'

'That is as may be, though it will serve him not at all, for my daughter will not return any such interest. Furthermore, as it does not concern Miss Celia, I should like to talk to her before I return to my many pressing matters. If you would be so kind,' she finished acidly.

Alice reddened again and bit her lip, while tears came to her eyes. She had not reckoned that this would be so difficult. And she was suddenly intensely aware that she had overlooked one crucial fact: her ladyship had had little real contact with her daughters in the last several months, and knew nothing of substantial events in their young lives. But she also knew that she must make one final effort. This one would be win or lose.

'If Your Ladyship would permit me one last opportunity to explain.'

'Very well, Alice,' said her ladyship, wearily, 'but please hurry, for I am very busy, as you saw for your self.'

'Well, Madam,' taking a deep breath before entering on the last-ditch effort, 'Miss Celia believes that the professor is in love with Miss Lucy, although almost certainly in vain, as you say. What she does *not* realize is that she is in love with him her self, and cannot meet him without appearing to betray her sister.'

'Impossible!' retorted her ladyship. 'How can you possibly know such a thing!'

Alice felt a great weariness come over her in turn.

'I cannot explain it, Madam, it is just so. Miss Celia cannot face him. She does not yet know why, though she soon will. If she is not carefully prepared for that event, believing as she does that her sister's happiness is at stake, the consequences flowing from it may seriously hurt or even destroy her.'

'This is incredible, Alice; you cannot possibly be right in this matter. Now, I have listened to enough. Please ask Miss Celia to join me here, *immediately!*'

Alice was now very pale, for no position of retreat or redress remained to her.

'I know that I am right, Madam. However, I am also aware that I have trodden where I should not, between your self and your daughter. To my shame, I have also revealed Miss Celia's confidences in a most ill-advised manner, for which I may not ask her forgiveness.'

Ashen faced and trembling now, she continued:

'It was simply my love for her that made me want to spare her from such a terrible hurt. As I have utterly failed to convince Your Ladyship, and as I will be unable to face Miss Celia for my betrayal,' here she drew a shuddering breath as the tears rolled down her cheeks, 'I request Your Ladyship's permission to withdraw from her service and to leave early in the morning.'

Lady Etheridge opened her mouth to protest this incredible statement, but no sound emerged, and it would not have mattered if it had, for at those final words, Alice had whirled 'round and departed in a flood of tears, leaving her in a virtual state of shock.

The silence of the room after the so recent tumult of emotion was broken only by the gentle tick of the mantel clock, which proceeded to chime eight, as if on cue.

'Dear me,' exclaimed her ladyship, to the room, for there was no-one else in it. 'This matter seems to have gone badly awry. Alice cannot be right, for it is not proper for Celia to be any thing to the professor, nor he to her. And certainly that should have no bearing on her attendance or otherwise.'

And she rose, resolved to speak to her daughter and get to the bottom of this ridiculous situation, then paused to decide how to address the subject. Still undecided, she resumed her seat once more. However, the longer she dwelt on it, the less and less certain she became of any thing. After all, how well *did* she know her daughters? Better than Alice? – who spent most of every day with one or the other, if not both? Was it possible that Alice was right? No, it could not be. Quite impossible!

But, then again, how could Alice be wrong with such intimate connections to them, for she had heard of Celia's nightly discussions on *all* subjects – perhaps even some of questionable propriety. Could it be true?

It was at this point in her introspection of the interwoven problems of Celia and Lucy and the Ball and the professor, and how they might be resolved, that the message of most import truly sank in.

Alice was leaving 'early in the morning'.

It was then that those other issues simply paled into insignificance. That was too unthinkable for contemplation, for she knew in her heart that once departed, Alice – and for a certainty her daughter with her – would never return.

And suddenly she 'saw' the scene when Celia awoke in the morning, waiting in vain for Alice to attend her, only to find that she – and Mildred with her – had already left her service for ever! And then that *her own mother* was responsible for this unbelievable, incredible event!

Heavens! And she realized – with a sickening lurch – that Celia would not excuse her if, however inadvertently, however innocently, she had been its cause, for she was aware that her daughter thought the world of Alice, and also very highly of Mildred's capability and artistic spirit. To lose them both in an instant? *Horrors!*

Now, with a shudder of increasing awareness, she knew that Celia would, in truth, never forgive, never forget. Indeed, the anger in her daughter's heart would be of such magnitude that she was more than capable of doing some thing equally drastic as Alice, some thing that she dare not put into words – even in her own head.

And then would Lucy choose also to . . . ? And the Quartet? Oh, no, this was too . . . and she had no words to even begin to imagine what the next twenty-four hours would bring if the situation were not immediately amended.

Enough of procrastination; time for action; the deed must be undone. For all she knew, Alice could be packing her few things at this very moment. Gracious, if Celia happened upon her and got even a *hint* of such a move – and she became aware of that dread feeling of some one walking on her grave, her tombstone reading, 'Never to be Forgiven'.

'Cook,' she exclaimed, surprising that worthy in her own kitchen. 'I have been hasty and ill-tempered, and have upset Alice dreadfully. And worse, without good cause. Would you please prepare tea for two and have Mildred bring it to me in the Morning room?'

'Thank you, Mildred, please put it on that table, Mildred, and sit for a moment, for I need to talk to you.'

As she uttered these words, she realized that she had not really spoken to Alice's daughter since her shocking arrival in the middle of the night, several months before. Yet *Celia* knew her talents and aptitudes intimately. Could – indeed *had* – described her capabilities in considerable detail, while Lucy was currently in the process of training her to be a personal maid. And she thought she knew her daughters?!

What madness had possessed her; for she really knew very little of any thing concerning their daily *lives*, much less the affairs of their *hearts*! Now she could only pray that she was not too late to right the terrible wrong she had done Alice.

Composing her self again, she said, 'Mildred, my dear,' looking at her for almost the very first time and noticing that apart from being very pretty, she was very creditably attired, almost the equal of her own daughter at that age. Celia had told her that Mildred made her own dresses; no wonder she was impressed.

'After you have poured me a cup of tea, I have a confession to make,' and was quite amazed at the skill with which the task was performed by one so young, the tea delivered without spilling a drop, with a little curtsey, too; and then remained standing, waiting. A quite remarkable child.

'Mildred, I am afraid that I have upset your mother badly, indeed *very* badly, and without cause at that. Would you please go to her and tender my sincere apologies – tell her that I am most sorry to have upset her, and that I wish to tell her so *personally*. You understand?'

'Yes, Madam,' responded Mildred politely, with a perfect curtsey.

'Good. I expect you to return *with* your mother, is that also understood?'

'Yes, Madam,' with another curtsey.

'Very well, you may go, Mildred, and thank you.'

Mildred stopped at the door, turned, and with a most graceful deep curtsey said, 'Thank *you*, Madam,' and the door closed noiselessly behind her.

What an unusual child, reflected her ladyship; no wonder Celia was taken with her. Her very movements, even her walk, were like those of a ballerina, and she wondered whence this natural grace emanated. She had just finished drinking her tea when there was a knock on the door and Mildred entered, followed by a very pale and forlorn Alice.

'My mother, Madam,' announced Mildred, with great solemnity, curtsied, and retired.

'Do come in please, Alice, and sit and have tea with me. I specially ordered it for you.'

But Alice remained standing by the door.

'Oh, Alice, Alice! How can we resolve our difficulties if you are going to stand there all stiff and starchy,' and, despite her self, Alice was moved to smile.

'That is much better,' said her ladyship. 'Now do sit down and have a cup of tea, or we shall be here all night. Firstly, Alice, you do not look well; it is entirely my fault, and I do sincerely ask your pardon. And, by the by, I have no intention of accepting your notice; it is absolutely and irrevocably denied. I do not wish it, and my daughter would certainly never speak to me again if I permitted it – if she even consented to remain under my roof!'

Alice managed a smile through tight lips, 'Yes, Madam, but you were not at fault.'

'I most certainly was, Alice,' responded her ladyship, firmly. 'You had some thing important to communicate to me, *concerning my very own daughter*, and I turned you away. Now the tea, and then to Celia.'

'Now I would like to understand a little better, so that I can help find a solution to this . . . difficulty,' and Alice nodded, surprised at the generosity of tone from her ladyship.

'First, you are sure of her affection – love, I think you said – for the professor?' Alice nodded. 'Very well. Does she know him well? Have they met often?'

'No, Madam, since his Christmas visit here she has met him only once, briefly, quite by accident, when we were out riding one morning. He was most courteous and assisted her dismount, but she sent him away with a flea in his ear when she thought he was being disobliging to Miss Lucy.'

'And was he?'

'I was not of that opinion, Madam.'

'And from this brief encounter, my daughter is *in love* with him?'

'Yes, Madam, I my self was puzzled at first, but now I am quite sure of it.'

'Yet she is not aware of this love her self; how can that be?'

'Well, Madam, Miss Celia has never been in love. Oh, she has had her little flirtations with the young gentlemen, and one or two of them have, regrettably, quite lost their heads over her. She is quite a one, Madam, when she wants to be,' ('do I not know it!' echoed her ladyship, softly). 'But in love, Madam? Never.'

'Not even with Reginald?' and Alice shook her head.

'Oh no, Madam. Poor Mr. Reginald. He is desperately in love with her, quite worships the ground she walks on, but I am afraid he has no hope in that quarter.'

'But to return to Professor Werner. It is different there, you say. How so?'

'May I be frank, Madam?'

'But of course, Alice. That is why we are sitting here drinking tea together. Mother to mother, is it not?' and she smiled.

'Yes, Madam, mother to mother,' her eyes shining again at last at the special recognition. 'Miss Lucy was quite swept off her feet by the professor, but only when he was near her, so she is not in love with him.

But now I know for a certainty that this infatuation is over for good. Also, there may be a serious interest from a *most* acceptable suitor.'

'Indeed, Alice, that may well be so. As early as tomorrow, perhaps.'

'Very good. Now; my elder daughter?'

'There are two causes for her malaise, Madam; Miss Lucy, and a danger to her self, both of which are quite difficult to comprehend. Firstly, she is convinced that her sister is in love with the professor, and that any thing she undertakes with him will betray her sister, and thus cannot attend the Ball. While this is untrue, even were I to try I could not convince her otherwise.

'I reason that Miss Celia takes this attitude to cover the confusion of her own feelings toward him, and is deliberately denying her own self – and her attendance – to reinforce her "betrayal" feelings of Miss Lucy. I understand that this has little reason behind it, but we are talking here of the heart not the head,' and her ladyship nodded her understanding of that from her own experience.

'Now, as clever as the professor undoubtedly is, your elder daughter wraps him 'round her little finger every time he addresses her. But, *for the very first time in her life* she sees a man she is strangely attracted to. She knows that she can easily outsmart him but, as a woman – begging your pardon, Madam – her natural wiles have recently come to the fore, and she would like to try these on him. That she could conquer him, I have not the slightest doubt, but in this new awareness, Miss Celia has become *over-protective* of her beautiful younger sister.

'However, for her own self, she sees the professor as a cat sees a mouse, as some thing to play with. But women are not cats, and men are not mice; they have wiles of their own and sometimes let them selves be caught so as to catch in their turn. Perhaps it would be better phrased to say that women, to their mortal peril, are some times enmeshed in their own snares.

'This is now the second aspect, and a true danger to Miss Celia, for the professor, underneath his very strange exterior, is a man of considerable fortitude, one very sure of him self when he is in his own element of leadership. Miss Celia, despite her effort to appear otherwise, has an extremely soft and vulnerable heart, which none has yet reached in the pursuit of romance. Thus she could be terribly hurt if the recipient of her suddenly released devotion is not compassionate, and I believe she is, without realizing it, perilously close to that point with regard to the professor.

'Before tomorrow evening, Madam, Miss Celia must be somehow made aware of the dangers of such playful amusement, especially as far as the professor is concerned, for she does not realize that it is not Miss Lucy, but her self – though she is quite convinced it is otherwise – who is in the greatest danger from him.

'You see, Madam, Miss Celia is, in her innocence, looking for pure love, whereas the professor is currently intending only upon that . . . that other thing. To her, love comes first, the self follows as it will. With him, it is the other way round. Unless they can meet on a common ground of the former, it can only end in devastation for Miss Celia.'

And here her ladyship nodded gravely, understanding for the first time the true nature of the difficulty, as her memory returned to her own early days when innocent love was paramount over all.

'And that is it, Madam. I was simply hoping that Your Ladyship would have some occasion in early womanhood that could be used to alert Miss Celia to the dangers of allowing one's feminine nature to run untrammeled, in the unquestioning belief that, once started, such a course can easily be put aside. For my self, once I had set my Richard on the path that I so artfully yet innocently contrived, I could no more have stopped him than I could a runaway horse by standing in *its* path.'

When Alice looked up, she was astonished to see tears in her ladyship's eyes, which then trickled down her cheeks.

'Alice,' said her ladyship, 'that was most beautifully told. I see now where Mildred gets her own fine spirit, and why my daughter is so taken with her – and with your self. I must thank you once more for having the courage and determination to stay the course – despite my rejection – for Miss Celia's sake.

'On a somewhat related matter, my daughter is, I believe, in the habit of discussing many things of a quite private nature with your self. Can you perhaps explain to how and why this is so?'

'The issue is quite simple, Madam, for like most daughters, I suspect Miss Celia is a little embarrassed. As we are not that apart in age, I am able to answer these matters of the person, while tempering them with counsel for caution and discretion.

'Miss Celia would be *most* reluctant to ask your counsel for fear you thought she was about to try them her self and commit some indiscretion.'

'Has my daughter committed an indiscretion, Alice?'

'No, Madam.'

'But she may in the near future, with the professor, if *he* has a mind to. Is that what you are trying to advise me?'

'Yes, Madam, it is possible – indeed, highly likely, if she continues on her present ingenuous path.'

'Your counsel, then, Alice, is for me to discuss the matter with my daughter?'

'Yes, Madam, but with a careful manner, for if she is *ordered* to do or not to do some thing as your "obedient daughter", she is most likely to proceed only as her heart dictates. That is where the guide from Your Ladyship's own past would be of inestimable value.'

'It does so happen, Alice, that as a young woman, though not quite as young as your self, I was attracted very strongly to a young man, and it would have ended in wantonness except for another circumstance. I think that, with a little womanly ingenuity on my part, I might find in it a parable for our daughter. As to the professor, can we ensure that there are no indiscretions in the future?'

'Not without employing a barbaric, mediæval custom, Madam. However, I intend to keep a close watch on all activities and proximity. If I find the professor overstepping the mark with Miss Celia, I will make him aware of his obligations to propriety.'

'But if he is as commanding as you say, Alice, will he heed your counsel?' responded her ladyship, doubtfully.

Alice lowered her eyes for some moments as if to consider her reply. When she raised them again, her ladyship saw a clear, intense flame burning there that brooked no denial.

'I believe, Madam,' she said softly, but with an edge of bright steel to her voice, 'that it can be couched in such terms that the professor will see it *to his advantage* to properly respect Miss Celia.'

'Very well, Alice,' said her ladyship, withdrawing a little from the intensity of the furnace she had witnessed in Alice's soul, 'I think that is now clear. One final question, though, if you would be so good. How do you read the auguries in terms of the professor and my daughter: is there a "future"?'

Alice paused for such a long period, that it seemed she would not answer at all. Finally she responded.

'How would Your Ladyship view a proposal from the professor for Miss Celia's hand?'

'With grave misgivings, Alice.'

'Then suppose the liaison were to occur without the benefit of clergy?'

'Alice! Whatever are you saying! Such a suggestion is monstrous and wicked.'

'Exactly so, Madam. However, I believe that if Miss Celia determines that the professor is her one chance of happiness, she will put her self in way of that chance whether he formally requests her hand in marriage or not. However, she must know nothing of our discussions on the matter or most certainly all will be lost.'

'Well, if it is to be, then we must make the best of it. But please keep me advised of events for I shall need much time to accustom my self to any "arrangement".

'If you would tell Miss Celia that I will visit her in a few minutes, to inquire after her health, I should be much obliged.'

'In the circumstance, Madam, it might be preferable for Miss Celia to visit your self if you have some confidence that you wish to divulge, for Miss Celia perceives her quarters to be the inner sanctum wherein she reigns and where her dictum rules. Sometimes I am ordered out simply to demonstrate that very thing!'

'Dear me! But I believe you to be right, Alice. That is most insightful, and I will follow your advised course. Please allow me some fifteen minutes or so to order my thoughts, then bring my daughter to my room.

'I will leave the explanation of the occasion to your undoubted wisdom.'

Ensconced now in her own quarters before a warm fire, her ladyship had recalled the situation concerning her own early behaviour that she wished to convey to Celia, and was satisfied that it could indeed form the basis of an appropriate caution.

That accomplished, her thoughts returned to Alice. In retrospect of the discussions that were still echoing in her head, it was abundantly clear that Alice was by no means a typical servant. She had been acquainted in some degree with Alice's early life and the tragedy of her interrupted education. However, in response to some of her questions, Celia had politely declined to reply in deference to Alice's privacy regarding some highly personal and privileged disclosures. She had accepted that without demur as being a confidence between companions, not to be broached.

All that she understood. What she was only now grappling with, was the unambiguous evidence that Alice was a truly remarkable young woman, with views and opinions and observations that she her self was unlikely to exceed. Indeed, could even her own closest acquaintance have provided as intelligent and insightful a discussion? That was a certain 'no', for most of those were more in the nature of gossip!

But it was more even than that. The insight into her daughters' lives – into their very inner feelings – was quite astonishing. What other 'servant', however experienced, would have had the perception that Alice had brought to the dialogue. And such dialogue; quite impeccable in both words and their use – to say nothing of its wisdom! No wonder Celia availed her self of the opportunity for discourse with Alice on such a wide variety of topics – and those were only the ones about which she had heard!

Now, at last, she comprehended why Celia had constructed those generous quarters for them in the new East Wing, with conveniences quite equal to her own, for it was abundantly clear that was how Celia regarded Alice – as a virtual equal. Certainly Alice's vocabulary and manner of speech and – yes, her very air of confidence and the way she carried her self – demonstrated that . . . And suddenly she grasped the full reality of it!

Alice had modelled her self upon Celia! On her mode of address, her deportment – at least the best part of it, recalling now some quite riotous behaviour from her daughter – even her knowledge of literature, art and music. Not only that, but she had apparently understood the necessity to do so from her very first arrival at the Hall, when she was only a simple scullery maid with little contact with any of the household outside the Servants' Hall. Remarkable, quite remarkable.

And as it all became clear as crystal, *that* is where Mildred received her own inherent in born abilities; from the most obvious of places – her mother! That explained why . . .

But a tap on the door interrupted her reverie.

'Miss Celia, wake up; her ladyship wishes to see you!'

Alice was apprehensive, for the centre of the past hour's attention was fast asleep on her bed and her ladyship waiting. Had she 'cried wolf' too soon? A damp cloth applied to her mistress' neck brought fairly quick results, however.

'Alice, what on earth are you doing? Are you trying to drown me, you stupid girl? Just as he was about to . . . it was a *beautiful* dream; one that I have been trying to have for months, and you got in the way. You are always getting in the way, Alice. What is the matter with you tonight?'

'Her ladyship wishes that you visit her in her room, but if you are going to be in that sort of temper, I had better tell her to leave it until you can be civil,' and she strode to the door.

'Come back here this instant, you foolish girl, and tell me what this is all about. A person cannot sleep undisturbed these days, and you were the very one urging me to do more of it.

'Her ladyship wants to see me, in her room? But she never invites me in there. What is it about, Alice, and this better be sensible.'

'All I know, Miss, is that when I told her ladyship that you did not intend to be present at the Ball tomorrow, she wished to discover more directly from your self. Am I to be blamed for every thing around here?'

'All right, Alice, do not get so excited, and help me out of bed. What shall I wear?'

'Your blue night-gown with the yellow roses, and Miss Lucy's Chinese robe. You need those soft colours tonight.'

'Do I indeed! Well, you are going to have to undress me, Alice, for I am simply too tired to do it unaided.'

'Very well, Miss,' and as she entered Miss Lucy's empty room for the gown she rang the bell, meeting a very alert Mildred in the doorway on the way back.

'Mildred,' she said quietly to her daughter to avoid being overheard by her still sleepy mistress, 'please ask Cook to prepare coffee for two immediately, and take it to her ladyship's room.

'As for you, young lady,' returning again to her mistress, 'let's get you into this gown and robe, and then dress your hair a little. But I should be respectful to your mother if I were you; she is extremely busy and likely to bite your head off if you so much as squeak. I will also lead you there my self to be sure you arrive, though why I should bother with such an ingrate the Lord only knows.'

'Alice, do you know you are turning into a domineering bully?'

'And you, Miss Celia, are turning into a bad tempered grouch. If I wasn't so fond of your sister, I would probably leave tomorrow.'

'And if I did not perceive some thing was afoot here, Alice, I would probably just let you go. As it is, I believe all you need is an old-fashioned hug. There, is that better? I can see I am going to have to find some one to do that for you, and often; some one who will replace your Richard.'

'You could never do that, Miss,' replied Alice, softly, 'for such a person does not exist. Besides, do we need men?'

'Well, I do not know about you, Alice, but I decidedly do, and it is time I went out and caught one for my self. I hear the woods are full of them.'

'I advise against it, Miss, for with rare exceptions, they are not worth it. And recall if you will that the forests are also full of wolves.'

'Are they now! Well, well. I might even manage to catch one of those, too,' replied her mistress, stroking an imaginary beard in contemplation of such fortune.

'Be forewarned, Miss. They have long teeth, sharp claws, and are quite immune to the wiles of young ladies even as they desire their charms, so I should steer clear of forests altogether, or you may lose more than you bargained for! There, almost presentable.'

Then she took her mistress' hand.

'Let us go and find her ladyship, and when you have finished being nice to her, I shall be down to tuck you in. Here we are,' and as she tapped lightly on her ladyship's door, she gave her mistress' hand a tight squeeze of encouragement, which was as tightly returned.

'Good evening, my dear, come in and sit in the comfortable chair there, by the warmth of the fire. I have had it made up because I do not have your radiator heating. You may also have a cup of coffee, which has miraculously just appeared in the hands of Mildred. A remarkable child that, so accomplished – as you have observed to me on more than one occasion.

'Now, I understand from Alice that you have some qualms about attending the Dinner Party tomorrow. May I inquire the reason for this sudden change of heart for I have been most pleased with all your efforts to ensure its success?'

In her room directly over Miss Celia's, Alice was asleep. Nevertheless she heard her mistress' door open and close, having told her self to listen for it, as a mother listens for her baby's slightest cry. So she descended, tapped on the door and entered before the dressing gown was even removed.

'Let me do that, Miss,' taking the gown and hanging it in the cupboard. 'Would you like some thing, Miss?'

'I would, Alice, but what?'

'Suppose I get you a glass of sherry to help you sleep. Then I will brush your hair while you tell me about your talk. It has been well over an hour.'

'On one condition, Alice: that you also massage my shoulders and neck, for you are very good at that,' and Alice nodded. 'Mother practically *insisted* that I tell you, though I do not see why I should, for you have been quite beastly to me of late.'

'Yes, Miss, I have, and do not deserve to be told, so please do not bother.'

'Oh, stop that do, Alice; it is no fun at all when you give in. Mother,' Celia proceeded, blithely ignoring the capitulation, 'had an illicit liaison with a young man when she was much younger than I – only seventeen. His name was Lorenzo, which made him Italian, and he called her Lottie, short for Charlotte, you see.' Alice, combing her hair behind her, nodded.

'She was so desperately in love that she was ready to elope and be his paramour – or whatever they were called in those far off days – which would have finished her, of course. Strange, I had somehow never thought of mother having those sorts of feelings – you know, the intimate ones we have talked of – but she made it very plain that she desired him in the most salacious way, and suddenly I saw my self in her eyes.

'She related in much detail how they arranged to meet in order to . . . though I shall not bore you with that. Anyway, the plans were all laid and she was to meet him in the garden after a Ball at her house, and there would be a coach waiting at the gate to whisk them off to his little love nest. It was all quite fascinating, especially when she revealed the secrets and mutual intimacies partaken in their little trysts. I never thought mother had that sort of spirit in her. And you accuse *me* of being a little wild! But I could see that crises could be survived, no matter how insurmountable they appeared at the time.'

'Well?' said Alice impatiently after the longest pause. 'What happened?'

'Oh, nothing happened,' said Celia, nonchalantly, studying her long fingernails. 'Shall I cut them a little tomorrow, before the Ball? If I decide to go, that is. Mother thinks I should, but it really is up to me, she says. Perhaps I will do both, or neither.'

'All right,' said Alice, 'I do not care to hear, anyway.'

Celia whirled 'round in her chair; 'You *do* want to know, I *knew* it!'

'Quiet or you will wake Miss Lucy. She needs her sleep as much as you do, or more, for she has to be her best ever tomorrow.'

'Is she going to get a proposal at the Ball, Alice?'

'I expect so, Miss. Would that bother you?'

'Why should it bother me? Who do *you* think she would be happier with, Alice, the Professor or the Captain?'

'How would I know, Miss, I am always kept in the dark on *personal family* matters.'

'Oh, very well, if you are going to sulk. It did not happen because, at that Ball, mother met a charming and handsome Colonel of the Dragoons who put all thoughts of the pretty young subaltern completely out of her head. In just one evening she was truly in love. And guess who he was!'

'The General, Miss?'

'Alice, you have been listening at keyholes again,' said her mistress, crossly. 'Now you have to answer *my* question. Which one?'

'Very well, Miss,' said Alice, now massaging neck and shoulders with a soft, scented cream. 'My answer is that she would most like to be with the professor, but she would be most attended and respected by the captain. Now, I am not at all certain that happiness is the most important aspect of a marriage – not that he would ask her to marry him. So, for a while, she would regret not going with the professor, but that would soon pass, especially when she has a baby of her own by the captain. Will that do?'

Celia had sat bolt upright in the middle of this statement, and turned to stare at Alice in disbelief. 'He would not ask her to marry him, Alice? Why do you say that?'

'Because the professor is not of the marrying sort. He is one of those who want their currant bun without paying for it.'

'That is a dreadful expression, Alice, if it means what I think it does. You also accuse him of being a man without honour, and I do not believe that.'

'As you wish, Miss, but one is able to read men after a while, and that is how I discern the professor, not that it affects you at all, of course.

'Now I will get you that sherry, Miss.'

When Alice returned, Celia was brushing her hair over her naked self in front of the mirror. 'Do you think he would admire my body, Alice?' parting her hair to display it to its reflection.

'I am quite sure he would, for I have seen him looking wonderingly at it; on the sly, of course,' she responded. 'I assume you mean Mr. Reginald, Miss?' she added, innocently.

'You are the most infuriating *child* sometimes, Alice! Reginald would not have the slightest notion of what to do with my body if I offered it to him as you see me now – having first fainted dead away, of course!'

'Then who can you mean, Miss?' draping the robe over her mistress' bare posterior again to keep out the cold, then taking the brush to gently continue the treatment.

'Well, who do you know that would like to be doing that brushing to my body?'

'That is easy, Miss. There must be half-a-dozen at least who have dreamed of being me just now. Shall I name them for you?'

'Don't you *dare*! Besides, it is none of those *boys*. I would not let them within one hundred yards of that brush handle. Can you not guess?' she added, plaintively.

'No, Miss, I can not. It cannot possibly be the professor for you hate him. You told me so your self only a few days ago, and scolded me roundly for even suggesting it! So it must be some one I do not know.' As she brushed, two tears slowly made their way down her mistress' cheeks and dropped onto her hand.

'Don't you see, Alice,' staring at her own pale face, 'if my sister is to receive a proposal from the Captain, it is no longer obligatory that I chastise the professor for his conduct of her? That makes all the difference, doesn't it? Then perhaps we, the professor and I, that is, might be able to meet some where, just occasionally, to talk about many things that I have in my mind. Surely there could be no harm in that, even if he is not the "marrying kind". Besides, if Lucy is no longer here, I shall need *some one* to converse with.'

'Meeting and conversing is one thing, Miss,' Alice responded, firmly. 'Meeting to have him stroke and titillate your body, *like this*,' applying the brush suggestively over her exposed upper body, 'and goodness knows where else,' she continued, softly, 'is some thing quite, quite different, and not to be countenanced. Which is it you desire?'

'I want all of them, Alice,' her mistress said softly to her reflection, 'meeting and talking and stroking, and just being with him, always,' and she turned and put her hands on Alice's shoulders, then lowered her head and Alice could feel the hot tears soaking through her own gown. 'And much more besides. I even crave what you designed, Alice, with Richard, and in just such a manner.' Her voice was now just a faint whisper in Alice's ear; '*I want his baby*!'

Alice mounted the stairs slowly and thoughtfully to her own room. So the crucial moment had arrived: Celia understood her self to be in love with the professor. While that was the good part, there was not the slightest indication that he understood any of what his present attitudes could do to her mistress if his actions were any thing even close to those with Miss Lucy.

She must find some way to meet with him, to reach an understanding with him concerning Miss Celia. But where was the time, the occasion? Why would he even listen to her – as her ladyship had queried.

And a grim foreboding darkened her heart, making the night long and full of sinister dreams of grim forests and sharp-toothed wolves, of a mistress destroyed by lust where she sought only love.

13

Exposure

'Tell me your thoughts about last night, Alice,' said Celia as they passed through the apple orchard on Jasper and Sally, 'then I will tell my side of it.'

It was well past noon, for they had danced and celebrated until the small hours, and then had difficulty sleeping with the excitement of it all.

'Cook thought it was the best Ball ever at the Hall,' responded Alice, 'and she has been there nigh on thirty-two years! At first she did not welcome the idea of all those different tables, for she had always thought that eating belonged in the Dining room. But when she saw it all laid out, she changed her tune, for she could see it was going to make the dinner guests so much more interesting to each other, especially as they were chosen out of a hat – with a little bit of adjustment in one or two cases. But, *mostly*, I think Cook suddenly realized she could show off her skills by making a lot more dishes, though less of each.'

'That *was* very well done, and I had many compliments on the food. Please make sure that Cook hears that. What else?'

'All below-stairs, Miss, were delighted to have those extra maids from Houghton Hall. They were very efficient, and the serving of the dishes and the removal of the plates was most expeditiously performed.'

'And pretty, too. But that was your doing, Alice. I put you in charge of it – so I must compliment you, for I noted it my self.'

'Thank you, Miss; I enjoyed doing it and would like to again, if the occasion arises.'

'Then perhaps we should make you Housekeeper, Alice. What say you?'

'Oh no, Miss! I should not like that at all! Thank you Miss, for your confidence, it is most appreciated; but I am very happy being personal maid to you and Miss Lucy – although that not much longer, unfortunately.

'But as to pretty, Miss, well that is as may be, but they were as empty-headed as they were pretty, and that does not rate in my book!'

'Well said, Alice.'

'But I will tell you one more thing, Miss; your paintings of Miss Lucy and my Mildred were wonderful. I saw many people stop and look at them more than once, and their comments were *most* complimentary. I saw them look at Miss Lucy then stare again at the painting, remarking how life-like it was. With Mildred it was the same, especially when Mr. Reginald danced with her. I told her that she should not have accepted, but she replied that he would not take "no" for an answer! But she was in heaven, of course, in her new off-the-shoulder dress and dancing shoes. And it was quite the same when the professor was her partner!'

'Well, I thought *you* were looking very pretty in the dark green taffeta showing a good deal of your own self,' and Alice blushed, but with pleasure, too. 'I am sure that some of the young men did not recognize you. You could have danced, too, you know?'

'But I did, Miss! Twice with the professor and then with Mr. Reginald – who is a very fine dancer. Perhaps you were talking to the guests at that moment. Mr. Reginald was the perfect gentleman, of course. And then several others who simply would not take no for an answer! But the professor, well, he held me very close – just like to your self, Miss; well, almost like.

'And now I think I understand it a little better, Miss, for it is both delightful and disturbing at the same time. I tried to engage him in conversation; but he was not really listening, his mind being on other things. And thank you for the compliment. I did enjoy watching all the young ones dancing, even if I was a little occupied my self with seeing that it all went well.'

'The professor overstepped the mark with you, Alice, as is his custom, although Mildred deserved the opportunity, for she worked hard on the table placements and getting a good *mélange* of dinner partners – and sorting out a few mismatches! I had many comments on that, too, and that it was all-together a most delightful evening.

'And the young people, Alice. What of them?'

'Well, Miss, both Misses Georgina and Geraldine seemed to be having an especially wonderful time. It would not surprise me at all if we did not hear some good news from that quarter quite soon. And Miss Alexa, too, if I perceived it aright. It seems that, as the Quintet, they are already exceedingly well-known to all the young gentlemen of the County for their beauty – though at a distance – and well respected by the sires and dames for their musical talent and appropriate decorum – making them most acceptable as prospective daughters-in-law.'

'That is an interesting perspective, Alice, indicating that the Quintet had significant benefits to all its members – other than my self, that is. They must all be quite pleased with that little manoeuvre.'

'Indeed, Miss, as I have been. And as to your self, Miss, I noted many of our guests – young and old – admiring you discreetly. And some very openly, for you had a very special "air" surrounding you last night. Very regal, Miss, if I may be permitted to say so.'

'Well, thank you, Alice. I confess I did feel . . . some thing. *Je ne sais pas quoi*. And those conducted tours of the new East Wing?'

'Wonderful, Miss. I was with one group led by Master Jeremy, and he could not praise you enough, Miss, for the marvellous ideas you had. Made all the difference, he insisted. I also overheard several complimentary remarks by Sir Richard Crimble him self, on your account. And many of the guests were most intrigued by your clever placement of the radiators and the efficient hot water system.'

'Come, come, Alice. That was Jeremy's work, not mine. I added very little.'

'Is that so, Miss? Then why was Sir Richard so complimentary on your arbitration settlement? I heard it my self. *I* think we shall be having a number of very similar schemes in the County before the year is out. Mark my words.'

But Celia did not reply this time; as if she had just stopped listening, or was overtaken with other, more intimate, more challenging thoughts. But then Alice had already noted the mistress subdued this morning, even allowing for all the excitement of the long evening and night. Also that the subject uppermost in her own mind, Miss Lucy, had not been broached; but she could wait. And they rode for quite a while in silence, until . . .

'At least the professor stuck to his agreement concerning behaviour,' offered Celia, finally. 'How about the protagonists them selves, Alice?'

'That did not amount to any thing as I could see, Miss – and I was keeping a close eye on that scene. We know the professor is aware of the captain, but I believe it not to be the other way round. Miss Lucy danced with the professor at least twice, probably more, but she did not seem more excited by that than when she danced with the captain – if as much – and that she did most of the evening! One might argue that she had little choice, but we both know that an overeager swain can be avoided if one wishes. So I believe the captain to be her clear partner of choice.

'After her piano recital, Miss, I do not think I have ever seen her so happy; she was positively glowing, and the captain almost as much – which the professor observed with a distinctly sour countenance!

'Did Miss Lucy receive a proposal, Miss?'

'As good as, Alice. And I think I have convinced mother to include in the Marriage Agreement that Lucy be permitted to continue development of her piano and other music skills. The captain has invited her – through her ladyship, of course – to visit his part of the county early next week, for he has three aunts who all desire to make her acquaintance, which will take her away for quite some time.

'There will also be an opportunity there for Mildred, Alice, if you choose to see it that way, for Miss Lucy would like to take her on the journey. That will mean that we will be unable to continue Mildred's education until they return, and perhaps not even then.'

Alice made a wry face at this.

'That would be a pity, Miss, for after I had introduced Mildred and explained that she was wishing for more formal learning, the professor did spend quite a time with her asking many questions. He expressed his appreciation of her afterwards and said he would be very happy to plan some lessons – a "syllabus" he called it.

'But I understand, Miss. It is a wonderful opportunity for her to accompany Miss Lucy. She has never been in any other big house, and will learn a lot of things just being there, for she is very quick. I shall miss her, of course, but it is too advantageous not to accept with good grace, and there may yet be an opportunity for the tutoring, so I thank you kindly for that thought.'

They had reached the upland and were slowly making their way along the ridge, for they were in no hurry to return, having brought a small hamper of food. At the glade, Celia paused for a moment.

'Perhaps we could lunch here in a few minutes, so put down the hamper on our thrones, and then let us make our way to the end.'

As they reined in at the end of the ridge, looking down on Greville House, Alice explored an area that was very much on her mind.

'While we are talking of the professor, Miss, after our little conversation the other night, I was fearful that you would have difficulty in meeting
him again.'

'That is the strangest thing, Alice. I had been dreading it, too, and it
was making me quite ill, as you well know,' as Alice nodded. 'But I think
our talk, and the one with Mother, set every thing to rights. The story
of Lorenzo had the opposite effect than I think she had intended. For
me, the professor is the subaltern and the colonel rolled into one – he
excites my physical nature at the same time as he challenges my intellect
and the nobler aspects of social intercourse. And when I poured out my
heart to you, Alice, on the eve of the Ball – for which forbearance, by
the way, I owe you another large boulder to my considerable debt-moun-
tain of gratitude – I think I removed my fears with the tears. Now I am
quite calm about it,' and she turned her mount to return to the glade.

'That is what shoulders are made for, Miss, and I was delighted to be
of service,' her blush of pleasure still shewing. 'But did you enjoy dancing
with him? I noticed that he stood up with you a number of times.'

They were seated now on what they regarded as their 'own' tree
trunks, the higher being the mistress's throne, and the lower and smaller
for 'hand-maiden' Alice, who was unpacking the luncheon basket.
Although the sun was out, it was a cold day, and they retained their capes
and hoods.

'I did, Alice, very much, but not more so than the captain and Reginald, and one or two of the other guests. Well, that perhaps is not quite
true,' with a little blush, 'for he holds me in a very special way. But I was
able to be much more my self with him than I had expected,' and here
she gave a little laugh. 'I had thought my knees might turn to jelly. Again,
I think mother's little episode helped me understand that it is all part of
growing up, whether one is seventeen or nearly twenty-two.'

'Talking of guests, Miss, I think we are about to have one that is unexpected.'

'No, Alice, he was more or less expected by me,' responded her mistress.
Then, a little more loudly; 'He may join us if he has a mind. *Wie geht's?*'

'Good-day, Mistress Celia. Well, thank you'

'And a good day to you, Master Manfred. Wouldst thou share a light
repast with us? 'Tis but a humble dish we offer.'

'Verily, Mistress, would I gladly,' and he dismounted, tethered his horse,
and seated him self on a tree stump.

'Alice, I believe we do have an extra platter, please serve a little some
thing for our guest.'

There was mostly silence during the eating, other than politeness concerning the excellent cold collation Cook had put up.

'Alice, please offer the professor a choice of pie, apple or pear.'

'"Manfred",' corrected the professor, looking steadily at Celia, 'and pear would be most welcome.'

'Is it?' queried Celia returning his gaze, calmly.

'It is, if you will have it so.'

'Alice?' and she nodded to them both.

'Will you have a little clotted cream with that fruit pastry, *Manfred?*'

'Alice, the answer is "yes", if I may address your mistress as "Celia".'

Alice glanced towards her mistress, and perceived the faintest inclination of her head.

'You have been accepted and may so address my mistress.'

'I thank you most kindly, though I will resist the temptation to inquire as to what matters the acceptance applies. Do you ride this way often?'

'When the mood so takes us, and the weather be passing fair. And you, Manfred?'

'I usually ride the hills on the other side, but there I meet no-one. Here I meet such engaging company that now it is my choice.'

'Are we, perchance, included in their number?' queried Celia mildly.

'My dear Celia, you and Alice *are* the number, and I shall make it my habit to ride here to this magic place every day from henceforth.'

'Please do not do so on our account, Manfred, for we do not come nearly that often, more like one in several weeks,' and she presented him a warm smile. 'But on another matter, Professor, while we have your attention. We had thought to engage you, Alice and I that is, to instruct her daughter, Mildred, in the arts and sciences. However, Miss Lucy, as perhaps you may have heard, will shortly be on an extended visit to the West end of the county to stay with aunts of Captain Allison, and Mildred is to accompany her.'

The professor shook his head.

'Perhaps, then, you have not heard,' said Celia, watching his expression with a measured interest, 'that my sister and Captain Allison are to be wed?'

The professor paused in mid-sip of drinking the cup of coffee that Alice had passed to him.

'No,' he replied, raising his head to observe Celia directly, 'I had not heard. Please convey to Miss Lucy my pleasure at the announcement.'

'Pleasure? You are not disappointed that she is no longer "available"?'

'Should I be?'

'You had expressed a considerable interest in certain physical aspects of my sister on more than one occasion. I thought perhaps you would be desirous of further exploration. Was I wrong in that assessment?'

With these words and the return to the 'Professor' mode of address, he detected a distinct chilling of the atmosphere, the very last thing he needed now.

'Miss Celia, I confess that I find your sister most desirable; and which red-blooded man would not!'

Here he paused, realizing too late that he had just set a trap for him self, which Celia could be relied upon to spring, for she was very prickly where her sister was concerned, especially if a comparison between the two of them were involved. He took a moment to finish his coffee, and settled on dissemblage as his only hope of escape from a certain verbal broadside which just might sink him.

'Alice, that was quite excellent coffee, for which my thanks to your Cook.'

Out of the corner of his eye he observed a frown forming on Celia's fine features, but he continued to Alice without a pause.

'Now, while you must agree that Miss Lucy has many admirable qualities, it is as surely indisputable that, should she ever leave the county, the crown would instantly pass to your mistress. And is it not also a matter beyond question that your mistress is as talented as Miss Lucy is beautiful?'

'A pretty speech, sir,' responded Celia, dryly. 'Your flattery is open to question, however, as I could suggest several to you who are both more than passing fair and truly accomplished.'

'I beg to differ on that matter, Mistress Celia, for I have never been known to err in the measure of talent. But we shall meet where and as often as you shall choose, and I shall give you the opportunity to discourse on any subject under the sun to demonstrate my point,' and he rose.

'Now I must take my leave, for I have German lessons to prepare for Master Otto. I shall be at this place, or near to it, every morning that my duties do not preclude. Perhaps I shall have the pleasure of your company at one of those. Until such time, I thank you for the delicious and most welcome luncheon, and the pleasure of your delightful company. I bid you farewell, and *auf Wiedersehen.*'

Bowing to each in turn, he mounted and galloped along the crest,

Celia rose to watch in silence until he reached the end, turned and waved, and disappeared. But she did not respond, seemingly deep in contemplation of some weighty matter. Alice, meanwhile, busied her self clearing and packing the remains of the provisions.

As they wound their own way homeward, Alice addressed her mistress a little awkwardly.

'Perhaps I should not tell you this, Miss, but you do have a right to know. Late last evening, in the midst of festivities, I was visiting my room, and I noticed your door ajar. When I checked, there was the professor in your room, as large as life.'

'Really!' exclaimed Celia, 'whatever next. Did he gain access to the studio?'

'No, Miss, for both doors were locked, as you instructed.'

'Thank goodness for that precaution! I suppose he was testing my bed to see if it would fit him?' she responded sarcastically.

'No, Miss. I gave him the rough edge of my tongue, I can tell you, and warned him severely not to do any thing so foolish again. But I do not think he was listening properly, he was so intent on studying the radiator and piping and the wash basin, and the style of your cupboards.'

And they rode on in silence because the mistress did not know quite what to make of that.

Shortly before descending to the orchard, Alice offered her mistress one last query.

'Well, Miss, were you well met? Shall we then journey here more often than heretofore? He did offer to meet and discuss any thing at all with you, just as you were wishing so fervently he would only two nights ago.'

'Perhaps, Alice; on the other hand, perhaps not. I do not relish being taken for granted, especially by him. I will decide what we do when we meet. And I do not need a memory lesson on what I may have indiscreetly and foolishly opined, recently or otherwise,' and she would not be drawn further.

Alice set this unkind response at naught, for she was firmly of the opinion that matters at the glade had gone well; exceeding well. She made several further remarks to draw out her mistress, eventually receiving a dispiriting 'cease and desist' message for her efforts.

This was strange indeed. It was going to entail a good deal more understanding on her part to resolve what she regarded as an inevitable outcome, before any plain sailing was in sight. Her mistress seemed to have no interest at all in him; indeed, even a general distaste for his mention, yet she was quite certain it was to the contrary. Puzzling.

Of the professor's feelings, however, she was in no doubt at all. In which case, Miss Celia was in as great a danger as ever. Indeed, the more so for her failure to realize her true inner feelings – even though she had done exactly that before the Ball. Most perplexing.

This was going to take some careful and conscientious handling if the worst of her own and her ladyship's fears were not to be enacted.

And she resolved to be more alert than ever of her charge.

'Tomorrow, first thing after rising, Alice, I want you to take my chaise into the studio. We shall manage it between us, for I want no-one else involved.'

'Yes, Miss,' replied Alice.

'Lucy and I will breakfast in my room so that we shall not be required to dress for it. After that, Alice, we shall be engaged all day. You may bring us some luncheon to my room at one o'clock, and then tea mid-afternoon when we ring, but no-one is to enter the studio. Is that understood?'

'Yes, Miss.'

Lucy was to leave in two days, and before she did Celia had one more painting, in oils, to be attempted. She was uncertain about many aspects of it, and said so to Lucy, who simply replied,

'Leave it until the moment, and the inspiration will emerge. We will do it together, as we usually do.'

What Lucy did not divulge, was that when Celia was out riding with Alice, she had stolen into the studio to study some of her sister's art folios to settle on a pose. Of course, the Artiste would decide what was to be painted and how the model was to appear, that she did not question. However, she wanted, at least to her self, to get the feel of how it *might* be composed, and given a choice how she would like it to be executed. As her beloved sister's model, she had long ceased to have any qualms of appearing *déshabillée*, although she understood that on this occasion Celia was in all probability going to require that she be *sans vêtements*.

At first embarrassed by the paintings, she had decided it was better to be prepared, for this could well be the last time for such intimacy; and already knew she was going to greatly miss these sessions. Even went so far as to lock all doors, for she intended to study as she was going to be portrayed, walking from her room wearing only an open robe – then quickly discarded. She was thus able to study the poses while reclining on a rug, folio in front of her, critically regarding her bare self in the mirror to compare female forms.

Of these, she determined that although the pose was rather vulgar, her own form was most like the Goya – except for the unusual bosom, breasts wide spread; hers she decided on self-examination were much closer to the Correggio. But she preferred the manner of the Giorgione, with its somewhat shielded hand positions. That settled, she returned every thing as it had been, and simply waited for her sister to name the day and time, happy in her heart that all was going to be well. And she was amazed at her calmness in appearing totally without attire; indeed, looking forward to exhibiting her charms. And she smiled at the swiftness she had become accustomed to showing her body, even now to exhilarating in it.

Celia was already in her smock arranging the red satin fabric on the chaise when Lucy entered from her own room, immediately exclaiming:

'I like the setting, it is lovely. Where did the flowers come from?'

'Mildred scoured the countryside first thing this morning, I believe, then displayed them in your favourite bowl. Quite professional.'

'Quite lovely, too; I am glad she will be accompanying me. She has learnt very quickly how I like to be dressed and coifed, and with every one around me being a stranger, I shall feel much more at home with some one I know to attend me.

'But to the matter in hand,' she continued, eagerly. 'If your work is to be in oils, Celia, we do not want to repeat the last time, where by my silliness I wasted all your effort in preparing the canvas, so let's get straight to it,' and she shed her Chinese gown to reveal her best silk night-gown. 'How would you like me to pose? Like this, perhaps?' stretching out on the chaise, one arm along its back, the other behind her head, examining the result in the long mirror. When satisfied, she rose again and, in a most languid and sensuous manner, removed her nightgown to reveal her natural self, all the while studying her reflection and its responses, as she imagined Alice to have done in seducing Richard.

After a few moments of stretching and turning slightly, hands on hips then on head, to gauge the effects of the movements on her body, she resumed her pose, as completely unself-conscious now as she had been reserved before. But she was not unaware of the effect this performance was having on Celia.

'Will I do, Sis?' smiling sweetly at her.

'You need to bend this knee a little, like so,' said Celia, when she found her voice, quite amazed by the exhibition Lucy had just put on and that it had all started so smoothly. 'One hand under your bosom, there,' as she adjusted it to her satisfaction. And perhaps a cushion behind your head,' and she left to bring one from her room, still shaking her head and thinking to her self, 'and this is my shy sister?' Thus she was unable to observe the amused smile of self-satisfaction on Lucy's countenance. She was getting to like this feeling of winning a hand now and then, and resolved to do more of it.

After settling the pillow and giving her sister a little kiss of encouragement on the forehead, Celia continued.

'One other thing, though, before we get too far. Your lying there so comfortably makes me feel positively overdressed,' and she peeled off her dress and other wear, leaving only her gold necklace. 'Much better, though I ought to have some thing to wipe my hands on, other than skin,' seizing a small apron to tie 'round her waist with a silk tie from her robe. 'There; now to work!'

They stopped and donned their gowns for luncheon when they heard Alice leave the tray in Celia's room, on the stroke of one.

It was a pleasant spring day, so they took their plates out on to the small table on Celia's South terrace to sit in the bright sunshine, sheltered by the new season's growth of ivy and the climbing roses that peered over the balcony edge.

Luncheon finished, Celia rang for coffee, which was brought by Mildred to the terrace and, at Celia's request, two small rugs, and a pillow each.

Celia positioned a rug on an area of stone paving already well warmed in the sunlight, placed the pillow against the wall, and lay down.

'For the first time this year,' she commented as she opened her gown and apron to savour the sun's warm rays, 'and it feels wonderful. My skin is alive again.'

Lucy, not to be outdone, immediately imitated her.

'It is not going well, is it, Sis? Why is that?'

'Not particularly,' replied her sister. 'I have the background very nicely already, although I really prefer to do the central figure first. I have the outline, of course, but today I do not seem to be able to "see" you very clearly at all. As to why, that is more difficult to say. I believe it is a question of passion. Things have changed for each of us, but especially for you, dear Sister.'

'But we still mean as much to each other. Surely that has not changed?'

'Yes, and no, Luce. You have received a proposal for your hand – an eminently acceptable one, I might add – and quite properly embraced it. For you it is a fork in the path of life, one that will increasingly take you in a different direction. While we may not have changed in our selves, you must now attune your ear to a different piper. But as I continue on my now solitary path, my melody will become discordant to you, as my own fortunes swell or diminish.'

'Never,' broke in Lucy, shaking her head violently. 'I know a lot has been happening of late and I have had so little time to think, but your song will be always in my heart.'

'Perhaps, but even when you do have time,' replied her sister, without enthusiasm, 'you may find your tune directed to a special person. Now, time for one more cup of coffee, then it is back to work.'

'Strange that you should call it that,' mused Lucy, as she took her place once more, 'when before – once I had got over my silliness, that is – posing for you was really a great joy.'

'You may have just put your finger on the life force, the secret behind the greatest art: Passion and Joy,' Celia replied, taking up her palette and brush. 'And if my efforts are to be fruitful, we need to recreate the passion in your soul and the joy in your expression. I *could* recite you a fable, but because we are working in oils, I doubt that I could keep it up that long – or you for that matter, however entrancing a tale I spun,' and she stood for a moment in thought.

'Though perhaps there is another way. This time you could do it for your self. I am sure you remember the tale; all you have to do is put your self back in it. So close your eyes for a moment, Luce, and imagine that you are back in your magic orchard, in your half-draped gown, with the apple just plucked in your fingers.

'Your prince is approaching,' she continued, warming to the subject as she mixed her colours, 'that is now Charles, of course, to make lo . . .' and her voice trailed away, for Lucy, to Celia's astonishment, had quite the opposite reaction. Instead of smiling and blossoming as intended, she had grown quite pale, eyes wide, and seemed to shrivel on the couch.

Indeed, she moved a hand involuntarily to partly cover her nakedness.

'Whatever is the matter, Luce,' exclaimed Celia in consternation as her precious model wilted before her very eyes.

Lucy opened her mouth to say some thing, but no sound emerged. She tried once more, but still without success. Then before Celia could intercede, she sprang up, snatched up her robe, and ran into her room, banging the door behind her.

It was some minutes before Celia could marshal her own whirling thoughts, recover her gown and follow her sister, to find her curled up on the bed, gown tightly wrapped around her, sobbing quietly.

'Whatever did I say, dear Sister, to upset you so,' sitting on the bed and resting her hand on Lucy's damp forehead, but Lucy simply shook off her hand and buried her face in the pillow, leaving Celia dazed and more perplexed than ever, trying to recall the exact words she had used, playing them over in her mind.

'Oh, my God,' she whispered to her self as the inwardly reiterated words echoed in her head: 'your prince – that is now . . .' 'Oh, my God,' and she rose to her feet, struck dumb in the dread of what she had so innocently perpetrated.

Stunned, she retraced her steps to the studio, standing for a moment seeing nothing.

'You idiot,' she said through clenched teeth as the full import crowded in on her; 'you stupid, half-witted *dolt!*'

And at these words, seething now with an uncontrollable rage at her thoughtlessness, she seized the jar of turpentine and brushes she was using and hurled it with all her strength against the wall, where it smashed into a thousand rainbow fragments and then, her anger spent as quickly as it had arisen, she sank to her knees and buried her face in her hands and sobbed uncontrollably.

There was a knock on the passage door, and Alice's voice inquired,

'Is every thing all right, Miss?'

'No! Every thing is *not* all right, Alice. Just leave me alone.' But thus distracted, she rose to re-enter Lucy's room. 'I am dreadfully sorry, Sister, dear,' tears streaming down her face, 'I just do not know how I could be so stupid. I never thought.'

'Shh,' whispered Lucy, pulling her down to sit on the bed, 'you mustn't upset your self so. It is all right, really. And it wasn't your fault; I was simply not ready to make that leap, that is all. Just because some body says he wants me to be his lifelong companion, doesn't mean that all my desires are suddenly transferred to him.

'When you spoke one name back there just as the "Prince" of my dreams were conjuring up another, I took fright, that is all. Suddenly I thought it was all going horribly wrong, that I had made a terrible mistake. Because, as you must already know, I still suppose Manfred fulfilling those fantasies, especially as he is the only one to have touched me in that intimate manner,' and she observed the flicker of pain as it crossed her sister's tear-streaked face. 'Does that shock you?'

'No,' replied her sister, dejectedly, eyes downcast, 'it doesn't shock me. One cannot forget the only one, and I know you need time to . . . to . . .' and her voice just drifted away into sadness.

'Does it wound you then, that I still have longing for him, in memory of those touches?' she said, softly.

Celia looked at her with large, melancholy eyes, 'Wound me?' but seemed unable to grasp the meaning or to form any words of her own.

'Do you think I do not *know*?' whispered Lucy.

'Know?' echoed Celia. 'Know *what*?'

'Why, about you and Manfred, of course; how you feel about him.'

'How *could* you know,' gasped Celia, 'when I do not – except angry and frustrated, of course!'

'Because, you silly goose, I have eyes, and a heart. I have known for some time.'

'But you can not have. I mean . . . he . . . that is . . . we, mean nothing to each other. He is using me I know, first to get to you, and now pretends to have some feelings for me just to . . . to . . .'

A long pause, then, with some force, a rushed,

'The proposal might still be a mistake, you know. It might still go awry, in some inexplicable way,' and she wrinkled her brow in contemplation. After some moments' further reflection, she switched back to the root of the question.

'And you do not mind, if I . . . if we . . . I mean, you are not hurt, after what he was . . . to you?'

'Mind? Of course I do not *mind*, you foolish girl. I am just so happy for you, for now we both have some one. And no, I am not making a mistake,' she responded quietly, taking her sister's hand in both of hers. 'I have known for some time that he was not for me – although I had incredibly strong feelings for him and what he could do to me, inside. Indeed, that was when I realized that he was indeed *bad* for me, because we did not see the same things in each other, and that mismatch was bound to end in disaster, especially for my self.

'And believe it or not, dear Sister, I owe that insight to your studied and practised education of me in body and spirit; belatedly recognized on my part, I confess, but very successful in the ultimate.

'One more thing before we leave Manfred. I also know, somehow, deep inside me, of your conflict, of the struggle within your self to protect me from what you knew was not right, while at the same time denying your self, disavowing your own feelings, even to the point of making your self ill for fear of wounding me. I treasure all that you have done for me, sweet Sister, and the sacrifices you have made in my honour.'

Celia opened her mouth to protest, but Lucy put a finger on her sister's lips.

'As for Charles, I also know he is very *right* for me. Although I do not yet love him, I do treasure him and believe I may in the fullness of time, for we start on an even footing, learning each of the other.

'But I misspoke a moment ago, for Manfred is *not* the only one to have touched me in that intimate way. Which brings me at the last to the one most precious to me of all,' and she paused, expectantly.

'And that one is?' queried Celia, with a shocked expression, for she knew of no other young man, certainly not one who had partaken of her charms as Manfred had. And she would have known, if it were Charles or one of their other young cohorts.

'You really do not know?' exclaimed her sister in surprise, sitting now, her gown fully open, her pain and its memory all dissipated with the lively conversation. But still Celia shook her head, wonderingly.

'No, I have no idea who he could be. I thought I knew all of your . . .'

'Then let me provide you a hint,' broke in Lucy, stroking her sister's face and throat with soft fingers, then gently down to her bosom, which swelled to the familiar touch. 'It is no-one but your self, silly! Did you suppose I would instantly forsake my own true companion; forget all that we have been – may still be – to each other? The pleasures and joys we have made together? Unless, of course,' eyeing her sister gravely, 'you so crave Manfred's passion – or have already experienced it to your person – that you no longer have love for your little sister?' And she raised her eyebrows in mock question.

Celia did not reply, except to stroke Lucy's cheek and slowly shake her head, while a solitary tear rolled down her cheek, to be quickly swept away by Lucy.

'No, not with him, yet; and certainly not with any other. It was only you he wanted, and I was certain he was not the right one. Besides, I do not believe he feels that way about me, as he did so powerfully with you.'

'That is not at all how I see it, dear Sister, as I observed him at the Ball, where he rarely took his eyes off you, although he was very discreet about it. You will, I am certain, experience that for your self at the appropriate time, although I feel honour bound to caution you as you did for my self.

'But that is all over now. Come, you silly child,' renewing her gentle stroking once more, 'it is time to be happy, not sad. You could not be my true sister and believe that I would forget you so quickly; ready to give my self to Charles before the ink is even put to the marriage contract – let alone dried? *Que sera, sera*; but that is for then; this is for now, just us, together.

'So let me comfort you as we shall always be in our innermost hearts,' and she ran her hands caressingly once more inside Celia's gown. 'Besides,' she whispered, kissing the damp cheeks and eyelids, 'it is you that I have enjoyment in and who grant my yearnings in answer. That other can come later, if it comes at all,' as she eased her sister's gown over her shoulders and pulled her gently to her own self, before reclining.

'There is one thing more, dearest Sister, to illustrate that you care for me still, for that you have yet to affirm', she continued in a whisper made breathless by her fondling of Celia, 'to demonstrate that he has not already supplanted me in your affections. And that is . . .'

But her words ended with a sharp intake of breath as Celia's lips consumed her breasts, then passionately replicated her own actions, caressing with such consummate skill inside the gown as to draw an involuntary cry of pleasure from Lucy's lips, before removing the garment entirely, and with it, all further restrictions to their ensuing impulsive intimacy.

'That was wonderful, simply wonderful, Luce,' in a whisper, her breathing still irregular. 'I do not know what to say.'

'For me, too,' whispered Lucy in equally breathless return, 'but I *do* know. It amazes me that you always perceive so wholly what I crave and then delight it to perfection,' and Celia simply flushed with pleasure at this knowledge of her mastery of her sister's gratification. 'It may be this pleasurable one day with Charles,' Lucy continued more soberly, 'or it may not. I only pray,' she whispered, 'that he is half as gentle with me as you. For to tell the truth, Sis,' holding her bosom to throbbing bosom in a fierce embrace once more, 'I am not really looking forward to that other thing with a man.

'But until then, whatever the future holds, I shall always celebrate the joy we occasion in each other,' and with a final playful rub and squeeze, she rose and put out her hand to her sister.

'Come, Celia Michaelangela, we have a painting to finish while the passion and joy are extant, assuming that you left any thing intact in the studio,' and arms around each other they entered laughing, neither finding a gown necessary to resume their interrupted session.

In mid-afternoon they broke for tea on the terrace, for Lucy to relax to a more natural posture and Celia to ease her fingers and spine, both welcoming the sun, gowns open to receive its spring warmth on their exposed bodies. They were thus relaxed when the tea and fresh-baked scones arrived, courtesy of Mildred, who greeted them properly and then retired, showing no element of surprise at their casual lack of attire, although the young ladies did exchange raised eyebrows.

In the studio once more, Lucy surprised her sister.

'Before I recline, let us replenish that special mood,' opening her gown to position her sun-warmed body against her sister's, curve to curve, enjoying the feeling of it quickly coming to life against her own, before eagerly settling into position. And the session continued.

'There,' said Celia, 'I believe I have captured the essence of your inner sensual spirit, and I can finish it by my self, now. I think I have some thing we can both be pleased with.

'Before we bathe, though, let me light these candles and show you some thing,' and she took her sister's hand to stand side by side before the large mirror, placing her arm around her sister's shoulder while Lucy did the same.

'Notice, Luce, though I am the taller by almost two inches, how your waist is at the same level as mine. It is your long legs, one of your loveliest features. And here,' running her fingers over Lucy's hip from waist to mid-thigh, 'you are beautifully curved, especially just there. See how my bone pokes out a bit at the side and the front, while yours is perfectly smooth. And your belly,' laying her hand on it, 'nicely curved here, not too flat or rounded, into a truly tiny waist.

'But this is your best part,' she concluded, moving her mirrored hand slowly upward to cup Lucy's bosom in one palm. 'Firm and exquisitely shaped, with a good division, too. I envy you there. While I am larger in form, you are larger here than me,' turning slightly, so that they touched at that point, 'and more pink; mine are more nearly brown. And your desire is more evident, and harder,' circling with her finger to demonstrate that very fact before turning her sister's body fully until they touched and responded. 'It is no wonder you drove Manfred to behave so badly,' and Lucy blushed at the memory of feelings she was still trying to master.

'But do not worry, sweet Sister, you will drive Charles just as wild, probably have already if we but knew it, but he has his position to think of. When he sees you like this, though,' running a finger down each side, 'you are in for quite a time of it, mark my words. But remember this, Sis: never take him for granted; men like to be teased, too – especially husbands.

'Recall if you will, how Alice did it; nothing at all on under her thin dress, and open at that to his *accidental* touch? That sort of thing drives them wild, just as it did her Richard. Remember, also, when you were in your private orchard waiting for your prince? You were undressed just enough to show what pleasures were in store for the right man. Not too much or too little, but it must retire easily, just like Alice's dress – and your drape,' and she gave her sister a big hug.

'But I am truly envious that you are already embarked on your journey of requited love, while I . . .' and her voice trailed away as she saw some thing in the mirror.

'Stay right there, Luce,' and she rushed back to her easel, returning with her palette and a fine brush. 'Now, turn around for a minute, while I . . .' and Lucy felt the faint tickle of the brush on her throat.

'No, do not move. I shall be only a second.' But it was more like several minutes. 'There, now you can look.'

And Lucy found to her astonishment that she now had an emerald necklace with a fine gold chain around her throat. But she was too overwrought to comment.

'Thank you, Sister; this is a day I shall remember forever,' was all she could manage, but that was enough to bring tears to both their eyes.

'Bath time!' Celia declared, and arms around each other in the candlelight that each carried, they passed into the bathroom to indulge themselves before going down to dinner.

Kneeling and facing the other, first came the careful soaping and massaging of every curve and hollow – mutually and impulsively under-taken and in carefully orchestrated unison.

Afterwards, it was a time of sensual play in the hot water, during which Celia whispered:

'I hope you realize now, Lucy, the importance of your own body, both to your self and to your Charles. He will appreciate it the more if you know how to use it to the maximum for your self. Then you must teach him how you want to be pleasured, as we have just done for each other. Men, being engrossed with their own gratification, do not understand that a woman's needs are different, and will not care to, unless you instruct them, and it will be just so with Charles.'

'Thanks to you, Sis, I am now much more aware of that. Also now that I have some experience in these personal matters of one's inner being and emotions and how they can be delighted and assuaged, I shall feel so much more confident with Charles and, as you said, show him how it is for me. I only hope that he listens. Do men listen, Cel?'

But Celia shook her head. 'I really do not know, Sis. I have a feeling that they are too involved in their own conquest of our bodies – even when we have made them freely available – that they hear very little. Perhaps we need to ask Alice about that. She must certainly know, even if it *was* only the one time for her. In fact, now that I think of it, there are several things along that line that we need of our Alice.'

The drying and powdering was equally attentive, and they silently revelled in each other, knowing that it was perhaps for the last time. After one final last embrace, they parted for their own rooms – ringing their respective bells as they did so – to be dressed for dinner; Celia by faithful mother Alice, Lucy by apprentice daughter Mildred. The latter had become as accustomed to her mistress' natural form as her mother had, sometimes wishing aloud – to Lucy's considerable embarrassment – that her own developing body would ripen as beautifully in its 'curves and hollows'.

And from Celia, while she was being dressed:

'Alice, I have a very special bedtime subject for you tonight.'

'Yes, Miss. And what might that be?'

'It concerns your Richard.'

'Really, Miss? But I have already told you every thing about him, Miss.'

'Well, not quite *every thing*, Alice; but I will provide the exact nature of the questions later. Also, for the very first time, there will be two of us asking and listening, so you need to be wide awake.' All of which puzzled Alice considerably, as the two young ladies proceeded arm-in-arm down to dinner.

When Alice arrived to prepare her mistress for bed, she found the two of them seated comfortably at Celia's small table, drinking coffee, chatting animatedly and giggling frequently as at some shared hidden thing.

'Please attend Miss Lucy first, Alice; she has brought her things with her.'

And indeed she had – except that it was hardly night attire. For the top, a light summer frock that had seen its best days and was now minus its sleeves, had been cut off just at the bust, but so as to be wholly inadequate of coverage. Below, the skirt had likewise been brazenly removed well above the knee and with a large opening to expose the belly. And, surprise, there was no more.

All the while she was attending her, Miss Lucy pranced around as her mistress was wont to do, frequently examining her body in the mirror and teasing it, before twirling away again. This was a Lucy that Alice had no idea even existed!

When it was Miss Celia's turn, Alice was thus not the slightest surprised when *she* chose two silk scarves and two velvet ribbons. *This* was going to be an interesting evening!

But the two young ladies had not finished for, after a whispered conversation between them, Miss Celia announced,

'We, Alice, are of the opinion, that as we are going to discuss our feminine selves,' and here they broke into unrestrained giggles again, 'that, to be fair and so that we are equal, you also should be in your night attire, although you may add a dressing gown, if you so choose.' And they would not budge from that position until she acquiesced.

Alice was initially bewildered by all this sudden high-spirited behaviour from both young ladies (especially Miss Lucy), but, hearing their laughter floating up from the room directly below her own, thought to rise to the challenge and play their little game, wherever it was leading – and she had a pretty good idea where Miss Celia would take it concerning womanly feelings!

But Miss Lucy? That was some thing she could not fathom, and found her curiosity piqued to the point of being unwilling to resist. Besides, she was not going to be bested by her young charges in that manner; she was not *that* much older than they, and two – or in this case three – could play at that game. After all, they were all young women, unmarried and thus equal in that respect, and if they could not talk openly of that sort of thing in the intimacy of a boudoir, then who could, and she smiled once more.

As she disrobed – this time 'down to her skin' (and she smiled at the connection) – she lit an extra candle and, holding it close to illuminate her self, examined her body in the half mirror her mistress had so thoughtfully provided.

'Passable,' she mused, not the equal of either of the young ladies, of course, but then, neither had borne and nursed a child. Considering every thing, her figure was a credit to her – for she tried to look after her self properly for their sakes, and Mildred's.

Now, nodding to her reflection as fresh laughter rose from below and feeling more than a match for them, she entered into the spirit of whatever the two of them had in mind.

'Just the thing,' she murmured as she chose a short, low-cut, light summer frock from which she had removed the sleeves and replaced them with shoulder straps. Indeed, it did look good, the mirror smiled back, perfect for the occasion, for it was a mild evening and quite warm in Miss Celia's room.

The young ladies were already in bed, sitting cross-legged with several pillows behind them for comfort, looking at one of Miss Celia's more explicit art books. There was also another pillow at the bottom of the bed, which Celia indicated was for her to sit on, cross-legged.

'You have taken so long, Alice, that we quite thought you were not coming!' said Celia, petulantly. 'And you have on that dreadful old cotton dressing gown that should have been burnt long ago!'

'If that is the welcome and consideration I am to receive, Miss Celia, perhaps I should not be here at all,' in a pretended sulk, and she turned to leave.

'Alice, Alice, do not be so huffy; now that you are here, you had better *stay*. But I must say, I am a little disappointed in your attire.'

'You would like me to sit here, Miss?' she inquired sweetly, indicating the cushion, and Celia nodded. 'Cross-legged, like your selves?' another nod, 'and preferably without my one-and-only dressing gown, is that right?'

'Well, yes, Alice. But only if you would feel comfortable that way, of course,' she replied, curious as to the meaning of all this unusual courtesy, for these days Alice usually gave as good as she got. But she understood immediately when Alice, now sitting cross-legged as were them selves, emerged in her short gown that revealed all too clearly that she was wearing no more under her light dress than they.

'Does this satisfy your requirements of suitable attire for this special conversation, Miss Celia?' she inquired impishly.

'Indeed, Alice, I must say that I am greatly astonished. I did not think you had it in you to be so . . . so *daring* as to be otherwise only in your skin. So, yes, I am more than satisfied, and thank you for being so agreeable in the matter. I trust that we can retain that feeling for the remainder of the evening, for we have many challenges of the spirit for you.'

'Thank you, Miss. I always try to accommodate these woman-to-woman matters, if I am able,' Alice replied with a smile – although it was a little more cautious than she had intended it to be. But, in for a penny, in for a pound.

'Now, we wish to ask you some questions about your Richard; personal questions. We know what makes us happy with regard to our bodies,' and she turned to smile at Lucy. 'But you see, Alice,' who did not see at all for the moment, 'while we know many things about men, we know nothing about their *bodies* and how to pleasure them, or how they make love to a woman – and you do.' And it was instantly crystal clear what all the hilarity was about.

'But I can not talk about that, Miss,' gasped Alice. 'It is not . . .'

'Proper?' prompted her mistress.

'Yes, Miss. I mean, no, Miss. It isn't proper, and I shall not do it.'

'That is very mean-spirited of you, Alice. I did not expect you to deny us your wisdom and experience on this delicate matter. Should I inquire then of her ladyship?'

Alice paled. 'Oh, no, Miss. Not that.'

'So how shall we acquire the knowledge? Do you suggest that we ask Reginald what would please him? Or do you prefer that we remain ignorant until our wedding night?'

Alice was silent for several minutes, thinking over the matter. They decidedly had a point, for neither her ladyship nor Mr. Reginald was an imaginable candidate. Indeed, she shuddered at both those thoughts. She was certainly in possession of the 'facts of life', as they say. Was it right then to withhold what they sought to know, quite reasonably, on the grounds of some vague 'impropriety'? She had been in that position her self, and much regretted that there was no-one to whom she could turn.

She knew the answers, of course, but how to frame them? That was the difficulty, the embarrassment of description. Returning to the present, she found her self unconsciously shaking her head – and saw the young ladies looking to her in some anxiety, hanging onto each other in apprehension of her impending refusal.

'Very well, Miss,' and at their huge sigh of relief, she relaxed into a smile, returned in full measure by each as they hugged each other in anticipation and delight.

'I will respond to your questions as best as I can, although you must give me time to express them in my own way. But only if we extinguish all the candles, so that we remain masked to each other. There is a good moon tonight, for I saw her rising from my window while I was changing,' and she rose and plunged the room into as dark as it could be with a full moon joining their little gathering through the panes.

It was a while before their eyes accustomed them selves to the moonbeams cascading across the counterpane and before they ceased giggling. But in the meantime they observed her full silhouette through the gown against the moonlight, head haloed by that very moon, confirming her body to be as unclothed as their own, occasioning another little giggle and a suggestive hug between them.

'Now,' began Alice, unaware of the saucy picture she presented, 'I shall tell my story again, starting with my dress, but adding some of the little details that earlier modesty dictated should be left unspoken. Then you can interrupt me as you think fit, with any question you wish answered. Will that satisfy your curiosity?' and they both nodded eagerly, eyes shining in the moonlight.

While the silvery light shortened as the moon rose, higher and higher, until it was no longer directly illuminating the bed, or the rug, or even the room, they did indeed ask all their questions.

'How did this happen, why was that so, how did that feel?' mutually checking each others' bodies to verify Alice's projected feelings. 'How many times could he do that, how would they know when he was satisfied, what if he wasn't?' 'til finally they were silent. And Alice rose to light a single candle before returning to her position.

'Thank you, Alice,' said Lucy, speaking almost for the first time, for Celia had asked the most penetrating questions, 'that was most explicit, and most valuable, though I will probably only fully appreciate it when I experience it for my self in a little while with my betrothed,' to which

Alice nodded in agreement. 'However, I must add that, without the further womanly knowledge that Celia has so kindly bestowed upon me,' (and here they gently stroked each other's bare bosom, their flimsy coverings long gone), 'I would have been like a frightened rabbit before my new husband on the wedding night. A very bad start to the marriage. But, a further question if I may.' And Alice nodded her acceptance.

'How did *you* know to do all this with your Richard, if no-one had instructed you?'

'A very good question, Miss, though much of it comes quite naturally to a young woman. However, you forget, Miss, that Richard and I both lived in the same cramped house, so that not only we were very comfortable with each other's presence, we also knew a little of the other's body from the sheer proximity of it all. Besides, when you are that close to some one you love, Miss, some things are just "felt", you do not need explanation.' And Lucy nodded her understanding in the pale candle glow.

'Now, Miss Lucy, may I add some thing which I think will be of great value to you, even though it may shock you a little?'

'Please do, Alice, though I did not think there could be much more to shock us after that *most explicit* undertaking of your conquest – or was it a seduction?'

'It was both, Miss, because we had the same intention and the same desire at the same time – which indeed helps to make my point. Do not expect Mr. Charles to make love to you that very first night, for he may be quite shy, too – and I note your surprise. Men can be very shy, indeed – is that not so, Miss Celia? Think if you will of your Mr. Reginald. Do you think he knows or is prepared for any of this?' to which Celia simply snorted in derision.

'So again I make my point. Thus it is not to be assumed that Capt. Charles has had any experience of his own with a woman – experience of the full and complete nature we have been discussing between my self and my lover.

'Now recall that proximity I spoke of,' and they both nodded, Celia as interested as her younger sister. 'Further, imagine the scene, Richard and I living in the same two rooms, cooking and eating together, reading and learning together at the same table – oft-times from the same book – being no more than a few feet apart for all of two years as we grew to love each other in the spiritual sense.

'But some where along the line, we gradually became aware of each other in a different way, some thing was stirring in each of our bodies. It took only his statement of my being a mere child to break those bonds of restraint. To me, that was the challenge – and the opportunity – for which my maidenly body was waiting.'

And the silence was broken only by their breathing as the listeners were once more drawn into Alice's private world of love and the feelings of the body, while she experienced it again to her self, needing for some long moments to wipe her eyes with the hem of her night-dress, careless in her reverie that she was wearing nothing under it, charming her audience to the point that they were compelled to stroke each other to assuage their mutual excitement.

'Where was I? Oh, yes, I was talking about Captain Charles. So you see, Miss Lucy, that nothing even approaching that can occur between your self and the Captain. You will enter the marriage bed – each from his or her own side – meeting in that sense as complete strangers, neither knowing what to expect from the other – a *very* poor start to a new life of togetherness!

'So here is my counsel. I strongly recommend, Miss Lucy, that you *insist* on having your own bedchamber and bathing facilities before the start of your marriage. You are both shocked, I can see, but let me explain my reasoning, and then you will see that my judgment is the correct one. And to demonstrate that, I will give you four examples, three old and one new.'

'You naturally wish your marriage to be a successful one in the bedchamber sense. But if it is full of disappointment – especially after this beautiful one with your sister – nothing will seem right, and you will become sour and disgruntled with every thing and every one around you, sorry you ever married. But handled properly, it could be near as joyful as you now have.'

'So, the first example of a successful and happy one is my own, where we lived side by side, getting to know and be comfortable with each other for more than a year – and you know the rest.

'Now the second is your self and the Captain. Suppose Richard and I had met only two or three months before, had never really been together except as guests at a soirée or two, and then always chaperoned so that he never touched me in a sensual manner – or any thing close to it. Given that, each as ignorant as the other, do you think we could have made love like that? A complete disaster even before we started! I probably never would have loved him, and even though still married, might have soon sought an understanding paramour to satisfy my *real* needs as a woman. And that situation is most probably the cause of failure of many such marriages!

'Understood so far?' and they both nodded.

'Good. Now, next comes one much, much closer to home, two young ladies I know well, one called Celia, the other called Lucinda. Look at you now, body to bare body, as close a union as two ladies can get. Would this have been acceptable, Miss Lucy, say a few weeks – or even some months – after your arrival? Not only would it have been impossible for you to agree to Miss Celia's amorous advances, it would almost certainly have caused you to flee in shock of such indecency.

'Note that it has taken almost a year for each of you to reach this state of caress, after much closeness – and little by little at that. The scene that I witnessed on the island so recently, takes a long, long time to achieve. Most married couples I suspect *never* reach what you have, even after twenty or thirty years of marriage. Either it is achieved as your selves have done or never.

'Now do you understand my meaning?' and Lucy and Celia looked at each other with a sense of wonderment. 'And well you might, for you are both extraordinarily fortunate to have achieved such a state of mutual joy.

'The last is some thing quite shocking; couples with a truly *bad* start to their marriage such as a poor choice of partner, financial difficulties to the point of poverty, or in the bedchamber sense finding they did not even like each other.

'In one married couple I know of, he forced his new bride night after night simply to satisfy his desires – and that in a matter of minutes, with no thought or consideration for her feelings. It was only animal lust; she was there simply for his male pleasure, and she quickly grew to hate him, and finally just left.

'I know this will upset you, Miss Celia, but this is not just the poor. You might well find your self forcibly married (and equally nightly assaulted) to an older Earl or Duke, who neither loves nor cares a fig for your sensual feelings,' at which her mistress went quite pale, knowing full well that it could be so.

'You see, Miss, men are quick to passion, eager to satisfy their carnal desire for it has nothing to do with love as we know it; nothing at all, and we will have received nothing in that brief and dreadful union. We might just as well be women of the street for all he cares about us – and you may easily see how hateful that would be, especially after your own increasingly passionate intimacy.

'So it is up to you, Miss Lucy, to see that it does not happen that way. I know the Captain is not like that, but the point has to be made. However, I shall advise how to ensure your mutual love in a little while,' and Lucy gave a small gasp of relief!

'Now, the other side of that horrid picture is that we women are *leisurely* to passion; we delight in coming to our pleasure slowly, gradually rising in enjoyment over quite a long period until we reach that point when we are ready for that final moment of ecstasy. I know, for I have watched you find that the greatest enchantment; the gradually teasing and titil-lating of each other until that peak is reached, when it *must* be released,' and they both nodded to that, smiling at each other in acceptance of that remembered joy.

'So my firm counsel, Miss Lucy, is give him time to get used to you as a person. Just be pleasant, and whatever you do, Miss, do not frighten or shame him by showing your self to be more "aware" in these matters than he is.

'There is one last requirement for your satisfaction. There must be a place where you can teach your new lover. Let me explain. While he is Master of the house in the accepted sense, *you* must be the mistress of the bedchamber and all that occurs between you.

'So, where is all this to take place?' looking directly at Lucy, who only remained silent.

'Simply that you must have a separate boudoir as part of your suite of rooms and bedchamber, and some where nearby for Mildred. It becomes another of those requirements necessary for him to gain your affection, little by little, in the manner you desire it and have grown to love with your sister. After all, you two do not wait for midnight to mutual discover each other, so why should the Captain and your self?

'It is here that you gradually get closer, personally and physically, as you make your self "available" little by little, so it may take several months or more to find your selves in bed together. Even then you may – perhaps even should – draw the line, for it must be in *your* bedchamber, not his, thereby remaining mistress of the ensuing joy, then or later as *you* choose.

'I might add that there is one good ploy to ensure his understanding of your needs as a woman, and that is to insist that he remain clothed, or mostly so, while he brings your self to the peak of fulfilment – or as close to it as you wish – to your choosing. Repeated a few times will ensure his understanding, you may be sure of that.'

'But you said there was a new example, which you have yet to reveal to us?'

'Quite right, Miss Celia, but I have just done so, which is that the future Miss Lucy must manage, arrange, plan – with guile – to a successful conclusion. Do you think you can achieve that, Miss Lucy?'

'I do not know, Alice, to be quite honest. But I see that I must – or live a miserable life for as long as I live.

'Well spoken, Miss. Make sure he understands it is for *your* pleasure, too, and he will soon realize that if he wishes to make you happy as his bride and life-long companion, he will understand that he is being taught the way *things must be* for that success.

'I judge him to be a sensitive, generous, gentle and thoughtful man. I believe you are most fortunate, Miss Lucy, to have such a man love you as he quite evidently does,' at which compliment to her betrothed, Lucy blushed most prettily.

'Which reminds me; one other thing before we close. You remember my answering your question as to whether it hurt, and I said "yes"?'

Here they both nodded.

'Well, although that was so in my case, it will not happen to your selves for reasons that I do not have to explain. I realize that is a good deal to absorb and remember, and I shall be available to answer any further questions you may have. But do you understand all that, Miss?'

'Indeed I do, Alice,' said Lucy, 'and that is a most timely warning, for which I thank you most humbly. The last thing I would wish to portray is any knowledge of such intimate things, and I shall be as circumspect as you suggest,' and she leaned forward to give Alice a kiss on both cheeks, followed by a big hug, dislodging Alice's gown strap from one shoulder in the process.

'Now, all that was addressed to Miss Lucy,' said Alice, turning to Celia. 'None of that will apply to Mr. Manfred, Miss, if I am any judge of such things,' and Celia simply smiled and nodded her agreement.

'Alice, how would you like me to paint you?'

'Like what, Miss?'

'Well, just as you are, for now we understand why Richard was so captivated by your natural form as to find it irresistible. We are quite delighted by it and approve of his excellent taste. Indeed, in this candle-light we find you especially appealing with one strap off your shoulder, so that one side of your adorable bosom is presenting it self to *our* private viewing.'

Alice was horrified as she looked down to find that was indeed the case, while they simply giggled happily to each other at her obvious embarrassment.

'Further, do you recall that, a while past while you were telling of your self and Richard, you were drawn to wipe your moist eyes?'

'Uh, no, Miss,' in some surprise. 'And . . .'

'With the hem of your night-dress?'

For a moment she was mystified by this remark – until she glanced down, instantly reminded of how careful she had been upon seating her self that her private person remained completely covered, for now it was any thing but, revealing all.

'That is quite all right, Alice, my sister and I were quite delighted by your further explicit display, and why Richard was unable to resist bestowing his gift unto you that night.'

'As you have already fully observed my natural charms,' and they both nodded, 'it seems I have little to lose, so I shall join you,' and to their astonishment, Alice peeled off her only garment so that she was as naked as they.

'Now that we are as three equal sisters, do you approve, ladies? Do I have a form that is worthy of a woman's enviable glance and a man's desiring?'

'Alice, you do indeed. Any man would be most fortunate to get you into his marriage bed.'

'Thank you, Miss Celia, I do appreciate that. Now to the last points. There are three, and, unhappily, I do not have the answer to any of them. One is for each of you but different, and one for you both together.'

'First is to Miss Lucy. Do not expect to achieve that level of love-making you have with your sister. The reason is quite simple: only a woman can read another woman's feelings, and respond to them.

'So do not seek some thing that is not within your reach. Just enjoy that which he can give you,' and she bent forward to give Lucy a reassuring hug and a kiss on the cheek, forgetting that she was as much without clothing as Lucy. Thus at the moment of contact, it was their bosoms that first touched, so that each felt a sudden shock at the contact; Lucy because it was no longer quite that way with her sister, Alice because that was the first touch since Richard those many long years ago, and she returned to her place with a deep blush on her cheeks, the heat of Lucy's hands on her body, and a decided throb in her breast.

'So I see that you are not quite so "dead" as you thought in our Sylvan Glade, Alice,' said Celia in her softest voice, 'for do I note a clearly discernable level of excitement in your bosom?'

Alice's blush deepened as she covered her bosom with her hands, then realizing that it was not only futile, but decidedly foolish.

'Yes, Miss, you do indeed, and I am as surprised as your self.'

'Then I am pleased for you, Alice.'

'Thank you, Miss. However, now I come to a subject with which you will *not* be pleased, but it must be said. It concerns the professor, Mr. Manfred. First, I know that you are in love with him, second, that you desire him to your person – the which he clearly returns in a most salacious manner – and third, he is not in love with you.'

'How can you say that, Alice!' replied Celia hotly. 'How can you know what is in his heart? And do you know what salacious means? It is quite insulting.'

'Firstly, I know he is not in love with you because love is easy to recognize. It is in the eyes, the manner, in every aspect of a person's being – as the Captain is with Miss Lucy,' at which the latter blushed, but pleased, just the same.

'Secondly, yes, I know that it means "lustful, lecherous", and that is his intention toward you, Miss. Love has no part in it, being replaced by lust in his eyes, his manner, and is clear in all of those other things.'

'Alice, you are speaking nonsense, and I shall not listen any more,' putting her hands over her ears.

'Miss Lucy, would you like to comment, or would you rather stay out of the matter?'

'No, I can comment,' and turning to her sister, 'Alice is quite correct, Celia. Manfred seems not to know the meaning of love. While I dreamed of it, he desired only my body, all of it, at once, to use and abuse as he wished. Love had no part in it,' and she reached for her sister's hand but was rejected.

There were many, many moments of silence, except for faint sobs from Celia, whose eyes were now covered to hide the tears that ran down her cheeks. Finally Alice found the courage to embrace her sad mistress, fully aware – or so she thought – of what it might do to her emotions.

'There, there, Miss,' as their bosoms touched, again with that shock of contact, but this time much stronger as Celia pulled her in even closer, cheek to cheek, hands firmly around her bottom, unable to break it even if she had wanted to, wondering whether 'lustful' could apply to women as well as men.

Gradually the tears grew less, and Celia became calm as she began to realize the truth of Alice's assessment and her sister's confirmation of it. Then, still held tight, bosom to bosom, Celia spoke in her ear.

'Alice, I asked how you would like to be painted, and you did not answer. Do you have an answer now?'

'No, Miss, I haven't had time to think about it.'

'Then how about as you are now?'

'You mean with nothing on, Miss? Oh no, I do not think I could do that.'

'Well, it would not be with nothing on,' pushing Alice away a little, hands on her shoulders, to gaze directly at her bosom, her belly, down to her private area which was now distinctly throbbing, for Alice realized a little too late for discretion – but not so for pleasure – that her mistress' knee was pressed against her inner thighs and beyond.

'Hm, let me see,' running one hand down Alice's side, sending a distinct tremor through her whole being.

'Yes, I think I see it,' turning her a little to one side, then the other with her shoulder.

Alice knew that this was just the artiste speaking now, assessing her personal 'charms', but that did nothing to quiet the powerful feelings surging through her.

'Yes, I think I see it. You have a beautiful body, Alice. How to capture it, to get the right mood of happiness . . . or . . . perhaps . . . sadness. Yes, of course. Yes, that is it. You would be perfect, Alice, just as you are. Bosom somewhat in shadow,' putting her hand on the left breast to create just that effect, 'and down here, hand just here,' placing it on her lower belly, at which Alice jerked perceptibly.

'If I am going to paint you, Alice, you are going to have to be less sensitive,' taking Alice's hand to place it just above that same area. Perfect,' she exclaimed joyously. 'You will be in front of the fire, of course, and we will use the one here in my room so that you can feel comfortable and secure.

'Perfect,' she repeated, happily hugging Alice to her bosom once more before releasing her to resume her seat, but Celia was not finished.

'Alice, would you get up please and stand at the foot of the bed. Yes, that is it. Just relax,' though Alice was feeling as tight as a drum!

'Now walk up and down a bit. Yes, that is it. Now sit in my chair, good, now stretch out on the chaise longue. Yes, quite beautiful. Thank you, Alice. Now you may return and tell us the last thing that was on your mind.'

But to Alice, parading about naked was never part of her bargain. And as for those fierce bosom to bosom hugs, with Miss Celia's hands all over her body, sparing very little, well, she was mentally speechless, although her body was full to overflowing with desire, close almost to how she had felt with Richard. And she had thought she was immune to those feelings; heavens, this was going to be difficult to forget!

Hopefully a little calmer, she resumed her position at the foot of the bed.

'Well, the last item I have in mind concerns the two of you. Miss Lucy, you will be leaving the day after tomorrow, and be gone for many weeks. You will have my Mildred to attend you and keep you company, of course, but you have not been separated from your sister for any thing more than a day or two since you arrived early last year,' and Lucy went pale, for she knew what was coming and she dreaded it.

'Also for you, Miss Celia, the same applies. While your sister will be occupied satisfying three elderly ladies for the Captain's sake, none of that applies to you. So you will miss each other dreadfully, and you need to prepare for that moment of departure and the endless silence that follows it.'

'But I shall be returning, Alice, I am not going to stay with those Aunts forever. Then all will be as before.'

Alice merely smiled and raised her eyebrows. 'I do not think so, Miss. It will never be the same again, you mark my words. So any thing you want to say or do between you and your sister had better be tonight – or not at all.

'Well, that is the evening as far as I am concerned, unless you have more questions.'

'Just one, Alice,' spoke up Celia. 'You said one of the reasons you took off your dress was to be as we were. What was the other?'

'It is very simple, Miss. You two seem to enjoy running around wearing very little – or nothing at all. I just wanted to feel what it was like, that is all.'

'And did you like it?'

There was a long pause, then, 'Some of it, Miss. I liked the feeling, certainly, but I am not sure about being looked at while I was doing it.

'Well, it is time you two young ladies went to sleep, though I suppose you will want to converse and caress for a little while, so I will leave you to it,' and she rose, picked up her dress, hung it over her shoulder and walked toward the door, but at the mirror stopped and examined her self in its reflection. Satisfied with what she observed, she turned to the door once more and opened it.

'Good night, Miss Celia, Good night, Miss Lucy,' gave a little curtsey and was gone, closing the door softly behind her.

As she mounted the stairs, still without attire, she smiled to her self at the thought that just flitted across her mind: that was the first and certainly last time she would curtsey quite naked, and she had a quiet chuckle to her self, for it had been a good evening; the telling, the feeling, but especially the touching. That was exquisite, and at that thought she tingled all over again.

However, once in her bed, she found her self sad, too, at the thought that she would miss her younger mistress. And worse, for she would miss her Mildred, too, and at that she shed a few quiet tears.

Both sisters were cuddled against each other, but quiet for some minutes after Alice left. It was Celia who broke the silence.

'What did you think about Alice's strictures to you, Luce?'

'I do not know, Sis. It all made sense, there is no doubt about that. But do you think I could really ask Charles to do all those things for me? To wait for me to become his true bride little by little?'

'I do not know what you could do, Luce, but if Alice is right then it is make the effort or pay the price. Personally, I thought her wisdom incredibly sound. I could not have said any where near as much, nor spoken greater truths and quite spontaneous at that. I must congratulate her tomorrow on her clarity of thought to see you as comfortable as she could help make it. And I thought her boudoir idea quite brilliant.

'However, a thought has just struck me. I shall visit Charles' Althorpe Manor in place of Mother, to see that her daughter's comforts are well met. She has that right – indeed, obligation to you – especially considering your relative youth. One way or another and before the wedding day, I could get in place most of what Alice has proposed; will that do?'

'Beautifully, my dearest Sister. Now I feel confident I can meet all Alice's guidance and strictures.'

'Excellent. Then tomorrow I will seek out Alice and write it down so that is as clear in my head as it seems to be in hers. Now where were we in those other matters?'

Both entwined now between the sheets, it was Lucy's turn to break the silence.

'I am going to miss you dreadfully, dearest Sister, not just for this,' running her hand over her sister's body, 'but for every thing. Will you miss me as much, in the same way?'

'Of course, my love, do you doubt it?'

'No, but I shall have to stand being scrutinized by those dreadful Aunts of Charles'. In a way, I almost wish they would reject me, then we could be as we always were.'

'Hush, dear Sister; they may not be as bad as you suppose. Besides, Charles loves you. The way he looked at you when you were dancing together was quite unmistakable, but especially when you were with some one else. And why not, for you are very beautiful.

'I shall miss you, too, Luce. However, the real loss will be you as a person, the one I have had with me for seeming years, the one who has posed for me, played the pianoforte with me, been a major factor in the Quintet, and on and on. That aspect I shall miss dreadfully.'

'So shall I, dearest Sister. And to think that it will be many months before I can be this way with Charles – even if I wanted to, which I am beginning to doubt.

'But did you notice how Alice was when you were discussing how to paint her?'

'That is just the way I look at all my models. It was no different when I was painting you.'

'While that may be true, did you not see how she was while you were holding her and then studying her figure, assessing her charms?'

'No, not particularly, Sis. I will admit she did seem a little excited, but then she was not wearing any thing, so that must have had some effect.

After all, we are quite used to it while to her it was quite new – and unexpected into the bargain.'

'Well, all I can say, dear Sister, is that from my own observation, when she was in your arms held tight while you recovered, she was in seventh heaven. And then when you were proposing the various poses you considered suitable, at the slightest touch she wriggled all over. At the end of it all, she could hardly contain the passion you had engendered in her body – and I know only too well from my experience as a model with you, *exactly* how that feels, so watch out!

'After all, she is a woman, more mature than we, certainly, but her charms are more than adequate for loving to the full, and they came abundantly to the surface tonight. So, deep inside, the timid and shy Alice we have known no longer exists. She may surprise you one day with a raging desire for that bosom to bare bosom contact that you have just conjured in her body to be appropriately requited by your own.

'Indeed, as she expressed, we were as three sisters at that moment, and she may take advantage of my absence to seduce you into making love to *her* body in place of mine.'

'But you will be gone only five or six weeks.'

'Then so much more the urgency of her body to feel your special touch to her own. If you doubt that, then you did not perceive the adoring looks she was giving you as you caressed her impassioned body, but I have more to say on that later.

'Now cuddle *my* body all over to show that you really care for me and me alone; that there is no other. Bestow some thing special upon me this night, my dearest one, some thing of the greatest intimacy to my person that you have not yet dared to perform. Take me to the greatest heights for as long as I can stand it and beyond, then I shall return it to your beautiful body in overflowing measure.

'My greatest wish is to have that special thing that no-one but my beloved sister can provide. Some thing to remember you, us, together, for all time. And when Alice hears our cries as we reach those ultimate joys of full release, she will know we have indeed said our own special farewells, each to the other.'

At first Alice thought sleep would come easily, but the more she thought about it the less certain she was about any thing, especially that business of Miss Celia painting her in front of the fire, wearing nothing but her skin. Was she ready for that sort of exposure, all captured on canvas, even to her excitement? She did not think so.

And yet . . . those feelings surging through her bare body at the contact between the mistress' breasts and her own, then the soft touch of her hand . . . and she buried her head under the pillow. She would think about later, except that those cries of shared passion from her charges below did nothing to calm her spirit; indeed, just the opposite, until she pounded the pillow in the frustration of ecstasy denied to her own body, one that was as eager and passionate as those below!

But even in the ensuing silence her head was still revolving with all the excitement of the telling, the exquisite touch of those bare bodies, and the evidenced joy they received from each other that she might never enjoy. And a great sadness crept over her.

It was then that she heard the click of the door latch and became aware that some one had entered the room.

'Are you awake, Alice?' came the soft voice of Miss Lucy.

'Yes, Miss. Is there some thing I can do for you?'

'No, Alice, there is perhaps some thing I can do for you. May I sit upon your bed?'

'Certainly, Miss.'

'You remember, Alice, after our witnessed passion on the island, that I believed you were owed recompense for having your spirit innocently reawakened from its slumber?'

'Yes, Miss, I recall it only too well and much regret that you were interrupted.'

'So did I, Alice, but I have a suggestion. Would it help if I were able to provide you some relief for your passion denied? It can only be this one time and right now, for I leave in two days, as you are aware.'

'Do I understand correctly, Miss Lucy, that you are offering to make love to my body, and at this moment?'

'That is so, Alice. Of course you may wish to decline an offer which can not be repeated, perhaps making your inner self more dissatisfied than ever. Also be aware that my sister and I are quite satiated, thus it will be giving only, in complete darkness and without a word being spoken. So what is your answer?"

'Then it is a decided yes, Miss,' astonished at the generosity of what was being proposed.

'Very well, then give me your hand and I shall guide you to our bedchamber.' Taking it and moving to the door.

'Before we go, Miss Lucy, there is some thing that I should have added to our discussions of earlier, when I said that you could not receive the same level of joy to which you have become accustomed. With Miss Celia present, I could not give the correct answer to that, as you will soon see, for I have not that authority.

'It could – and perhaps should – be available, if on occasion you visit your sister here for a brief stay of a night or two, or perhaps together occasionally undertake a visit to Town for new gowns and such, staying with Aunt Julia in those guest rooms that I am sure you remember well. That would not, in my opinion, negate your promise to be true to your betrothed, and I am quite certain that Miss Celia would be delighted to welcome your self – in every sense of the word.'

'Alice, that is a wonderful thought, which I shall review with my sister as soon as may be, and here is my hug of appreciation. But you are in your nightgown, and that will not do at all!' bending to lift it over Alice's head, brushing Alice's bosom lightly as she did so. 'There,' and to Alice's astonishment, Miss Lucy's hands were on her bottom, that luscious body pressed against her own for some long moments, while each came alive to the other, with delighted quivers passing through each.

'But come,' releasing her, 'we have perhaps some further joy awaiting.'

Afterwards, Alice could only recall it as if in a dream. The large bed was open and she was invited to lie upon it, hands over her head, after which Miss Celia sat on one side and Miss Lucy on the other.

At first their hands were soft on her bosom and quivering belly, but gradually the tempo was increased as her face, neck and upper body were massaged by two pairs of hands uniquely experienced in providing love of the deepest and most experienced nature to the female body, some thing quite unknown to her experience.

In no time she was wriggling with the increasingly massaging of breasts and nipples, first with delicate fingers then with smooth lips, then to urgent fingers and hungry, consuming lips both at the same time and in unison. Finally after much delicate exploration of her lower body the action was increased all over until it seemed that there were a dozen hands and half that many mouths devouring her, and the ecstasy was beyond anything she could ever have imagined.

Then, with her entire being on fire, it culminated with increasingly urgent massaging of her most intimate inner self until she was forced to cry out, not once but thrice, and there was only quiet – except for the quiet closing of the Studio door.

She did not remember climbing the stairs to her room, but she must have done so for the next thing she knew was the sun shining on her face, so that she rose to raise the sash to its maximum, heedless of her bare bosom as she leaned to greet it and the wonderful day it promised.

And suddenly she felt a tremor run through her from the soles of her bare feet to the very roots of her hair as she realized she was liberated, at last free of the shame of the unwed coupling, of an out-of-wedlock child, of guilt of her poverty as a young woman. The sharing and telling of it all – especially the intimate and private details – had made it no longer a dishonourable thing that she must hide. It now could be one to celebrate. She must find and thank her mistresses for the splendid opportunity they had provided her, and for that incredible dream of joy beyond joy.

14

Release

But Alice was to be denied that opportunity, what with the impending departure of Miss Lucy and Mildred as her personal maid, and all the things needed to be prepared for it. Besides, the mistress was in a distinctly low humour, so that Alice's spirit sank with it.

After they were gone, Celia was unable to settle to any thing, and her mood soured by the day. The parting had been painful to each sister, with many tears, for they had hardly been out of each other's company since Lucy returned, so many years ago, it seemed, though a twelve-month would better measure it. Now that they had found each other, they were separating, almost certainly for good, though each vowed that it would not be so.

Alice was equally upset, for she was losing two of her most special people. Though she kept most of it inside, she was not her usual cheery self to be able to offset her mistress' blue mood, although she tried. Attempted to interest her in the Island. Even went so far as to pack a luncheon hamper before rowing her there. But all she got for her trouble was a scolding, her mistress declaring after only five minutes that she was ready to return and that she could not comprehend 'for the life of me what you see in this place', and returned to her room where she sat and moped.

Once they set out for the glade, hoping to meet with Manfred, only to return because of inclement weather. It was on the eighth day that the mistress insisted on a second trip – against Alice's considered advice as she studied the lowering skies. They had reached the ridge and were in sight of their destination when a cold rain swept over them. Without shelter, for the bare trees offered little, they drove for home as fast as they dared in the treacherous conditions, reaching it only after they were thoroughly drenched, even through their capes.

'This is most infuriating and provoking, Alice,' she complained loudly as they dismounted, as if to imply it was all her fault. 'First I lose my beloved sister to her affianced, then Manfred is not at hand for any thing pleasurable; even the discourse he pledged me is denied by this rain. It really is too tiresome to be borne,' and she stamped into the Hall, advising every one of both her return and her ill-humour by banging the doors as she went.

Alice said nothing, though feeling the same loss of companionship. Yet she was unable to shake the sinking feeling that she was letting down Miss Celia badly, for the situation regarding the professor's designs on her mistress – and her acceptance of the danger he posed – remained unattended.

'Get these wet things to the laundry, Alice,' shivering as she stepped out of the dripping pile on the floor of her room and donned her bathrobe. 'But run me a hot tub first, and be quick about it. I need to soak the cold and damp out of my bones before they rot within me, and then I shall be good for nothing and nobody. And you are looking downright miserable, Alice,' she added petulantly, 'I do not need *you* with a cough or a sniffle.' And Alice winced at the unkind remark.

'Especially now,' her mistress continued, in the distortion of her own unhappiness, 'when I have just lost my most special friend in the whole world. And when I can not make *him* mine either in this hideous weather. I am going to recline and forget every horrid thing that has happened of late,' and she flounced into the bathroom.

Immersed in the hot water to her neck, her ill-humour gradually subsided and calm settled upon her. Soothed and relaxed with a glass of light spirits thoughtfully provided by Alice, she recalled to her self some of the splendid times she and Lucy had contrived between them, and then even dozed a little.

All the while, Alice, wrapped now in her dressing gown, waited on her.

As she was patted dry and powdered, to be dressed in her Chinese robe, the sun broke through the remnants of the rain clouds, providing a brilliant double rainbow, and reflecting its dazzling colours in her dressing mirror.

'Alice, you are *still* looking awfully cold and pinched,' but this time Celia caught the strained expression in the mirror, and as suddenly grasped its meaning. 'But,' she temporized, as the awareness engendered a novel idea, 'I believe I have the ideal solution.

'Yes, indeed I do. Alice, why not use that hot water to soak *your* bones. It really is *very* refreshing, and I have some of those special bath salts in there that Lucy gave me for Christmas.'

'I am sure it is, Miss, but I could not do that, for it would not be right,' replied Alice, resenting her mistress' display of bonhomie now that she was warm and contented once more, in contrast to her own loss of companionship in her beloved daughter and her own postponed comfort, for she was still damp through to her skin underneath *her* gown.

'Right or not, you do it,' Celia said determinedly. 'When you are finished,' she added more softly, 'you may get into Miss Lucy's silk blue-bird gown. The one you admire so much,' she appended, to sweeten her argument. 'I believe it is still in the cupboard.'

But that appeared only to stiffen Alice's resolve; 'til her mistress turned and placed both hands on her damp shoulders, belatedly realizing for her self Alice's true condition.

'Alice, I am just a bad-tempered grouch, as some one once so rightly said. I was too selfish to notice that *you* are still in your wet under-things, while I am cosy and warm. You deserve better of me than that, I know. I am sorry I was so rude and inconsiderate. Just go and soak your wet bones, and add some more hot water, for I have need of your services that require a cheerful and pleasant countenance.'

Alice hesitated still, not wishing to be won over by flattery, though she thought the gown magnificent. '*Please?*' said Celia, relieved as Alice finally smiled then nodded, reminded of her mistress as a little girl. She could not resist her then, either.

'All right, Miss, if it will make you happy.'

'It will, and you too, you will see. Take as much time as you like. I shall be in the studio sketching a new thought; you can join me there, so there is no hurry. And use Lucy's special shampoo to wash your hair; I may need it for what I have in mind. And thank you, Alice,' giving her shoulders an extra squeeze.

'Now, doesn't that feel oceans better?' said her mistress, smiling as she looked up from her easel, when Alice entered some thirty minutes later, hair piled high. 'The gown suits you well, too.'

'Yes, Miss, I confess it was wonderful, just as you promised. I am very grateful. I love the sweet scent and softness it imparts to my skin, too.

And this gown is very lovely,' as she preened her self in it before the mirror – a little for her mistress' benefit as well as for her own.

'I believe I could get used to the feel of the silk on my body,' she added with a big smile, running her hands over it from bosom to hips, for she had secretly chosen not to wear her nightgown under it for just that reason.

'And you shall, Alice,' smiling in return. 'But first I need you to select a pose, for the inspiration is returning now that you, too, are refreshed in spirit and in body,' correctly interpreting Alice's remark regarding 'the feel of silk'. Indeed, as she was quite bare beneath it, her undisclosed purpose would be much more easily achieved.

'I am afraid I will not make a very good picture, Miss, however inspired you feel.'

'On the contrary, Alice, you are a very compelling subject. I have painted your daughter – and you admit that was very good – so why not the mother? Might she be even better? So, how do you see your self portrayed this evening after that warm soak and the silk against your skin?'

'I do not know, Miss, I have not had any time to think about it. Perhaps we should leave it until I have.'

'As some one is fond of saying, "Never put off 'til the morrow what can be done today".'

'Yes, Miss,' blushed Alice, hoist on her own petard.

'So, what is it to be. Mildred was a sprite, Miss Lucy was a fairy queen, what will you be?' and she opened her cupboard to withdraw one of her special books and place it on the table.

'Here,' she said, 'how about some thing full of innocence, like this "Girl with the Broken Pitcher".'

'Could you really make me look like that, Miss?' exclaimed the spell-bound Alice, leaning to examine it, innocently exposing most of a shapely white breast.

'Hardly, Alice,' laughed her mistress; 'Greuze was a superb painter, well beyond my puny skills, but I would give it my best effort – that is what art is all about, just doing your intelligent best. Here is his "Milk-maid", a very saucy one, that,' standing and looking at her thoughtfully. 'That would be easier for my talents and would suit you admirably, too.'

'They are wonderful, Miss,' whispered Alice in awe, 'just wonderful. I could see my self, 'specially in that one.'

'Or how about "Mrs. Siddons" by Thomas Gainsborough?' continued Celia as she turned the pages. 'We have that sort of society lady clothes some where around, although personally I think there is too much cloth and too little Siddons. I want to paint the person, not the clothes she is wearing!'

'Now you are making fun of me, Miss,' exclaimed Alice in dismay. 'And I took you for serious about painting me.'

'I am deadly serious, Alice. That is the special joy of painting, for in it one can be any thing one wants to be – except for *Alice*, apparently,' she added, pointedly, 'who can be a *water maid* or a *milkmaid*, but not a *society lady*. Shame on you, Alice, I thought you were made of sterner stuff. My sister could be Athena, for example. It was simply a question of establishing the passion, and it turned out to be one of my greatest successes.

'Would you care to see it?' and Alice nodded, suddenly feeling quite small for her pettiness of inverted pride. 'If I show it to you, though, you must never even mention its existence, unless I give you permission. Agreed?' and Alice nodded again.

'Very well, close your eyes,' as she unlocked the cupboard and drew out the picture, placing it against the chair back. 'There, what do you think of that?' queried Celia, as Alice gasped in astonishment. 'Do you like it?'

'It is lovely, Miss, though very revealing, exposing almost every charm that Miss Lucy has. It does capture her to perfection, though, as only my self and Mildred would know her. What a shame it must always be hidden from view, for no-one could ever be allowed to see Miss Lucy in such a state of undress; it is simply too lifelike to be anyone else.'

'Thank you, Alice; you have just paid me the greatest compliment.' Then she sighed. 'But you are quite right, of course, it is so very *revealing*. My best work always seems to be like that, when all frippery and persiflage is dispensed with,' continuing to turn the pages.

'Perhaps I could do you as Deirdre,' as that painting was at hand. 'She was turned into a tree. You might make a very good tree, Alice.'

'Oh no, Miss!' gasped Alice, 'I could not have people looking at my picture and seeing every thing I possess. I would never be able to hold up my head again. Besides, who would want to look at me that way?'

'Richard would, for one,' replied her mistress, 'if he were still here. But you do not have to be undressed to be painted. The one I did of mother with the bowl of roses came out rather well, I thought. I work best when I can reveal the hidden element in the subject, and it just so happens that roses are her passion and I was able to capture that.'

'Well, there is not much hidden to that one, Miss,' responded Alice, dryly, referring to 'Athena'.

'That is where you are quite wrong, Alice. Just because the subject has little in the way of clothing, does not mean that there is no deeper significance to the painting, as I can demonstrate to you quite easily if we are successful with your pose.

'Remember, we are talking of the hidden *beneath* the surface, that which exists within each of us. That is the challenge for the artiste. Clothes are easy to paint, but I aspire to a subject in whom I can bring out the implicit emotion – not the explicit wearing apparel. One might as well paint a clothes horse!

'Now, Alice,' looking her over thoughtfully, while Alice blushed at the candid appraisal, and glanced down to ensure that she was still properly attired. 'I wonder what your passion is. Where does your hidden element lie?'

'I do not think I have any "hidden element" Miss, or passion that I am aware of,' she replied guardedly, for she mistrusted that word.

'Nonsense, Alice. I noticed from when you last were with Lucy and my self a great deal of passion emerging from you. Besides, I am equally certain that we all do, I just have to find it, that is all. Now let us start by seeing what you look like under that robe.'

'Oh no, Miss,' responded Alice quickly, as she drew the gown more tightly around her, 'for there is nothing underneath but my skin!'

'So much the better, Alice, for then there is no artifice – especially after that same night.' But Alice did not move. 'Oh, very well, I can get the general idea, anyway, and it does give me a thought. Today I will make some general outline sketches as you move around, but I would like to continue tomorrow after breakfast, provided the weather is just as awful as today, and provided you are willing, of course,' and Alice nodded, but her eyes were uneasy.

Much as she had enjoyed their boudoir session, this business of baring every thing in broad daylight was, well . . . Besides, that was in the intimacy of Miss Celia's private chamber, and by moonlight, at that. Now to stand here and have it all captured on canvas for any one . . . that was unthinkable – even though the artiste was Miss Celia. In comparison, it was like having a bucket of cold water thrown over you, and her skin prickled at the thought.

Fortunately for Alice's troubled spirit, the weather made a remarkable recovery, and the mistress spent most of the day in the rose garden, studying 'Painting in Oils: The Human Form'. This was an art treasure newly arrived from Town, consisting mostly of the undraped female – as Alice discovered at a glance while providing the mistress her al fresco afternoon tea.

Happily, the next two days were no different, and her mistress' study continued unabated.

For Alice, this was her dilemma: if the weather continued as the present, her modesty was secure, but then her portrait in oils would remain an unfulfilled dream, and suddenly her ambivalence was out in the open. Yes, she would like to have her likeness taken; but no, she did not wish it to be unclothed – or at the least to retain some semblance of modesty. However, Miss Celia was quite enchanted with the folios – clearly indicating in which direction her artistic spirit was heading. Oh dear!

Then it turned quite cold, and it rained. The moment she had been dreading was at hand.

'Have you thought yet how you would wish to be portrayed, Alice?' inquired her mistress, breakfast and chores completed. 'We shall be using crayon for this initial sitting, and perhaps oils later if you are able to adequately express your "hidden" talents – for I am knowledgeable of those outer ones, as you are well aware,' with a little smile, to which Alice replied only with a blush.

There was a lighted candle on the bookcase shelf, for Celia had closed the blind over her large skylight to provide the effect she was hoping to achieve.

'No, Miss, I really can not decide. I shall have to let you choose the subject, but,' she added with a tense expression, 'I would like to remain dressed, if it is all the same to you, Miss.'

'Perhaps we may agree to that, Alice. Not in your usual attire, of course, for there I have only the face and hands to work with. Hals was brilliant at that – as was Dürer – but they well exceed my modest skills. No, I have need of a good deal more of you than . . .' and she stopped as a brilliant thought struck her.

'Alice, did you perchance retain that dress with which you bewitched Richard?' becoming excited when Alice nodded. 'Wonderful; please fetch it for me.' And when she returned, added, 'Will it still fit, do you think?'

'I am not sure, Miss, for I never wore it again after that special time; somehow it did not seem right,' her voice here dropping to a whisper, 'it was just . . . too precious. I am not sure that I want to now, for it seems disrespectful of his memory, you see,' she added, doubtfully.

'Please, Alice, for me, and for him too,' pleaded Celia; 'he would like to see it again, I am very sure of that. Just try it on and then decide.'

'Very well, Miss, if you really want me to. But my figure is not what it was then, you know,' she added defiantly, 'and it may look just awful on me, where it once was . . .' sorrowfully now, and in a whisper, 'and I am not sure I could abide that,' as a tear welled up and trickled to her chin.

But Celia shook her head and moved to lift Alice's face up to her own, to wipe away the tear before it dropped.

'It will not, Alice, believe me; I promise it will not. Why not use the bathroom to change, and we will see what it looks like,' with a gentle smile, 'but this time from the artiste's point of view.'

Still Alice hesitated, before exclaiming in a quiet uncertain voice,

'Do you want me as I was that night, Miss?'

'Would you *like* to be that way again, Alice – for remembrance – of your own Richard?'

'But I only did it to encourage his love, Miss, and without him I just do not see the point of it. Nothing can come of it without him,' she repeated almost to her self, her eyes swimming with yet-to-be-spilled tears. 'Just the dress, Miss? With nothing on at all under it? I do not think I could do that now, Miss. It was special for just that one time, for him,' shaking her head sadly.

'Whatever you feel comfortable in, Alice,' said Celia, with a squeeze of her hand. 'But we have to start with the dress,' she added firmly. 'I think that you and he enacted a great love story that night, and I would like to try to recreate it. I cannot guarantee to succeed; that will happen only if you *make it happen.*

'I leave it to you, Alice; we can always try some thing simpler, but it will be the less in meaning, too,' she added, looking directly into Alice's sad and liquid eyes. 'My sister's picture is only as good as it is because she *dared* to be that good her self.'

'Very well, Miss, if *you* want it. I will try to do it, for you,' holding it against her body. 'But if I can not . . .' shaking her head as she looked into the mirror before moving slowly into the bathroom, closing the door quietly behind her.

While she waited, Celia changed into her usual attire, her light gown open down the front, with only a loose tie.

It was many minutes before she emerged, hesitant, barefoot, head and eyes downcast. It hardly seemed the same Alice, for her dark hair was now brushed and glistening down her back to her waist and below, something Celia had not seen since she her self was a child. The dress was simple enough and quite modest, but it clung and revealed now where her figure was more mature, transforming her being completely.

'Beautiful, Alice,' whispered Celia in awe, 'exquisite beyond all belief. And the buttons?' Alice flushed slightly and nodded, unable to raise her head to look at her mistress for fear of divulging that it would not have fitted otherwise.

'Good, very good,' she continued, softly. 'No, do not look up, just stand there for a few minutes while I get the feel of you and the dress,' and she sketched in a few outlines to get the shape she knew to be there.

'The challenge is not you, Alice,' she commented softly, drawing rapidly now, 'but the absence of Richard. As you so rightly said, he was the reason for it all in the first place, I know, and without him it makes little sense. Unless . . . unless,' she repeated, in a whisper of excitement, 'his *absence* is the theme. I think I see it. No, do not move, you are perfect just as you are. We have need, however, of two things more.'

She placed her own silver-backed hairbrush in Alice's hand, and moved the candelabra to a small table in front of her.

'There. Now, I hope this will not pain you too much, Alice,' whispering in her ear to avoid breaking the spell, 'if it does, I shall stop immediately. All right?' and Alice nodded, though the pain showed clearly enough. 'Perfect,' thought Celia; this was not the moment to change a thing.

'Alice,' she said softly, 'please move a little closer to the mirror, put your right hand on the top and look into it, head bent forward a little. That is it. Now brush your hair over your left shoulder, down the front, all of it on the one side, my side, and turn just a little towards me. Left knee bent, just a little. That is it. Wonderful.

'As you brush your hair, you are thinking of that happy time, so long, long ago, and of dear Mildred, his gift to you that night. You are not really seeing any thing there in the mirror as you brush, because it is all so misty, but the feeling of excitement of you as a young emerging woman is returning as you brush, just as it did that night, urging you to reveal and explore your new abundant self with him for the very first time, as you have long wished to do, but have not dared. Your need is desperate now to recapture once more that feeling of togetherness, that feeling of being as one with him, but the dress prevents your reunion, and it needs only one thing more.'

And now came the challenge for both artiste and model, but she pushed on in hope.

'The final button, as you reach to release it, a twist of the shoulders, as you return to the brushing, brushing, brushing, down and down, over your swelling bosom, feeling the tension rising there once more, as it did then, as you brush.'

Celia captured the tear that slowly slid down one cheek and dropped into her dark hair, as Alice continued the slow movement, even as the dress slid slowly down her form until it became a dark pool at her feet; releasing and revealing the generous milky curves of both swollen breasts, and below the bewitching, intimately dark hollows in the candlelight, perfectly matched in their shimmering, excited reflection. And Celia held her breath in check so as not to break the spell.

'Now you feel as you did then, as you did when you went to him to unveil your chaste, maiden self, to be irresistible once more, to feel his admiring gaze devouring your womanhood, his intimate touch exploring your bounty, his ardour ignited by the open declaration of your own awakening, your clear longing for release driving him to an overwhelming fulfilment of his own suppressed desires; for the pleasures frankly offered and joyfully accepted, to be joined in a mutual passion until at last you feel him with you, against you, taking you eagerly, breathlessly, into him, and him unconditionally into you, as he was before, and you know that nothing in the world will ever be this wonderful again. And at the ending of it, he leaves forever a part of himself within you, your precious Mildred, to have and to hold in his place, your dearest possession after his memory, and your hair and the dress a further part of that beautiful memory, endlessly held close in your heart, just as he will always be.'

The silence that followed was broken only by the swish of the brush over dark hair, the faint hiss of Alice's animated breathing, and soft glide of Celia's crayon on paper, until that, too, ceased.

'Thank you, Alice,' she whispered, not daring to move herself, 'that was quite wonderful. You may use the bathroom to dress again, if you wish,' as Alice stepped out of the dress as if in a trance, and slowly left the room, apparently oblivious of her naked state.

Celia continued with her work, but when Alice had not emerged after some ten minutes, she picked up the dress and entered the bathroom, to find it empty, clothes still draped over the chair. Concerned, she proceeded quietly up to Alice's room, to find her curled up on the bed, still unclothed except for where her hair reached, the hair brush in one hand, sleeping quietly, so she laid the dress gently over her and tiptoed out, returning to put the finishing touches to her latest triumph.

So preoccupied was she, that only when she sensed a presence did she raise her eyes to find Alice standing in the studio doorway, still barefoot, but clad now in the light night-dress of their boudoir séance, only lightly fastened, her bright eyes contrasting oddly with her poignant expression.

'Yes, Alice?' she said softly, with a smile.

'I just wanted to thank you, Miss,' whispered Alice, 'for what you did earlier, making my Richard live again for a few minutes; I did not think that was possible – not even for one second. But Miss,' her voice strength-ening now with a diffused happiness, 'you *were* right, it *was* wonderful to have him to me again, just as you said it would be, and not awful at all. I even dreamed of him a few minutes ago, a thing I have not been able to do for many years, and it was beautiful . . .' pausing as if uncertain if she wanted to say more or not.

'Yes, Alice,' said Celia softly, moving to take her hand. 'Was there some thing else you wished to tell me?'

Alice blushed and swallowed hard before replying.

'Yes, Miss. I would like to say that, although I know I can never replace Miss Lucy, if you would like me to . . .' and she paused to find the courage, 'if you have need of a model again – until Miss Lucy returns, that is,' she added, all in a rush, 'I should be very happy to pose for you.'

Now with that difficulty overcome, she was finally able to smile as she felt her mistress squeeze her fingers in encouragement.

'And in any manner you choose, Miss. I do not know when I removed my dress, but I must have done, for I was wearing nothing when I awoke on my bed. And I did enjoy it, after all.'

So saying, she turned once more to the mirror, hands on hips to admire her form as she had presented it to him, satisfied only when she opened the dress so that both white breasts were fully exposed so as to feel his lips upon them as on that special occasion.

It was some moments before she noted her mistress standing behind her, smiling at her openness of attire, returned in full measure by Alice,

'And now that you have observed my upper body once more, Miss, but this time in the full light of day, do you approve of it – in the pursuit of Art, that is?'

Celia's reply came in an unexpected manner, for she pulled the gown back slightly to expose both shoulders so that the gown opened fully. Then she whispered in her ear.

'Now raise your right heel, tilt your hips and turn your self . . . just . . .

so,' hands on her bare hips to create the pose. 'Excellent. Now your right hand on your belly, just there,' placing it as she wished, 'and your left hand on your head – just so, shoulders back to lift the bosom. Perfect.

'There, Alice, study that mirror-figure, carefully, commit it to memory. Remember, that is not Alice; it is a well-endowed young woman in her prime. She might have a hair brush or some thing . . . but those are mere details. As a model you *assume* that personality, so that nakedness is not yours, it is simply who you are obliged to be,' and she stepped back to her easel.

'Now that is your portrait for whenever you wish me to paint it in oils,' at which Alice smiled again to her self in the mirror, and left as quietly as she had come.

It was nearly bath time before Celia saw Alice again that day, and she was shy to the point of being tongue-tied.

'If you have some thing you want to tell me, Alice, out with it; you know we do not keep secrets from each other.'

'Yes, Miss, I do, but I do not think I can express it,' replied Alice, with an expression born of love.

'Well, just try. I shall respect it, whatever the subject.'

'It is just that you released some thing inside my self when you were painting my likeness this morning, that I have bottled up all these years, ever since that night. I think I can remember him now with complete joy after your wonderful words to me. Thank you, Miss, for being so kind, for you spoke to my very soul then.'

'There is no need to thank me, Alice,' softly taking her hand. 'I was glad to do it. But I do very much appreciate your sentiments. It *is* encouraging to know that one can be of help, now and then, beyond creating a mere painting, that is.'

'I have also thought', continued Alice, in an even softer voice, filled with considerable emotion, 'about the manner I would like to be painted for some one very special to me, just as you said Miss, though not a tree. I do not think I would want that; nor would he. I think he would want me to be all there – as he alone knows me,' and she smiled nervously. 'But I would like you to do some thing else of me, if you have the mind.'

'Well, well, quite the model,' said Celia, in a softly mocking voice, 'and you did not think you had any "hidden elements"!' and Alice blushed at the memory of her ignorance. 'But now that we have seen your special places, too,' she continued, 'you would like to show off their passion further; is that it?' and Alice blushed more deeply still.

Celia laughed and squeezed her hand. 'Silly Alice, I am only teasing. Certainly we will do it. Do you have any thing special in mind for this special some one?'

'Yes, Miss,' said Alice, her courage returning, 'I would like to be painted curled up on a pouf, brushing my hair in front of a fire.'

'Indeed, you remember again that special night with Lucy, when I was holding you and looking at you as an artiste does?' and Alice nodded, smiling, remembering only too well. 'Well, that is exactly as I pictured you, but I wanted you to feel it, too. And if I recall correctly,' smiling, taking her by the shoulders, 'that you were *very* excited that night,' and Alice blushed deeply at the thought. 'That is all right, Alice, we all get those feeling now and then.

'So, am I to assume that it is to be *"au naturel"* as they say in polite circles?' with a little smile at her.

'Yes, Miss, that is, if *you* do not mind me being that way. I do not mind any more for my self after that "mirror" pose.' smiling in return, 'now that I see how freeing it can be. I suddenly feel alive again inside; and where my Richard is concerned, it is as if I have him back again. Who knows, perhaps he will be with me again at my feet, before the fire, and perhaps I could even get those feelings of excitement again?'

'Wonderful, Alice; we shall do it as you wish, and he may indeed join you in spirit, although only you will be able to see him. It could be an excellent pose and setting for you, if we can get the firelight right. I do have one, as you well know, though I have never used it. However, there is no reason why it could not be lit – indeed, there is every reason now why it should!

'If you will arrange to have it laid – with logs, of course – we will do it whenever you are ready. Agreed?'

'Oh yes, Miss, most willingly,' with her biggest smile.

'Do you realize, Alice,' said Celia, sitting up in bed, 'that you have now been released to choose another if you will, and that you go with Richard's blessing?'

Alice stood stock still, contemplating these words.

'No, Miss,' she responded, slowly. 'I hadn't thought of it that way,' and she turned it over in her mind for several moments. 'No, but now that I think of it, I see what you mean. I shall always have him, even if there were another who wanted me in that way. But I am content. Anyway, Miss, it is too late for me, now.'

'What *arrant nonsense* you do talk sometimes, Alice! I might have been fooled into accepting that, had I not just seen you preening in that mirror, positively revelling in your own body. You are a woman in the prime of life, with much to offer a man. If you do not believe me, go over to the mirror and tell me what you see in it? No, not with the robe on, silly, that will not tell you any thing except what a beautiful robe *it* is! I want you to see the beautiful person *inside* it.

'Now, as you are so evidently determined to display your full talents, Alice, please bring that pouf to the side of the bed and kneel on it. Excellent; you really have chosen a very attractive pose. I am getting quite excited about it,' and Alice beamed with pleasure. 'We need a little more light – no, you stay right there,' and she got out of bed to bring a candelabrum and a small drum table.

'There, that seems to get the idea admirably. The shadows are quite fascinating,' as she moved it from side to side before selecting one that satisfied her. 'The firelight will look very much like that, except that it will flicker, of course,' shaking the candles a little to achieve that very effect. 'I like that area in shadow,' indicating the hollow of her lower body, 'and you are naturally dark there, anyway. We must get to this one as soon as we may.

'That is it, Alice, bedtime. You can stop parading your mastery of your own delights so openly and tuck me in. You can show it off again in your new model role the very next rainy day, which will undoubtedly be the morrow.'

But the morrow was bright and warm and, mastery or not, the disturbed night for Alice – with its waking and sleeping dreams of youthful desire that she had not experienced for many a year – were not to be expressed on canvas that day.

Celia woke with the rising sun, refreshed and eager at its promise of a fine day. She was down early to breakfast, meeting her mother entering as she was leaving.

'Well, my dear, what do you have planned for this beautiful day?'

'I thought I would go riding, Mother, perhaps for the whole day, ride right out of the county even, for there are several places I have been meaning to visit. And, then . . . who knows what we shall encounter? But I will ask Alice to meet me with a luncheon hamper.'

'Quite ambitious, my child. Do not overdo it, for the weather can change suddenly, as you know.'

'Not today, Mother dearest, not today,' planting a kiss on her wondering cheek, and was gone.

Coming out of her room, she met Alice. 'I am off riding, Alice, as you can see. You can follow a little later if you like on Sally, but bring a goodly luncheon with you, for I shall be hungry for food afterwards. I expect you will know where to find me.'

Alice, sharply disappointed at seeing her first formal day as a model go swinging across to the stables, said nothing other than 'Yes, Miss.'

It was almost mid-morning, with the washing and ironing for her mistress done and while she was preparing the luncheon, that she had time for several little things to piece them selves together in her head. Her mistress' mood was almost *too* extravagant, as if she was up to some mischief, playing some game. Had indeed seen that expression in her many times as a child. She knew Alice would find her with the luncheon for she was going to the glade, of course. Inevitably, Manfred would arrive, and stay for lunch, certainly, if he had no other duties for Master Otto.

How was it she expressed it? She remembered now that it sounded a little odd at the time. 'Hungry for food afterwards' – *after what* Alice wanted to know, but she did not have to ask to know the answer, and her heart leapt into her throat.

'Good heavens,' she exclaimed involuntarily, dropping the carving knife and startling Cook. 'Sally!' but to her self she was saying *'why not Dolly'* as she raced outside, nearly knocking James over in her undue haste.

'Yes'm,' replied Carter, ''Er took both 'uns, a'ridin' Jas an' leadin' Doll. Said she'd be gorn aw't day.'

'Thank you, Carter,' she called as she reached the stable door again, before turning again.

'Saddle Sally, please, Carter; and hurry,' and then she was gone in a whirlwind to throw on some riding clothes, narrowly missing James again on the way back in.

The bag her mistress was carrying, she reflected as she flew down the stairs to her mistress' room, what did it contain? But she knew even before she confirmed the items missing from the closet as she remembered the words 'a simple scarf, seductively draped', as well as her mistress' equally saucy smile. Then she realized with dread precisely what 'game' her mistress had in mind, and it could not have been more utterly *devastating*.

As Carter led out Sally, her heart sank at the head-start her mistress had, and the fact that she her self would have to ride Sally side-saddle, and she was not as good as her mistress in that mode. Pray to heaven that she was in time, as she galloped out the yard and drove forward as fast as she dared without falling.

Celia rode side-saddle on Jasper, leading Dolly. She was not hurried, for she had until lunchtime; and anyway he was likely to be tutoring as he usually did for the first two hours or so.

At the glade, she led Dolly in and tied her to a tree with plenty of grass within reach, and then relaxed on her favourite stump to catch her breath and prepare her thoughts for the near future. Now that Lucy was settled, all conflict in that area had been resolved. Thus it was time to test her self, her own feelings in the matter of love, and his feelings toward her. And to calm her jangling nerves, she brought out her favourite book of poems and forced her self to read to pass the day until he arrived.

In the perfect stillness she would have heard his approach, but there was nothing. Perhaps she had misread his intentions at the Ball. Perhaps he charmed all who stood up with him. Certainly Alice and Mildred were enthralled, as was Alexa. And she suddenly found her self doubting her ability to reach him. She could wait no longer and rose to settle the matter.

As she sat on Jasper looking down on Greville House, she detected a movement in the trees.

'Well, he is out at last,' she said to her self as he neared the top of the rise, 'but now he must wait for me.' She wheeled Jasper and set off for the glade at a fast trot, rounded it, and returned at a near gallop to pull up a short distance from Johnson, her face and skin now glowing from the effort, and her breathing quite fast and her pulse racing.

'Good morning, Celia, a beautiful day, is it not?'

'Indeed, Manfred, a day to remember.'

'You rode beautifully there. You are to be congratulated,' and he rode his horse in until they were knee to knee.

'Thank you, Manfred,' as she looked levelly into his pale blue eyes. 'I do enjoy riding, the faster the better, as you shall see when I have regained my breath and cool off a little.' And she threw back her hood and riding cape over both shoulders, enjoying the sight of Manfred's eyes widening as he took in her manner of dress and before he took control once more.

'You also look the very picture of health, Celia, and I very much admire that lovely blouse; the lace is really quite exquisite. May I?' and he reached to run his fingers over the almost transparent fabric where it clung damply to the mounds that gave it shape and to circle their dark centres through the cloth so that they swelled and hardened immediately to his touch.

'Quite exquisite,' he repeated, continuing the gentle fingering. 'I should like to see more of this,' as he probed the fasteners for entry.

'Then wait here, Manfred, and you shall,' Celia exclaimed excitedly, wheeling Jasper and setting off for the glade at a canter.

He did not have to wait long, for Celia emerged riding Dolly, but astride instead of side saddle, racing in the other direction before turning in a tight circle and galloping back, to slide to a halt only yards from him, then walking Dolly up alongside Johnson again.

'How was that?' she smiled, looking up at him from the much smaller Dolly. Capeless, her chest heaving with the effort, she was glowing freely with the exertion, her long hair now free and streaming behind in the faint breeze.

'Magnificent, though I fear you overtax your self, for you are quite out of breath. But you are correct regarding the garment; there is more, indeed much more to be seen, and I cannot help openly admiring it once more.'

So saying, he reached out to the fabric, opened almost to her waist now by the wind of the gallop and the exertion, exposing her only apparent under-garment, a silk scarf tied so carelessly with a bow across her bosom that one side was already free to his gaze.

'Quite beautiful,' was all she heard as from a great distance, for after caressing the lace, he had released the bow to fully expose her upper body to his examination, fingers directly upon her, massaging with delicacy, masterfully stoking her already hard desire to fever pitch until she closed her eyes and leant into the glorious feelings they sent surging through her body, surrendering to the shivers of pure ecstasy that throbbed through to the very saddle leather.

Marvelling at her submissiveness, he placed the scarf on his saddle and, softly leaning his cheek against hers, tested her still further as he gently released the belt of her riding skirt and the fasteners beneath to circle her belly button before squeezing her white, softly rounded belly that elicited from her parted lips a soft cry of longing as his hand gently slid inside her riding skirt to stroke her inner thigh, 'til she could scarce breathe for the exquisite thrill of it.

"Perhaps we should return to the glade. Once there we can relax while you regain your breath,' he continued, opening his own shirt, anxious to make better contact than was possible while they were separately mounted. He took the reins from her limp hands and gently guided both animals, the while stroking from gorge to belly the bareness of her smooth curves and hollows in appreciation of their total accessibility under her open blouse.

She opened her eyes only when he reined in the horses and dismounted, and smiled when she saw where they were.

'Allow me,' he said, and reached up and swung her from the saddle, her toes barely touching the ground, his hands sliding up her soft skin until they once more firmly encircled and moulded her bosom, hard with desire and yearning anew for the pleasure of his touch.

'You may put me down, Professor, I shall not . . .' but got no further, as his lips closed hers in a fierce and passionate kiss, while she felt his hands slide down to her waist and beyond. How they got inside her riding skirt she could not fathom, but she loved their touch on her bare bottom as they pulled her relentlessly into him, her throbbing bosom against his cool, bare chest. And time ceased to exist for Celia.

She only dimly recalled that this wasn't her intention. She had thought only to tease and excite, to measure the depth of her feelings and his response in return. But enmeshed now in a web of powerful emotions that she did not begin to comprehend, here she was willingly opening her intimate body to his pleasure and consummation, swept on an inexorable current of ecstasy, powerless to withdraw.

Surely there could not be within these glorious feelings the humiliation of ruin and a life of misery, as Alice, dear Alice, had warned would be the inevitable reward.

'Perhaps,' said Alice's voice sharply inside her head, 'you should be a little more warmly dressed, Miss Celia, for we are not in summer yet?'

Celia pulled back, gasping for breath, to discover that it was the real Alice, riding Sally, and she was indeed speaking the truth. For glancing down, she was mortified to find her blouse remained only on her wrists which he now held; otherwise she was naked down to the waist – as she now discovered was he.

Even that was a charitable description, for her riding skirt and under-clothes were more nearly off her belly and bottom than on, and she struggled desperately to cover her nakedness and shame before the two of them.

'Good morning, *Professor,*' exclaimed Alice in an acid tone, breathing hard as she dismounted, slapping her riding crop hard across her boot to emphasize her displeasure. 'Perhaps you would be good enough to release my mistress that I may attend to her clothing. Also, it would be appreciated if you would retire and wait beyond the clearing aways.'

Manfred bowed, with a 'Good morning, Alice', and turned his back, though he did not venture far.

'Out of earshot, if you please, *Professor!*' commanded Alice in a whiplash voice that brooked no resistance.

'What are you doing, Miss,' she whispered to Celia as he left. 'If I had not come along at that very moment, where would you be now? And you think *I* did wrong?'

Celia said nothing as her clothing was restored, but then buried her head in Alice's shoulder and sobbed uncontrollably.

'There, there, Miss, do not take on so. I am sorry, I should never had said that, it was wicked of me, but I was so shaken at what I witnessed, and in another half-minute – well, let's not talk about it now, there will be time later,' and she gave her mistress a fierce hug and a kiss on the cheek, before putting on her cape and hood and leading her to the favoured stump.

'You just sit there, Miss, while I go and have a word with the professor,' and she mounted Jasper and led Johnson out to the professor.

'Please mount, Professor; we will ride a little ways up the ridge.'

Manfred was still recovering from the sensual shock of being so rudely parted from Celia, and by the suddenness of his changing fortunes, though he had restored his clothing – regretfully – to its normal state. One moment he had the object of his desires in his arms, offering her soon-to-be-naked self freely and openly for the taking; the next – virtually at the moment of that taking – he was being shooed away by her *maid*.

'I do not intend to go far,' he stated sourly, hopeful that Celia would still be a willing partner when Alice was through.

'Just out of earshot,' replied Alice quietly, but she rode in silence a good furlong before halting and moving toward the professor until they were only a few feet apart. On Jasper, a large horse of some sixteen or more hands, she appeared almost as tall as he.

'Professor,' she exclaimed, in a tight, controlled voice, white faced, looking directly into his eyes. 'How *dare* you treat a lady that way!' and he realized that she was white with rage, not the dismay he had thought. 'Would you please explain your *disgraceful* conduct back there, and your total lack of respect for the person of Miss Celia?'

'*My* conduct?' he responded in astonishment. 'Your mistress rides up half-naked to taunt me, her obvious intention to excite me. Her body was afire, crying out to be made love to, and I took her at her word in answering the urgency of that desire. Can you blame me for wanting to pleasure and satiate that demand for intimate love?'

'Yes, Professor, I *do* blame you, for only an utter cad would take advantage of her desire in such a contemptible way,' Alice replied, coldly now. 'Miss Celia is not always as wise in her associations or as controlled in her responses as she might be, for she acts straight from her heart. But you took advantage of that openness, that spirit so freely given, and abused it in a most despicable manner as would a knave.

'If,' she continued with a harsh growl in her throat, 'Miss Celia chooses to wear a riding garment of unusual design and construct,' reaching out with her riding crop and retrieving the silk scarf, 'you are bound as a *gentleman* not to comment on it in any fashion *whatsoever*. That you should have the audacity to *touch* it, let alone *actually remove it*,' her voice now almost a shriek, 'is beyond even the most outrageous behaviour ever witnessed toward a lady. You may yet be called to account by others for that *despicable* action.

'But above and beyond all that, *Professor*, and here mark my words *very, very, carefully*. If you ever, *ever again* do any thing so *utterly humiliating*,' her voice low and cold in absolute fury, 'so *wretchedly vile*, to the person of Miss Celia,' and it was now only a venomous hiss, 'This is my promise: *I will kill you. Is that completely understood?*'

Manfred opened his mouth to protest, or laugh, at this torrent of sound, he did not know which, until he looked at Alice, and any utterance died on his lips. For there burned in her eyes a light, a bright blue fire such as he had never witnessed before in man or woman. And even as his voice died in his throat he knew that this was no jest, no idle threat to be laughed away. For she was, at this precise moment, quite prepared and capable of it. And he shrank back in respect at the ferocity displayed there, until it slowly faded, to be replaced by a look of utter contempt, until she backed away Jasper to quell the growing restlessness he had exhibited during the intense discussion, and walked him several times in a circle, all the while patting his neck to calm him down.

'I am glad we are in concord, Professor,' she observed, upon her return, calm, once again in control of her self. 'You have some unbelievably disgraceful flaws in your character which are to be utterly despised in a so-called gentleman. Nevertheless, I do not dislike you, for you can be charming and gracious when the mood takes you. Indeed, I regard you more with pity. You must clearly understand, however, that my mistress comes first, before every body, *more precious to me even than my own daughter.*

'I admonished you once before, as an intruder in Miss Celia's room – which warning you obviously chose to ignore. I trust this time, *Professor,* I have truly reached your full and complete understanding of my promise, for I shall assuredly act upon it if your conduct is this grave again,' and for a brief moment the fire was back, receding as quickly as it had arisen.

'We shall talk again, soon, Professor. I will send a message to you. However, I must look now to my mistress, for you have delivered a most terrible shock to her soul, for which you may yet live to be sorry, or you may not – *live*, that is. I shall explain it to you one day in simple terms that shall reach your full comprehension. But you shall promise me, here and now, that you will *never* do any thing as extreme as that again, unless you receive my consent; is that clear? *My* consent, *Professor*, not Miss Celia's. *My* consent. You are clear now on that score? Yes?

'There will be no further warning, I assure you, before I act on my promise if yours is ever broken,' and this time Manfred merely nodded, avoiding her eyes, fearful of what he might find buried in their depths.

Alice turned Jasper and rode forward a dozen or so paces before she halted and addressed him again.

'Keep in mind, Professor, *without my permission* you promised you would not, as did I promise that I would. Remember that – as you value your very life, now go, before I use my whip on you,' indicating with it the direction whence he came.

When he was out of sight, she laid her head upon Jasper's neck to stroke it.

'But come, we must see to Miss Celia,' and she galloped away to take charge in the glade.

As she mounted her horse and they headed home, she whispered in its ear:

'Thank you, Sally, for getting us here in time, for what I feared is now upon us.' And now, mostly to her self, 'he has turned that awesome power of the Hollow onto Miss Celia, so that she makes her self naked in the same manner as he did Miss Lucy, seemingly without a word or gesture. And the dreadful thing is that I know not how to thwart it. It seems even that I must visit that dreadful place to find the secret of its power, though I hate it with as great a passion as I do him. The difficulty is that it I fail, then the Mistress is without any defence whatsoever.'

'Madam, could you spare a moment in the Morning room?'

'Why yes, Alice. Is it important?'

'I am afraid it is, Madam.'

'Oh, dear,' replied Lady Etheridge as she led the way, 'I do not like the sound of that at all.'

Once the door closed she asked, 'Is it about Miss Celia?' to receive a nod of the head. 'Then it is not good news.'

'No, Madam.'

'Very well, Alice, but please sit down and give me a moment to ring for some coffee; I have a dreadful feeling about this. I can read it in your face that the worst has happened,' and she buried her face in her hands.

'No, Madam,' said Celia, softly. 'Bad, very bad, even, but *not* the worst.'

'Thank God for that,' whispered her ladyship, sitting for a moment in silent prayer. 'Tell me what happened, but please make it quick for I must know how bad it is right away. Did she . . . has she allowed . . .'

'No, Your Ladyship, not that, although it was very, *very* close. I am ashamed to admit that in another few minutes I would have been too late,' and she in turn buried her face in her hands as the spectre of the scene she had witnessed returned to her inner eye.

'I really know very little, Madam,' when she had recovered enough to speak. 'Miss Celia left early this morning and asked me to bring a lunch basket. When I arrived, Miss Celia had . . . she was . . .' and she had to pause 'til the catch in her throat disappeared. 'She was not completely dressed, Madam,' she whispered, 'but nothing serious had happened beyond some extremely intimate contact. I spoke sharply to the professor, and sent him away after a thorough scolding, then brought Miss Celia home.'

'How is she?' queried her ladyship, anxiously.

'She is sleeping now, Madam, but she has had a considerable shock, and I think it may take a little while to overcome it.'

'A shock? Did he force her?'

'No, Madam, Miss Celia was a willing participant in the affair, of that I am sure. It was, unfortunately,' she said wearily, 'rather as I feared; indeed, exactly as we discussed only so short a time ago. She is unable to resist him now that Miss Lucy has been removed from his attentions and she is free to give him her heart – and her body. I must make him understand when I speak to him next – when he *shall* listen to me.

'I should have seen it coming; but there was no warning, just the impulsive action that I feared. But no warning,' and she wept at her own failure to forestall the very thing she dreaded and had so accurately divined.

'Shall I visit my daughter, Alice?'

'Perhaps later this evening, Madam, when she has rested; or better tomorrow morning. Then, when she is more her self, we can perhaps discuss what is to be done about the affair.'

But Alice's diagnosis was incorrect, for Celia was not 'more her self' in the morning. Immediately after the event while Alice was bathing her and putting her to bed, she recovered her spirits a little, but after that the decline was quite marked, until by the third day she was listless to the point of not even wanting to leave her bed, let alone the room.

She did not refer to the event in any way, or mention the Professor or Manfred. She did not even *enter* the studio, where she normally spent all morning. Even when Alice led her there by the hand, she showed not the slightest interest in either the easel or her sketches for works in hand.

She would, in fact have stayed in bed all day if given the chance by Alice.

'It is bad for you to lie around like that,' Alice would say, and make her rise and dress. But nothing made much difference, for then she sat in her room all day in the chair or chaise, unless Alice led her to the terrace, where she sat and stared, apparently at nothing. She refused entirely to go downstairs.

In the hope of sparking a renewed interest in painting, Alice reminded her one bath time that she had thought to do a painting of her in the bathroom brushing her hair.

'In here, Alice? I wanted to paint you in the bathroom? Why would I want to do that?' she asked.

'Because you wanted to do a picture of me stepping into the bathtub.'

'I did?' was all Celia could manage. 'How strange. Surely you do not mean without any clothes on, Alice? Why would you want other people to see you like that!' And that terminated the discussion.

Alice was now genuinely concerned, for the pattern was becoming clear. Any thing to do with the body was anathema to her mistress. It wasn't so much that she had lost interest in the subject, as that she had almost forgotten the *very existence* of the female form, and Alice found that most challenging and instructive. The worst part was, that having elicited the likely cause, she could find no solution to correct it. Perhaps it would take Manfred to unlock the puzzle, but she was not about to risk that. Not until the situation was desperate, anyway, and after a great deal more preparation.

'Do you think we should send for Dr. Jameson, Alice? It has been a full week, and there is no change, except that she has become much thinner and grown even more pale.'

'How would we explain it, Madam? Dare we tell him the truth: that Miss Celia was . . . well, like she was, with . . . some one, in the woods? If we did not tell him, we would be wasting his time, and every body else's. Besides, Madam, even if he knew, I do not see what he could do, she is not ill in the usual way. It is her *spirit* that has been damaged. I think perhaps I should meet the professor and find out more of what happened *before* I arrived, that might provide some thing of a clue to this mystery.'

'How is Miss Celia, Alice? Is she well? I was quite worried when I neither saw her nor heard from her, or anyone else.'

'And well you should be, Professor, for she is quite ill. She does not eat well, or sleep well, and she is listless and tired at all times.'

'Perhaps she is in love,' he responded with a smile, 'those are the usual symptoms.'

'Professor,' snapped Alice, fingering her riding crop and slapping her boot so purposefully that he leaned a little away from her. 'I did not leave Miss Celia alone and come all this way to listen to you spout arrant nonsense! Please have the goodness to treat this matter with the seriousness it warrants!'

'I apologize for my unwarranted levity, Alice; it is simply a manifestation of my own concern. Would it help if I visited her?'

'*No it would not!* You have done enough damage to Miss Celia's mind and in some way that I have yet to fathom. Until I do, you will *not* be admitted into her presence, and probably not even then. However, you *can* assist by telling me what happened between my mistress and your self *before* I arrived. I am sure you can remember when and how that was!' she finished in an angry tone.

'There is no mystery,' he responded, innocently, 'it was all very simple and straightforward. We met, and she was already virtually naked under that half-opened transparent blouse, so it was obvious what she intended I should do, so we went to the glade where you saw us embracing. That is it.'

'*Professor*,' hissed Alice, 'for a supposedly intelligent man, you are certainly the most *appallingly stupid being* I have ever had the misfortune to meet, and I have seen a number quite damaged in the head. You are a complete *buffoon*, and if it weren't that I needed the information in your doltish head, I would dispose of you now, on this very spot!

'Now,' she almost shrieked, 'start at the very beginning and tell me *what happened*, and *do not* miss out a *single, solitary, thing!*'

The telling took longer than the event it self, for Alice would not let him omit a single action.

'*Where* did you touch her, *precisely*?' '*How* did you touch her, *exactly!*' she would bark. 'Miss Celia, what was *she* doing while you conducted this lewd exploration of her innocent body?' 'But you have not said when you loosed her riding skirt', and on and on until the last titillation was explained and examined.

At the telling, the professor was pale and shaken, with the demeanour of a whipped hound, for Alice had humiliated him almost beyond endurance. But he respected her determination to leave no stone unturned to restore her mistress to health. He was also more than a little afraid of her, for she demonstrated a fearlessness and a savagery he had never experienced in any man, let alone a slip of a woman.

Alice, on the contrary, was red in the face and breathing hard.

'Wait here,' she snarled as she dismounted Jasper to stride across the leafy clearing to the far side. Stooping, she picked up a large fallen branch, examined it carefully for a moment, and swung it suddenly and so violently against a stout tree trunk that it shattered into a dozen fragments, the largest of which she picked up, contemplated for some moments, then flung to the ground again before standing facing away for several minutes more.

Turning, she strode back to Jasper and leapt into the saddle in one incredible bound.

'That should have been your stupid head,' she snarled. 'Wait here, and do not move until I return,' then swung Jasper recklessly out of the clearing and was almost at a full gallop even before she had cleared the trees.

It was some considerable time before she returned this time at a fast trot, noting to his credit that he was still mounted, and where she had left him.

'Professor, I have come to one conclusion, at least,' she barked at him. 'That you are either an unmitigated scoundrel or that, whence you originated, your disgraceful behaviour is somehow normal.'

'I can assure . . .' he began, before he was silenced.

'Quiet!' she snapped, 'I have no time for your silly prattle. This time you will listen to *me. In silence.*'

'You were fortunate to be loved, *yes, loved, Professor,*' as she saw his eyebrows rise in astonishment, 'by one of God's gentlest creatures. She thought not of her self, only of you, otherwise you would have been horse whipped until . . . by those who truly love her,' and she whacked her boot hard to emphasize that preferred treatment.

'She has the most beautiful nature I have ever encountered, and is generous to a considerable fault. She is intelligent and talented to a significant degree in many ways: art, history, classical literature, music, architecture – even to settling a building dispute that defied the architect him self. That she is also beautiful of body is a simple act of nature.

'She is, or was before you passed her way, innocent of life, wanting little for her self, and her soul reflects all these things.

'In your callous *stupidity*, you mistook them all to be sweet fruits for the taking; for your sole amusement and pleasure, thinking nothing of the giver and caring even less. In your selfish greed, you were prepared to take every thing her body freely offered, without a second thought as to what your actions would cost her, how they might destroy her, mind and soul, now and forever.

'Perhaps in your world, *Professor*, these things are commonplace; here they are not. Great store is placed on virtue of the kind that Miss Celia has in abundance, and behaviour in the manner exhibited by you during that entire sordid episode is simply not tolerated. Such persons are regarded as a curse on society and are simply removed – with little regard or ceremony, and even less regret.

'I find you to be an evil and greedy person – for man you are not – unfit for association with gentlefolk, and totally unsuited to even clean Miss Celia's boots. I have had recourse to London street sweepers with more kindness and thought for others in their little finger than you possess in your whole loathsome body. It is you, *Professor*, who have been sullied by this despicable affair.

'I will return now to my mistress, to care for her, and hope to nurse her back to some semblance of who she was before you savagely betrayed her.

'My considered opinion is that you should also return whence you came, for you are only a force for evil and destruction in this place,' and she savagely wheeled her horse.

'Come, Jasper, we shall find the air less foul out of this wood than in it,' and she departed in a thunder of hooves that lasted well into the distance.

Manfred, however, remained rooted to the spot for a long, long while, pondering all that had just taken place, for while clearly out of his element, he was not a stupid man.

15

Rapprochement

'How was he, Alice?' inquired Celia, from her chaise on the terrace where Alice had just brought afternoon tea.

Alice jumped. 'To whom are you referring, Miss?'

'Why, Manfred, of course. Who else would I inquire after?'

'I can think of several dozen for whom you might inquire, Miss. Certainly you should not include the professor in that number!'

'But I *do* think of him, Alice, now and then. Why should I not?'

'Because, Miss, he did terrible things to you,' replied Alice firmly.

'Nothing that I did not deserve for my disgraceful conduct, Alice. I taunted him shamelessly, and he responded as you said a man would; so what should I expect of him other than what happened?'

'He could still have been a gentleman, Miss,' said Alice, hotly. 'Mr. Reginald would have behaved perfectly.'

'Ah, yes, dear Reginald, he would. Except that I would not have taunted *him*, would I?'

Alice had no reply, but she did not give up that easily.

'Then why not restore your friendship with Mr. Reginald, Miss, if he is always the perfect gentleman. You could do a lot worse than marry him. And the very *worst* you could do is to ever see the professor again.'

'But that is where you are quite wrong, Alice. I do not love Reginald; I never could, so there it is. But I do love Manfred, or I would if . . .'

'How could you possibly love some one who was going . . . who was so little concerned for your good name, Miss?,' cried Alice, in despair.

'I do not know, Alice. Why do we love at all, tell me that! Why did you love Richard? I do not think we are supposed to know these things; they just are, that is all. And come to that, I was the one who proposed it by dressing heedlessly, without much regard for my own good name, if you recall. But that is all over now; I see it quite clearly. I have sullied my self to the point that I am not a fit companion for any man – and especially him.'

'What are you *saying*, Miss!' replied Alice in utter dismay. 'He is the very one who defiled you!'

'No, Alice, you have it all wrong. I was the one who nourished his natural instinct to fondle me by revealing my self to him; after that he was unable to draw back. I deserved that humiliation; now I am not worthy of his love – or anyone else's, if ever I was.'

'Oh, Miss, do not say that, you have it all wrong in the head. You must forget him. In time you will find some one truly worthy of you to love, I know it,' and she flung her self on her mistress, clinging to her and sobbing.

'There, there, Alice, it is not that bad; I can still find some good works to do to keep me occupied,' at which Alice sobbed all the more, and Celia held her tightly until she had recovered her self somewhat. 'Do not fret so, Alice, it will turn out well enough, I expect. Think about it and you will see that I am right. Now, I am of a mind to rest for a little while.'

'You quite tired me out this afternoon, Alice, so much so that I have had to retire to my bed. Also, I did not get an answer to my question. How was Manfred?'

'How should I know, Miss?'

'Because you saw him this morning, Alice. I saw it in your face the moment you returned,' and she waited. Finally, she continued, 'Well, do I get an answer, Alice, or must I wait all day. How was he?'

'He was his usual selfish self, Miss, totally unconcerned for anyone but him self.'

'Alice, are you sure that is true? He did not inquire after my health at all?' to which Alice made no reply. 'You see, Alice, you deliberately mislead me. He did inquire, then. He is not as entirely selfish as you aver. Did he look well?'

'When I left him, Miss, he did not look well at all, thank goodness!'

'You were unkind to him, Alice? That is not like you, and it does not please me. What *would* please me is for you to respond to two requests that I have of you. First, I would like you to call him Manfred rather than "The Professor",' and Alice opened her mouth to protest, but her mistress continued. 'Second, I would like you to arrange for him to visit me, for I have need to apologize for the mischief I have done him.'

Alice almost exploded. 'No, Miss, I will do no such thing! Not the first, nor the second, and certainly I will not permit you to do the third.'

'Very well, Alice. I cannot force you, for I am much too weak. But you disappoint me greatly. I had expected greater loyalty from you and more concern for my well-being. If you cannot provide me with either, I have no further need of you and you may leave me.' and she turned over in her bed to face the other direction, from whence Alice thought she heard quiet sobbing.

She had no choice but to leave, for she had been dismissed. And she retired to her room and sobbed her heart out on her own bed.

The situation continued all next day, when neither would give in. Alice would bring her mistress' food, and wait to talk as they usually did, but Celia dismissed her until she rang for her, which was infrequently.

At bath time Celia insisted on bathing her self, although Alice would not leave the room. But she would not let Alice touch her.

'You will see that I am right eventually, Alice. Now it is time for my bed,' though it was barely past eight o'clock.

'How is Miss Celia this morning, Alice?' inquired her ladyship, preparing to visit her daughter as usual but, equally as usual, expecting nothing material of it.

'Not improved, Madam. That is because she wants me to ask the professor to visit her,' and here she took a deep breath, 'So that she can *apologize for inciting him to abuse her!*'

Her ladyship gasped, 'Utterly impossible! And what did you reply, Alice?'

'As you have just said, Madam, that it was not possible. However, Miss Celia is very obdurate, Madam, and she shows no sign at all of changing her mind on the matter, but I will not relent.'

'Quite right, Alice. I will visit my daughter in a few moments to see how she is, but I will say nothing on that subject, unless she does, that is.'

'Yes, Madam, that would be best, I believe.'

'Very well, Alice. I must point out, though, that you are looking far from well your self. Are you sleeping and eating properly?'

'I am having difficulty with both of those things, Madam, I am so worried for Miss Celia.'

'I understand, Alice, but it will do no good if you are also confined to your bed, so you must take more care of your self.'

'Yes, Madam, I will try.'

The trouble was that she would lie awake and feel compelled to visit her mistress to see that all was well, only to find her as restless as her self. When she did finally get some sleep, it was to be disturbed by haunting dreams of dark riders on even darker horses, brandishing stout staves to destroy all who were foolish enough to come within their reach, and she would awaken sweating, or shivering, or both.

It was also quite evident that the stalemate which existed could not be resolved by talking, although she tried many times, when angry words and looks were exchanged.

However, of late, her mistress would simply not discuss the subject further.

'You know my wishes; Alice,' she would declare, 'if you will not carry them out, there is nothing more to be said. But I shall not regain my health until I have made my apologies to Manfred.'

The most dreadful part for Alice was that the statement was coming true. She could not tell whether her mistress made it deliberately so or not, but she was getting thinner and more drawn by the day. Some accommodation clearly needed to be made, and there was little doubt who would be compelled to make it.

'Supposing I visit the professor, Miss, and explain your point of view to him. Would that make you feel better?' but all she got for that suggestion was a withering look of disbelief.

'But I cannot let you prostrate your self before him, Miss, that would be just too awful to witness. Besides, her ladyship would not permit him to come, I am quite sure of that!'

'I do not exactly propose to "prostrate my self", as you so crudely phrase it, Alice. But you do not have to be present if it pains you so.'

'*Oh, yes I do*, Miss. I will not permit that monster to be alone with you, not even for one second.'

'If by "that monster" you mean Manfred, Alice, I would be obliged if you be more polite to his name, at least in my presence. If you cannot convince her ladyship, then that is an end to the matter, and there is no hope for me. Now please leave me, for I must rest,' and Alice was dismissed once more to brood over a situation that she was not winning; in fact was decidedly losing, which was much the more disquieting.

More importantly still, her mistress was clearly intent on sacrificing her self, and it was a late hour before Alice had made her decision.

'Professor, I have with great difficulty obtained her ladyship's permission for you to visit Miss Celia at three o'clock this afternoon,' and ignored his raised eyebrows. 'She was *most* reluctant to have you in the Hall under any pretext whatsoever, for she believes that you have grievously harmed her daughter, and she is of a mind to involve her solicitor in the affair. It would greatly cool your ardour to spend a few months in Wandsworth prison. However, although you most deservedly warrant such treatment, I do not support that course for the whole matter would then be a subject of public debate. In her present invalid condition, Miss Celia would not survive such an ordeal.'

Alice raised her hand to silence his attempt to speak.

'Before you indicate your desires in the affair, there are several points which I must make clear. Miss Celia has requested that I explain some issues to you.'

Suddenly she was trembling so violently that she had difficulty in controlling Jasper. 'Quiet!' she barked, giving him a slap with the heavy end of her whip, some thing he had never seen her use before, and her eyes were blazing with anger.

'She feels strangely impelled to *apologize to you, Professor*, for *your* disgraceful conduct! I may not be able to prevent her from offering that apology. *But, if you accept that apology*, if you *crow*, if you *laud* it over her *in any manner whatsoever*, by God, you shall have a day of reckoning with me, even if I swing high on the gallows for it. It will be worth it, for I will not stand by and see you humiliate her anew!'

And her knuckles on the riding crop were white and trembling with the effort of control.

At these words, Alice was surprised to see the professor wheel his mount and take several paces away, holding there for some moments.

'Can you then not face the enormity of your crime against a helpless young lady?' she called.

'On the contrary, Alice,' he responded quietly, turning once more to face her. 'I can face it because I have gone through purgatory my self this past week and more; since our last meeting in fact, when you most admirably laid out the depths to which I had sunk.'

Alice looked sceptically at him for evidence of duplicity, but to her surprise found none.

'After you left me, it took some time for your message to sink through, but it did, finally. Thus you may be surprised to learn that I am in agreement with her ladyship, and do not deserve to enter the Hall ever again, for I have indeed grievously harmed her daughter. But I am also honour bound to rectify my mischief through my own actions, if it possibly can be repaired.'

Alice was appeased not at all by this statement, for she mistrusted his motives altogether, considering that he aspired to return to her mistress' good graces only to serve his own base purposes. But she had to admit that his contrite demeanour seemed genuine. He also appeared to be thinner than when they had last met, and the jauntiness was gone from his posture. Was it possible that he had learnt some thing after all?

'I also agree with you, Alice,' he continued, 'that I deserve a horse whipping for what I perpetrated on your mistress,' wonder of wonders, thought Alice, 'and pray that I may not have created permanent damage to her, for I would then deserve a *lifetime* of prison.

'Further, please rest assured that I have *no intention whatsoever* of accepting *any* apology from your mistress for my disgraceful conduct, and I shall prevent her making any if I possibly can. I shall also be most assiduous in my own abject apologies,' and he sat quietly on Johnson waiting for his message to be fully absorbed by an almost incredulous Alice.

'How was he this morning, Alice?' inquired Celia, eagerly. 'Is he coming? Oh dear, whatever shall I wear? What shall we have . . . ?'

'One question at a time, Miss! He was not his usual self, Miss.'

'Alice! Was he ill or some thing? Is he not coming? Oh dear, what have I done to . . .'

'Hold, Miss; he was in fine fettle. What I meant was that he has changed, Miss – for the better,' she hastened to add before her mistress got the wrong end of the stick again. 'And *I* shall take charge of all arrangements. As for your dress, we shall think about that directly; we do have some three hours.

'Firstly, you must have a good luncheon,' brushing aside protestations that she was not the slightest bit hungry, 'a good hot soup, *that I shall make my self,* so you had better eat it. Then bathe in Miss Lucy's special bath salts, and we will have to put a little colour in those cheeks.'

At Celia's eager acceptance of these suggestions, she added,

'Is he *that* important to you, Miss?' and Celia blushed a very pretty colour, as if to deny the need for such deception.

'Yes, Alice, I am ashamed to admit that he is, although I expect he will find me unworthy of those sentiments.'

'He better not,' Alice rejoined, stoutly, 'or he will get his face roundly slapped by me.'

'Oh, Alice,' laughed her mistress, 'I believe you would, too!'

'I would indeed, Miss, if he treats you any less than the finest lady in the land,' and gave her mistress a big but gentle hug, for that was the very first laugh since that most dreadful day. 'We shall make you so pretty, that he will fall in love with you on the spot.'

'Do you really think he might, Alice? Perhaps just a little? Oh, I do so want him to, Alice,' she rushed on, a tear forming and dropping to the bed sheet.

'Do you want my *honest* opinion, Miss?' said Alice, softly.

'Do I dare say "yes", Alice?' replied Celia in a whisper.

And Alice drew near, put her arms around her neck, and whispered the reply in her ear:

'I hold, my dearest mistress, that he does already.'

'Really?' cried the disbelieving Celia.

'Really and truly, Miss. I am quite sure of it. Besides, if he doesn't, why I will box his ridiculous ears, that is what!'

'Oh, Alice, you are a silly goose, and I think his ears are quite nice, but I love you for it anyway,' laughing and holding her close while they shed a considerable number of tears between them.

Alice waited for the professor in the apple orchard, for she had directed him to make that approach, and he was early.

'Professor, Miss Celia has requested me to address you as "Mr. Manfred", and I shall do so in her presence as a special consideration to her. However, if you behave correctly, as you have promised, then I shall continue to do so afterwards, if that is acceptable to you.'

'*Most* acceptable, Alice, and I deeply appreciate your thoughtfulness. Thank you.'

'And one thing more, Mr. Manfred; Miss Celia is quite weak, so I shall be the judge as to when she tires, and I shall be glad if you would take my indication as your acknowledgement that it is time to depart. Is that agreed?'

'It is agreed.'

'Very well, then. Let us proceed indoors. First, I will take you to her

Ladyship in the Drawing room, but you must not approach her. A "Good afternoon, Your Ladyship", will suffice and which she will most likely refuse to acknowledge. Then we will proceed to Miss Celia's room. You have been granted *very special permission* to visit her in her boudoir – and that only because she is too weak too be moved. Please understand that *most* clearly.

'You must maintain an appropriate distance there also, and I have the *strictest* instructions not to leave the room while you are in it. I bring this to your attention now, Mr. Manfred, because I do not wish to appear discourteous to you should the occasion arise, for I have been left no choice in the matter.'

'I understand perfectly, Alice.'

'We will find Miss Celia on her South Terrace on her chaise, and the conversation will occur only there. Her ladyship is *very* concerned about the propriety of this visit. Is that also quite clear?'

'Perfectly clear, Alice. I am most appreciative of your advising me of these affairs.'

Alice knocked before entering.

'Mr. Manfred, Miss. Shall I ask him to approach?'

'Yes, please, Alice. Good afternoon, Manfred. I am sorry that you find me in such condition that I cannot rise to greet you, but I have been rather poorly, as you may have heard,' and she extended her hand to him, which he took and held for a long moment.

'I had expected to find you pale and wan, my dear Celia, but to me you are as beautiful as the first rose of summer,' and the object of his homage did her best to emulate one such of rose pink hue.

'Please sit there, Manfred,' she managed, after a pause to regain her poise. 'Is tea ready, Alice?'

'Yes, Miss, it will be here directly.'

'Thank you, Alice. Manfred, I have invited you here that I might . . .' but she got no further.

'Mistress Celia, I would like to offer you these humble wild flowers, which I my self picked in a place that is very dear to me. I know that they are insignificant and far less than grow in your own garden. But they come with my heart,' and he positioned him self before her on one knee as he presented them, head bowed low.

'Manfred, they are quite the most beautiful I have seen all summer long.' and she blushed again. 'Alice, please get a vase for these lovely flowers.'

Alice, mindful of her obligations, replied only, 'Yes, Miss. As soon as tea arrives, I will have one brought up,' at which there was a knock on the door.

Alice returned with the tea tray to find them already holding hands, although at a considerable stretch. The tea table between them soon put a damper on that activity, and Alice arranged the flowers to place them at her mistress' feet.

After the small talk of the tea, Celia began:

'Manfred, I have been thinking that I may have . . .' whereupon Manfred jumped to his feet.

'Mistress Celia, before you utter a single word of reproach, I must confess that I have been dying with humiliation at the great iniquity I wrought you, an injury so great as to place you in this present distressed condition. I could not bear to hear any words from your sweet lips other than those of utter condemnation at my disgraceful conduct. If you should in any manner seek to pardon it, my shame would cause me to depart immediately, never to return out of complete humiliation.'

'But, Manfred, I only wished to . . .'

'Say no more, my dearest,' at which phrase Celia blushed again, 'or I shall be compelled to flee in dishonour.'

'Very well, Manfred, if you are sure I may not even . . .'

'I positively insist, my love. We shall not speak of the affair, ever.' And there the matter rested as he skilfully turned the conversation to other affairs.

'More tea, Manfred?' but when she tried to lift the pot, her hand trembled so that she was forced to set it down again. At this, Alice immediately jumped to her feet.

'Mr. Manfred, thank you for coming. It was most thoughtful of you.'

'Must you go so soon?' said Celia in a pained tone. 'You have only just arrived.'

'I must not tire you further, my love, but I would willingly return, should you command it,' he added, eagerly.

'Tomorrow?' responded Celia, quickly.

'Tomorrow, certainly,' and he looked at Alice, who nodded. 'At the same hour. Until then, farewell, and sweet dreams,' and he kissed her hand as he bowed.

'I will see you out, Mr. Manfred,' said Alice, and she smiled at her mistress as she departed.

To her ladyship, on return to the Drawing room in answer to her anxious question, Alice responded,

'Yes, Your Ladyship, it went well; indeed *very* well, Madam. He proposes to come again at the same time tomorrow, and I took the liberty – begging your pardon, Madam – I took the liberty of accepting that request, having judged that Miss Celia improved remarkably while in his presence.'

'And did she insist on . . . ?'

'No, Madam, he simply *would not* permit her to utter a word on the subject. He described his own conduct as disgraceful, to be utterly condemned, and if Miss Celia offered one single word, he would be forced to flee in complete dishonour – never to return. A very clever ploy, if I may say so, Madam, for Miss Celia will not risk that.'

'But was he sincere in his apology, Alice, or was it simply another guise to . . . you know what I mean?'

'Yes, Madam, I know precisely what you mean,' now with a puzzled frown on her thoughtful face. 'But it is very strange, Madam. I do believe he is sincere, indeed, *most* sincere. And to my astonishment, Madam, he loves Miss Celia in the accepted sense of the word. Of that I now have no doubt whatsoever – begging your pardon, Madam, for that is your prerogative to accept or dismiss. I am here merely to report to you as honestly as I can what I have just witnessed.

'And now, if I may have Your Ladyship's permission, I would like to visit my charge again, for she will be most anxious to discuss the visit, and I am most anxious to continue her improvement of spirit and health.'

'Certainly, Alice, for you have done splendidly. But then you always do, my dear. Please give my daughter my love, and let me perhaps have another report before you retire for the night?'

'Certainly, Madam,' and with a deep curtsey of acknowledgement of the trust bestowed upon her, she left quietly, but ran up the stairs to arrive breathless in Miss Celia's room again.

'Alice,' said her mistress, severely, when she returned. 'What on earth took you so *long*? I could have died of a chill in the time you have been away. I suppose you took tea below stairs and tattle-taled all you know of my dreadful conduct.'

'Yes, Miss. They were all agog, particularly at the news of how you made him crawl at your feet!'

'Alice! You didn't!'

'No, Miss, because I do not tattle in the servant's hall, as full well you know; and if you do not, then I will withdraw forthwith,' and she turned to go in pretended indignation.

'Not so fast, Alice; for I have a bone to pick with you! You put him up to that confession,' her cheeks once more a delicate pink, which pleased the secretly happy Alice immensely.

'On my honour, Miss, I did not. I was going to, I admit, but he would not let me speak, just as he would not let you speak, so we were both thwarted. But no more, Miss. Now you must rest.'

'But I am too excited to rest, Alice. I want to laugh and sing.'

'Rest you shall, Miss, for tomorrow he must see that you are improving, or he may not return at all!'

'You really believe so, Alice?' said Celia, in a troubled voice.

'No, Miss, I was only making light of it. He will be back tomorrow, and many a morrow thereafter, I will be bound. Sleep now until I bring your dinner, or I shall send him away without admittance!'

'You would not dare!'

'Oh, yes I would! We will see how much you sleep, first, and I shall tarry 'til you do.'

'One question first please, Alice. Do you think he does? I mean, really and truly?'

'Yes, Miss,' laughed Alice, 'of that I am quite, quite certain. He is truly, madly in love with you – and I know all about that, Miss Celia. Soon you will see and feel all of that for your self. But, *but*, he is going to want a healthy lady love, not one who is always sickly and pining, so off to slumber land with you, or I really shall send him away, saying you are still too ill to receive him!'

'Alice, you chased him away again, just as I was enjoying having him so close to me. I think he is really beginning to like me and you dispatched him like a supplicant. Worse, you would not let him come tomorrow. You have a most cruel nature, Alice, to act so.'

'Yes, Miss, I have, for I do not like to see you happy.'

Celia regarded her suspiciously.

'You are making jest of it again, Alice. How could you be so horrible to me, just as I am beginning to get better. Now I shall pine away once more, you will see.'

'Very well, Miss; but shall I divulge the purpose?' and Celia nodded impatiently. 'If Mr. Manfred comes a third time in as many days and finds you *still* lying on that chaise, he is going to wonder if you are not, perhaps, already an invalid and doubt whether you will ever get out of it?

'Now, by Saturday, you will have exercised and got some natural colour back in your cheeks, and you will be walking again. If you are, *if* you are, and it is a warm day, I shall row the two of you 'round the lake. And if you are very, *very* good, I shall take some tea to the Island for the two of you. Does that sound like a better idea than lying on that silly chaise all the time?'

'Would you do that for me – for *us*, Alice?'

'Aye, Miss, and much, much more. But only if the two of you are good, mind!' and they both laughed and set to planning the events for recovery until the next visiting day.

Tea was over, and Alice was putting the plates and other things back in the hamper as Celia turned to Manfred.

'Please help me up into the hammock, Manfred. I am still not quite strong enough for that.'

'Certainly, my love,' and he bent and picked her up in his arms. 'Good gracious,' he exclaimed, 'you are no more than a feather,' and he held her in that position until she put her arm around his neck and leaned her head on his shoulder, while Alice found it necessary to take something to the boat.

'This is most agreeable,' she whispered, 'I could linger here a goodly while, perchance forever.'

'Then perhaps you should,' he responded softly, kissing her cheek, while she kissed his neck.

'Perhaps I will,' she replied, 'but there is much to discuss first,' and she looked up into his eyes with a very serious expression.

'We shall,' he replied, 'whenever you feel hale enough to do so,' and there it stood 'til that day.

'Thank you, Alice, for rowing us, you must be very tired.'

'No, Miss, not at all. Firstly, because it was so gentle; and secondly because it did my heart good to see you so happy.'

'It is all because of you, Alice,' who smiled her appreciation at the words. 'So to the most important question remaining – where do we live? Do you think it could be here?'

'This "we", Miss, is who, exactly?'

'Why, Manfred and my self, silly. Who else?'

'Has he asked you, Miss, when I was not listening?'

'Does he have to actually ask? Is it not enough to listen to my heart?'

'Perhaps, Miss, if you are sure you are hearing *his* heart correctly. When you were in his arms, perhaps?'

'Then it was most clear. But there were other times also, when he held my hand in that special way of his, and the way he played with my fingers. He doesn't have to ask, and I do not have to say "yes", to some thing we both know, do I? But if it makes you feel any better, will you please contrive to oblige him to ask?'

'You may be quite sure I will attend to that, Miss.'

'Thank you, Alice, that is very kind of you. Now, where to live?'

'Not here, Miss, that would be a poor substitute for the avocation of making a home. How about a little – not too little – cottage, with a few fields surrounding it, a few animals, a copse for picnics, and a fishing river meandering along one side.'

'Sounds just idyllic, Alice. Is it real, or just a dream?'

'It exists, Miss. Just the two of you, Miss?' accompanied by an anxious look, which her mistress interpreted correctly and responded accordingly.

'Yes, Alice. I am sure I could manage a small cottage by my self, with Manfred helping with the heavier things, of course. But if it gets too much when the babies start arriving, then I suppose I might get some help in the kitchen. Now, where is this perfect cottage you conjure?'

'It would not suit just a couple, Miss; it is too big for that, so you should not inconvenience your self with it after all,' her face a mask of confused emotions, while her fingers twisted her apron corner into a knot.

'Some thing the matter, Alice?' enquired her mistress, innocently. 'Have I upset you in some way? And you really must stop that nervous habit you have with your apron!'

'No, Miss, nothing very important. I just thought . . . that perhaps . . . when . . .' and looked as if she were about to burst into tears.

'Alice, come here you foolish child,' as she folded her in her arms. 'Of *course* the "we" includes you! *Whatever* made you think that I could live without *you*. You shall be part of me, wherever I go, always; for as long as I live, and for as long as *you* wish it to be so. There, will *that* satisfy you – or do I have to throw in the moon?' And Alice hugged her mistress and laughed and cried at the same time, until they were both doing it.

'Now, about this Dream Cottage of *ours*, Alice. Shall we visit it tomorrow, perchance, as soon after lunch as maybe?' Alice smiled and hugged her mistress all the more tightly, as if to say she would have never let her go, anyway, adding only:

'As to the moon, Miss, you just did, and the stars, too,' providing her a kiss on the cheek, happily – and wonderingly – content to lie in her mistress' arms for a good while longer, such was her contentment at the special feelings it engendered in her bosom.

'Is it not pretty, Miss,' said Alice, after she had obtained the key from the neighbouring farm, 'with all those roses growing 'round the door?'

'A little too abundant for my liking, Alice, but you are quite correct, it is quaint – though perhaps a little too large for just two people as you so rightly said.'

'I will have them trimmed, Miss; and you are forgetting about the thirteen children.'

'Heavens, Alice, do not wish that on me!'

'It isn't big enough for that many anyway, Miss, but there are three nice-sized bedrooms, and room for quite a large bathroom in the roof space here. The kitchen is dreadful, but a decent cook would want a new one anyway.'

'But I was intending to do the cooking my self, Alice, or Manfred will think me most unsuited to the wifely tasks.'

'I will get a cook for you, Miss, one that I already have in mind. Manfred will find your soft hands more to his liking and be the more loving of you for it, believe me.'

'Very well, Alice, if you say so. However, that "river", as I believe you called it, has not been properly instructed, for it behaves more akin to a brook.'

'Yes, Miss, but it is several hundred yards long, and you have both banks, out to that line of willows. There are several places where you could widen it with a little dam, perhaps a waterwheel. And the fishing is quite good, I hear. The copse is behind that windrow there, and up the rise.'

'I do not think I want to see that, Alice, for there is really only one copse for me.'

'But you must see it, Miss, for if you do not like it, you must not purchase the property.'

'Oh, very well, Alice. How you do push a person,' Celia grumbled, remounting her horse and proceeding to the place indicated. Alice followed more slowly, holding back a little and waiting 'til her mistress entered the trees. She did not have long to wait, for there was a sudden loud cry followed by a squeal of delight.

'Alice, come quickly, for this you will not believe.'

As Alice drew alongside on Sally, her mistress pranced around the clearing until both horse and rider were quite giddy.

'My Sylvan Glade, Alice, now *my very own* – and Manfred's too, of course. So that is why we never saw anyone here. This is just too much to comprehend. Now I must take a closer look at that Cottage, for this puts an altogether different complexion on the matter,' as she turned and hurried Jasper down the slope. 'There will be a lot of planning and altering to do, Alice, but we are most fortunate, are we not?'

'Yes, Miss, we are indeed,' she replied a little dryly, as they reached the Cottage again.

'Alice?' said Celia, pulling up Jasper, 'are you telling me that you knew it was there?'

'Yes, Miss, I knew it was your glade.'

'But how can that be, Alice; I have never seen this Cottage before.'

'Because that is where I started, Miss. I also wondered why we never saw any body near, so one day I rode down here to find out who owned it and whether they would consider selling. And you know the rest.'

'Alice, why am I always so surprised when you do some thing quite wonderful; for you are always doing it,' and she closed her horse to hold Alice as tightly as she could reach.

'Now I will never be able to let you go, Alice,' she whispered in her ear.

'No, Miss, you never will, and I am so glad that you are pleased.'

'Come then, we must look at it all again,' dismounting, 'for I believe I would like to live here, once it is all shipshape and Bristol fashion.'

'Supposing he doesn't ask you, Miss, what then?'

'What indeed! If he doesn't, he doesn't, and more fool he. That is why I would take it only if you were in agreement, Alice, for it will certainly require at least two to manage it.'

'I liked it the moment I set eyes on it, Miss, dirt and all. Somehow I knew it would suit you, even if it hadn't had the special glade. For good measure, it also has a nice big vegetable garden at the back that is not too overgrown, and we could soon have it all looking most presentable.'

'But who is this "we" you speak of, Alice?' and they both laughed, and entered the Cottage together.

'This could be a very nice sitting room, Alice,' as she sat on an old settle that Alice had quickly dusted. 'After that inglenook fireplace is repaired, it should be quite charming, and this bay window hardly needs any work – once the windows are cleaned! Those two rooms, I would knock down the dividing wall and turn it into a dining room; and there is space for a cosy study in that corner. And you were certainly right about the kitchen. It is perfectly *horrid!*'

'If you would like to look at the other buildings, Miss, I will do a little work here.'

'Very well, Alice, I do need to poke around a bit to get the lie of the land,' and she departed in a most sprightly manner for one so recently quite ill.

'What is this, Alice; tea cups? And plates and cake? How is this possible without a kettle or a fire?'

'We have a small fire in the kitchen, Miss, and a kettle – which I believe I hear boiling, so I shall return directly with the tea. You see, Miss,' returning with a large steaming teapot, 'I asked James this morning to bring over kindling and a few logs, together with an old kettle and a few cups and the like. And Cook had just baked, so that was at hand, too.'

'Alice, you are a marvel! Even before I have seen the Cottage, you have it already provisioned. Bless you,' reaching to provide a lingering kiss to her cheek; whereupon Alice positively glowed with pleasure.

'And I see you have cleaned a few of those small window panes. They are going to look most handsome when all is done.'

'It was just a quick rub, Miss, but they have come up rather well, for so little effort.'

'All in all, Alice, a most delightful proposition. I will speak to our solicitor the first moment that I can to obtain the details of the property. If there aren't any restrictive hereditaments, I could perhaps rent it with the option to purchase and start cleaning up and repairing immediately. You are in agreement?'

'Yes, Miss, completely. I know that we could be very happy here.'

'That is settled, then. But before we depart, I will have another cup of that most admirable tea, and I do believe another slice of Cook's excellent plum cake would keep the wolf from the door, for I am suddenly hungry once more,' receiving Alice's nod of appreciation – and an extra-thick slice of cake.

'While we are relaxing and contemplating, Miss, and by way of under-standing, may I ask a question, even one perhaps quite personal?'

'Certainly, Alice, what would you like to know of my heart's desire?'

'Well, Miss; all of a sudden you seem quite well again. Not only that, but now you seem to be able to accept – with a clear heart – that Mr. Manfred may indeed not ask for your hand in marriage, or even accompany you here? How can that be when, only yesterday, he was your only hope of happiness?'

'That is very perceptive of you, Alice. I confess it has puzzled me some, too. In response, I think I have crossed some sort of Rubicon – you know the word, Alice?' – surprised and gratified to receive a nod and a murmured 'a river in ancient Rome, Miss' (was there *no end* to her capabilities?).

'Somehow, having quite shamelessly set my cap at Manfred, I have apparently and irrevocably charted a course. I am not sure yet to where, but I have set forth and there is no turning back. I do not fully comprehend it, but in some measure I have set my self free.

'I have somehow just "grown up", some where deep inside me. Yesterday I was a child with dreams; today I am a woman with hopes. Not in the usual sense with a man, but emancipated, nonetheless.

'I love Manfred dearly, of that there is no doubt. And I always shall. It is required that he should join us and I would be deeply hurt should he choose not to. But, somehow I would survive – with your wonderful assistance of course – because this Cottage I deem to be my destiny, our destiny – provided we can manage to hold onto it. Does any of that make sense to you?'

'Oh yes, Miss, completely. Somehow I have known it, too, and we *shall* succeed. However, I do have another question.

'As I understand it, you feel free to follow your own course. That means you will buy the Cottage and make it your home, whatever you – or he – decides about marriage. If that is so, why not simply let nature take its course, for I am sure he will ask in the fullness of time?'

'A most interesting question, Alice, and the answer is rather involved. I am not quite as free to order my life as you presuppose. Her ladyship would be *most* reluctant to allow her only true daughter to live alone (and for this purpose, the hired help do not count) in an unmarried state. It would simply be too shocking.'

'But if you have the means to do so, Miss, why could that not be done?'

'Ah, the means. And what do you know of my "means", Alice?'

'Well, Miss, really very little, and it is certainly none of my business, as you are aware. But the talk in the Servants' Hall has it that you are a wealthy young woman. So if you – that is we – are to be fully happy and accomplished in our new venture, then sufficient means would eliminate the possibility of failure for the lack of it.'

'That is well reasoned, Alice, and as to the "wealthy young woman", I acknowledge to you – and to you only, for it is not for below-stairs gossip – that it is so, and irrevocably so.'

'Thank you, Miss, for that instruction. Yet if the means are secure, does not that make you truly independent to travel your own path?'

'Yes, it is more than adequate for any thing the Cottage could possibly require. I will also add that the new East Wing was all to my account, which gave me virtual *carte blanche* with regard to design and quality of finish. The investment here is as naught compared to that. But this is for your private ear alone, Alice. Even my sister knows nothing of this.'

Alice blushed deeply as she realized her debt of gratitude for her own and Mildred's quarters – which far exceeded any thing for the rest of the household – was due solely to her mistress.

'Thank you, Miss, that is most generous and gracious of you. I would say more . . . but I cannot speak,' for her throat was restricted and her eyes swimming with unshed tears.

'Then come, Alice,' taking her arm, 'let us retire now that we are rested, and on the return journey talk about that last "we". If it is to be two, then we shall have to learn to be farmers. I will collect the eggs, and you, my dear Alice, will have to learn to slop the cows and milk the pigs. Or do I have that the wrong way?' and they both laughed as they mounted their horses.

'I believe it is the other way, Miss, but I shall confirm it for you,' as they rode through the yard and up toward the glade.

'Let us then return to "independence", Alice, now that you have raised the subject, because you have a sound mind for this sort of thing. Now, it does not depend solely on sufficient means. When one is from a good family – as are both Miss Lucy and my self – it is assumed that wealth goes hand-in-hand with social position.

'You see, if I were to live an unwed life, society would conclude that I had a lover some where hard by. Besides, young ladies of good fortune do not live in mere *cottages* – especially tumble-down ones! Where should we hold our first Ball? In the hay barns? With the orchestra in the loft?' And they both had a good laugh at the ridiculous pictures that conjured.

'Not only that, but all my friends and associates would be considered contaminated by association, and suspect of the same malady. And so, quite soon, we would become isolated and alone, with the Quintet quite unthinkable. Can you see Lord Houghton's face at the thought?'

'Oh, yes, Miss, I can,' responded Alice with a laugh. 'And it is most dismaying.'

'Yet there is actually more, for mother would also be suspect for having such a peculiar daughter – and especially for permitting her to do such an odd thing.'

'I am so glad, Miss, that I am not a society lady! I know I would not have the patience for all those petty restrictions.'

'Then brace your self, Alice, for there is yet still more! You see, like it or not, I would still be eligible for being married off to a gentleman of high position in society and of the landed gentry – especially one of noble birth such as an Earl – who could not be denied. Mother would be unable to resist the demand for my acceptance – once I had been suitably chastised and cleansed of my errant ways, of course! And absolute refusal to such an eminent proposal would bring ruination to my entire family.'

'Now I see, Miss, that marriage would remove you from our Cottage as if by force.'

'Exactly, Alice. It would be lost to us, even as we lived in it.'

'At nearly twenty-two, I should have been successfully married some time ago. And the longer I wait, the older and more displeasing my husband will be. So if you have even half a solution to the conundrum, I shall be delighted to hear it, for I do value your opinion quite highly.' And the object of these words blushed most prettily at the generosity of the compliment.

'Thank you, Miss,' with a little bow and a grateful smile. 'Then it would seem, Miss, we have to get Mr. Manfred to desire to marry you, to ask to marry you, and then in truth to marry you! That would place you beyond reach of even the most determined suitor, and would also secure the Cottage for all time.'

'But how do you conjure that dilemma? Do you believe that we could achieve all that within the next several months? Otherwise tenure could be, in the words of Thomas Hobbes, "Solitary, nasty, brutish, and short"!' and there was a long silence as they wended their way from the open ground down towards home.

'That was most instructive, Miss. In turn, I may be able to offer some thing of value to your self, although it may prove more challenging than welcome, for it is not a solution.'

'Please, Alice, express whatever is on your mind, welcome or otherwise.'

'Well, Miss, you recall with the Quintet that we visited many – if not most – of the Great Houses in the County. While I did not reside in the Servants' Quarters, I did take meals with them. Thus I heard the gossip of the Household, much of it related to your self.'

'Is that so?'

'Yes, Miss. Some of it salacious and based on envy, but some also to your marriageability to the young scions of the house. But there was also a number concerning the Master of the House when he was in a widowed state, and some of an unmarried son – also well advanced in years, who were desirous of offspring to continue the family fortunes through the male line.

'Some of those were as you have just described. All-in-all, a most unhappy prospect, Miss, and one perhaps closer than you are aware.'

'Thank you, Alice, that was a most valuable intercession. A sudden thought, Alice. Were any of these "names" at the Ball?'

'Yes, Miss, many, for the guests represented the cream of your society, including all the lords and ladies of those Great Houses. I now recall more than one regarding your person inappropriately – if you under-stand my meaning, Miss.'

'Do you perhaps mean "lewdly", Alice?'

'Yes, Miss. Of course, I was not then aware of a threat to your status. Now I see it *quite* differently, for if they are aware of your fortune they may choose to add it to their own, together with a most handsome bounty – your private self – to sweeten the arrangement. So we must succeed, or both lose our fortune in every sense of the word.'

'Not a pretty thought, Alice, as you did earlier inform us,' making their way to Celia's room by way of the side entrance, where Celia paused.

'I shall ask mother to be excused from dinner, and have a plate sent up. Would you do that for me?' Please say that I am well, but a little fatigued after the day's events and my recent indisposition. Then perhaps you could bathe me a little earlier than usual to provide more time for our bedtime chat. You know what the subject will be, for we must succeed or, as you stated, "lose our fortune"?'

'Now that you have been so open, Miss,' as Celia relaxed on her chaise, 'I believe I see a way to achieve all three of your challenges, for it must be all or nothing – although more unto several weeks – and all conducted in the utmost secrecy. As Mr. Burns put it: "The best laid schemes of mice and men go oft awry".'

'Very good, Alice, to know your Burns, although I do believe it was "gang aft a-gley". He was a great poet – even if his Scots was at times incomprehensible!' and they laughed at so accurate a remark.

'Thank you for finding my future home for me, Alice, that has made it a truly wonderful day, and I see hope for the future, after all. It is high time I settled and made some thing of my self and my talents – with your help, for it could not be done alone.

'Then I shall see you in the bathroom in an hour or so. Which reminds me, Alice, do I recall a promise to do more of your self as a model? If so, I still intend to honour that. And it also seems that I was rude to you over a painting I had suggested concerning bathing. Is that correct?'

'Yes, and no, Miss. There was a bathroom pose that we discussed, but you were not rude, Miss, just a little not your self, that is all. It can wait, and is of no consequence in comparison to the weighty issues that currently oppress your self.'

'Thank you, Alice, but I shall not forget my promise, and a return to my easel will certainly help my full recovery.'

And with another deep curtsey, Alice withdrew to attend to the next affairs for her beloved mistress.

Sister Lucy was required to spend most of two weeks with each of the Earl's sisters in turn – first with the oldest, maiden Aunt Augusta, now with the next senior, Aunt Beatrice (widow of the late Sir Archibald Montrose of the Manor of that name), and then with the youngest, Aunt Cicely, a 'campaign widow', for her husband was serving with his regiment on the Northwest Frontier, not expected to return for at least a further year.

Now Lucy was tired, and worse, quite annoyed, having spent the last three weeks or more traipsing around the County with Charles' Aunt Augusta – and there was at least another fortnight to go! Not that Aunt was unpleasant or difficult; on the contrary, she was most attentive. It was simply that she was very dull company.

Being Charles' oldest relation, she was also quite advanced in years, and Lucy was unaccustomed to having such people around her, still needing to develop the patience that living with them required. Nor did Aunt know any thing of matters musical, and, although she did play the piano a little, it was without style or grace.

It was only when Lucy heard her sing for the first time, that she realized the poor lady was tone deaf, and simply unaware of the wrong notes she played or sang – and at that felt more than a little guilty at her own ill humour.

She had also come to realize that the introduction to Charles' extended family had been a decidedly rude awakening. She might have welcomed it in contrast to her own quiet lifestyle after her father had passed on – were it not for those exhilarating days with Celia and the Quintet, which seemed now to compose her entire life! At that discouraging thought, a tear trickled down her cheek as she laid her head on her arms on the little writing desk in her private suite.

She had retired after dinner to pen a letter to her sister and had progressed but little. Indeed, 'My Dearest Celia' was its totality. Somehow, nothing would fix itself long enough in her mind to put it on paper, much as she longed to write – for she missed her sister terribly. Not only that, but their way of life, too.

It was not any one thing; it was *every* thing. She missed especially their evening bathing session, when they spent the most time together, talking, planning and, yes, the caring, too – she especially missed that. And on that thought shed a few more silent tears into her lace handkerchief.

While she understood that the purpose of the visit was to make them certain that this was the proper wife-to-be for their nephew, it was not her intention to be submitted to other than the most cursory of inspections, for she regarded Charles as the only proper one to make that judgment.

And as far as she herself was concerned, it had already been made, and she almost wished they would reject her so she could return to her former happy life in the East Wing.

16

The Cottage

As he wound his horse slowly up the hill to the crest for the first time for almost two weeks, Manfred was puzzled. He had thought Celia was growing warm toward him again, forgiven for the event on the hill. Thus he had expected to visit her ever more frequently. Instead, several days had gone by before he even heard from Alice, only to be told that it would be more nearly a week before he could visit again, and this time it would be at the glade: Three o'clock sharp for an 'Art Study' class.

That was the best he could make of Alice's description, and its obscure message and its implications had kept him awake most of the night.

'Bring your own charcoal and paper if you choose, but supplies will be on hand,' was the way she had put it.

The strangest part, though, was that he was warned not to visit the glade before then, or even ride to the top of the ridge, or he would be trespassing, as it was now Miss Celia's private domain. Wishing was one thing, he thought, but calling it your 'domain' was going a bit far.

And now he took a moment to recall the few additional words Alice had uttered. They added up to a message that Miss Celia was planning her affairs, and the train was about to leave the station, so not to delay if he wanted to be aboard. Of course, she hadn't used those words, but that was her pretty clear intent. 'All Aboard' as they would say in the New World. And some odd thing about prizes being awarded to all?

The 64-dollar question was: did he want *to be aboard? He thought he had a ticket to ride, or would, perhaps by the end of the day. If not, there was always Plan B; he had a ticket for that all right, but that could be a solo ride, destination unknown, perhaps to the back end of a black hole!*

Thrilling as that would be to experience, oblivion was not his idea of a bright future, especially as it was guaranteed to be a one-way ride. Of course, it might be the return trip. A bit like standing on the edge of an abyss, the other side an easy jump away – but that was last time you did it. Now it was pitch black; you thought you were in the exact same place, but hard to tell when you can not see your hand in front of your face! In those circumstances it took a lot of nerve to jump out into the darkness; certainly a lot more courage than he had.

Besides, he liked it here in many ways. On balance, there really was not much of a choice. A bird in the hand, and an intelligent and beautiful, warm loving one at that, was worth a whole bush-full of time jumps.

At the top he paused, for he was intentionally still a few minutes early. The copse in the distance looked as always in the mid-morning sunshine of a beautiful early summer's day, and he was mindful to move slowly ahead, but checked himself. Better a few minutes late in this case than ten minutes early.

Nor did he intend to disturb the genuine new friendship growing between them – if it was destined to be only that in this more stately-paced era. Besides, he was enjoying the intellectual nature of her company – and she with him, he had thought. The physical aspect could wait its turn. Indeed, that could only be described as a disastrous beginning, moving much too fast even for his own time, recalling one partic-ular blow to his right eye. Here it was based on his dreadful misunderstanding of the social mores of this culture, in which he was the alien intruder – and inevitable loser.

Yes, he liked that word; Alien. How would he have felt if some real, all-powerful aliens had come into his world and turned it upside down socially, but especially sexu-ally, and he shuddered at some of the images of mayhem his fertile imagination turned up.

Suddenly, he felt like Attila the Hun, who he could indeed be related to, and was deeply ashamed of his behaviour. Alice was exactly correct in her description of his actions toward Lucy – and especially to his – and her – beloved Celia. Some of the words she had uttered, all now burned indelibly into his memory, returned: 'A force for evil and destruction' and 'Sweet fruits for the taking', which made him a thief of virtue, a capital offence in this world. All true, and he felt so unworthy of meeting with either of them that he almost turned about.

Instead, he urged Johnson on to avoid being late. He had an appointment to keep, whatever fate came with it, or to paraphrase Boswell's 'Dr. Johnson', when a man is facing the gallows, 'it concentrates his mind wonderfully'.

He slowed as he neared the glade, and stopped as he heard faint laughter. That was Celia's; which meant she was recovered. That was good news, certainly. Then another indistinct voice that sounded like Alice's, so he dismounted, tethered his horse, and walked softly through the trees.

The sight that met his eyes was quite remarkable. At the back of the clearing there was now a small tent with an easel to one side, at which Celia was busily sketching. She was wearing a simple, cotton dress with thin shoulder straps, that came only to the knee, leaving her legs and sandalled feet bare, her beautiful golden hair streaming down her back to the waist, something he much enjoyed. And she seemed to be completely preoccupied talking to Alice, but without changing position she called to him softly.

'Good morning, Manfred. Please make your self at home where you are, but no closer. We are decidedly informal this day, as we are when in our studio. The only difference is that today it is *al fresco*, and Alice is an Indian Maiden at her ablutions.'

Only then did he look toward the centre of the clearing. There, kneeling on a tree stump was Alice, Indian-like after a fashion with a black and white feather, brushing her astonishingly long dark hair in front of her. The most remarkable feature was her golden back where the shafts of bright sunlight struck her body; the coloured beads around her neck and ankles, with a waist band of similar beads forming a brief skirt front and back, emphasizing the fact that otherwise she had not a stitch on her body.

All the while, Celia was weaving a fantastic tale of this Indian maiden greeting the morning sun by brushing her hair and praying that the love for her Indian brave would be returned. Alice appeared not to notice his presence. In any event, her hair effectively covered the private areas of her body, except for the brief, entrancing moment when, the story concluded, she brushed back her hair for Celia to wrap a gown around her and lead her into the tent.

'Manfred, you have been away too long. So, while Alice is dressing, you may advance and sit. We are, as you see, at our first outdoor art class of the summer, and you are invited to join us and sketch a little. Now, Alice, please pour us all a drink.

'I cannot show you the "Indian Maiden" I am currently doing, Manfred,' Celia continued in a soft voice, 'for it is unfinished. But, in any event, considering the explicit nature of the pose, it would require Alice's express prior approval. However, as I am aware from my sister that you are fond of sketching, perhaps you would care to view some of my earlier work in the same vein?'

'That would be delightful. In a moment though, if you please, Celia, after I have quenched my thirst a little with this quite excellent lemonade.'

In truth, Manfred was only just beginning to get his breath back since he first arrived and they both seemed to know it, for neither of them was making it any easier. Strange how these young women could be so casual and open about displaying their bodies, and yet so closed in other ways, so that he was frequently caught on the wrong foot. No wonder he stumbled so often!

'Thank you, Alice, that was most refreshing,' returning the empty glass to her hand. Small wonder that she was out of the tent almost as soon as she had entered, for she had merely slipped on a light tunic similar to her mistress, though halfway up her thighs, leaving little to his imagination! From the clear thrust of her body, this demonstrated she was wearing little other than necklace and ankle beads, for even her brief bead skirt was not evident through the light fabric.

Then suddenly he realized where he was and what he was doing – staring at Alice's body through her tunic, and he reddened in embarrassment to realize that they were both watching his reactions with amused smiles.

'I am dreadfully sorry,' he exclaimed to Celia, 'that was unforgivably rude of me, and, yes, I would like to examine them,' with what he hoped was not too false a note of calmness, for the 'in a similar vein' had set his pulse beating faster than it already was by their intentionally sensuous apparel.

Simply nodded her acceptance, Celia said, 'Alice, please bring out the canvas art satchel. Thank you.'

'Now, the first is of Mildred, Alice's daughter, which you have already seen. The second, of Lucy, you have also seen,' giving him a moment to appreciate them.

'Quite exquisite, Celia,' he said, a little breathlessly, for they were indeed stunning. 'They should both be exhibited.'

'And these also?' indicating to Alice to bring forth her 'Richard I' scene before the mirror, and then the very latest of 'The Coiffeuse', followed by 'Contemplation', showing a very explicit and delectable Alice on a cushion before the fire.

There was a slight gasp from Manfred, then silence.

'How about this one of my sister?' said Celia, as Alice propped 'The Apple' against a tree trunk for his viewing, neither missing a single change of colour in Manfred's face, from pale to red and back again, as he struggled to contain and conceal his emotions.

'Beautiful,' he finally whispered, 'quite exquisite. Somehow, though, I think none of these will be appropriate for other than the most private of viewings.'

'Unfortunately, there you are quite correct, Manfred; and that does seem to be the nature of my best work. Somehow, I seem not to be able to get the most out of the subject when her spirit is hidden from view by an excess of clothing. Now, please note, you are seeing Miss Lucy and Alice in these explicit poses for the first and last time. They are not to be mentioned or referred to, ever, is that understood?' and he nodded, without taking his eyes off it, thus failing to observe the smile exchanged between the other two.

'Time now for a little exercise of art. We have both charcoal and crayon, and plenty of parchment, though I perceive that you have your own tablette. Would you care to participate, Manfred?'

Manfred took this as an offer to join Celia at the easel, and an opportunity to compliment her charming attire which, as it so often did, greatly disturbed his equilibrium.

'I am still in admiration,' he continued softly, 'of your long and beautiful hair,' at which she turned and smiled at him. That, and her personal scent, sent his senses reeling, while her full, soft lips so close to his own were nearly his undoing all over again.

'I would . . .' he stammered, 'I think . . . that is . . .' and he was lost in a whirl of her nearness.

'Why not use my easel,' she whispered, taking his hand. 'I could use a rest from sketching for a while,' and she placed him in front of it, brushing her self sensually against his bare arm while doing so. Then she stretched up to whisper in his ear, 'We have missed you,' and her bosom momentarily settled its softness on his forearm as she took the opportunity to kiss his cheek with soft lips before withdrawing that self, ever so slowly.

'Perhaps you wish for Alice to model for you in some manner? Or would you rather I did, as she has already posed for us this morning and may be a little weary?' she continued with a bright smile.

He stood trying to concentrate on the proposition, but at last able to answer with an equal smile.

'If you are willing, I would indeed like to try my hand at portraying your charms,' wondering whether those words meant the same thing now as they did in the early part of his century.

'Very well; in what pose would you care to liberate my spirit?' and she stood waiting for his response.

'Any manner you choose would be most satisfactory to me,' he responded gallantly, suddenly enjoying the warm sunshine flooding through the canopy overhead.

'Alice, let us hie our selves to the shelter, and see what artefacts we have to provide Manfred some thing worthy of his talents as an artist.'

He was examining the assortment of crayons and charcoals in Celia's box, when she appeared at the tent opening.

'Alice and I think that a woodland sprite would be most appropriate to the setting, although I am perhaps a little too grown for such a pose,' her mouth assuming a pretty pout. 'Will that do?' she added sweetly.

'Admirably,' he returned, and they disappeared again.

Celia emerged a few moments later wearing a robe, and moved to the centre of the clearing, where, with her back to him, Alice spent some moments adjusting the garment beneath before Alice removed it. Then she turned to show her self in a short sleeveless tunic, caught at the throat by a gold chain, the thin muslin fabric leaving little to his imagination as to what lay underneath – for it was clearly the essential Celia.

'We are having some trouble with the pose because the filmy gauze that sprites wear is barely adequate for me. As I suspected, my charms are a little much for it,' and she smiled at him. 'Nor can I ask Alice to hold it there until you are finished, Manfred, so she has pinned it in place.

'Now,' she continued calmly, 'you can portray me as flying over the ground, with my silken gown in my hand,' and she slipped off her tunic and raised her hand so that it fluttered most attractively in the light breeze, and was quite motionless.

Manfred was equally motionless, charcoal in hand, but quite unable to take his eyes off the beautifully sculpted body before him, for she was now draped only in a strip of cloth that started at one shoulder, wound across her bosom, leaving one side barely covered, across her belly and around one smooth thigh. It seemed to stay there only by the good graces of Alice behind her, completing the pinning.

'There, Miss, that is the best I can do with it, for it is very light, and the pins we brought are quite small. Do you still wish to continue, or shall we attempt some other thing?'

'What say you, Manfred? Does this seem a suitable garb?' providing him a wide smile.

'I think,' he whispered, hoarsely, 'that we must postpone the session for a little while, as I seem not to be able to concentrate on the pose.'

'Really?' said Celia, lowering her arm, and turning her glowing body to face him completely, where in the bright sunlight she knew the fabric she had selected for the task of discovery made the most of her form.

'Well, perhaps it is getting a little late,' and she raised her hand to shield her eyes from the sun to judge its position, knowing instinctively that her thrusting bosom sent shivers of delight through her artist admirer, turning him to jelly and destroying any objectivity that might remain.

'Alice, please fetch my gown, for I do believe that the master is correct. He must be able to concentrate. Perhaps after our repast,' and she smiled at him again, as Alice returned to place the garment over her mistress' up stretched arms.

'Just a moment,' exclaimed Manfred, excitedly, 'that is *exactly* the pose!'

'Like this?' said Celia, as she stepped up onto the stump once more, arms high over her head, fingers entwined, on her tiptoes, bosom teasingly exposed for a moment and bathed in liquid gold sunbeams.

'Yes,' breathed Manfred, 'Not a sprite at all, a Golden Goddess. "All the world should see such a glorious sight as heaven has vouchsafed me"', safely stealing a line from Kenneth Grahame's 'Willows'; and he sketched as if he were on fire. Inside, he certainly was.

'Bring me a piece of that broken branch, Alice, for I shall never be able to maintain this pose without some thing to support my heels.'

Alice did as she was bid, reflecting on the nature of life, for that was the very one with which she had threatened to make an end to Manfred, and she smiled at the strangeness of it.

Her mistress, exposed innocently to him for the first time – for the fabric around the hips was every now and then lifted enough in the breeze to set his pulse racing – all in the legitimate pursuit of art, while he was required to maintain his detachment from an adequate distance.

'There,' he exclaimed, at last, as her strength was all but giving out, though she was not about to display any sign of it. 'Finished.'

'Good,' was all she offered, as she slowly lowered her arms and relaxed her body. 'My gown now, please, Alice,' and as it slithered down over her, Alice unpinned the fabric, and Celia helped it by smoothing her body with her hands in a manner calculated to leave him breathless all over again.

'Now we can go down to tea, for I am hungry for some thing,' and she took his arm and tucked it inside hers to hold it against her sun-warmed softness. 'Please bring *all* the paintings, Alice,' she called over her shoulder, 'for we cannot leave those around for prying eyes,' and they set off down the hill arm in arm.

Tea over, Celia addressed him: 'Now we will answer the questions you may have.'

Manfred, who had been forced to wait for this moment by their self-appointed protocol, immediately asked his first question.

'Is the glade really your private domain, and this Cottage?'

'It is, although at the moment for we are only leasing, but the papers are being drawn as we speak. Though it is not a large farm, it extends over the ridge to include the glade. But then, we do not wish to be farmers, do we Alice?'

'No, Miss, just enough to keep our selves in provender.' Turning to Manfred, she added, 'So you will require Miss Celia's permission to visit or ride there.'

'And the two of you are going to handle all the work of running it?'

'Indeed no, for we shall need the usual assistance. Perhaps you would explain, Alice.'

'Certainly, Miss. We have already engaged a carter – for the horses, ploughing and the like – and a cook to start as soon as we move in proper. Then there will be a scullery maid to clean and do the milking as well as the odd jobs and, of course, a farm lad to help Carter with the outside chores.'

'And when will that be – the moving in, I mean?'

Alice looked at her mistress, who nodded. 'As soon as matters at the Hall are arranged, and her ladyship gives her approval.'

'And upon what does that depend?' continued Manfred, still quite amazed that these two enterprising spirits could go out on their own to run a farm, neither of them being his idea of the farming type.

'Her ladyship is concerned that Miss Celia will not have a man about the place for the proper security of person that her social position requires,' replied Alice.

'But you said you had already engaged a carter. Would he not do?'

'For the farm, certainly. But we are talking of Miss Celia's *person*, a completely different matter. She believes that before young ladies make an establishment of their own, they must be settled, by which she means married. Besides, ladies do not possess property in their own right, that is the new husband's obligation from the marriage contract.'

'Otherwise, you would move soon?' continued Manfred.

'Tomorrow,' interjected Celia. 'But if I do not receive her consent within a month or so, I shall make my own course,' and she rose to her feet.

'And that would grieve her ladyship sorely,' added Alice.

'Alice, please bring my gown, for I think I will take advantage of this beautiful evening sun. Now, please see that Manfred concentrates his attention in the opposite direction for a few moments,' and when Alice indicated that was so, she peeled off her dress and stood naked – save for the gold chain – for the brief moment Alice required to enrobe her.

'Thank you, Alice. Briefly clad posing for the beauty of art is one thing, Manfred,' she added, in a louder tone; 'observing a lady disrobe down to her natural beauty is some thing altogether different and not to be borne.'

Together they positioned an old settee so that it was bathed in the bright sunshine pouring through the open windows and, placing a cushion at one end, stretched her self upon it.

'Alice, please ensure that Manfred keeps his eyes in a proper direction; one other than this,' and opened the gown wide to allow her body to drink in the golden liquid as Alice drew a small screen across the head of the chaise to provide some semblance of privacy.

'Wonderful. Manfred, pray continue with your questions. I shall answer as appropriate, although Alice has as much knowledge of the matter as my self,' and she sighed in delight as the warmth penetrated her skin, and closed her eyes.

'Now you may be seated – facing away from my mistress, if you please,' and it was all Manfred could do to prevent him self from turning.

'Where was I?' he asked, trying to engage his mind and drag it from what he knew to be a wonderful sight. He did so only by concentrating his full attention on Alice, only to become aware that, at only a few years his junior in age, her choice of dress on her full figure was hardly less stirring than that of her mistress. Her bare bosom was evident against a fabric so thin that the aureole was clearly visible, despite the light shawl she had thrown over her shoulders and tied across the front. And he could not fail to notice the heightened colour in her cheeks from his probing glance.

'Oh, yes,' dragging his eyes down to the table top and concentrating on his fingertips to lessen her embarrassment – or was it pleasure – at being sensuously observed? 'Ah, yes. Your mistress was explaining what she would do if her ladyship refused to grant her consent. "Make her own course", I think she said. What did she mean by that?'

There was a brief pause while Celia left the question for Alice to field.

'She meant that . . . Are you sure you wish me to answer this question, Miss?'

'Yes, Alice. Please express it any way you choose. Manfred is evidently a man of the world, judging by his past actions, and has no need to be shocked.'

'Very well, Miss. I will do so while I prepare some lemonade,' and she rose to make the arrangements, providing Manfred with the briefest of opportunities to peep out of the corner of his eye. That perfect golden body was displayed even more gloriously than he had imagined, for the screen was pierced sufficiently to permit her general outline to be observed. Her earlier posing and his own imagination filled in the rest. Once more seated, Alice was facing him again to require his attention.

'Miss Celia meant that she would marry a man who could satisfy the conditions for obtaining her ladyship's consent.'

'Any man?' retorted the incredulous Manfred, struggling to refocus his mind. The thought that this gorgeous creature could be wasted on just any male was horrifying. 'Even if she did not love him?'

'Firstly, love does not enter into it at all; it is simply a matching of societal standing,' replied Alice. 'Secondly, he would have to pass muster before her ladyship – not an easy task, for she has exacting standards and obligations. But, given that approval, it would then be a quite straightforward matter.'

'And these young men; would they be willing to come forward, and how would she choose one?' persisted Manfred.

'Most assuredly they would, Sir!' replied Alice, a little hotly, rising to convey a glass of lemonade to her mistress, but this time keeping a wary eye on Manfred. 'Miss Celia's hand has been requested on many occasions that I know of, and I am sure a good number more of which I am completely unaware. She has rejected them all, for while her ladyship may reject a suitor, she cannot command one,' and Celia nodded; impressed with Alice's grasp of the subject of marriageable society daughters.

'As to the choosing, the mistress would prepare a list of young gentlemen of her acquaintance whom she would find acceptable as consorts, put them in order of desirability, and submit it to her ladyship, who would probably delete a number as "unsuitable" partners for her daughter, and perhaps add some – whom Miss Celia would probably as promptly expunge. The final prepared list would then be the subject of consider-able emotional debate between mother and daughter as to the order in which suitors would be approached – a vital point, as you will note later.'

'Would they then be asked if they wished to marry your mistress?' continued the wondering Manfred, his mind on the winner of the prize of the century – any century.

'Indeed not!' snorted Alice. 'Nothing of the sort. It would be made known to their sires or guardians that such a match would be favourably viewed, etc, etc. You should know that these matters are conducted with the utmost decorum and good taste.'

'The ending presumably being a wedding,' continued Manfred, unabashed. 'That must consume a goodly amount of time?'

'It would be accomplished in two months, at the most,' broke in Celia.

'Really; that quickly?' pondered Manfred. 'This list and its origins,' he continued, his mind desperately seeking a brake on those events; 'it inter-ests me greatly. Is it possible to suggest a name? Might I propose one, for example? That is,' he added, hesitantly, deciding that the plunge must be taken, 'could *my* name be proposed for inclusion on it, if your mistress were so inclined? More importantly, might her ladyship be persuaded not to take a heavy pen to it?'

The silence following this remark was complete.

'Shall I answer that, Miss?' queried Alice.

'Please do,' came the calm voice from over his shoulder, and he would have given any thing to observe the object of that voice at this moment. Well, almost any thing, mindful of Persephone; a pillar of stone – even a golden one – not being his most cherished desire!

Alice hesitated, and looking steadfastly into his face, took a long, slow drink from her glass.

'Firstly, names are *never* proposed; they emerge only from the heart of the bride-to-be. Secondly, I do not believe her ladyship could be dissuaded from exercising her right of refusal. There are two issues involved: the proposal and its acceptance, and the swain's eligibility and acceptance.

Besides, the young gentlemen are already well known, having been vetted for acceptability together with expectations of inheritance, or worth in their own right.

'Your position, Mr. Manfred, arising from your recent arrival in our community, would of necessity be different, requiring you or your proposer to present your credentials of suitability for the hand of Miss Celia as a suitor above all other claimants.'

'Please, could you not just call me "Manfred"?'

Alice shook her head.

'No, Sir, that would not be at all proper. Only the mistress may address you in that manner.'

'Very well, Alice, if you say so. And if I cannot make the list, is there no hope for a shattered man, Alice?'

'Mr. Manfred, may I be frank with you?'

'Certainly, Alice; I have never noticed you any thing else in the past when, on occasion, you have been most brutally frank!'

'Ah, yes; but then, you see, I was angry with you. Now I am merely patient. You doubtless recall my intimating that for a supposedly educated man you were . . . well, not as astute as you might be.'

'Vividly!' responded Manfred.

'It still applies. But,' and here she dropped her voice to a whisper and bent her head toward his, 'while you may not propose to be on the list, young gentlemen *have* been known to propose directly to the object of their heart's desire, which would leave only the second step to be considered. Do I understand that such a course might be of interest? Think carefully before you answer!'

'I do not have to think at all, Alice,' was his whispered response, 'for I do indeed love your mistress.'

'Have you told her so?' responded Alice.

Manfred blushed. 'Unfortunately, your mistress and I, we . . . well, we got off to a poor start – all my fault I hasten to add, and I am fearful that my words might be misconstrued as an attempt to . . . to . . . you understand?' he finished lamely.

Alice nodded.

'I understand,' she whispered, 'and well they might have, had you expressed them at that time. Now you may see your hasty and inconsiderate actions have not served you well,' to which he nodded, glumly. 'However, having acted with appropriate decorum of late, your true feelings might shine through and be regarded in a different light.

'Shall I inquire for you, how such a course might now be weighed?

That is, if the person of Miss Celia is your heart's most ardent desire?'

'She is, Alice, most decidedly,' to which Alice nodded acceptance.

'What are you two whispering about over there,' inquired a loud voice. 'Do you not know that it is rude to whisper in company?'

'Yes, Mistress. We thought you asleep and chose not to disturb you,' she dissembled with an innocent expression.

'Mistress, Mr. Manfred has some personal matter he wishes to say. Would you please attire your self appropriately so that he may approach, for this must be said directly,' and she rose to place her self between the suitor and his desired one, arms folded. With her anklet and necklace of beads, she became for all the world like an undeniably feminine Indian Warrior.

'Very well,' said Celia, drawing her robe around her and sitting up. 'Yes, Manfred, what is it you wish to declare?'

Manfred rose and approached, and, dropping to one knee, took up her hand and uttered the magic words:

'Dearest Celia, I love you with all my heart, and wish to spend the rest of my life with you. Will you marry me?'

Celia went pale, flushed, went pale again, withdrew her hand, and struggled to reply, without success.

'Miss Celia, before you respond, please recall that a proposal cannot be accepted, or even considered, until the suitor's eligibility has been examined. Mr. Manfred, will you please return to the table. Mistress, you may listen, but this time you may not question or comment.'

And Celia turned, pulled her robe even more tightly about her, lay down and sobbed quietly into the cushion.

'Mr. Manfred, you will please allow Miss Celia the courtesy of being unaware of her distress – quite understandable in the circumstances of your past actions regarding her person.'

Manfred nodded, not understanding in the slightest, and fearful that the tears and withdrawn hand signalled an equally withdrawn heart.

'Take courage, Sir,' whispered Alice, noting his pale visage. 'All may not be lost if you are willing to discuss matters here and now, more formally?' And Alice noted his eager nod of acceptance.

'Very well,' now in normal voice so that Celia could overhear the conversation. 'Now, you are unfamiliar with our customs, so be aware that Mistress Celia has no comment in this affair whatsoever. It should also be understood that I, Miss Celia's personal maid, have no standing to make a judgment in these matters, although I can certainly explain the required formalities and elicit the information essential for making that judgment, while she may not. Is that also clear?'

'Perfectly.'

'Splendid. Now, I shall assume the role of one qualified to perform the necessary investigations, – for example, her ladyship's legal advisor. I shall therefore address you as "Sir", and you will oblige me the courtesy of "Madam".

'I shall take notes as we proceed, as they may form the basis of a Marriage Agreement, should any ensue from your suit,' and again he nodded.

'Let us then open at the very beginning. Is it your intent, Sir, to seek Miss Celia's hand in matrimony?'

'It is, if she will have me.'

'That is as may be, Sir, and qualifies your response. You are only required to confirm your intent.'

'Very well, Alice – that is, I do seek it, Madam.'

'Thank you, Sir. Now to the essentials of the inquiry. How do you propose to support Miss Celia in the style and manner to which she was born and raised?'

Manfred had always assumed that the question now put to him was some thing of a rhetorical one. He soon found out otherwise, for Alice was as thorough in her interview as any he had ever had. Fortunately, he had been considering the problem of what to do with his life for some time, and had a plan laid out to use his advanced knowledge of what to him was simple history. It was as well that he had, otherwise he might have appeared a simpleton, with neither skills nor purpose.

But even here he was caught often unawares, for he had thought that it was just a wife that he was expected to find for, and children in due course. He was thus very surprised to learn that, in addition, there would be a whole entourage of servants, with carriages, stables and the like, and a sizeable estate to boot. This simple Cottage was out of the question. He was used to earning a generous monthly salary, but this was of no avail to him here and, with a distinctly sinking feeling, found that he could supply no evidence of means to support any of these.

On the question of farming and whether he was prepared to contribute significantly to its growth and development, he also considered that his general knowledge of modern farming methods would serve Miss Celia well. But his detailed knowledge of animal husbandry was not well received, for in the minutiæ sense he knew next to nothing.

The interrogation lasted a full hour, and covered his family history for several generations back, as well as his and their education – none of which could have had any meaning to Alice, but she noted all in her neat hand. It also included his plans for fatherhood and the matter of marital fidelity while Celia was unavailable for conjugal relations, on which subject he was left in no doubt whatsoever, especially as his plans for work involved frequent visits to London, whereupon Alice wanted to know where he would stay and of which clubs he was a member.

He was further required to permit the mistress to pursue her art and music in whatever manner she chose, and admonished never to mistreat her in any way, if he were fortunate enough to be selected for the role of consort.

It all sounded so stilted that he wondered how any young man survived the business successfully – until he reflected that there were no alternatives for one of standing. If it wasn't this father's daughter whose hand he sought, it was the other's! He had assumed, in a light-hearted sort of way, that it was just a game they all played.

Now that he was enmeshed in it himself, he saw it for what it truly was: a gauntlet, one they seemed to have to run no matter what, to receive whatever blows were directed, unflinching and decidedly to the end – hopefully sweet, not bitter.

At last there were no more questions, though whether he had satisfied Alice and passed or not, was not indicated. He had not long to wait.

'Mistress, I believe I have obtained a sufficient understanding of your suitor's capabilities and desires on the subject of supporting you materially and spiritually. If you would care to join us at the table, we could conclude matters, at least as far as can be today in this simple forum, though you may have no formal voice in the discussion.'

'Sir,' when Celia was seated opposite Manfred, 'you will recall that I said that her ladyship will evaluate the suitors – after her own fashion – from that final list prepared by Miss Celia.' Manfred nodded as Alice continued.

'While it is true that no formal list currently exists, it is my opinion that her ladyship will construct one the moment she hears of your interest in Miss Celia's hand. Considering the prior demeaning treatment of her elder daughter, she would relegate you to a position at the bottom. Only Miss Celia's insistence would move it more than half way.

'That would place you no better than a fourth or fifth position, and I need hardly add,' giving Manfred a decidedly cool look, 'that Miss Celia's hand would be most eagerly sought by any ranked suitor.

'The information provided her advisor is the only virtue that could raise or lower this standing. While you may love Miss Celia as you profess, these matters of the heart carry no weight whatsoever. Indeed, recall there were no questions concerning your feelings toward her, nor any concerning Miss Celia's to you. They have no bearing on the union of the two persons involved. Is that quite clear to you, Sir?' receiving his formal nod of acceptance, though with a distinct frown.

'Good. Now, these enquiries would rank the first two contenders, and perhaps even the third. Discussions would then be conducted with the full expectation of selecting the first suitor. If no agreement is reached, it would pass to the second suitor, though this is *most* unlikely with a young lady of Miss Celia's eligibility.

'Thus your suit, Sir, would not even be addressed, being too low on the list to be considered. However, to be fair and open in the matter, let us now deal with it.

'From all the testimony received – and here I have no option but to be forthright with all parties – and commencing from such a lowly position, it is considered that you have no agreeable chance of being a potential suitor for Miss Celia's hand. Furthermore, even if you were, your suit would fail on the support grounds alone. I am truly sorry, Sir, to have to put it to you in this manner, but it is so.'

At these words, Celia burst into tears and laid her head on the table.

'Pray, Sir, ignore this unseemly interruption.'

'How can I?' retorted Manfred, in a flash of anger at his impending loss. 'A man and a woman should marry for love, not baubles.'

'That may be your opinion, Sir, but many an arranged marriage has survived when a love match has not. I am sorry that you cannot be rated more highly, but on that list will be several gentlemen of title, or position in society, or wealth of landed estates – and most certainly some of all three – not one of which, sadly, you possess.

'Some without heirs of the line, would see in the mistress a fine chance of a healthy son to ensure it, as well as a regarded beauty in the fullness of feminine youth to parade to the Balls and grace their dinner tables and soirées. In society, this is not a trivial opportunity to be rejected out of hand. Need I say more?'

'Indeed not,' said Manfred, hotly, 'for I can see that the real values of living with one another are missing entirely.'

'Unfortunately, those values count for little with the landed gentry of our time,' at which words Manfred rose abruptly and strode out into the sunshine, leaving a calm and composed Alice, and a pale and trembling Celia.

'Did I handle it fairly and honourably, Miss?'

'Indeed you did, Alice, although I dearly wish you could have been more understanding of my feelings in the matter, and directed it that way.' Then she whispered from across the table, 'But do you not see any hope, at all?'

'Not much, Miss. I tried to be as even-handed as I could, for I could not mislead you, nor could I be in any part less than truly honest, for to do so, my dearest Mistress, would be to mislead him into hope – and more importantly your self, too, for we are not the final givers of this judgment. I had to be as true to what that Solicitor would determine as I could be – as I told Mr. Manfred.

'He has no heritage that counts, no title, no lands, he has not even a humble abode and must come to live in yours, cap in hand. That will sit *very poorly indeed* with her ladyship, as well it should. I need hardly remind you of the fine match that Miss Lucy has just made. Could you realize less, Miss?' noting the tears trickling down her mistress' cheeks once more.

'Could you expect her ladyship to be any thing but most dismayed if you did not marry at least to your station? Your acknowledged beauty, intelligence and wit should enable you to strike well above it. At least a Baron, if not an eventual Earl.'

'But I do not love any Barons or Earls, Alice,' Celia wailed. 'I love Manfred!' resting her head on the table again to hide her flowing eyes.

'I know, Miss, more's the pity. So is it to be heart or duty?' I am not sure that her ladyship would forgive you the former.'

Celia said nothing, knowing it to be true, except to sob, quietly now, on her sleeve.

'Let me talk to Mr. Manfred, Miss,' reaching to squeeze her cold fingers. 'Meantime, why not lie down again and rest. He should not see you looking as upset as this,' and she led her mistress to the chaise, and brought a blanket to cover her.

Alice found Manfred, now shirtless, coat and waistcoat hanging on a tree branch, at a wide point in the river, skipping flat stones across it to the farther bank.

'Well, what now, Alice; have you not done enough damage today, that you want to inflict more?'

'I Sir?' said Alice, surprised. 'I have done nothing but elicit the truth as her ladyship will undoubtedly see it. Indeed, my questions would be as honey in contrast to her ladyship's undoubtedly hostile legal advisor. The simple truth, Sir, is that you do not have a legitimate suit for Miss Celia's hand. Others of power and title may love her less – or even not at all – but claim her simply for what she is, a beautiful and desirably ripe young woman, her position secured by theirs, a due reward for the marriage bed.'

'Thank you, Alice, for that brutally frank description of what is in store for your mistress and what I am losing.'

'You cannot lose some thing you never had, Sir, can you?' replied Alice, softly.

'Alice,' said Manfred, turning solemnly to face her, 'why is it that whenever I converse with you or your mistress I seem to lose. I lose the argument, the logic, and now the very person of Miss Celia her self, whom I adore beyond all understanding. Somehow I cannot put it together so that I even get half a loaf. It is just too cruel.'

'Mr. Manfred, come sit on this bench, for my neck aches looking up at you,' as she spread her shawl on the bench for them both. 'Now, would you please tell me some thing of your love for my mistress?'

'Do you want it in poetry, Alice? I am not very good at that syrupy stuff,' said Manfred, the sarcasm arising from the pain of loss that he felt deep inside.

'No, Mr. Manfred, just tell me how you feel about her in ordinary words.'

'I am sorry, Alice, that was very rude of me. I know you are trying to help in what is clearly a very difficult situation,' and she nodded. 'I just think she is the most wonderful person in the world. I would say that I cannot live without her, but I am a little too old for that sentimentality. However, whenever she is near, the day seems to brighten immeasurably, and I cannot imagine ever being out of her presence. It is that simple. I do not quite know what I will do without her to cherish and, hopefully, return it to me.'

'Ah, yes, that! Is it not then her body that you truly covet? You have made that amply clear on more than one occasion, as I my self have witnessed. She is certainly well endowed in that area.'

'Alice,' he smiled, 'for a self-professed simple person, you do not miss very much! Should I lie to you?' and Alice shook her head. 'Besides, you would not believe me if I did.' Another shake. 'So, yes, she has the most gorgeous body I have ever seen – including Miss Lucy's if you force me to it – all right? But that is natural to a man. That is what he sees, what I see, first. It is the way we are made – and with a deliberate purpose.

'But then, as I got to know your mistress a little better, I found there was much more, for she has an outstanding mind, and there is some thing very special about her, some inner quality that I cannot define, some natural goodness of spirit or soul that comes shining through so suddenly that I am almost blinded. I am talking a lot of gooey nonsense, aren't I, Alice, but you did ask me.'

'Manfred, and I will call you that for this time only; you have indeed seen Miss Celia for what she truly is, inside, and the reason why I love her so dearly that I was prepared to do dreadful things to you should you ever hurt her again. Would you always love her like that, tenderly, forsaking all others, as you would be required to swear before God? Could it be possible?'

'Without any difficulty at all, Alice.'

'Do not be too sure, Sir, for she can also be very trying when she is in one of her moods. You haven't seen them, but you would,' she finished quietly.

But Manfred simply laughed.

'You cannot frighten me off that way, Alice. I have those, too, as do you, assuredly far more threatening than mine. I would just love her the more until she came out of it, and if love would prevent them, then she would never have another as long as she is in my arms.'

'A pretty speech, Sir, but what will you do if Miss Celia marries another, one whom you positively dislike.'

'My first impulse would be to kill him; and the second. But in reality I would go away some where, for I could not bear to see her in the arms of another man. Reginald, I might be able to stomach, for he would treat her with the respect she deserves; let her continue her art even, for she is very talented,' and Alice nodded. 'Might it be him?'

But this time she shook her head, and tears formed in her eyes. 'It would be an older man, I fear,' she whispered, 'much older; titled, with much power and influence, for she cannot abide the young "boys" as she calls them. She will not give her self to them.'

'So what are we to do, Alice? Let her be married off like some prize cow because she has not the power to marry of her choice?' he responded, angrily. Then, in apologetic tone, 'I am most sorry, Alice, for the way I expressed that; it was ungracious of me.'

'You are forgiven, Sir,' she answered, quietly, 'for I fully understand your feelings on the matter. Remember that I, too, stand to lose my mistress in an equally distressing manner,' and she shook her head at this horrid thought and wiped her now freely-flowing tears, leading him to assuage the sadness by putting his arm around her, drawing her near to comfort her, whereupon she laid her head on his shoulder to shed a few more tears there.

'I am sure I do not know, Sir, what can be done,' she whispered, when she had recovered her spirits a little, surprised by his warmth against her own self. This was some thing she had not known for the longest of times, and was so entranced by the feeling as to let it remain, comforted and soothed by the encircling arm of one she had quite recently threatened to . . . This was madness, but a very pleasant form of it, she could not deny, and so she remained, cocooned in delight.

'I only know that,' she added softly, looking up into his gloomy face, 'if she is precluded from delighting in artistic expression by her possession of a title, her new position in society, or an over-bearing or possessive lord and master, her heart will be broken in no time and her spirit will wither away to become old well before her time.'

With that grim foretelling of a likely future for the one they both most adored in all the world, she laid her head against him once more, and they lapsed into complete silence, heavy almost as the grave, which seemed natural to allies in their joint desire for the same person, together in a light embrace and thus accepting of its intimacy.

But that was only at first glance, because Alice found, to her great surprise, a growing awareness of his bare chest against her thinly veiled bosom and, despite her best attempts to quell it, her spirit rose until it was almost on fire.

As Manfred sat looking at nothing in particular, he became aware of the gradual stirring in Alice's body and, glancing down, was surprised to see her loose gown now gaping wide. Caught in a sudden shaft of light from the lowering sun, he was intrigued at the open display of one soft white breast, with its deep pink circle and darker prominent center, becoming swollen even as he admired it, and below that, illumined through the thin fabric, a perfectly white, rounded belly with a hint of dark fringe below.

And at the same moment, he became acutely aware of the other breast crushed against him, as its warmth and hardness penetrated to his own.

Further, clearly visible beneath her short smock were her soft white inner thighs which, in her excitement to be ever closer, had risen to where it hid very little. So this is what her body revealed up close – very close – recalling that as the Indian Maiden he had been required to keep his distance.

Surprised by this intimate revelation, he paused momentarily to assess his own feelings in response, disturbed to find himself nowhere near as detached as he had thought.

When she had regained some control of her confused emotions, she finally queried through the tingling silence, 'You would return to your own place?'

She raised her self a little against him, not yet ready to relinquish the delighted feelings newly aroused in her body by the contact as she did so, care-less that her short dress was now higher than ever, fully exposing every thing she possessed in that region of her body.

Manfred shook his head in turn.

'No,' he responded. 'I have been gone too long now to go back. Besides, I like it here, or I did until your cross-examination this afternoon. No, that was very wrong of me and undeserving to you, Alice,' giving her shoulder a gentle squeeze in apology, inadvertently causing her bosom to rise tanta-lizingly close and – unbeknownst to him – her emotions to lift with it.

'I cannot blame you, for you only did what had to be done, which, by the way, I know was performed as well and as thoroughly as any thing I have witnessed in my life. As you said, "it is the custom".

'I would probably go on loving your mistress from afar, and in vain, of course. I would not compromise her marriage; that would be too dreadful. That is why I would have to try to be some where else, as far away as possible. Perhaps, when I am a successful man in the City, one of "Power and Influence" as you so aptly put it, I would seek Miss Celia again, hoping that by then she was rid of the senile old fool she had married.'

He was silent for a further moment as he dwelt on that dreadful prospect, as was she, but her thoughts had turned in an altogether different direction, following her emotions, which were becoming increasingly difficult to control.

'And what will you do, Alice, when she marries that drunken sot, for you will lose her, too, as surely as I.'

As she raised her face to reply, her luminous dark eyes querying his, he felt a *frisson* race through her body so that it moved submissively into his. In response, his encircling arm instinctively pulled her softness in and up towards him, causing her shoulder strap to fall away and reveal her upper body, her full moist lips now partially open and only inches away from his own, even as soft fingers gently massaged his bare chest, exciting him equally as she knew it would.

Involuntarily, his unengaged hand found her warm inner thighs, which at his touch, opened to invite his caress to her inner private self. At this intimacy, her body flowed liquidly into his own, her open soft belly rising and moving with it to encourage his roving fingers, now gently assisted by hers as she sought to promote their inevitable stroke of ecstasy, her engorged and willing breast and lips moving ever closer, waiting only for his, to move toward the inevitable union of their bodies.

Suddenly becoming acutely aware of what was truly happening between them, he quietly released her, rising to hurl stones again into the river in his frustration and equal emotional confusion while, unseen, she put her hands to her face as if to stem the hotness of her blushing cheeks, fore-arms crushing her throbbing bosom to quell their riotous feelings and those of her fully aroused lower body, aware of his full view and access to her as she surveyed her state of undress, as well as his equal arousal as she had brushed lightly against his manhood to declare her total availability and encourage his conquest of her open body.

After a little while with no reply, he turned to repeat the question, but the bench was empty.

'Damn it, that was close,' he whispered to his inner self. 'Why are all these women firstly so confoundedly attracted, *then so* available, *so damnably* willing, *seemingly having no limits to his explorations – even to assisting his desires? There was Lucy opening her gown, Celia riding with her open body, and now Alice!'*

But there was no logic in that line of reasoning, for they were correct almost to a fault with others. That left only one alternative: he *was the guilty party!*

17

Introspection

He had always thought himself an honourable man; now, seemingly, was he the one who caused all the confusion and uncontrolled excitement in them? If so, he was in deeper trouble than he had thought – and of a quite different and much more perilous nature!

As he searched for flat skipping stones, that thought matured, and he recalled something from his early career. When a distant star system was behaving strangely, erratically, apparently disobeying the natural laws of the universe, it was almost always because there was an unknown rogue element. It could be an unseen planet, perhaps an invisible brown dwarf star.

And he suddenly saw it all quite clearly. Of course, that must be it; he was the 'brown dwarf' that upset all their careful calculations of how to avoid being entrapped by a man!

The nearly two centuries of development that separated them was evident in his better health and subsequent physique – amongst many other things. But he had overlooked the sociological side. It was now apparent that he – and the rest of his era – had advanced in that direction also. Probably his people had a heightened awareness of each other – and a suitable defence mechanism to counter it – neither of which was matched by his present company, but especially not the ladies.

Excited by the discovery, he likened it to pheromones. Presumably we had them, too; certainly not as powerfully as did some insects to attract a mate, but faintly there, all the same. If that were so, then his were developed considerably beyond theirs, making his 'invisible' powers virtually irresistible, while negating their customary defences.

Alice was a perfect example of it. She of that strong command and determination had literally melted into his arms and his body with her own yielding one. When she turned her face to his just moments ago, she was offering her self up for much more than a passionate kiss. That was to be just the appetizer to her breasts, even as she guided his hand to arouse and stimulate her inner softness to its ultimate thrill!

In his world he had been there many times, was attuned to those unmistakable signs – and taken full advantage of them when presented. However, though many were willing to be his partner for some things, for some titillation, that did not necessarily include their entire bodies! They would, and did, lay down clear limits to his exploration. They knew when to say no, and they meant it.

But in this *place, his special appeal apparently short-circuited their normal line of defence. That was too incredible, and yet her strange and erratic – if not to say erotic – behaviour would have led to* his *satisfaction in less time than it took to tell, and the stark reality of it all struck home with full force. Horror of horrors! If he had simply met her soft lips with his that would have been deadly, fatal for all concerned. If he needed further proof of his new theory, he could not recall ever having a young woman so eager, so willing to make herself his plaything. And could he have restrained himself? – never in a million years.*

And it was all total and utter madness!

Shaken now by this evidence, the enormity of it thrust upon his struggling senses. In his world it had always been accepted that they *were the ones to say 'no'. He simply wasn't used to women – all* women, *apparently – desiring to be his toy; eager for any thing (which inevitably meant every thing) he chose to take from them. And, yes,* he had been about to make love to Alice. *The stalwart, incorruptible Alice!*

If that wasn't enough evidence of the unconscious powers of his magnetism then nothing was.

By now his brain was spinning in so many directions at once, that he sought the bench again, putting his head in his hands for long, long moments to think it through.

Following his line of reasoning then, he *was the one to say no from the very beginning, not her, and he broadened his theory to the young Quintet to provide further evidence. So, after Lucy and Celia, could those pheromones have seduced the rest of them?*

He suddenly recalled dancing with them at Celia's Ball. Alexandra, the oldest of the three whom he partnered only once, was decidedly alluring in her manner. Geraldine, who was probably eighteen, was certainly very affectionate in his arms and normally worthy of a follow up. But it was her younger sister, Georgina, at only seventeen who seemed to have fallen already!

He had thought nothing of it at the time; after all, she was barely more than a girl. Yet when he was on the terrace alone for a few moments taking a little fresh air, she suddenly appeared at his side. He remembered saying something about the Ball being very successful, to which she did not reply, simply looking up into his eyes, her own shining.

With his new insight, he suddenly understood: she was waiting, willing him to take her in his arms, eager for his kiss. Even more, she had taken his hand with some unknown intention. Somewhat embarrassed, he had suggested they return to the Ballroom even as he sensed her reluctance to do so. Now he realized that she wished it on her slight bosom!

All young and attractive in their own way, each clearly innocent, that was the irresistible challenge. For any man it was a special treat to be the very first to caress and arouse a young woman to open her perfect body to full exploration and then final union. And this despite the fact that he had no interest in them at all!

And suddenly he saw himself as the earlier Alice had, the pariah of the county, every county, hounded out of every place. 'A curse on society' she had called him — until some one's fatal arrow found its mark, or, as she so aptly described, 'simply removed with little regard or ceremony, and even less regret!'

This required some very cool, very level-headed thinking. And he rose to return to the brook once more, kneeling to splash his face liberally with its cold water.

Refreshed, he sat cross-legged on an old flat grindstone, and turned his thoughts inward. He was a scientist — and a good one at that. So, examine it and analyse it properly.

Starting with emotions; first, Alice. Was she in love with him? Of course not, for she would have regretted it immediately. Simply overwhelmed by the emotions of the day — and there had been much of that, recalling the art poses in the glade. So that was entirely his wilful doing — pheromones or not.

Second, Lucy. Was she in love with him? Perhaps a little, at first. No, that was not so, for all the evidence of their brief first encounter was to the contrary. Afterwards might have been a little different; but then she left with little or no regret. His doing again. Two strikes, no hits.

Lastly, Celia. Ah, she probably was in love, genuinely in love, but there were many important factors stacked against him. So, call that equal, for the moment. But it was still a strike against him. Three strikes and you're out, Manfred, in shame and dishonour.

Now for Consequences. For Alice, undoubtedly quite fatal. It was really rather straightforward. They could then have gone away together, 'riding into the sunset'. In actuality, Alice would have been compromised beyond any possibility of redemption. She would have found her self so humiliated — not by his actions — but by her own reckless taking of her mistress' desired one as the lover unto her own body; an act so perfidious as to preclude being able to face her mistress — probably even Mildred and certainly himself — ever again.

Thus it was complete and utter disgrace for her; disaster of a magnitude he simply could not comprehend. That would be a living hell for Alice – if she chose to remain on this plane at all – for her love for Celia was absolute. At that he felt as if a cold hand were clutching his heart, and he waited for it to subside before resuming his analysis. That had been close; too damned close!

Lucy was already safe from his apparently deadly embrace; though, as to that, it had been an incredibly narrow escape. If the Baroness had, without her word of warning, strolled onto the terrace, where he had reduced Lucy to a quite shocking state of undress, her ruin would have been instant and complete, for the Baroness was not one to mince words or actions! Thus her present happiness would have been destroyed by his *total lack of any consideration for* her *position and* her *honour, in the satiating of his own (here he almost,* almost, *wanted to say 'evil') desires.*

The exact same question applied to Celia. Should a stranger – master or servant, it mattered not – have happened by and observed even one second of his attentions to her naked upper body and – but for Alice's timely arrival – the rest of her intimate self as well, his beloved would have been equally ruined and cast out.

But there was yet more for her. If Alice were forced to depart – especially in the final form of it – Celia would have probably lost her mind.

As for the Quintet, while that was all imagined, he knew within himself that it could be equally true. Humiliation and ruin, if they even survived his attack – for that is what it truly was – upon each of them.

So, what was the final score: misery and complete ruination all round for them all – because any one was condemnation of all, and he had to wipe the cold sweat from his brow. And for himself? Equal misery, losing every thing he had grown to love here – especially his adored Celia. To cause her a life of despair because of his stupid and thoughtless actions, was a tragedy beyond any thing he could imagine, and he hung his head in the realization of his own humiliation and depravity.

In this innocent and respectful world, his thoughtless actions amounted to nothing less than serial rape of any woman, all women who crossed his path; a deadly contagious pathogen.

And with that, he dipped his face in the cool water for a long while to cool his fevered brain and refresh himself once more.

Calmer now, it was time to consider a remedy to this apparently unbridgeable gulf between them – and he suddenly remembered Jane Austen! She was of this time, the young ladies would almost certainly have read her and, strange and quaint as the customs depicted in the novels were to him, to them they were life itself.

He had enjoyed her works, and especially the videos, vividly recalling that Mr.

Darcy, having proposed to Elizabeth and finally been accepted, did not even hold her hand, let alone kiss her. That came only after they were married. Yet they were, and had been for quite a time, in love with each other; he almost from their first meeting at that local soirée. And the man, Mr. Darcy, had not even touched her. Amazing!

As for the social niceties of the time, it was Lady Catherine who questioned with the same vehemence that Alice had used in excoriating his conduct: 'But who are your Aunts, who are your Uncles . . . ?' These things were real then . . . that is, now. While what Alice said about suitors and order of selection sounded unbelievably quaint to him, it was in deadly earnest to them! No wonder Alice found his suit unacceptable on every count. So would Mr. Bennet!

Now it was clear what a fraud he was. A shallow and contemptible betrayer of every thing honourable. Alice had been justified in every aspect of her denunciation of his conduct. And he rose in fury at his own superficial, selfish actions, and was of a mind to hurl the grindstone as far as he could, then thought better of it; that sort of anger would not help. Time for some corrective action.

The key seemed to be, once more, Ms. Austen – or, at least, her characters. Mr. Darcy was a good deal too haughty for his taste, but Bingley might make a good model. Yes, he rather liked that thought. He would ask Celia – if he still had the chance – if he might borrow her copies. Reading them in the original English would be entertaining, and he could ask her opinion on the various niceties of decorum. He would enjoy that immensely, putting their love on a base firmly rooted in her dimension. Yes, a capital idea, capital. He would start tomorrow – if there was to be a tomorrow with his darling!

But first he must apologize to Alice; that would be difficult enough. Celia would be an even more delicate task.

As she returned to the Cottage, Alice's thoughts – not to mention her emotions – were in complete disarray. If this is what his touch could do to her innermost being – hands still pressed to her bosom to calm their agitation – it was little wonder that the young ladies were completely carried away. They had no experience or defences to deal with it, while she, a grown woman and a mother, with a rapidly developing daughter, had considered her self immune to such frivolous nonsense.

Yet here she was, had been, filled with a wantonness and abandon that now positively shocked her. Alice, the 'iron maiden' as she was wont to consider her self, ready to give her body and every thing it had to offer, her lips waiting only for his to finally enrapture hers, her bosom already fully exposed . . . Heavens, that was . . . and she had to lean her forehead against the cool stone doorway before going further.

Then an additional thought thrust itself upon her. Manfred seemed no longer the same person, taking advantage of all women. It was true that she had just felt his power over her, yet she was clearly as guilty as he, both having their passion risen to dangerous heights by the events in the Glade. Certainly, as she glanced down at her own shameful lack of attire, swollen breasts plainly visible, what man could have resisted the temptation to make love to her excited and willing body.

He truly loved her mistress – in the accepted sense of their society – which was not so with Miss Lucy or Miss Celia on those earlier occasions, and there was perhaps a change. So if his power came from the Hollow, perhaps it had been modified, or directed elsewhere, and he was no longer under its spell.

As for elsewhere, she had heard from Andrew through James, that Horst's evil power over the household appeared to have grown. That was some thing to think on; but for now her attention must be to her mistress.

'I am back, Miss,' she called as she entered, in a sudden panic, other guilty thoughts thrust aside as she found the room empty. 'Miss,' she called again more sharply, and this time with a genuine fear of some thing amiss.

'Yes, Alice?' Celia replied quietly, looking pale and tired as with a heavy load, as she emerged from the bedroom behind her. 'You have some news for me?'

'Oh, Miss,' spinning around to face her, 'I was afraid for you; I do not know why.' Then contradicting her self, 'Yes, I do. Miss, can I give you a hug, if you will hug me, too? For I am all of a sudden very frightened.' And they met in the middle and remained in a strong embrace for some time before Alice whispered to gain her attention.

'Yes, Alice?' came the choked reply.

'Some one has to be disappointed, Miss; I mean really, bitterly disappointed?' and she felt the nod of response. 'It is either her ladyship, who may find it so impossible to forgive that you will lose her – and all your other friends and acquaintances with her. Or it is your self, and Mr. Manfred, too, I am in no doubt, who may lose each other, for it could go very badly for him at the Blackmoor estate.'

Again an answering nod, then silence, except for the trembling that Alice felt for a long while before it subsided.

'Miss,' whispered Alice again in her mistress' ear, 'I was praying that it would not come to this pass. We have succeeded in the first two of our endeavours, and all in a single day, but this last is not in our hands, for her ladyship may take it all very badly indeed and deny your course absolutely. So are you sure of what you are doing, and that this is the card you wish to play?'

'So was I, Alice,' came the whispered response. 'And, no, I am not sure, for my vision is so clouded that I cannot tell whether it is an ace or a deuce. Are you?'

'No, Miss, not at all, and I feel dreadful about it,' and she relayed the conversation with Manfred, and felt her mistress' hot tears soaking through her gown to wet her shoulder long before she had finished.

'Very well, Miss. Then will you go through with it, trusting that the card will not be trumped after you have played it? That would be the very worst of consequences, for then you lose twice,' and Celia nodded so delicately as to be almost imperceptible; but her eyes indicated the same acceptance.

'Remember though our agreement,' said Alice softly, as they drew apart, stroking her mistress' cheek. 'If you fail in that, except it be no fault of yours – and I do not see that in the offing – I cannot face her ladyship, and I must go, and also endure that bitter parting.'

'I shall remember, Alice, and pray that I am strong enough, for both our sakes,' she whispered.

'If it is to be so, Miss, then let it be. I shall talk to Mr. Manfred to give you plenty of time to settle your self and look as pretty as I know you can be.' Celia nodded, still pale and tearful, not trusting her voice.

'Miss?' continued Alice, as she turned at the door. 'Please smile and be happy, for it may also be that yours is the ace of hearts – which in this game are trumps – whereby you win, though all the other players in the game be very angry indeed.

'Whatever happens, dearest Mistress, simply remember that I shall always love you, and I shall never, never, *ever* leave you, no matter the sky shall fall,' and she was gone, leaving the memory of a sudden radiant smile to warm Celia's sad heart.

'Manfred?' finding him with a thoughtful countenance and still contemplating the river.

'Yes, Alice?'

'Pray come sit with me on the bench once more, for I have some thing more to say.'

'Alice, I do not think I can offer any more than I have already this day, I am quite depressed by it all and by my own stupidity, my own actions of the past, and of a mind to quit the race for ever. On the other side, I cannot receive more blows than I already have.'

'Is it that bad, then, Sir? Is your love for Miss Celia that great?' to which he nodded.

'But before that, Alice, I have need to apologize to you for my most recent disgraceful conduct.' And he fell on one knee to perform that obligation. To his horror, she went dead white, shrank back against the seat, then covered her face with her hands.

'Oh, no,' came the muffled cry through her palms. 'Not like that! Not like that! Oh dear.'

'But, Alice I only wanted to . . .'

'Please, Sir, please stand up!' at which command he rose to his feet. 'Are you risen, yet?'

'I am, Alice, but what on earth is the matter?'

Uncovering now her eyes, she took some moments to recover her poise.

'But, Alice, what did I say? What did I do that upset you so? I apologize most humbly if I have offended you.'

'No, you have not offended me, it is just that . . . you see,' and she took several shuddering breaths. 'You see, Sir, that posture, and especially down on *that* knee, signifies only one thing. Do you understand?'

As the significance broke in on his consciousness, he turned once more to the river, and let out a violent but wordless curse. Ye gads, this was a devilishly difficult place to get it right! Like so many things here, the significance of a simple action was totally lost on him. Indeed, he had regarded it almost as a joke! But, like Darcy, he would conquer this! And he strode yet again to the river to moisten his brow, before returning to Alice, who completely misunderstood his heavy frown as being directed at her self.

'Oh, dear, have I made you angry? I am sure I did not mean to.' Whereupon he smiled, relieving her trembling spirit.

'No, Alice, not in the slightest. I am just upset with my self, that is all. And I still wish to apologize.'

'Well, if you find it necessary to do so, but I have not been offended by you; not that I am aware of.'

'Believe me, you have been done a grave disservice, Alice, by me, and I hereby apologize most sincerely for that,' taking a seat now at a suitable distance, neither near nor far.

'Firstly, I want you to know that I now fully understand what you were trying to instruct me in the glade, when last we met there, just you and I. And the other times also when you have had occasion to chastise me for grossly inappropriate behaviour.

'Secondly, I have also realized the most shocking nature of my behaviour toward the persons of Miss Lucinda and Miss Celia. It was abominable, and it shall never happen again.

'Thirdly, and this one is very difficult for me to express,' and he reddened in embarrassment. 'Last time we were sitting on this bench, together, I caused you great embarrassment by touching your . . . uh . . . person as I did, and by my . . . uh . . .'

'Manfred,' she said softly, leaning forward and looking him squarely in the face, both hands resting upon his knee 'I know *exactly* what happened that last time, for I was here, my self, if you will recall. So I do not accept your apology on that account. The others, most assuredly, but on that one, it is neither necessary nor accurate. If there was fault, then I was equal party to it.

'Furthermore, I welcomed and thoroughly enjoyed your touch to my person. My daughter, Mildred, is just thirteen. It has been that long since anyone held me in that special way, and my body was thrilled by its nature and intent, with that special feeling of . . . shall we admit to, admiration? It shall be treasured forever, whatever else befalls.

'However, like your self, I am more than aware of the dangers of such contact, and what it would do to those around us should we fail to heed them. I shall therefore strive to direct my self more appropriately in the future. And I suggest that you do likewise if we are to seal a bargain. Shall we shake hands on that?' putting out her hand to him.

'Alice,' reaching out to take hers in both his, whereupon she added her other hand, too, 'I do not know what to say, except, you are one of the most amazing people I have ever had the privilege to know. I salute you,' and he gently kissed the fingertips of both hands, at which she blushed most prettily.

'Thank you for that gentle acclaim, Manfred, I appreciate your generosity, and I propose to give you a sisterly hug, and a kiss on both cheeks,' surprising him anew with her warm softness against his breast, accompanied by the lingering delicacy of her soft lips on each cheek.

'We have an understanding, then, Manfred?'

'Indeed we do, Alice. Thank you for that; I enjoyed it, too. As to the other, that was very foolish of me, but very enjoyable, too. If circumstances had been different, I could well have . . . But there it is. Perhaps we can be brother and sister? I hope so.' And she nodded her acceptance, dark eyes shining with pleasure. Only then did she gently release his hands.

'However, this new relationship requires that I apologize to you for the terrible words I used to describe your actions and your self.'

He opened his mouth to dissent, but Alice continued.

'I know what you are going to protest, Manfred – that they brought you to your senses – and that may indeed have been so, and I am content that they did. Nevertheless, now that they have completed their purpose, they must be withdrawn. So, please accept my sincere apologies for having uttered them. They are dissolved and we will not speak of them ever again.'

'Alice, that was admirably expressed, and I am grateful to you for using them in the first place to effect the drastic change necessary in my self, and now for withdrawing them. And now it is my turn,' rising to bow low with a click of the heels, giving her hand a prolonged but gentle kiss, for he dare not touch her otherwise.

'Now, to business, if we may, Manfred?'

'Certainly, Alice. What is it that you propose?'

'Returning now to the matter of your Proposal of Marriage. If I should offer you a card that could perchance improve your fortunes with Miss Celia – not knowing whether it be ace or joker – one that may entitle you to be received more favourably, what would be your response?'

'If you are suggesting some thing of an ephemeral nature, Alice, I could not accept.'

'Well, that is honourable. And if it were more, much more? Then how say you?'

'If it were an eternity, Alice, then I would most gladly accept it. Can you promise me that?'

'No-one can promise you that, Manfred,' she returned, softly. And then, softer still:

'But if the card be an ace, will you promise me here and now that you will be faithful to Miss Celia; to her mind, to her spirit, to her body, and to put aside all other temptations of the body, and to all such things for your eternity; and that is what you offer for her hand in yours?'

'Most assuredly I do, Alice, without reservation.'

'Now, I find your position in this matter of two hearts beating as one to be an honourable one, Manfred, and I have so commended it to my mistress on those grounds alone. Although in the normal course they count for naught, as you are now fully aware, they also contain a considerable power of their own, as we may yet demonstrate.

'So, I have ascertained that Miss Celia has considered your suit and is not adverse to it. I cannot say more, for that would be well beyond my position. That is hers alone to demonstrate to you in whatever manner she chooses, if you will but accept it as it is presented to you.

'However, I believe there to be a way by which you may both be rewarded – if you will follow what I now say,' and he nodded, curious as to how this could possibly be when it had appeared to be a closed chapter.

'You recall our promise, yours not to do, and mine to do if you failed in yours?'

'I do indeed, Alice, and I shall be faithful to that promise until you, and only you, release me from it.'

'Well spoken, Manfred. Now, please give me your right palm,' and she laid her right hand on his, saying, 'here is that card,' folding his fingers upon it. 'With it I now release you from that promise, excepting only that final, special act of union, to which you alone are now to be the judge. I require nothing more of you than that. If you but remain bound on your honour to me – and to Miss Celia – regarding that final act, I believe we may see an end to all these difficulties. Are we in accord on that, Manfred?'

'We are indeed, Alice, and I am most eternally grateful. I shall not fail you.'

'Very well,' reluctantly releasing his hand.

As she turned away, he saw that there was nothing more in his open palm than before; except the warm imprint and memory of her own palm upon it. Meanwhile, she held hers together to quiet the powerful tingling sensation that his had induced in them.

'Manfred, let us now repair to my mistress once more, but first you must dress more formally. I will wait for you at the Cottage door,' as she turned toward it.

'Thank you, Alice.'

'Thank *you*, Manfred. Now I know how Prometheus felt upon his release – which I trust you do also upon your discovery of your own errant ways.'

Manfred followed after only a little while, mystified by this last remark, for his Greek mythology was woefully lacking.

18

Forever

'Mr. Manfred is here, Miss,' speaking to her through the bedroom door.

'Let me first make some tea, and then you shall address him. Please be seated, Mr. Manfred. Miss Celia will be with us shortly, for she does wish discourse with you,' and she busied her self with the kettle and teapot.

'There is your tea, Sir, and a generous slice of Cook's excellent currant cake,' with a little curtsey, returning to her normal formality of manner.

'Miss?' as she tapped on the bedroom door, 'tea is ready, and I have brought it to you,' as she entered the bedroom, closing the door behind her.

'Miss, I have given Mr. Manfred the card you wish to play. It is yours if you wish to match it.'

'Thank you, Alice, you are very kind to me. It is well then, on that which we are embarked?'

'As well as we can make it, Miss, for we are both of a single mind. It is done with honour, and more than that we cannot aspire to.'

'Good; let us now join Manfred,' as she opened the door.

'Manfred, I shall drink the tea with you both on the little terrace in the sunshine, for Alice must share it with us.'

Manfred could scarcely contain his surprise, for here was a Celia barely recognizable from only a short while ago. Now she was radiant and sparkling, face aglow with good health.

'Manfred,' she exclaimed briskly when seated, 'I was afraid you had left after that dismal report of Alice's. But I am delighted you remained, for there are some things that have been left undone, and I should like to get to those as soon as you are available.'

'It would have been ungracious of me,' he replied in a subdued tone, 'after your kindness of the day. First modelling most excellently, then providing me the opportunity to explain my background and purposes, not to mention my . . .' he paused, a little uncertain, as if regretting raising the subject. 'Especially for giving me the opportunity to tell you how much . . . how very, very fond of you I am,' he finished quietly, putting down his cup.

'Yes,' said Celia, offhandedly. 'I am sorry that your offer was not more politely received, but we do have our protocol to see to such matters. However, when we have finished our tea, I may have a more appropriate response, for I have some thing to show you, and also some thing to share with you,' closing to him and linking her arm through his, and she talked of the weather and her plans for the garden, as if she had not a care in the world.

'Besides,' she added brightly, 'it has been a lovely day and it is not yet done.'

Manfred was completely baffled by it all, especially Alice's final comments. What was all that supposed to mean, and where was it leading?

'Come, Manfred,' and she led him through to her room, closing the door behind them. 'Alice has worked very hard to make it even partially respectable as a bedroom, so you must be sure to compliment her on it as soon as you have the opportunity.'

Manfred, very conscious of the warmth and softness of her bosom on his arm through her light gown, pulled his thoughts back to look around. Although small, it was indeed nicely decorated, predominantly in pink, a very feminine room, though a little sparse on furniture.

'It suits you well, Celia,' he said, in as well-modulated a tone as he could manage, his mind and body off balance once more at her closeness. 'The counterpane is very pretty, and I see that you look out onto the river,' his words sounding so trite in his own ears that he wondered whether she would find them similarly contrived, leading her to the conclusion that he was dull company.

'Yes, it will do well enough for the moment; at least until we renovate the upstairs portion of the Cottage. There is quite a lot of work to do up there. I will show you that later.

'Alice tells me that you have a card for me,' and held out her right hand to him, whereupon he placed his right hand over hers, while she placed her other hand over his.

'And you accept this card, not knowing its value, or whether it brings fortune or its sad cousin?'

'Indeed I do, dearest, for better or for worse, whatever shall be, for it cannot be less than I have at this moment.'

'Very well, Manfred,' smiling warmly in response, while he hid his disappointment when she disengaged her arm and walked to the window to gaze out at the tranquil scene before turning and leaning back on her elbows against the sill, looking at him with a soft loving expression that seemed to carry an invitation within it.

But surely that was not possible after Alice's dismal verdict; and he was suddenly all at sea again, very unsure of his standing with this lovely young woman. He had just proposed marriage – for the very first time in his life – but she had remained silent and aloof as to her feelings about it, so that he had no idea whether he was still even in the running – and last man at that. Not his choice of the way to win the prize he so desperately sought – although he suddenly recalled that Alice had intimated that there were prizes to be had at the end of the day.

Yet, through his confusion, it seemed that her robe was more loosely fastened than when she left his side, and surely there was a message in that, for beneath it she was certainly wearing very little. Swallowing hard in an unsuccessful effort to control his racing pulse, he would have responded to the apparent invitation – except that he could not formulate any thing suitable. Besides, he wondered how sincere he would sound, for his gaze and overreaching imagination were on the deep cleft revealed by her stance, where her gown had parted almost to the waist as she shifted her position slightly, revealing the cleft and inner curves of her bosom.

She paused for a moment, as if pulling her own mind back to the scene.

'You like to see my hair down?'

In response to his nod she raised her hands to unpin her hair, the movement causing her robe to further loosen so that it opened all the way to the hem, permitting a generous portion of self to shine through, confirming his assessment of a considerable deficit of underclothing before the tresses cascaded around her shoulders and covered her upper body again.

'Now, if you will remain where you are, I promised you some thing to see,' and taking up a hairbrush from the window sill, she brushed her long hair sensuously over her upper body, before parting it then to let the bosom thrust through.

'Now,' she whispered softly, 'I do owe a reply to your formal offer, to which I have now given due consideration. So, my formal response is that I now accept your request for my hand in marriage, and this goes with it,' lifting her arms to touch the ceiling beams over her head so that the gown slithered to the floor, and her body glowed fully and softly in the rays of the setting sun, except where a silk scarf draped it self carelessly across her lower belly.

'And the some thing to share?' he continued, hesitantly, almost not daring to ask for fear of saying the wrong thing and sending her back into her shell.

'As to that, Manfred, judging from your past interest in my intimate person, I thought perhaps you would care to share what you see before you,' pulling her hair aside, and running her hands lightly, suggestively, over her body, from bosom to belly to hips, and back again.

Manfred was so surprised that for the moment he stood stock-still, unsure of the reality of what he was being invited to share.

'And this is your response?' to which she inclined her head, seductively, 'and that is what you wish to share?' he whispered, not believing that it could be so.

'It is, as you see,' her hands moving across and under her breasts, to cup and lift them to his gaze through the curtain of hair.

'A truly wonderful response,' he whispered in return, moving to her gloriously open form, lifting her silky veil of hair with gentle fingertips to reveal the softness beyond and marvelling at their perfect formation, his gaze fascinated by, yet not daring to touch, their swollen dark centres.

'But I never dreamed of such an incredible acceptance. You are sure, truly sure that this is what you wish?' recalling his most recent concerns and his firm resolution.

'More sure than any thing I have *ever* done,' as she tilted her head to meet his mouth in a gentle kiss. Then, standing on tiptoe to him and locking her hands behind his head, she pulled him down onto her bosom as she whispered,

'Is this what you have been dreaming of?'

Suddenly his body came to life with the passion that was already flowing in hers as any lingering doubts in his mind as to the nature of her sharing vanished, belatedly realizing that she was all available, every exposed part of her, and he avidly accepted her breasts as the first sampling of it.

With the contact, the fire flowed through her ever more strongly as his hungry lips and hungry mouth explored her, and she dug her fingers into his back to crush her self more fiercely into him and increase her own pleasure at the touch, before realizing quite suddenly that he was still as fully dressed as she was the opposite.

'Now it is my turn to disrobe you as you once did me,' she whispered as she nibbled his ear, 'and I shall enjoy it as much as you did. But,' she warned, 'you are not allowed to touch me until we are dressed – or undressed – exactly alike, or I shall vanish into thin air.'

And she teased him unmercifully as she slowly removed his garments one by one, allowing her excited body to freely engage his as she did so, secure in the knowledge that he dare not lay a hand on her, much less a mouth, then dancing around the room with them, each in turn before discarding it and returning for the next soft encounter.

His waistcoat in particular fascinated her, and she tried it on, buttoning it sensually under her bosom to proclaim her self, taunting him in a voluptuous dance, as close to him as she dared without driving him beyond the point of control.

But finally the tenuous soft brushes against him worked their magic and her own desires rose hot within her again, so that she hurriedly removed the final garment, and he was at last as unadorned and as so evidently excited as her self.

'There, isn't that better,' she whispered, as she returned to his embrace. 'Now I can feel you, too,' she added, fingering his chest and gently teasing him. 'My, you are so hard here; I did not know that happened to you, too,' as she leaned forward and raised her self until they touched, her bosom playing with his, sending shivers through them both.

'Just like you,' he whispered in return, before enveloping and enjoying her once more. And she responded by placing her hands on his bottom, pulling her self into him, to instantly experience his hard pulsing manhood against her belly.

'And here, too,' she whispered, almost in awe, leaning back once more in examination.

'Is this some thing else we can share?' for he was nothing like the Michelangelo David that she had studied in her art classes, while Alice's description did not begin to do justice to that excited part of him. So this is what she longed to have deep inside her – wonderingly, for she doubted that she would be able to accommodate him, although Alice had assured her that it could be so. And she could hardly wait for that moment, so great was her exhilaration!

Eagerly lowering her hands to feel its excitement, she stroked him, thrilled to feel a quiver run through his entire body at her touch, and then become quite rigid as she fondled him with greater intensity there and below.

His response was to pick her up, holding her for a long minute while their lips met in a passionate and probing kiss, her arms tightly around his neck, while her legs instinctively wrapped themselves around his waist, so that their private parts were in such intimate contact that she settled down on him even more to increase the thrills it sent deep into her body.

But he was not ready for that ultimate intimacy and, still holding her, advanced to the bed, carefully depositing her there to gently remove her silk scarf, the final barrier to her bareness, to which she raised no objection, giving only a soft sigh of satisfaction. Then he leaned over to gently kiss those parts that were once more desperate for his attention.

'But where I am hard,' he whispered back, 'you are incredibly soft,' as his fingers gently probed her body, before concentrating their exquisite touch, until she would surely have screamed out in the ecstasy of the fire that drove into her, had not his lips been consuming hers.

'And yes,' he responded softly, 'it is for sharing, too, if that is what you truly wish. But only if you are *quite* sure. I can wait 'til you are.'

'Yes, oh yes,' she cried out, 'but I can not. You do not know how desperately I have wanted you, to feel you as part of me, and I am ready now, please, right now,' and she pulled him down on top of her in an instinct of complete submission to his will. Then as suddenly pulled back again.

'No, not that, my dearest, for I have promised. Every thing else is yours for the taking. But that one thing must needs be held in trust until we are wed.'

To her surprise, he did not challenge and pursue her as she suddenly feared, but also withdrew a little, whispering, 'I, too, have promised that this – but only this – shall wait.'

Her eyes opened wide at this sudden cessation of intense passion.

'How can that be,' she said, 'for you knew nothing of this!'

'Indeed, that is quite true, my sweet, but I made a solemn promise to Alice – on pain of death, I might add – that I would not abuse your perfect form again. Now she has released me from that promise, excepting this one last thing.'

'Oh that Alice,' she mocked, 'I shall have serious words with her.'

'No, my darling, for it was she who made me see, finally and completely, how much more you mean to me than that which we are sharing so intimately now. She was so entirely correct in her approach to it all, that I believe this very precious moment we owe entirely and exclusively to her.

'Now let us resume where we were before your Alice came between us, my dearest one. Excepting that one last thing – important as we may feel it – I am all yours, and you are all mine.' And his mouth and lips and tongue and probing fingers devoured and explored her until she could take no more without expressing it all to the whole world.

In the kitchen clearing the tea things, Alice was tidying up generally, heard the murmured voices, the sounds of their love-making, the sharp cry, and her hot body suddenly rebelled, and picking up her hairbrush she fled out to the garden, suddenly halting, unable to resist the over-whelming urge to peek through the window at the entwined lovers, before wrapping her self tightly in the shawl to stand with her back against a tree, staring straight ahead, perfectly still.

With this talk of husbands and marriage and the passion of love-making, it was certainly time that she looked to her own needs as a woman. It had been much too long since she had felt the intimate touch of a man – though she blushed at the thought of that most recent contact, but that made the point exactly.

In her early days after Richard, she had entertained salacious thoughts about one or two young men, but they either already had entanglements, were not interested in one already some other's property – with a child to prove it, or had simple lust in their eyes. But now she was fearful that it really was too late, despite what her mistress – and Manfred – thought of her form. She seemed to be lacking the courage.

More importantly, unless she found some way to provide release, she was at considerable risk of that bench scene recurring – next time perhaps to the cost of her very way of life.

All the while, her reverie was invaded by the increasingly urgent sounds of the lovers through the open windows, ending in that sharp cry once more, then silence. She was happy for her mistress, with her very real lover, but envious, just the same.

Suddenly, unable to absorb any further intimate play of man with woman, so perfectly re-enacting her own virginal ecstacy with her first and only lover, so consumed by the fire inside her entire being, she could stand no more.

Frantically she threw her shawl to the ground and wrenched off her dress to expose her pale body, releasing her throbbing bosom with its hard, thrusting desire to the warm dusk air. Now she was as free as her fully naked mistress, though she must rely on her own inadequate methods, pretending that her sensual stroking was that of the passionate, well-endowed lover she had just vividly witnessed. And she feverishly brushed her long hair over and against her body hoping to achieve what her mistress was now thrilling to, but it was woefully short of that.

Then she brushed her hair back over her shoulders, and stood for some moments examining and appraising her own quieting body in a shaft of light from the rising moon through the trees, moving into it until it fully illumined her still throbbing self.

No, not nearly as fine as her mistress', she judged with dismay. Perhaps adequate to entice a man, but how to get close enough to win him. How then to display her charms, without appearing wanton, as any watcher to her recent action must conclude.

She gave a deep sigh, then slid into her gown once more, in a sad and depressed state of mind. In spite of all the assurances she had received – even Manfred's so clearly demonstrated need of her, recalling his rising manhood – she lacked the courage to attempt it. And she sighed deeply. Dealing with others' problems seemed immeasurably easier than her own, somehow.

Putting those gloomy thoughts behind her, Alice turned to the lovers once more, startled to find her mistress leaning out the widow, regarding her quizzically, and finger to lips, directed her to return. Now she was doubly dismayed. Had some of her own release and lack of restraint been observed – and how much? What would her mistress think of such shamelessness?

'We must be gone before he wakes again, Alice, I quite wore him out,' she whispered as they met at the Cottage door. 'Besides, he has not been sleeping well since . . .' This surprised Alice to comment on her willingness to abandon her lover almost as soon as he had satisfied her passion.

'My lover, as you call him, is quite capable of fending for him self, so stop looking so glum,' misconstruing Alice's sombre countenance. 'Just light a candle and bring it behind the screen so that you can dress me quickly. My clothes are on the settee, and he cannot see the light from there.'

Alice moved as fast as she could in the uncertain light but it was not accomplished speedily enough for her mistress.

'Leave some of those hooks undone, Alice; we are not going to be seen, and we must be away. Quickly gather up our model things and the paintings and store them in that cupboard until we return in a day or two. I have had a stout lock fitted to ensure our privacy. I will see to the horses,' and reached the door as Alice quickly pulled off her own garment to complete her attire.

'Just a moment, Alice!' came the sharply whispered command; and she looked up in surprise, believing her mistress had already left the room, caught unprotected in the candlelight in the act of finding a place for her dress.

'Perfect,' whispered Celia, returning to where Alice stood motionless to study her pale figure intently before continuing. 'This could be the most exciting painting yet – if I can capture it. One more thing is needed though, the focus, the central element.'

She looked around the room and selected a red rose from the mantelpiece vase to replace the dress in Alice's fingers, dropping that on a convenient chair.

'This will do very fine, a memory; or rather the *echo* of a memory, a study in red, for the rose; white, your body; and blue – for the melancholy spirit,' and stood in silent contemplation for a moment.

'Just a single candle!' she whispered to her self, 'I never thought so small a flame could render so powerful an image. How beautifully it flickers on the body, yet so difficult to capture,' as she moved first left then right, composing the picture in her inner eye. 'In shadow here, in soft light there. But we need just a *hint* of light, *here*, Alice, to create the mystery, perhaps from a mirror as Rembrandt was fond of doing,' placing a finger on Alice's firmly rounded belly to turn her slightly away from the candle-glow.

Light as the touch was, Alice reacted instantly, tightening her muscles in reflex, even though her downward gaze had anticipated the contact, her skin prickled just at the thought of it.

'My, you *are* sensitive, tonight, Alice,' said Celia, not missing the heightened colour at this remark. 'Now, to make the most of the light,' she continued to her self as she studied her quiescent model, 'we would also need to twist the upper you a little in the other direction,' turning her gently by the shoulder.

'Now your best feature is part in shadow and part in light,' indicating the shaded part on one side and the lighted area on the other, 'yes, and with a deeper shadow in the cleavage just *there*,' she concluded emphatically, running her finger between.

Alice reacted almost as if shot, stiffening her entire body and trembling as an unexpected thrill surged through her even as she watched in fascination her mistress' stroking finger. And, despite her determination not to be embarrassed during the artistic positioning, to remain calm before her mistress, she could sense her self coming alive again with a deep throb of desire. Could now feel the tingle and discern the surge of her passion, powerless to arrest the automatic response once set in motion or prevent the erratic breathing that accompanied it.

'Gracious,' whispered Celia, 'Models are not supposed to react to a simple touch.' Alice nodded, and tried to concentrate on being the perfect model. 'We must reflect the rose in your cheeks and lips,' her mistress continued, focusing on those areas, 'but the most important,' moving her hand adjacent to her bosom and studying again, 'will be to echo your natural dark pink. So; perhaps the flower would be better nestled in the centre for greater contrast and balance.'

As she moved the rose against the white softness of Alice's bosom to study the effect, she was surprised once more at the violent reaction its soft petals elicited.

'You do not usually get this excited, Alice. I thought we were over all that?, And Alice coloured again.

'I am sorry I got so jumpy, Miss, but you see, while your self and Mr. Manfred have exercised and exhausted your passions quite freely and openly, I have had to contain and control mine. And now they seem to be beyond my rule,' holding her mistress' hand and rose against her swollen breast for a moment, then reluctantly releasing it.

'Well . . . but now you really must dress in a hurry, Alice,' whispering once more, 'or your stimulating performance will have a wider congregation! Come, we have been too long here already. We will talk about it all on the way home,' she added more softly as she hurried to the door. 'Put the candle on the kitchen table as you leave, so my darling will be able to find his way home,' and she turned quickly and left, surprised as she mounted to find Alice so close behind her.

'I am sorry, Miss, I should have been more controlled as you require,' as she closed the gate softly behind them and quickly mounted. 'I was carried away by all the emotion of the day, and it suddenly boiled over.'

'I understand, Alice, believe me I do. However, a model has to learn to be detached, as I observed when I was in Town at the Art School – unless she is the central element of the passion, of course. But best forgotten now,' and she set her mount to as fast a pace as she dared in the dim light – for they had chosen the much longer route to avoid the darkened copse – while Alice trailed behind.

He awoke suddenly, disturbed by something, but though he listened carefully expecting to hear Celia's laughter, the Cottage was in complete silence. He perceived a light from under the door; perhaps they were hiding from him, but when he opened the door and searched, there was no-one.

He took the kitchen candle back to the bedroom and dressed quickly, for they must be somewhere, perhaps in the garden, but that turned out to be a false assumption. Only then did he note their horses were missing and was disappointed; he had every intention of taking his beloved to the heights once more before they parted. So the day was really over.

Now in the saddle, he rode slowly, waiting for the still-rising moon to light the path, giving Johnson his head; it knew the way home. Free of that concern, his thoughts turned to the day in which he had just participated. In retrospect it was all completely amazing, unlike any in his experience. From a puzzled arrival, to the art class and the sensual excitement of their scantily clad bodies – Alice included – to the marriage proposal, acceptance and then that wonderful episode with his beloved Celia.

That was incredible; from despair to overwhelming joy in almost less time than it took to tell. And it was all due to Alice, he had no doubts about that, for somehow he knew it to be so. A remarkable young woman that, reflecting on his near disaster. And yet, he was decidedly and genuinely attracted to her. Yes, to her voluptuous body, certainly, but also to her excellent and logical mind, equal to his bride-to-be (oh, he liked that phrase) in some way he could not define. She would make someone a damned fine wife – if his Celia could bear to part with her, and she likewise.

So he was engaged to be married and soon, as he understood it, otherwise it was still possible that he could lose her. But that thorough Solicitor's questioning had him thinking, and he turned his mind to briefly examine the issue.

He was expected to provide his wife with an appropriate estate and all that went with it. While here that was not possible, he could certainly have achieved it in his world – and at that thought he halted Johnson quite abruptly, for he suddenly understood the challenge: if he was capable of it there, why could he not do it here?!

He had the skills. Indeed, the more he thought about it the more he convinced himself that not only was it possible, it was some thing he had to do to provide his new bride the respect and honour she deserved from himself, as well as that expected of him by her society.

Moving forward once more, his thoughts turned to how this might be achieved, indeed must *be achieved. After all, he knew far more than any one in this era, for much had been achieved in the two centuries between them.*

The problem was that no-one must suspect that he was from their future; unusually bright perhaps, but knowledgeable of what was to happen? Never! If any discovered that, his life would be made a misery by unscrupulous scoundrels. But he considered himself more than capable of handling that by implying that society in his Prussia (in this era a great power) was much more advanced than their own.

He had not got his Ph.D by being stupid, and as that thought matured, he realized the issues were quite similar. He had studied far distant star systems by projecting present knowledge well into the future. Here he was doing that backwards, but instead of some thoughtful and calculated prognostications, here he had the answers at his fingertips, and he suddenly became very excited.

Already in possession of these, this could be one of the most electrifying periods of his life, being required only to move them forward at an acceptably suitable pace, based on a logical advancement. Of course, he would have to be careful how he went about it. Whilst he thought their candles were incredibly quaint, he wasn't about to invent electricity or the light bulb!

No, it was energy of a different nature that seemed to be the key, and engines were the centre of that. Whilst he was not a mechanical engineer, he was more than adequately acquainted with their means of performance. In that case, his first step must be the steam engine and its early use in railway engines, to contact the inventor, James Watt, of Birmingham as he remembered it.

With his Prussian background (and if challenged, he did speak the language), he should be able to help him in a subtle way with the design of shaft drives, gear boxes and the like. That should be relatively easy. Secondly, his economics and finance were sound enough to make something of himself in London as an unusually astute businessman – even a banker!

He would have to attire himself appropriately, of course, but a good tailor would solve that problem. He had seen a number of gentlemen visitors at Greville Hall – and Mr. Darcy, of course. He supposed he could manage that – though a top hat wasn't his preferred head covering, nor those inevitable gloves!

And the more he thought about it the more excited he became, for he could see himself becoming wealthy in a relatively short period of time, urging Johnson forward now that the moon had risen sufficiently to light the way.

Yes, as soon as he got to his room he would lay out some principles on which to work, and a timetable to set against it. By George, he would make his glorious Celia proud of him, and yes, he would provide all those things she clearly deserved, and his head was now spinning with the multitude of possibilities before him.

The only other thing necessary was to leave a note for Alice explaining that in order to establish his beloved to the level of society that her Ladyship required, he had gone to Birmingham at short notice, etc., away for at least a week to establish that. Andrew could take that in the morning, and in his eagerness, he put Johnson into a fast trot.

At this very precise moment, but riding in the opposite direction, Celia reined in her horse to face her companion, unable to contain her delighted feelings any longer.

'Oh, Alice,' she exclaimed, 'it was wonderful, even more wonderful than I ever imagined, even though you told me that it would be,' and she leaned over and gave Alice a kiss on the cheek. 'But I am not yet a full, complete woman, Alice, like your self.'

'I am so glad, Miss. Was that difficult?'

'Oh, yes, Alice. I failed at the first, for it was so glorious that I nearly forgot all about that. I wanted him so much; just as you must have wanted Richard. But suddenly I knew what must be withheld and just gave the rest of my self to him. And it was still wonderful, the excited feelings he produced in me.

'Besides, Manfred, the sweet darling, would not enter me at all, even though I was begging him to at the start. He said we should wait. Indeed, he told me that he had promised you that he would not perform that final act that so enthralled you. Is that so?'

'It is indeed, Miss, for I did not want to leave that challenge entirely to your self, hoping that in this case two "noes" might still make a "no".'

'Well, you were quite right, Alice, and though you told me what his body would be like, I am still in disbelief that my own will accommodate him; that we shall see in the fullness of time. And when I held and stroked him there, he was as agitated as I was pleased to provide him joy, and he . . . oh, it was so wonderful,' and the tears so streamed down her face that she had to wipe them with the hem of her dress.

'He did things with my body, too, that quite startled me, as you said they would. He called it "foreplay", meaning to play with each other's bodies and special parts, before . . . you know. But I did not mind, for he so enjoyed doing it, that I enjoyed it, too. Whatever he wants, Alice, is what I want, you see. Just to see him so happy is wonderful to me, as it must have been with your self.'

'Indeed, Miss, it was just so, for I confess that I did take a peek for a moment or two through that other small window to assure that all was well with you. And, yes, it was so with Richard, for he was all over my body, just as was Manfred at that very moment, illumined by the last dying rays of the sun.'

'And for how long were you a spectator, Alice?'

'Judging by the sun, Miss, perhaps two or three minutes?'

'Long enough to have witnessed much of our loving, then.'

'Yes, Miss, and as you stated, he is well endowed, and that will be a special joy when that moment comes. Nothing quite compares, and you will find your self unwilling to let him go, wishing he could remain there forever. And yes, your intimate body will accommodate his.'

Then I am quite delighted that you are more fully aware than I had thought. Now we are truly sisters in that regard,' taking her hand to squeeze it. 'And I am so relieved.'

'Relieved, Miss?'

'Yes, Alice, because now I do not have to be concerned about protecting my body any more. I have had to guard it so carefully all those years that I was growing up, sometimes wanting to give it just to see what the fuss was all about, but it was not to be sanctioned. Now I am so glad I waited, keeping my self just for him, for he does seem to adore my body so. I was afraid he might not covet it, but he really does, especially the privy parts,' she rushed on excitedly, unselfconsciously. 'Now I have availed it to him alone, it shall always be his to regard as he chooses.

'But I do have a confession I must make to you, Alice, that may make you angry,' in a whisper. 'It was when he picked me up and my legs just wrapped themselves around his waist of their own accord . . .'

'And then, Miss?'

'Well, that is the embarrassing part, for then we were in full contact with each other, even to his entering me, and despite your entreaty I lowered my self further upon him as the feeling was so wonderful that I wanted more of him. Does that break our understanding, Alice?' and now in her softest whisper, gripping Alice's hand tightly, *'and could I have his baby?'*

To her surprise and confusion, Alice simply laughed.

'Oh, Miss! Firstly it does not count nor break our contract. Secondly, no, it is not possible to bear a child from that light contact, he must enter you fully, and you will know for a certainty when he does that! I shall tell you why as we resume our journey, but I am delighted that you experienced that joy,' providing her a kiss on the cheek, receiving one in return, hands held tight.

'Strange thing, Alice, I had always thought that surrendering my maid-enhood was losing some thing very precious. Now it is so clear that I will gain manifold my supposed "loss", for it is not a loss I will suffer, but a gift I shall make on our marriage bed. I shall secure him as the guerdon for the relinquishment, and have not to concern my self further about making love.'

'You are not going to make love any more, Miss?' cried the astonished Alice.

'No, silly. I am going to enrapture my darling every moment that he says we can without having babies, for he seems to know more about a woman's body than I do; and I shall savour every minute of him, inside or out.

'But do you not see that, having opened my self for *his* pleasure and passion, with only one delicacy of constraint – and that soon to be released – I am now set free to pursue those other things that are *my* passion: painting and drawing, and exploring colour and shape, and how things work? My darling says he will tell me all about such matters, just as much as I want to know, and he seems to know infinitely more than anyone I have ever met.

'I can throw away my old hair brush, too – unless, of course, I gift it to you – for when I get too tense he will be there to pleasure me, and I him. Oh, Alice, I had such fun removing his attire all the way to his skin,' and amidst lots of giggles she told her story of tormenting him almost to distraction. 'Next time, though, he says he is going to seek retribution and keep me waiting for him. But I really do not think he will. I could not stand that, for I would insist on that wonderful foreplay once more.'

'And we talked of so many things, Alice, when we were making love and afterwards, and in between. He would like to have three babies – two girls and then a boy – just as I do, except I would have two boys and then a girl to spoil. They would come later, of course, because I have so many things I want to do first. But he, the sweet darling, wants them right away.'

'There is some thing that you *do* have to do right away, Miss, before the two of you make any babies.'

'Really, Alice?' said Celia in surprise. 'And what is that?'

'Get married, Miss!'

'Oh, Alice,' giggled Celia, 'of course we will get married, and right away, for he is as determined in that as I – for fear of losing me, I believe. And Alice,' Celia went on after a moment of silence, then averting her eyes briefly to study her hands, 'you were also quite correct; all those other horrible memories are washed away to be replaced by beautiful ones with my darling Manfred, just as you said they would be – though I could not accept it at the time. While he did many of the same things, he was so gentle and loving, and he lay on me as light as a cloud,' and suddenly she moved closer to weep on Alice's shoulder.

'Time we were going home, Miss,' whispered Alice in her ear, holding her mistress tight to her.

When they had put the Cottage a goodly distance behind them, Celia slowed to a walk in order to ponder her companion's recent behaviour. It must have been a very trying day for her. Indeed, now that she thought about it, Alice had behaved splendidly in the circumstances, taking all in her stride, including a quite spirited petition to her suitor. What other *maid* could have even dared to assume so much and then perform so magnificently.

But that was only on the society side, for her Indian Maiden pose, together with only her skin beneath that essential scanty dress to arouse her would-be lover, must have tried her spirit sorely. That was well beyond her expected duties, and though she knew Alice to be a gem, she was only now beginning to appreciate the true worth of her devoted admirer. That must be looked into and a suitable reward gifted.

With regard to that little incident of the candle, she had been unjustifiably sharp, and now sincerely regretted it. After all, Alice had not expected to be called upon to model just then, caught by mere chance in her natural state when they were supposedly rushing to leave. And she was acutely aware of her own emotional and libertine excesses with her new 'lover', so it was small wonder that Alice was overwrought! Could she her self have performed so admirably? And suddenly she felt guilty and quite small in comparison.

'Is that what I have, Alice,' she called softly, to break the ice, then dropping back to ride alongside once more. 'A lover?'

'That is what he is until you are married, Miss,' relieved that her mistress was no longer cross. 'I had a lover, too, of course,' she confessed, warily. 'Do you mind me calling him that?'

'No, Alice, not a bit. Indeed, I rather like it. It gives it a saucy edge,' and she laughed. 'So we are akin in having lovers; and good ones, at that! Although I sincerely hope mine will tarry awhile before planting his seed. And she laughed again as she reached for Alice's hand to give it a squeeze, surprised once more at the fierceness of Alice's answering clasp, but gratified that all was well between them.

'And Alice, I owe you an apology for my sharpness back in the Cottage; I see now how very careless that was of me. I should have been more understanding. In my own delight and joy of release, I had not thought of your stoic self-denial. We must certainly find a way to ease those tensions, and soon,' recalling the hunger so eagerly demonstrated in that silent room. 'And I shall find a suitable reward for your devotion.'

For her part, Alice was all the time wishing it had been more and much deeper but not daring to indicate it to her mistress (still in thrall of her own exhilaration), or that she already knew the way and could name her reward!

As the moon ascended further to bathe them in its silver light, they trotted for a while in meditative silence, then set their pace to a steady walk again.

Suddenly, 'There it is, Alice,' cried Celia, 'the little church I shall be married in,' as she reined in, quickly dismounted, and tiptoed to the side door. It gave with only a slight squeak to her push as they entered, their eyes taking some moments to adjust to its dimness.

'Is it not beautiful, Alice? I knew it would be, although I have never been in here before. It will be so pretty dressed up, and big enough for a small wedding, just my particular friends as bridesmaids, with some thing special for Lucy.'

'She should be your Matron of Honour, Miss,' whispered Alice, in awe of the stillness.

'Oh, no, Alice, it will have to be some thing other than that, for that shall be your role, and Mil . . .'

'Me, Miss?' squealed Alice, and put her hand to her mouth as the sound reverberated through the vaulted nave. 'I would love that. I have never been in a wedding, Miss,' she finished, timidly.

'Then this will be your very own as well, Alice. We shall dress you for the part, and Mildred will be there as a flower girl for me and as a witness for you and Richard. And we shall say a special prayer for your Richard so that he can share in it, too. With music from the quintet – or rather, quartet,' with a little laugh, 'for I shall be rather preoccupied.'

'Thank you, Miss,' replied Alice, wiping her eyes and squeezing her mistress' hand, 'that would be lovely. For Mildred, too, for she has never been in a wedding, either,' as the thought of her daughter as a flower girl for her mistress brought a smile to her lips, dropping then to her knees at the altar rail for a moment's prayer.

Rising, there was more silence, and perhaps a silent prayer or two, during which they held hands and listened to the peace of the soft moonlight cascading through the rose window onto the altar rail, just where the happy pair would soon be standing, *Deo Gratia.*

'He said he would design my dress, too, Alice,' as she mounted again. 'Just fancy, a man designing a bridal gown! And that is not all. He thinks our under-things are needlessly cumbersome – with which I heartily agree – so he will design one I will like much better than the bodice, and you shall sew it, and if you like it, one for your self. What do you think of that?' she laughed. '*I* think he just wants access to me more quickly than is possible now!'

Alice was inclined to agree, though she thought it better not to comment; mainly because pictures of her self and Mildred in their wedding finery kept drifting across her inner vision, for she knew instinctively that her mistress would spare no expense to make it a most beautiful occasion.

Listening to a nightingale in the otherwise still air, they travelled without speaking, 'til Celia broke the silence once more to address the issue that still lay between them before it became too heavy to broach.

'Alice, I know I surprised you back in the Cottage, but did you object to my touching you in the interest of artistic endeavour?'

'Is it all right, Miss, to confess even that I liked it? Indeed,' she added, more softly still, 'that your gentle touch was quite wonderful, even though as a model I should not have reacted that way at all.'

'That is true, Alice, you should not; but they are your feelings, and you should never be ashamed of them; for what they are, you are. And in the solace of this magic moonlight, we should be able to say what we feel without undue regard for who we are, or think we are. Do you understand, Alice?'

'Yes, Miss, I understand. Now can I answer the question you asked about maidenly release in the glade, so long ago?' and Celia nodded. 'The simple truth, Miss, is that there was never a need to liberate my tensions, for I was all dried up inside. Being your model has now released me from my self-made prison and awakened me to joy once more. Yet despite that, I seem unable to achieve that feeling, that release for my self as you do, Miss, and I was too shamed to reveal it,' – and suddenly she simply had to know.

'Did you witness me in the clearing, Miss, when I shamelessly . . . exposed my self?' she whispered, receiving a nod. 'All of it?' and blushed when her mistress nodded again. 'I believed you to be still engaged with your betrothed, Miss; otherwise I would not have displayed and pleasured my self like that.'

'That is why I am so surprised, Alice, at what you are telling me now, for I thought that an imaginative and spirited release that served you well in the moment of need. And in the moonlight, too. That would make a wonderful painting – without the release, of course – for there you were the Silver Goddess without peer. We must try that one day – or rather, one night.'

'Thank you, Miss, I would like to be your model for it sounds wonderful; firstly because I now enjoy the sun or moon upon my skin and the freedom it provides the spirit, and secondly because . . . because it gives me great pleasure to see your beautiful self so happy in your artistic mode,' she rushed on, suddenly embarrassed by her expressed love. 'Besides, I receive much joy at being the only model – at the moment, of course – able to provide the explicit and sensual needs that your spirit requires.

'There, I have expressed some thing that I have long felt, but had never the courage to vent. But this night, Miss, was very challenging because of my viewing your open love-making, and I just had to express my self or explode! And, yes, the moonlight was indeed glorious, and yes I would love to have such a painting of my self. I would wish also to include that special moment of arousal and release to capture the fullness of my joy and the memory it invoked. You might call it "Richard III", and you have only to name the night.'

'Well, that was all beautifully expressed and shared. I know now, dear Alice, just how very thoughtless of me that was. My darling is *very* enthusiastic to my person, and now I have no secrets left to me, as you have none from Richard, so we are allied in that.

'But in my desire to satisfy afresh my own craving, I had not considered how it might affect you, and I am truly sorry to have put you through that,' but she smiled as she took Alice's hand for a tight squeeze.

'I shall instruct him to be more considerate of his audience next time.' And she was surprised to feel Alice trembling as the hold tightened on her fingers.

'That is quite all right, Miss, I was so pleased for you, except for one other thing that I must now reveal to you. That is why they were so strong, so urgent, so undeniable that I could not restrain my self.'

So there were to be more revelations. This was indeed intriguing, but Celia maintained her silence.

Alice paused for a further moment, fiddling with the reins, before shyly continuing.

'That is also why I enjoy posing so much for you, Miss, because you make me aware of my natural body again, cause me to come alive as I used to when Richard was close to me even before that wonderful night. And that is what I would like to experience again, Miss,' she concluded in a whisper, 'when we do that forthright painting, the one with the single rose and candle at the Cottage. Then my spirit shall be very happy, too.'

They continued in silence while Alice discreetly observed her mistress deep in thought.

'Alice, as I understand your message, you require a certain physical stimulation in order to achieve the "hidden meaning" that I need for it to be a successful painting. Is that so?' watching Alice carefully nod her head.

'Well then, suppose I preferred you fully attired as in, say, "The Milk-maid" or worse, a "Mrs. Siddons" pose that did not require any contact, and certainly none of an intimate nature?' and Alice's only reply was to cast her head downwards. 'I see. Would it then concern you if I could not find the time or the necessity for you to pose for me, ever again?' There was no audible response from Alice except for a long drawn-out sigh, followed by two tears trickling slowly down her cheeks.

'This modelling business is of some consequence to you, then,' said Celia, softly, and Alice nodded, wiping her eyes but neither replying nor raising her head.

'I do not see how that can be, Alice, unless there is some thing of importance that you are not disclosing.'

'That is true, Miss,' and she forced her self to look into her mistress' eyes, her own swimming with tears, 'but I had hoped you would not notice the omission,' as her voice dropped to a whisper. 'I am mortified to confess, Miss, that I had thought to gratify my newly awakened self by importuning a man. But to have my overtures spurned perchance he found my physical charms wanting would be too humiliating to endure.

'I know what you told me, Miss,' as she sensed her about to interrupt, 'but that is not the only thing that stays my course,' and she rode in close to take her hand gently. 'I consider you a very fortunate young woman, Miss; I could not believe my self to be so favoured. I have heard many dreadful tales of how some men treat their women, harsh and cruel, even when – sometimes particularly when – they are being passionate. I could not, indeed *will* not accept that from any man,' she concluded firmly. 'Thus I do not intend to lay my self open to it, and I must therefore make my own solitary course.'

Celia raised her head, surprised by the gentleness in Alice's voice and her considerable insight into some thing she had only recently discerned for her self.

'That was excellently said, Alice. If it helps you any, I have assembled my own reasoning concerning passion and love. They are similar in some purely physical ways, but in the emotional sense they are almost direct opposites. Passion is closely linked to lust, which, as you know, is one of the seven deadly sins. And lust has no love component or tenderness at all. We women can sometimes be lustful, but very soon our tender feelings negate the harshness, and it turns to love.

'As regards the former, my lover has been most passionate with both Lucy and my self. But it is to you, Alice, that I owe an immense debt of gratitude for curing Manfred of that serious shortcoming.

'Love is quite, quite different, and very difficult to put into words, so I shall not even try. You and I both knew it when we received it from our lovers; and, to my shame, I have also known lust. Perhaps I could sum it all up in two words: Lust is "taking", love is "giving". And that makes all the difference. Manfred was consideration it self in loving me today – quite unlike that previous horrid experience in Town.'

'That is wonderfully put, Miss, and it is indeed most helpful, for now I know what to look for in a man – one who will respect me. Happiness can only be obtained for me with that obligation on his part.'

The silver stillness returned once more, while, continuing at a leisurely walk, both young women struggled with their emotions. For Celia, she had suddenly been made aware – and not a little ashamed – of her own fortune in such matters of heart and body, compared to the trials and tribulations that her faithful servant bore with outward equanimity. She would have responded in some such manner, except that she knew she could not trust her voice 'til she had overcome the lump in her throat, nor could she as yet formulate a coherent reply.

For Alice, it was a struggle between openness and concealment. She decided on the former, knowing that in any event, it would not be long before the mistress suspected her secret. Thus it was Alice who recovered her poise first, but there was a certain weight on her heart that must be unburdened before the other could be broached.

'Miss, I have a confession to make, one that must be aired before I can speak of other affairs of the heart. It is very personal, but as it involves your self, I must first request your permission. May I do that?'

'You may, Alice, though I cannot imagine what it could be.'

'It concerns Mr. Manfred, Miss. That is why.'

'Oh, I see,' though that was the last thing she was able to do. 'But please proceed, just the same,' though she thought there was nothing about Manfred that she did not already know.

'Well, Miss, it was while I was talking to Mr. Manfred after his Marriage Proposal. I was trying to offer him some hope, and the conversation turned toward your self, Miss, and to those other suitors, the older ones of power and title who would want you not for your fine qualities of mind and spirit, art and music, but just for your . . . uh . . . fine . . . uh . . .'

'My fine body, Alice? Is that it?'

'Well, yes, Miss, just so. I shed a few tears, and the next thing I knew, Mr. Manfred was holding me to him by way of comforting me.'

'That would certainly be a surprise, Alice.'

'That it was a surprise, Miss, was not the problem. It was my reaction to it. Perhaps it was the posing we had done earlier; perhaps all the talk of marriage and such. Certainly my wearing very little under my gown did not help – well, nothing at all, of course, because I had no time to change and I had dispensed with my shawl to sit upon it. But suddenly I felt my self coming alive against him, despite my best efforts to . . . No, that will not do. I am ashamed to admit, Miss, that I did not really try, because that was the very first time since Richard, you see, that a man had held me to him self, and it was such a glorious feeling once more.'

All the while of this emotional telling, Celia was regarding Alice with a carefully-listening air knowing this was to be some thing unusual. But now she raised her eyebrows in considerable surprise. Alice, her faithful

Alice, with feelings for Manfred. This was incredible! And now she simply had to know.

'Did any thing happen, Alice?' she rushed out. 'Any thing untoward, that is?'

'No, Miss, nothing.'

'Well, thank goodness for that!' with a great whoosh of relief. 'So where is the problem, Alice? Why the necessity for the apology, for the down-cast looks, if Manfred did not touch any intimate part of you?'

'You see, Miss, it was me. I *wanted* it to happen. I had no idea how powerful his allure was, none at all. Now I understand how Miss Lucy and your self were so attracted, so irresistibly drawn to him, unable to deny your selves in his presence, for I was suddenly there, too, unable to . . . resist.'

'But if he did not touch you, Alice – even though you were wearing next to nothing – did nothing to you, as he did to Lucy, and earlier to my self, I still do not see the need for any apology?'

'Oh, Miss, do you not *see!*' she cried, 'I *wanted* him to! I was *willing* him to kiss me, passionately, to *hold* me, to *touch* me, to . . . to . . . Oh, Miss, I am so ashamed of my self!' and she burst into tears, laid her head on Sally's neck so that it paused mid-stride, and cried as if her heart would break.

Celia was so amazed at this tremendous outburst of contrition, that she was too stunned to react. Alice had felt considerable emotion, certainly, but nothing had happened; so why . . .? And then she understood. Alice thought she had been unfaithful to her mistress not in her actions but in her *intentions*, and in the most perfidious way. What a dreadful, awful thing to happen to Alice, gentle Alice, whose heart was quite as soft as her own, despite the hard shell that she had formed to protect it, and that most people never penetrated.

Now she moved Jasper alongside, and gently, ever so gently, raised Alice up until she was able to hold her, hug her to her own bosom, to stroke her and kiss her wet cheek, much as she had done with Lucy so long ago, or so it seemed, when Lucy had a similar challenge to the spirit. And, she noted wryly to her self, with the very same person! So they were now, all three, victims of his power over their most intimate emotions and especially their persons.

'Alice, please do not cry so, I can not bear to see you so unhappy.

Nothing happened, so you owe me nothing, even if you did feel some strong emotions.'

'But I . . . I . . . so *wanted* him to, Miss, I really, *really* did, *desperately*,' sobbed Alice, still very distraught.

'Remember what I said, Alice? Your feelings are your feelings; they are indeed you. Your *actions* may sometimes be considered inappropriate, but your feelings – never!'

'But do you not see, Miss, if some thing *had* happened, I would have been forced to leave you for having ruined your love and your life – and my own when I was turned out,' looking quite miserable once more.

'Alice, look at me! What do I see in those beautiful dark eyes of yours? Alice simply shook her head. 'I see love, Alice, pure love. And the object of that love, Alice?' and again a shake of the head. 'Why, none but my self, Alice; me. Now, I do not know what you understand, but I cannot blame you for your desire even though you wanted to act upon it, desperately.

'But, and more importantly, Alice, you are suggesting that, should there have been any thing of a serious and intimate nature between the two of you, the options presented to my self were: Manfred or my faithful companion, and further that the choice was an obvious one – Manfred, of course.

'Then let me assure you, Alice, in the utmost sincerity of my inner being,' blue eyes probing into dark brown, 'that, difficult – impossible even – as it would be in that final moment of decision, I could never let *you* go. You have become such a part of me, Alice, that Manfred would needs go his way. Though with the utmost difficulty and regret. Him I could live without; you I could not.'

'Oh, Miss, that is the loveliest thing I have ever had said to me!' eyes shining in the moonlight. Thank you, Miss, for I do indeed love you, more even than my own Mildred, as I told Mr. Manfred in defence of your honour,' as she raised her mistress' hand to kiss it gently, 'for you are part of me, too.'

And they shed a few more tears on each other's shoulder, before setting off again.

'Alice, now that you have relieved your soul of that unnecessary burden, there was some thing else that you needed to tell me.'

But even as she was speaking, another thought broke through to Celia's mind, suddenly, and it was devastating, so that she reined in Jasper quite suddenly, causing Alice to do likewise.

'What is it, Miss? Is there any thing I can do?'

'No, it is just me, some thing I have realized, out of the blue – or rather, the black.'

'But, Miss, if you could just tell me what it is, I am sure I could help in some way.'

'I am not sure I should, Alice, because my relief may be your distress. Are you so sure in that circumstance your course is the right one?'

'Yes, Miss, quite sure. Your suffering is my suffering, so it cannot get worse with the telling.'

'Then, as your anguish sank through to my heart, Alice, I realized that you must have suffered dreadfully through my joy.'

'How so, Miss?'

'Moments ago you revealed to me how, in the service of securing my lover to my self, you desired Manfred to satisfy the most urgent needs of *your* body Then almost immediately, had to acknowledge that I was the one receiving that very thing denied you. My joy was your despair – and with the same lover! And several times at that! That must have been agony for your spirit, Alice, the which you cannot deny – especially when it was openly enacted before your very eyes! I am so dreadfully sorry, Alice, but I was not to know, although if my eyes had not been blinded I might have seen it so.'

'Thank you, Miss, for your concern, but it was not as bad as you conjure. Firstly, in response to a question, he confirmed your opinion that my form was more than adequate to intrigue a man to desire me in that special way. He was *very* specific about that, Miss, in his usual direct manner, But you are not upset or disappointed in me?'

'Should I be? Nothing happened of any substance between Manfred and your self, so I can have no quarrel with it. Indeed, without your presence in a most intimate and challenging assignment, Alice, none of what has been achieved today would have been remotely possible, and I owe you a deep debt of gratitude.'

'Thank you, Miss, you cannot know how much it is balm to my soul. The only other thing when all settled is that we agreed we could be brother and sister, which put the matter on an altogether different plane.

'Another little thing has come to my remembrance, Miss, of little import, but when I said that we were as three sisters, he replied that there was an excellent play about three sisters living in the countryside then moving to the city, and that we should read it. It was when I asked him the author, his reply was couched in uncertainty. It was by Chekhov, he said, an Anton Chekhov. I said I had never heard of him and did he have a copy. He said it was with his other things, and anyway it was in Prussian so it would not be useful to me. Have you heard of him, Miss?'

'No, Alice, I have not. Perhaps I should ask him about it.'

'Oh, please do not do that, Miss, for he seemed embarrassed at having mentioned it. Somehow it is not for us,' and Celia nodded her assent.

They were now close to home, yet still Alice had not taken the opportunity to reveal the other matter. It was now or never.

'So, Alice, before we enter our own domain, there is still time to avail your self and claim the moment for your revelation.'

'Well, Miss,' she said hesitantly, pausing once more as her throat momentarily constricted, her heart pounding loudly in her ears, her cheeks burning. 'May I really take advantage of the privacy offered by the night and your insistence on knowing it?' and she was able to breathe again at her mistress' nod.

'Then I beg to reveal my true thoughts and confess some thing intensely personal, Miss, but please do not make light of it or mock me; I could not bear for you to think so little of my sacrament.' And she had to pause again to control her overwhelming emotion, while Celia held her breath.

Indeed, this was an Alice that she was only beginning to know, with feelings and depths of emotion she had been oblivious to, now more than a little ashamed at her lack of awareness of one so close to her in every physical aspect of living. She could not have obtained any where a more devoted and true companion, in every sense of the word, and wondered whether she was as true and constant in return. But she already knew the answer to that.

'I have conjectured of late, Miss,' she whispered, holding her mistress' hand tightly, 'what it meant to have another woman's caress, in the intimate sense, I mean,' and the mistress' hand was tightened by hers 'til it almost hurt, 'in places that we rarely if ever make available to each other. This evening I found out; for my self-release among the trees – outspoken though it was – could not be compared to your own demonstration of light and shadow on my body; to what *your* touch meant to me. I think it must be a little like being tickled. You simply cannot do it to your self.

'But that really thrilled me, deep inside, Miss. Now I know that a woman's caress can be quite as powerful to the inner emotions and deep longings as ever it is with a man – except for that one last special thing. And while I am being transparent with you, Miss, and revealing my inner secrets, your intimate touch is what I long to surrender to again.

'But now that you have such a passionate lover, Miss,' closing Sally in tight so that they were in contact once more, 'I understand that my yearnings can only be explicitly requited if you paint me, and then only if I am cast in a completely candid pose, so that my natural charms can express them selves frankly and honestly as they have craved ever since that first re-enactment with Richard. And then your touch as you adjust my body will be a joy to experience.'

They approached a path that required single file, and Celia was glad to fall back to give Sally the lead while she tried to make sense of the tumult of confused emotions in her head and her heart at this unabashed confession of longing for *her* caress, *her* soft touch. She was struggling with them still as they reached the edge of the trees on the slope leading down to the orchard, when Alice reined in her mount.

'May I then entreat one last favour, Miss,' she said, in a ragged whisper, her face turned away into shadow, 'before we go down through the orchard?'

'Yes, Alice,' responded Celia, still in a whirl over the open passion in Alice's startling disclosure. 'If I can.'

'Before we left, Miss, you said that we would talk about it more, and indeed we have. You also said that we must find a way for release, and soon.'

Celia nodded slowly, turning her mount to face her directly.

'And you have found such a way, Alice?'

'Yes, Miss; that is, it was *you* who showed me the way. And as for "soon", I would choose right now before we descend the hill to whatever awaits us,' and she rode Sally in as close as she could to reach and hold her mistress' hands on her body. 'Please, Miss,' now in a whisper.

'And your way is that you want them inside your cloak, Alice, is that it?' whispered her mistress in return. 'On your self?'

'Yes, Miss, if you would,' was the huskily whispered response. 'If it shocks you too much, I will try to understand,' but her eyes sparkled in the moonlight as never before. 'Just this once, Miss, if that is what it has to be, and I will not ask again, even if you never paint me,' and so saying, pulled her urgently forward and upon her, closing her eyes in anticipation.

'My, you are already all undone, Alice,' exclaimed Celia, softly, as her hands were placed by Alice inside the cloak and upon her readily receptive bosom, surprised at the already opened blouse, with no undergarments that she could feel. 'Now I understand how you dressed so quickly, Alice – because you did not; and already so excited, too!'

Alice made no reply except for a sharp intake of breath to express her pleasure at the touch as she was caressed and stroked until the fire in her breast spread completely through her body. Meanwhile, she had opened her riding skirt to provide easy access to that which she truly desired.

That completed, she could not restrain her self from leaving the one hand in place while taking her mistress' other hand and thrusting it down to her now opened and exposed belly, desperately wishing but not daring to go beyond. At that touch she felt compelled to throw her cloak back over her shoulders to evidence her excitement to the bright moonlight, leaning back against Sally, stretching her arms upward until she was lying fully upon her, just as open and exposed to the moonlight and to the thrills racing through her body as she could make her self.

And the silence was broken only by the sounds of her sensually derived pleasure as her mistress acceded to Alice's invitation 'til she relaxed and was silent.

'Have we then found the way, Alice?' whispered Celia as she drew her upright and pulled the cloak back over her shoulders to cover the moonlit nakedness.

'Oh yes, Miss,' whispered Alice, 'now I am ready and calm again. Thank you for your consideration of my intimate feelings and for releasing them for me. It was wonderful, and I am eternally grateful for your caring of me.'

'I am glad it comforted you, Alice, and confess I enjoyed it, too. But we should go now,' moving down the slope, 'for we have quite a scene to face in the morning, first with mother, and after that Manfred, then the solicitor and all the plans for the wedding.

'But we are arrived. Please see to the horses, then join me in the bath-room. And make no noise, for I am not ready for a tête-à-tête with Mama this night. Then a hot bath to soothe my tired body, for though I am physically, emotionally and spiritually quite exhausted, as you will readily appreciate, we still have much to do this night.'

'Please top up the water, Alice, then recite what you believe I should say to Mother?'

'I think the less said the better, Miss. Perhaps that Mr. Manfred proposed marriage to you, and you accepted. If I am asked, I shall say that the acceptance was in such a manner as to make it irredeemable, and there is an end of it, although her ladyship will not thank me for it!'

Celia nodded acceptance.

'I think you are right, Alice, less discussion and argument that way. However, from the information you elicited, I believe we can make a very plausible case for Manfred as an acceptable suitor. He *does* have property – indeed two, town and country. He *does* have substantial means and investments, even if they are not readily to hand. His heritage is *more* than adequate, and he is *abundantly* educated and cultured. How many among our acquaintance can call them selves 'Professor'? It might go better than we first perceived, when we put our minds to it.

'Further, we may need a little time for contemplation before we say too much to her ladyship. I will make some notes in the morning, and would be glad of your contribution, Alice.

'Thank you for this wonderful hot water and that generous glass of spirits to warm the inside as well as the out. It seems neither of us has taken a chill prancing around the Glade only in our natural state.'

'You are welcome, Miss, and for my self, my inner spirit has kept me well warmed. Now, may I sit on the edge of the bath-tub?'

'Certainly, Alice, unless you would prefer to bring in a chair.'

'I am very comfortable here, Miss, thank you.'

'And you have lit the fire?' receiving an answering nod, 'for there are a number of things I wish to examine before I sleep this night. And the cocoa?' Another nod, this time with a gentle smile, for she loved doing these little chores for her mistress. It made her feel an indispensable part of her, almost as if they were one and the same being.

'Now that we are relaxed and refreshed, let us consider the Cottage in a little more detail – on the understanding that Manfred will be with us there at the appropriate time.' And Alice nodded her agreement.

'In the next days we have much to do to get it ready. We – because, if I understand your position, you refuse to allow me to travel there alone,' to which Alice nodded emphatically. 'We are going to have to meet with Manfred to discuss his very novel ideas – for he may not come here until mother and I have reached our agreement.' A further nod from Alice.

'Now, my lover was quite entranced with the Cottage, for it much resembled one he visited as a boy in Thüringia – Königshofen I think he said – which brought back delightful memories of childhood, so that was a most pleasant surprise.

'He also admitted to being very impressed with my new heating system in our apartments. Now he wishes to build an engine driven by steam from a kettle that will do work for us on the farm, as well as pump the water from the stream instead of bringing it in buckets. That is where he has need to talk to the village blacksmith, and to a Mr. James Watt of West Bromwich – although I thought he was some thing to do with canals.

'So you may note, Alice, that I did not waste my time with my lover by engaging only in mutual pleasure; a little of it was directed toward more constructive pursuits. But it is all very exciting and I cannot wait to get started.'

'If I might comment, Miss?' and Celia nodded. 'You do need to be careful how often you meet now, together and alone, for I have seen that my function as a chaperone is rapidly losing its effectiveness. For all the notice you two took of me yesterday, I might just as well be invisible.'

'Oh, Alice, you fuss. We shall get on well together, Manfred and I.'

'Yes, Miss, that is *exactly* what concerns me; because you might then undo all the effort that you have put into his worth as a suitor. That would be a great pity and could lose our cause completely.'

'I believe you are only intent on spoiling my fun, Alice. But it does behove me to be considerate of others' ways of thinking, as well as to secure his standing in our society. So I shall need a diversion, and the Cottage can be it – with your omnipresence, of course – to keep me out of his intimate embrace. But, never mind, I believe I can wait now that it is almost settled.'

She splashed the scented and newly reheated water over her self by way of comfort, and stretched out again.

'So I promise to be careful with my self, if you will promise to keep him at a safe distance from me – as long as we can steal a little kiss every now and then.'

'Agreed, Miss, and I shall monitor those – and make sure they *are* little.'

'I believe you would, Alice,' laughing gaily, 'I do believe you would. But now I am ready to be bathed – gently, please – for in some places I am a little sore; well, perhaps more than a little. You may well imagine where those centres might be!'

'Yes, Miss, I know *exactly* where they will be!' and they both enjoyed a merry laugh.

'That was wonderful. Now please help me out and dry me carefully. Then jump in and make your self sweet-smelling, too. There is lots of hot water left,' as Alice fitted her Chinese robe.

'But, Miss, I should not take advantage of . . .'

'Do stop arguing, Alice, and do as you are told! My, how you do fuss. I have to spend at least twenty minutes in the Studio making some rough sketches of the things we have discussed this evening. I am sure it is better relaxing your weary spirit in there than waiting around for me in the bedroom.

'And speaking of spirits, here is a glass of the one you poured for me. I found it very beneficial and calming. I will tap on the inner door when it is time for you to join me. You may use Lucy's yellow bath towels and her special powder, and I will see you in my room for the usual routine.'

Celia was relaxing on the chaise when Alice had joined her in the bedroom with two steaming cups of cocoa.

'I believe my Cottage sketches and those of "Alice and the Rose" have gone well, and I see them both quite clearly now. But before you brush my hair, Alice, I think we should discuss the challenges before us. I have to face mother in the morning, and I suddenly find my self very anxious at that prospect, frightened that I shall lose my beloved at the very moment of triumph after all – just as you did, and I do not think I could bear that.' And a tear trickled down her cheek.

'There, there, Miss,' responded Alice, gently stroking her hair. 'There is no need to get upset, for that will not happen.'

'How could you possibly know that, Alice,' sitting upright once more. 'You do not know her ladyship. Where do you think I get *my* determination?'

'I understand, Miss, and perhaps a good cry will release more of your earlier dismay when I played the role of Solicitor, for Mr. Manfred did not release the tensions of your mind when he dissolved those of your body.'

'That is as may be, Alice, but the music is still mine to face – and pay the piper!' raising her face once more to Alice's – surprised at finding her smiling.

'So what is it that you find so amusing, Alice, for it all looks rather grim from my position?'

'May I speak plainly, Miss?'

'Of course, Alice, I thought that is what we were doing here between us, and when you made your bold request in the orchard.'

'Yes, Miss, quite so. But this is different. This involves her Ladyship, and on that subject I need to have your understanding before I do.'

'Will it help me, Alice?'

'Yes, Miss.'

'Will it ensure that Manfred is mine forever?'

'Well, I am not a magician, Miss, but yes, if that is possible in this uncertain world.'

Celia looked at her thoughtfully, wondering how Alice was going to conjure this one out of her hat.

'Do I have any thing to lose, Alice?'

'No, Miss, you have nothing to lose – although her Ladyship will be very cross with you, and perhaps for quite a while, but it will come right soon enough, for she cannot still be cross on your wedding day, Miss. You will retain your self-respect – if you follow my strictures on meeting with your lover – and he too,' and Celia had to smile at this reference.

'Very well then, Alice, you may proceed with your conjure,' reclining once more, while Alice added another log, creating a shower of sparks, and then adopting her favourite pose on the pouf, delighted with her new light dressing gown.

'It is like this, Miss. You do not have to speak to your mother – her Lady-ship, that is – at all,' at which Celia raised her eyebrows at this bit of magic – knowing it to be impossible to avoid – but said nothing.

'My thought is that you suggest, when asked, that she first speak to me as the neutral observer, and then if she has further questions, you will be glad to address them your self in a day or two. Naturally, her ladyship will then ask you to summon me while you depart to your Studio. I shall explain what has occurred between you and . . .'

'Alice, you could not tell her lad . . . I mean, mother, all that! How I was in my skin and he in . . . Oh no, Alice, that would be just too humil-iating!'

She recoiled now in horror as the scene in the Cottage replayed it self in her mind, but this time with her mother almost being there, watching her daughter make passionate love to a man – and he to her by return – comprehending a little of what mothers go through to protect them.

'Do you trust me, Miss Celia?'

'What you mean, Alice,' looking solemnly into Alice's dark and lumi-nous eyes, 'is, do I trust you with my future happiness, with my very life – which is the same thing,' and waited for the answer.

'Yes, Miss, that is what I mean,' calmly returning the gaze.

There was a long moment before Celia replied.

'In which case, Alice, I find that I already have, several times today, so why should this be any different? So yes, Alice, I trust that if a thing can be done, then you will find a way to achieve it. Pray continue.'

'Thank you, Miss, for your confidence. You see, I shall advise her lady-ship all that has happened, but it will be in "clothed" words – if you get my meaning,' and now Celia merely nodded. 'Your mother – and if it doesn't bother you, Miss, I would prefer that form of address for this discussion, being a mother my self and knowing fully what that means. Your mother needs to know, above all – and she will ask this of me very directly – if your virtue is still intact, to which I can reply that it is most assuredly so, to my certain knowledge.

'Now do you see, Miss, why that was so important to retain?' And Celia nodded once more, thoughtfully, for Alice seemed almost to have already worked this all out in her head, even before any thing had transpired. Quite amazing!

'Naturally, she will conclude that if I can be so sure, then I must have played an intimate part in the affair, otherwise I could not possibly know such a thing. And I shall receive a severe reprimand for my pains, you may be sure – especially if she believes that I connived in it – mayhap even *created* the opportunity for you to misbehave. And then even more so, when she recalls that I said I would keep her informed . . .' and her voice trailed away at that, leaving her with a feeling of betrayal that lay heavily upon her.

'But, Alice, that will be most distressing to you – and to my self – after all you have done for me today. She might even discharge you for your dishonour of me. So the choice is you or Manfred, and you already have my answer on that subject!

'No, Alice, it will not do. When I owe you all my happiness – even though it be short-lived – I cannot and will not let that happen, you are much too dear to me. I must confess my self to mother and take what comes as a just return for my waywardness.'

'Please, Miss, do not distress your self. It was *not* wayward, nor will it come to that, I am quite certain. It will be severe, very severe, and I shall be hurt, but I am prepared for that – at least I hope I am. It will not last but a day or two, and I shall be buoyed by the certain knowledge of your impending wedding and your – our – life of happiness together.'

'Alice, I marvel at your composure over this most difficult issue; but I have said that I trust, and I will. If there is more, pray continue.'

'Thank you, Miss, and yes, there is more. When she gives me an opening – and I fully admit there is an element of chance here, but she and I have been through this before – I shall explain to your mother how carefully and thoroughly the formal investigation of your suitor's claim to your hand in marriage was conducted – for we spent almost an hour on just that – and how it was considered insufficient. I shall even offer her my many pages of notes, in their original form, to demonstrate that it was all most sincere and no mere charade – which is the truth.

'Following that will come a discussion of the formal request, fully and properly executed, for your Hand in Marriage which, after a considerable amount of thought and discussion you did formally accept. Then to seal the agreement once and for all, you acted upon it – and I am *quite* sure your mother will understand what that amounted to, Miss!

'I believe she will finally understand that it was your love – and his – making the bargain, and not just wanton and irresponsible behaviour on your side or his. I will certainly encourage her in that direction of thought, for I deem that to be truly the case.'

'The one thing paramount above all considerations of conduct or morality or any such matters, Miss, is your safety and well-being. For a mother, all else pales into insignificance. Yes, she will be cross, and yes, more than a little sad that she was not a part of your decision to choose your future husband – just as I may be one day with Mildred.

'But I will further explain that there is no other way to ensure her daughter's happiness; that your choice is Manfred – or nobody – and you will reject all other suitors, out of hand. Then I believe she will see that it was your clear decision – which I could not sway – and that her choice is now a simple one – happiness or loneliness for her only true daughter. Either she has faith in your upbringing from childhood – and the wisdom of your choosing – or she does not.

'I further believe, Miss, that the knowledge that you are happy – and without that ultimate shame (which I did not avoid), all else will be forgiven and soon forgotten in the joy of that happiness. And I know for certain in my heart, Miss, that she will soon enough embrace your choice of a mate, though she may need a deal more time than did I. Mr. Manfred has certain qualities that none of your other suitors could offer – his undoubted love for you – excepting only Reginald, and he was never in the running.'

And Celia's blush of pure happiness was her full reward.

'Alice, this is unbelievable! You have thought it all through so brilliantly. When did all this happen?'

'When I was bathing, Miss. You took almost forty minutes in your Studio, and during that whole time I was relaxed in solitude in that lovely scented hot water with that glass of spirits, waiting for your call, marshalling my thoughts, and constructing in my head the meeting with her ladyship in the morning. Then it all just fell into place.'

'Amazing! And to think, Alice, that you did not want to avail your self of that luxury; thank goodness I insisted. And, Alice?'

'Yes, Miss?'

'I really do not know what I would do without you, for I can see it will all be just as you say, and mother will not scold, and her sadness I believe can soon be smoothed away by telling her of my plans for our Cottage – *our* Cottage, Alice, as in *you and me* – and perhaps Manfred? Should we, perchance, invite him to join us? What say you?'

'I think we might just find a corner for him, Miss,' she replied, mischievously. And, holding hands, they had a good laugh, a good hug, and a few soft tears together over their resolution.

'Now I am ready for sleep, Alice. I know that you have things you wish to discuss and discover with me, but we must delay those until the morrow, for my answers and actions would lack the spontaneity they require.'

'That is quite all right, Miss. It can wait, for rest and recovery for you are far more important than my simple needs.'

Later as she wended her way to bed, she was surprised to find that she could indeed wait, for it seemed in some way that her mistress understood. It was the letter that she had just opened that tipped the scales, for though she could wait, it could not be for much longer.

Mildred, who was Miss Lucy's personal companion and travelling with her, had just written to provide her mother some details of the voyage to visit Capt. Charles' three Aunts. Whilst the journey was going well, she wrote, Miss Lucy was not too pleased with some things, particularly the second, Aunt Beatrice. She was a very prim and proper widow with a sour disposition according to her mistress. The last was to be with Aunt Cecily, whom they had met briefly, a rather jolly lady, and they were looking forward to staying with her.

For Alice, the most important item was the day of return. From the date of the letter, it seemed that Miss Lucy could be back in as little as ten days, though two weeks was more likely. Mildred also mentioned that they might be visiting the Captain's seat, Althorpe Manor, escorted by Aunt Augusta, so it could even be a little longer.

While Alice longed to see her daughter again and equally Miss Lucy, it was the latter that was troubling her spirit. Upon her return, there was little doubt where and with whom she would spend her bathing and her bed, which meant that the mistress would no longer be able to spend much time with her self – and certainly nothing of an intimate nature. Miss Lucy would probably elect to stay several months, delaying the promised portraits also for some time, and she had been counting on those. Not a particularly pleasant prospect for her hopes.

If she was going to succeed in her posing endeavours – and with it the emotional aspect of her mistress' touch, there was surely not a moment to lose.

While Alice was fairly certain that Miss Celia now knew of her emotional needs to pose, it was not as clear that the intimacy provided on their return journey was to be part of that compact. Yes, she had stated that "we must find a way for release, and soon", and this was part of the new understanding.

But whether Miss Celia understood the *depth* of those not so simple needs was a matter still to be plumbed. Only the dozen or so morrows would reveal that, and she fully intended that they would – even to overflowing – for there had been more to her bathroom planning than she had just revealed!

19

Divertimenti

'Whilst I was sleeping until almost the noon hour, then working in my studio 'til dinner was sent up, how did it go with you, Alice?'

'Very much as I was expecting, Miss. Her Ladyship was very cross with me, that is for certain, but when I showed her the Solicitor papers, I believe she understood that I had done what I could.'

'Oh, my poor Alice; what an ordeal I put you through,' rising from the tub to give Alice a hug as she had a warm towel placed around her. 'Let us retire then to the bedroom to see what we can conclude.'

With her gown now wrapped around her, lying on the bed, Celia turned to Alice. 'Well, what do we conjure?'

'That the matter is over, Miss, finished, for what has been done cannot be undone. No-one can do that. So in a day or two you may show her Ladyship your sketches. Whether she will scold you I cannot say, but I rather think not, for she still loves you. Wayward or not, you are still her true daughter.'

'Thank you, Alice. Well what is, is, so let us move forward and talk about the future,' settling in her bed as Alice added a pillow behind her mistress as a preliminary to the hair-brushing routine, 'But before we do, please add another log or two to the fire. And if you are not too weary, another cup of cocoa?'

'It will be my pleasure, Miss.'

'Of the several things on my mind, the work to be done on the Cottage is foremost. Firstly, we have need of some one to undertake the considerable alterations necessary to make our cottage even habitable, much less comfortable, and to see what it might cost, how long it will take, and so forth. That will affect the wedding day, of course. I did ask Carter what he thought and who might be available.

'He suggested the young man whom you may remember I engaged to clean up the cottage and the barns. Apparently he is a Carpenter who lives with his mother in the village,' and she noted immediately Alice's interest, though said nothing.

'If he were available,' she went on, casually, 'I suppose he could be engaged. The renovations will take many months, and he could stay in one of the outbuildings, the shepherd's cottage, perhaps – unless, of course, you have some one else in mind,' with a sidelong glance at Alice.

At the very first reference, Alice remembered him only too well, and was already conjuring sensuous images of the virile carpenter. He was about her own age, or perhaps a little older, and she had been wondering whether she could persuade her mistress to engage him.

'Oh no, Miss, I mean, yes, Miss, he will do fine,' with a sigh and a blush that revealed her intimate thoughts.

'Well, well, Alice,' as she discerned Alice's aspirations from her brightened eyes. 'How then blows the wind from that quarter?

'Alice?' bending and peering at her lowered face, 'I thought we did not keep our feelings from each other. Do I err in that opinion?'

'No, Miss,' whispered Alice.

'Then please raise your face and look at me so that we may examine this matter carefully and thoughtfully. You surely are not afraid that I would condemn your thoughts?'

'Oh no, Miss,' looking at last directly into her mistress' eyes. 'It is just that . . . that you caught me by surprise – a little bit like in the Cottage with the candle. You were ahead of me in that direction of thinking, and I am having to catch up. But there,' she smiled, 'I am back with you, Miss. What would you like to know?'

'Firstly, is he of interest to you?'

'Yes, Miss.'

'Of great interest?' receiving an answering nod. 'And he is one who might, could perhaps, replace your Richard – acknowledging that *he* will always have that special, secret place in your heart?'

'Yes, Miss.'

'Very well. Remembering that "faint heart ne'er wan fair laddie" – to paraphrase your Mr. Burns again – shall we then proceed to obtain him for you, Alice?' but received only a further downcast face in response.

'Come, come, Alice, yes or no, before we waste a lot of our very valuable time on an idle pursuit.'

'It is not idle, Miss, but before I say "yes", are we not being, perhaps, a little bold in our presumption that we can?'

'Alice; look at me,' tilting that face up to her own with her forefinger. 'Did we not – the two of us – achieve that very thing, only yesterday?'

'Indeed we did, Miss, but . . .'

'But me no buts, and sigh me no sighs, Alice. Will you have him to be yours?'

'Yes, Miss, I will!'

'Good; consider it done, for I have a brilliant idea.'

'In your quest for a beau, I will hire him and set him up in the shepherd's cottage immediately, to which the improvements will be his first task – for we must have him comfortable and settled. Yes?' And Alice smiled her acceptance.

'Good. There will be cleaning work for a scullery maid or two – whom you must needs find – getting the place shipshape and Bristol fashion, which will require your frequent attendance there.

'Then, once he starts work proper, I shall give him instructions for the necessary renovations and alterations, and sketches indicating the nature and style of the work. But because I shall be busy here, I will ask that he accept instructions from your self, as you represent me in my absence.

'Between the two duties, that will give you ample opportunity to review and keep me informed of progress, and to report back any problems or issues that arise. Also what other workers we shall need – such as roof framers, thatchers, plasterers and the like. Can you do that, Alice?'

'Oh, yes, Miss. With confidence and pleasure to satisfy the two of us!' now positively glowing with happiness at such a wonderful opportunity, when only a day ago (was it only that?) she had given up all hope of finding a "stranger" to woo her as beyond her powers. Now, it was quite . . . well . . . overwhelming!

Celia missed none of these emotions openly crossing her face. 'Now do you see, Alice? Are we too "bold"?'

'Oh no, Miss; together we shall gratify my needs, as we have just accomplished for your self,' and she was so happy she wriggled with the delight of it.

'Well said, Alice. Now, one day, if all goes well, you may find it necessary to set up your own home on the property with your new husband,' and she observed Alice's pretty blush, eyes still glowing with pleasure, 'in which case, you will need a suite of rooms for your selves.' And here a squeal of delight from Alice.

'During my inspection, I noted that there are two or three fairly sound rooms over the stables that I thought of giving over to my new Carter. Instead, they would be most suitable for you and your lover (giggles from Alice), while Carter moves into one of the old feed rooms. If that be the case, once the main house is attended to, we can then get him to work on your suite.

'If he hasn't by then been seduced by your natural charms – and I shall be very surprised if he has not, for they are ample as I have oft observed for my self – why then we might leave your "Reflections" picture in a corner where he could get a glimpse of it as he worked around the apartment. And perhaps a little later, "The Rose" – if we have painted it by then. *That* should spark his enthusiasm to *know* you better!'

'Would you do all that for me, Miss? And could I do that for my self? Is that not too . . . saucy? though it would certainly leave him in no doubt as to what the *real* me looks like underneath,' giving a quiet inner smile at the thought of his surprise and pleasure on finding such an explicit pose.

'But only if you judge him to have a kind heart, Miss, and an interest in the inner me as well as the rest.' And she smiled happily at the thoroughness of her mistress' 'brilliant idea'.

'Excellent; then you shall visit him in the village in your search for suitable maids, requesting that he meet with us at the Cottage to discuss the work I have in mind. Will that suit, Alice?'

'Oh, yes, Miss. It will suit me very well, very well *indeed*,' and she leaned forward to give her mistress a hug and a kiss on both cheeks – unknowingly flaunting to her mistress' wondering eyes a good deal of bare bosom through her open gown as she did so, which Celia, puzzled by the implications of that display, resolved to examine before she slept.

'However, before we leave the Cottage matters, there is one last thing to mention. It is not concluded yet, so I do not wish any comment at this time, for some thing could still go wrong. But I need to make you aware – as you are with most of my affairs. My other heritance was legally well protected at the time it became mine, and I wish this one to be, also. So good, so far?' and Alice nodded.

'Now, I have been talking to mother's Solicitor about the property. It was some thing you said, Alice, that brought it to my mind concerning ownership if I marry. If it be the wrong man, as my legal husband he could take it from me, or sell it, or some other horrid thing. Therefore,

I shall sign a Property Agreement with my Solicitor to the effect that, in the event of my impending marriage to any other person than Manfred Werner, twenty four hours prior to the hour of that marriage, the property will be transferred to a person nominated in the Agreement as the new and rightful owner, lock, stock and barrel, although I will retain the usufruct. It will also state that this right cannot be reassigned, even by my self.

'So now, Alice, please tell me what you understand from all that – in simple, plain terms.'

'Well, Miss, that no-one other than Manfred can inherit it, though if some other did marry you – good or bad – it would be no longer yours, becoming that of your nominee, although you would have the legal right of use.'

'Excellent, Alice, exactly so. There is of course a possibility that I might actually like that "other", but it would be too late as the nominee would already own it, for the Contract is irrevocable.'

'If I may inquire, Miss, I presume that the nominee would be her lady-ship, or perhaps Miss Lucy?'

'I am still thinking about that, Alice. Mother doesn't really need more property – certainly not an old cottage! Neither in truth does Lucy, with the Captain as her spouse. But I will let you know – in strict confidence of course – when that moment arrives.'

'Very good, Miss.'

'Now, as you continue your routine, Alice, I have a question for you. You like to bathe me and then to brush my hair, is that so?'

'Yes, Miss; it is so silky soft and a gorgeous colour. Besides, I know how you like it.'

'That is why you must teach my dearest to do it before we retire, as a prelude to more intimate delights.'

'Oh no, Miss,' exclaimed Alice in dismay, 'that is *my* pleasure to provide for you.'

'Very well, Alice, if it is your pleasure rather than a duty, let it be so. Yet as I reflect on it, is it just the brushing?' queried her mistress, softly, 'or is there more that you seek?' and Alice blushed and shook her head.

'Just the hair, Miss,' she whispered, though she had gone quite pale. 'Why do you ask?'

'Because you have been looking at me strangely, Alice, especially while I soaked just now, almost as if you have never set eyes on my body before. There is a reason for that?'

'I am sorry, Miss, I did not intend to,' she stammered, quite flustered.

'And when you were bathing and drying me, you seemed more gentle, more attentive than is the usual.'

'But you your self asked me to be gentle, Miss, for you were still sore in some places, and I tried to be that for you.'

'Quite so, Alice. And yet . . . there was a sensuous caress that I have not been aware of before. Perhaps it was my own changed nature; perhaps Manfred has some thing to do with heightening my awareness, my sensuality. And yet . . . there was some thing.'

'But every thing is the same as always, Miss, I believe.'

'Really, Alice? Then why are you sitting on the edge of my bed instead of using the chair as we usually do? That is some thing that is not your wont, surely?'

'I thought to be more comfortable, Miss,' replied Alice, unable to meet her mistress' glance.

'And in your dressing gown? That is not the same as always, is it?'

'This is because – at your insistence, Miss – you had me bathe in your tub, and it seemed to me more sensible to put on this robe than dress my self once more. It is a new one that I wanted to show you. I altered a summer robe Miss Lucy gave me before she left. Also, as I am tired I thought to get ready for bed, too,' but her explanation did not seem to convince even her self, as she flushed and her hand trembled in the brushing so that it became entangled.

'I am sorry, Miss,' she whispered, in a low frightened voice, head down.

Celia regarded her steadfastly, so that the brushing ceased.

'Your blushes are very becoming, Alice, yet I still find my self puzzled. All your answers have excellent logic and are clearly based on facts that I cannot refute, yet some thing does not fit,' looking her straight in the eye, receiving a flushed and lowered gaze in response.

'You see, Alice, there is some thing. However, I have no intention of badgering you over the matter after your magnificent performance on my behalf yesterday, all you did for me this morning, and will do in the succeeding morrows. So let us say no more about it. Please finish my hair and then we can perhaps take an early night,' and she closed her eyes, deciding that it was perhaps the best advice of all.

But Alice did not move, so she opened her eyes once more. 'Alice?'

'Yes, Miss?'

'Are you indicating that you do not wish the subject closed? That you would rather I proceed until we reach the end of this mystery?' Alice gave the faintest of nods, for otherwise her purpose would be thwarted, and she would needs retire to bed unfulfilled – and that was the very *last* thing she wished.

'Then to continue – but please stop me if I overstep the mark, for I do not wish any thing of substance between us, now, or in the days and weeks to come. We are perhaps only halfway through our challenges, with much more to accomplish before our goose is ready for the pan, and the pan ready for the oven.

'So, contrary to your assertion of normality, I am not sure, Alice, that *any thing* is the same as always. For example, while you have adequately explained the new gown, does that also necessitate dispensing with the usual night-dress, for I have observed not the slightest evidence of one?' and Alice blushed more deeply still and wriggled uncomfortably.

'Could I further hazard a guess, Alice,' continuing the unbroken gaze, 'that you are wearing very little,' and seeing her knuckles go white on the brush handle, 'other than your skin under that robe?' and Alice's body became quite rigid. 'And might that be related to a prior request, that was granted, I might add without reservation and with considerable indulgence? And that after some one said, "Just this once", and "I will never ask again". Does my memory serve me correctly?'

Alice blushed crimson and slid off the bed, yanking her gown savagely around her as she did so. 'If you want me to leave, Miss,' she said gruffly, her eyes brimming with tears, 'I shall be *happy* to do so,' and she made her way furiously toward the door and opened it. Then paused in confusion and vacillation, unsure what she was even doing there, and, closing the door, looked to her mistress once more, her expression a contradiction of love and pain and longing.

'Did I indicate that, Alice?' replied Celia, quietly. 'I am simply endeavouring to establish why you are acting so strangely, the which I believe you cannot deny.

'So, you may now resume your pleasure of brushing my hair while we further explore your feelings or wishes– and we *never* keep those from each other, Alice. Unless, of course,' this with a soft smile, 'you *choose* to get all huffy about it and retire, so we can both get the sleep and rest we need for the morrow?'

Alice turned in her new uncertainty of purpose, but not toward the bed. Instead, she strode angrily to the window, breathing hard, opening the heavy curtains in pretence of admitting the last of the moonbeams, in reality covering her own dismay at detection. Her subterfuge had been fully exposed, and she could neither deny it, nor as her mistress had teased, get all huffy, for her adult body was clearly advising that this was not the moment for that sort of childishness.

As she gazed out over the silent night she took several deep breaths, and found that the moonlight and breathing combined had a distinctly calming effect. Now that her game was lost, perhaps there was a simpler way to achieve what she yearned – if she had the nerve to carry it through. She sought the moon's acceptance as she loosened her gown before returning and placing a candelabrum and a vase of roses on the bedside table, then resumed her position on the bed.

'I am back, Miss,' she said quietly. 'Thank you for asking me to return.'

As she leaned forward to resume the brushing, Celia easily observed the smooth inner curve of bosom in the now bright candlelight. 'Then my eyes did not deceive me, Alice,' she remarked casually, 'concerning the absence of night attire.'

'No, Miss, they did not,' said Alice softly, 'I never could keep much from you. As you surmised, I am quite without modesty under the gown, as you may see for your self,' straightening to open it to the waist and beyond to demonstrate the point unequivocally.

'But have I asked for a favour or any other thing, Miss – except to brush your hair, as is my charge?' she concluded in a whisper, for her voice would not give forth more. And she remained sitting, gown still open, regarding her mistress as evenly as her rapid heartbeat would permit.

'Not in words, Alice, that is true,' Celia replied calmly. 'But if actions mean any thing – and they usually do – they cry loudly that this all has a very deliberate design. Am I supposed to conjure that?' she asked, innocently.

'If you like, Miss,' responded Alice huskily, trying to control her emotions but without much success. 'I shall grant you three guesses.'

'I see,' said Celia, softly, 'so we are to play games to add a little excitement to this mysterious affair?' and Alice blushed but held her gaze nonetheless. 'And if I fail in my attempts?'

'If you do not succeed, Miss, then I shall have *my* wish granted,' the last in barely a whisper, her heart fluttering wildly in anticipation of what she fervently hoped was a now sanctioned dream.

Celia gave her a long look.

'Alice; if I prevail in resolving this puzzle, what then? Is there a prize to be awarded?'

Alice blushed more deeply and lowered her eyes, belatedly remembering that she was no match for her mistress in games of the intellect. She had courted humiliation for overreaching, and should have been satisfied with the attention she had already received in full measure. She swallowed hard and pulled her gown around her again to salvage what remained of her self-respect.

'Why, Alice, you have gone all pale, and your hands are trembling,' stated her mistress, in mock concern. 'Has my reluctance to play your game upset you?' and Alice shook her head. 'It was just that it occurred to me, Alice, that if I succeed in the quest, I suspect you are the winner. But if I fail, you triumph equally over me; is that not so?' and Alice nodded again, unable to utter a word in her own defence.

'But then,' noted her mistress, more kindly, 'as you have asked for nothing and I have promised nothing, my losing seems to be of little consequence other than pretentiously wounded pride. But perhaps even though I lose, Alice, I have some thing to gain? Could it be so?'

Alice was silent for a moment, to recover her poise in this glimmer of reprieve. 'My happiness, Miss, that is your gain, if you choose to see it that way,' she finally managed to whisper, 'and there may be some in it for you, too, Miss, if I may be so bold as to venture that.'

'So; the contest appears to be that should I lose, there may be a measure of joy for me, there is delight for you, and your prize for winning is again your pleasure.'

'I find this contest a most intriguing one, but I have a question. Although on the same subject, it is really two questions. Are you willing to answer these before I accept or decline your little charade?'

Alice was silent for a long moment trying to conjure to what the questions might pertain, but her mistress broke in.

'This is no time for debate, Alice; is it yes or no?'

'Yes, Miss, I will answer them,' for to say no was to shatter all her hopes and dreams.

'Very well. So, does this puzzle relate to that moonlit release of yesterday?'

Alice blushed before replying, holding her breath, but eventually managing a whispered, 'Yes, Miss,' fingers crossed, just in case.

'Good. So to the first question. Now, I have known this quiet – sedate even – Alice for many, many years as one always sailing on an even keel. Now, of a sudden I find her aware of her body in a most salacious way, requiring much titillation. So when did this sudden change of heart come about and why?'

'Well, Miss, it was gradual rather than sudden. But I know clearly when it started, for that was the day I arrived on the island to find you and Miss Lucy engaged in . . . Well, Miss, I watched you for some ten minutes or so, and I was very surprised to find the tension growing in my bosom. I am sure you remember the occasion, Miss.'

'I do, indeed, Alice, for that was also the start of some thing very special between my sister and my self, some thing I shall never forget, nor Lucy either, of that I am quite sure. And then?'

'Well, after that came all the nightly questions Miss Lucy and your self had about Richard and his . . . body. But what really made the aware-ness, Miss,' now in a soft and gentle voice, 'was when I took off my dress to match the two of you having already viewed all I possess. Then, as naked as your self and Miss Lucy, I took much joy in it, especially when you bade me walk about and undertake certain poses. Then my senses were much awakened all over my body.

'But the moment of final truth, Miss, was when I hugged Miss Lucy to help her overcome her dismay – quite forgetting that I had nothing on, like Miss Lucy, and our bosoms touched quite by accident. Despite all our talk and descriptions of love-making, no-one had actually touched me, and it was almost like a spark passed between us – like those new machines they have, and for those few moments I thrilled at the contact between our bodies.

'But the next one – which I am almost too embarrassed to relate, Miss, but it must be said, was when you got very cross. I leant forward to hug you, too, but this time I *knew* what I wanted: your soft bosom pressed against mine, body to bare body. I was in seventh heaven, such was the thrill that surged right through me, to every place a woman can feel these things, a joy I had never known, even with Richard. And when you proposed to paint me as I was, in the natural state, well, I could have cried for joy.

'After that, Miss, you know the rest; the modelling where your every touch sent thrills through me. Then the Richard pose really opened my eyes, and yesterday the "Indian Maiden" scene before Mr. Manfred was quite thrilling, his eyes on me, admiring my almost naked body.

'The climax was the love-making of your self and Mr. Manfred, which drove me almost wild. In desperation I tried to release my self there in the moonlight but it wasn't the same, the feeling was just not there, no matter how I tried.'

'Well, well, I do not know what to say, Alice. I had no idea of your feelings, or your suffering. You should have advised me of it.'

'I could not, Miss, although when you suggested the "Rose" pose, I did slip and held your hand to me. But that almost made it worse, because I wanted so much more than you were ready to give. Besides, I was so mixed up inside, embarrassed by your viewing my self-loving so that I could not then admit my further need.'

'But there is one thing more from that same special night, Miss, when I said that we were now all sisters and we hugged. For the first time in my life, I felt a real live, flesh and blood woman against me, breast to breast, belly to belly, and that was when I coveted *your* beautiful body against mine, in the same manner and without reservation.

You see, Miss, I discovered that another woman could both generate the passion and satisfy its urgency, and also what heaven it could be.

'It was superior even to that with Richard – except for that last thing – knowing she was feeling exactly as did I at each moment, how to satisfy it, because I knew what satisfied me. And that is where I am at this moment, Miss, wishing, hoping, desperately that you will satisfy my cravings.'

'There is only one thing more, and that is, at the same time I shall be wanting, wishing to satisfy you, Miss, in the same manner, at that same moment.

'There, I have said it all, and it is such a burden lifted that I could cry for joy,' shedding a few tears even as she spoke.

'Well, I do not know what to say, Alice, to that torrent of emotion – except that I had no idea of it, failing to recognize your true feelings being so preoccupied with my own lover. Now that I understand, I could not but accept your challenge.

'Besides, I could not have you leave looking sad after all you have done for me, now could I?' pleased to note a ghost of a smile play on Alice's lips.

'Very well then, come a little closer, sit up straight, hands on top of your head,' she stated briskly, and Alice managed a genuine smile at last as in this position, shoulders back, she felt her gown open wide.

'Now,' said Celia, more softly, 'my first guess as to your purpose of grooming my hair on my bed in your new yellow dressing gown *sans chemise de nuit*, while baring most of your delectable bosom, is this,' and she slipped her hands inside it to circle Alice's waist. At the first touch Alice's body stiffened, then mellowed to welcome the touch while her face softened with a sweet joy.

'Judging by your response, that appears to be the correct answer,' Celia said gently, as she tenderly massaged belly and lower chest with her delicate fingers and thumbs 'til Alice's throat constricted to almost stop her breathing.

'In which case, Alice, my second guess as to your quite brazen lack of attire,' her voice also dropping to a whisper, 'is this,' opening the gown to expose her full upper body then sliding her hands upwards to cup the clearly excited breasts so that Alice arched her back at the sensuous touch, giving an inadvertent cry of pleasure before moving her self against her mistress' palms as the ecstasy grew within her.

'Again I seem to have guessed correctly. But I am having trouble with the third; I just wonder what it could be? You will have to provide me a sign.' In response, Alice, eyes now closed, put her own hands on her mistress' and moved them to her shoulders.

'In that case, could the third one be some thing to do with this,' she whispered, as she caressed and fondled until the bow loosed itself completely at the waist, then eased the gown off altogether, unknowingly liberating Alice to play her trump card for, with a sigh of expectant pleasure, Alice reclined to lie back on the bed, with the full intent of encouraging her dearest wish.

With knees bent, Alice's most private self was now fully open to her mistress view, so as to make perfectly clear the nature of her ultimate prize, surprising Celia, momentarily taken aback with that *fait accompli!*

Could this be possible? Was this what Alice had been longing? And she hesitated, temporizing by placing one hand on Alice's belly to elicit a responsive wriggle. She had explored her sister in this manner many times – though rarely so explicitly viewed – so why not Alice, the one who had just brought her own dearest wish and its accompanying intimacy into being. Could she do any less for her beloved companion?

In answer to her own soliloquy, she placed both hands on belly and hips, gently massaging to her soft moans, running fingers through her dark fringe and inner thighs, steadily moving toward her yielding moistness with exploring fingers for long, long moments so that Alice was wriggling in delight at the exploration, but stopping short of that ultimate thrill. Withdrawing, she ran her hands up Alice's body to massage her breasts once more before pulling her upright again to receive a huge hug, at which she whispered in her ear.

'I am sorry, Alice, that I could not provide that ultimate thrill your body was clearly wishing. You see, it is a little too close to Manfred's delight in my self, but I shall in time; do you understand?'

'Completely, Miss, but in any event, it was a true joy, and thank you for accepting my open body, and for pleasuring it as I had hoped.'

'Looking at you now, who would believe that this is the same Alice, that shy, bashful young woman who had to be coaxed to show even a bare shoulder. And there she is, sitting unguarded fully contented without a stitch to her body, without a care in the world, openly soliciting titillation and adoration. What more could any one want!'

For reply, and in an automatic response to her own pleasure, 'Just this, Miss,' with a sly smile under lowered lashes; 'to return it to your self,' and she leaned forward to slip a hand inside her mistress' gown in return, only to have her wince at the light touch.

'Oh, I am so sorry, Miss, I forgot,' she exclaimed, jerking her self back to reality, rising to add a log to the fire – for her plans that night included its role – and to bring a lotion from the dressing table.

'It happens when you are suckling a baby, too,' as she opened her mistress' night-dress and gently applied the balm. 'Fortunately, it doesn't remain so for long,' as she tenderly caressed her mistress' now open body, beyond even those regions requiring it.

'Thank you, Alice, that was very comforting. You may now close my gown, if you will.'

'Must I, Miss?' Alice pleaded, ignoring the request by adding further lotion in order to continue her stroking. 'You have such a lovely softness, and a velvety skin that I have long wished to caress as you did to mine – as long as it does not hurt, of course.'

But Celia suddenly sat up as the light dawned: '*Now* I see what all this is about, Alice; *you are envious of Manfred?*'

Alice looked up in confusion, returning also to sit and face her mistress.

'No, Miss; I mean . . . I do admit to being envious of his freedom to love you and at will,' she returned, hesitantly.

'And those strange looks and sensuous touches you provided while bathing me, then towelling and powdering me dry, Alice. *You were coveting my body!*'

'Yes, Miss; I mean no, Miss,' in even greater confusion. 'It is not like that at all. I am not quite sure why it is so, but I think you expressed it perfectly when you said, 'We want only that which we can return'. You see, Miss, I long to touch your body *in just the same manner* as you have just touched mine. That other by moonlight, although quite wonderful, left me feeling as if I have some how . . . well, *cheated* unless I can return it in full measure.

'It seems to me, Miss,' as she strengthened her resolve, 'that we women cannot be one-sided – it must be giving and receiving in kind – otherwise it becomes a purely a selfish act. Is that not how you and Miss Lucy saw it, Miss, to your mutual delight?'

'My, my, Alice, that was a pretty speech indeed. I did not think such understanding was within you – although I know not why I think it, considering that I owe the whole of that wonderful yester day and its hoped-for future to your steadfastness and your generosity.

'And yes, since you ask, that is exactly how Lucy and I regard each other. We can not take without giving equally in return, for I honestly can not say which is the more pleasurable of the two. Let us just say that the pleasure is doubled, whereas it might otherwise be halved.

'So, to consider this further, Alice, do I now understand from all that insight into the deepest feelings of your body and my satisfying of them, that you wish to replace Lucy in my affections?'

'Oh, no, Miss! I could never do that, nor would I ever wish to! It is just that . . . that . . . if you become lonely – if you see what I mean – and I do likewise (for I have no Manfred to comfort me), then perhaps it is some thing that you might . . . you know . . . consider . . .' and she lowered her eyes to cover her embarrassment at such a naked disclosure of the desires of her own body and the coveting of her mistress'.

'So you believe that Manfred will not completely satisfy the urgings of my spirit – despite yesterday's considerable evidence to the contrary?'

'Oh no, Miss, it is not like that at all. I mean . . . it is just in case . . . whenever . . .' and Celia could see the tears beginning to form in Alice's pleading eyes.

'That is all right, Alice, I understand your meaning. Pray continue, for this interests me greatly,' in little doubt as to where this stark confession was leading, and where it might finally arrive, but curious to follow it, nonetheless.

'Well, it seems to me, Miss, that we should be close to each other just now, if for only a little while – until you and Mr. Manfred are wed, that is. It also concerns me greatly that neither of you will be able to control that final urge to consummate your love, whatever I, or her Ladyship, or anyone else for that matter might say to dissuade you. All of our remonstrations and arguments would be as naught compared to the urgency of that precious moment.

'I know it, Miss, because I was there. Despite my better inner judgment and Richard's sensible words – all was swept away by the accessibility of my openly proffered body, just as you risked with Mr. Manfred.

'There are some things, Miss, that cannot be resisted, because we are not meant to refuse them – once the appropriate conditions of love and honour are met, of course. We are made for coupling, else why would we be made to fit one into the other as easily as we do. I am convinced that there is no more powerful force on this earth than the desire to mate, as God intended.'

'Now where did all that come from?'

'Well, since you ask, Miss, from your self.'

'Really? I do not remember saying those words.'

'Well no, Miss, it is not quite like that. You see, I have been studying, too. I have been with you for nigh on ten years, and almost from my very first day (I was then just Miss Lucy's age now), I decided that in order to improve my self I would study some one close to me, your self.

'Even as you were growing into the beautiful, accomplished young woman you are today, I was listening to you and trying to understand your manner of thinking. Then, any thing I did not comprehend I would look up in my dictionaries – for I have two, my own and Richard's, as well as his many books from his father on history, poetry, art and such. He was quite a scholar and very quick at learning new things.

'Also, since Miss Lucy has been here, Miss, there has been much more to take note of in the discourse between the two of you – and that was very important to me, how to converse with ladies – as well as *her* way of thinking. Then there were the Misses Georgina and Geraldine, and

Miss Alexa, and many others; at the Quintet Balls, for example. Then there was your mode of dress and deportment, and gowns, and on and on.

'So you see, Miss, there has been plenty of opportunity for anyone with an inquiring mind. I have always had a good memory and been quick to learn, so I do not miss very much.'

'Indeed you do not, Alice! Nevertheless, you do embarrass me more than a little. I had no idea I was anyone's role model, or I might have behaved better than I did. But a philosopher? Have you been reading my *Essays* by David Hume? Or Locke, or George Berkeley's *Essays* and *Dialogues*?'

'No, Miss; I have never even heard of him, or the others. That just comes to me naturally; it is just the way things are. If we try to fight them or set them at naught, we make enemies of our selves, of our bodies, and then we become sick in both body and mind.

'As to the other, Miss, I think you are just perfect as you are, and I would not have you change a single thing,' she cooed happily, eyes shining in the delighted memory of it all, taking up her mistress' hand to caress it.

'Well, Alice, we must explore that original philosophical thinking in much greater depth in our nightly chats. I will get out my volumes on Socrates and his pupil, Plato, mentor to Aristotle, for amongst them they changed the world. In our discussions we might even include his friend, Euclides, who gave it all a mathematical dimension.

'I must also inquire how Manfred regards all this. Perhaps we should converse with him, pitting our wits against his to lay him low, as was Socrates' wont. And in preparation, we might read together from Plato's *Republic*. What say you to that, Alice? Is it enough of a challenge for your scholarly bent?'

'If you think I could master some of what you speak, Miss, I shall be pleased to try. As for Mr. Manfred, if you believe I could add some thing to such a discussion, Miss, I would be most happy to join with you.'

'Well said, Alice. Now, in return, what can I do for you?'

'The carpenter will do just fine, Miss, if you can manage to land him on my plate.'

'Very good. Just let me know whether that should be boiled or stewed.'

'I will take him just as he comes, Mistress!' and they both had a good laugh together, holding hands, and washing away all fears and concerns.

'Consider it done, Alice; for that whole glorious yesterday – and now, I believe, my happiness with my beloved – is owed all to your tenacity of purpose.'

'We did it together, Miss; I could not be the generator of it.'

'That is as may be, Alice, but did you not willingly become my Indian Maiden – exposing your self to a man without any qualms – or none that showed?'

'Well, I did have *some* qualms, Miss.'

'And well you may have, but you did it, notwithstanding. I could not have performed similarly without your setting the stage. It was you who led the way, Alice, and made the rest possible.

'Who was it, Alice, who constructed the setting in which my future lover actually proposed to me – and on one knee as custom dictates – formally requesting my hand in marriage? Without that, I could not have played my Ace of Hearts, and all that posing would have been mere cinders and ashes.

'And who, pray tell, accomplished the essential role of Solicitor so admirably – even to rejecting my suitor! – to educe the necessary information from my beloved and to convince mother of my sincerity, to make it even *possible* to discuss marriage, let alone receive a genuine proposal! I certainly could not.

'Indeed, if it had been left to *mother's* Attorney, do you think Manfred would have had as fair a hearing as you provided? – even if he had any hearing at all, which I very much doubt.'

'But, Miss . . .'

'Yet there is more, Alice, for who has now explained it all away – and, I might add, received a thorough scolding into the bargain – such that mother accepts her daughter to marry for love?

'And you call all that of little consequence, Alice? I should call it honest devotion above and beyond any call of duty. Would I have performed such delicate services for George, or Alexa? I think not; for you know as well as I that it would all have gone very badly indeed for every one involved in the charade.

'My health, my happiness, my art – which is so dear to me – all were entrusted to you, although at the time I did not understand that. But *you* did, Alice; to you, they were as clear as the morning sun.'

Embarrassed by this eulogy, Alice tried once more. 'Yes, Miss, but . . .' and failed.

'No, I shall not give way, Alice, for I have not finished. Think of it as a steeple-chase, each hurdle to be surmounted one at a time and in sequence, a failure at any one being a failure at all. Those were five difficult hurdles, Alice, some very high, some very wide, with scarce a pause between any of them. But you took them all in your stride, surmounted them, and at the winning post delivered the only prize that my heart and my whole being desired, asking nothing in return. No reward for your loyalty, your sincerity of endeavour, or your clarity of thought over it all.'

'Not entirely correct, Miss, for there was your happiness. That is all the reward I need; and as I am already assured of that, there is nothing more to be said. Also, I hope to receive your love, Miss, by way of return, and that is by no means "nothing".'

'Well, as to that, Alice, you had it before, during and after from the thousand and one things you do for me, so there must be some little addition to your well-being that would please your heart?'

'There is, Miss, but that comes later,' and would not be drawn further.

'May I ask the one question, Miss, that you have not addressed?' And Celia nodded.

They were now around the fire, to which Alice had added a further log or two; Celia on her chaise, which had been pulled into a position more in front of it, while Alice knelt on her pouf before the floor-length mirror so they could still be close. Both had resumed their gowns, though more for warmth than any sense of a shield, for each remained almost fully open to view. And Alice had procured a further cup of hot cocoa and some gingersnaps for each, this time enriched with a few drops of brandy at the mistress' request.

'I believe this will complete my understanding of it all, Miss, for it also relates to why you were so eager to leave Mr. Manfred before he could join us.'

'I rather thought you knew the answer to the latter, Alice?' and when she received an answering shake, continued.

'It is really quite simple. I value my independence almost more than any thing, as you should know. Just because Manfred accepted the openness of my body is no reason to surrender my true spirit to him as well. Contrariwise, it is every reason to retain it, as I fully intend to.'

'Yes, Miss; knowing you as I do, I see that. But if you are so happy in his loving of you and you of him – as I was clear witness to – why do you still humour . . . the other course?' she continued, a little shamefaced at her boldness, 'even though I have just been the delighted recipient of it. I had thought that pleasure now to be behind you, your desires proceeding in only the one direction?'

'I think you answered that one for your self, Alice,' looking intently into her dark eyes, 'when you gave me *your* reasons for not wanting the first.'

'You mean when I said men could be so rough, Miss?' and Celia nodded. 'So, by the same measure, we women are gentle and tender with each other. Yes, I see that clearly now. Men have some thing they want *from* us, and they will take it whether we give it freely or not, whereas we want only that which can be equally returned, especially as we are identical in body,' she exclaimed, happily.

'And in that same sense, Miss, we surrender nothing of our spirit to each other, because nothing is asked of us.'

Celia nodded, surprised at the clarity of insight.

'True, Alice. However, one might also consider it the opposite way, wherein we surrender *every thing*, receiving it then in return in equal measure. The only thing I would add is that men do not really understand us – certainly not as we wish to be cherished – their own urgent rush to that final act blanketing every thing else, of which your Mildred is the demonstrable proof.

'On the other hand, we women naturally complement one another to perfection, because that is what we our selves are seeking, having no end point to achieve as they do. Besides, would you have me reject Lucy on a matter of principle?'

'Oh, no, Miss, and thank you for making every thing seem so right between us,' and she kissed her mistress' cheek in her own pleasure of discovery.

Then she jumped up, pulled a rose from the vase to whirl her self around the moonlit room with the flower pressed to her bosom.

Meanwhile, her mistress arose to lie on her bed in preparation for a well-earned sleep, whereupon Alice returned to curl, cat-like, on it for her to judge the pose.

'Perhaps you could call this one "The Rose", Miss,' stroking her self, trying to achieve a rise in spirit but not succeeding.

'Do I take it, Alice,' exclaimed Celia upon observing this new effusion of spirit, 'that we have inaugurated a new nightly custom of brushing my hair in bed, you in nothing but your new gown, which in any event soon gets discarded to facilitate sensual diversions with soft candlelight, flowers and the rest?'

'Would that bother you, Miss, if it were?' she replied impishly, if every time I needed consoling I wore a rose in my hair, naught under the gown save my charms, and offered you a trio of guesses?'

'I really do not know what has got into you tonight, Alice; you are quite wild. Perhaps it is a touch of the sun?'

At this, Alice rose on one elbow to regard her mistress, solemnly. 'Do you realize, Miss, that your exquisite touch – especially in that most intimate area – is the first in those many years since Richard? And for all that time a mature, capable woman with dreams of fulfilment, yet all of them empty? Do you wonder that I am filled with a wild delight at the return of that dimly-remembered joy?'

At this, Celia simply took Alice in her arms and they shed many tears together.

It was Celia who broke the quiet moments of togetherness.

'Thank you, Alice for that insight, I shall treasure and act upon it as possible.

'Now, a sudden thought. Do you realize, Alice, that you now know Manfred in the same sense that I know Richard?'

'Not until you mentioned it, Miss, but I see what you mean. Mr. Manfred was indeed very . . . uh . . . excited, just like my lover. So now we are equal in our knowledge of the other's lover, both as to form and purpose yet still both unwed, while Manfred is equally knowing of each of us, although yours is, well, intensely *intimate*.'

'Well said, Alice. Perhaps that is the reason – other than love it self – why I feel so comfortable with you when we are together like this, for we have no secrets of each other's bodies – or even those of our respective lovers. Surely that must be a very rare and enviable position to be in with the some ones you love, knowing their mind, body and intimate spirit, with almost nothing being left to chance?'

'Indeed, Miss, I feel it is exactly so, and thank you for explaining it so lucidly,' laying her self against her mistress' warmth. 'It is indeed wonderfully comforting to have some one know you even better than one knows oneself,' giving the soft cheek a gentle kiss, 'for it follows that every thing then may proceed to perfection.'

'Alice,' rising once more, 'this fire has failed in its duty to warm us, so please add another log or two; good,' when Alice had obliged and it was blazing merrily again, for she had made certain that the split logs were dry, as well as to include a goodly supply of kindling. Then she returned to cuddle her bare self into the warmth of her mistress on the rug before the fire, and for some minutes there was a warm and happy interlude, during which a new thought struck her.

'Do you believe he is aware of us, Miss? As we are now and have just been with each other?'

'Manfred?' receiving a nod. 'Why do you ask? Would it bother you if he did?'

'Yes, Miss, greatly, for then I could not . . . that is . . . I would be so self-conscious in his presence that I would . . .' and she felt the impending tears stinging her eyes, the thought too awful to contemplate.

'That is quite all right, Alice, for I have not the slightest intention of informing him. I shall act as I choose in all such things pertaining to my inner spirit, so please dry your tears; they are quite unnecessary.

'After Manfred and I are married, we shall see what we shall see, but I do not intend to abandon you, Alice, to turn you out into the cold, unloved and unrewarded, as I trust I have made clear. You shall always have my love and care,' providing a warm cuddle and a kiss on the cheek, returned in full measure.

'Thank you, Miss, for your kind words, and I hope we may both be happy in that outcome,' her heart encouraged, her hopes for that ultimate thrill rewarded before this night was concluded now closer than ever.

20

Mirrors

'Now, in the silence of this perfect moment, Alice, I would like to present you with a little memento of my appreciation of all the things you do – and have done – for me, yesterday, today and all the days, but you will have to approach my dresser to receive it,' and Alice arose as directed, shedding her gown as she did so, trusting that nature would take the course she wished for it.

'It is in the centre drawer, a little box in blue velvet, with my crest on it. Yes, that is it. You may add a further log, and then open it.'

Alice stood before the mirror, candle in one hand, the box in the other, quite in awe of the occasion. She had never received a present as formally as this. It was indeed a beautiful box, with silver trimming and Miss Celia's crest on it, too.

'Are you not going to open it, Alice?' came the soft voice.

'No, Miss, I mean, yes, Miss. It is just that I have never received any thing so beautifully presented. I am almost afraid.'

'That you will not like it?'

'Oh no, Miss; nothing like that. I know that I shall, for you have such exquisite taste. It is . . . that I am sure I shall be so overcome with emotion, that I shall be dreadfully embarrassed and will not know what to do with my self,' and there was a long, long pause.

'Very well, Miss,' as she opened the silver latch and lifted the lid, careful to avoid spilling hot wax on it. And there was complete silence, until:

'Oh, Miss,' she whispered, 'it is just as I thought; truly *beautiful*. And you *remembered*. But you have already replaced that which I had to surrender.'

'True, Alice, but this is some thing a little more than an exact replacement which the other was intended to be. This time it has a diamond as reminder of what a jewel you have been and are to me.'

433

'It is too precious for me to touch; you must take it out and adorn it on me, Miss,' eyes pleading through the mirror.

'If you wish it,' and she rose to oblige her faithful servant, standing behind to reach over the shoulders, her bosom through the open night-gown touching the bare back as she did so, innocently sending thrills through Alice. The necklace was removed and draped, where it settled on her smooth skin, sparkling in the candlelight, Celia's hands remaining lightly on the shoulders.

Meanwhile, Alice's tears flowed freely, coursing down her cheeks to run unheeded over her bosom and belly so that she took her mistress' hands and placed them directly on her bosom, pressing them to her.

Then, overcome at seeing her self adorned with gold and jewels, her very own for the first time in her life, Alice sank to the pouf in her accustomed pose while she tried in vain to stem the tears, in complete distress as she had foreseen, before placing the candlestick on the floor to touch the pendant with careful fingers.

The effect on her mistress was only slightly less dramatic as she knelt behind to offer her faithful servant a little comfort, chin on Alice's shoulder. She reached to the pendant to turn it slightly so that it sparkled red in the fire glow and bright in the candlelight in order to study their effect, becoming acutely aware of the tingles pulsing through Alice as she did so.

And as they looked into the mirror together, Celia's bright blue eyes focused on Alice's sparkling brown, noting them widen, some signal invisible to the naked eye was exchanged, whereupon she slowly and deliberately brushed her hand lightly across Alice's bosom, one side to the other. Then she lowered her mirrored gaze to the bosom, watching, fascinated as it came alive to the gentle touch, Alice instinctively swelling her self to enhance the contact, while pressing her back into her mistress so that Celia came alive also, rotating her self against Alice to heighten the rapidly growing excitement in them both.

In response, Alice put her hands behind to hold her mistress' bottom, then on to her smooth hips and thighs, finally to the soft belly, down to mould her triangle, and on to her inner thighs, delighted almost beyond measure when Celia replicated her movements, one by one, before returning to stoke the fire consuming her bosom with soft hands and gently massaging fingers until she thought her breasts, with their hard, swollen tips would burst as Celia played with them.

Then, to her utter fascination, while one hand massaged and titillated her breasts, she saw in the mirror and felt in her inner being the other hand creep gently, ever so slowly down, massaging as it did so, over her navel where it paused briefly, then on to her quivering belly, till it met her dark triangle, where it stopped again to mould and squeeze, then to Alice's incredulous delight, on and over to stroke and massage her white inner thighs once more. At this, Alice opened her self wider and still wider to welcome the delicate fingers, each exquisite movement mirrored to her widened eyes and throbbing spirit.

Alice was now moaning in sheer delight at the softness of touch and delicacy of movement, eyes closed, allowing her emotions to flow freely until her "lover" found what she sought, and Alice squealed in pleasure at the touch and was forced to remove her hands from her mistress' body to thrust one knuckle deep into her own mouth to muffle the scream that she knew was inevitable, opening her eyes once more to participate fully in the unfolding prospect of ultimate delight.

Meanwhile Celia, continued the caressing and massaging of both upper and lower regions, all actions vividly displayed and mirrored to her wondering gaze as she did so, doubling the thrill to both giver and receiver.

Just when Alice thought she could take no more, Celia became more urgent in her actions, until Alice thought to explode with the enormous build up of impending fulfilment, arching her back to receive it all, until with a final shuddering climax she did shriek out, muffled though it was, and with a great quiver almost collapsed in her mistress arms, as she half tuned to face her, and for some moments, knew no more.

When she regained her senses cuddled to Celia's bosom, she could barely speak, but Celia, with fingers to lips shushed her to be quite and still, and so for some while they remained in that position until Alice was somewhat recovered, when Celia rose to add another log to the fire.

'I do not know what to say, Miss.'

'Then say nothing, Alice.'

'But you have done all the giving, Miss, while I have done nothing, no giving in return.'

'That is quite all right, Alice, there will be other times for me – with some one.'

'Perhaps, Miss,' resenting and rejecting the switch of lovers, 'but there may never be another quite like this, and with my self, so I shall attend to it in just a little while,' and Celia smiled her gentle acceptance, for she had been delighted with her own requited feelings in the exchange of emotions.

It was when the logs were burning brightly once more, that Alice arose, pulling her mistress-lover up with her, providing her a brief embrace, thrilled by the intimate well-warmed bosom and belly to belly contact, before seating her new lover on the pouf in the same manner as she her self had just been.

Now it was her challenge and delight to replicate every detail her lover (for that is how she now thought of her) had provided to her own intense passion, step by step, bosom to triangle, each in turn, massaging, fondling, squeezing, stroking, feeling the passion rising and overflowing into every part of her body as she did so, responding to the urges and needs as she felt them through her supple, probing fingers.

But much as she enjoyed it all, it was the final act that she loved the best and took the most pleasure in, for while the rest of the mistress' body was well known to her; this was to be the ultimate thrilling *dénouement*, the prize that she sought in return for her own thrilling experience and the many months of longing.

She adored the fair, downy triangle, so contrasted to her own dark covering, extending the exploring as long as she could, feeling her mistress' urgency growing more intense with the delay, and continued until she was wriggling and jerking her body, urging the final contact. At last at the height of movement and soft cries, Alice felt the moment to have arrived. So she increased the caressing until the climax was reached, her mistress burying her hand in her mouth as she screamed her pleasure, though Alice did not cease, further increasing the intensity, repeating it several times, so that each cry was louder than the last, until with a violent shudder she was still, collapsing in Alice's arms.

What surprised Alice the most was that when her mistress' body was close to reaching its peak, so suddenly was her own, although she had scarce noticed the rising level until that last moment. Indeed, her release was so fierce and at the same instant, that she, too, cried out in ecstasy, burying her face in her mistress' shoulder to muffle the cry as best she could, also with a great shudder to end it. After some moments to recover, Alice drew her mistress up to stretch out before the fire, both as crushed together as they could be.

For some little while they must have slept, for when they awoke, one stir arousing the other, the fire was quite low. Alice corrected this by placing on more logs, then gently raised her adored companion to the chaise where she reclined, covered with a blanket, while Alice, now loosely robed, left for some moments then returned to kneel at her side.

Senses almost back to normal, Celia would have spoken, but Alice was there first.

'Hush, Miss, take your time. I have here some of your brandy, also some cold ham from the kitchen larder, tomatoes, several slices of fresh-baked bread and butter, strawberry jam, and a large cup of cocoa. We shall eat together while you rest there quietly, eating and drinking as I talk.

'That was quite wonderful, Miss; I simply cannot express just how wonderful,' she whispered. 'And as you see, we were, after all, both winners.'

'For me, too, Alice; but first tell me how it was for you.'

'I am not sure I can, Miss, it was so breathtaking – and so different. You see, it was so long ago, that although I remember every thing we *did* together those were mostly the actions, which remain quite clear; a touch here, a caress there, and so on. But the *emotions* them selves – what with the thousand different ones piled on just as we go through life – have been dulled by time.

'To try to say how it felt with your self, Miss, is . . . well . . . nigh on impossible, it was so glorious. Your touch, your caresses were so exquisite that my desire swelled like a mountain until I thought I would erupt as a volcano, it was so thrilling.

'I know comparisons are odious (and that is what I think Mr. Shakespeare *meant* to say in Much Ado), but it is now in memory as the most wonderful experience of my entire life. Did it surpass that with Richard? That is harder to say, because that final act has its own unique joy, and partly because of the dimness of memory. Yet if I am honest with my self and true to your self, Miss, it did, and by some margin.

'But it was also so different from that with him, Miss, because of your gentleness. I could feel the passion flowing through your body, so that it enhanced mine. Also, anticipating your movements, knowing your desires would lead you to produce my desires, one leading the other, or equally the other way around.

'Yet of equal pleasure, Miss, was seeing it all take place, mirrored, with my own eyes on my own body. Seeing what I was feeling, wanting, needing, all at that same time, at the exact moment it was happening – and going to happen in the next few seconds.

'Then to cap it all, there was the supreme delight of re-enacting it all, Miss, but this time being the one that achieved it, rather than the receiver who felt it, although as to that, I found it difficult to separate receiver and giver, they both seemed to so meld together.

'Then I was further astonished to once more experience it to my self at the very same instant,' as the tears started in her eyes. 'That was beyond any thing I have ever experienced, Miss, a joy beyond joy.' And Celia reached to hold her tightly until the tears ceased.

'Now what of your own feelings, Miss; did my touch meet and satisfy your own desires?'

'Well, you have already said it all, Alice,' was the equally soft reply. 'It was glorious, indeed – as you well must know, for you were both a close observer and the creator of it. But if I were to say any thing beyond that, it would be to repeat what you have just spoken, word for word, and I see little point in it.

'However, to answer your unspoken question – which lies in your breast exactly as it does in mine – was it better, more delightful, more exquisite than with Manfred? My answer there will be different, because the two experiences for me were only hours apart. His was more robust, yours more gentle. Sometimes he seemed not to quite "understand" me, while you always did, providing exactly what I craved, where he was sometimes just off the mark.

'Of course, you had a special advantage in that mirror. I fully admit that was quite wonderful, feeling and seeing my self touched at precisely the same moment, especially when you deliberately withheld it for excruciatingly long moments before reaching that peak. That seemed to swallow me up inside – and several times at that,' and her listener positively glowed with pleasure at the success of her endeavours.

'So, while the two are different in many ways, I would have to give the accolade to . . . This is very good cocoa, Alice,' watching Alice's face fall as she switched subjects. 'Will that do?'

'Oh, Miss, you know only too well that it will *not* do! You were perfectly correct; I do want, need to know how I was as your giver, even if it fell far short of the other,' tears starting once more.

'Well, if you insist, Alice, I shall tell you, but be it on your own head,' and with these words Alice went quite pale.

'I have to be honest with my true feelings, and do love him greatly,' and here Alice simply held her breath, 'and therefore I give the accolade to . . . Miss Alice Marlowe, with an "e".'

'Really, Miss?' squealed Alice, with a whoosh of exhaled breath, quite unbelieving.

'Really and truly, Alice; you were quite beyond compare.'

'Oh, Miss, you make my heart overflow with joy, with pure love.'

'Where did you find it, Miss?'

They were lying together on the chaise, a joint pillow behind their heads, warmed by the still-bright fire, with a single candle on a table beside them casting flickering and fascinating shadows on their openly bare bodies, choosing to hide nothing, each from the other.

'I did not, Alice, I had it made. Mother had a very old one as a keep-sake from *her* mother, and when I explained my intention, she considered that she had saved it for just such a purpose. Of course, I exchanged it for one of my own guineas so that the gift could still be mine.

'Nothing I had seen suited me, so I designed the filigree frame my self – for I wanted it to be delicate – and then my pretty sketch informed me that a solitaire diamond was the perfect finishing touch where the chain joined it. That, too, was to my own design. I confess that I am more than pleased with both the design and its execution by one of the jewellers recommended by Aunt Julia as the best in Town.

'And as I now see it lying on your flawless skin, I know that is the perfect choice. It shall be in the next pose we do together – although capturing its beauty will be a considerable challenge. Head and shoulders, I think,' studying her model closely, 'including your delectable bosom, of course,' providing each side a gentle touch to arouse them. 'Yes, and suffused like that, if you prefer,' and Alice smiled in pure joy at the thought.

'And you went to all this trouble, Miss, just for me? It must have . . .'

'*Alice!* Don't you *dare!*'

'No, Miss. It is just that I haven't thanked you properly.'

'Really, Alice? I thought you just did, and in a most appropriate and all-encompassing manner – and more than once, at that. Certainly in that last I was most appreciative of its urgency,' gently running a finger down Alice's cleavage to her belly, so that she wriggled at the touch, nearly falling off onto the rug – which favour was quickly returned so they had need to hold on to each other to avoid a tumble.

'I do love you so, Miss,' with a kiss on the cheek and a gentle fondle of the bosom, receiving the same in equal measure.

'Since we have this quiet moment, Alice,' she said, softly, 'can I add a little to your store of knowledge from a book the doctor provided me at my insistence?' and Alice nodded.

'Well,' now in a whisper, 'those intimate parts that protect our secrets, that very special tip of passion,' reducing now to the barest of whispers, 'although it is quite tiny, is homologous to that of a man, becoming erect as does he when excited – as you have now observed directly with both your male admirers. So you see, Alice, we women have both our own organs and his, which I believe makes us wonderful beings indeed, for he has none of ours.

'Well that is not quite true, for I was speaking of the lower body. As you already know, his chest is almost as sensitive as ours, growing quite hard, and he adored my soft lips upon them,' and Alice smiled at her remembrance of that.

'You see, Manfred could not have created that mirrored-self scene on the pouf; firstly because his growing need would not have permitted his being behind me, but more importantly because he could not feel what I was feeling – which our mutual enjoyment has just confirmed. Manfred could never achieve that no matter how he tried. And that is the difference between men and us women.

'And that brings another thought, which I am sure will please you, Alice. While I adore my Manfred as a lover, when I feel the need for that special thrill I must needs turn to your precious self for fulfilment, as I shall return it to you.'

'Thank you, Miss,' returning to a whisper. 'Now you have warmed my heart of hearts, knowing that I am that precious to you, as you are to me, knowing that I can truly love you in that perfect intimacy. Also, those other things of knowledge are quite exciting to know, for I do like to understand these things, even if they are intensely personal and can only be discussed in a whisper with some one exceeding close both in being and spirit.'

'However, a caution, Alice. One thing you may have to accept is that it may never be this exquisite again, try as we might, nor as oft as you would wish. But we shall see what we see when the next opportunity arises. I am certain that Manfred will want my body all over again and often. Does that disappoint you, Alice?'

'Indeed it does, Miss; however, I shall make the most of the next seven and more days to have you make love to my body as you did tonight, and mine to your self, Miss, and I have some thoughts on the manner in which to provide that "special thrill" you desire, to make it even more exciting to each of us.'

'Really, Alice? I do not see how that can be with Manfred now as my betrothed. Are you aware of some thing that I am not?'

'Yes, Miss. Earlier today, I received a message addressed to my self from Mr. Manfred by way of Andrew, that friend of James from Greville Hall,' and Celia's brows rose sharply at this knowledge.

'I was greatly surprised also, Miss, for that has not happened before. In it he says that he now understands and appreciates what I informed him in my Solicitor's role regarding the manner in which his bride must be provided by way of an estate, carriages, servants and so forth.

'Then he continues that to do so, he must visit a Mr. James Watt, and he will be away some seven days before his return. He ends by saying to tell you of all this and to say that he loves you greatly, and that I must keep you well 'til his return.

'So you see, Miss, we really do have at least seven days for our joint pleasure, and I can think of no better way to "keep you well" than to love each other to distraction!

'Well, thank you for that advice, but we shall have to see about that loving, Alice, remembering that we have much to accomplish regarding the Cottage and the Wedding in those seven or more days free from distraction. Besides, on return Manfred will expect to see progress to at least match his, for there are two of us.'

'Now I do not know what to think, Miss.'

'Well I *do*, Alice. You might think about going to *bed*!'

'On, no, Miss, I am much too excited to sleep.'

'Then do you think *I* might be permitted a few moments of slumber, Alice, while you cavort in your skin and roses some more?'

'I am sorry, Miss, I was so excited I quite forgot that we still have much to do.' Then she giggled; 'But it would be an excellent idea if you slept a little before the sun gets it into his head to be here first.'

'Thank you, Alice; excellent, indeed. Yesterday it was Manfred who was every thing to my inner spirit, and today it was your self. I shall not realize every thing that has happened for at least a week. But the sooner I start that week the better. Though, come to think of it – judging by your wild antics – I had better get Cedric working *tout de suite*, to see if *he* can tame that wild tiger that I seem to have awakened in your private self.'

'Who is this "Cedric", Miss?'

'Why, none but your handsome carpenter, Alice. I thought you would have winkled that out of him,' but Alice shook her head, then nodded as she whispered 'Cedric, the tiger tamer'.

'Now, do not wake me too early in the morning,' as she climbed into bed, waving away the proffered night-gown then giving her hand a final encouraging squeeze.

'Remember, though,' she added, with a sleepy smile, 'that whenever you take it into *your* head to require some intimate caressing and passionate frolicking, that tiger may have to be muzzled, for I am not to be taken for granted. That applies to you, equally as to Manfred, although, as I reflect back upon it . . . there may be times when . . .' and her accompanying smile was one of warmth and happiness – and gratitude.

'I will not forget, Miss, and thank you for my special prize,' touching her lower body, now loosely protected by a silk scarf, and this, which engendered it, fingering her pendant, then kissing her mistress' hand in final salute. 'I shall try to be less abandoned – perhaps with a little help, although . . . there may be times . . . and that quite soon when . . .' and she indulged a secret seductive smile.

'Now perchance may I sleep, Alice?'

'Yes, Miss, you may. But now you do not have to wake early in the morning and I shall provide you tea when you do. I will simply advise her Ladyship that there was much to be achieved to bring the Cottage to the standard you require for your new home, and that you are going to sleep as long as possible to recover from all the excitement.

'Then that you are going to do some sketches in your Studio as to how you would like the interior to be and the alterations that it will require, plus lists of things that need to be done over the next several weeks which will occupy you all day. After that, you would be glad if her Ladyship could find a little time to discuss it all with you, so as to get her ideas on how it should be.

'I shall hold the fort meanwhile. Would that suit you, Miss?'

'Alice, you are a complete marvel! I do not know what I should do without you. Well, I do; and I do not like the thought of that one little bit.

'Have we concluded our games then, Alice? Have I satisfied all the most intimate wishes and desires of your body and spirit?'

'Completely, Miss – except for one that my newly awakened being suddenly finds itself yearning.'

'Oh? I had thought with our mirrored selves there was nothing left to explore; so what is the last mystery?'

'A very simple one, Miss; to spend one night with your beautiful self, in your bed, asleep and awake, just as with my last lover, Mildred's father.'

'As you are aware, Alice, that is reserved for one very special person' and there was a soft silence, while Alice merely held her breath.

'However, as you have successfully granted all my wishes over these last days, I shall equally grant yours; and you shall choose the night to your own entire satisfaction.'

'Thank you, Miss, for being so wonderful and understanding of my woman-to-woman needs and attending to them, and acceding to that final joy, which I shall plan for our mutual and ultimate pleasure.

'Goodnight, Miss. Sweet dreams.'

'Oh, one last thing before you go, Alice, I have made a decision on the nominee for the Cottage, but if I reveal the name to you, it must remain our private secret. Also that you must make no comment. Agreed?'

'If you wish it so, Miss; agreed.'

'Good. Then the Nominee is Miss Alice Marlowe, with an "e".

'Goodnight, Alice. And the same to you.'

Alice stood stock still, looking at her mistress – or at least where she had been, for she had already turned over and her breathing was becoming soft as she entered the land of nod.

Lit now only by her single candle and the last moonbeams crossing the floor and illuminating the bed, she stood gazing out the window for some while before she drew the curtains to keep out her day companion.

Miss Celia was quite right; it had been such a day as never before, unlikely to be as wonderful ever again, excepting only that night-to-be of exquisite togetherness. She would probably need a week her self to absorb it all. She could tell by the breathing that her mistress was already asleep, and she did indeed make a solitary light waltz around the room, stopping at the large mirror for one last self-appraisal.

'Yes,' she whispered to her self, as she studied the effect of the light and shadow on her supple body by moving the candle from side to side to highlight her 'most beautiful feature', as Manfred had described it. 'Miss Celia was quite correct; it is truly wonderful what one little candle can achieve.'

And then another thought swiftly followed. Tiger? – tigress, more like it. Her mistress was unbelievably perceptive, for that is exactly how she might have expressed it her self – had she thought of it. Then, gently adjusting the sheet around her mistress, she silently withdrew, and the latch clicked softly behind her.

Languidly mounting the stairs to her own room, gown carelessly trailing behind her, a rose in her hair, she could not comprehend her own exhilaration and her sense of freedom; whence they came or why, though it mattered not, as long as they remained to her.

The wedding before her, with her self as Matron of Honour, Mildred as Flower Girl, an inclusion even of Richard, and hope for her own future happiness – it was almost too much to comprehend. And if it should go terribly awry with the mistress – heaven forbid – even a Cottage and every thing in it to her own name? It was all too much for one day or even a month of days.

The cool sheets on her excited body; vividly recalling that special night that had started it all. So *this* was what her mistress was on about when she spoke of her skin being free to breathe. She was understanding so many things for the first time.

As she settled into hopeful sleep, perchance to dream of Cedric and his taming of her tigress, she knew only that a new era had begun, one that, thanks to her benefactor, was freer than any in the past.

And she was content that the future was as bright as it was unknowable, that her place in it was set to be warm and secure for the very first time in her memory.

And she offered a simple prayer in gratitude.

Want to read more? Turn the page for the opening to Part 2 of *The Hollow: Silla*

1

Recital

'Mildred, I'm feeling all at sixes and sevens this evening, so I would be grateful if you would dress my hair again.'

'Certainly, Miss,' she said with a little curtsey, unpinning the flowing locks and brushing deeply prior to creating a new style for this special evening, while Lucy attended to the streaked, solemn face that presented itself in the dressing mirror, occasionally taking a quick peek at Mildred's movements. She was still amazed at the delicacy Alice's young daughter gave to these tasks, never at a loss to tackle anything requested of her. Always so willing, always attentive and thoughtful, even to anticipating the request itself on numerous occasions as if reading her mind.

She had discussed the current obligation with Celia at some length, and one of its most important elements had been Mildred and her situation. Celia (who, with good reason, thought the world of Mildred's capabilities) was apprehensive – although 'determined' would better describe it – that Mildred was properly received and regarded wherever she went as the companion for Charles' affianced, as if some sixth sense had warned her that it would not be so unless special provisions were made. It was most likely her experience with the Quintet that had forewarned her, thus the deliberations were most carefully recorded in Celia's neat hand.

Alice was especially consulted regarding her daughter's mode of dress, so it was agreed that Mildred would be attired in dark blue and white, with a change to dark green and white for evening wear, to add an air of distinction from the other servants who were – like Alice herself – invariably and unchangingly in black and white.

Thus Mildred was sewing for a considerable period before they proceeded on the journey, grateful for Miss Celia's insistence on adding a sewing maid to the household for a week beforehand. The personal touch to the uniform came from Celia's fertile mind in the form of a monogrammed 'E', set in a circlet of oak leaves, taken from the Etheridge coat of arms.

Mildred was in seventh heaven when she was dressed in it for the first time – though hardly more so than her mother – especially when Miss Celia commissioned a similar design for Alice's own outfit in navy for day wear, and maroon for evening. 'Any thing but that drear black' she was wont to say, for it was a colour she abhorred – protesting even that it was a 'colour'. The final touch for Mildred was a tiny monogrammed MM set within the circlet, and an AM for Alice's soon-to-be outfit.

Aunt Beatrice, the second of Captain Charles' aunts, and with whom Lucy was now staying, was a very prim and proper widow whose every attitude and action was conducted from the viewpoint of one to whom life had dealt a decidedly sour hand. Celia would have termed her 'desiccated'.

For Lucy, this evening was of particular importance, with all three aunts in attendance, together with many of the more distant family as well as a number of important and influential guests who had not been in attendance for the early formal dinner. It was also – thankfully – the last night of her stay, for she was leaving with Aunt Cicely in the morning.

There now remained only the recital that had been arranged to intro-duce her to that extended family and its acquaintance. Having been guided and guarded by Aunt for the whole of her ten-day residence, on this last occasion Lucy intended to take charge, shewing the person she now was and decidedly who she intended to remain. Accordingly, she had laid her plans most carefully.

Gown and coiffure accomplished, she descended the main staircase with its delicately figured balustrade and ornate panelling, pausing to examine herself in the half-landing mirror. She had selected one of her finest gowns, the ecru with tiny seed pearls. It was modestly low-cut, shewing her figure to its full advantage, together with the emerald tiara and emerald drop earrings - and a fresh rosebud in its little silver holder pinned close to her bosom. She had to smile to herself at the last and its significance in her growth to young womanhood. Aunt Beatrice would indeed be shocked if she were to know the story behind that little trinket!

'Creditable' she half-smiled to her reflected self, then adding a wider one to Mildred behind her. 'Beautiful' mouthed Mildred, reading her mistress's mind, providing her own conspiratorial smile as she followed two steps behind her mistress.

'Are you nervous, Mildred?'

'A little, Miss; but I believe I have it all committed to memory,' at which Lucy smiled once more and nodded her encouragement.

Thus it was that Lucy entered the Salon with head held high, in a more confident mood than at any time since she left Etheridge Hall, followed at the appropriate distance by Mildred, who acknowledged the assembled hosts and guests with a deep curtsey, before retiring to a chair adjacent to the piano. It was set aside especially for her, so as to be always available should her mistress have need for any thing during the remainder of the evening, or until her mistress quietly signalled that she might retire, which she would achieve with a discreet manner and a small curtsey to the assembly.

Lucy noted with relief that her request for the chandeliers to remain unlit had been granted, though Aunt had grumbled about it at the time of application and much since.

Aunt Beatrice then introduced Lucy to the some two dozen or so newcomers to the party, so that there were now perhaps forty-five to fifty persons present. In particular, Sir William Barton and his lady interested her. His glance was piercing and his hand firm and purposeful, but there was also a hint of doubt in both that this slender young woman could do justice to the serious musicianship that had been promised for this special evening. Indeed, several seemed surprised by her youth and delicate beauty, as if that excluded any possibility of artistic talent. She merely smiled shyly at all the remarks and unspoken questions.

Introductions complete, Lucy moved to the piano – which was a very fine and well-tuned full concert grand. She had practised on it discreetly when assured that her aunt was not at home, though most had been on a much smaller instrument in an unused suite. Even there she had been prudent so as not to give Aunt any inkling of what was in store for this last evening.

Now the moment she had been craving – and that had kept her spirits high – had finally arrived, and she would have to be at her best to do justice to such a fine instrument. But she had prepared well and was ready for the challenge.

She surprised her hostess by remaining standing as she beckoned Mildred forward.

'I would like to introduce my *companion* (here with deliberate emphasis, noting out of the corner of her eye the slight frown from Aunt), Miss Mildred Marlowe," who presented the gathering a deep and gracious, long-held curtsey, then rose to address them in a clear well-modulated soprano.

'Ladies and Gentlemen, Honoured Guests, Miss Lucinda wishes me to inform that first she will be playing without a break between compositions; second, that she prefers not to be interrupted by approbation, however polite; and last, that she chooses to play by subdued light so as to limit the distractions that occasionally occur during such séances,' and she finished with an equally graceful curtsey before withdrawing to one side.

This presentation produced a murmur of surprise from around the large conservatory, and a deepening frown from Aunt Beatrice, who thought it all much too pretentious and in a setting already too dim for her liking. But there was a gentle smile from Aunt Cicely - now barely discernible for, by this time, Mildred had quietly snuffed all the candles in their holders save those at the piano itself, and one at a small table alongside. Even these were strictly unnecessary, for Lucy intended to play from memory.

In the quiet hush that followed this extraordinary statement, Lucy leisurely seated herself, relaxed her fingers by playing a few soft, simple scales, gradually increasing the tempo and complexity until she was satisfied with the feelings of her body and receiving the complete attention of the assembly, well aware that she was the focus of it, being the only illumined being in the large room.

She opened softly with Beethoven's Sonata Opus 13 in C minor, the 'Pathétique', lyricizing the slower passages, moving suddenly into the glittering *glissando*, then providing a crashing finale, for she had decided that this evening she was playing for herself, in whatever manner took her mood – and at this instant it was decidedly defiant!

As previously announced by Mildred, without pause she moved effortlessly into a spirited Scarlatti and a lighter-than-air Corelli, followed by W A Mozart's Rondo in A major played without the repetition but delivered very slowly and moodily. Then followed a thoughtful third and a thunderous fourth movement from the Appassionata by Herr Beethoven, and finally, while those echoes were still filling the ears of the assembled guests, the Rondo once more, this time both parts full of energy, expression, smooth-as-silk glissandi, and crashing chords, and as fast as her fingers could fly – which was fast, *very* fast, indeed!

Even as these last notes were bouncing off the walls, Mildred quickly extinguished the remaining candles, quietly led Lucy to the door and through the hall to the staircase, where she indicated to the footman stationed there that candles were required in the conservatory, and they were gone.